Renewals can be made

by internet   www.fifedirect.org.uk/libraries

in person   at any library in Fife

by phone   03451 55 00 66

ON
AT FIFE
LIBRARIES

Thank you for using your library

Also by Frank Schätzing

Death and the Devil

FRANK SCHÄTZING
[LIMIT]

PART TWO

TRANSLATED BY

Shaun Whiteside,
Jamie Lee Searle
and
Samuel Willcocks

Jo Fletcher

BOOKS

First published in the German language as *Limit* by Frank Schätzing

First published in Great Britain in 2013 by Jo Fletcher Books
This edition published in two parts, this part in 2016 by

Jo Fletcher Books
an imprint of
Quercus Publishing Ltd
Carmelite House
50 Victoria Embankment
London EC4Y 0DZ

An Hachette UK company

A CIP catalogue record for this book is available
from the British Library

PART 1 PB ISBN 978 1 84916 517 4
PART 2 PB ISBN 978 1 78429 420 5
EBOOK ISBN 978 0 85738 540 6

10 9 8 7 6 5 4 3 2 1

Typeset by Jouve (UK), Milton Keynes
Printed and bound in Great Britain by Clays Ltd, St Ives plc

For Brigitte and Rolf
who gave me life in the world

For Christine and Clive
who gave me a piece of the moon

What Went Before

2025: The United States found Helium-3 on the Moon and the Earth's energy needs are now secure. Orley Enterprises' breakthrough technology has revolutionised space travel, and as the oil industry collapses and entire corporations go under, the Americans and the Chinese go head-to-head in a desperate race to stake their claims on the Moon. Even the Canadian oil giant EMCO is threatened with bankruptcy.

EMCO Manager Gerald Palstein is trying to save his company by getting into the Helium-3 business when unknown assassins attempt to kill him. Palstein narrowly survives, and joins forces with environmental journalist Loreena Keowa to track down the people behind the attack – an undertaking that soon proves to be just as dangerous for Loreena.

It's dangerous for cyber-detective Owen Jericho too, who's ended up in Shanghai after an unhappy love affair. He needs to find the dissident hacker Yoyo, who's gone underground, for his client Tu Tian, who has to take her under his wing. What sounds like a routine case turns out to be the prelude to a nightmarish chase. He is not the only person seeking Yoyo; the authorities have Yoyo in their sights, for she has accidentally come into possession of some closely guarded secrets and is in mortal danger. An organisation called Hydra, alarmed by Yoyo is also doing everything possible to withdraw her from circulation. When Jericho finally tracks down the girl, they both make the unwelcome acquaintance of the killer Kenny Xin, one of Hydra's emissaries. It's not looking like they're going to be able to escape the cunning psychopath, so instead, the hunted decide to counter-attack. They must solve Hydra's identity, and the trail is leading them to Berlin.

Meanwhile, Julian Orley, the billionaire boss of Orley Enterprises and builder of the space elevator, which enables the production of Helium-3 on a grand scale, is about to take a life-changing step. He offers his technology exclusively to the USA, but other countries are striving for the space elevator too – especially China, which is falling behind on the Moon. Orley is fully aware of his own power, but he also knows that America's monopoly of Helium-3 is not just against his own business interests, but also his vision of a space-faring humanity. Determined to stimulate competition between nations, he sets out for the Moon with a group of international investors to open up Gaia, the first Moon Hotel, and to use the occasion to negotiate the finance for the construction of a second elevator. During the breathtaking trip, it looks like Orley's strategy is working.

He has no idea that Carl Hanna, one of his guests, is pursuing his own dark plans – and that his fate is inextricably linked with the dissident hacker Yoyo, the cyber-detective Owen Jericho, the environmental journalist Loreena Keowa and the Canadian businessman Gerald Palstein.

29 May 2025

THE MERCENARY

Night Flight

There was one good thing you could say about Teodoro Obiang Nguema Mbasogo: after he'd come to power in August 1979, the human rights situation in Equatorial Guinea had visibly improved. From that point on, there were no more mass crucifixions along the highway to the airport, and the skulls of the opposition were no longer impaled on stakes for all to see.

'A true philanthropist,' scoffed Yoyo.

'But not the first,' said Jericho. 'Have you heard of Fernão do Pó?'

Heading towards Berlin at twice the speed of sound, they travelled backwards in time, from the Shanghai dawn to the Berlin night, from the year 2025 to the beginnings of a continent in which it seemed everything that could go wrong, always did. Africa, the unloved cradle of humanity, characterised by dead-straight borders which severed its ancient tendons and nerves, creating countries of bizarre geometry, the smallest of which lay patchwork-like on the western fringes, its history reading like a chronicle of continual rape.

'Fernão do Pó? Who on earth is he?'

'Another philanthropist. After a fashion.'

As Tu had insisted on flying his company jet himself, Jericho and Yoyo had the luxurious, twelve-seater passenger cabin to themselves. They were using two monitors, supported by Diane, to familiarise themselves with Equatorial Guinea in the hope of finding answers to the questions of the last two days. The picture only became more and more confusing with each piece of information the computer provided, and the only thing that had become clear was that the events in Equatorial Guinea could only be understood if one looked at their development from the very beginning. And that beginning started with:

*   *   *

Fernão do Pó.

A stagnant lake. Dead calm. Curtains of rain billow out over the coastline.

Sweat and rainwater mix on skin, making it look as though it's been boiled in steam. Orchestrated by the cries of small seabirds, the boats are lowered into the water. The oarsman pulling, a man upright in the bow. The shore comes closer, vegetation takes shape against the deepening grey. The man walks onto the shore, looks around. Once again, an area's transformation into a state-like zone starts with a Portuguese man.

In 1469, do Pó's caravels anchor beneath the elbow of Africa, right where the continent tapers off dramatically. The discoverer, the legitimate successor of Henry the Navigator, lands on a small island and calls it Formosa on account of its beauty. Bantus live here, the Bubi tribe. They welcome the visitors in a friendly manner, unaware that their kingdom has just changed hands. From the very moment when do Pó left his bootprints in the sand, they are now subjects of his majesty Alfonso V of Portugal, to whom Pope Nicholas had handed over the entire African island, along with monopoly on trade and sole maritime law, a few years before. At least, the Pope believed that Africa was an island, sharing that misconception with Western Christianity. Do Pó provided proof to the contrary. It was discovered that Africa was in actual fact a continent, and one with a long and fertile coastline, inhabited by dark-skinned people who seemed to have very little to do and who were in dire need of Christianisation. This, in turn, corresponded perfectly with the crux of the papal bull, which decreed that non-believers were to be steamrollered into slavery – a recommendation with which Alfonso and his seafarers were happy to comply.

The day that do Pó arrived changed everything. And yet, ultimately, nothing. If he hadn't come, then sooner or later someone else would have. Many followed in his footsteps, and the slave trade thrived for three hundred years. Then the Portuguese crown exchanged its ownership of African territory for colonies in Brazil, and the Bantu changed masters. Spain was the new owner. The British, French and Germans began to get involved, all of them fighting for the areas from Cape Santa Clara right up to the Niger Delta—

'And then they tried to oppress the natives, a task which was made easier by the discord amongst the Bantu, or to be more precise, the growing rivalry between the Bubi and Fang.'

'Fang?' grinned Yoyo. 'Fang Bubi?'

'It's no laughing matter,' said Jericho. 'This is Africa's traumatic past.'

'Yes, I know. The colonialists thought about everything, just not about ethnic roots. Look at Rwanda, Hutu and Tutsi—'

'Okay.' Jericho massaged the back of his neck. 'On the other hand let's not pretend that it's a purely African invention.'

'No, you Europeans of all people should keep quiet on that matter.'

'Why?'

Yoyo's eyes widened. 'Oh, come on! Look at Serbia and Kosovo. There's still no peace even seventeen years after independence! Then the Basques, the Scottish and the Welsh. Northern Ireland.'

Jericho listened, his arms crossed.

'Taiwan,' he said. 'Tibet.'

'That's—'

'Different? Just because you lot don't want to discuss it?'

'Nonsense,' said Yoyo, irritated. 'Taiwan belongs to mainland China, that's why it's different.'

'Well, you lot are the only ones who believe that. And no one is overly pleased that you're threatening the Taiwanese with nuclear missiles.'

'Fine, smart-arse.' Yoyo leaned forwards. 'So what would happen if, all of a sudden, let's say Texas, the Cowboys . . . if they suddenly declared their independence?'

'Now that really is different,' sighed Jericho.

'Oh sure. Completely different.'

'Yes. And as far as Tibet is concerned—'

'Tibet today, Xinjiang tomorrow, then inner Mongolia, Guanxi, Hong Kong – why can't you Europeans grasp the fact that a One China policy is best for security? Our huge kingdom will fall into chaos if we allow it to fall apart. We *have* to keep China together!'

'With force.'

'No, force is the wrong way. We didn't do our homework there.'

'You can say that again!' Jericho shook his head. 'Somehow I just can't figure you out. After all, you're the one who's so passionate about human rights. That's what I thought, anyway.'

'And it's true.'

'But?'

'No buts. I'm a nationalist.'

'Hmm.'

'That doesn't compute with you, right? That the two can coexist. Human rights and nationalism.'

Jericho spread his hands out acquiescently. 'I'm happy to learn.'

'Then learn. I'm not a fascist, not a racist, nothing of the kind. But I am absolutely convinced that China is a great country with a great culture—'

'Which you yourselves have trampled all over.'

'Listen, Owen, let's get one basic thing straight. Give it a rest with all the *you, you lot, your people*! When the Red Guards were hanging teachers from trees, I wasn't even a twinkle in my father's eye. I'd rather you tell me how the whole thing with Bubi Fang carries on, if that's even relevant.'

'Fang,' Jericho corrected her patiently. 'The Bubi lived on their island. They didn't care two figs about the coast until Spain united the mainland and islands into the Republic of Equatorial Guinea. And the Fang dominated on the mainland: another Bantu tribe, who greatly outnumbered the Bubi and were less than pleased at being thrown in a pot with them overnight. In 1964, Spain gave the country full autonomy, which in practice meant that they fenced two groups who couldn't stand each other inside a state border and left them to their own devices. Something that could only end in disaster.'

Yoyo looked at him with her dark eyes. And suddenly, she smiled. So unexpected and untimely a smile that he could do little else but stare back at her, confused.

'By the way, I wanted to thank you,' she said.

'Thank me?'

'You saved my life.'

Jericho hesitated. The whole time, while he had swum so bravely through the hot water that Yoyo had got herself into, he had contented himself with his own sense of reward. Now he felt taken by surprise.

'No need,' he said feebly. 'It's just the way things turned out.'

'Owen—'

'I didn't have any choice. If I had known—'

'No, Owen, don't.' She shook her head. 'Say something nice.'

'Something nice? After all the trouble that you've—'

'Hey.' She reached out. Her slender fingers clasped around his hand and squeezed firmly. 'Say something nice to me. Right now!'

She moved closer to him, and something changed. So far he had only seen Yoyo's beauty, and the small flaws in it. Now, waves of unsettling intensity washed over him. Unlike Joanna, who controlled and regulated her erotic potential like the volume dial on a radio, Yoyo could do nothing else but burn seductively, relentless, a bright, hot star. And suddenly he realised that he would do everything in his power to make sure that this star never burned out. He wanted to see her laugh.

'Well.' He cleared his throat. 'Any time.'

'Any time what?'

'I'd do it again, any time. If you ever need saving, let me know. I'll be there.' More throat-clearing. 'And now—'

'Thank you, Owen. Thank you.'

'—let's carry on with Mayé. When does it get interesting for us?'

She let his hand go and sank back in her seat.

'Difficult to say. I'd say that in order to understand the relations in the country, we need to go back to independence. With the change to—'

Papa Macías.

In October 1968, the same damp and humid climate reigned in the Gulf of Guinea as on any other day of the year. Sometimes it rained, then the land, islands and sea would brood in sunshine that made the beaches glisten and brought all activity to a standstill. The capital city, located on the island and little more than a collection of mildewed colonial buildings with huts gathered around them, was seeing the advent of the first State President of the independent republic of Equatorial Guinea, chosen by the people in a memorable election campaign. Francisco Macías Nguema of the Fang tribe promises justice and socialism, and forces the remaining Spanish troops to retreat, an action which had already been agreed in any case, although they had imagined a slightly more conciliatory end. But 'Papa', as the president named himself out of his love for his people, is accustomed to having a good and hearty breakfast. The defeated colonialists were horrified to discover that he was a cannibal, with a tendency to eat the brains and testicles of his enemies. You couldn't expect a teary goodbye from someone like that.

And yet that's exactly what happened.

A sea of tears, a sea of blood.

The young republic was defiled almost as soon as it was born. No one there was prepared for something as exotic as market economy, but at least they had enjoyed a flourishing trade in cocoa and tropical woods. Macías, however, enflamed with glowing admiration for Marxist–Leninist-supported despotism, was interested in other things. The last units of the Guardia Civil had barely cleared their posts before it became clear what was to be expected from testicle-eating Papa and his Partido Unico Nacional. The army reinforced Macías' claim to god-like absolute dictatorship with clubs, firearms and machetes, prompting the remaining European civilians to flee the country in terror. Numerous posts were taken by members of his Esangui clan, a sub-tribe of the Fang. The fact that the island, the most attractive part of the country, seat of the government and economic centre, was Bubi territory had been a thorn in the side of the numerically superior Fang for a long time. Macías fanned the flames of this hate. At least he had had the decency to annul the constitution before breaking it.

From that point on, the Bubi felt the full force of his paternal care.

More than fifty thousand people were slaughtered, incarcerated, tortured to death, including all members of the opposition. Anyone who was able to fled abroad. And because Papa didn't trust anyone, not even his own family, even the Fang became a target for the president. Over a third of the population was forced into exile or disappeared in camps, while hundreds of Cuban military advisors were given free rein to prowl around the country; after all, Moscow was a reliable friend. By the mid-seventies, Papa had managed to annihilate the local economy so thoroughly that he needed to bring Nigerian workers into the country. But they too soon take to their heels and flee. Without further ado, the country's father enforces compulsory work for all, thereby unleashing a further mass exodus. Numerous schools are closed, something that doesn't stop Papa from calling himself the Grand Master of the People's Education, Knowledge and Traditional Culture. In his delusion of divinity, he also bolts up and barricades all the churches, proclaims atheism and devotes himself to the reinvigoration of magic rituals. The continent is now experiencing the heyday of dictatorship. Macías is referred to in the same breath as Jean-Bedel Bokassa, who also had himself crowned and was utterly convinced he was Jesus' thirteenth apostle; he is likened to Idi Amin and the Cambodian Pol Pot.

'At the end of the day, he was an even bigger criminal than Mayé,' said Yoyo. 'But no one cared. Papa didn't have anything that would have been worth caring about. As a good patriot, he renamed everything that didn't yet have an African name, and since then the mainland has been called Mbini, the island Bioko and the capital city Malabo. By the way, I also looked into Mayé's native background. He's from the Fang tribe.'

'And what happened to this splendid Papa?'

Yoyo made a snipping motion with her fingers. 'He was got rid of. A coup.'

'With support from abroad?'

'It seems not. Papa's family values got out of hand; he even started to execute his close relatives. His own wife fled over the border in the dead of night. No one from his clan was safe any more, and in the end it became too much for one of them.'

*   *   *

In 1979, there was singing and dancing in Equatorial Guinea.

A man in a plain uniform stands in the entrance to a vault, where glowing ghosts dart over the walls and ceiling, generated by the crackling fire in the middle of the room. He is inconspicuousness personified. From time to time, he gives instructions under his breath, prompting the guards to give the dancers, who have been hopping around the fire and singing Papa's praises in grotesque liveliness for hours, a helping hand with red-hot pokers. It smells of decadence and burnt flesh. Mosquitoes buzz around. In the gloomy corners and along the walls, the scene is mirrored in the eyes of rats. Anyone who tips over the brink into exhaustion is dragged up, beaten until they bleed and hauled outside. Almost all of them, apart from the uniformed men, are undernourished and dehydrated, many show signs of mistreatment, and others have yellow fever and malaria written on their gaunt faces.

Black Beach Party: just a normal day in Black Beach Prison, the infamous jail in Malabo that makes America's Devil Island look like a relaxing spa resort.

The man watches for a while longer, then leaves the dance of death, his face filled with worry. His name is Teodoro Obiang Nguema Mbasogo, nephew of the president, Commander of the National Guard and Director of the Black Beach Institution. He is responsible for scenes like these, so highly valued by Papa – just as the president enjoys spending his birthdays shooting prisoners in the Malabo stadium with 'Those Were the Days, My Friend' blasting out at full volume. But Obiang's concern wasn't for the prisoners, most of whom would never get out of this shabby, car-park-like fortress alive. It was his own life he feared for, and he had every reason to do so. These days, everyone in Papa's clan had to confront the possibility of suddenly falling victim to the president's paranoia and being sent off into the eternal rainforests to a soundtrack of Mary Hopkin.

So even Obiang was afraid.

And yet his own family values weren't very different from those of his cut-throat uncle. Macías' fear of clans was part of his blood, a fear of the preferential politics which saw clans give their sons and daughters to other clans in order to stay in power. Papa himself felt the full force of it when Obiang staged a coup and chased the Unique Wonder out of office. Papa, deprived of his power, fled headlong into the jungle, but not before first burning the remaining local currency. More than one hundred million dollars go up in flames in his villa, literally the very last of the State money. By the time Obiang's henchmen tracked down the weakened Macías amongst the huge ferns and piles of apeshit, Equatorial Guinea was as bare as a bone. They drive the man to Malabo, play him 'Those Were the Days' and bullet by bullet deliver him to the ghosts of his forefathers, a task taken care of by Moroccan soldiers – his own people are too afraid of the cannibal's dark magic.

And so the highest military council takes command of government business. Like all newly enthroned leaders, Obiang makes well-meaning promises to the people, proclaims a parliamentary democracy and, at the end of the eighties, even allows elections. Numerous candidates are suggested: but by him. Obiang wins, primarily because his Partido Democrático de Guinea Ecuatorial runs without competition, the representatives of which celebrate with a big party in Black Beach Prison. The government regrows like a lizard's tail: the same blood, the same genes. Esangui-Fang even. It's a family business. Anyone who criticises it will soon be dancing and singing around the fire, the only thing that's changed is the wording. Obiang's temper isn't anywhere near as bad as Papa's; he's much more preoccupied with re-establishing trust abroad, making tentative links with the enduringly snubbed Spain and informing the Soviets that they are no longer friends. Equatorial Guinea begins to look more like a state again, and less like a subtropical Dachau. Money flows into the country. Annabon, Bioko's sister island, is large and beautiful, ideal for the disposal of nuclear waste, something for which the First World is prepared to pay a pretty penny. The only problem is that Annabon is inhabited, but it won't be for much longer. Illegal fishing, arms smuggling, the drugs trade and child labour: Obiang pulls out all the stops and transforms the green patch in the Gulf of Guinea into a lovely little gangsters' paradise.

Foreign creditors put the pressure on. Democracy is a necessity.

Obiang reluctantly accepts opposition parties, but despite using all his criminal talents, he is still 250 million dollars in the red. Then something inexplicable happens, something which gives the future a completely new shine overnight. First near Bioko, and then off the mainland coast. Something which makes the president round his lips reverently, as round as one needs to shape them in order to articulate a certain word.

'Oil.'

'Exactly, said Jericho. 'The first sites were detected at the beginning of the nineties, and after that the race was on. There's a constant stream of companies interested in the Gulf. Not one of them makes any more references to human rights. All of a sudden, mining licences are more popular topics of conversation.'

'And Obiang cashes in.'

'And cleans up, because of the low prices.' Jericho pointed at his screen. 'If you want to see the list of people who were imprisoned or murdered—'

'Show me.'

'Spain was the exception, I should add. Madrid clearly does get worked up about human rights infringements.'

'Respect to them.'

'No, it was motivated by frustration. Some opposition forces had found shelter in Spain and railed against Obiang's clan, so he was a little reluctant to grant licences to Spanish companies. The Spanish government reacted bitterly and suspended foreign aid in protest. Heart-warming really, because Mobil opens up another oilfield near Malabo just a little later, and Equatorial Guinea's economic growth shoots up by forty per cent. Then it's one after another: there are discoveries near Bioko, near Mbini, a building boom in Malabo; oil towns such as Luba and Bata spring up. Obiang has no more political opponents; he is the oil prince. His re-election in the mid-nineties turns into a farce. The only competitor who can be taken seriously, Severo Moto from the Progressive Party, is sentenced to a hundred years' imprisonment for high treason and escapes to Spain by the skin of his teeth.'

'Interesting.' Yoyo looked at him thoughtfully. 'And who held the most licences?'

'America.'

'What about China?'

'Not at the time. The US companies took the lead. They were the quickest and forced outrageous treaties on Obiang; he had very little understanding of the trade and signed everything they put in front of him. The ethnic shambles between the Fang and Bubi reached a new peak. There were very few Bubi on the mainland, but they're the majority on Bioko, where the coastline was suddenly spluttering with oil. They all used to be poor, and in theory this should have made them all rich, but Obiang only lined his own pockets. The protests started in 1998. The Bubi founded a movement, fighting for the independence of Bioko, and there's no way Obiang was going to allow that.'

'Soviet troops have hauled the tanks out of the garage for far lesser reasons than that.'

'Chinese troops—'

'—too.' Yoyo rolled her eyes. 'Yes, I know. So how did Obiang react?'

'He didn't. He refused to enter into discussion. Radical Bubi mount attacks on police stations and military bases. They're in despair, made to feel like second-class citizens every day. Which isn't to say that the Fang are having a better time of it, but it hits the Bubi the hardest. And yet there's technically enough money around for each person to build themselves a villa in the jungle. On the other hand—'

'—there's a hell in every heaven,' as the people of Malabo said back at the beginning of the millennium, and by that they meant that heaven stands out against hell like a gold ingot swimming in a sea of shit.

Right before the boom, Equatorial Guinea topped the list of poorest countries. The coffee export industry collapsed in Bioko, and a number of coffee plantations along the coast disappeared under the chummy presence of all manner of weeds. Precious wood species are said to be profitable, so they start to fell obeche and bongossi trees and then just stare at the fallen trunks, because there are no machines to take them away, not to mention no transport routes. Malaria, the mistress of the jungle, conspires with the miserable healthcare to reduce the average life expectancy to forty-nine years, backed up by an up-and-coming epidemic called AIDS. All across the land, the only thing flourishing besides fame, orchids and bromeliads is corruption.

Four years later, the sweaty region in Africa's armpit registers a yearly GDP growth of twenty-four per cent. The oil and dollars flow, but there is little change to the living conditions. Obiang suspects that he was taken to the cleaners during the negotiations for the licence contracts. Not even the sentencing of popular Bubi leaders to imprisonment and death improves his mood. It's not that the president is struggling financially; after all, he gets rich while black Africa perishes of AIDS, signs a trade agreement with Nigeria for collaboration in oil mining and launches an attack on the exploitation of natural gas resources. It's just that other dictators have made more lucrative deals. In 2002, a year before the elections, dozens of alleged rebels were arrested, including numerous opposition leaders, which has a wondrous influence on poll attendance. No one of clear mind had any doubt that Obiang would be re-elected – but the fact that he won 103 per cent of the votes amazed even the most hard-boiled analysts. Strengthened by experience and referendum, Obiang assigns licences under stricter conditions, and the coffers are finally rewarded. Teodorin, his eldest son and Forestry Minister, is able to jet around between Hollywood, Manhattan and Paris, buy Bentleys, Lamborghinis and luxury villas by the dozen and spends his time at champagne parties, dreaming of the day when his father will lose the battle against his prostate and hand the presidency over to him.

In the meantime, his father is given a helping hand by a bank in Washington, which discreetly reallocates thirty-five million dollars from the State account to private ones. When the whole thing gets blown open, the president acts offended, although not particularly bothered. You can have a good life with a ruined reputation in 'Africa's Kuwait', as Equatorial Guinea has become known by then. The country is amongst the most significant oil producers in Africa and records the biggest economic growth in the world. The dictator almost lovingly nurtures his reputation for taking after his uncle in culinary matters, of not being averse to the crisply fried liver of an opponent if the right wine has been selected to accompany it. It's all play-acting of course, but the impact is considerable. Human rights organisations are outraged, dedicating articles to him, and at home no one dares to pick an argument with Obiang. The idea of being tenderised and then devoured in Black Beach is not appealing.

Elsewhere, people are not so sickened. George W. Bush, usually less than fond of Africa on account of it being full of epidemics, fly-covered, starved faces and poisonous creatures, starts to change his mind. Profoundly upset by the attacks of 9/11, he is striving for independence from the oil of the Middle East, and more than a hundred billion barrels of the best petroleum are alleged to be stored in West Africa alone. Bush plans to cover twenty-five per cent of America's needs from there by 2015. While Amnesty International gets overwhelmed, drowning in horrendous reports, Bush invites Obiang and other African kleptocrats to breakfast in the White House. Meanwhile, Condoleezza Rice gives a press conference and publicly expresses solidarity: Obiang is described as 'a good friend', whose engagement for human rights is valued. The good friend smiles modestly, and Ms Rice smiles along with him. The other side of the cameras, the managers of Exxon, Chevron, Amerada Hess, Total and Marathon Oil, are smiling too. By 2004, Equatorial Guinea's oil mining is entirely in US hands; the companies transfer seven hundred million dollars directly to Obiang's accounts in Washington each year.

Which is rather odd.

Because no one visiting Malabo will see any sign of this wealth. The four-lane Carretera del Aeropuerto which leads from the airport right into its colonial centre is still the only tarmacked road in the country. The old town, partly renovated, partly disintegrated, is ridden with brothels and drinking holes. Extravagant cross-country vehicles are parked in front of the air-conditioned and ugly government palace. The only hotel exudes all the charm of an emergency accommodation building. There's no school anywhere worthy of the name. There are no daily papers, no smiles on the faces, no public voice. Here and there, scaffolding leans against scaffolding like drunk men huddling together, but only on constructions carried out for the Obiangs; apart from the villas of the kleptocracy, hardly any building work gets finished. Those are the only new structures: monuments of monstrous tastelessness, just like the warehouses and quarters for foreign oil workers which spring out of the ground overnight. As if embarrassed to be there, the American Embassy cowers between the surrounding houses, while a little further on, the other side of the cordoned-off Exxon grounds, the Chinese Embassy flaunts itself brazenly.

'So they did start to court Obiang,' said Yoyo. 'Even though almost everything was owned by the Americans.'

'They tried, anyway,' said Jericho. 'But they weren't that successful to begin with. After all, Obiang's new circle of friends didn't just include the Bush dynasty. Even the EU Commission was eagerly rolling out the red carpet for him, especially the French. What did a ban on religion or torture matter? The fact that the only human rights organisation in the country was controlled by the government, along with the radio and television; they couldn't care less. The fact that two-thirds of the population were living on less than two dollars a day; *mei you ban fa*, there was nothing that could be done. The region was of vital interest, anyone who comes too late loses out, and the Chinese were just too slow.'

'And how did the locals react to the oil workers being there?'

'They didn't. The workers were flown straight into sealed-off company grounds. Marathon built their own town not far from Malabo, around a gas-to-liquid plant, and at times there were more than four thousand people living there: a highly secured Green Zone with its own energy grid, water supply, restaurants, shops and cinemas. Do you know what the workers called it? Pleasantville.'

'How sweet.'

'Indeed. When a dictator gives you permission to plunder his mineral resources while his own people are butchering monkeys out of sheer hunger, you don't exactly want to let those people catch sight of you. And *they* certainly don't want to see you. But they aren't even put in that awkward situation, because the companies are self-sufficient. The local private economy doesn't benefit in the slightest from the fact that several thousand Americans are squatting just a few kilometres away. Most of the oil workers spent months in ghettos like those or on their rig, fucking AIDS-free girls from Cameroon, gobbling down piles of malaria tablets and making sure they arrived back home without having made any contact with the country. No one wanted contact. The main thing was that Obiang was firmly in the saddle, and, therefore, the American oil industry too.'

'But something must have gone wrong. For the Yanks, I mean. By Mayé's time they were practically out of the game.'

'It did go wrong,' said Jericho. 'The decline began in 2004. But that was actually down to an Englishman. I'd hazard a guess that our story and the mess we've got mixed up in really started after the Wonga Coup.'

Wonga Coup. A Bantu term. Wonga meaning money, dosh, dough, moolah. A flippant way of describing one of the most ridiculous attempted coups of all time.

In March 2004, a rattling Boeing of prehistoric design lands in Harare Airport in Zimbabwe, packed full of mercenaries from South Africa, Angola and Namibia. The plan is to take weapons and ammunition on board, fly on to Malabo and meet up with a little group of fighters smuggled in ahead of them. Together, they plan to overthrow the government in a surprise attack, shoot down Obiang or throw him into his own prison, the main priority being a change of power. The day before, and as if by magic, the leader of the oppositional progressive party, Severo Moto, arrives in nearby Mali from his Madrid exile, thereby enabling him to get to Malabo within the hour to have his feet kissed by the grateful hordes.

But it didn't quite turn out like that. The South African Secret Services – on the alert against the now unemployed henchmen of apartheid – got wind of the plan and warned Obiang. Simultaneously, the Zimbabwe government was informed of the arrival of a bunch of dreamers convinced they could rewrite history by letting rip with some decommissioned Kalashnikovs. The trap snaps down on both sides: they were all arrested and given immediate prison sentences, and that was that.

Or that *would have been* that.

Because unfortunately – for those behind the coup – the people questioned betrayed their confidentially vows in the hope of lighter sentences. And so the full force of the law makes itself felt. One of the ringleaders of the unlucky commandos was a former British officer and long-time leader of a private mercenary firm, which had links with a certain Jan Kees Vogelaar. The officer, imprisoned in Zimbabwe, is able to tell them that a dodgy oil manager with a British passport is behind the whole thing, and above all a relative of a British prime minister, who is alleged to have put up considerable sums of money for the operation. Just this information alone is enough to elicit statements from Obiang, hinting at handing over certain parts of the perpetrator's anatomy to his cook, if they ever get their hands on him. Pretty soon Simon Mann is threatened with extradition. This, and the prospect of dance lessons in Black Beach – and worse – contribute immensely to the loosening of the mercenary leader's tongue. Then the truth comes out.

The real financers are British oil companies, the crème of the trade, who were disgruntled at the sputtering wealth being divided up between American companies and the impossibility of getting a foot in the door with Obiang. No offence intended, but they wanted to change a few things. Severo Moto had been chosen to undertake the distribution of the cake. A puppet president who, amongst other things, had promised to favour Spanish oil companies too.

And then the mercenary drops the real bomb:

They all knew about it!

The CIA. British MI6. The Spanish Secret Service. They all knew – and they all helped. It was said even Spanish warships had been en route to Equatorial Guinea, an infinite loop of colonialism. Obiang was outraged. Even his brunch buddy from Washington stabbed him in the back. No longer willing to stabilise him, Bush was prepared to divide up shares amongst the English and the Spanish in the interest of a puppet government, and to negotiate more favourable mining conditions in turn. Obiang rages against the whole sorry lot of them – and decides to help put their plan into action: he really does redistribute the mining rights – just in a completely different way from how the global strategists imagined. American companies get the boot, and in their place the South Africans get the lot. Relations with José Maria Aznar, Severo Moto's friend and host to forty thousand Equatorial Guinea residents in exile, are suspended. France, on the other hand, is alleged to have helped to prevent the coup, and so Obiang looks favourably on the Grande Nation.

And wasn't there a country on the starting blocks, waiting for America to go it alone?

'China comes into play.'

'Yes, although treading delicately. Obiang seems prepared to forgive and forget at first. Aznar has been voted out by then, making Spain approachable again, so he launches into a charm offensive. By the same token, Washington tries its hand with diplomatic reparations. Smiling competitions with Condoleezza Rice, new contracts, all of that. By 2008, the companies are pumping half a million barrels a year from the sea off Obiang's *own country*, the country that records the highest income per capita in the whole of Africa. Analysts estimate that there is more oil stored in Equatorial Guinea than in Kuwait. The bulk of it flows into the USA, a little to France, Italy and Spain, but the real winner—'

'—is China.'

'Exactly! They caught up with America. Slyly and quietly.'

'I get it.' Yoyo looked at him, her eyelids drooping. Jericho felt strangely spaced out too. The lack of sleep and the jet gliding at twice the speed of sound were starting to have a narcotic effect. 'And Obiang?'

'Still angry. Furious! He realises, of course, that high-ranking members of his government must have known about the plans to overthrow him. You can only arrange a coup like that with support from the inside. So heads roll, and from then on he doesn't trust anyone. He gets himself a Moroccan bodyguard out of fear of his own people. At the same time, though, he demands to be courted in a bizarre way. When the Exxon bosses arrive, they have to address his ministers and generals as

Excellentissimo. Former slaves encounter former slave traders, everyone detests everyone else. The board members of the oil firms hate having to sit at a table with the jungle chiefs, but they do it regardless because both sides stand to make a huge profit.'

'And the country is still on its knees.'

'There are some benefits for the Fang, but generally speaking the economy is corrupt. Sure, there are a few more nice cars parked in the slums, but running water and electricity are still in short supply. The country is paying for the curse of having natural resources. Who would still want to work or educate themselves if money were flowing into their accounts of its own accord? The wealth transforms some into predators and others into zombies. Bush states that he plans to pump the sea floor near Malabo empty by 2030, and promises Obiang he'll leave him in peace with regard to human rights and coup plans, as well as reward him appropriately.'

'That sounds like a good deal. For Obiang, I mean.'

'Yes, he could have contented himself with that. But he didn't. Because good old Obiang—'

—is an elephant: unforgiving, mistrustful. As elephants tend to be. He just can't forget that Bush, the Brits and the Spanish wanted to do the dirty on him. The pistons of his lubricated power machine rise and fall cheerfully, everything running like clockwork, including his sparkling re-election in 2009. There's such immense wealth that lesser quantities finally spill over to the middle and lower classes too, enough to anaesthetise any revolutionary ideas for the time being. But Obiang still plots his revenge.

Ironically, of all things it's the change of government in Washington that heralds the new era. In a way, it was possible to rely on Bush, who lacked the same amount of morals as he endeavoured to fake in his speeches. Barack Obama, on the other hand, the high priest of Change, dreaded the thought of tucking into hard-boiled eggs in the company of cannibals behind closed doors. Eagerly attempting to re-establish America's worse for wear image around the world, he hauled terms like democracy and human rights out of the sewers of Bush's vocabulary, listened courteously to the UN when sanctions against rogue regimes were the topic of debate, and aggravated Obiang with his humanitarian demands.

In the fanfare of changed American rhetoric, Obiang is probably the only one to notice that two heavily armed US military bases have sprung up in São Tomé and Príncipe overnight, right in front of his nose. Oil is suspected around this small island state too. By now, China and the USA are engaged in a real race in the resources market. The treasures of the earth seem solely destined to be divided up between the two economic giants. Officially, the two bases are supposed to secure trouble-free transport of gas and oil in the Gulf of Guinea, but Obiang senses betrayal. His fall would make things a great deal easier for the Americans. And they will force his fall, as long as he continues to go to bed with each and every whore instead of marrying just one of them.

Obiang looks to the East.

In 2010, Beijing ascended to become Africa's biggest financial backer, ahead of even the World Bank. The president figures out two geostrategic equations. The first is that China is least likely to carry out a coup against him, so long as he favours them in commodities poker. The second is that Beijing is most likely to overthrow him if he doesn't, so he gives more licences to China. The alarm bells start to ring in Washington. Just like before, they still try to maintain close relations with states that have something they want. US representatives travel to corrupt meetings under the soaking skies of Malabo. An unblemished cosmopolitan on the surface, Obiang assures his American friends of his undiminished appreciation while, behind their backs, he puts an end to contracts, redistributes mining rights at will, commences licence fees and stirs up public opinion against the Western 'exploiters'. These actions result in infringements on US institutions, imprisonments and the deportation of American workers. Washington considers it necessary to threaten Obiang with sanctions and isolation, and the climate rapidly deteriorates.

Then, drunk on power, Obiang crosses the line. Peeved at the extension of the American military bases, he has Marathon's oil town

'Pleasantville' attacked in the dead of night. This culminates in a real battle at Punta Europa, with casualties on both sides. As always, the president denies any part in it, expresses deep consternation and promises that he, like his uncle before him, plans to nail the guilty parties to stakes along the side of the highway. But in doing so, he makes the mistake of casting the blame onto the Bubi, a spark that triggers an explosion. Distracted by geostrategy, Obiang failed to notice that the ethnic conflict had long since overstepped the border of controllability. The Bubi defend themselves against the accusations, attack Fangs of the Esangui clan, and are riddled with bullets by Obiang's paramilitaries, but this time his intimidation tactics don't have the usual impact. Marathon people identify the corpse of a fallen attacker as an officer of the Equatorial Guinea army, a Fang who was loyal to the party line, and one who was also related by marriage to Obiang. Washington doesn't rule out taking military action. Obiang pointedly has Americans arrested and accuses Obama of trying to engineer his overthrow, a statement which encourages Bubi politicians to send signals to Washington. Severo Moto, the unlucky almost-president, who has little else to do but chew on the bones of failure in Spanish exile, conveys the details: if Malabo, the capital city, can be successfully brought under control, then – and only then! – can a coup have any chance of success. The hearts of the Bubi beat for America. And so a new equation is made: America plus Bubi equals coup equals China out and America in. Officially, the Americans turn down a coup, of course, but the trenches are dug.

Obiang gets nervous.

He tries to unite the Fang to support him, but their belated rage at his failings puts paid to that. Most Fang had no better a time of it under his regime than the Bubi. By now, they are discontented and disunited. The ruling clan in particular shows itself to be a stronghold of Shakespearean plotting. Barricaded behind his puppet guard, the president fails to notice that America has begun to buy Fang and Bubi leaders off in secret, urging them to shake hands and make peace. China makes a bid too. The Equatorial Guinea parliament is up for auction, a Sotheby's full of corruption. The scattered Bubi parties at home and abroad find themselves in shaky alliances. Obiang responds with terror; civil-war-like conditions shake the country and draw the attention of the foreign media. The USA finally drops the oil prince. He is ordered to call a re-election or, preferably, to step down immediately. Beside himself with rage, Obiang threatens the Bubi with genocide and expresses his desire to eat a whole lot of fried liver. But by now the resistance can no longer be contained.

To add to the confusion, Fang clans from the less than wealthy hinterlands unexpectedly join the Bubi side. Obiang shouts for military helicopters, Beijing hesitates. The hands-off principle, the most important cornerstone of Chinese foreign policy, won't tolerate military intervention. At the same time, the UN assembly strives for resolutions against Equatorial Guinea. China exercises its veto, the EU demands Obiang's resignation. Cameroon wants to mediate, but both sides of the Atlantic are in agreement: Obiang's time is up. The guy has to go. One way or another.

In 2015, a year before his time in office is up, weakened by both politics and his prostate, the dictator finally buckles. A tired old man is shown on State TV describing his health, citing it as the reason why he is no longer able to serve his beloved people in the reliable way they have become accustomed to. Ergo, for the good of Equa-torial Guinea, he is now handing over his power to younger hands, and in particular to – to – to—

According to the script, Obiang's eldest son Teodorin was supposed to rush out from behind the curtain in full presidential regalia, but he had planned ahead, making himself scarce in the Bermuda triangle of the jet set. In any case, the majority of his uncles and cousins wanted to see Obiang's second-born in power instead: Gabriel, who managed the oil trade. The USA – a bitter opponent of Teodorin since he had boasted years ago of wanting to renegotiate all the oil treaties to America's disadvantage – spread rumours that Teodorin was planning Gabriel's murder. Suddenly, no one seems to want to take the reins any more. Obiang, disgusted by the whiff of cowardice, decides without further ado to nominate an interim candidate, one who will lead government business for the duration of his office and then organise fair elections with the inclusion of all parties and candidates. The chosen one is the commander in chief of the armed forces, a cousin of Obiang's, whose chest is covered with medals for loyal service, including the prevention of numerous assassination and coup attempts as well as the imprisonment and torture of innumerable Bubi and Fang. He is—

Brigadier General Juan Alfonso Nguema Mayé. Huge and bald-headed, with a broad, captivating smile. Mayé, running a store for oil tankers in Berlin and devouring Yoyo's eyeballs with relish, while Jan Kees Vogelaar—

'Owen.'

Mayé transforms into Kenny, comes closer, black against a wall of flames, raises his arm, and Jericho sees that he's waving Yoyo's eyeless skull.

Give me your computer, he says.

Give me—

'Owen, wake up.'

Someone is shaking him by the shoulder. Yoyo's voice snuggles into his ear. He breathes in her scent and opens his eyes. Tu is standing behind her, grinning down at him.

'What's going on?' Jericho gestures towards the cockpit with his thumb. 'Shouldn't you be sitting up front?'

'Autopilot, *xiongdi*,' said Tu. 'A wonderful invention. I had to stand in for you temporarily. Do you want to hear how the Mayé story continues?'

'Erm—'

'That might have been a yes,' whispered Yoyo, turned towards Tu. 'What do you reckon, did he say yes?'

'It sounds more like he wants coffee. Would you like a coffee, Owen?'

'Hmm?'

'Would you like a coffee?'

'I— No, no coffee.'

'He's in another world, our innterrrrimm candidaaaa,' whispered Yoyo conspiratorially.

Tu chortled. 'Innterrrrimm candidaaaa' he repeated, against a backdrop of Yoyo's melodic giggling. Both seemed to be highly amused, and Owen was clearly the source of their merriment. Disgruntled, he looked out of the window into the night and then back again.

'How long was I out for?'

'Oh, a good hour.'

'I'm sorry, I didn't mean to—'

Yoyo stared at him. She tried to keep a straight face, then she and Tu burst out out laughing. They cackled idiotically at the tops of their voices, nervous and breathless.

'Hey! What's so funny?'

'Nothing.' They were still panting and laughing.

'There's clearly something.'

'No, nothing, Owen, it's nothing. It's just that—'

'What?'

Altitude sickness, he thought. The beginnings of hysteria. You hear of people who start laughing after traumatic events and then just can't stop. Astonishingly, even though he didn't have the faintest clue what it was about, he felt a painful longing to laugh along, whatever it was. That's not good, he thought. We're all going crazy.

'So?'

'Well.' Yoyo blew her nose and wiped the corners of her eyes. 'Oh, it's silly really, Owen. I lost you in the middle of a sentence. Your last word was—'

'What?'

'I guess it was meant to be interim candidate. You said, Obiang had an inteeeeriiim—'

Tu was making bleating noises.

'Candidaaaaaa—'

'You've both lost your minds.'

'Come on, Owen. It's funny,' grunted Tu. 'It's really funny!'

'Why, for God's sake?'

'You fell asleep in the middle of the sentence,' giggled Yoyo. 'Your head fell forward in a funny way, your lower jaw dropped down, like . . .'

Jericho waited patiently until her re-enactment of his degradation had reached its drooling conclusion. Tu dabbed the sweat from his bald head. In moments like these, the English and Chinese senses of humour seemed to be galaxies apart, but Jericho suddenly realised he was laughing too. For some reason it felt good. As if someone had put the furniture inside his mind in order and let some fresh air in.

'Right then.' Tu patted him on the shoulder. 'I'm going up front again. Yoyo will tell you the rest. Then we can draw our conclusions.'

'Where did we get to?' asked Jericho.

'To interiiiiiim—' chirruped Yoyo.

'Enough now.'

'No, I'm being serious. To General Mayé.'

She was right, that was where they had left off. Obiang had named his highest commander in chief as his successor. Mayé was supposed to use the time the outgoing president had left in office to prepare for democratic elections, and yet—

No one trusted the brigadier general. Mayé was seen as a hard-liner and as Obiang's puppet. There was no doubt that the elections would result in either Mayé himself or one of the president's sons seizing power. Definitely not the kind of result anyone would like.

Apart from Beijing, that is.

What happened next was so surprising, both for Obiang and Mayé, that even weeks later they were still convinced it was a bad dream. On the day when office was to be handed over, a boldly soldered-together alliance of Bubi and Fang, including members of the armed forces, simultaneously stormed numerous police stations in Malabo as well as the seat of government, taking the dictator and his designated successor prisoner. They drove them to the Cameroon border and threw them out of the country without any further ado. America's investment had paid off: practically every key position in government circles had been bought. This even turned out to be to Obiang's advantage, because America refused to tolerate any cases of lynch justice for the logistic and strategic support of the coup.

For the next few hours, the country seemed to have no leader.

Then Severo Moto's successor emerged from an aeroplane, a university-educated economist by the name of Juan Aristide Ndongo, from the Bubi clan. He had once been forced to reside in Black Beach for a number of years for his criticism of the regime, and for that reason had gained the trust of a large proportion of the population. Ndongo was known to be clever, friendly and weak, the ideal Manchurian candidate. The Fang and Bubi agreed on him in advance with the USA, Great Britain and Spain, expecting to be able to spoon-feed good old Ndongo to their heart's desire, but he surprised them by having his own plans. The speedy dissolution of parliament is followed by the equally speedy formation of a new government, in which the Bubi and Fang are equally represented. Ndongo promises to create the long overdue infrastructure, a pulsing educational system, to reinvigorate the economy and to provide healthcare and prosperity for everyone. But, above all, he rails against China's bloodsucking vampire capitalism, which he sees as having destroyed Equatorial Guinea in collaboration with Obiang's recklessness. He also puts a stop to Beijing's licence treaties and puts the American ones back in force, without forgetting – with wise foresight – the Spanish, British, French and Germans.

But reality catches up with Ndongo like a pack of hungry dogs. His attempts to put his plans into action aggravate the Fang elite, who hadn't reckoned with his political survival instinct. He puts oil income into trust funds instead of transferring it to private accounts, and by doing so keeps the money out of the reach of corruption. He keeps to his promise and builds streets and hospitals, kick-starts the wood trade, and relaxes censorship. In doing so, he provokes the hate of the Obiang clique who, they now realise, let themselves be bought without taking into consideration that the preaching Bubi politician intended to take the lead. Within the first year after the coup, the hard-liners move over to the opposition. Ndongo's successes just feed their hatred, so they try to sabotage him wherever possible, denouncing his inability to rid the world of ethnic resentment and stirring it up in the process. They claim that Ndongo is just another Obiang, a puppet of the USA, and that he will discriminate against the Fang. Many bravely initiated projects grind to a halt. Aids grows rampant, crime is rife, and Ndongo's parliament proves itself to be just as corrupt as his predecessor's, while the president, hobbling around defiantly on the crutches of legality, begins to lose touch.

In the second year under Ndongo's rule, radical Esangui-Fang launch attacks on American and European oil institutions. Bubi and Fang go for each other's necks as they have since time immemorial, terrorist cells thwart every attempt at political stabilisation, and Ndongo's idea of a better world collapses with a crash. He has gone too far for his opponents, but not far enough for his friends. In a painful act of self-denial, Ndongo takes a harsher stance, carries out mass arrests and loses what was once his only capital overnight: integrity.

Meanwhile, Mayé is warming up on the sidelines in Cameroon.

'From the outside,' said Yoyo, 'it looked like this: Obiang, sick and bitter, hangs around in the neighbouring country and pressures Mayé to force Ndongo out of office at the next available opportunity. But the old man doesn't want Mayé himself to rule, but rather to prepare the ground for Teodorin and Gabriel, who have sunk sobbing into one another's arms at the mere thought of Ndongo. Rivalry is no longer the issue. The country is destabilised and Ndongo is for it. All Mayé would really need to do is travel in and say Boo! Aside from the fact that he can't enter the country of course.'

'But because putschists don't need a visa—'

'—he agrees and sets off. It's common knowledge by then that Mayé has already made contact with a private mercenary firm, African Protection Services, APS for short. And they' – Yoyo paused for a short, dramatic moment – 'are of interest to us!'

'Let me guess. This is where Vogelaar comes back into the picture.'

Yoyo smiled smugly. 'I've found the missing years. Does the name ArmourGroup ring any bells with you?'

'It does. It's a London security giant.'

'In 2008 ArmourGroup took on a mandate in Kenya. Around that time, a smaller company, Armed African Services, went through a de-merger. Vogelaar's Mamba was operating in the same crisis area. They crossed paths, perhaps one of them approached the other and borrowed some ammunition or something, but to cut a long story short they took a liking to one another and formed APS in 2010, with Vogelaar at management level. Do you see?'

'I do. So Mayé overthrew Ndongo with the help of APS. But who paid APS?'

'That's exactly the point. Mayé was incredibly friendly with China.'

'You mean—'

'I mean that we assumed the whole time that the coup attempt discussed in the text fragment was the one from last year. But Beijing would have had far more reason to pull the strings in 2017.'

'And how did Mayé's coup go?'

'Without a hitch. As a precaution, Ndongo was out of the country. But no one seemed particularly surprised by it. No resistance, no fatalities. The only one who was shocked was Obiang. Mayé had numerous opposition members imprisoned, including Obiang's closest confidants, Teodorin supporters, Gabrielists—'

'Because he had no intention of stepping down.'

'Bingo.'

'And Vogelaar became his security boss.'

'Yep.'

'Is there proof that China was tied up in it?'

'Owen, what's wrong with you?' Yoyo reprimanded him. 'There's never proof, you know that. But on the other hand you would have to be a zombie to overlook the fact that Exxon, Marathon and Co. got the chop immediately after the putsch, whereas the Chinese company Sinopec was suddenly swimming in oil from Equatorial Guinea. Then there's Mayé's speeches: they owed the Chinese their gratitude, China had always been a brother, blah blah blah. When it came down to it, he wholeheartedly agreed to his country being sold out to China.'

Jericho nodded. It was obvious that Yoyo was right: Mayé had taken power with the help of the Chinese and, as agreed, hadn't forgotten to reward them. But then why did they later want to kill him?'

'And if it wasn't the Chinese . . .' said Yoyo, as if she had read his thoughts. 'Last year, I mean.'

'Then who?'

'Is it that hard to guess? Mayé doesn't miss a single opportunity to snub the Americans. He has their representatives imprisoned, breaks all contracts, aids and abets terrorist attacks on American institutions, even though he denies it outright in diplomatic circles. In any case, it was enough that Washington was threatening him with sanctions and invasion.'

'It sounds like sabre-rattling.'

'That's precisely the question.'

'So what then? The guy ruled for seven years. What happened in that time?'

'He held his hand out. Finished the economy off. Made opposition members disappear, had them tortured, beheaded, who knows what else. Before long, Obiang looked like a philanthropist compared with Mayé, but now they had him by the neck. Mayé didn't get involved with cannibalism, witchcraft and the whole black magic scene, but he was certainly developing considerable delusions of grandeur. He built skyscrapers that no one moved into, but he didn't care, the important thing was how the skyline looked. He planned Equatorial Guinea's own version of Las Vegas and wanted to set up an opera house in the sea. The final straw was when he announced that Equatorial Guinea was promoting itself to become a Space nation, to which end, and in all seriousness, he had a launching pad built in the middle of the jungle.'

'Wait a second—' It slowly dawned on Jericho that he had read something about it at the time. An African dictator who had built a space-rocket launch base and bragged to the rest of the world that his country would be sending astronauts to the Moon. 'Wasn't that—?'

'In 2022,' said Yoyo. 'Two years before he was overthrown.'

'And what happened?'

'Well, do you see any Africans in space?'

'No.'

'Exactly. He did send one thing up though. A news satellite.'

'And what on earth did Mayé need a news satellite for?'

Yoyo circled her finger over her temple. 'Because he wasn't all there, Owen. Why do men get penis extensions? They're nothing but space-rocket launch bases on a smaller scale. But the whole thing became a mockery because the satellite broke down just a few weeks after the launch.'

'But it *was* launched.'

'Yes, without a hitch.'

'Then what happened?'

'Nothing really. Two years later, Mayé was liquidated, and Ndongo came back.' Yoyo leaned back. Her entire posture said she was ready to call it a day and unwind. 'You probably know more about that than I do. That was the part you researched.'

'But I don't know much about Ndongo.'

'Oh well,' Yoyo shrugged. 'If you want to find out who footed the bill this time then you'll need to take a close look at Ndongo's oil politics. I've got no idea whether he has been as loyally devoted to China as Mayé was.'

'Definitely not.'

'How do you know?'

'You said yourself that he would have attacked China pretty heftily. I don't think there's any doubt about that. Ndongo was put in there by the USA and taken out by China.'

'So who took Mayé out?'

Jericho gnawed on his lower lip.

statement coup Chinese government

'Something in this story doesn't make sense,' he said. 'In the text fragment it's about a coup that China is tied up in, but they can't mean the coup of 2017. For one thing, that's eight years ago. And in any case, everyone suspects Beijing was involved in it anyway, so why would they be hunting us down because of that? And another thing, it was explicitly about Donner and Vogelaar. But Vogelaar only comes up in connection with Mayé.'

'Or was placed there by Beijing back then. Maybe as a kind of guard for Mayé. A spy.'

'And Donner?'

'Think back, it wasn't just a coup last year. It was an execution. A concerted effort to get rid of witnesses. Mayé must have known something, or rather, he and his staff must have. Something so explosive that someone was prepared to kill him for it.'

'Something about China.'

'Why else would China have cleared someone out of the way that they themselves put in power? Perhaps Mayé became a liability. And Donner was one of his staff.'

'And Vogelaar was the one who had contact with Beijing. As security chief, he was closest to Mayé. So he recommends decapitating Mayé's regime.'

'And they do. Apart from Donner.'

'He gets away.'

'And now Vogelaar is supposed to find him and give him the same send-off he gave Mayé. That's why they're after us. Because we know that Donner's cover has been blown. Because we could beat Vogelaar to it. Because we could warn Donner.'

'And Kenny?'

'He might be Vogelaar's Chinese contact.'

Jericho's brain was throbbing. If the yarn they were spinning was actually true, then Donner's life was hanging by a silk thread.

No, there had to be more to it. It wasn't just about them preventing Donner from being killed. That was part of it, certainly, but the real reason for the brutal hunt of the last twenty-four hours was something else. Someone was worried that they could find out what Donner *knew*.

He stared out into the night and hoped they weren't too late.

Berlin, Germany

A glowing circuit board. A mildewed spider's web against a black background. Colonies of endlessly interwoven deep-sea organisms, the neuron landscape of an endlessly sprawling brain, a cosmos slipping away. At night, and seen from a great height, the world looks like anything but a globe illuminated only by streetlamps, neon signs, cars and house lights, by exhausted taxi drivers and shift workers, by the perpetual search for diversion and by worries which find their expression in sleeplessness and apartments lit up into the early hours. What – in the eyes of an extraterrestrial observer – might look like a coded message, actually means: Yes, we *are* alone in the universe, everyone for themselves and all for one, and we're here in the dark wilderness too, except that we're underdeveloped, poor and cut off from everything.

Jericho stared indecisively out of the window. Yoyo had dozed off in her seat, the jet was preparing for landing. Tu didn't like engaging in conversation while he was at the controls. Left to his own devices, Jericho had tried for a while to wring information about Ndongo's current time in office out of the internet, but the media interest in Equatorial Guinea seemed to have vanished with Mayé's departure. He suddenly felt his motivation ebbing away. Yoyo's light, melodic snoring had the air of a soliloquy to it. Her chest rose and sank, then she gave a start and her eyes rolled under her eyelids. Jericho watched her. It was almost as though the confusing moment of intimacy they had shared had never happened.

He turned his head and let his gaze wander out over the ghost of light as it become steadily denser. At a height of ten kilometres, he had felt a gnawing loneliness, too far from the Earth, not close enough to the skies. He was grateful for every metre that the plane sank closer to the ground, allowing the strange pattern to form familiar pictures again. Buildings, streets and squares created the illusion of familiarity. Jericho had been in Berlin a number of times. He spoke German well, not perfectly, because he had never made the effort to learn it, but what he could say was accent-free. As soon as he put his mind to swotting up on a language he mastered it in a matter of weeks, and, in any case, just listening was enough to be able to understand.

He fervently hoped that they would find Andre Donner still alive.

At 04.14, they landed in Berlin Brandenburg airport. Tu set off to arrange a hire car. When he came back he was morosely waving an Audi stick.

'I would have preferred another make,' he moaned as they crossed the neon wasteland of the parking lot in search of their vehicle. Jericho trotted behind him with his rucksack slung over his shoulder, accompanied by a shuffling and sedated-looking Yoyo, whom they had barely managed to wake. Apart from Diane and some hardware, he had nothing else with him. Tu had refused to take him to Xintiandi before their departure so he could pack a few essentials. Not even Yoyo had been permitted to go back to her apartment, although she been bold enough to protest, making Tu see red.

'No discussion!' he had scolded her. 'Kenny and his mob could be lying in wait. They'd either finish you off right on the spot or follow you to me.'

'Then just send one of your people instead.'

'They'd still follow them.'

'Or just let me—'

'Forget it!'

'For God's sake! I can't just run around in the same smelly clothes for days on end! And nor can Owen, right? Or can you, Owen?'

'Don't try ganging up on me. I said no! Berlin is a civilised city; I hear they have socks, underwear, running water and even electricity there.'

There was electricity; that much was true. But beyond that a hot shower or the scent of fresh laundry seemed light years away in that deserted, car-packed hangar. Tu hurried past dozens of identical-looking metal and synthetic-fibre bodies, swinging his full to bursting travel bag, chivvied the others along and finally spotted the dark, discreet limousine.

'The car's not bad at all,' Jericho dared to comment.

'I would have preferred a Chinese make.'

'What are you talking about? You don't drive a Chinese car. Not even when you're in China.'

'Funny,' said Tu, as the car read the data from the stick and obediently opened its doors. 'Such a talented investigator, but in some respects you're from the Stone Age. I drive a Jaguar, and Jaguar is a Chinese make.'

'Since when?'

'Since three years ago. We bought it from the Indians, just like we bought Bentley from the Germans. I would just as happily have taken a Bentley of course.'

'Why not a Rolls?'

'Under no circumstances! Rolls-Royce is Indian.'

'You two are nuts,' yawned Yoyo, and lay down across the back seat.

'Listen,' said Jericho, as he slid onto the passenger seat. 'They don't automatically become Chinese models just because you buy them. They're English. People buy them because they like English cars, and that's precisely why you buy them too.'

'But they belong—'

'—to the Chinese, I know. Sometimes the entire globalisation process just seems like one big misunderstanding.'

'Oh, come on, Owen! Really!'

'I'm serious.'

'Comments like that didn't have any punch even twenty years ago.'

Tu steered the car in slalom through the aisles, whose uniformity was only outdone by the fact that they seemed so infinite in number. 'I'd rather you told me whether you've found out anything else that might be of interest to us.'

Jericho gave him a brief overview of Ndongo's unsuccessful attempt to reform the country and do business with the United States again, and of Mayé's subsequent coup, Beijing's obvious implication in it and Mayé's China politics. He also mentioned the dictator's growing delusions of grandeur, his failed space programme and his violent removal from power.

'The official story is that Mayé and his clique fell victim to a Bubi revolt which was supported by influential Fang groups,' he said. 'Which would be plausible. But Obiang certainly wasn't behind it. Since his expulsion to Cameroon he's become quite a hermit and, according to rumour, is fighting his final battle against cancer.'

'And it wouldn't have been the sons either?'

'No.'

'Well,' Tu clicked his tongue. 'There's surprisingly little information about what's been happening there over the last year, don't you think?'

Jericho gave him an appraising look. 'Is it just my imagination, or do you know something that I should know?'

'*Oída ouk eidós*,' said Tu innocently.

'That's not Confucius.'

'I know, are you impressed? It's Plato, Socrates' apologia: I know that I know not.'

'Show-off.'

'Not at all. It's perfectly fitting for what I'm trying to say. I do know that there's an explanation for the diminished interest in Equatorial Guinea, but I just can't work out what it is. I know it's something obvious though. Something that's right in front of our noses.'

'Does it also explain why there was hardly any public speculation about involvement from abroad?'

'Ask me after I've figured out what it is.'

Jericho listened to the navigation system for a while.

'Look, the problem is that the coup wouldn't have been possible without outside help,' he said. 'It's clear that Mayé was installed there by the Chinese, so one would assume that America did it. But our text fragment says something different, that China had its finger in the pie too. If that's correct, then the submissive servant wasn't submissive enough when it really came down to it.'

'You mean he was no longer willing to comply with Beijing's wishes?'

'Yoyo and I are leaning towards the view that he and his inner circle could even have become dangerous for China.'

'Which would explain why the Chinese build him up first and then kill him,' concluded Tu.

'And accept the considerable disadvantages too.'

'How do you mean?'

'Oil. Gas. Ndongo had never been Beijing's friend.'

Tu opened his mouth. For a moment he looked as though he had grasped something which had far-reaching implications. The he clapped his lower jaw back up. Jericho raised an eyebrow.

'You wanted to say something?'

'Later.'

They fell silent. Yoyo had fallen asleep on the back seat again. Once they were finally on the autobahn, dawn began to break and the traffic became busier. The navigation system issued muted directions. They approached Berlin Mitte, were directed towards Potsdamer Platz and, by 5.30 a.m., had secured spacious rooms on the seventh floor of the newly renovated Hyatt. An hour later, they sat down to breakfast. The choice was more than ample. Yoyo had overcome her tiredness and was shovelling immense quantities of scrambled eggs and bacon into her mouth. Tu, much less picky, instead made his way diagonally through what was on offer, managing to combine smoked fish and chocolate spread in such a repulsive way that Jericho had to avert his gaze. As usual, Tu didn't even seem to register what he was eating. He noisily watered down the melange with green tea and started to talk:

'You can't still be tired, you slept enough in Shanghai, so—'

'I didn't even get a wink of sleep,' groaned Yoyo. 'Only just then on the plane.'

'The same with me,' admitted Jericho. 'Every time I thought I was dropping off it felt as if I was falling into an electrical field.'

'God, that's it!' Yoyo opened her eyes wide and touched his hand, as though in reflex. 'That's exactly what it feels like. As if someone's running a bolt of electricity through you.'

'Yes, you jump—'

'And then you're awake again! The whole night through.'

'Interesting.' Tu looked at them each in turn and shook his head. 'I mean, I went through the little Depression of 2010, the Yuan Crisis of 2018, the recession two years ago – and I didn't let any of it rob me of my sleep.'

'Oh no?' drawled Yoyo. 'Did someone slaughter your friends in front of your eyes too, and then almost hound you to death afterwards?'

Tu cocked his head to one side.

'So you think you're the only person who's seen others die?'

'I have no idea.'

'Exactly.'

'I mean, I have no idea what *you've* seen.'

'If you don't have any idea—'

'No, I don't!' hissed Yoyo. 'And do you know why not? Because you and my father brood about your miserable pasts by yourselves! I don't care what you've both been through. Maggie, Tony, Jia Wei and Ziyi were shot into shreds in front of my eyes. Xiao-Tong, Mak and Ye are dead too. I don't even want to start on Grand Cherokee; and the fact that my father, Daxiong and Owen are still alive is bordering on a miracle. So I've allowed myself to lose a little sleep over it. Do you have any other clever comments?'

'You should keep your outbreaks of emotion—'

'No, *you* should!' Yoyo waved her hands around wildly in the air. 'Hongbing, tell your child the truth, you have to trust her, you can't keep up this silence any longer, blah blah blah. God, you're the master of blah blah blah, Tian, you're sooo understanding and constructive! But when it comes to you, you keep things under wraps, right?'

'If I could just—' interjected Jericho.

'You're no better than Hongbing, do you know that?'

'Hey!' Jericho leaned over. 'I've no idea why you guys came to Berlin, but I want to find Andre Donner, is that clear? So sort your issues out somewhere else.'

'Tell *him* that.'

Tu kneaded his hands morosely. He slurped tea, took a bite of a sausage, shoved the rest in after it, scrunched up his serviette and threw it carelessly onto the plate. Clearly he wasn't anywhere near as untouchable as he liked to imply. For a while, hurt silence reigned.

'Fine. As far as I'm concerned you can have a nap. But at some point in the course of the morning it would be advisable for you to stock up on the essentials, underwear, T-shirts, cosmetics, whatever. Perhaps we'll be back home again by this time tomorrow, but perhaps we won't. There's a shopping mall just opposite. Go and get what you need. After that we'll pay Muntu a visit. Is the place open at midday?'

'From twelve until two. According to the website.'

'Good.'

'I'm not sure.' Jericho tore a croissant to pieces indecisively. 'We shouldn't just all rock up there at once.'

'Why not?'

'We want to warn Donner, not make him take flight. A European-looking guy, a Chinese girl, fine. In the city we'd just look like a normal couple. But add another Chinese guy and Donner could get suspicious.'

'You think? Berlin is full of Chinese people.'

'Do they go to African restaurants?'

'Please! We're the most culturally open people in the world.'

'You're as open as a vacuum cleaner,' said Jericho. 'You suck up everything that isn't screwed on and riveted, but gastronomically you're all ignorant.'

'You're confusing us with the Japanese.'

'Not at all. The Japanese are culinary fascists. You lot, on the other hand, are just ignorant.'

'I'm sure things would look different at McDonald's.'

'Oh, come on!' Jericho couldn't help but laugh. Discussing food with Tu was almost as absurd as explaining the benefits of vegetarianism to a shark. 'When you guys are abroad you always go to Chinese restaurants, right? All I'm saying is that the man who now goes by the name of Donner has had bad experiences with Chinese people, if our theories are correct. He's being hunted. The organisation that Vogelaar and Kenny belong to want to kill him.'

'Hmm.' Tu pursed his lips. 'Perhaps you're right.'

'Of course he's right,' said Yoyo to her plate.

'Fine then, you two go to Muntu. I'll hold the fort here.'

'You could amuse yourself with Diane in the meantime,' suggested Jericho. 'Try to find out more about how Mayé was overthrown. And more about Ndongo. What drives him, what are his interests, who's supporting him? And why has there not been any more news from Equatorial Guinea?'

'I think I already know.'

Jericho stopped. Even Yoyo seemed to have overcome her hurt pride and was looking at him expectantly. Tu stretched out his fingers and massaged the globe of his belly.

'And?'

'Later.' Tu got up. 'You have things to do, I have things to do. Have a good sleep. After that you can go and exhaust my credit cards.'

Jericho would have preferred to track down Donner as soon as they landed and, if needs be, turn up on his doorstep and get him out of bed, but there was no private address on record for him anywhere. He instructed the hotel computer to wake him at 10 a.m. He feared he'd relive the nightmare of the previous night, interspersed with phases of just staring at his eyelids from the inside, but instead he slept a deep and dreamless sleep for two hours and awoke in a much better mood and full of purpose. Yoyo seemed more cheerful too. They made their way through the mall, purchased underwear, shirts and toothbrushes and commented on the everyday life going on around them. Yoyo bought several bottles of spray-on clothing. It was hot and sunny in Berlin, so they didn't need more than just a few things. Jericho avoided asking her about her private life. He didn't really know how to act around the girl in this relatively normal setting; for a change there wasn't anything to research, nor was there anything to run from. Yoyo displayed an almost dismissive lack of concern by skipping around in front of him in the tiniest of tops, touching him every few minutes, pulling him here and there and getting so close to him that the only possible explanation for her actions seemed to be her complete lack of sexual interest in him.

That's exactly what it is, concurred the pimply boy hiding in the shade at the corner of the playground, seeking comfort from Radiohead, Keane and Oasis. That's what women are like; you're just a thing to them, not someone who can express desire or intentions. A conglomerate of cells only spat into life to be a friend to them. They would rather be seduced by their teddy bears than acknowledge the possibility that you could fall in love with them.

Bite me, Jericho told him. Pussy.

After that, the pus-filled, pubescent-stubble-covered ghost retreated, and Yoyo's company really began to grow on him. Nonetheless, he was still relieved when it got closer to twelve and it was time to drive to Oranienburger Strasse. Muntu was on the ground floor of a beautifully renovated old building just a few hundred metres from the banks of the Spree, where Museum Island divided the water like a stranded whale. They almost walked right past it – the tiny restaurant was crammed furtively between an evangelical bookshop and a branch of the Bank of Beijing, as if it wanted to make a surprise attack on passersby. Over the door and windows was a cracked wooden panel with MUNTU in archaic-looking lettering, and underneath, *The Charm of African Cuisine*.

'It's cute,' said Yoyo as they stepped inside.

Jericho looked around. Ochre and banana-yellow coloured walls, offset with blue on the skirting boards. Batik-patterned tablecloths, above which paper lamps hung down like huge, glimmering turnips. Wooden pillars and ceiling beams were painted and decorated with carvings. The end wall of the square room was dominated by a bar of rustic design, and to the left of that swing doors covered with mythical images led through into the kitchen. There was no trace here of the battle sculptures, spears, shields and masks commonly found in similar establishments, an agreeable omission which suggested authenticity.

Only a few of the tables were occupied. Yoyo headed towards a table near the bar. A figure broke away from the half-shadow behind it and came over to them. The woman might have been in her early forties, possibly older. Wrinkles came late to African women, which made guessing their age a challenge. Her slim-fitting dress was hued with powerful, earthy colours, and a matching headdress unfurled from an explosion of Rasta locks. She was very dark and quite attractive, and had a laugh that didn't seem acquainted with the compromise of a smile.

'My name is Nyela,' she said in guttural German. 'Would you like a drink?'

Yoyo looked at Jericho, confused. He mimed bringing a glass to his lips.

'Ah, okay,' said Yoyo. 'Cola.'

'How boring.' Nyela switched to English instantly. 'Have you ever tried palm wine? It's fermented palm juice made from flower bulbs.'

Without waiting for an answer, she disappeared behind the bar, came back with two beakers of a milky-looking drink and laid out English menus in front of them.

'We're out of ostrich steak. I'll be back in a moment.'

Jericho took a sip. The wine tasted good, cool and a little sharp. Yoyo's gaze followed Nyela to the neighbouring table.

'What now?'

'We order something.'

'Why aren't you asking to see Donner? I thought it was urgent.'

'It is.' Jericho leaned over. 'I just don't think it's a good idea if we blurt it out just like that. In his position I would be a bit mistrustful if someone asked for me for no reason.'

'But we're not asking for no reason.'

'And what do you want her to tell him? That he's going to be killed? Then he'll slip through our fingers.'

'We'll have to ask for him at some point.'

'And we will.'

'Okay, fine, you're the boss.' Yoyo opened her menu. 'So what do you fancy today, boss? Ragout of kudu-antelope perhaps? Monkey penis with skinned-alive frogs?'

'Don't be silly.' Jericho let his gaze wander over the starters and main courses. 'It all sounds really good. Jolof rice, for example, I had that back in London.'

'Never had it.'

'All it takes is a little courage,' Jericho teased her. 'Think of how we Europeans have to suffer in Sichuan.'

'No, I'm not so sure. Adalu, akara, dodo.' Her eyes flitted back and forth. 'Look at the crazy names these things have. How about some nunu, Owen? Some nice nunu.'

Jericho paused. 'You're on the menu too.'

'Eh?'

'Efo-Yoyo Stew!' He laughed loudly. 'Well, we know what you're having then.'

'Are you insane? What on earth is it?' She wrinkled her brow and read: 'Spinach sauce with crabs and chicken and – ishu? What the devil is ishu?'

'Yam dumplings.' The black woman had come back over to their table. 'No party without yams.'

'What are yams?'

'It's a root. The queen of all roots! The women cook them and then pound them with a pestle and mortar. It really builds the muscles.' Nyela gave a deep and melodic laugh and showed them a well-sculpted bicep. 'Men are too lazy for it. Probably too dumb too, no offence, my friend.' Her hand clasped Jericho's shoulder in a familiar way. A spicy scent came off her, a raw seduction.

'You know what?' said Jericho cheerfully. 'Just put something together for us.'

'He's no fool,' said Nyela, winking at Yoyo. 'Letting the women decide.'

She disappeared into the kitchen. Not even ten minutes later, she came back bearing two trays groaning with dishes.

'*Paradise is here,*' she sang.

Yoyo, her face full of mistrust, watched as Nyela put down little plates and bowls in front of them.

'Ceesbaar, pancakes made from plantain. Akara, deep-fried dumplings with shrimps. Samosas, pastry parcels with minced beef. Those are moyinmoyin, bean cakes with crabs and turkey meat. Next to that is efo-egusi, spinach with melon seeds, beef and dried cod. Here, nunu, made from millet and yoghurt. Then adalu, bean and banana stew with fish. Brochettes, little fish skewers. Dodo, roasted in peanut oil, and – tapioca pudding!'

'Ah,' said Yoyo.

Jericho stretched out his finger and sampled the akara, samosas and moyinmoyin in quick succession.

'Delicious,' he cried, before Nyela could get away again. 'How is it possible that I'd never heard of this place before?'

Nyela hesitated. Catching sight of a raised hand at the neighbouring table, she excused herself, took their order, delivered it to the kitchen and then came back.

'That's easy,' she said. 'We only opened six months ago.'

Jericho was stuffing his mouth full of nunu while Yoyo nibbled timidly at one of the fish skewers. 'And where were you before that?'

'Africa. Cameroon.'

'You speak excellent English.'

'I can get by. German is much harder. It's a strange language.'

'Isn't Cameroon French-speaking?' asked Yoyo.

'African,' said Nyela, with a facial expression that implied Yoyo had just cracked a good joke. 'Cameroon *was* once French. A large part of it at any rate. Many languages are spoken there: Bantu, Kotoko and Shuwa, French, English, Camfranglais.'

'And you're the one who cooked all these wonderful things?' asked Jericho.

'Most of them.'

'Nyela, you're a goddess.'

Nyela laughed, so loudly that the paper lamps shook.

'Is he always this charming?' she wanted to know. 'Such a charming liar?'

Yoyo didn't answer, coughing instead. She seemed to have just realised that the spiciness of the pancakes struck with a malicious delay. Jericho took a slug of palm wine.

'Nyela, we've been play-acting a little. Muntu was actually recommended to us. So we're not here completely by chance. We would like to include you in a food guide. Would you be interested?'

'What kind of guide?'

'A virtual city guide,' said Yoyo, who had got a grip of herself again and, her eyes sparkling, picked up on Jericho's idea. 'People could get a three-dimensional experience of your restaurant in it by putting on holo-glasses. Are you familiar with holographics?'

Nyela shook her head, visibly amused. 'My speciality is the law, my child. I studied law in Jaunde.'

'Picture it like this. We produce a walk-in image of the restaurant as a computer program. With the necessary equipment, people can even take a peek into the cooking pots. But there is also a simpler version, just an entry online.'

'I can't say I fully understand, but it sounds good.'

'Are you in?'

'Of course.'

'Then we just need to take care of the formalities,' said Jericho. 'If I've been correctly informed, you're not the owner?'

'Muntu belongs to my husband.'

'Andre Donner?'

'Yes.'

'Oh, you're Mrs Donner?' He raised his eyebrows, feigning sudden realisation. 'May I ask – your husband – I mean, Donner isn't an African name—'

'Boer. Andre is from South Africa.'

'No, what a love story!' cried Yoyo in delight. 'South Africa and Cameroon.'

'And you two?' grinned Nyela. 'What's your story?'

Jericho was just about to reply when Yoyo's fingers flew nimbly across like a squirrel and covered his.

'Shanghai and London,' she whispered happily.

'Not bad either,' said Nyela cheerfully. 'I'll tell you what, my girl. Love is a language that everyone can understand. It's the only one you'll ever need.'

'We—' said Jericho.

'—are in love, and we work together,' smiled Yoyo. 'Just like you and your husband. It's so wonderful!'

Jericho could almost hear the string section warming up. He didn't know how to pull his hand back without making it look suspicious. Nyela looked at them both, visibly moved.

'And where did you meet?'

'In Shanghai.' Yoyo giggled. 'I was his tour guide. To be more specific, he had the glasses on, the holo things. Owen fell in love with my hologram, isn't that sweet? After that he did everything he could to get to know me. I didn't want to at first, but—'

'Amazing.'

'Yes, and you? Where did you meet your husband? South Africa? Or was it in Equatoria—'

'Sorry to interrupt,' interjected Jericho. 'But we still have a lot of things to do. So, Nyela, in order to prepare the entry we need to speak to your husband. We need his signature. Perhaps he's here now?'

Nyela looked at him thoughtfully with her shining white eyes. Then she pointed at the tapioca pudding.

'Have you tried it yet?'

'Not yet.'

'Then you're not going anywhere, not for the time being at least.' Her grin lit up the room. 'Not until you've eaten everything up.'

'No problem,' purred Yoyo. 'Owen loves African food. Don't you, poppet?'

Jericho thought he must be hearing things.

'I sometimes call him poppet,' Yoyo confided in Nyela, who seemed interested and not at all embarrassed. 'When we're by ourselves.'

'Like now?'

'Yes, like now. What do you think, poppet, shall we stay a little longer?'

Jericho stared at her. 'Of course, you old bag. Whatever you say.'

Yoyo's smile frosted over. Her fingers made their retreat. Jericho felt a mixture of regret and relief.

'Andre isn't here right now, by the way,' said Nyela. 'How long will you be in Berlin?'

'Not long. We've got an early flight.' Jericho scratched the back of his head. 'There isn't any chance that we could meet him at short notice, is there? This evening perhaps?'

'We're actually shut this evening. Although—' Nyela put a finger to her lips. 'Okay, wait a moment. I'll be back shortly.'

She disappeared through the swing doors.

'Did you really call me an old bag?' asked Yoyo under her breath.

'I did. And I meant it.'

'Oh. Thanks.'

'You're welcome, poppet.'

'But why?' she protested. 'What I said was nice! I said something nice, and you—'

'Consider yourself lucky I didn't say something worse.'

'Owen, what's all this about?' A steep fold was building up between Yoyo's brows. 'I thought you knew how to joke around.'

'You nearly let the cat out of the bag, you twit! You were about to say Equatorial Guinea.'

'I wasn't.'

'I heard it!'

'But she didn't.' Yoyo rolled her eyes. 'Okay, I'm sorry, calm down. At the very most she would have thought I said the equator. And that makes sense, right? Cameroon is on the equator.'

'*Gabon* is on the equator.'

'Daft know-all.'

'Toad.'

'Jerk!'

'Are we having a relationship crisis?' mocked Jericho. 'We shouldn't push it, darling, or we might as well leave right now.'

'So I'm the one that's pushed it too far? Because I was nice to you?'

'No, not because of that. Because you weren't being careful.' He knew he was reacting too harshly, but he was boiling over with rage.

Yoyo looked away morosely. They were still silent when Nyela came back to the table.

'What a shame,' she said. 'Andre is obviously on the move. And can't be reached. But he should be giving me a call sometime in the next few hours. Can you give me your mobile number? I'll call you.'

'Of course.' Jericho wrote his number on a paper serviette. 'I'll make sure my phone's turned on.'

'We'd like to be in this guide of yours.' Nyela laughed her throaty, African laugh. 'Even though I don't have a clue what hologoggles are.'

'We'll put you in,' smiled Jericho. 'With or without the goggles.'

'Wow, a restaurant guide. What a great idea!'

Yoyo fidgeted along behind him resentfully as they left Muntu. The midday light was crystal clear, a hot early summer Berlin day, the sky an upside-down, sparkling blue swimming-pool. But Jericho didn't stop to take it all in. He crossed the street, marched into the shade of the row of buildings opposite and halted so suddenly that Yoyo almost ran into him. He turned round and stared at the restaurant.

'She didn't notice anything,' Yoyo assured him. 'I'm sure she didn't.'

Jericho didn't answer. He gazed thoughtfully over at Muntu. Yoyo paced on the spot, planted herself in front of him and then waved her hand around in front of his eyes.

'Everything okay, Owen? Is there anyone at home?'

He rubbed the bridge of his nose. Then he looked at his watch.

'Fine, you don't have to speak to me,' she warbled. 'We can write to each other. Yes, that's a good idea! You can write everything down on a little piece of paper and give it to someone to give to me. And I—'

'You can make yourself useful.'

'Oh, you do have a voice!' Yoyo bowed in front of an imaginary audience. 'Ladies and gentlemen, the moment you've all been waiting for. The man has spoken. It is with great pride that we present to you—'

'You can shadow Nyela.'

'Excuse me?'

'I've no idea whether she noticed your slip or not, but there's one thing I don't buy: her claim that Donner couldn't be reached.'

'Why?'

'She was in the kitchen too long.'

'You mean that Donner would be suspicious if someone wanted to include his restaurant in a guide?'

'You said it yourself – a great idea,' Jericho flashed back at her. 'Your irony was clear enough.'

'Could you stop being mad at me for just a minute?'

'There are two possibilities. Either she bought it. Which doesn't necessarily mean that he did. But it doesn't really matter what story we dished up. Donner will be suspicious by nature, towards everyone and everything. The second possibility is that she didn't believe a word we said. Either way, he needs to find out who we are, what we want from him and what we have to tell him. He needs to make quite certain. I'd hazard a guess that they've already spoken on the phone. If Nyela leaves the restaurant it could be that she's going to meet him. Either that or he'll turn up here.'

'What for?'

'To get here before someone can surprise him on his own premises. Or maybe just because he has garlic to chop. Things to do, whatever.'

'Which means you'll watch the restaurant?'

Jericho nodded. 'Did you notice the camera?' he asked, trying to make the tone of his voice more gentle now.

'What camera?'

'There was one installed above the bar. It didn't look like one, but I'm familiar with them. Muntu is under surveillance. Perhaps Donner will want to look at the recording before he agrees to a meeting.'

'And what if none of that's right? What if you're wrong?'

'Then we wait until Nyela calls us. Or until she leads you to Donner's private residence.'

'I mean, if he's not suspicious at all. If he really does want to meet us about the food guide, just not until this evening. Aren't we frittering away the chance to warn him *in time*? Shouldn't we tell Nyela the truth?'

'And have him take off? We didn't come here to save his life, but to find something out from him. And to do that we need to *meet* him!'

'I know that,' retorted Yoyo irritably. 'But if he's already dead he can't tell us anything anyway.'

'Yoyo, for God's sake, I know that! But what are we supposed to do? We have to take a risk. And, believe me, he *is* mistrustful! He may even mistrust Nyela.'

'His own wife?'

'Yes, his wife. Do you trust her?'

'Okay, fine,' murmured Yoyo. 'So I'll shadow Nyela then.'

'Do that. Call me if you notice anything.'

'I might need the car.'

Jericho looked around and spotted a Starbucks. They had parked the Audi a few metres further down, in full sight of Muntu.

'No problem. We'll sit over there, have a coffee and keep our eyes on the restaurant. If she goes anywhere, you follow her. On foot, by car, whatever's necessary. I'll hold the fort here.'

'We don't even know what Donner looks like.'

'White, I guess. It's a Boer name, South African—'

'Great,' said Yoyo. 'That narrows it down considerably.'

'I could easily widen it again. Donner might be from a mixed marriage. He wouldn't be the first black person on the Cape to have a white surname.'

'You sure know how to look on the bright side, don't you?'

'I'm renowned for it.'

Jericho had committed the faces of the other guests in the restaurant to memory. After he and Yoyo left, three more couples had gone in, as well as a lone old man accompanied by his incessantly yapping alter ego. In the time that followed, they watched as Muntu emptied person by person. The man and dog were the last to leave, and after that Jericho was convinced there were no guests left inside. More time passed. Yoyo drank tea by the bucketful. Shortly after three, a dark-skinned man came out onto the street, unchained a bicycle and pedalled off. Clearly one of the kitchen staff, perhaps Nyela's sous-chef.

'So this is what you do?' Yoyo asked, somehow managing not to sound scornful. 'Spy on people for hours on end?'

'Most of the time I'm online.'

'Uh-huh. And what do you do there?'

'Spy on people.'

'It's so *dull*.' She pulled a dripping teabag from her cup. 'One big, long, boring wait.'

'I don't entirely agree with you. There are a lot of fun aspects and it's certainly lively. From time to time someone sets a steelworks on fire. There are lovely little chases, you get to save people and fly halfway across the world at the drop of a hat. Is your life so much more exciting?'

Expecting her to protest, he stared back out of the window, but Yoyo seemed to be giving it serious thought.

'No,' she said. 'It's not. But it is more social.'

'But society can do your head in,' said Jericho, then brought up his hand to silence her. Nyela was just leaving Muntu. She had swapped the colourful folklore of her dress for jeans and a T-shirt.

'Time for your mission,' he said.

Yoyo dropped her teabag, gathered up the car keys and her mobile and ran outside. Jericho watched as she started the car. Nyela paced away in lengthy strides and disappeared around the corner of a house. The car followed her slowly. Jericho hoped Yoyo wouldn't be too obvious. He had tried to give her a brief overview of the basic rules of a subtle observation, which included not ramming your bumper right into the behind of the person you were observing.

She phoned just ten minutes later.

'There's a parking lot two streets down. Nyela just left it.'

'What's she driving?'

'A Nissan OneOne. SolarHybrid.'

A small, nimble town car, designed for heavy traffic, which could reduce its floor space by shortening the wheel base. Against that, the Audi was a cumbersome monstrosity, only superior on highways.

'Stay close to her,' he said. 'Let me know if anything happens.'

After that he rang Tu and brought him up to date.

'And how's it going there?'

'I'm having fun with Diane,' said Tu. 'A lovely program. Not top of the range any more, mind, but we're having a good time nonetheless.'

'The program is completely new,' protested Jericho.

'New is something that hasn't been built yet,' Tu advised him.

'Get to the point.'

'So, with regard to Ndongo: he seems to be striving for more balance than during his first time in office, and is resisting influence from the Chinese, but this time without snubbing Beijing. His sympathies clearly lie with Washington and the EU. On the other hand, he made it known at the beginning of the year that he wants to consider the interests of all countries equally, as long as they don't show tendencies towards economic annexation. He also pushed a few scraps over to Sinopec. Other than that, he's trying to clean up the pigsty that Mayé left behind.'

'He sounds like less of a puppet than before.'

'That's right. And do you know why? We all know! They've got oil and gas down there. And by the tonne. The answer to questions that no one's asking any more. That's where the problem lies, and it seems it became Mayé's problem too. Do you see?'

'Helium-3?'

'What else?'

Of course! Everyone knew it. It was just that they also quickly forgot who was affected by the shift in circumstances brought about by the Moon business.

'At the start of 2020 it was clear that helium-3 would supersede fossil fuels,' said Tu. 'The United States put all their eggs in one basket. Into the development of the space elevator, the extension of the infrastructure on the Moon, the commercial backing of helium-3, Julian Orley. He, in turn, worked feverishly on his fusion reactors. Orley and the USA created an immense bubble back then. It could have all gone horribly wrong if it had burst. The biggest company of all time would have exploded like a cluster bomb, the USA would have suffered painful losses in fossil poker with their unilateral arrangement on the Moon, millions and millions of people would have lost their money. Africa would have been able to continue swimming in wealth, financing the never-ending civil wars from oil income and dictating conditions to the rich nations. Think back to the barrel price in 2019.'

'It was still up then.'

'For the last time. Because we know it worked! Orley and the USA built their elevator, and the first one ever at that! I've researched it in detail, Owen. On 1 August 2022 the moon base was put into operation, and a few days later, so was the American mining station. Two weeks later the mining of helium-3 officially began. A month and a half later, on 5 October, the first Orley reactor went onto the network and fulfilled all expectations. The fusion age had begun; helium-3 became the energy source of the future. In December, the barrel price of oil was a hundred and twenty dollars, the following February it sank to seventy-six dollars, and in March China followed suit and sent its first helium-3 deliveries to Earth, albeit with conventional rocket technology and in minute quantities. Nonetheless, the two most commodity-hungry nations were on the Moon. Others panted along behind them: India, Japan, the Europeans, all obsessed with staking their claim. It's not that oil didn't play a part any more, but the dependence on it was dwindling. The summer of 2023, fifty-five dollars a barrel. Autumn, forty-two dollars. Even that was fairly high, but it kept going down. People expected brisk trade, that it would never be that cheap again, but they were wrong. The important consumer nations had stocked up their supplies in good time. No one sees the need for more depots, and in the car sector electricity becomes a serious option. The countries that export fossil fuels, which have relied exclusively on their income from the oil and gas trade and therefore neglected their native economy, feel the full impact of the resource curse, particularly in Africa. Potentates like Obiang or Mayé see the end dawning. Now they have to pay the price for milking their countries to death. They don't make the rules any more. Their pals from overseas, who they played off so wonderfully against each other for decades on end, have had enough of being messed around and having very little to show for it, and now, to top it all off, they aren't interested in oil any more either! That, my friend, is the reason why Washington's indignation over Mayé sounded more and more scripted as time went on. For China it's a done deal, catching up with America and freeing itself from the fossil fetters. So what does the crazed man go and do?'

'You're not seriously suggesting that Mayé started his idiotic space programme in order to land on the Moon and develop helium-3?'

'Yes. Precisely that.'

'Tian, please. He was a madman. The torturer of a country where the greatest technological achievement was the painstaking maintenance of a functioning power network.'

'Of course. But he said it.'

'That he wanted to go to the Moon? Mayé?'

'That's what he said. Diane found quotations. He was clearly an idiot. On the other hand, experts attested to the launch pad being in good working order. He sent a news satellite into orbit with it, at any rate.'

'Which broke down.'

'Regardless. The launch was successful.'

'How did he finance even the launch pad?'

'I guess he used the national budget. Shut down hospitals, I don't know. The interesting thing is that Mayé's overthrow definitely wasn't the result of other countries' interest in his oil. So what worried Beijing so much that they felt it necessary to get rid of the ruling clique of a tiny little country which had become entirely uninteresting, both economically and politically – and right down to the very last man? With this question in mind, I kept looking – and I found something.'

'Tell me.'

'On 28 June 2024, a month before his death, Mayé publicly chastised the exploit-ative nature of the First World on national television and directed explicit accusations at Beijing. He claimed that China had dropped Africa like a hot potato, the money promised to them had never materialised, and above all, that they were responsible for the entire continent withering away.'

'Who did he think he was, Africa's lawyer?'

'Yes, it's laughable, isn't it? But then, while he was saying all this, he let something slip that he shouldn't have. He said that if Beijing didn't fulfil its obligations, he would be forced to hawk information about that would incriminate China all over the world. He publicly threatened the Party.' Tu paused. 'And a month later he was no longer able to talk.'

'And he made no indication of what that information was?'

'Indirectly, yes. He said that his country wouldn't let anyone bring it down. And, in particular, that the space programme would be extended and another satellite launched, and that certain contemporaries would be well advised to offer their full support unless they wanted a rude awakening.'

Jericho paused. 'What did China have to do with Mayé's space programme?'

'Officially, nothing. But even the dumbest person can figure out that no one in Equatorial Guinea was in a position to build something like that. I mean, physically speaking maybe, but not to make the whole thing a reality. The only thing Mayé came up with was the idea. He waved his millions, and they came from all around: engineers, constructors, physicists. French, German, Russian, American, Indian, from all over the world. But if you look a little closer, one name in particular stands out – Zheng Pang-Wang.'

'The Zheng Group?' Jericho blurted out, amazed.

'That's the one. Large parts of the construction were in Zheng's hands.'

'As far as I know, Zheng is closely connected with the Chinese space travel programme.'

'Space travel and reactor technologies. Zheng Pang-Wang isn't just one of the ten richest men in the world, and one with an enormous influence on Chinese politics at that – he also seems to have decided to become Julian Orley's Chinese counterpart. The cadre are resting their biggest hopes on him. They expect that, sooner or later, he'll build them their own space elevator and a functioning fusion reactor. So far, though, he hasn't delivered either of them. There's a rumour that he's putting much more energy into infiltrating and spying on Orley Enterprises. In official circles he's trying to get Orley to collaborate. There's even talk that Orley and Zheng like each other, but that doesn't necessarily mean anything.'

Jericho thought for a moment. 'Mayé's assassins acted fast, don't you think?'

'Suspiciously so, if you ask me.'

'Conjuring Ndongo up out of nowhere, and then the logistics of the attack. You can't plan something like that in four weeks.'

'I agree with you. The coup was prepared just in case Mayé said the wrong thing.'

'Which he did—'

'Excuse me, Owen,' said Diane's voice. 'May I interrupt you?'

'What's up, Diane?'

'I have a Priority A call for you. Yoyo Chen Yuyun.'

'No problem,' said Tu. 'I've told you everything I needed to anyway. Keep me posted, okay?'

'I will. Put her through, Diane.'

'Owen?' Yoyo's voice came through, embedded in street sounds. 'Nyela got out of the car in the city centre. I followed her for a bit; she was looking in the shop windows and speaking on the phone. She didn't look particularly worked up or concerned. Two minutes ago she met a man, and now they're both sitting in the sun in front of a café.'

'Doing what?'

'Chatting, having a drink. The guy is dark, but not black, perhaps mixed race. Around fifty years old. You saw the photos of Mayé and his staff. Did any of them look like that?'

'There aren't that many photos. And none of them show all of his staff. There's always someone or other next to him, but you could try searching for the list of his ministers that died during the attack.' Jericho tried to remember the pictures. 'None of them had that skin-colour, I think.'

'What should I do?'

'Keep at it. How are they acting around each other?'

'Friendly. A little kiss when they met, a hug. Nothing extreme.'

'Do you have a rough idea where you are?'

'We drove over that river twice – the Sprii, Spraa, Spree – one crossing right after the other. The café is in an old railway station, one built in brick with round arches, but nicely renovated. Wait a moment.'

Yoyo marched along the brick façade and looked out for any markings, street signs or the name of the station. Hordes of people were streaming down from the steps of the subway station. Owing to the beautiful weather, the forecourt looked as if it were under siege: young people and tourists were pushing the turnover in the numerous pubs, bars, bistros and restaurants sky-high. Clearly Nyela had led her into one of the hip quarters of the city. Yoyo liked it here. It reminded her a little of Xintiandi.

'Don't worry,' said Jericho. 'I think I know where you are. You must have driven over Museum Island.'

'I'll be able to tell you in a second.'

'Okay.'

Yoyo spotted a white S on a green background. Next to it, something was written in light green lettering. She opened her lips and hesitated. How did one pronounce s, c and h one behind the other?

'Hacke – s – cher – Mar—'

'Hackescher Markt?'

'Yes. It could be that.'

'Okay. Keep your eye on both of them. If nothing happens here I'll come and join you.'

'Okay.'

She ended the call and turned round. The station was excreting an even bigger contingent of travellers, most of whom seemed to be trying to catch up on the time they had lost. The rest, chattering away, spread out amongst the folding chairs and tables of the outdoor eateries, on the hunt for free seats. Suddenly, Yoyo found herself staring at a battery of backs. She stuck her elbows out and pushed her way forward. A waiter circled over like a fighter jet and made a move to run her down. With a dart, she managed to escape behind a little green and yellow tree. Scribble-covered boards were obstructing her view. She ran out past the tables into the square, and approached the café with the blue and white striped awning, under which Nyela and the light-skinned black man were sitting.

Were *supposed* to be sitting.

Yoyo's heart skipped a beat. She ran inside. No one. Back out again. No Nyela, no companion.

'Shit,' she mumbled. 'Shit, shit, shit!'

But cursing wouldn't bring them back again, so she rushed back out onto the main street, to where Nyela had succeeded in securing a parking place in rush hour and where she herself had parked the car beneath a strict 'No Parking' sign.

The Nissan was gone. Breaking down both physically and mentally, she ran on, issuing pleading looks in all directions, up and down the street, begging fate for mercy, just to curse it the very next moment, and then finally gave up, out of breath and with sharp pains in her sides. None of it helped. She had cocked it up. All because of a lousy sign. Just because she had insisted on being able to tell Jericho where she was.

How was she supposed to tell him *this*?

A lighter-skinned black man around fifty years old. Jericho tried to imagine him. He could fit in with Nyela in terms of age.

Andre Donner?

Indecisive, he looked over at Muntu. It was all quiet. The lights were out, as far as he could tell through the mirrored glass anyway. After a few minutes he pulled out his mobile, logged into Diane's database and loaded the photos of Mayé they had found on the internet.

Almost all of them came from online articles about the coup. The whole thing had made waves only in the West African media, where sumptuously illustrated biographies of the dead dictator had appeared as a result of the putsch: Mayé on a visit to a waterworks, Mayé inspecting a military parade, Mayé orating, patting children's heads, flanked by oil workers on a platform. A man who, even in the pictures, oozed physical presence and narcissism. Anyone who managed to make it into a picture with him seemed strangely out of focus, insignificant, overshadowed, irrele-vant. Aided by the captions, Jericho identified ministers and generals who had died in the coup. The others pictured remained nameless. What united them was their dark or very dark skin colour, typical of the equatorial regions.

Jericho loaded the film which showed Mayé with Vogelaar, various ministers, representatives from the army and the two Chinese managers at the conference table. He zoomed in on the faces and studied the background. A uniformed man sat two seats behind Vogelaar, following the Chinese presentation with an arrogantly bored expression; he might have passed for lighter-skinned, but then again it could just have been down to the effect of the overhead lighting.

Was one of them Donner?

He looked up and stopped short.

The entrance door to Muntu was open.

No, it had just swung shut! Behind the glass, a tall shadow became visible and disappeared into the reflections of the building opposite. Jericho suppressed a curse. While he had turned his attention to the idiotic task of trying to recognise a man he had never seen amongst a group of complete strangers, someone had gone in over there. If he really had gone in, that is, and not opened the door from the inside. Hastily, he pushed his chair back, tucked away his mobile and walked outside.

Was it Donner he'd seen?

He crossed the street, cupped his hands around his eyes and peered in through the small window. The restaurant lay in darkness. No one to be seen. The only thing of note was a blue flicker from a defective emergency light, behind the small windows in the swing doors that led to the kitchen.

Had his senses been playing tricks on him?

No, there was no chance of that.

He pushed against the door. Cool, stagnant restaurant air wafted towards him. He glanced quickly around at the tautly pulled tablecloths, the motionless ferns and the bar. From the other side of the swing doors he heard a machine start up, possibly an air-conditioner. He froze and listened. No more sounds. Nothing to suggest that anyone was here apart from him.

But where could the man have disappeared to?

Automatically, his right hand grazed the hilt of his Glock. It was resting in its usual place, narrow and discreet. Even though he had come to warn Donner, there was no way of predicting how the man would respond to his visit. He paced lightly over to the bar and looked behind the ornate counter. No one. Behind the swing doors, the gleam of light flickered icily. He went back into the middle of the room and turned his head towards the bead curtain in front of the toilets. Thinking that he saw some of the cords swinging softly, he looked more closely. Like naughty children caught in the act, they froze into motionlessness.

He blinked.

Nothing was moving. Nothing at all. Nonetheless, he went closer and peeped through the bead lattice into a short, gloomy corridor.

'Andre Donner?'

He didn't expect any answer, nor did he get one. The door on the left led, as far as he could tell, to the men's toilets, and opposite them was their female counterpart. At the end of the corridor was another door, marked 'Private'. He pushed his hand between the cords, awakening them to a lively murmur, then pulled them further apart. He hesitated. Maybe he should put off the inspection of the toilets and the private room until later. His gaze wandered back to the swing doors, and at that moment the hum of the generator stopped. He could now clearly hear—

Nothing.

He had preferred the sounds of the machine.

'Andre Donner?'

He was answered by dry stillness. Even the noises from the street seemed to be cut off here. Slowly, he walked over to the swing doors and peered through one of the tiny windows. There wasn't much to see. A little world of its own, made up of chrome and white tiles, chopped up in a strobe effect by the defective fluorescent lamp. The archaic body of a gas cooker with dark attachments, covered by a tarnished cooker hood. The corner of a workbench. Roasting pans and pots were piled up in a cupboard.

He walked in.

The kitchen wasn't that small after all. It was surprisingly spacious for a restaurant like Muntu. Three walls were taken up with shelves, cupboards, fridges, a sink unit, oven and microwave. Along the fourth wall were storage surfaces and struts, draped with casserole dishes, pans, soup ladles and splatter screens. A longish work table took up the centre of the room, occupied at the stove end by two huge pans, bowls of finely chopped vegetables under cling film and closed polystyrene boxes. As if to balance it out, a huge slicing machine was enthroned at the opposite end. The kitchen smelled of stock, congealed frying fat, disinfectant and the cold sweetness of thawing meat. The latter was resting half-covered on a baking tray, pale brown in the pulsing light and coated with iridescent skin, its bones protruding. It looked like the hind leg of some huge animal. Kudu-antelope, thought Jericho. He couldn't picture the breed, but he was sure he was staring at the leg of an antelope. He suddenly pictured the whitish tendons and ligaments under the fur of a living creature, a masterpiece of evolution which enabled the animal to take such stupendous leaps. A highly developed flight mechanism, but ultimately useless against the smallest and quickest of all predators, the rifle barrel. Cautiously, he went closer to the stove. The bluish flicker was increasingly reminiscent of an insecticide device, every flicker a record of death. Smeared wings and little legs, compound eyes, staring unfazed before they boiled in the electronic heat and exploded. In the crystal silence, he could now hear the humming of the lights too, their stumbling clicking when they sprang on and then died again, like some strange code. His gaze fell on a cas-serole dish on the stove. The contents gripped his attention. He looked in. Something was wriggling in it, something that seemed to be alive and squirming in the pulse of the lights, a headless, rolled-up snake.

Jericho stared at it.

He suddenly felt the temperature fall by several degrees. Pressure exerted itself on his chest as fingers encircled his heart, trying to bring it to a standstill. The hairs on the back of his neck stood up. He felt someone breathing behind him and knew that he was no longer alone in the kitchen. The other person had stalked in without a sound, appeared from nowhere, a professional, a master of disguise.

Jericho turned round.

The man was considerably taller than him, dark-haired, with a strong jawline and light, penetrating eyes. In an earlier life he had had a beard and been ash-blond, something which was only detectable from his light eyelashes and brows, but Jericho recognised him at once. He was familiar with the faces of this man; he had seen them again just a few minutes ago, on the display of his mobile.

Jan Kees Vogelaar.

Alarmed thoughts came in a rush: Vogelaar was waiting for Donner in order to kill him. Had already killed him. A body in the freezer cabinet. And he was in the worst possible position, much too close to his opponent. Unbelievable stupidity on his part, to have gone into the kitchen. The ghostly effect of the flickering neon light. The weapon in Vogelaar's hand, pointing at his abdomen. Talk or fight? The failure of rational thinking.

Reflexes.

He ducked and aimed a blow at Vogelaar's wrist. A shot freed itself from the weapon, echoing into the base of the cooker. Springing back up, he rammed his skull against the man's chin, saw him stagger, grabbed the saucepan and hurled it towards him. A twitching alien whipped out, the skinned body of the snake. It smacked Vogelaar in the face, the casserole dish scraped his forehead. With all his strength, Jericho kicked out at the hand holding the gun, which clattered to the floor and slid under the workbench. He reached for his Glock, grasped the hilt and tumbled backwards as if he'd just been hit by a ram. Vogelaar had got a grip of himself, turned on his own axis as quick as lightning, flung up his right leg and given him a kick in the chest.

All the air drained from his lungs. Helpless, he crashed into the cooker. Vogelaar whirled up to him like a dervish. The next kick got him in the shoulder, another, his knee. He fell to the floor with a cry. The huge man leaned over, grabbed his lower arm and rammed it hard against the edge of the cooker, again and again. Jericho's fingers twitched, opened out. Somehow he managed to maintain his grip on the Glock and sink his left hand into Vogelaar's solar plexus, but it had zero impact. His opponent hit his lower arm again. A sharp pain flooded through him. This time, the pistol flew out of his hand in a wide arc. He punched Vogelaar's ribs repeatedly with his free hand, around his kidneys, then felt the grip around his arm loosen. Released, he crawled sideways.

Where was the Glock?

There! Not even half a metre away.

He threw himself forwards. Vogelaar was quicker, pulling Jericho up and hurling him towards one of the huge pans. Instinctively, he tried to get a grip on it, buckled over as Vogelaar kicked him in the back of his knees, and ripped the pan down with him as he fell. A torrent of greasy broth gushed down over him, hailing bones, vegetables and meat. Filthy and wet, he writhed around on the kitchen floor, then saw the other man leaning over him, saw his fist coming down towards him, grabbed the empty pan with both hands and rammed it as hard as he could against Vogelaar's shins.

The South African tried to suppress a cry of pain and stumbled. Like an amphibian, Jericho glided through the pool of liquid, grabbed a bowl of finely chopped tomato and threw it at Vogelaar, then another, fruit salad relieved of gravity: mango, pineapple and kiwi in free fall. For a few seconds his adversary was busy with dodging manoeuvres, giving him enough time to gain a metre of distance before the giant attacked again. Jericho fled around the workbench, grabbed the struts of a high cabinet, bringing pots, tins, bowls and sifters, pans, casserole dishes and cutlery drawers crashing down to the floor. Vogelaar sprang back, away from the avalanche. In no time, half of the kitchen was blocked. There was only one route left, along the opposite side of the workbench.

But Vogelaar was closer to the swing doors.

You idiot, Jericho cursed to himself. You've backed yourself right into the trap.

The South African bared his teeth sneeringly. He seemed to be thinking exactly the same thing, except that Jericho's predicament was visibly cheering him. Eyeing each other, they paused, each clasping their end of the workbench. In the flicker of the neon light Jericho had the opportunity to get a good look at the man for the first time. His short-term memory simultaneously unearthed the birth date of the former mercenary, and he suddenly realised that his opponent was long past sixty. A fighting machine of pensionable age, against which the privilege of youth withered away, a farce. Vogelaar didn't seem in the slightest bit tired, while he was puffing like a steam engine. He saw the man's eyes light up, reflecting the flicker of the neon light. Then, without any warning, it went dark.

The light had given up the ghost. Vogelaar faded into a silhouette, a black mass emitting a low, triumphant laugh. Jericho narrowed his eyes. The only light still coming in was through the gaps in the swing doors, just enough to see the only remaining escape route. Like a crab, he shuffled out from the protection of his cover. As if mirroring his movements, the silhouette of the South African set itself in motion too. An illusion. He wouldn't get to the doors fast enough. Perhaps a little conversation was advisable.

'Hey, let's cut the crap, shall we?'

Silence.

'We won't achieve anything like this. We should talk.'

The disheartened tremolo in his voice wasn't good at all. Jericho took a deep breath and tried again.

'This is a misunderstanding.' That was better. 'I'm not your enemy.'

'How stupid do you think I am?'

An answer, at least, albeit croaky and threatening and not exactly emanating a desire for understanding. The silhouette came closer. Jericho backed off, grappled behind him, got hold of something jagged and heavy and closed his fingers around it in the hope that it was suitable as a weapon.

With a dry bang, the lights sprang back on.

Vogelaar stormed over, swinging a worryingly long kitchen knife, and Jericho was paralysed by a déjà vu. Shenzhen. Ma Liping, the paradise of the little emperors. At the very last second, he pulled up what he was holding in his hand. The knife sliced the radish in two, whizzed through the air and missed him by a hair. Jericho stumbled backwards. The giant chased him around the table towards the upturned cabinet. On a wing and a prayer, he reached into the pile of kitchen utensils that had poured out from it, grabbed hold of a baking sheet and held it in front of him like a shield. Clanging steel screeched over aluminium. He wouldn't be able to fend off Vogelaar's enraged attacks for long, so he grabbed the tray with both hands and went on the attack, swinging it around wildly and landing an audible hit. Vogelaar swayed. Jericho threw the tray at his head, fell to the floor, rolled under the table through to the other side, sprang to his feet and started to run. Vogelaar would have to go around the table—

Vogelaar went *over* the table.

Just centimetres before the door he felt himself get grabbed and pulled back with such force that he lost his footing. Effortlessly, Vogelaar spun him around and knocked him down. He crashed against something hard, making him lose his hearing and sight, then realised that the South African was holding his head against the meat slicing machine. The next moment, the blade began to rotate. Jericho wriggled, trying to break free. Vogelaar turned his arm behind his back until it made a cracking sound. The blade sped up.

'Who are you?'

'Owen Jericho,' he wheezed, his heart in his throat. 'Restaurant critic.'

'And what do you want here?'

'Nothing, nothing at all. Donner, to speak to Donner—'

'Andre Donner?'

'Yes. Yes!'

'About a restaurant review?'

'Yes, damn it!'

'With a gun?'

'I—'

'Wrong answer.' The South African pressed his head against the metal and pushed it towards the racing blade. 'And a wrong answer costs an ear.'

'No!'

Jericho gave a howl. Burning pain shot through his outer ear. In fear and panic, he kicked his feet out and heard a muffled blow. The pressure on his shoulder suddenly gave way. Vogelaar slumped over him. He pulled himself to his feet, saw his torturer stagger and rammed his elbow into his face. The other man sank his fingers into his belt, then toppled over. Jericho held onto the edge of the table to avoid being dragged down with him. Something big and dark landed on the back of Vogelaar's head. The man collapsed and didn't move again.

Yoyo was staring at him, both hands clasped around the bones of the frozen antelope leg.

'My God, Owen! Who is this arsehole?'

Dazed, Jericho felt behind his ear and touched raw, ripped-open flesh. When he looked at his finger, it was red with blood.

'Jan Kees Vogelaar,' he mumbled.

'Damn it! And Donner?'

'No idea.' He drew air into his lungs. Then he crouched down next to the motionless body. 'Quick, we have to turn him over.'

Without asking any more questions, Yoyo threw the antelope leg aside and helped him. With combined effort, they managed to roll Vogelaar onto his back.

'You're bleeding,' she said, casually.

'I know.' He opened Vogelaar's belt buckle and pulled it out of the loops. 'Is there any of my ear left?'

'Hard to say. It doesn't really look like an ear any more.'

'That's what I was afraid of. Back on his stomach.'

The same sweat-inducing process. He bent Vogelaar's lower arms behind him and tied them tightly together. The unconscious man breathed heavily and groaned. His fingers twitched.

'Clobber him again if necessary,' said Jericho, looking around. 'We'll manoeuvre him over to the fridge over there. The one next to the microwave.'

Together, they gripped the heavy body under the arms, dragged it across the tiles and lifted it up. Vogelaar weighed around a hundred kilos, but his groaning and blinking suggested that he wasn't far from regaining consciousness. Hastily, Jericho whipped his own belt off and tied him to the fridge door handle with it. Sitting upright and with his head dangling down, the South African now had a martyred look about him. The flickering of the neon light became a constant, sterile brightness. Yoyo had found the light switch. Jericho crept over the kitchen floor, spotted his Glock and his opponent's pistol and seized both.

'Bastard,' spluttered Vogelaar, as if he were spitting snot into the gutter.

Jericho handed Yoyo the pistol and fixed his gaze on the restrained man.

'You should choose your words more carefully. I might be offended. I could, for example, think about the fact that my ear hurts, and who I have to thank for that.'

The South African stared at him, with a look full of hate. Suddenly, he began to tear at his shackles like mad. The fridge moved forward a centimetre. Jericho released the safety-catch on the Glock and pressed it against Vogelaar's nose.

'Wrong reaction,' he said.

'Kiss my ass!'

'And a wrong reaction will cost you the tip of your nose. Do you want to go through life without a nose, Vogelaar? Do you want to look like an idiot?'

Vogelaar ground his jaw, but stopped his attempts to free himself. Clearly the idea of a noseless existence bothered him more than the threat of losing his life.

'Why all the fuss?' he asked sullenly. 'I mean, you're going to shoot me anyway.'

'Why do you think that?'

'Why?' Vogelaar laughed with disbelief. 'Man, don't bother messing around.'

His healthy eye wandered over to Yoyo. The glass eye stared straight ahead. 'What's with you guys anyway? I thought Kenny would insist on finishing off the job himself.'

Inside Jericho's brain, cogs interlocked, circuits loaded up, and the Department for Astonishing Developments and Incomprehensible Activities started its working day.

'You know Kenny?'

Vogelaar blinked, confused. 'Of course I know him.'

'Now listen here,' said Jericho, crouching down. 'We have a document, only fragmentary admittedly, but I'd have to be a real idiot not to realise that you're here to kill Andre Donner. So, first things first. Let's start with Donner, okay? Where is he?'

Something in Vogelaar's gaze changed. His rage gave way to pure, complete confusion.

'You're wrong,' he said. 'You'd have to be a complete idiot to believe that I'm here to do that.'

'Where in God's name is Andre Donner?'

'Are you completely stupid, or what? I'm—'

'For the last time!' screamed Jericho. 'Where is he?'

'Look!' the man tied to the fridge screamed back at him. 'Open your eyes.'

Well, said the manager of the Department for Astonishing Developments and Incomprehensible Activities, it looks like we'll miss out on the award for lateral thinking again.

'I don't understand—'

'He's sitting in front of you! I – *am* – Andre – Donner!'

Mercenary

The wars of the modern age, explicitly the First and Second World Wars, are regarded as international conflicts, established on the basis of the laws of war and executed by state-owned forces. In many parts of the world, this has led to the mistaken notion that soldiers have in actual fact always been armed civil servants, who earn money even when there is no one to attack and nothing to defend. It's un-imaginable that divisions of the US Army, the Royal Air Force, the *forces armées* or the Bundeswehr would rampage through their own country plundering and raping. The introduction of compulsory military service actually seemed to herald the end of the forces which had decisively shaped warfare until then. King David's Kerethites and Pelethites, the Greek hoplites in Persia's army, the marauding hordes of late mediaeval Brabants and Armagnacs, mercenaries in the Thirty Years War and private armies in colonialist Africa: they all served whoever happened to be the most generous master at the time. They were paid for fighting, not for sitting around in barracks.

In the twentieth century, the retreat of the colonial powers lured many mercenaries into the turmoil of post-independence Africa, where persecution and expulsion, coups and genocide were the order of the day under the new, ethnically disunited rulers. Ordered not to intervene, the West began to secure its interests with the help of private troops rather than on an official level – for example their efforts to oppose the establishment of communism on African soil. The communists' approach was no different. States like South Africa also got themselves paramilitary task forces like Koevoet, and procured lucrative long-term positions for the contract soldiers. The old-style mercenary seemed to have found his niche in amongst the dictators and rebels.

Then everything changed.

With a sigh from history, the Soviet empire collapsed; without a whimper, banal and irretrievable. East Germany ceased to exist. London's U-turn called the IRA into question, apartheid came to an end on the Cape, the Cold War was declared over, Great Britain and the USA reduced their troops, and political change in South America discredited thousands in the armed forces. All over the world, soldiers, policemen, Secret Service workers, resistance fighters and terrorists lost their jobs and their raison d'être. That was nothing new. Years before, unemployed Vietnam War veterans had founded private military and security services in the USA, ones that ventured where Washington didn't dare get caught. Serving the CIA, these firms hunted unpleasant rulers out of power, trafficked weapons and drugs and, incidentally, also relieved the strain on the defence budget. Now, though, the market was collapsing under a surplus of trained fighters fighting each other for the last crisis zones in the era of Nelson Mandela and Russian–American chumminess. The remaining despots could only do so much to encroach on human rights; there simply wasn't enough for everyone.

And then the curtain rose on a new act.

The new players were Saddam Hussein, arrogant and voracious, and Slobodan Miloševi´c, delirious with nationalism. Perfect antagonists of an otherwise peace-loving humanity, one which yet again speedily agrees to permit war as a continuation of politics, but this time with other means. Foolishly, a few soldiers too many had been laid off in the frenzy of reconciliation. The mercenaries were on the march again. Authorised by the United Nations, they polish up their tarnished image by helping to conquer the lunatic in the Gulf and the monster of the Balkans, and secure peace. Then, one day, two passenger jets fly into the Twin Towers and send the final remains of the pacifist mindset up in flames. Determined to bring the axis of evil to its knees, George W. Bush, otherwise known as the biggest political bankruptcy in American history, bestows on the USA thousands of dead GIs and a fiscal hole the size of a lunar crater. Practically all its allies are forced to learn how terribly expensive war is and how much more expensive it is to win peace, especially with the employment of regular armies. But on the other hand, given that the way war is led is no longer up for debate, commission after commission goes to the efficient and discreet private security firms.

Fittingly, Africa uses its raw materials to enter the playing field of globalisation. Wounds that were long believed healed burst open, petrodollars split whole nations, and the gravitational forces of East and West pull at everything. Somalia becomes synonymous with blood and tears. Millions of people die during the civil war in the Democratic Republic of Congo. Barely recovered from the wrangling between the government and liberation armies, the Sudan staggers into the Darfur conflict, the pull of which grips the whole of central Africa. With France as a silent partner, Chad's dictator invests trillions of oil money in arms purchases and destabilises the region in his own special way. The parties of the north and south are smashing each other's head in on the Ivory Coast, while violence is rampant in oil-rich South Nigeria. Senegal, Congo-Brazzaville, Burundi and Uganda top the scale of inhumane acts. Even supposedly stable nations like Kenya sink into chaos in just a short time. Almost everything that was supposed to improve just gets worse.

The only people things improve for are the likes of Jan Kees Vogelaar.

At the beginning of the millennium, his Mamba supports the peace troop of the African Union in Darfur, reduces the popularity of the

Arabic Sudanese in the guerrilla camps and takes on lucrative mandates in Kenya and Nigeria. After the foundation of African Protection Services, Vogelaar is able to expand his activities to more crisis areas. APS develops for Africa in a similar manner to how Blackwater developed for Iraq. By 2016, the group of companies makes a name for itself in the safeguarding of oil plants and transport routes for raw materials, the conduct of negotiations with hostage-takers and the exploration of exotic locations for Western, Asian and multinational companies, which are increasingly acquiring a taste for hiring private armies.

But it remains a painstaking business, and Vogelaar gets tired of changing sides again and again. After years of instability on all fronts he begins to long for something more lasting and solid, for that one, ultimate commission.

And then it comes.

'In the form of Kenny Xin,' said Vogelaar. 'Or rather Kenny's company, which practically handed me the future on a silver platter.'

'Xin,' echoed Yoyo. 'The name doesn't exactly suit him.' Jericho knew what she meant. Xin was the Chinese word for heart.

'And who's behind the company?' he asked.

'Back then, it was the Chinese Secret Service.' The South African rubbed his wrists, which were marked by the welts of the belt. 'But as time went on I started to have my doubts about that.'

The revelation of Donner's identity had thrown everything off-kilter. Adjusting to the new situation, Jericho had first seized the opportunity to take a quick look at his ear in the toilet mirror. It looked awful, drenched in scarlet; the blood had run down his neck in streaks and into the neckline of his T-shirt, where it had congealed and was now encrusted. Bleeding, drenched with fish stock and covered in the remains of squashed root vegetables, he was a wretched sight. After he'd washed the blood away, though, things looked a little better. Instead of finding himself faced with a problem of van Gogh proportions, he discovered he had actually only lost a carpaccio-thin slice of ear muscle. Yoyo, directed by Vogelaar to the kitchen's first aid box, had bandaged him up. It had felt as if her touch was much more tender than the task required; if he were a dog, one might have referred to it as petting, but he wasn't a dog, and Yoyo was probably just doing her job. Vogelaar had watched them, suddenly looking very tired, as if he had years of sleep to catch up on.

'If you're not here to kill me, then what in God's name are you here for?'

'To warn you, you stupid bastard,' explained Yoyo in a friendly tone.

'About who?'

'About the people who are planning to kill you!'

Jericho pulled his mobile out and silently projected the text fragment and then the film onto the wall, the clip which showed Vogelaar in Africa.

'Where did you get that from?'

'We don't know. We stumbled across it on the internet, but ever since then your friend Kenny has been trying to kill us.'

'My friend Kenny.' A sound somewhere between a laugh and a grunt came from Vogelaar. 'Let's be frank now, there's no way you came here because you were seriously concerned about my survival.'

'Of course not. Especially not after the meat-slicer incident.'

'Well, how was I supposed to know who you were?'

'You could have asked.'

'Asked? Are you right in the head? You forced your way into my kitchen and attacked me!'

'Well, after you—'

'Good God, what was I supposed to do? What would you have done in my position? Nyela phoned and told me that two clowns were sitting in my restaurant pretending to be restaurant critics.'

'See!' said Yoyo, triumphantly. 'I told you—'

'*That* wasn't the problem, little one! You were the problem. Your little slip of the tongue. No one here knows anything about our time in Equatorial Guinea. Nyela is from Cameroon and I'm a South African Boer. The Donners were never in Equatorial Guinea.'

Yoyo looked embarrassed.

'Did you watch the films from the security camera?' Jericho wanted to know.

'Aha, so you noticed the camera?'

'I'm a detective.'

'Of course I looked at them. I'm prepared for everything, boy. I had actually hoped to live out the rest of my life in peace here. New identity, new home. But Kenny doesn't give up. The bastard has never given up yet.'

'Do you think the text came from him?'

'What I think is that you should untie me right away, or you can figure the rest of it out by yourself.'

And so, with an uneasy feeling, he had untied Vogelaar while Yoyo covered him with the gun. But the only thing the South African did was go next door and put palm wine, rum and coke on the table. He then proceeded to listen to their story as he led one cigarillo after another to its cremation.

'What kind of deal did Kenny offer you?' asked Jericho as he gulped down a glass of rum he felt was more than well-earned.

'A kind of second Wonga coup.'

'Not exactly a good omen.'

'Yes, but the circumstances had changed. Ndongo wasn't Obiang, and he certainly wasn't as closely guarded. Practically all the key positions in his government had been bought by the USA and Great Britain. It's just that money doesn't make a good building block, not in the long term, anyway. You have to constantly replaster it, otherwise the place will collapse above your head. And besides, Ndongo was a Bubi. The Fang only got involved with him because they'd been having just as bad a time of it, and things threatened to be even worse under Mayé. Back then, APS operated along the entire west coast of Africa. In Cameroon, we were protecting oil plants against the resistance. It was in Jaunde that I met Nyela, by the way, the first woman who inspired me to bring some kind of order into my life.'

'Is she really called Nyela?' asked Yoyo.

'Are you crazy?' snorted Vogelaar. 'No one uses their real name if their life is at stake. In any case, one beautiful day I arrive in my office, and there sits Kenny, waiting to explain the Chinese interests to me.' Vogelaar puffed away, veiling himself in smoke. 'He had this strange way of switching terminology when it came to his clients. Sometimes he spoke about the Communist Party, sometimes about the Secret Service, and at others it sounded like he was there in the service of the State oil trade. When I demanded a little more clarity, he wanted to hear my thoughts on the difference between governments and companies. I thought about it and realised there wasn't one. Strictly speaking, I haven't found one in over forty years.'

'And Kenny suggested a coup.'

'The Chinese were quite bitter about the American presence in the Gulf of Guinea. Remember that we're talking about the time before helium-3; the area was like pure gold back then. Besides that, they felt they were entitled to something that Washington had helped itself to since time immemorial. I tried to make Kenny realise that there was a difference between *protecting* governments from guerrillas and actually overthrowing them. I told him about the Wonga Coup, about Simon Mann, how he was rotting in Black Beach because of it, and how the Briton had made himself look like a complete fool. He responded by sharing information about the overthrow of the Saudi Arabian royal family the year before, and I almost passed out. It had been obvious to all of us, of course, that China had supported the Saudi Islamists, but if what Kenny told me is true, then Beijing did more than just provide a little assistance. Believe me, I can smell bullshit from ten miles away upwind. Kenny wasn't bullshitting. He was telling the truth, and so I decided to carry on listening to him.'

'I guess he was on excellent terms with Mayé.'

'They were certainly in contact. In 2016, Kenny was still in second rank, but I knew right away that the guy would soon pop up in a more exposed position.' Vogelaar laughed softly. 'If you meet him, he actually seems like a nice guy. But he's not. He's at his most dangerous when he's pretending to be nice.'

'Can anyone be nice in this business?' asked Yoyo.

'Of course. Why not?'

'Well, take mercenaries for example.' She shrugged. 'I mean, aren't they all more or less – erm – racists?'

Good God, Yoyo, thought Jericho, what are you playing at? Vogelaar slowly turned his head to face her and let smoke billow out of the corner of his mouth. He looked like a huge, steaming animal.

'Don't be shy, speak your mind.'

'Koevoet. Apartheid. Do I need to go on?'

'I was a professional racist, my girl, if you're directing that at me. Give me money, and I hate the blacks. Give me money, and I hate the whites. It's real racists who screw up the fun. By the way, there are racists in the army too.'

'But you're for sale. As opposed to regular—'

'We're for sale, sure, but we don't betray anyone. And do you know why? Because we're not on anyone's side. Our only loyalty is to the contract.'

'But if you—'

'We're *unable* to commit any kind of betrayal.'

'Well, I see it differently.'

Jericho was fidgeting uneasily on his chair. What was Yoyo thinking, impaling Vogelaar on the stake of her indignation, and now of all moments? He was just opening his mouth to interrupt when a trace of realisation flitted across her face. With sudden humility, she slurped on her cola and asked:

'So who made contact with whom? Mayé with the Chinese? Or the other way around?'

Vogelaar looked at her, debating his answer. Then he shrugged his shoulders and poured an almost overflowing glass of rum down his throat.

'Your people approached Mayé, as far as I know.'

'You mean the Chinese,' Yoyo corrected him.

'*Your* people,' Vogelaar repeated mercilessly. 'They came and knocked the doors down, doors that were already wide open. After all, the point was that Obiang had dramatically misjudged things with Mayé.

He wanted someone he could direct from behind the scenes, but he picked the wrong guy. Without helium-3, Mayé would probably still be in Malabo.'

'But he did end up being a puppet just recently.'

'Sure, but for the Chinese, the buffoon of a ranking world power. That's different from letting yourself be spoon-fed by a terminally ill ex-dictator. When Kenny turned up at my place, he had already done his research and decided that we were the best match. So I listened to him calmly – and then refused.'

'Why?' wondered Jericho.

'So he would come down from his high horse. He was disappointed of course. And uneasy too, because he had opened up and made himself vulnerable. Then I told him that perhaps there was a chance after all. But for that he would have to throw more on the scales than the commission for a coup. I made it clear to him that I was tired of the trench warfare, this constant haggling for jobs, but that, on the other hand, I would bore myself to death if I went off to live in some villa somewhere. I was nearing some sort of retirement, but I didn't want it to be of a retiring nature.'

'So you asked for a position in Mayé's government. That's quite an unusual request for a mercenary.'

'Kenny understood. A few days later we met with Mayé, who banged on at me for two long hours about his lousy family, and Kenny had to make all kinds of promises to him. There was no way there was a position in it for me too! He kept me in suspense for hours on end, then he switched sides, to cuddly old Uncle Mayé, and pulled the rabbit out of the hat.'

'And offered you the position of security manager.'

'The funny thing is that it was Kenny's idea. But he buttered the old guy up so much he thought it was his own. So the deal was done. The rest was child's play. I took care of the logistics, put commandos together, organised the weapons and helicopter, the usual rigmarole. You know the rest. The Chinese were adamant that the whole thing had to go off without any bloodshed and that Ndongo had to leave the country unscathed, and we managed all of that.'

'Beijing didn't seem to have that many concerns last year.'

'There was much more to play for last year. In 2017 it was just about an adjustment to the power relationships.'

'*Just*, sure.'

'Oh, come on! Everyone knew that clever journalists would write clever articles sooner or later. Beijing's role was clear just from the redistribution of the mining licences. And so what? People are used to "arranged" changes in government. But they're less used to killings. Especially when you're trying to clean up your image. The Party hadn't forgotten the Olympic gauntlet-running of 2008. That's also why the House of Saud got off so lightly in 2015 when the Islamists captured Riyadh. It was Beijing's condition for financing the fun. Anyway, we advanced into Malabo, Mayé squeezed his fat ass into the seat of government, I built up EcuaSec, the Equatorial Guinea Secret Service, had the entire opposition imprisoned, and that was that.'

'And that didn't make you sick?' asked Yoyo.

'Sick?' Vogelaar put the glass to his lips. 'I only got sick once in my life. From rotten tuna.'

Jericho shot Yoyo a look like daggers. 'And then what?'

'As expected, Kenny landed on his feet shortly after we heaved Mayé into power and ended up with more authority. Equatorial Guinea became a playground to him. Every few weeks he would relax in the lobby of the Paraíso, a hotel for oil workers, where he treated himself to hookers and waited for my reports. We had agreed in Cameroon that I would keep an eye on Mayé—'

'So that was the deal.'

'Of course. As I said, it was Kenny's idea. No one got as close to Mayé as I did. He accepted me as a close confidant.'

'A confidant who also happened to be spying on him.'

'Just in case the fatty escaped our leash. I was being watched too of course. That's Kenny's principle, how he builds up his clique: everyone keeps an eye on everyone else. But I always had one more pair of eyes than the others.'

'Yes, made of glass,' scoffed Yoyo.

'I see more with one healthy one than you do with two,' retorted Vogelaar. 'I quickly found out who the moles were that Kenny had set on me. Half of EcuaSec was infiltrated. I didn't let on that I knew of course. Instead, I began to watch Kenny myself; I wanted to find out more about him and his men.'

'All I know is that he's completely insane.'

'Let's just say he loves extremes. I found out that he lived in London for three years, assigned to the Chinese military attaché, and spent two years in Washington, specialising in conspiracy. Officially, he belonged to Zhong Chan Er Bu, the military news service, the second department of the General Staff of the People's Liberation Army. Unfortunately my contacts there turned out to be scarce, but I did know a few people who had worked with Kenny in the past in the fifth office of the Guojia Anquan Bu, the ministry for state security. According to them he had outstanding analytical abilities and an instinct for how people's minds work. They also commented that when it came to sabotage and contract killing, he handled things with quite a – well, uncompromising attitude.'

'In other words, our friend was a killer.'

'Which in itself isn't any cause for alarm. But there was something else too.'

Vogelaar paused to light another cigar. He did it slowly and elaborately, switching from the spoken word to smoke signals and immersing himself in his own thoughts for a while.

'They thought there was something monstrous about him,' he continued. 'Which my gut instinct had told me too, although I couldn't really say why. So I tried to delve deeper into Kenny's past. I found the usual military service, his studies, pilot training, arms certificate, all the normal stuff. I was just about to give up when I stumbled on a special unit with the beautiful name of Yü Shen—'

'Lovely,' said Yoyo sarcastically.

'Yü Shen?' Jericho wrinkled his forehead. 'That rings a bell. It has something to do with eternal damnation, doesn't it?'

'Yü Shen is the Hell God,' Yoyo explained to him. 'A Taoist figure based on the old Chinese belief that hell is divided up into ten empires, deep inside the earth, each of which is ruled by a Hell King. The Hell God is the highest power. The dead have to answer to him and the judges of hell.'

'So that means everyone goes to hell?'

'To start with, yes. And everyone appears before a special court, according to his or her actions. The good ones are sent back to the surface and are reborn in a higher incarnation. The bad ones are reborn too, after they've served their time in hell, but as animals.'

Jericho looked at Vogelaar.

'So what was Kenny Xin reborn as?'

'Good question. A beast in human form?'

'And what was he before?'

Vogelaar sucked at his cigar.

'I tried to collect information about Yü Shen. It was a difficult task. Officially, the department doesn't exist, and it's actually very similar to the hell court. It recruits its members from prisons, psychiatric institutions and clinics for brain research. You might say they search for evil. For highly gifted people whose psychic defect is so far over the inhibition threshold that they would normally be locked away. But, with Yü Shen, they get a second chance. Not that they want to make them into better people there, mind, it's more about how to *use* their evil. They carry out tests. All kinds of tests, the type you wouldn't even want to hear about. After a year, they decide whether you'll be reborn in freedom, for example in the military or Secret Service, or whether you'll live out your life in the hell of the institution.'

'It sounds like an army of butchers,' said Yoyo, disgusted.

'Not necessarily. Some Yü Shen graduates have gone on to have incredible careers.'

'And Kenny?'

'When Yü Shen tracked him down, he had just turned fifteen and was in an institution for mentally disturbed young offenders. Most of what happened before that remains in darkness. It seems he grew up in bitter poverty, in the corner of a settlement where not even tramps dare to go. A father, mother, and two siblings. I don't know much more detail than that. Just that one night, when he was ten years old, he poured two canisters of petrol onto his family's corrugated iron shack while they were all sleeping. Then he blocked up all the escape routes with barricades he had spent weeks making out of rubbish, hooked them all up so that no one could get out, and set the whole thing on fire.'

Yoyo stared at him.

'And his—?'

'Burnt to death.'

'The whole family?'

'Every one of them. It was pure chance that some shrink got wind of it and took the boy away with him. He declared that Kenny possessed outstanding intelligence and well-developed clarity of thought. The boy didn't deny anything, didn't utter a single word in attempt to explain why he had done it. For four years he was passed around circles of experts, each of them trying to get to the bottom of his behaviour, until ultimately Yü Shen became aware of his existence.'

'And they let him loose on humanity!'

'He was declared to be healthy.'

'Healthy?'

'In the sense that he was in control of himself. They didn't find anything. No mental illness that features in the textbooks at any rate. Just a bizarre compulsion for order, a fascination with symmetry. Classical symptoms of compulsive behaviour, but overall nothing that could brand him as being insane. He was just – evil.'

For a while, there was an uneasy silence. Jericho thought back over what he knew about Xin. His love of directing the action, the eerie ability he had of reading people's minds. Vogelaar was right. Kenny *was* evil. And yet he had the feeling that wasn't all there was to it. It was as if some dark code underlay his behaviour, one that he followed and felt bound to.

'Now, in the meantime I had no reason to mistrust Kenny. Everything was running like a well-oiled machine. Beijing kept to its promise not to get involved, Mayé was enjoying the status of an autonomous ruler. Oil flowed in return for money. Then the decline came. The whole world was talking about helium-3, everyone wanted to go to the Moon. Interest in fossil resources kept falling, and Mayé couldn't do a thing about it. Nothing at all. Neither executions nor fits of madness could help.' Vogelaar flicked ashes from his cigar. 'So, on 30 April 2022 he called me to his office. As I walked in, he was sitting there with a number of men and women, who he introduced to us as representatives of the Chinese Air and Space Travel Ministry.'

'I know what they wanted!' Yoyo waved her hand eagerly as if she were in a classroom. 'They suggested building a launching pad.'

Jericho was jerked from his thoughts. 'So it wasn't Mayé's idea at all.'

'No, it wasn't. He wanted to know what it was for of course. They said it was to shoot a satellite into space. He asked what kind of satellite. They said: "Just a satellite, it doesn't matter what kind. Do you want a satellite? Your own, Equatorial Guinea news satellite? You can have it. The only important thing to us is the launch, and that no one finds out who's behind it."'

'But why?' asked Jericho, dumbfounded. 'What did they have to gain from shooting Chinese satellites up from African soil?'

'That's what we wanted to know too, naturally. They told us there was a space treaty agreed in the sixties at the initiative of the United Nations, then signed and ratified by the majority of member states. It's about who outer space belongs to, what they can or can't do, and who can permit or forbid things. Part of the treaty is a liability clause, later put in concrete terms in a special agreement, which regulates all the claims regarding accidents with artificial celestial bodies. For example: if a meteorite falls into your garden and kills your chickens, you can't do a thing. But if it's not a meteorite but a satellite with a nuclear reactor, and it doesn't fall on your chickens but right smack bang in central Berlin, then that would cause damage of astronomic proportions, not to mention the dead and wounded and the soaring cancer rate. So who would be liable for that?'

'Whoever caused it?'

'Correct. The state that sent it up, and the treaty dictates that the liability has no limits. If Germany can prove it was a Chinese satellite, then China has to cough up. The decisive factor is always whose territory something was launched from. So the more a nation launches, the higher the risk they run of having to pay up at some point. That's why, according to the delegates, they were now negotiating with states who were willing to allow China to build launch pads on their territory and pass them off to the world as being their own.'

'But that would make those states liable!'

'Guys like Mayé don't have any issues with driving their own people into ruin. He had long since piled the millions from the oil trade into private bunkers, just like Obiang did before him. The only thing he cared about was what was in it for him. So Kenny named a figure. It was exorbitantly high. Mayé tried to stay calm, while all the while he was pissing himself with joy under his tropical wood desk.'

'Didn't the whole thing seem completely absurd to him?'

'The delegation claimed that Beijing was concluding deals like these for minimisation of risk. That the danger of a satellite falling was becoming less and less, and that it wasn't to do with military operations, it was merely about the testing of a new, experimental initiative. The only thing Mayé had to do was strut about as the father of Equatorial Guinea space travel and pledge his lifelong silence about who was really behind it. And for that, they were prepared to pay for his satellite.'

'What an idiot,' commented Yoyo.

'Well, think about it. Equatorial Guinea, the first African country with its own space programme.'

'But didn't anyone notice that loads of Chinese people were running around when they were building the launching pad?' asked Jericho.

'It wasn't like that. There was an official announcement. Mayé informed the world that he wanted to get in on the space travel scene, invited specialists over to Equatorial Guinea, and of course the Chinese came too. The whole thing was organised perfectly. In the end, Russians, Koreans, French and Germans all ended up working on the launch pad too, without noticing whose tune they were dancing to.'

'And the Zheng Group?'

'Ah!' Vogelaar raised his eyebrows admiringly. 'You've done your research. That's right, a large part of the construction was developed by Zheng. They had a team on site the whole time. They started in December and a year later the thing was up. On 15 April 2024, Mayé's first and only news satellite was shot into space in a festive ceremony.'

'He must have practically burst with pride.'

'Mayé was obsessed with the thing. There was a model of it hanging in his office, it rode along the ceiling on a rail and then circled around him at his desk, the sun of Equatorial Guinea.'

'But not for very long.'

'Not even three weeks. First a temporary failure, then radio silence. The news spread of course. Mayé became the subject of ridicule and malice. It wasn't that he really needed a satellite; after all, he had coped perfectly well without one before. But he had taken his place in international circles, he wanted to be part of it all and now he had to contend with this major fall. He made a proper fool of himself, and even the Bubi in Black Beach were rolling around in their cells with laughter. Mayé was frothing with rage, screaming for Kenny, who informed him that there were more pressing concerns. And there were. The Chinese and Americans were threatening each other with military action, each of them accusing the other of having stationed weapons on the Moon. I advised Mayé to hold back, but he kept on and on. Eventually, at the beginning of June, when the Moon crisis was just starting to defuse, Kenny travelled to Malabo for talks. Mayé refused to restrain himself, demanding a new satellite immediately. But then he made a mistake. He mentioned his suspicion that there was more behind the launch than the testing of some experimental initiative.'

Jericho leaned forward. 'What did he mean by that?'

Vogelaar blew smoke, in memory of bygone times.

'It was something he'd heard from me. Something I had found out. About the whole project.'

'So you had the whole thing investigated?'

'Of course. I kept a closer eye on the building of the ramp and the launch than Kenny would have liked, but in such a way that he didn't notice. In the process, I stumbled upon inconsistencies. I told Mayé about it and impressed upon him the need to keep it to himself, but the idiot had nothing better to do than threaten Kenny.'

'How did Kenny react to it?'

'In a nice manner. And that was what concerned me. He said that Mayé didn't need to worry, that there would be some way of agreeing on things.'

'That sounds like a pre-announced execution.'

'That's exactly what I thought. A lot of fuss had been caused by that point. So the only option was to find out the whole truth, to increase the pressure on Kenny so much that he couldn't simply get rid of us. And I did find out. When Kenny next turned up, Mayé received him in the company of his most important ministers and military staff. We confronted him with the facts. He was silent. For a long time. A very long time. Then he asked us if we realised we were playing with our lives.'

'The beginning of the end.'

'Not necessarily. It showed that he was taking us seriously. That he wanted to negotiate.' Vogelaar laughed joylessly. 'But Mayé messed the whole thing up again by demanding horrendous sums, practically a genuflection. Kenny couldn't give him what he wanted. He seemed to be making things easy for Mayé though, and I genuinely got the impression that he didn't want things to escalate, but Mayé, in his arrogance, was unstoppable. By the end he was screaming that the whole world would find out about it all. Kenny stood up, hesitated. Then he gave a broad grin and said, Okay, I give in. You'll have what you desire, Mr Dictator, give me two weeks. He said that and then left.'

Vogelaar watched the smoke from his cigar float away.

'At that moment I knew that Mayé had just condemned us all to death. He may have been basking in the belief of being the victor, but he was already dead. I didn't waste any time convincing him otherwise, and just went home. My wife and I packed our bags. I always have a few identities up my sleeve, an escape plan or something. The following morning we disappeared from Equatorial Guinea. We left all of our possessions behind, everything apart from a suitcase full of money and a pile of false papers. Kenny's henchmen were on our heels right away, but my plan was perfect. It wasn't the first time I'd had to go underground. We dodged them again and again until we had thrown them off. Once we got to Berlin, we became Andre and Nyela Donner, a South African agricultural engineer and a qualified lawyer from Cameroon with a gastronomic background, and looked for some premises. The day we opened, Ndongo was filling his pants in Malabo, and Mayé was dead. Everyone who knew about it was dead.'

'Apart from one person.'

'Yes.'

'So what was the space programme really about?'

Vogelaar stretched out a finger and pushed a half-full glass over the tablecloth. The rum sparkled in the light of the paper lamp, a frenzy of movement and reflection.

'Come on, don't make me keep asking. Why did it all happen?'

The mercenary propped his chin in his hands meditatively.

'It should be me asking who's coming after the two of you.'

'Oh, sure!' Yoyo glared at him angrily. 'What do you think we've been doing the whole day?'

'Obviously I'm asking myself the same thing.'

'Probably Zhong Chan Er Bu,' conjectured Jericho. 'The Chinese Secret Service. After everything you've told us.'

'I'm not so sure any more. I've since started to believe that Kenny's strange delegation represented neither the Chinese government nor the Chinese space travel authorities. Both of them are probably still none the wiser that they were used as a pretext.'

Jericho stared at him in amazement.

'They were very convincing, Jericho.'

'But the Party must have realised what was happening in their name. Mayé must have mentioned it on official state visits.'

'Nonsense, think about it! There were no Chinese government visits to Equatorial Guinea, just as Mayé was never invited to the Forbidden City. No one wanted to be seen with him. A little minister of the energy authorities might pop up coyly here and there, but otherwise Chinese oil people kept their heads down. Beijing had always emphasised the fact that its only relationship with Equatorial Guinea was strictly trade-related.'

'But they didn't have any problems with being photographed with dictators in Mugabe's era.'

'They didn't overthrow Mugabe. After a coup, it's not the done thing for the initiators to draw attention to themselves. The Chinese are more careful nowadays.'

'But what about Zheng?'

'What about him?'

'The Zheng Group works for the Chinese space travel authority. Scrub that, they *are* the space travel authority, and they did construction work for Mayé too. It must have come out then that official positions had been used as a pretext.'

'Who says Zheng was consulted? Inside an authority, there are those that know and those that don't. His company accepted a commission on the free market. And so what?'

'The Party allowed their most important construction company to build a foreign launch pad.'

'You can't control companies like Zheng or Orley; not even the Party can do that, nor do they want to. The Chinese prime minister has shares in Zheng, so that would have meant keeping an eye on himself too. On the contrary, Beijing welcomed the fact that Zheng responded to the invitation to tender, because it made espionage there easier.'

'So why did you become suspicious?'

Vogelaar smiled thinly.

'Because I'm always suspicious. That's how I found out that Kenny left Zhong Chan Er Bu in 2022. He now works purely on a freelance basis for the military Secret Service.'

'Just a second,' said Yoyo. 'The coup that brought Mayé to power—'

'Was financed by Chinese oil companies, ratified by Beijing and executed by the Chinese Secret Service, with our help.'

'And the launching pad?'

'That had nothing to do with it. The launching pad just brought new protagonists onto the scene. Beijing was only ever concerned with commodities. The people that talked us into the launching pad had other interests.'

'So Kenny changed camps?'

'I'm not sure whether he did or not. Perhaps he just broadened his circle of activity. I don't think he explicitly contravened Beijing's interests, rather that he saw someone else's interests as being more important.'

'And the Mayé coup?'

'The launching pad people were to blame for that. It's possible that the Party approved of it. But they were certainly never asked.'

'Is that what you believe or what you *know*?'

'What I believe.'

'Vogelaar,' said Yoyo insistently. 'You have to tell us what you found out about the launching pad, do you hear?'

Vogelaar put his fingertips together. He fixed his gaze on his thumbs, brought them towards the tip of his nose and then looked at the ceiling. Then, slowly, he nodded.

'Okay. Agreed.'

'Tell us.'

'For a quarter of a million euros.'

'What?' Jericho fought for air. 'Have you gone insane?'

'For that you'll get a dossier, everything's in it.'

'You're crazy!'

'Not in the slightest. Nyela and I have to go underground, and right away. A large part of my fortune is frozen in Equatorial Guinea. What I was able to take with me is tied up in Muntu and the apartment upstairs. By tomorrow I'll have flogged whatever I can, but Nyela and I will have to start again from scratch.'

'Damn it, Vogelaar!' exploded Yoyo. 'You truly are the most filthy, ungrateful—'

'One hundred thousand,' said Jericho. 'Not a cent more.'

Vogelaar shook his head. 'I'm not negotiating.'

'Because you're not in a position to. Think properly now. It's a hundred thousand or nothing.'

'You need the dossier.'

'And you need the money.'

Yoyo looked as though she wanted to drag Vogelaar straight off to the slicing machine. Jericho kept an eye on her. If it came to it he was prepared to give the South African a good going over with the Glock, but he doubted that Vogelaar would let it go that far again. They had to reach an agreement with him somehow.

He waited.

After what felt like an eternity, Vogelaar breathed out, long and slow, and for the first time Jericho sensed the big man's fear.

'One hundred thousand. In cash, to be clear! Money in exchange for the dossier.'

'Here?'

'Not here. Somewhere busy.' With a nod of his head, he gestured outside. 'Tomorrow at midday in the Pergamon Museum. That's right around the corner. Take Monbijou Strasse down to the Spree, then go over the river to Museum Island and to the James Simon Gallery. That's where the stream of tourists divides between the museums. We'll meet at the Ishtar Gate opposite the Processional Way. Nyela and I will leave immediately afterwards, so make sure you're on time.'

'And where do you plan to go?'

Vogelaar stared at him for a long time.

'You really don't need to know that,' he said.

'Fantastic! So where are you going to get a hundred thousand euros from?' Yoyo asked as they crossed the street to where the Audi was parked.

'How should I know?' Jericho shrugged. 'It's still better than a quarter of a million.'

'Oh, much better.'

'Okay.' He stopped abruptly. 'So what do you think I ought to have done? Tortured the truth out of him?'

'Exactly that. We should have beaten it out of him!'

'Great idea.' Jericho felt his ear where it had been bandaged up. It was thick and puffy. He felt like a plush toy rabbit. 'I can just imagine the scene. I hold him down while you beat him to a pulp with an ante-lope haunch.'

'Good of you to mention it. I—'

'And Vogelaar would have just let us do that to him.'

'But I *did* beat him to a pulp with the antelope haunch!'

'So you did.' Jericho walked on, and opened the car door. 'How did you get here anyway? Weren't you supposed to be keeping an eye on Nyela?'

'That just about beats everything.' Yoyo flung open the passenger door, flopped down in her seat and twisted her arms into a knot. 'You'd have ended up as cold cuts if I hadn't come along, you arsehole.'

Jericho kept quiet.

Had he just made a mistake?

'I don't know where we're going to get the money either,' he conceded. 'And I don't want to count on Tu's help, not automatically.'

Yoyo grumbled something he didn't catch.

'Well then,' Jericho said. 'Let's go to the hotel, shall we?'

No answer.

He sighed, and started the car.

'I'll ask Tu, in any case,' he said. 'He can lend it to me. Or give it as an advance.'

'Whver.'

'Maybe he's got some news for us. He's been playing about with Diane since this morning.'

Silence.

'I called him before I went into Muntu. Very interesting stuff he's found out. Confirms everything that Vogelaar said. Should I tell you what Tu told me?'

''f y'wnt.'

He couldn't get anything else out of her. All the way to the Hyatt, all she would do was spit out knotty strings of consonants. Jericho reported his conversation with Tu, in the cheery tones of a man pushing water uphill, until in the end he couldn't keep up the pretence that nothing was wrong. In the Hyatt's underground garage, he finally gave up.

'Okay,' he said. 'You're right.'

Arms folded, she stared dead ahead.

'I behaved very badly. I should have thanked you.'

'N'wrries.' On the other hand, at least she wasn't jumping out of the car.

'Without you, Vogelaar would have killed me. You saved my life.' He cleared his throat. 'So, umm – thank you, okay? I mean that, really. I'll never forget it. It was extremely brave of you.'

She turned her head and looked at him, her brows drawn down like thunder.

'Why exactly are you such a halfwit?'

'No idea.' Jericho stared at the steering wheel. 'Maybe I just never learned.'

'Learned what?'

'How to be considerate.'

'I think that you can be, though. Very considerate.' Her arms, folded tight, relaxed a little. They even slipped apart a bit. 'Do you know what else I think?'

Jericho raised his eyebrows.

'I think that you're least considerate towards people you actually care about.'

He caught his breath. Not stupid, this one.

'And who helped you with that little insight?' he asked, nursing a suspicion.

'What do you mean?'

'I was just thinking it's the kind of thing that Joanna might have said.'

'I don't need Joanna for that.'

'You didn't happen to talk to her about me, then?'

'Of course I did,' she admitted straight away. 'She told me that the two of you were an item.'

'And what else?'

'That *you* cocked it up.'

'Ah.'

'She said it was because you didn't like yourself – you're never nice to yourself – *not at all* nice to yourself.'

Jericho pursed his lips. He lined up some counter-arguments, and each looked more threadbare than the next. He held them back. God knows they had better things to do here than rummage through their emotional baggage, but somehow he suddenly felt as if he'd been caught with his trousers down. As if Joanna had stripped him bare and was marching him about by the ring in his nose. Yoyo shook her head.

'No, Owen, she didn't say anything bad about you.'

'Hmm. I'll think about it.'

'Do that.' She grinned. The way he surrendered seemed to have smoothed her ruffled feathers. 'We mustn't rule out the possibility that we'll have to save one another's lives a few more times.'

'As I believe I've already said – any time!' He hesitated. 'About Nyela—'

'My fault. After I screwed it up, I thought the best thing to do would be to come back quickly.'

Jericho felt his ear.

'To be honest,' he said, 'I'm glad you did screw it up.'

Calgary, Alberta, Canada

Pounding the streets of Calgary and showing people the photograph of a possible gunman was more or less like knocking down an anthill and looking for one particular ant. Just a moment ago one and a half million people had been hard at work here, busy making more goods for the shelves and building more blocks on the streets of Canada's fastest-growing city, industrious citizens flooding the streets, but now they seemed to have lost all sense of direction in an instant. Loreena welcomed the switch to helium-3 in the energy industry, but for all that she couldn't bear the grim spectacle of mass unemployment, the decline of whole cities and provinces, the impending bankruptcy of countries which had made their money almost entirely from oil and gas. Ecologists had always had an idealistic vision of a smooth and manageable transition, with Mr Fossilosaurus given a gold watch and sent packing to a nice quiet retirement home, where he would then draw his last breath after a dignified decline, while ten billion people cheerily got their electricity from helium-3 generators. But transition had never gone smoothly, never in history. Not in the Cambrian epoch, not in the Ordovician, the Devonian, not at the end of the Permian, Triassic or Cretaceous, and not in the Upper Pleistocene either. That was when a new species called mankind appeared, a self-aware creature who added war and economic crisis to the catalogue of boundary events that already included volcanic eruption, meteorites, ice ages and epidemics. So the brave new world of clean fusion came hand in hand with a full-blown global economic crisis, whether the heralds of the new dawn liked it or not.

She put fruit, yoghurt and bread rolls onto her tray and took it over to the table, where the intern was already piling into his second stack of pancakes.

'Yesterday was a damp squib then,' he said.

Loreena shrugged. The Westin Calgary had the advantage of being near the Imperial Oil building on 4th Avenue Southwest, so after she had telephoned Palstein she had decided to take rooms for the night there for herself and the kid. After that they retraced the mysterious fat man's steps. It was a dispiriting business. On Bruford's video, he came in from the north. Most hotels were to the south, west or east though. He could have been staying in any one of them, *if* he had been staying in a hotel at all. Perhaps he even lived in the city. There was a clear Asian presence here. Just a walk away from the Bow River, the third largest Chinatown in Canada after Vancouver and Toronto stretched down Calgary's lively Centre Street. In the Sheraton, not far from Prince's Park Island, the staff thought that they remembered a tall, shabby-looking Asian man with a paunch on him, but he hadn't been a guest. They had showed his picture around shops and restaurants, and had even paid a visit to Calgary International Airport, all to no avail. The only good news this morning for Keowa was her breakfast, a filling but not fattening tray of pineapple, sunflower seed rolls and low fat yoghurt.

Just as she was pouring a cup of herbal tea, Sina called, from the Vancouver desk for high society and other gossip.

'Alejandro Ruiz, fifty-two years old. Last heard of as a member of the strategic board for Repsol, or more exactly Repsol YPF to give it its full name, incorporated in Madrid—'

'I know all that already.'

'Wait though! They're market leaders in Spain and Argentina, for a long while they were the biggest energy corporation in private hands, they're focused on ex-ploration, production and refineries, they're also world number three in LNG. They've never held any stake in alternative energies. Just to make up for it, the Mapuche Indians in Argentina have been bringing lawsuits against them like clockwork for the past twenty years, accusing them of polluting the groundwater.'

It was news to Loreena that this tribe was so litigious.

'Are there even any Mapuche left?'

'Oh yes! They're in Argentina and Chile. Even if the Chilean government stubbornly denies that there's *ever* been any such thing as the Mapuche. Makes you laugh, eh? Anyway, Repsol's one of those companies where the lights are going out floor by floor. And Ruiz wasn't just vice-president for strategy, which is what I thought yesterday, he was also directly responsible for petrochemical activities in twenty-nine countries, as of July 2022.'

'That's odd,' said Loreena.

'Why?'

'I mean, given the way the company's set up. Why would they make somebody strategic director who demands they diversify into solar power, and uses funny words like ethics?'

'Most of the time they just put him on the payroll as their ecological conscience so they wouldn't look dumb in public. He was a second-ranker in the corporate hierarchy, so he could bark but he couldn't bite. But by 2022 the tanker was well and truly headed for the rocks. In a situation like that, you could have appointed an Andalusian donkey to the top job. Once it was obvious that Repsol was going to be one of the big losers, they needed a scapegoat at the helm, that's all.'

'By 2022 Ruiz had no chance of preventing catastrophe.'

'I know. Still, he tried pretty much everything he could. He even tried striking a deal with Orley Enterprises.'

'Say what?' said Loreena, taken aback.

'I watched a couple of videos. He gives a good impression, this guy. His wife and daughter in Madrid are distraught over whether he'll ever turn up again. I'll send you contact details for them, and for some of his colleagues at Repsol. Best of luck.'

'You're gonna call Ruiz's old lady?' the intern asked once she had finished speaking to Vancouver.

Loreena got up. 'Any reason why not?'

'The time. Also, you can't speak Spanish.'

'It's half past five in the afternoon in Madrid.'

'Hey, really?' He licked grease off his fingers. 'I thought it was always night in Europe when it's day here.'

Loreena opened her mouth to answer, stopped, shook her head and went up to her room. She was pleased to get through on her first attempt. Señora Ruiz looked distracted, and tried to rebuff her at first but in the end was very helpful; above all, she spoke excellent English, as Loreena had secretly been hoping, since indeed she didn't speak Spanish. They talked for about ten minutes, then she called one of the strategic team at Repsol, who had also been a friend of Ruiz out of the office. Sina had hunted down numbers for some more of his colleagues, but they were all newly unemployed.

She was interested by what she found out.

She looked out of the window. A grey sky brooded over the city, warning that all things must pass. Drizzling curtains of rain blurred the lines of the Calgary Tower, one hundred and ninety metres tall, built by the oil companies Marathon and Husky Oil back in the day. There was something skeletal about the high-rises. A once-prosperous city was shedding weight fast, devouring its own reserves of stored fat. After thinking things over for a while, she called Vancouver again.

'Can you reconstruct the last few days before Ruiz disappeared?'

'Depends what you want to know.'

'I've just been speaking with his wife, and one of his colleagues. Ruiz's last stop before he flew on to Lima was in Beijing.'

'Beijing?' asked Sina, surprised. 'What was Ruiz doing in Beijing?'

'Yes, indeed. What?'

'Repsol has no stake in China.'

'Not quite true. There was definitely a joint venture with Sinopec – it had been planned for a while. Some kind of exploration deal. They spent a week bashing it into shape. I'm more interested in what he did on the last day, right before he left China. On 1 September 2022, to be exact. Apparently he was taking part in some conference that his colleague I spoke to knew next to nothing about. All he knew was that it took place outside Beijing. He reckoned there had to be some papers about it lying around somewhere, and he'll have a look.'

'Nobody knows what the conference was about?'

'Ruiz was strategic director. Autonomous. He didn't have to sit up and beg for every little thing. Señora Ruiz tells me that her Alejandro was a very warm-hearted, easygoing person—'

'Sobs.'

'I'm getting somewhere. He wasn't the type to get upset over nothing. They had spoken on the phone just before the conference, and he was all smiles and sunshine. He had helped get the joint venture on its feet, he was in a good mood, he was cracking jokes and looking forward to Peru. But when he called from the plane to Lima, he seemed fairly downcast.'

'This was the day after the mysterious conference?'

'Exactly.'

'And did she ask him why?'

'She supposed that something must have gone wrong in Beijing, something that really got to him, but he didn't want to talk about it, she tells me. All in all he seemed like a different person, he was in a very uncharacteristic mood, upset and nervous. Then he called her one last time from Lima. He sounded desperate. Almost scared.'

'This was just before he disappeared?'

'The same night, yes. It was the last she heard from him.'

'And what am I to do now?'

'Dig around, as usual. I want to know what kind of meeting he was attending in China. Where it happened, what it was all about, who was there.'

'Hmm. I'll do what I can, okay?'

'But?'

Sina hesitated. 'Susan wants another word with you.'

Loreena frowned. Susan Hudsucker was the Greenwatch number one. She had an idea what was coming, and come indeed it did, just as she expected: when, Susan asked, did Loreena expect to be done with her documentary about the oil companies' environmental sins? If at all possible, they wanted to broadcast *Trash of the Titans* while there were still titans around, and didn't she think she might be barking up the wrong tree with Palstein?

Loreena said she was trying to solve an attempted murder.

Susan said that Greenwatch wasn't the FBI.

But it could be that the shooting had a lot to do with the subject of her documentary.

Susan was sceptical, although on the other hand Loreena wasn't someone that even she could push around.

'Maybe you should bear in mind that what you're doing could be dangerous,' she said.

'When has our work ever not been dangerous?' snorted Loreena. 'Investigative work is always dangerous.'

'Loreena, this is about an attempted *murder*!'

'Listen, Susan' – she paced up and down the hotel room like a tiger in a cage – 'I can't give you all the details right now. We'll take the first plane to Vancouver tomorrow morning and call an editorial conference. Then you'll all see that this is an *extremely* hot story, and that we've already got a whole lot further than the darn police. I mean, we'd be fools not to stick with this one!'

'I don't want to stand in your way. It's just that we have an awful lot else to do as well. *Trash of the Titans* needs to be finished, I can't take you off that task.'

'Don't worry about that.'

'But I do worry.'

'Apart from all that, I did a deal with Palstein. If we solve this case, he'll give us the deep dirt on EMCO.'

Susan sighed. 'Tomorrow we'll decide what happens next, okay?'

'But by then Sina has to—'

'Tomorrow, Loreena.'

'Susan—'

'Please! We'll do everything you want, but first we have to talk about it.'

'Oh, shit, Susan!'

'Sid will come fetch you. Let him know in good time when you're landing.'

Gritting her teeth, Loreena paced the room, thumped her clenched fist on the wall several times and then went back down to the restaurant, where the intern was digging into a huge portion of chocolate mousse.

'Why do you stuff your face like that all the time?' she snarled at him.

'I'm having a growth spurt.' He raised his eyes sluggishly. 'That doesn't seem to have been a particularly good call to Señora Ruiz.'

'No, that was fine.' She slumped down sulkily into her chair, looked into the empty cup and rattled the empty teapot. 'The not particularly good call was with Susan. She thinks we should be concentrating on *Trash of the Titans*.'

'Oops,' said the intern. 'That's not good.'

'All the same, we fly to Vancouver first thing tomorrow and we'll sort it out. I'm not going to let it slip through my fingers now!'

'So we're still working on *Trash of the*—'

'No, no!' She leaned down. '*I* will be working on *Trash of the Titans*. You take a good look at Lars Gudmundsson.'

'Palstein's bodyguard?'

'That's the guy. Him, and his team. I found out that he worked for an outfit in Dallas called Eagle Eye – cute name, huh? Personal protections, mercenaries. Check Gudmundsson out, tell me his shoe size and his favourite food. I want to know every-thing there is to know about the guy.'

The intern looked uncertain. 'What if he notices something? Catches us sniffing around after him?'

Loreena gave him a thin smile. 'If he notices anything, we've made a mistake. And do we make mistakes?'

'I do, sure.'

'I don't. So eat up before I get sick from watching you. We've work to do.'

Grand Hyatt, Berlin, Germany

They were sitting in the lobby by the fireplace. Tu listened to their report as he guzzled down nuts by the handful. He was scooping them from the little bowl by his vodka martini faster than he could gulp them down, so that his cheeks filled out like a squirrel's in the autumn.

'One hundred thousand,' he said thoughtfully.

'And that's his final price.' Jericho fished around in the bowl. A single remaining peanut sought to escape his clutches. 'Vogelaar won't be beaten down.'

'Then we'll pay him.'

'Just so we're all on the same page here,' said Yoyo, smiling sweetly, '*I* don't have a hundred thousand.'

'So what? Do you really think that I flew the whole way here just to give up because of a measly hundred thousand? You'll have the money tomorrow morning.'

'Tian, I—' Jericho managed to catch the nut between finger and thumb, and popped it into his mouth, where it rattled around on his tongue, lonely. 'I wouldn't like to see you shell out the money.'

'Why not? I'm the client.'

'Well, as to that.'

'Am I somehow not your client?'

'Actually that's Chen, and he doesn't have a—'

'No, *actually* it's me, and I'll pick up the tab!' Tu said emphatically. 'The main thing is that your friend hands over the dossier.'

'Well that's very – noble of you.'

'Don't fall on my neck weeping. This is what we call expenses.' Tu dismissed the topic. 'As for myself, I can report that after some hours spent in the pleasant but somewhat sexless company of your Diane, we've identified the provider who hosted those dead letter boxes.'

'You decoded the message?' Yoyo yelped.

'Shhh.' Tu twinkled merrily at the waiter, who had come to exchange the empty bowl for another, brimming with nuts. He chomped away and waited until the man was out of earshot. 'First of all I tracked down the central router. Very sophisticated system, that. The web pages were bounced from server to server until they appeared to be hosted in several different countries. If you track them all back though, you end up at one single, common server. And that – marvellous to report! – is in Beijing.'

'Blimey!' Yoyo exclaimed. 'Who's the host?'

'Hard to say. Mind you, I'm afraid that this server might turn out not to be the last link in the chain either.'

'If we had some way of tracking each and every page routed out from there—'

'There's no list, if that's what you mean. Anyway, Diane is working with the latest miraculous software from Tu Technologies, so she found some more dead letter boxes in the web which respond to the same mask.' A reverential look passed over Tu's features. He looked at each of them in turn. 'The text is now a little longer.'

Jan Kees Vogelaar is living in Berlin under the name Andre Donner, where he runs an African private and business address: Oranienburger Strasse 50, 10117 Berlin. What should we continues to represent a grave risk to the operation not doubt that he knows all about the. knows at least about the but some doubt as to whether. One way or another any statement lasting Admittedly, since his no public comment about the facts behind the coup. Nevertheless Ndongo's that the Chinese government planned and implemented regime change. Vogelaar has little about the nature of

Operation of timing Furthermore, Orley Enterprises and have no reason
to suspect disruption. Nobody there suspects everything. I count because
I know, Nevertheless urgently recommend that Donner be liquidated.
There are good reasons to

'Orley Enterprises.' Yoyo frowned quizzically.

'Interesting, isn't it?' Tu grinned slyly. 'The world's biggest technology corporation. We were just talking about them! If you ask me, that throws a whole new light on the matter. It seems to have less to do with some violent handover of power in Equatorial Guinea and much more to do with who's top dog—'

'—out in space.' Jericho felt his ear. Right now he felt as though he'd been slogging and stumbling along a rutted country road for hours, and had just found out that the main road was running along-side. According to Vogelaar, their problems had begun in 2022 when a delegation paid a visit, supposedly from the Chinese aerospace ministry; Mayé had seen all his hopes dashed and was ready to take any deal. He signed a contract which could hardly have been more absurd, but Kenny stood for Beijing, and so Mayé had believed that he was dealing with an official delegation.

'Good.' He steepled his fingers. 'Let's forget Mayé for a moment. Yoyo, do you remember what Vogelaar said about the launching pad? Who built it?'

'The Zheng Group.'

'Exactly, Zheng. And who is Zheng's biggest competitor?'

'America.' Yoyo frowned again. 'No. Orley Enterprises.'

'Which more or less amounts to the same thing, if I'm not mis-taken. Orley helped the Americans towards lunar supremacy, and he's always just ahead of Zheng, any way you look at it. So Zheng turns to espionage—'

'Or to sabotage.'

'I see that you've got it.' Tu scrabbled around in the Brazil nuts and pistachios. 'They're talking about an *operation*, and the fact that Vogelaar *continues to represent a grave risk* because he *knows all about* something.

But what kind of operation could this be where people have to die in droves to keep it secret?'

Yoyo's face clouded over.

'An operation that's not been carried out yet,' she said slowly.

'I think so too,' Jericho said, nodding. 'Vogelaar doesn't seem to know anything about the *nature* or its *timing*, but he could send the whole thing sky-high if he made a *public comment about the facts behind the coup*. The whole world still believes that Ndongo got the presidency back under his own steam, or with Beijing's help—'

'Quite, and just for once we're not going to fall into the usual trap,' said Tu. 'Then there's more. *Furthermore, Orley Enterprises* – blah blah – *have no reason to suspect disruption*. And—'

'*Nobody there suspects everything.*'

'So they suspect something.' Yoyo looked from one to the other. 'Isn't that right? I mean, that's what you'd say if they know *something*.'

'We can't assume that the second phrase is actually complete, just because it looks it,' Jericho said. 'What's quite clear is that Orley Enterprises is part of the picture somehow. Then Zheng stands on the other side. The disaster in Equatorial Guinea is all down to some faked-up space programme that he got onto its feet. Zheng represents Beijing, although he could be acting on his own account. Julian Orley stands for Washington, he's the saviour of the American space programme and Zheng's natural enemy—'

'That's only true to a limited extent,' Tu butted in. 'Julian Orley is English himself, if I'm not mistaken, and he only plays that game with the Americans because they're useful to him. Even he's just acting on his own account.'

'So what's going on here? A proxy war?'

'Possibly. We've known since last year if not before that the Moon's got the potential to cause a crisis.'

'Vogelaar sees things differently,' Yoyo threw in. 'He reckons that Beijing was just a bluff on the part of whoever was actually behind the Equatorial Guinea satellite programme.'

'Call it Beijing or call it Zheng.' Tu shrugged. 'Do we really want to rule out the possibility that if a global corporation planned an attack on a rival, its government would give tacit approval?'

'Do dogs get in dogfights?'

'Wait a moment.' Jericho put his fingers to his lips. 'Orley Enterprises – haven't they just been in the news? There was a report about the Moon crisis a few days ago, and—'

'Orley is always in the news.'

'Yes, but this time there really was something new.'

'Of course!'A spark of recognition lit up in Yoyo's eyes. 'Gaia!'

'What?'

'The hotel! The hotel on the Moon! Gaia!'

'That's right,' Jericho said pensively. 'They're planning a hotel up there.'

'I think they've even built it by now,' Tu said, frowning in thought. 'It was supposed to be ready last year, and then there were delays thanks to the helium-3 flare-up. Nobody knows what it looks like. Orley's big secret.'

'You can find all kinds of speculation on the net,' said Yoyo. 'And you're right, it *is* ready. Sometime round about now there's even sup-posed to be— Hmm.'

'What?'

'I think there's supposed to be an inaugural trip. Some gang of filthy rich guests are flying up there. Maybe even Orley himself. Utterly exclusive.'

Jericho stared at her. 'Are you saying that the operation might have to do with this hotel?'

'Interesting.' Tu ran his fingers through the sparse growth at the sides of his head. 'We should get to work straight away. We'll have to learn all the latest about Orley Enterprises. What's up right now? What's planned in the near future? Then we'll have a look at the Zheng Group. Once we have Vogelaar's dossier on top of all that, we'll prob-ably be one giant leap further. When were you going to meet this guy, anyway?'

'Tomorrow noon,' said Jericho. 'At the Pergamon Museum.'

'Never heard of it.'

'Of course you haven't. Three thousand years of Chinese civilisation puts everything else just that little bit out of focus.' Jericho rubbed his jaw and looked at Yoyo. 'By the way, I don't think it's a good idea if we both turn up there.'

'Now wait a moment!' she protested. 'So far we've been through everything together.'

'I know. Nevertheless.'

'I see!' She tightened her lips into a hostile line. 'You're still pissed off because of Nyela.'

'No, not in the least. Really, I'm not.'

'Do you think that Vogelaar will try to shove you into the meat-slicer again?'

'He's unpredictable.'

'He wants money, Owen! He chose to meet in a public place. What's going to happen there?'

'Owen's right,' Tu put in. 'Do we know whether Vogelaar even has this dossier?'

Yoyo frowned. 'What do you mean?'

'Just what I say. He *told* you about a dossier. Did he actually show you one?'

'Of course not, he wants us to give him the—'

'So he could have been bluffing,' Tu interrupted her. 'Precisely *because* he wants the money. He could try to get the drop on Owen in the museum and make off with the hundred thousand.'

'Get the drop on him how?'

'Like this.' Jericho stretched out an index finger and put it to his temple. 'It works, even in crowds.'

'Well great!' Yoyo squirmed in her seat from rage and frustration. 'So that's why you want to go into the museum on your own?'

'Believe me, it's safer.'

'It would be safer with me and my haunch of antelope.'

'I'm faster and more adaptable on my own. I don't have to watch out for anyone but myself.'

'Like you can look after yourself, bunnikins.'

'I can look out well enough to save your skin twice.'

'Oh, so that's what it's about,' Yoyo huffed, turning red. 'You're worried you'd have to save my skin a third time. You think I'm a nitwit.'

'You're anything but a nitwit.'

'So what am I?'

'Could it perhaps be that you're trouble?'

'I should hope so!'

'Yoyo,' Tu said gently but firmly, 'I think the decision's been made.'

Yoyo had got herself worked up into a storm of indignation, and now came the cloudburst. Fat tears like raindrops gathered in the corners of her eyes, brimmed over her eyelids.

'I don't want to just sit about!' she said in a ragged voice. 'I got all of us into this mess. Don't you understand that I want to do something?'

'Of course we do. You'll be doing something if you help me with the research.'

The waiter appeared and checked their table. Tu plunged his hand into the bowl, as though afraid that he hadn't been giving due attention to the nuts.

'We'll haff to fime oup emryfing abou' Orley,' he muttered indistinctly. 'On fop of all vat' – he swallowed – 'I want to know more about Zheng's solo projects. After all, he's the only Chinese entrepreneur who could go building a satellite launch pad anywhere on Earth without prior state approval. You see, my dear Yoyo, even if Owen were to beg me on bended knee to let him take you with him, I'd still refuse.'

Yoyo glowered at him. 'You eat like a pig, just so you know.'

'Are you going to help me or are you not?'

'Have you two alpha males even considered letting Orley Enterprises know?'

'I have,' Tu said. 'All the same, I don't know exactly what we could tell them.'

'That something is going to happen, at some point in time, though we don't know what it is or what's the target, but that they are possibly the victim.'

'All admirably specific. Shall we also tell them that Zheng is behind the whole thing?'

'Or Beijing. Or the Chinese Secret Service.' Yoyo was visibly calming down. For the time being, it seemed that the dams would not burst. 'We don't know when the attack is going to take place – if indeed it *is* an attack. Mayé was deposed right around the time of the Moon crisis, it could even be that the crisis *was* the operation, but our text tells us something quite different. It's still to come. But when? How much time do we have? We zoomed over to Berlin at Mach 2 to warn Vogelaar. We should send word to Orley Enterprises at the speed of light, even if our message is very vague.'

'Excellent strategic argumentation,' Jericho put in.

Yoyo leaned back. She looked only halfway mollified. Jericho knew what she was going through, the rage, the shame and the helplessness of a child who isn't even allowed to clear up the mess she's made; he knew that her father's reproachful silence loomed up somewhere inside her. Like so many children, she had learned early enough that she wasn't up to some unspoken standards.

There was a pimply boy who knew all about such things.

Like the goddess Kali, the Orley conglomerate had many arms growing from its torso, so many that at some point Tu got fed up with following links and flowcharts. The company presented some excellent targets for attack. The hotel project was nominally part of Orley Space, which was responsible for the space programme and ancillary technologies, but then again it wasn't, because private travel to the Space Station and the Moon came under Orley Travel. For helium-3 mining and freight, NASA and the US Treasury were the people to talk to, but then again so were Orley Space and Orley Energy, whose main business was building fusion reactors. The further they delved into the labyrinthine structures of the company, the less they felt they knew about where the 'operation' might be aimed. Orley Entertainment produced films such as *Perry Rhodan*, which had made the Irish actor Finn O'Keefe one of the top earners in the movie world; it was also experimenting with the next generation of

3D cinema, and had built an Orley Sphere in several cities around the globe, each a huge spherical arena for grandiose concerts and events, seating thirty thousand visitors. Currently a concert on the OSS was in the planning stages, to be given by David Bowie – almost eighty years old – and this of course was Orley Entertainment's brief, but Orley Space and Orley Travel were also part of the project. There was a division for marketing and communication, Orley Media, as well as an innovation incubator where young researchers tweaked tomorrow's world into shape – this was Orley Origin. Once you got to the internet, the conglomerate grew and ramified like a spiral galaxy. When Diane tried the simple keyword *news*, it came up with a complete agenda for the twenty-first century. Everything was new, and everything really did mean *everything*, since there was hardly a field of human endeavour where Orley Enterprises wasn't trying to plant their flag, all of course with fervent belief and noble intent. There seemed no end to their search by the time they found OneWorld, an initiative which Julian Orley had founded to prevent global collapse; it poured forth projects for prevention and adaptation as reliably as the gushing geysers of Iceland, constantly testing new fuels and reagents, new kinds of engine, new this that and the other, all the way up to the meteorite shields which were being developed aboard the OSS in collaboration with Orley Space and Orley Origin.

And all of this under the aegis of Julian Orley, icon, philanthropist and eccentric, more like a rock star than a business mogul, smiling youthfully, the promise of endless adventure on his lips; he was America's ally and at the same time nobody's partner, a concerned citizen, generous patron, unpredictable genius, a master of time and space, the high priest of what-if, a man who seemed to hold the patent on planet Earth and interplanetary space, even on the future itself.

Diane also informed them that Gaia, the hotel on the Moon, was now open for a select group of guests led by Julian and Lynn Orley. The trip was organised by—

'That's enough for me,' Tu declared, and called company headquarters in London, asking to be put through to Central Security. Jennifer Shaw, the chief of security, was in a meeting, and her deputy, Andrew

Norrington, was travelling. In the end Tu spoke to a woman called Edda Hoff, number three in the hierarchy, who wore her hair in a pageboy cut like a crash helmet. She had all the personality and approachability of an electronic voice menu: if you want to report a terrorist attack, please say 'one'. For bribery, corruption and espionage, say 'two'. If you wish to attack us yourself, please say 'three'. She spoke as though Orley Enterprises spent the whole day fielding calls from people warning of dark deeds or announcing their own.

Tu sent her the text fragment. She read it carefully, without a flicker of expression passing across her mask-like face. She listened calmly to his explanations. It was only when Tu started talking about the hotel that her features came to life, and she raised her eyebrows so that they almost met her black fringe.

'And what makes you so sure that the attack is going to target Gaia?'

'I heard that it was open for business,' Tu explained.

'Not officially. The first group of visitors arrived there a few days ago, Julian Orley's personal guests. He himself—' She stopped speaking.

'Is up there?' Tu completed the sentence for her. '*That* would make me nervous!'

'There's nothing in the document about the timing of the operation,' she said somewhat pedantically. 'It's all rather vague.'

'What's not so vague is that innocent people have lost their lives because of this document,' Tu said, almost cheerfully. 'They're dead, dead as doornails, definitely dead, nothing vague about it, if you see what I mean. As for ourselves, we've also risked our lives so that you can read it.'

Hoff seemed to consider. 'How can I reach you?'

Tu gave her his phone number, and Jericho's.

'Do you plan to do anything about it?' he asked. 'And if so, when?'

'We'll let Gaia know. Within the next couple of hours.' The corners of her mouth lifted slightly, giving the illusion of a smile. 'Thank you for letting us know. We'll call you.'

The screen went dark.

'Was that a woman?' Yoyo wondered out loud. 'Or a robot?'

Tu snorted with laughter. 'Diane?'

'Good evening, Mister Tu.'

'Just call me Tian.'

'I shall do so.'

'How are you, Diane?'

'Thank you, Tian, I'm very well,' Diane said in her warm alto voice. 'What can I do for you?'

Tu turned back to the others. 'I've no idea who or what Edda Hoff is,' he whispered. 'But compared with her, Diane is *definitely* a woman. Owen, I owe you an apology. I'm beginning to understand you.'

Gaia, Vallis Alpina, The Moon

'Is there someone close to you whom you can trust unreservedly?'

Lynn thought about this. Her first instinct was to say Julian's name, but suddenly she felt uncertain about this. She loved her father and admired him, and of course he trusted *her*. But whenever she saw herself through his eyes she was terrified by the image of the woman with sea-blue eyes, the woman Julian called his daughter, and the worst of it was that she could only ever see herself through his eyes, that even as a child she had yearned for his approval as a plant turns towards the sun. But she wasn't that woman. So how could she trust *him*, since clearly he knew nothing at all of how she felt, didn't know that she was just a puppet on strings, a shape-shifting monster, a mimic, a tumour, a thing?

'Who are you thinking of at the moment?' asked ISLAND-II.

'Of my father. Julian Orley.'

'Julian Orley is your father?' the program asked, just to be sure.

'Yes.'

'He's not the person you trust, though.'

It wasn't a question, it was a statement of fact. The man sitting across from her leaned forward. Lynn breathed heavily, and the sensors in her

T-shirt dutifully registered her breathing and stored it in the database. The polygraph measured her body temperature, pulse, heartbeat and even her neuronal activity; the program scanned her voice frequencies as she spoke, measured her gestures, the way her pupils expanded or contracted, every movement of her eye muscles, each drop of sweat that formed. With every passing second of measurement, Lynn supplied more information for ISLAND-II, giving the program more to work with when it made statements about her.

The man seemed to stop and think for a moment. Then he smiled encouragingly. He was strongly built, completely bald, with friendly, thoughtful eyes. He seemed to be able to look through every veil that Lynn had wrapped around herself, her diorama of concealment, to pierce every layer with his glance but without that cool invasive gaze that psychologists so often used to put their patients under the microscope.

'Good, Lynn. Let's stick with the people around you right now. Tell me the names of the people you feel close to right now. And please leave a couple of seconds between every name.'

She looked at her fingernails. Talking to ISLAND-II was like walking a tightrope in the darkness to an unknown goal – along a torch-beam. The trick of it was to think of yourself as just as unreal as the program. The best thing was that there was no way of making a fool of yourself. For instance, Lynn had no idea at all whether there had ever been a real person who had served as the model for the bald man; the only thing she knew for sure was that it was impossible for him to feel contempt for her concerns. ISLAND-II – the *Integrated System for Listening and Analysis of Neurological Data* – was only as human as the therapists had programmed it to be.

'Julian Orley,' Lynn repeated – although the program had already struck him from the list of people she trusted – and she obediently included a brief pause. 'Tim Orley – Amber Orley – Evelyn Chambers – that's all of them, I think.'

Evelyn? Did she really trust America's most powerful talk-show queen? On the other hand, why not? Evelyn was a friend, even if they hadn't spoken much since the trip began. But the question had been about people she felt close to. What did 'close' have to do with trusting a person?

The man looked at her.

'I've learned a great deal about you in the past quarter of an hour,' he said. 'You're afraid. Less because of any actual concrete threats than because you have thoughts which make you horribly afraid. For as long as you do that, you can't feel anything else. And then because you've lost that ability to feel, you lurch into a depression, this makes you more afraid, and most of all you're afraid of fear itself. Unfortunately, when you're in this frame of mind, every one of your thoughts grows to monstrous size, so you make the mistake of imagining that there's some substance to what you're thinking and that's to blame for your condition. So you try to get rid of them at the level of substance, and you end up doing entirely the opposite. They only look like monsters, but the more seriously you take them, the bigger and stronger they grow.'

He paused to let his words sink in.

'But in point of fact the substance is practically interchangeable. It's not the substance of your thoughts that makes them frightening. Fear is a physical phenomenon. It's the fear that creates the substance. Your heartbeat speeds up, your chest tightens, you tense up, stiffen, you become rigid. Your inward horizons shrink down and now you feel helpless and no longer free. You rage against it, like an animal in a cage. All these physical symptoms taken together make you give your thoughts such weight, Lynn, that's why they have such horrible power over you. It's important that you learn to see through the mechanism. It's nothing more than that, you see. As soon as you manage to relax you'll be able to break the spiral. The more intensely you feel yourself, the less power your thoughts have to torture you. That's why any sort of therapy will have to begin with physical exercise. Sport, lots of sport. Exercise, feel the burn, make your muscles ache. Sharpen up your senses. Hearing, sight, taste, smell, touch. Leave all these projections behind and get out into the real world. Breathe deeply, feel your body. Do you have any questions?'

'No. Actually, yes.' Lynn wrung her hands. 'I understand what you mean, but – but – it's just that these really are very specific fears. I mean,

I'm not just making this up! What I've done here, what I've let myself in for. My thoughts only ever have to do with – destruction, disaster – death. Other people, dying. Killing, torturing them, destroying them! – I am so horribly afraid of turning into something, suddenly slipping my leash, that I'll leap on the others, tear them to shreds, people I love! Something eating away at me from inside, until there's nothing left of me but a shell, and inside that shell something awful, something strange, and – I don't know who I am any longer. I don't know how much longer I can take all the pressure—'

Suddenly there were tears in her eyes, drops of sheer despair. Her chin trembled. There seemed to be fluids spouting from everywhere, from her nose, the corners of her mouth, spilling over her lower lip. The man leaned backwards and looked at her from under lowered eyelids, maybe expecting that she would add something, but she couldn't say any more, she could only gasp for air. She wished she could vanish from this world, back to the womb, not to Crystal's though – the woman had never been able to offer her safety or warmth, all she had done was pass on her melancholy poison, the bad code written in her genes. She wished she had a father who would tell her that it had just been a bad dream, but not Julian – he would take her in his arms and comfort her, yes, but he wouldn't have the least idea of what her problem was, any more than he had been able to understand Crystal's depression and her later mental illness. That didn't mean though that Julian despised weakness, he just couldn't *understand* it! Lynn wanted to be back in the loving arms of parents who had never existed.

'I have very high expectations of myself,' she said, straining to sound businesslike. 'And then – I feel sure that they're too high, and I hate myself for falling short – for failing.'

She felt herself become transparent, and clutched her arms tightly around herself though it did nothing to make the feeling go away. She was talking to a computer, but she had rarely felt so exposed.

'I'll just suggest another way you could look at it,' ISLAND-II said after a while. 'These aren't *your* expectations. They are other people's expectations, but you've bought into them so completely that you *think* that they are yours. So you try to bring your actions into line with these expectations. You don't place any value on who you truly are, but rather on how other people would like you to be. But you can't deny your real self for ever, you can't spend for ever running yourself down. Do you understand what I mean?'

'Yes,' she whispered. 'I think I do.'

The man looked at her for a while, friendly, analytical.

'How do you feel right now?'

'Don't know.'

'The person you really are knows. Try to feel that feeling.'

'I can't,' she whimpered. 'I can't do something like that. I can't get – close to myself.'

'You don't have to conceal anything here, Lynn.' The man smiled. 'Not from me. Don't forget, I'm just a program. Albeit a very intelligent one.'

Conceal? Oh yes, she was the queen of concealment, had been since her childhood, when she had spent hours in front of the mirror, herself and her reflection practising concealment together, until she was able to project any possible expression onto her pretty face: confidence, when she was about to fall to pieces, easygoing calm when the winds of stress were screaming all around her, bluffing with an empty hand. And how quickly she had learned what such tactics could achieve, when the man she most wanted to please disapproved of the very idea of such concealment. But he couldn't see through her mimicry, and in the end even she couldn't see through it. In the hectic attempt to keep up with the pace he set, she developed a deep-seated aversion to finer feelings, her own included. She began to despise her fellow man's maudlin moods and public passions. Souls stripped bare, suffering on display, the clingy confidentialities of unearned intimacy. Letting the whole world know what side of bed you'd got out that morning, letting them all peer in at the bubbling chemistry of your mind – all this was repulsive. How much she preferred her own clean, hygienic concealment. Until that day five years ago when everything changed—

'What you're feeling is rage,' ISLAND-II said calmly.

'Rage?'

'Yes. Unfettered rage. There's a Lynn Orley trapped inside who wants to break out at last, and be loved, wants herself to love her. This Lynn has to tear down a great many walls, she has to free herself of a great many expectations. Are you surprised that she wants to maim and kill?'

'But I don't want to maim and kill,' she sobbed. 'But I can't – can't do anything to stop—'

'Of course you don't want to. Not physically. You don't want to do anything to anyone, Lynn, have no fear on that front. You're only torturing one person, yourself. There's no monster inside you.'

'But these thoughts just won't leave me alone!'

'It's the other way around, Lynn. You won't leave them alone.'

'But I'm trying. I'm trying everything I can!'

'They'll become weaker the stronger the real Lynn grows. What you think is some monstrous transformation is really just a new birth, a beginning. We also call it liberation. You kick and bite, you want to get out. And of course as you do that, something else dies, your old self, the identity that was forced upon you. Do you know what the three childhood neuroses are?'

Lynn shook her head.

'They're as follows: I have to. I mustn't. I ought to. Please repeat.'

'I – have to, mustn't – ought to—'

'How does it sound?'

'All fucked up.'

'From today, they don't count for you any longer. You aren't that child any longer. From now on, all that counts is: I am.'

'*I am what I am*—' Lynn sang in a wavering voice. 'And who am I?'

'You're the one who knows what you think and what you're doing. You are what's left when you have shucked away all those people you think are you, until all that's left is pure awareness. Have you ever had the feeling of watching yourself think? That you can see the thoughts rising up and then vanishing again?'

Lynn nodded weakly.

'And that's a very important truth as well, Lynn. You are not your thoughts. Do you understand? You are *not* your thoughts. You are not the same as what you *imagine* the world to be.'

'No, I don't understand.'

'An example. Are you aware right now that you can see the holographic image of a man?'

'Yes.'

'What else can you see?'

'Furniture. The chair I'm sitting on. A few gadgets, technology. Walls, floor, ceiling.'

'Where are you, exactly?'

'I'm sitting on a chair.'

'And what are you doing?'

'Nothing. Listening. Talking.'

'When?'

'What do you mean, when?'

'Tell me when this is happening.'

'Well, now.'

'And that's all we need. You are well aware of the world that's really there, around you, you can cut through to the world as it is. To the here and now. Then after that there's another now, and another now, and now, now, now, and so on and so forth. Lynn, everything else is just projections, fantasy, speculation. Do you find the here and now threatening?'

'We're on the Moon. Anything could go wrong, and then—'

'Stop. You're slipping away into hypotheticals again. Stay with what really is.'

'Well then,' said Lynn, unwillingly. 'No. Nothing threatening.'

'You see? Reality is not threatening. When you leave this room, you'll meet other people, you'll do other things, you'll experience a new now, then another now, and then another. You can look at each moment as it comes, and ask if it's threatening, but there's only one thought not allowed here – *What if?* The question is – *What is?* And then you'll find, nearly all the time, that the only threat is in your imaginings.'

'*I'm* dangerous,' Lynn whispered.

'No. You *think* that you're dangerous, so much so that it frightens you. But that's just a thought. It pops up and goes boo, and then you fall for it. Eighty-five per cent of everything that goes through our heads is rubbish. Most of it we don't even register. Sometimes, though, a thought comes along and goes boo, and we jump with fright. But *we are not* these thoughts. You needn't be afraid.'

'O-okay.'

The man was quiet for a while.

'Do you want to tell me any more about yourself?'

'Yes. No, another time. I'll have to end the session – for now.'

'Good. One more thing. Earlier I asked you whom you trust.'

'Yes.'

'I assessed your physiological responses as you named each name. I recommend that you confide in one of these people. Talk to Tim Orley.'

Confide in a *person*.

'Thank you,' Lynn said mechanically, without even thinking whether ISLAND-II cared for the common courtesies. The bald man smiled.

'Come again whenever you like.'

She switched him off, removed the sensors from her forehead, took off the T-shirt and put on one of her own. She stared at the empty glass plate for a while, unable to stand up, even though standing up was easier here on the fucking Moon than anywhere else.

Had it been wise to come here? To sweat and strain in front of a mirror that she really didn't want to look into? Famously, ISLAND-II could deliver some astonishing results. Since it had come along, manned space-flight without regular psychotherapy was unimaginable. During the 1970s, of course, the age of hero-worship, people would have been more likely to believe that Uncle Scrooge McDuck was real than they'd have believed that astronauts could suffer from depression, but now, in the era of the long-haul mission, everything depended on the mysteries of the human mind. Nobody wanted to screw up grotesquely expensive undertakings such as the planned missions to Mars just because of neurotic compulsions. The greatest danger didn't come from meteorites or technical failure, but rather from panic, phobias, rivalry displays and the good old sex drive, all of which urgently demanded a psychologist on board ship. Simulations had been tried, which yielded much food for thought. In two cases out of five, the psychologist lost his mind before anyone else, and began to drive the other crew members mad with his analytical skills. But even when he managed to keep it together, his presence didn't have the desired effect. It became clear that the other astronauts would rather swallow their own tongues than confide their troubles to a living, breathing fellow crew member, who could pass judgement on them. There were tragically obvious reasons for such self-censorship: men were worried for their careers, and women were scared of judgement and scorn.

Which was how virtual therapists had joined the game. At first, simple programs ran through questionnaires and gave advice straight out of the self-help shelves, then later came scripted exchanges, then finally software capable of complex dialogues. There was nothing here that could replace a video-link and a chat with friends and family, but what could be done on Mars, where it was virtually impossible to get a connection? In the end, prize-winning cybertherapists had developed a program which combined advanced dialogue capacity with simultaneous evaluation of the most extensive corpus of knowledge that any artificial intelligence had ever had access to. Sceptics proclaimed that every individual human being had their own specific needs, that only another human being could ever understand, but results seemed to show quite the opposite. There might be many doors to the labyrinth of the human soul, but once you'd wandered around in there for a while you always reached familiar ground. There weren't millions of different psychological profiles, just a few basic patterns repeated a millionfold. In the end, you always hit the same old neuroses, complexes and traumas, and most of them were acute in nature, such as squabbles over who had eaten whose last pot of chocolate pudding. Since then, ISLAND-I had been used in space stations, remote research installations and corporate headquarters all around the globe, while the incomparably more advanced ISLAND-II was so far only installed in Gaia's meditation centres and therapy rooms. Even its programmers didn't quite understand this pseudo-personality, a creature with no Promethean spark but able to learn astonishingly fast and reach remarkable conclusions.

After a while Lynn summoned up the energy to leave the therapy centre. As she walked to the lobby, her body language shifted to exude good cheer and brisk confidence. Guests walked past, euphoric, fidgeting restlessly, eyes as wide as children's, back from their excursions to the lava caves in Moltke Crater, the peak of Mons Blanc or the depths of the Vallis Alpina. They chattered away about mankind's civilising mission in the universe (specifically through tennis and golf), about the thrill of water sports in the pool here, about shuttle flights, grasshopper trips, moon-buggy rides, and of course, over and over again, about the view they had of Earth. Quarrels and disagreements seemed buried in the regolith by now. They were all talking to one another. Momoka Omura actually used words like *creation, humility*; Chuck Donoghue said that Evelyn Chambers was a real lady; Mimi Parker giggled as she agreed to take a sauna with Karla Kramp. Good cheer hung like a miasma over any honest, straightforward resentments they might have harboured. They were all hugs and smiles, even Oleg Rogachev, who forced each and every one of his fellow guests into a round of judo and sent them flying through the air for metres at a time with a nage-waza, grinning like a fox, *and of course nobody got hurt*! It was enough to make her throw up, but Lynn the chameleon listened to all the stories as though she were learning the secret of life, accepted compliments as a whore accepts payment, smiled as she suffered, suffered as she smiled. Quarter to eight, time to look forward to dinner. In her mind's eye she saw the first course served and devoured, saw a fish-bone stick in Aileen's throat, saw Rogachev spitting blood, Heidrun choking, saw Gaia's faceplate burst open and the whole merry gang of bastards sucked outside, defenceless in the vacuum, popping open, boiling, freezing.

Well, you didn't go pop straight away.

But their own mothers wouldn't have recognised the corpses.

Dana Lawrence looked up as Lynn came into the control room. She glanced at the clock. There were a few minutes yet before feeding time, and she had to go down to the basement for a routine check. Normally Ashwini Anand would take over in the control room while she was away, but she was just now looking into why the robot had failed to change the sheets in the Nairs' suite.

'Everything all right?' Lynn asked.

'So far, yes. There's been a tech failure up on level twenty-seven, nothing important.'

Lynn's eyes flickered. It was enough to trigger Dana's analytical turn of mind. She wondered what was wrong with Julian's daughter. More and more, she was showing signs of uncertainty, irritability. Why had she so vehemently refused to show Julian the footage two days ago? She looked at Lynn searchingly, but the woman had pulled herself together by now.

'Can you manage, Dana?'

'No problem. Look, since you happen to be here, could I ask you for a favour? I have to go downstairs for ten minutes. There'll be nobody in the control room during that time, and—'

'Just route it all through your phone.'

'I do, usually. It's just I'd like to keep an eye on everything when it all gets going in the restaurant. Could you take over for a while?'

'Of course.' Lynn smiled. 'Go on then, never fear.'

You're acting, Dana thought. What are you hiding? What's your problem?

'Thank you,' she said. 'See you soon.'

The control room. Little Olympus.

There were so many buttons you could press here, systems you could reprogram, settings and parameters you could shift. Increase the oxygen level until everything burst into flame. Mix in a lethal level of carbon dioxide. Shut all the bulkheads and lock away the restaurant party until they all went mad, one after another. Pump the sludge into the drinking water so that everyone fell ill. Stop the lifts. Unplug the reactor. Increase the internal air pressure and then shunt it all out in one. All kinds of fun you could have. There were no limits to creativity here.

I am dangerous.

Lynn's eyes drifted across the wall of monitors, all the areas under surveillance.

No. You are not your thoughts!

'*I am what I am,*' she sang softly.

Another tune joined in. A call from London, Orley headquarters, Central Security. Lynn frowned. Her hand hovered indecisively over the touchscreen, then she took the call, feeling queasy. Edda Hoff's face appeared on the screen, with her pageboy cut. Her mask-like features gave no clue as to whether she had good news or bad to report.

'Hello, Lynn,' she said in a flat voice. 'How are you?'

'Couldn't be better! The trip's a complete success. And down there? Body count? Armageddon?'

Hoff took worryingly long to reply.

'To be honest, I don't know.'

'You don't know?'

'A few hours ago someone got in touch with us. A certain Tu Tian, a Chinese businessman, currently in Berlin. He had a rather convoluted story to tell us. Apparently he and some friends of his have ended up in possession of restricted information, and since then they've been on somebody's hit list.'

'And what does that have to do with us?'

'The text that caused all this kerfuffle is very broken up. There are only fragments, but from the little that they've been able to send us it doesn't read much like a bedtime story.'

'What is it, exactly?'

'I'll send it over to you.'

A few lines of text appeared on a separate screen. Lynn read the text, read it again, then once more, hoping that the name Orley might perhaps vanish, but it just seemed to grow bigger every time she read it. She stared at the document, paralysed, and felt a black wave of panic roll towards her as though the conversation with ISLAND-II had never taken place.

Nobody there suspects everything.

'And?' Hoff urged her. 'What do you think?'

'It's a fragment, as you say.' Just don't show any uncertainty! 'A puzzle.

As long as we don't have the full text, we may perhaps be reading more into it than is really there.'

'Tu is worried that there will be an attack on Gaia.'

'That's going a bit far, don't you think?'

'Depends how you look at it.'

'There's nothing here to tell us when this operation is even going to take place.'

'That's what I told him. On the other hand, we can't simply ignore what's going on.'

'What is going on though, Edda? To decide whether or not you're going to ignore something, you need to know what it is, don't you? But we just don't know. Orley has interests worldwide: if there really is something planned against us, it doesn't necessarily have to be aimed at Gaia. How did this Chinese gentleman get that idea?'

'Because the reports are in all the newspapers.'

'I see.' Her thoughts raced. The edges of the room seemed to be blurring and fading. 'Well, that's true, the hotel is certainly most in the news, but that doesn't automatically mean that it's most at risk. At any rate, we really can't afford any upset up here at the moment – you do understand that, don't you, Edda? Not with *these* guests! There's no way we can risk scaring away potential investors with this sort of thing.'

'I don't want to scare anyone away,' Hoff said, somewhat indignantly. 'I'm doing my job.'

'Of course.'

'Apart from which, I didn't want to bother you about it, I thought I would speak to Dana Lawrence, but you just happened to pick up. And I'm not daft, Lynn. I know that you've got a crowd of investors up there, all very important people, ultra-rich, famous faces. But isn't that exactly what might suggest that the hotel is in some sort of danger?'

Lynn kept quiet.

'Be all that as it may,' she said in the end, 'you did the right thing telling us so quickly. We'll keep our eyes open up here, and you should do the same. Stay alert. Have you already talked to Norrington and Jennifer Shaw?'

'No. First of all I checked out this character Tu.'

'And?'

'A self-made millionaire from the first wave. Extremely successful. He runs a high-tech holography and virtual environments outfit in Shanghai. I found a few interviews and articles about him. Definitely not a nutcase.'

'Good. Stick with it. Tell me if there are any developments, and – Edda?'

'Yes?'

'Speak to *me* first if anything happens.'

'I'll have to tell Norrington and Jennifer as well of course—'

'Certainly you shall. Until then, Edda.'

Lynn ended the call and stared dead ahead. A few minutes later Dana came up from the basement levels. She got up, smiled and wished the director good evening, without breathing a word about the call. She left the control room at a steady pace, took the lift up to Gaia's curved bosom, squirmed into her suite as soon as the door slid open and dashed into the bathroom. She tore open the packet of green tablets and gulped down three of them, and even as she choked them down she was wrestling with a dark glass jar full of little capsules the size and shape of maggots.

It slipped through her fingers. Fell.

She snatched and caught it. Two little maggots crept out into the palm of her violently quivering hand. She shoved them hurriedly between her lips and washed them down with water. When she raised her head there was a Gorgon staring at her, a fearsome face with serpent hair; she wouldn't have felt surprised if she'd turned to stone on the spot. She was gripped tight by the feeling that she was falling, and that the fall would never end. The stuff wasn't working, not fast enough, she was rushing onward, headlong into madness, she would go mad if it didn't work, mad, mad—

Sobbing, she ran into the living room, forgot the lesser gravity for a moment, slammed straight into the wall and fell on her back. Helpfully, she ended up where she had wanted to be anyway, even if not quite like this, but what the hell. There it was, the minibar, right in front of her nose. Cola, water, juice, everything out, there had to be a bottle of red wine here somewhere, or even better the whisky, the little emergency ration that she had smuggled in, even though you weren't supposed to drink alcohol up on the Moon, blah blah blah, get it down, neck it—

The bourbon burned her throat as it went down. She crept back to the bathroom on all fours as her ribcage quivered from the coming eruption. She just made it to the toilet, clutched the sides of the bowl and spewed out a jet of whisky, tablets and whatever else was in her stomach. The vomit splattered against the ceramic in front of her, and some of it splashed back onto her face. Where were the tablets? A sour stench assailed her nose, brought tears to her eyes. She couldn't see anything. She retched again, although there was nothing left to bring up, until at last she could wrench herself away from the toilet bowl and collapse beside it. Whimpering, motionless, she lay there bathed in sweat and vomit, staring at the ceiling – and all at once she could breathe again.

Tim. ISLAND-II had said that she should talk to Tim. Where was he? At dinner? Had they already started? It's twenty past eight, you silly cow, of course they've started, a quick hello from the kitchen staff, fripperies of foam and essence and whatever damn thing those fools served up; anything she ate would come straight up again, but she had to go there, she couldn't stay lying here for ever could she, somebody would come and break the door down.

Fear is a physical phenomenon.

Oh how true, you clever-clogs machine, you Socrates!

All these physical symptoms together make you give your thoughts such weight, Lynn, that's why they have such horrible power over you.

She sat up carefully. Something buzzed and boomed inside her skull. She felt as though she had lain in the baking Sahara sun for a year, but she could still think straight, and her nerves slowly settled back down from the hideous shock that had set them thrumming. She climbed to her feet like an old woman, and looked at herself in the mirror.

'God, you look like shit,' she murmured.

As soon as you manage to relax you'll be able to break the spiral. The more intensely you feel yourself, the less power your thoughts have to torture you.

Well then. They'd just have to eat the first course without her. What she saw in the mirror there couldn't be fixed with just a bit of blusher.

She would have to retouch, for sure, but she'd be able to do that too. Then she would turn up in the Selene just in time for the main course, glowing and beautiful, the queen of concealment.

A succubus dressed as an angel.

Berlin, Germany

Tu insisted on an evening's entertainment once he had shot off messages to all and sundry, hoping to get some inside information about the Zheng Group. Some of the people he wrote to were already lying in their beds in Shanghai or Beijing at this time of day, while others were in America – these he either spoke with, or he left a message asking them to call him back. He quipped that at the end of the day, any information he could get about Zheng from America was going to be better than anything from China.

'Why's that?' Jericho asked, as they were served their Wiener schnitzel in the legendary Restaurant Borchardt.

'Why?' Tu raised his eyebrows. 'America is our best friend!'

'That's right,' Yoyo said. 'Whenever we Chinese want to know anything about China, we ask America.'

'Fine friends you have,' Jericho remarked. 'That friendship of yours makes the rest of the world quake in their boots.'

'Oh, Owen, come on now. Really.'

'Seriously! Didn't you say yourself that the Moon crisis was as bad as the Cuban crisis?'

Tu lifted up his schnitzel with his knife where it spilled over the edge of the plate, and peered doubtfully underneath, as though perhaps he might find something there to explain why Europeans didn't cut their meat into bite-sized morsels like civilised folk. He would rather have gone to a Chinese restaurant, but he had given way in the face of a dual chorus of 'You cannot be serious!'

'Quite so,' he said. 'And I was as worried sick about it as you were. But you just have to remember that China and America simply *can't* go to war. They are the twin giants of the global economy, and they might be at odds but they're joined at the hip. Traditionally, arch-enemies have always done the best deals, there are advantages to not actually liking the guy you're doing business with. If you like your trading partner, deals are guaranteed to go wobbly, but antipathy puts you on your guard. That's why China does so extraordinarily well when it trades with the nations it likes least of all, meaning the USA and Japan. Of course, if I wanted to know something about America, naturally I would get in touch with the Zhong Chan Er Bu.'

'That's all a heap of platitudes.' Jericho began to eat. 'The idea that the citizens of totalitarian regimes can find out most about themselves if they ask the people whose job it is to spy on them. We're talking about something else. Even the Americans can't peer into Zheng Pang-Wang's mind.'

'True. It's still worth asking the CIA and the NSA though, if you want to know something about him. Or for my money you could ask the Bundesnachrichten-dienst, the SIS, or the Sluzhba Vneshney Raz-vedki, or Mossad or the Indian Secret Service. You're a detective, Owen, you believe in infiltration. So do they. Anyway, experience has shown by now that it's easier to infiltrate a government than a company.' Tu squeezed some lemon onto his schnitzel, though from the look on his face he seemed worried it might jump from the plate and run out of the door. 'You said earlier that Orley Enterprises and the USA are the same thing in the end. They are. But only to the extent that Orley can set the conditions for American space flight. Of course, they don't like that. They hate the idea, but the truth is that the USA is *totally dependent* on Orley. Their space programme and their whole energy plan is drip-fed from the world's biggest tech company; it's plugged in to Julian Orley's money and his boffins' know-how. To that extent, Orley might be the same thing as American space-flight, but Washington's a long way from being the same as Orley. Even if you knew everything about what the American government was planning, you still wouldn't have much idea about Orley Enterprises. That corporation's a fortress. It's a parallel universe. It's a state in its own right. Extraterritorial.'

'And Zheng?'

'Well, that's different. American presidents may have been in hock to the oil lobby, or the steel barons or the military-industrial complex, but they were never totally identical. Even if that's just because the big corporations are by definition private in democratic countries. It's different in China – historically, they're rooted in the State, but they do what they like.'

'Are you telling me that the Party has lost power to the corporations?' Jericho asked. 'I'd be surprised to hear that.'

'Rubbish.' Yoyo shook her head. 'Losing power implies that somebody has shoved you aside and now rules in your place. But you're still there, for all that maybe you're sitting in opposition. But nobody shoved anybody aside in China, it was more like a one-hundred-per-cent transformation, a metamorphosis. Every old communist who kicked the bucket made room for some bright young thing with a Party membership book in his pocket and a chair on the board of a profit-making company.'

'It's not much different in America.'

'But it is. Washington has lost power to Orley Enterprises, and that probably makes the government stare out of the window cursing on rainy days, but at least there's somebody to stare and curse. There are no State institutions left in China where that could happen. The whole shooting match might still call itself communism, but it's really just a self-appointed government by corporate consortium.'

'You can look at it the other way round though,' said Tu, as though the two of them were moderating a political talk-show. 'China is governed by managers who have a second job in politics. The Western world still has a few heads of state who'll say No when private enterprise is saying Yes. Maybe the great big No dwindles away to a hopeless little bleating No, but at least there's still something or someone defending a position. In China you just have to imagine what No looks like when it's made up of a whole load of Yeses. When Deng Xiaoping decided to allow some experiments in privatisation, lots of people wondered how much privat-isation would be allowed in future. Well, the question's obsolete by now, since in the end communism itself was privatised.' He put down his knife and fork, picked the schnitzel up in his fingers and bit into it. 'And that, Owen, is why it's simpler to get information about a Chinese company from abroad than it is in China. If you want internal details about Zheng, all you have to do is tap into the flow of intelligence in all the nations spying on Beijing. And as it happens, I know some people in the intelligence services.'

Jericho fell silent. He had no idea whom Tu knew, or when he had crossed paths with the Secret Services in his busy lifetime, but he knew that he had rarely been given such a clear picture of a world where either the governments had been taken over by the corporations, or the corporations had lifted themselves clear of all governmental control.

Who was their enemy?

Around ten o'clock he felt tired, drained, while Yoyo was suggesting that they check out the local night life and see what trouble they could get into. She was in frantic high spirits. Tu demanded a look at the Kurfürstendamm. Jericho logged into Diane and teased out a list of the hot clubs and karaoke bars. Then he said he'd go back to the hotel, using the excuse that he had to work, which even happened to be true. He had been neglecting some of his clients dreadfully these past two days.

Yoyo protested. He had to come along!

Jericho hesitated. He had basically made up his mind to go back to the hotel, but all of a sudden he felt like giving in. When she protested, some previously undiscovered reserve battery had flooded his system with energy. It felt like extra oil in his tank, a warm feeling around the ribcage.

'Well, to be honest I really ought to—' he said, for form's sake.

'Okay. See you later then.'

The battery spluttered and died. The world snapped back into the unending winter of his teenage years, when he had only ever been invited to parties so that people could say afterwards that they hadn't forgotten him. It flashed through his mind that Yoyo would have plenty of fun without him, just as everybody else had been able to have plenty of fun without him back then.

How he had hated his youth.

'Well?' she asked, her eyes cold.

'Have fun,' he said. 'See you later.'

Later turned out to mean after he had done absolutely none of the things that he had gone back to the hotel to do. He lay there wondering where he had taken that wrong turn in life, why he always ended up where he least wanted to be, as one did in a nightmare. He was like a traveller standing at the luggage carousel waiting for a lost suitcase, while it was probably being auctioned off somewhere at the other end of the world; he waited and waited, and the certainty crept over him that maybe all he would ever do in life would be to wait.

About two o'clock he was half watching a botched 3D remake of Tarantino's classic *Kill Bill* when there was a shy knock at his door. He climbed to his feet, opened the door and saw Yoyo standing in the hallway.

'Can I come in?' she asked.

Automatically, he looked at the digital clock on his video wall.

'Thanks.' She shoved past him and came into his room, not quite steady on her feet. 'I know how late it is.'

Her eyes were as sad as a dog's. A cigarette between her fingers sent up its curls of smoke, and she'd evidently had a good deal to drink. By the look of her, they'd even run into a minor tornado somewhere on their adventures, which had left her rumpled. Jericho rather doubted that she'd had fun that evening after all.

'What are you doing right now?' she asked inquisitively. 'Got a lot of work done?'

'Not bad.'

There would have been no point telling her that he had spent the last few hours wrestling with his inner eighteen-year-old. 'And you? Had a good time?'

'Oh, fantastic!' She spread out her arms and spun about, so that Jericho suddenly he felt he should hurry to catch her. 'We ended up in some karaoke bar that was playing pure shit, but Tu and I managed to liven up the joint all the same.'

He sat down on the edge of the bed. 'You sang?'

'And how.' Yoyo giggled. 'Tian doesn't know even one line of lyrics, and I know them all backwards. A couple of guys hanging around there told us we should come along to a gig in a club. Some band called Tokyo Hotel. I thought they'd be Japanese! But they were German, old guys, dinosaurs of rock.'

'Sounds good.'

'Yes, but I had to go and pee after half an hour, and I couldn't find the loo anywhere. So we had to go in the bushes, and then on to the next pub that was still open. No idea where that was.'

She fell quiet all of a sudden, and slumped down onto the edge of the bed next to him.

'And?' he asked.

'Hmm. Tian told me something. Do you want to know what?'

Suddenly he was seized by the idiotic notion of kissing her and finding out what Tu had said that way, simply sucking the knowledge out of her. Drunk and dishevelled as she was, pasty and drawn, she seemed lovelier than ever. He felt it briefly in his loins and then straight away felt the pain of knowing that Yoyo had come here to *talk*.

He stared at Diane, sitting there cool and sexless. Yoyo looked down and sucked the last life from her cigarette.

'I'd like to tell you, you know.'

'Okaaay,' Jericho said, drawing out the word. He was turning her down flat and there was no way she couldn't know it.

'Well only if you're not—' She hesitated.

'What?'

'Maybe it is a bit late though. Is it?'

No, it's just the right moment, the adult man in his head shouted, but he was on autopilot now, frustration and misery had taken charge and were consummately giving Yoyo the cold shoulder. They looked at one another across an emotional Grand Canyon.

'Well then – I probably ought to go.'

'Sleep tight,' he heard himself say.

She got to her feet. Jericho was baffled by his own behaviour, but did nothing to stop her going. She paused for a moment, drifted indecisively over to the computer and then back again.

'We might hate it now but some day we'll look back on this time of life and we'll love it,' she said, suddenly speaking clearly. 'Some day we'll have to make peace, or we'll go mad.'

'You're twenty-five years old,' Jericho said, tired. 'You can make peace with whoever you please.'

'What the hell do you know?' she muttered and ran from the room.

Calgary, Alberta, Canada

She felt like a Dobermann chained up in front of a butcher's shop. Loreena Keowa couldn't think of any other way to describe it; her instinct had taken her straight to Beijing, to the conference which had led to Alejandro Ruiz vanishing so completely. She had caught the scent, she was just about to bite, she could sink her teeth into it, and now Susan wanted to *talk*. Why? What about? Sina couldn't give her any more help for now, because Susan Hudsucker had reservations. What a pointless waste of time and of opportunity! Loreena didn't doubt for a second that the reason for Ruiz's disappearance would become clear as day if only she knew what the conference had been about, and that the mystery of the attempt on Palstein's life would be solved at the same time. She was *so* close!

And now Susan wanted to *talk*.

Listlessly, she typed a couple of sentences into the *Trash of the Titans* script on her laptop. Strictly speaking, she didn't even need Sina's help. Sitting here in Calgary, she could access the databases at Vancouver headquarters just as easily as she could reach her own computer back home in Juneau. If she wanted, she could *be* headquarters. She could have searched the network off her own bat. All that was keeping her playing by the rules was respect, and the fact that so far Susan Hudsucker had always covered her back when it came to it. So she was planning to bring the chief a good, well-researched treatment – for *Trash of the Titans, part 1: The Beginnings* – to sweeten her up before she wooed her over to her cause, setting out the facts that would force her to make Palstein a priority.

Loreena shut her laptop. She caught the eye of the Chinese waiter killing time behind the bar polishing glasses, and held up her empty glass to let him know that she wanted another Labatt Blue. It was oppressively empty here in the Keg Steakhouse and Bar at the Calgary Westin hotel. She was looking forward to a grilled salmon and a Caesar salad, and impatient for the intern to arrive. She was more and more cautious about eating with him, mind you, since she was afraid he could well explode, showering her with the vast quantities of sausage, steak and scrambled eggs she had seen him shovel down in the past few days. On the other hand, the kid was good at what he did. He'd certainly have some information for her, when he did turn up.

The waiter brought her beer. Loreena was just about to take a sip when her phone rang.

'Good evening, Shax' saani Keek,' said Gerald Palstein.

'Oh, Gerald,' she replied, pleased. 'How are you? Quite a coincidence you should call, we're just busy right now with your friend Gudmundsson. Have you slung him out yet?'

'Loreena—'

'Maybe we should keep an eye on him for a while first.'

'Loreena, he's disappeared.'

It took Loreena a moment to realise what Palstein had just said. She stood up, took her beer, left the bar and found a private spot in the lobby.

'Gudmundsson has disappeared?' she asked, keeping her voice down.

'Him, and all his team,' said Palstein, looking worried. 'Since today noon. Nobody knows where. Eagle Eye can't reach him at any of his numbers, but I learned that one of your people had called them and had been asking about him.'

Loreena hesitated. 'If I'm going to find out who shot you, there's no getting past Gudmundsson.'

'I'm not sure we still have a deal.'

'One moment!' she yelped. 'Just because—'

'No, you listen to me a moment, will you? You're not a professional investigator, Loreena. Don't get me wrong, I'm deeply indebted to you. I'd never have known otherwise that Gudmundsson was working against me! Believe me, I'll do everything I can to support your ecological reporting, that's one promise I will keep, but from now on in you should leave all this detective work to the police.'

'Gerald—'

'No.' Palstein shook his head. 'They've got you in their sights. Get out of their cross-hairs, Loreena – these are people who kill to get what they want.'

'Gerald, have you ever wondered why you're still alive?'

'I was stupidly lucky, that's all.'

'No, I mean why you're *still* alive. Perhaps it was never even about killing you. Perhaps you'd be alive now even if you *hadn't* stumbled on the podium like that.'

'Do you mean—'

'Or perhaps they couldn't care either way. Think about it! Gudmundsson could have taken pot-shots at you a thousand times over by now, but instead you're running around without a care. I'm sure that the attack was simply intended to get you out of the way for a while.'

'Hmm.'

'All right, one small correction,' she added. 'If you hadn't stumbled, that bullet would have hit you in the head. But everything else is right, it *has* to be. Somebody wanted to stop you from doing something. My guess is stop you from flying to the Moon with Orley. And that worked, so why should they kill you now? Could be that Alejandro Ruiz wasn't so lucky—'

'Ruiz?'

'Strategic director at Repsol.'

'Slow down, my head's spinning. I really can't see any connection between myself and Ruiz.'

'I can though,' she breathed, looking around to see whether anyone was within earshot. 'My God, Gerald! You're the strategic director of a company that has spent pretty nearly its whole existence doing exactly what you didn't want it to do. It was only when everything was far too late and it was all going downhill that they gave you the power to do anything, and there's hardly anything you can do. This is exactly how it was with Ruiz! He was a voice of conscience, he fouled their nest and got on their nerves. He kept up the pressure on Repsol to get into solar power, he wanted a partnership with Orley Enterprises just like you did! He was talking to a brick wall there. And all of a sudden, when the ship's already sinking, they make him strategic director. You and Ruiz both spent years arguing for a stake in alternative energy, you're ignored and then put on the throne, one of you gets shot, the other one disappears in Lima, and you don't see a connection?'

Palstein didn't answer.

'On 1 September 2022,' Loreena went on, 'the day before he flew to Lima, Ruiz took part in a mysterious conference somewhere near Beijing. Something must have happened there. Something that shook him so badly that his own wife barely recognised his voice. Does that ring any bells?'

'Yes. Warning bells.'

'And what does that tell you?'

'That you're in danger. When you tell me all this, I actually think your suspicions are right. We can't ignore parallels like this.'

'There you have it.'

'And that's exactly why I'm worried.' Palstein shook his head. 'Please, Loreena. I don't want you to come to any harm because of me—'

'I'll be careful.'

'*You'll* be careful?' He laughed harshly. 'I was duped by my own bodyguard, and believe me, *I* was careful! Are you going to leave the detective work to the—'

'No, Gerald,' she pleaded. 'Twenty-four hours, give me twenty-four hours – every good thriller gives the detective twenty-four hours! I'm flying to Vancouver first thing tomorrow morning, then the whole thing goes up to boardroom level. All of Greenwatch will be working on the story. Tomorrow night I'll know what the conference was about, who Gudmundsson is really working for, and if I don't, I swear to you we'll bring the police on board. That's *my* promise to you, but *give me that much time.*'

Palstein looked at her with his sad eyes, and sighed.

'All right then. How many people have you shown those photographs to, of Gudmundsson and the Asian guy?'

'A few. Nobody recognises Fatty.'

'And this business with Ruiz?'

'Three, maybe four people know about it. I'm the only one who knows everything.'

'Then do at least this much for me. Keep it that way until you land in Vancouver. In the meantime, don't go lifting up any more rocks.'

'Hmm. Okay.'

'Promise?' he asked, doubtful.

'Honest Injun. You know what that means, for me.'

'Of course.' He smiled. 'Shax' saani Keek.'

'Take care of yourself, Gerald.'

'And call me when you get to Vancouver.'

'I will do. First thing.'

She hung up. The picture of Palstein faded out. Somewhat surprised, Loreena discovered that she found him oddly attractive, even if he was melancholic, in love with mathematics in that abstract way of his, a man who listened to weird music by dead avant-garde composers. On top of all which, he was shorter than her, a trim little man, almost skinny, losing his hair, the exact opposite of the broad-shouldered masculine type she usually went for. He had regular features, but they weren't especially striking; there was just something reassuring in his dark velvet eyes. She was back in the bar, still looking thoughtfully at the blank screen, when the chair across from her scraped noisily back.

'I'm dying of hunger here,' said the intern. 'Where's the menu?'

She put her phone away. 'I hope you've been busy. Steaks for information. One to one.'

'Should be enough here for a kilo of T-bone.' He spread out a dozen sheets of paper in front of himself. 'All right, watch this. I called Eagle Eye, the security company that provided Palstein's bodyguard. Dished them up a story about a journalist in peril, working on a sensitive story, needs protection, told them you'd just recently met Gudmundsson, Palstein had told you a lot of good things about him, yadda yadda yadda. They told me that Gudmundsson's a freelance and fairly busy keeping an eye on the oilman, so they'd have to see whether he still had any spare capacity, if not, they could put together a tailor-made team for you. By the way, they knew about you.'

Loreena raised her eyebrows. 'Oh yes?'

'From the web. Your reportage. They were pretty taken with the idea of protecting Loreena Keowa.'

'Flattering. Do they use a lot of freelancers?'

'Almost exclusively. Half of them are ex-police, the others are a mix of Navy SEALs, Army Rangers and Green Berets, some of them were mercenaries, active right round the world. Then they use ex-Secret Service agents for logistics and information operations, they prefer CIA, Mossad or the Germans. They tell me that the Bundesnachrichtendienst have excellent contacts, and the Israelis of course, but sometimes they even get guys from the KGB wandering into Eagle Eye, even Chinese or Koreans. If you ask, they'll give you the CV of any of their agents. They don't keep these things secret, quite the opposite! The career histories are part of their reputation.'

'And Gudmundsson?'

'He's half Icelandic, hence the name. Grew up in Washington. Ex-Navy SEAL, trained as a sniper, he's got his hands dirty, you could say. When he was twenty-five he joined a mercenary army, Mamba.'

'Never heard of them.'

'They were operating in Kenya and Nigeria at the beginning of the century. Then he went on to a similar operation in West Africa called African Protection Services, APS for short.'

'Hmm. Africa.'

'Yes, but he's been back in the States for five years now. He offers his expertise to private security companies, Eagle Eye and others, usually as project manager.'

Loreena thought it over. Africa? Was it important where Gudmundsson had worked before? What was certain was that he had betrayed one of his employer's clients. She couldn't rule out that Eagle Eye was involved there, but nor could she assume that that was the case. It was a well-respected company and their services were used by a lot of well-known figures. Interesting that Eagle Eye was already employing Gudmundsson at the time Ruiz disappeared. So what had Gudmundsson been doing on the night of the second to the third of September 2022? Where had he been the night Ruiz went missing? In Peru, perhaps?

'Was that all?' she asked. 'Nothing else?'

'Hey, come on there, that's not bad.'

'Might be enough for a roast potato.' She grinned. 'Okay, okay! And a couple of spare ribs.'

30 May 2025

MEMORY CRYSTAL

Berlin, Germany

Exobiologists had come up with scenarios for extraterrestrial life where you would least expect it. Weird forms of life thrived in volcanic vents, braved oceans of sulphur and ammonia, sprouted under the icy crust of frozen moons or glided with splendid lethargy through the banded skies of Jupiter, giant creatures with wings like manta rays, buoyed up by hydrogen in their body cavities that kept them from crashing down to the gas giant's metallic core.

At 6.30, one such creature was approaching Berlin.

Its skin shone in the cold, hard light of dawn as it curved slowly about and lost height. Its wingspan was almost a hundred metres. Its body and wings flowed seamlessly together, ending in a tiny vestige of a head that seemed to point to only rudimentary intelligence, compared with the size of the whole thing. But appearances were deceptive. In fact, this head brought together the whole calculating capacity of four autonomous computer systems which kept the monstrous body aloft, all under the supervision of pilot and co-pilot.

It was an Air China flying wing, coming in to land at Berlin. There was room on board for around one thousand passengers. The engineers who had built it were fed up with screwing their lifting surfaces onto canisters, and instead had created a low, hollow, symmetrical craft packed with seating all the way to its wingtips, an aerodynamic miracle. The giant's engines were embedded in the stern. Because of the phenomenally large surface area, it generated thrust even at low engine speeds, while at the same time the ray-shaped wings made for increased lift and kept turbulence to a minimum. This reduced fuel consumption and kept engine noise to a socially acceptable sixty-three decibels. The designers had even done without windows for the sake of the aerodynamics. Instead, tiny cameras along the midline filmed the world outside and broadcast their pictures to 3D screens which simulated glass panes. Flying here was a feast for the senses. All the same, airsickness could strike those who had the cheap seats out in the wingtips, which could hop as much as twenty-five metres up and down when the aircraft banked, and bore the brunt of the turbulence.

By contrast, the man walking back to his seat from the on-board massage parlour with a spring in his step was enjoying the luxury of the Platinum Lounge. Here, the simulation showed him nothing less than the view from the cockpit, a fascinating panorama with perfect depth of field. He sank back into the cushions and shut his eyes. His seat was precisely on the aircraft's axis, which was a stroke of luck considering how late he had booked. For all that, the people who had booked the flight for him knew his preferences. Accordingly, they had made sure they made their own luck. They knew that rather than take a seat just next to the axis, he would prefer to travel in a wingtip – or in the basket of a hot-air balloon, be dangled from a Zeppelin's bag or clutched in the claws of the roc bird. A middle seat was a middle seat, and not up for negotiation. The closer a thing was to perfection, the less he could bear falling short of that ideal, and something inside him pushed him to set things right straight away.

He looked out at Berlin below him in the sunlight, surrounded by green spaces, rivers, sparkling lakes. Then the city itself, a jewel box containing many different epochs. Long shadows fell in the morning light. The flying wing banked in a 180-degree curve, then fell to earth, speeding over the tower blocks, the public parks and avenues, dropping quickly. For a moment it looked from his exposed vantage point as though they were headed straight into the runway, then the pilot lifted the nose and they landed, almost imperceptibly.

The mood inside the aircraft changed subtly. For the last few hours the future had been in abeyance, a matter of aerodynamics and good will. Now it came rushing back to them with all its demands. Conversation broke out, newspapers and books were hastily put away, the aircraft came to rest. Huge hatched gateways opened to let the passengers flood out to all corners of the airport. The man picked up his hand luggage, and was one of the first to leave the plane. His data were already stored in the airport security system here. Air China had sent his files across to the German authorities not twenty minutes after take-off in Pudong, and right now the footage from the on-board cameras was also being transmitted. As he neared the gates, the German computer already knew what he had eaten and drunk on board, which films he had watched, which stewardess he had flirted with and which he had complained to, and how often he had gone to the toilet. The system had his digital photograph, his voiceprint, his fingerprints, iris scan, and of course it knew his first stop in Berlin, the Hotel Adlon.

He put his phone and then the palm of his right hand onto the scanner plate, said his name, and looked into the camera at the automated gate while the computer read his RFID coordinates. The system compared the data, identified him and let him through. Through the gates, the manned counters were lined up in a row. Two policewomen passed his luggage through the X-ray and asked him about the purpose of his visit. He answered in a cordial but somewhat distracted manner, as though his thoughts were elsewhere, at the next meeting. They wanted to know if this was his first time in Berlin. He said yes – and indeed he had never visited the city before. It was only when they handed back his phone that he let genuine warmth enter his voice, saying goodbye to them both and telling them he hoped they didn't have to spend their whole day standing behind this counter. As he spoke, he looked the younger policewoman straight in the eyes, wordlessly telling her that for his part, he wouldn't at all mind spending this lovely sunny Berlin morning with her.

A tiny, conspiratorial smile shot back at him, the most she would allow herself. You're a good-looking guy and no mistake, it said, and your suit is wonderfully well cut, we both know what we're after, thank you for the flowers, and now get lost. Meanwhile she said out loud,

'Welcome to Berlin, Zhao *xiansheng*. Enjoy your visit.'

He walked on, pleased that in this country they knew the proper forms of address. Ever since Chinese had become compulsory at most schools in Europe, travellers could at least be sure that traditional Chinese first names and family names wouldn't get mixed up, and that the family name would be followed by the right honorific. At the exit a pale, bald man with eyes like a St Bernard's and hangdog jowls was waiting for him. He was tall, strongly built, and wore his leather jacket fastened all the way to the neck.

'*Fáilte*, Kenny,' he said softly.

'Mickey.' Xin gave him a hearty clap on the shoulder in greeting without breaking stride. 'How's the last remnants of the IRA?'

'Couple of them dead.' The bald man fell in step beside him. 'I hardly have contact with them these days. Which name did you fly in with?'

'Zhao Bide. Is everything organised?'

'All in place. Had a hell of a delay in Dublin, mind you. Didn't get in here until after midnight – what a shitty flight. Well, that's life, I suppose.'

'And the guns?'

'Got them ready.'

'Where?'

'In the car. Do you want to go to the hotel first? Or should we go straight to Muntu? It's still dark there, mind. So's the upstairs flat. Probably still asleep.'

Xin considered. Already, a week ago, once his people had cracked Vogelaar's new identity, Mickey Reardon had dropped by Muntu to check the place out for possible entrances. Alarm systems had been his speciality back in Northern Ireland. Since the IRA had fallen apart he, like many former members, was at work on the open market, and from time to time did jobs for foreign intelligence agencies as well, such as the Zhong Chan Er Bu. Ordinarily Xin liked to work with younger partners, but Mickey was in good shape even if he was in his late fifties; he knew his way around a gun and could navigate any electronic security system blindfold. Xin had worked with him several times before, and in the end had recommended him to Hydra. Since then he'd been on Kenny's team. He might not be a towering intellect, but he didn't ask questions either.

'Off to the hotel quickly,' Xin decided. 'Then we'll get it over and done with.' He squinted up into the sunlight and swept the long hair from his brow. 'They say Berlin's very nice. Maybe it is. I still want to be out of here this evening at the latest, though.'

*　　*　　*

But Jan Kees Vogelaar wasn't asleep.

He hadn't shut an eye all night, which was only partly to do with the headache left behind by Yoyo clouting him with a joint of meat. It was much more to do with talking to Nyela and agreeing on a plan to flee to France for the time being, where he had contacts with some retired Foreign Legionnaires. While Nyela began to pack, he organised their new identities. That evening Luc and Nadine Bombard, descended from French colonists out in Cameroon, would arrive in Paris.

At half past seven he called Leto, a friend of theirs, half Gabonese, who had come to Berlin a few years ago to help his white father fight his cancer. Nyela had met him the day before on the city's grand avenue, Unter den Linden. Leto had been in Mamba before the company joined the newly founded African Protection Services, and had helped them open Muntu. He was the only one in Germany they could trust, even if he didn't know all the details of why Vogelaar had had to get out of Equatorial Guinea. As far as he knew, Mayé had been toppled by Ndongo, financed by who knew which foreign powers. Vogelaar had avoided setting him right on the matter.

'We'll have to disappear,' he said brusquely.

Leto had obviously just got out of bed to answer the call, but was so surprised he forgot to yawn.

'What do you mean, disappear?'

'Leave the country. They're onto us.'

'Shit!'

'Yes, shit. Listen, can you do me a favour?'

'Of course.'

'When the banks open in two hours' time I'm going to empty our accounts, and then I'll have a few things to take care of. Meanwhile Nyela will go downstairs to Muntu and pack whatever we can take from there. It would be good if you could keep her company there. Just to be on the safe side, until I'm back.'

'Sure.'

'Best thing is if you meet her up in the flat.'

'I'll do that. When do you want to leave?'

'Right after noon.'

Leto fell silent for a moment.

'I don't understand it,' he said. 'Why don't they just leave you in peace? Ndongo's been back in power for a year now. You're hardly any threat to him any longer.'

'He's probably still not got over me putsching him out of office back then,' Vogelaar lied.

'That's ridiculous,' Leto snorted. 'It was Mayé. You simply got paid for it. It wasn't anything personal.'

'All I need to know is that the goons have turned up here. Can you be with Nyela by half past eight?'

'Of course. No problem.'

An hour and a half later Vogelaar flung himself into the stream of rush-hour traffic. The traffic lights took so long to change they seemed to be doing it out of spite. He crossed Französische Strasse, made it as far as Taubenstrasse, squeezed his Nissan into a tiny parking spot and went into the foyer of his bank. The temple of capitalism was full to the brim. There was a huge crush in front of the self-service computers and the staffed windows, as though half of Berlin had decided to flee the city together with himself and Nyela. His personal banker was dealing with a red-faced old woman who kept pounding the flat of her hand against the counter in front of the window to punctuate her harangue; Vogelaar caught his eye, and gave him a signal to let him know he'd wait next door. He hurried over to the lounge, collapsed into one of the elegant leather armchairs and fumed.

He'd wasted his time. Why hadn't he fetched the money the afternoon before?

Then he realised that by the time Jericho and his Chinese girlfriend had left, the banks were probably closed. Which didn't make him any less angry. Really, it was archaic that he had to hang around here like this. Banks were computerised businesses, it was only because he wanted to carry the money from his account home as cash that he needed to be physically present. Glowering, he ordered a cappuccino. He had hoped that his banker would call him in the next couple of minutes and ask him to come back to the foyer, but this hope was dashed to pieces under the red-faced woman's avalanche of words. All the other counters had queues snaking around them as well, mostly old people, very old some of them. The greying of Berlin seemed in full swing now; even in the moneyed boulevards a tide of worry backed up like stagnant water, the worry about old age and its insecurities.

To his surprise his telephone did ring, just as he raised the coffee to his lips. He got up, balancing the cup so that he could take it across with him, glanced at the display and saw that the call wasn't from the bank foyer at all. It was Nyela's number. He sat down again, picked up the call and spoke, expecting to see her face.

Instead, Leto was staring at him.

Straight away he realised that something wasn't right. Leto seemed distraught about something. Not quite that. Rather, he looked as though he had got over whatever had upset him, and had decided to keep that look on his face to the end of his days. Then Vogelaar realised that the end had already come.

Leto was dead.

'Nyela? What's up? What's happened?'

Whoever was holding Nyela's phone stepped back, so that he could see all of Leto's upper body. He was leaning, slumped over the bar. A thin trickle of blood ran down his neck, as though embarrassed to be there.

'Don't worry, Jan. We killed him quite quietly. Don't want you getting into trouble with the neighbours.'

The man who had spoken turned the phone towards himself.

'Kenny,' Vogelaar whispered.

'Happy to see me?' Xin smirked at him. 'You see, I was missing you. I spent a whole year wondering how the hell you managed to slip through my fingers.'

'Where's Nyela?' Vogelaar heard himself ask, his voice dwindling and dropping.

'Wait, I'll hand you over. No, I'll show you her.'

The picture lurched again and showed the restaurant. Nyela was sitting on a chair, a sculpture of sheer fear, her eyes open wide with terror.

A pale, bald man clamped her tight to the chair, his arm stretched across her. He was holding a scalpel in his other hand. The tip of the blade hung motionless in the air, not a centimetre from Nyela's left eye.

'That's how things are,' Xin's voice said.

Vogelaar heard himself make a choking noise. He couldn't remember ever having made a sound like that before.

'Don't do anything to her,' he gasped. 'Leave her alone.'

'I wouldn't read too much into the situation,' Xin said. 'Mickey's very professional, he has a steady hand. He only gets twitchy if I do.'

'What do I have to do? Tell me what I have to do.'

'Take me seriously.'

'I do, I take you seriously.'

'Of course you do.' Xin's voice suddenly changed, dark, hissing. 'On the other hand, I know what you're capable of, Jan. You can't help yourself. Right now there are a thousand plans racing through your head, you're thinking how you could trick me. But I don't want you to trick me. I don't want you even to try.'

'I won't try.'

'Now that would surprise me.'

'You have my word.'

'No. You won't really understand why you shouldn't even try until you've grasped the basic importance of saving your wife's sight.'

The camera zoomed in closer. Nyela's face filled the screen, twisted with fear.

'Jan,' she whimpered.

'Kenny, listen to me,' Vogelaar whispered hoarsely. 'I told you that you have my word! Stop all that, I—'

'One eye is quite enough for anyone to see with.'

'Kenny—'

'So if you could grasp the importance of saving what *remains* of her sight, then—'

'Kenny, no!'

'Sorry, Jan. I'm getting twitchy.'

Nyela's scream as the scalpel struck was a mere chirrup from the phone's speakers. But Vogelaar's yell split the air.

Grand Hyatt

Jericho blinked.

Something had woken him up. He turned on his side and glanced at the clock display. Almost ten! He hadn't intended to sleep this long. He leapt out of bed, heard the room's phone ringing, and picked up.

'I've got your money,' Tu said. 'One hundred thousand euros, just as our dog of war demands, not too many small-denomination notes, you'll be able to get through the museum door.'

'Good,' said Jericho.

'Are you coming down to breakfast?'

'Yes, I— Think I will.'

'Come on then. Yoyo's making a spectacle of herself with the scrambled eggs. I'll keep some warm for you before she eats it all.'

Yoyo.

Jericho hung up, went into the bathroom and looked into the mirror. The blond man with the three-day beard who stared back at him was a fearless crime-fighter who put his life on the line, but didn't know how to use a razor or even a comb. Who didn't even, come to that, have the decency to say No loud and clear, not even when he really wanted to say Yes. He had a nagging feeling that last night he had screwed everything up again, whatever 'everything' meant here. Yoyo had come along to his room, drunk as a skunk but in a chatty mood, she could hardly have found her way there by accident, and she'd wanted to *talk*. The pimply kid inside him hated that idea. But what was talking, except a little ritual that might lead who knows where? It was person-to-person, it was open-ended. Anything could have happened, but he had taken umbrage and had let her scurry off, then stubbornly watched the re-make of *Kill Bill* right to the end. It had been about as abysmally bad as he deserved. This arrested adolescence was like lying on a bed of nails, but at last he had fallen comatose into a restless sleep and dreamed of missing one train after another at shadowy stations, and running through a dreary Berlin no man's land where huge insects lurked in cavernous houses, chirruping like monstrous crickets. Antennae waved at him from every doorway and corner, chitinous limbs scuttled hastily back into the cracks in the wall in a game of half-hearted hide-and-seek.

Trains. What heavy-handed symbolism. How could he be having such ploddingly obvious dreams? He looked the blond man in the eyes, and imagined him simply turning away and walking off into the mirror, leaving him alone there in the bathroom, sick and tired of his inadequacies, the inadequacies of that pimply kid.

He had to get rid of the kid somehow. Anyhow. Enough was enough!

Vogelaar

His shout burst through the lounge like a nuclear blast, tearing to shreds all conversation, all thought. Sleepy jazz muzak tinkled away in the sudden silence. On the low glass table in front of him, an abstract composition in coffee and foamed milk surrounded a jagged heap of shattered porcelain.

He stared at the display.

'Do you understand me?' Xin asked.

His knees gave way. Nyela's muffled sobs sounded in his ear as he sank back into the leather chair. Nothing had happened. The scalpel had not plunged into her eye, had not sliced through pupil and iris. It had simply twitched, and then stopped dead still once more.

'Yes,' Vogelaar whispered. 'I understand.'

'Good. If you play by my rules, nothing will happen to her. As for what will happen to *you* though—'

'I understand.' Vogelaar coughed. 'Why all the extra effort?'

'Extra?'

'You could have killed me by now. As I left the building, on my drive across town, even here in the bank—'

The picture vanished, and then he saw Xin again.

'Quite simple,' he said, back to his chatty old self. 'Because you've never worked without a safety net and an escape hatch. You believe in life after death, or at least you believe in lawyers opening deposit boxes and releasing their contents to the press. You've made arrangements in case you die suddenly.'

'Do you need help?'

Vogelaar looked up. One of the lounge staff, with a startled look on his face, a hint of disapproval. No screaming and shouting in banks. At most, they were places were you could contemplate a dignified suicide. Vogelaar shook his head.

'No, I – it's just that I've had some bad news.'

'If there's anything that we can do—'

'It's a private matter.'

The man smiled with relief. It wasn't about money. Someone had died, or had an accident.

'As I say, if—'

'Thank you.'

The staffer left. Vogelaar watched him go, then got up and left the lounge hurriedly.

'Go on,' he said into the phone.

'Your sort of insurance rather depends on the idea that if anyone's out to cause you harm, they'll go after *you*,' Xin continued. 'So you can warn them to keep their hands off. If I don't turn up to take afternoon tea tomorrow at such and such a time and place, with all my bits and pieces intact, the bomb goes off somewhere. It's a lone wolf strategy, because for most of your life you were a lone wolf. But you're not any longer. Perhaps you should have changed your plans.'

'I have.'

'You haven't. That bomb will only be detonated if it's your life at stake.'

'My life, and my wife's.'

'Not exactly. You've changed your mind but you haven't changed your habits. Earlier you'd have said, get the hell back on the next plane out, Kenny, there's nothing you can do. Or, kill me and see what happens. But now you're telling me, leave Nyela alone or I'll make things hot for you.'

'You can be sure of that!'

'Meaning that you could still set off the bomb.' Xin paused. 'But then what would we do with your poor innocent wife? Or to put it another way, how long would we do it to her for?'

Vogelaar had crossed the foyer, and went out into the crowds on Friedrichstrasse.

'That's enough, Kenny. I see what you mean.'

'Really? Back when Vogelaar only cared about Vogelaar, life was hard for people like me. Back then you'd have said, go on, kill the woman, torture her to death, see where it gets you. We'd have played a little poker, and in the end you'd have won.'

'I'm warning you. If you harm even a hair on Nyela's head—'

'Would you die for her?'

'Just come out with it and tell me what you want.'

'I want an answer.'

Vogelaar felt his mind soar, saw his whole life spread out beneath his wings. What he saw was a bug, biting, pinching, stinging, playing dead or scuttling lightning-fast into a crack. A drone, a programmed thing, but one whose armour had been corroded these past few years by regular doses of empathy. His instincts had been ruined once he realised that there was in fact a purpose to life, that there could even be a purpose to dying so that others might live. Xin was right. His plans were out of date. This bug was sick and tired of creeping into cracks, but right now the future held nothing else.

'Yes,' he said. 'I would die for Nyela.'

'Why?'

'To save her.'

'No, Jan. You'd die because altruism is an egotist's crowning glory, and you're a deeply egotistical man. Nothing appeals more to a man's self-importance than martyr-dom, and you've always had a very high sense of your own importance.'

'Don't speechify, Kenny.'

'You have to know that you won't save anyone with your death, not if you try to cheat. You'd be leaving Nyela on her own. There'd be no end to her suffering. You'd have achieved nothing.'

'I understand.'

'So what's your escape hatch this time?'

'A dossier.'

'This is what Mayé wanted to blackmail us with?'

'Yes.'

'Where?'

'In the Crystal Brain. It's on a memory crystal.'

'Who knows about it?'

'Only my lawyer, and my wife.'

'Nyela knows what's in the dossier?'

'Yes.'

'And your lawyer?'

'He doesn't know a thing. He just has instructions to retrieve the crystal if I should die a violent death, and upload the contents to a distributor feed.'

'Why didn't you tell him what was in the dossier?'

'Because it's nothing to do with him,' Vogelaar snorted, growing angry. 'The dossier only exists to protect Nyela's life, and mine.'

'That means that as soon as I have this crystal— Good, fetch it. How long do you need?'

'An hour at most.'

'Is there anyone coming by here before then we should know about? Cleaner, kitchen porter, postman?'

'No one.'

'Off you go then, old friend. Don't dawdle now.'

Vogelaar was no tree-hugger. He drove a solar-powered Nissan because Nyela was concerned about the environment. He realised of course that more small cars meant less traffic in the city, but something in his genes cried out for a jeep. But now that he was crawling painfully through the government quarter, he cursed aloud every vehicle bigger than his own, and felt a sweeping rage against all the damned ignorant drivers hereabouts.

And in fact Germany was the country with the most innovative car technologies that had ever been left to slumber in a drawer. Hardly any market worldwide was fonder of petrol motors and speedsters. While in Asia and the USA the number of hybrid cars on the roads had been steadily dropping in favour of ever more sustainable designs, in Germany the hybrid itself had never even made a dent. Nowhere else were hydrogen, fuel cells and electric cars condemned to such a miserable waking death. And nowhere else in the world did men set such store by having a big, *imposing* car, and by driving it themselves – despite the availability of sophisticated and totally safe autopilots. It was as though whenever the Germanic national character set out to find itself, it always ended up, with tiresome predictability, behind the steering wheel. The only thing less popular hereabouts than the compact car was the future itself.

All of which explained why the Nissan crept along so slowly. Vogelaar swore, and slapped the wheel. When he finally turned into the car park at the Crystal Brain, he was bathed in sweat. He leapt from the cabin and strode hurriedly across to the main entrance.

Einstein looked him square in the face, briefly.

The building had been put up in 2020, not far from the government quarter, but it still looked as though it had just landed. It was a cubist glass UFO with dozens of perfectly faceted surfaces where the logo 'Crystal Brain' came and went, glowing like a passing thought. Worlds showed like ghosts in the façade as you approached, different from every angle: raptors loping across the Jurassic savannah, Stone Age hunters hurling their spears at mammoths, Assyrian kings holding court. He saw Greek hoplites, Roman emperors, Napoleon on horseback and Egyptian princesses, pyramids and Gothic cathedrals, the *Kon-Tiki* and the *Titanic*, satellites, space stations, moon bases, the stern face of Abraham Lincoln,

Shakespeare's bald head and smiling face, Bismarck, Niels Bohr, Werner Heisenberg, Konrad Adenauer, Marilyn Monroe, John Lennon, Mahatma Gandhi, Neil Armstrong, Nelson Mandela, Helmut Kohl, Bill Gates, the Dalai Lama, Thomas Reiter, Julian Orley, geocentric, heliocentric and modern representations of the universe, abstract diagrams of quantum worlds on the Planck scale, molecules, atoms, quarks and superstrings like model building blocks, the invention of the wheel, of printing, of curried sausage. All this and infinitely more was there, holographically embedded in the huge walls; it came to life, breathed, pulsated; the figures turned their heads, winked, smiled, shook hands, walked, flew, swam and vanished again as the viewer moved around them. The exterior alone was a masterpiece, a wonder of the modern world, and yet it represented barely a fraction of what was hidden within.

When Vogelaar stepped inside the Crystal Brain, he was entering the world's greatest concentration of knowledge in the smallest space.

He walked through the foyer's shimmering dome. Lifts rose and fell to either side of him, seemingly unsupported, a sophisticated optical illusion. They were a fractal representation of the building itself, just as everything in the Crystal Brain was built using the principle of self-similarity. The smallest component, the memory crystal, resembled the largest, the building itself. A crystal in a crystal in a crystal.

The world's memory.

The tales that mankind had to tell about the world could fit either in one single book, or into so many that even a whole extra planet full of libraries would not be enough to hold them. The Bible, the Qur'an and the Torah knew nothing of evolution, or of the tangled chains of causality, or of Schrödinger's cat, nothing of the uncertainty principle or standard deviation, nothing of non-linear equations and black holes, nothing of the multiverse, of extra-dimensional space or of how time's arrow could be made to point backwards. These books were sturdy, impregnable vehicles of faith driving down a one-way street to the absolute truth; they made vast claims, but they were compact.

Look beyond these, though, and the planet was bursting with information.

History alone was a vast academic discipline: millions and millions of works dedicated to deciphering the past, like a cloud chamber filled with the trails of fleeting elementary particles. It was almost impossible to determine their speed and direction, regardless whether they had to do with the colour of Charlemagne's hair or with whether he had ever even existed. There was huge variety in the fields of physics, philosophy, futurology. The dizzying number of all articles published to date, all the essays, novellas, novels, poems, song lyrics, the works of Bob Dylan alone and then all the commentary about them! The verbiage of assembly instructions for stainless-steel barbecue grills, the meteorological data that had heaped up since records began, the collected speeches of the Dalai Lama, the totality of every menu from every Chinese restaurant from Cape Horn to the Bosphorus, the avaricious words from every one of Uncle Scrooge McDuck's speech balloons, the angry, exasperated replies that his hapless nephew quacks in turn, the careful record of every leaflet from every packet sold of haemorrhoid cream or anti-depressives . . .

There was definitely a storage problem.

The book was definitely not the answer.

But CD-ROMs, DVDs and hard drives had also run up against the limits of their capacity, helpless in the face of the exponential growth of information. They were threatened by digital oblivion. Given how long chiselled stone slabs could last, Christianity could take comfort in the thought that the Ten Commandments still existed somewhere. Books could only last about two hundred years, unless they were printed with iron-free ink on acid-free paper, in which case their life expectancy was triple that. Celluloid film was estimated to last about four hundred years, CDs and DVDs maybe one hundred, while floppy discs lasted maybe a decade. Even so, floppies were still in theory better than USB sticks, which showed signs of amnesia after only three years, but then again there were no floppy disc drives any longer. There were thus three principal obstacles to a permanently accessible and truly compact global memory: limited storage capacity, rapid storage decay, rapid hardware obsolescence.

Holographics had solved all three problems at one blow.

The eight storeys of the Crystal Brain housed racks of crystals and laser reading desks, roomy lounges for historical sightseers; it was an El Dorado for an alien who might happen along one day far in the future, clearing away the rampant vegetation in search of human artefacts. Vogelaar, though, blind to the glories around him, made for one of the lifts and rode it down to the second sub-basement, where storage space could be rented for private data. He authorised himself – eye-scan, hand-print, all the usual – and was let through to an atrium glowing with diffuse light.

'Number 17-44-27-15,' he said.

The system asked him if he wanted a place at the lasers. Vogelaar declined, saying that he would take his data away with him.

'Aisle 17, section B-2,' the system said. 'Do you know your way about, or would you like directions?'

'I know my way.'

'Please retrieve your crystal within five minutes.'

A glass door slid back at the end of the atrium. Behind it, aisles branched off to either side, their walls apparently smooth and featureless. Lines ran along the floor, marked with aisle and section numbers. Vogelaar went to his aisle, stopped after a few steps and turned his head to the left. Only the closest examination revealed that the mirror-smooth wall was in fact divided up into tiny squares.

'17-44-27-15 is being prepared for delivery,' the system said.

A faint mechanical click sounded from the mirror. Then a thin, rectangular rod slid out. The transparent object inside was about the size of half a sugar cube. One of millions of crystals that made up the totality of the Crystal Brain, high-efficiency optical storage media with integrated data processing and encryption. They had no moving parts and were practically indestructible. Memory crystals had a storage capacity of one to five terabytes, and were readable at several gigabytes per second. Access time was well under a millisecond. The storage was written in by lasers, etching electronically readable data patterns into the layers of the crystal. A single layer could hold millions of bits; one crystal could hold thousands of pages. Vogelaar's dossier took up only a tiny fraction of that.

'Please remove your crystal.'

Vogelaar looked at the tiny object and felt his mood plunge. Suddenly he was overcome by despair. He sank down against the wall opposite, unable to pick up the little cube.

How could it all have gone so horribly wrong?

It had all been in vain.

No, it hadn't. There was still a chance.

He considered just how far he could trust Xin. In fact, incredible though it might sound, he *could* trust the killer, to a certain extent, at least within Xin's own strictly defined limits of madness and self-control. Vogelaar didn't doubt for a moment that, in the final analysis, Kenny managed to keep his madness at bay with his manic penchant for numbers and symmetry, his constant search for oases of order and his highly personal code of honour. Xin knew perfectly well that he was mad. On the surface, he seemed eloquent, convivial and cultured. But Vogelaar had some idea of just how hard Xin found it to hold an ordinary conversation, and how hard he tried regardless. There must be some final scrap of humanity left alive inside him, a yearning that he could not admit even to himself, a need to be something other than what he was. Something that prevented him from simply gunning down anybody in his way, from setting the world on fire, from becoming the final all-engulfing flame. If he gave Xin this crystal, he would have to make a deal with him for Nyela's life and his own, although perhaps it would only be Nyela. One way or another, he'd have to decide whether he was going to give the killer everything, this dossier—

And the *copy* of the dossier.

'Please remove your crystal within the next sixty seconds.'

He shrugged himself away from the wall, took the little cube between his finger and thumb and held it up to the light. He could see tiny fault-lines inside, history in miniature. He put it in his pocket. He left the basement as quickly as he had arrived, took the lift upstairs, quickened his pace as he came out onto the car park, and started the Nissan. By some miracle the traffic had ebbed away, so that he was able to park in front of the restaurant before his time ran out. This time he didn't allow himself a moment's delay but got out and walked to the entrance with his hands raised, palms outward. He saw the bald man through the glass pane of the door, a silenced pistol in his right hand. Slowly, he opened the door and peered into the gloom. Leto's feet were sticking out from behind the bar.

'Where's Nyela?'

'Went in there with Kenny,' said the bald man, in a thick Irish accent. He motioned with his gun towards the swing doors. Vogelaar didn't spare him a glance as he walked through the dining area and into the kitchen. The gunman followed.

'Jan!'

Nyela wanted to go to him. Xin held her back, a hand on her shoulder.

'Let her go,' said Vogelaar.

'You can say hello later. What happened, Jan? Your kitchen looks like it was hit by a herd of elephants.'

'I know.' Vogelaar looked at the chaos left behind by his fight with Jericho, his face expressionless. 'Do you want to clean up, Kenny? Put everything back? You'll find all you need under the sink: scourers, cleaning spray – I know that you can't bear to look at a mess.'

'That's in my own world. This is yours. Where's the crystal?'

Vogelaar reached into his jacket pocket and put the memory crystal on a clear spot on the worktable. Xin picked it up in his fingertips and turned it this way and that.

'And you're sure that this is the right one?'

'Dead sure.'

'I want to go to my husband,' Nyela said, softly but emphatically. Her eyes looked sore from weeping, but she seemed to be keeping it together.

'Of course,' Xin murmured. 'Go to him.'

He was gazing at the crystal as though under a spell. Vogelaar knew why. Crystals were one of those forms that Xin loved. Their structure and purity fascinated him.

'You've got what you wanted,' he said. 'I kept my promise.'

Xin looked up. 'And I never even gave one.'

'What did you do then?'

'I was just talking through the options. It's really too risky to let the two of you live.'

'That's not true.'

'Jan, you disappoint me!'

'You promised to spare Nyela's life.'

'Either he lets us both live or neither.' She hugged herself close to Vogelaar's chest. 'If he kills you, he can shoot me straight away as well.'

'No, Nyela.' Vogelaar shook his head. 'I won't let that—'

'Do you really believe that I'd just watch this bastard shoot you?' she hissed, her voice dripping with hate. 'He's a monster. How many years he came and went at our home, accepted our drinks, put his feet up on our terrace. Hey, Kenny, do you want a drink? I'll mix you a drink that will make the flames shoot out of your eyes.'

'Nyela—'

'You leave my husband alone, do you hear me?' Nyela screamed. 'Don't touch him, or I'll come back from the dead to have my revenge, you miserable wretch, you—'

Xin's face clouded with resignation. He turned away, shaking his head, tired.

'Why does nobody listen to me?'

'What?'

'As if I had ever minced my words. As if the rules hadn't been clear from the start.'

'We aren't here to follow your shitty rules!'

'They're not shitty,' Xin sighed. 'They're just – rules. A game. You played too. You made wrong moves. You lost. You have to know how to leave the game.'

Vogelaar looked at him.

'You'll keep your promise,' he said quietly.

'One more time, Jan, I never gave you a—'

'I mean the promise you're about to give.'

'That I'm – about to?'

'Yes. You see, there's still something you want, Kenny. Something I can give you.'

'What are you talking about?'

'I'm talking about Owen Jericho.'

Xin spun about. 'You know where Jericho is?'

'His life for Nyela's,' Vogelaar said. 'And spare me the rest of your threats. If we die, we die without a word. Unless—'

'Unless what?'

'You promise to spare Nyela. Then I'll serve you up Jericho on a silver tray.'

'No, Jan!' Nyela looked at him, pleading. 'Without you I couldn't—'

'You wouldn't have to,' Vogelaar said calmly. 'The second promise concerns myself.'

'Your life against whose?' Xin asked threateningly.

'A girl called Yoyo.'

Xin stared at him. Then he began to laugh. Softly, almost silently. Then louder. Holding his sides, throwing back his head, hammering his fists against the tall fridge, quivering with hilarity as though he was having a fit.

'Incredible!' he gasped out. 'Unbelievable.'

'Is everything all right, Kenny?' The bald man furrowed his brow. 'Are you okay?'

'All right?' spluttered Xin. 'That girl, Mickey, that detective, the two of them should get a medal! What an achievement! They took those few scraps of text and – incredible, it's just incredible! They tracked you down, Jan, they—' He stopped. His eyes opened wide, even more astonished. 'Did they actually come to *warn* you?'

'Yes, Kenny,' Vogelaar said calmly. 'They warned me.'

'And you're betraying them?'

Vogelaar was silent.

'You try to find fault with my morals, you reproach me with some promise I've supposedly made, and then you rat out the people who came to save your life.' Xin nodded as though he had just learned a valuable lesson. 'Look at that, just look at that. Unredeemed man. What did you tell the two of them about our adventure in Africa?'

'Nothing.'

'You're lying.'

'I'd like to be,' Vogelaar snarled. 'In fact I offered them a deal. The dossier, for money. We were just about to make the exchange.'

'That's priceless,' chuckled Xin.

'And? What now?'

'Sorry, old friend.' Xin wiped a tear of laughter from the corner of his eye. 'Life doesn't offer all that many surprises, but this – and do you know what's the best thing about it? I even *considered* that they might come and find you! Just as you consider the possibility that *perhaps* next week you'll be hit by a meteorite, that *perhaps* there's a God. I fly off to Berlin in a tearing hurry to prevent something that I never really – never! – thought would actually happen, but life – Jan, my dear Jan! Life is just too wonderful. Too wonderful!'

'Get to the point, Kenny.'

Xin threw his hands in the air in a gesture that said, let's all have a drink. A baron among his minions.

'Good!' he guffawed. 'Why the hell not!'

'What does that mean?'

'It's a promise. It means you have my promise! If everything runs on rails, no hiccups, no tricks from you, not even *thinking* about tricks, not even a wrinkle in the skin – *then* the two of you can live.' He came closer and narrowed his eyes. His voice took on that hissing note again. 'But if, contrary to my expectations, *anything* from that dossier becomes public, then I promise that Nyela will die by inches, you can't even begin to imagine how! And you'll be allowed to watch. You'll see how I pull her teeth out one by one, see me cut off her fingers and toes, gouge out her eyes, I'll flay the skin from her back in strips, and all that while Mickey here rapes her over and over again until there's nothing left for him to fuck but a whimpering lump of bloody meat, and by then she's still *a long way* from dead, Jan, a *long* way, I promise you that, and I'll keep every one of *these* promises.'

Vogelaar felt Xin's breath on his face, looked into those cold eyes, dark as night, felt Nyela tremble in his arms, heard his heartbeat in the sudden silence. He believed every word that Xin said.

With a dry crack, the faulty neon tube gave up the ghost.

'Sounds good,' he said. 'It's a deal.'

Museum Island

In satellite images of Berlin, the Museum Island in the river Spree stuck out like a wedge, a kilometre and a half long, driven slapdash into the neatly laid parquetry of the city's boulevards. An ensemble of imposing buildings, linked by broad paths and walkways, housing exhibits from over six thousand years of world history. Visitors could pass from huge halls the size of cathedrals, through quiet cloisters, to great court-yards flooded with light, could get lost in the megalomaniac grandeur of ancient architecture or lose track of time in silent galleries full of more human-scale artworks. At the northern end of the island, the Bode Museum towered above the water like some baroque ocean liner, its col-umned prow crowned with a great dome, while at the southern end of the whole complex a Classicist façade churned out crowds of visitors in its wake. Most imposing of all was the Pergamon Museum, a vast building like something glimpsed in a dream – if a bewhiskered German patriot of the nineteenth century had nodded off dreaming over a book of Greek myth. A huge, glowering central hall was flanked by two iden-tical wings to either side, colossal rows of pillars marching off to end in Doric temple façades. The ground plan had originally been a U-shape, but in 2015 a fourth wing had been added, glassed-in, that made the building into a square. Here, as in no other museum on Earth, visitors could walk through millennia of human history, Egyptian, Islamic, Near Eastern and Roman.

Jericho had often crossed the island during trips to Berlin, taking one of the many bridges that moored it to the city, without ever having set foot in one of the museums. There had never been time. Now, as he hur-ried along the banks of the Spree, the thought that the time had finally come was not a cheering one. His jackets bulged with all the packets of money which made up Vogelaar's payment. His Glock was in its holster, invisible to all. He looked like any other tourist, but he felt like the proverbial goose, off to meet the fox for dinner. As long as Vogelaar actually had the dossier, the two of them would make the exchange quite quietly and calmly, cash for information, and be on their way. If he didn't, there would be trouble in store. The mercenary would want the money by hook or by crook, and he would certainly not rely on a smile and a kind word to get it.

Jericho felt his ear and slowed his pace.

The Pergamon Museum's temple façade seemed to stare at him, each window a watchful eye. In the fourth wing, crowds of culture vultures jostled along the glass hallway, among the last surviving traces of lost empires. He walked on, glancing at his watch. Quarter past eleven. They had agreed on twelve o'clock, but Jericho wanted to get to know the location first. On his right, a long, modern building abutted the rest, its lower storey modelled after the older architecture while the top was a tall, airy colonnade: the James Simon Gallery, entrance to the museum island's web of walkways. Visitors bustled across to the island in a chattering, sweating throng. Jericho joined the crowd crossing this arm of the Spree and was carried along up a grandiose stairway to the top floor of the gallery. He bought his ticket in a spacious hall lined with terraces and cafés, and followed the signs for the Pergamon Museum.

His first impression as he entered the southern wing of the museum was that he had walked into nirvana. The only feature in the room which tied it to earthly time and space was the Romanesque arched window towards the river. The exhibits were lifted clean out of any historical context, displayed in a space so huge it could almost be hyperspace, and looked splendid yet lonely at one and the same time, a chilly, hypothetical view of history. Jericho turned right and walked along a kind of street, with walls on either side, its frieze and battlements glowing with rich colour, reading the explanatory captions as he went. The animals in the frieze represented the Babylonian gods, with stately lions for Ishtar, goddess of love and protector of armies, serpentine dragons for Marduk, god of fertility and eternal life, patron of the city of Babylon, and wild bulls for Adad, lord of storms. Nebuchadnezzar II had ordered an inscription for the walls, reading 'May ye walk in joy upon this Processional Way, oh ye gods.' He could never have dreamed that the moment would come when groups of Japanese and Korean tourists would mill about in confusion here, losing their bearings amidst the grandeur of the past, hurrying to catch up with the wrong tour guide, confused by identical tabards. There was a model of Babylon in a glass cube, with a truncated pyramid in the middle soaring heavenwards; this was the ziggurat, the temple of Marduk. So that was where the God of the Old Testament had poured out his wrath, onto this surprisingly low tower, where he had confounded their language. Right then. This street had originally led to the ziggurat from the Ishtar Gate, which dominated the next hall, blue and yellow, glorious, shining like the sun, covered like the walls of the Way with the gods' totem animals. The mass of visitors crowding the Way gave some idea of what it must have been like here at the time of the great processions.

Rush hour in Babylon.

Jericho went through the gate of Babylon and emerged 660 years later from a Roman gate that took up the whole wall of the next hall: the Market Gate of Miletus, two storeys high, a showpiece of transitional architecture, halfway between Hellenistic and Roman. He kept a constant lookout for exit routes. So far, it was easy to keep his bearings in the museum. The only thing that might slow him down was the density of the crowd of visitors, moving only at glacial speeds. Next to him, a Korean man was gesticulating furiously, telling his tour guide that he had lost his wife to the Japanese, only to learn that *he* had ended up with the Japanese. This was the modern equivalent of the Tower of Babel, with languages mixing in confusion: the tourist group huddled into a knot. Jericho edged his way around them and escaped to the next hall.

He knew where he was at once.

This was where Vogelaar had chosen for the meeting. The room was the size of a hangar, but more than half of it was taken up by the front of a colossal Roman temple. Even the stairway leading up to the colonnades had to be a good twenty metres wide. All around the base of the temple ran a comic strip in marble, twice the height of a man, which the museum signs announced as the famous frieze of the Gigantomachy, showing the story of the Greek gods' battle against the giants. It was the tale of an attempted coup, making it the perfect place to meet Vogelaar: Zeus had slighted Gaia by imprisoning her monstrous children, the Titans, in Tartarus – a sort of primordial Black Beach Prison. Gaia was determined to free them from the underworld and get rid of the hated father of the gods and all his corrupt crew, so she roused up to rebellion her children who were still at liberty. These were the giants, and Gaia knew that they could not be killed at the hands of a god. The giants were well-known ruffians, and just to make them scarier, they had giant snakes for legs. They leapt at the chance to protect their mother's honour, and this gave Zeus the pretext to indulge in yet another of his many dalliances with human women – *This is just a strategic move, Hera, it's not how it looks!* – and to father Hercules, a mortal, who would be able to sort the giants out. The giants put up a fight, chucking around hilltops and tree-trunks, so Athena rose to the challenge – *Anything you can do, I can do better!* – and flung whole islands at them, burying one of the ringleaders, Enkelados, under nothing less than Sicily; from that moment on, the giant blew his fiery breath up through Etna, while another, Mimas, was trapped beneath Vesuvius, and Poseidon scored a square hit on a third giant with the island of Kos. Most of them, though, succumbed to Hercules' poisoned arrows, until the whole serpent-legged brood was exterminated. The frieze told the same old story, of a struggle for power, with the same old weapons. Who were the Fang, who were the Bubi, and who were the colonialists? Who bankrolled whom, and why? Had there been a dossier back then as well, containing the whole story, something like 'The Truth about the Gigantomachy' or 'The Olympus Files'? A dossier like the one that the last surviving giant from Equatorial Guinea claimed to have?

Jericho's gaze turned to the stairway.

There were three entrances to the pillared central hall, where the altar had once stood. Vogelaar had said he'd be waiting there. He climbed the gleaming marble steps, went through the columns and found himself in a large, rectangular space, brightly lit, with another, smaller frieze running around its walls. From up here there was a good view of everything happening down at the bottom of the stairs, as long as you didn't mind being seen in turn. Further back in the room, and you were safely out of sight.

Jericho looked at his watch.

Half past eleven. Time to explore the rest of the museum.

He left the temple hall the other way and went into the north wing, where he found other examples of Hellenistic architecture. And what if Vogelaar *didn't* have a dossier? He paced along the façade of the Mshatta palace, a desert castle from the eighth century. He was increasingly worried that the whole thing might be a trap. Romanesque windows marked the end of the north wing, but he couldn't have said what he had seen in this part of the museum. As a scouting trip to learn the lie of the land, this was a wash-out. Stone faces stared down at him. He turned left. The way through to the fourth wing of the museum, the glass wing, led between rams and sphinxes, past pharaohs, through the temple gate from Kalabsha and beneath artefacts from the pyramid temple of Sahuré. Suddenly Jericho felt reminded of another glass corridor, the one where the ill-fated Grand Cherokee Wang had met Kenny Xin. An omen? With a grating sound, arms lifted, spear-tips were raised, granite fingers closed on the hilts of swords carved from stone. He went on, the daylight flooding in on him. To his right he could look through the windows that covered the whole wall, down to one of the bridges over this arm of the Spree, while to his left the inner courtyard of the museum stretched away. In front of him was an obelisk showing priest-kings gesturing strangely from the backs of glaring beasts, and in the corner was a statue of the weather god Hadad. Here the glass corridor joined the museum's south wing and completed the circuit, leading back to the Babylonian Processional Way.

Twenty to twelve.

He went into the Pergamon hall for the second time, and found it besieged by art students who had parked themselves on the landing with sketch pads and were beginning to turn the glories of antiquity into rough sketches for their own future careers. He started up the steps with a feeling of foreboding. In the inner courtyard with the Telephos frieze, visitors were shuffling from one marble fragment to the next, seeking history's secrets in the missing arms and noses. Jericho's head pounded as he paced among the crippled heroes, eavesdropping on a father who was lecturing his offspring in muffled tones, stifling whatever faint glimmer of interest they might ever have had in ancient sculpture. With every date he mentioned, the kids' frowns grew deeper. The look in their eyes spoke of honest bafflement – why were grown-ups so keen on broken statuary? How could anyone get through life without arms? Why not just fix the things? Their voices were older than their years as they feigned enthusiasm for smashed thighs, stone stumps and the fragmentary face of a king, without hope of escape.

Without hope of escape—

That was it. Up here, he was trapped.

Pessimist, he scolded himself. They had saved Vogelaar's life, and furthermore the Telephos hall wasn't the kitchen at Muntu. The exchange would take place, swift and silent. The worst that could happen would be that the documents didn't contain what the seller claimed. He tried to relax, but his shoulders had frozen solid with tension. The father was doing his best to enthuse his children for the beauty of a right breast, floating free, which must, he explained, have been part of the lovely goddess Isis. Their eyes darted about, wondering what was lovely or beautiful here. Jericho turned away, glad all over again that he was no longer young.

Vogelaar

His thoughts were a whirl. He was caught up on a merry-go-round of ifs and buts as his feet carried him mechanically along the Processional Way. *If* Jericho and the girl got there at the time agreed, *if* Xin kept to the arrangement, *if* he could actually trust the Chinese assassin – but what if he couldn't? Here and now, he was in danger of letting the last chance to free Nyela slip through his fingers, but she was in the clutches of a madman who quite possibly never even intended to let her, or him, live. He had decades of experience in finding his way out of tight spots, but it was no use. He was unarmed, without even a phone, in the middle of a crowded museum, and his chances of putting one over on Xin were slim – but it wasn't impossible. Could he really afford not to use any tricks? Just how dangerous was this Mickey who was currently watching over Nyela? The Irishman gave the impression of being just another hapless career criminal, but if he worked for Xin, he had to be a threat. Nevertheless Vogelaar reckoned he could get rid of the guy, but first of all he had to deal with Xin.

An attack, then. Or not? In the next couple of minutes, before he reached the Pergamon hall. Unarmed and with no plan.

Not a glimmer!

No, he *couldn't* attack. The only way to get one over that madman was blind luck, but what if Xin actually intended to keep his promise? What if Vogelaar failed in his attempt to put one past him, and in failing, actually *caused* Nyela's death, not to mention his own?

Trick him? Trust him? Trick him?

Five minutes earlier, in the James Simon Gallery.

'I understand you,' Xin says gently. 'I wouldn't trust me either.' He's close behind Vogelaar, the flechette pistol hidden under his jacket.

'And?' Vogelaar asks. 'Would you be right?'

Xin considers for a moment.

'Have you ever got to grips with astrophysics?'

'There were other things in my life,' Vogelaar snarls. 'Coups, armed conflict—'

'A pity. You would understand me better. Physicists are concerned, among other things, with the parameters of a stable universe. Or indeed of any universe which could come into existence at all, as such. There's a long list of facts to deal with, but it all comes down to two different points of view. One of them says that the universe is infinitely stable, that it never even had any choice but to develop in the form in which we know it. If things had been different, perhaps no life would have been able to arise. Pondering such matters though is as pointless as wondering what your life might have been like if you'd been born a woman.'

'Sounds fatalistic, boring.'

'Philosophically speaking, I quite agree. Which is why the other camp likes to speak of the infinite fragility of the universe, of the fact that even the smallest variation in initial parameters could lead to fundamental changes. A tiny little bit more mass. Just a very few less of this or that elementary particle. The first camp says that all sounds too contingent, and they're right. But the second viewpoint does come closer to the way we imagine existence to be. What if . . . ? For myself, I prefer a vision of order and predictability, grounded in binding, non-negotiable parameters. And that's the spirit in which we made our agreement, you and I.'

'Meaning that you can always come up with some reason you needn't keep your promise.'

'You have a petty mind, if I may be so bold as to say so.'

Vogelaar turns around and stares at him.

'Oh, I already see what you mean! I understand how you see yourself. Might the problem perhaps be that your' – he waved his hand in the air in a circle – 'idea of universal order doesn't hold true for your fellow mortals?'

'What's up all of a sudden, Jan? You were calmer just a moment ago.'

'I couldn't give a damn what you think about that! I want to hear you say that Nyela will be safe if I keep my side of the bargain.'

'She's my guarantee that you'll keep it.'

'And then?'

'As I have said before—'

'Say it again!'

'My goodness me, Jan! Truth doesn't become any more true just from being repeated.' Xin sighs and looks up at the ceiling. 'If you like, though. As long as Mickey's with her, Nyela's fine, she's safe. If everything else goes according to our agreement, nothing will happen to either of you. That's the deal. Are you content?'

'Partly. The devil never does anything without his reasons.'

'I appreciate the flattery. Now do me a favour and move your arse.'

The Market Gate of Miletus.

Xin's words in his ear. What if he turned round, right now, this moment? Ran through the museum full tilt, tried to reach the restaurant before him? That would definitely change the parameters! But to do that he would have to know exactly where Xin was. He had stayed behind as they went into the south wing. Vogelaar had turned round once to try to spot him, but hadn't been able to see him among the hordes of tour groups. He didn't doubt that the killer was watching his every step, but he also knew that from now on in, Xin would stay invisible until the time was ripe. Jericho and the girl were sitting in a trap in the Telephos hall. He would show up as though out of thin air, shoot twice—

Or would it be three times?

Trust him? Trick him?

Xin wasn't sane. He didn't live in the real world, he lived in some *abstraction* of reality. Which was actually a reason to trust him. His madness forced him to cling to order. Perhaps Xin wasn't even *able* to break a promise, as long as all the parameters were observed.

He shrugged his way through the crowds and approached the entrance to the Pergamon hall, a smaller gate in the Hellenistic façade, which was just now being cleaned and restored. To leave a clear view of the architecture, the museum had clad it with glass walls rather than shrouds. The glass reflected the spotlights from the ceiling, and the statues and the columns all around, the visitors, himself—

And someone else.

Vogelaar stared.

For the length of a heartbeat he was helpless against rising panic. Iron bands clamped his ribcage, and an electric field paralysed his legs. Rage, hate, grief and fear pooled like a thrombosis in his feet, which became numb, refused to take one more step. Instead of horror at all the things that could happen to Nyela, he felt the searing certainty of what had most probably already happened.

As long as Mickey's with her, Nyela's fine—

Then why was Mickey in the museum?

Because Nyela was no longer alive.

It could only be that. Would Xin have allowed her to stay in the restaurant unguarded? Vogelaar walked on as though drunk. He had failed. He had surrendered to the childish hope that the madman might keep his promises. Instead, Xin had ordered the Irishman to come along to the museum to share the work of killing. That was all. Just as Nyela had never had a chance, right from the start, he too would die along with Yoyo and Jericho, in the little room at the top of the temple, if not before.

The thought acted like an acid, dissolving his fears in a trice. Ice-cold rage flooded in instead. One by one, his survival mechanisms clicked into place, and he felt the metamorphosis, felt himself become once more the bug he had been for most of his life. He marched onwards, chitin-clad, through the gate and into the Pergamon hall next door. Watchful, he waved his antennae, saw the entire hall through faceted eyes: over there, at the opposite end of the great hall, another gate that was the partner of the one he had come through, tiny, almost ashamed to be so small but nevertheless bravely doing its work, one narrow little bypass in the flow of bodies through the museum, pumping tirelessly. To his left, isolated parts of the frieze standing alone on pillars and pedestals; to his right the temple with the stairway, up above the colonnade, leading through to the Telephos hall where Jericho and the girl would be, waiting for a dossier that they would never see now, that they would never need. It would have all been so simple, so quickly over and done with. He would have been a hundred thousand euros richer, and he would have handed them the second dossier. The duplicate that apart from him only Nyela had known about—

Had known?

How could he be *sure* that she was dead?

Because she was.

Wishful thinking. No part of a bug's existence.

Vogelaar's jaw worked back and forth. Platoons of tourists thronged the stairway to the colonnade, many sitting on the steps as though planning to have lunch there. Vogelaar spotted a younger group all armed with sketch pads and pencils, their faces fixed in concentration, rapt in their struggle with immortal art. A few curious passers-by were peering over their shoulders. He swept his eyes across the students, one by one, and stopped at a pale girl with a sharp nose who had gathered no admirers around her. He walked up to her, unhurried. On the white sheet of paper, Zeus fought the giant Porphyrion, and the two of them together fought the girl's artistic ineptitude, her inability to breathe life into the scene. She must have had a good twenty pencils in the case next to her, and the number was obviously inversely proportional to her talent. Clearly every euro of tip money from the evening job waiting tables went on her art supplies. She was throwing money away in the deluded belief that in art, having the right kit is half the struggle.

He leaned down to her and said in his friendliest voice, 'Could you perhaps – excuse me! – lend me one of your pencils?'

She blinked up at him, startled.

'Just for a moment,' he added quickly. 'I want to jot something down. Forgot my pen, as always.'

'Hmm, ye-e-es,' she said, slowly, obviously upset at the thought that pencils might be used for writing as well. In the next moment she seemed to have come to terms with the idea. 'Yes, of course! Pick any one.'

'That's very kind of you.'

He chose a long, neatly sharpened pencil which looked sturdier than the rest, and straightened up. Xin was watching him at this moment, he had no doubt. Xin saw everything and would draw his own conclusions from whatever Vogelaar did, meaning that he only had seconds.

He turned round, lightning-fast.

Mickey was only a few steps behind him, and stared at him like a surprised mastiff, then half-heartedly tried to hide behind a group of Spanish-speaking pensioners. Vogelaar was at his side with just a few brisk paces. The Irishman fumbled at his hip with his right hand. Obviously Xin had never given him instructions in the event anything like this should happen, since he seemed absolutely flummoxed. His jowls wobbled with fury, his eyes darted hectically to and fro, sweat broke out on his pate.

Vogelaar put a hand to the back of his head, pulled him in close, and rammed the pencil into his right eye.

The Irishman gave a blood-curdling scream. He twitched, and blood spouted from the entry wound. Vogelaar pushed the flat of his hand more firmly against the end of the pencil, drove it deeper into the eye socket, felt the tip break through bone and enter the brain. Mickey slumped, his bowels and bladder emptying. Vogel-aar felt for the killer's gun and tore it from the holster.

'Jericho!' he yelled.

Stampede

Jericho had chosen to wait for the South African on the other side of the temple, hidden behind a phalanx of free-standing sculpture exhibits, uncomfortably aware that Vogelaar could get the drop on him. He was even more frightened by what he saw now. It was worse than any of the scenarios his overheated imagination had dreamed up over the past couple of hours, since it meant that the handover had failed. No doubt about it.

Everything was going horribly wrong. With his Glock in his right hand, he broke cover. Shock-waves of horror and revulsion were spreading out from the scene of the attack; he could hear screams, shrieks, groans, noises that defied description. The immediate eyewitnesses had reeled back to form a kind of small arena, with Vogelaar and the bald man in the middle, like a pair of modern-day gladiators. Others had frozen with terror as though struck by a Gorgon's gaze, as motionless as the gods and giants all around. Pencils dropped from the art students' nerveless fingers. The girl with the sharp nose leapt up, bouncing on the balls of her feet like a rubber ball, and held her hands in front of her mouth as though trying to stop herself squeaking. Little yelps of fear slipped through her half-open lips, as regular as an alarm. Everywhere heads turned, eyes went wide with shock, people walked faster, groups broke apart. The fight-or-flight response was beginning to set in.

All structures were breaking down. And in the midst of it all, Jericho saw the angel of death.

He was running towards Vogelaar, who was buckling under his victim's weight. The dying man fell to the ground, dragging the South African with him. The angel was closing in from the northern wing, white-haired, ferociously moustached, his eyes hidden by tinted glasses, but the way he moved left no doubt as to his identity. Nor did the pistol that seemed to leap into his hand as he ran.

Vogelaar saw him coming as well.

Yelling, he managed to heave the bald man back up. The next moment the leather jacket covering his torso exploded, as the shots that had been meant for Vogel-aar smacked into him. Jericho threw himself to the ground. Vogelaar struggled to shove the dead man aside and opened fire in turn on Xin, who took cover among the screaming, running crowd. A woman was hit in the shoulder and dropped to the ground.

'No point!' Jericho yelled. 'Get out of here.'

The South African kicked at the corpse, trying to get free. Jericho dragged him to his feet. With a sound like meat slapping down onto a butcher's block, Vogel-aar's upper thigh burst open. He collapsed against Jericho and clutched him tight.

'Get to the restaurant,' he gasped. 'Nyela—'

Jericho grabbed him under the arms without letting go of the Glock. He was heavy, much too heavy. All hell was breaking loose around them.

'Pull yourself together,' he grunted. 'You've got to—'

Vogelaar stared at him. He sank slowly to the ground, and Jericho realised that Xin had shot him again. Panic swept over him. He scanned the crowd for the killer, spotted his shock of white hair. He only had moments before Xin would have another clear line of sight.

'Get up,' he screamed. 'Get going!'

Vogelaar slipped from his grasp. His face was going waxen, mask-like, horribly fast. He fell on his back, and a gout of bright red blood gushed from his mouth.

'Nyela – don't know if – probably dead, but – perhaps—'

'No,' Jericho whispered. 'You can't die on me . . .'

A few metres away, a man was lifted up and flung forward as though by a giant fist. He flew through the air and then crashed to the ground, spread-eagled.

Xin was clearing his way through.

Vogelaar, Jericho thought desperately, you can't just croak on me now, where's the dossier, you're our last hope, get up, for goodness' sake. Get up. *Get up!*

Then he turned and ran as fast as he could.

Vogelaar stared into the light.

He had never been a religious man, and even now he found that the promise of heaven sounded tawdry and hollow. Why should every fool who'd ever drawn breath find their way to the Other Side? Religion was just one of those cracks this bug had never scuttled into. He couldn't understand a character like Cyrano de Bergerac, who had spent a life-time scoffing at religion and then felt a pang of fear at the last moment, humbly seeking forgiveness on his deathbed in case there was a God after all. Life ended. Why waste what time was left to him believing in some paradise? This was only the neon white light streaming down onto him from the ceiling, the artificial daylight of the museum hall. The white light that people spoke of after near-death experiences. The Hereafter, supposedly. In truth it was nothing but hallucinogenic tryptamine alka-loids flooding the brain.

How stupid of him not to have given Jericho the dossier! Done with now. Dead and gone. He felt a faint flicker of hope that he had been wrong about Nyela. Hope that she was still alive, that the detective could do something for her – if he got out alive. Otherwise the situation was beyond his control, beyond his concern – but it wasn't the worst way to die, his last thoughts with the only person he had loved more than himself.

Now he was freed from his armour, his bug's shell. Free at last?

Xin came into view.

Gasping and grunting, Vogelaar lifted his gun, or rather strained every muscle to do so. He might just as well have been trying to fling a dumb-bell at Xin. The pistol lay in his hand, heavy as lead. He only just had strength enough left to shoot daggers from his eyes.

The killer curled his lips contemptuously.

'Parameters, you idiot!' he said.

Xin shot Vogelaar in the chest and stalked on past without giving the dead man a second glance. Did he have any cause to reproach himself? Had it been a mistake to order Mickey along to the museum at the last moment, so that nothing went wrong this time? Vogelaar had spotted the Irishman, had drawn the wrong conclusion – and all this time Nyela was hanging from two pairs of handcuffs in the cellar at Muntu. Unharmed, as Xin had promised.

Hadn't he *said* that he'd let her live?

He'd done that, damn it!

Yes, he would have let them *both* live! He'd have been *happy* to let them live! Vogelaar hadn't understood anything, the stupid ape. Now it was all past help, the laws cried out for vengeance. Now he *had* to kill the woman. He'd promised *that* too.

Xin began to run, driving the crowd before him like lowing cattle, dumb animals all trying to crush through the narrow gate at the same time. A girl in front of him stumbled and fell to the ground. He tram-pled her underfoot, flung another to the side, cracked the pistol grip against the side of an old man's head, fought his way through, charged like a battering ram at the ruck of fleeing tourists and plunged out the other side, his gaze fixed on the Market Gate of Miletus, where Jericho had just vanished through into the next wing. He squeezed off a burst of fire, sending splinters flying from two-thousand-year-old carvings. People screamed, ran, flung themselves to the ground, the same old tiresome spectacle. Swinging his pistol like a club, he followed Jericho, saw him melt into the crowd of visitors thronging the Processional Way, and then in his place two uniformed figures ran out from a corridor off to the side, their weapons at the ready but without the first idea of who their enemy really was. He mowed them down without breaking stride. A bow wave of panic washed before him, all the way to Babylon.

Where was that blasted detective?

Jericho ran along the Processional Way.

How absurd it was to be running away with a loaded gun in his hand, instead of using it. But if he stopped, Xin would shoot him before he could even turn round and aim. The killer was trained to hit small targets and to use any window that presented itself. He swung his Glock like Moses swinging his staff, shouting, 'Get out of the way!' parting the sea of people, and ran to the black statue of Hadad, past grinning sculptures of crouching lions. The beasts looked as though they had poodles or mastiffs somewhere in their bloodline. Had the cultures of the ancient world ever even seen lions, or had they only existed in the limited imaginations of sculptors working to order? Perhaps they'd just been bad sculptors. Not everything that found its way into museums necessarily had to be any good. And what the hell was he thinking about, at a moment like this!

A family scattered to all sides in front of him.

Beyond Hadad, a row of tall, slender columns marched away meaninglessly, no longer supporting whatever it was they had once held up. Following an inner impulse, he flung himself to the right, heard the dull crack of a pistol being fired and the shot thud into the storm god, ran towards the glassed fourth wing—

And stopped.

Stepping into that glass corridor meant that he would be trapped in the museum, running round the square all over again. He could get to the James Simon Gallery by going left here, and right now, just for a moment, he was out of Xin's sight—

He dropped to all fours like a dog, scuttled behind the pillars, seeking cover, then crept back the other way, and from the corner of his eye he saw Xin running into the glass hall. Jericho stuffed the Glock back into his pocket. From now on he was just one of many, trying like all the rest of them to avoid becoming a statistic on the evening news report. A tsunami of rumour and consternation swept through the museum entrance hall, so that nobody paid him any attention as he hurried outside, running rather than walking down the steps to the river. He crossed the bridge back where he had come this morning.

Nyela. The dossier.

He had to get to Muntu.

Things were calmer in the glass hall. Xin scanned the crowd for Jericho's blond hair. His pistol cast a spell of fearful silence all around, but something was wrong. If Jericho had come through here before him, armed, shouting, running, people would be a lot less relaxed. Obviously they thought that Xin was a policeman of some kind, on patrol. He glanced along the corridor, its western wall glowing with noon sunlight. In front of him an obelisk from Sahuré's temple, the pharaohs on their plinths, the glowering temple gate of Kalabsha – he couldn't rule out that Jericho might have the nerve to be hiding behind any of these. He'd had ten seconds' head start, maximum, but enough to get behind one of the pharaohs.

And if he'd gone north—

No. Xin had seen him run in *here*.

Cautiously, he pushed on, taking shelter among the museum visitors – who were growing visibly more nervous. He aimed his gun behind plinths, pillars, façades, statues. Jericho had to be *somewhere* in this hall, but there were no shots, nobody broke cover to dash away, there was no headlong frontal assault. Meanwhile the tension was building up to open terror, worry tipped over into the fear that perhaps this man was a terrorist after all. Armed men would be turning up shortly, he was sure of that. If he didn't find the detective in a hurry, he'd have to disappear himself, leaving the job unfinished.

'Jericho!' he yelled.

His voice fell unheeded on the glass walls.

'Come on out. We'll talk.'

No answer.

'I promise that we'll *talk*, do you hear me?'

Talk, then shoot, he thought, but all was silent. Obviously he hadn't expected Jericho to step out from the shadows with a look of cheery relief on his face, but what really enraged him was the total lack of any reaction – except, that is, that everyone around him was suddenly in a hurry to leave the wing. Seething, he stalked onward, saw a movement in among the pillars of the Kalabsha Gate and fired. A Japanese tourist staggered out of the shadows, hands clutching her camera and a look of mild astonishment on her face. She took one last picture as if by reflex and then fell headlong. Panic spread, unleashing a stampede. Xin took advantage of the confusion, ran to the end of the hall and looked wildly around to all sides.

'Jericho!' he shouted.

He ran back, stared down through the glass at the inner courtyard, turned his head. He could hear heavy boots approaching from the passage to the James Simon Gallery. His eye fell on the bridge leading away from the Pergamon Museum, swept along the pavement by the riverside—

There! Blond hair, Scandinavian almost, a good way off by now. Jericho was running as though there were devils after him, and Xin realised that the detective had tricked him. There was a crowd forming now between the statues of the pharaohs. Security personnel were trying to get through the rush of visitors coming the other way – and these guards had sub-machine-guns. He had wasted too much time, shed too much blood to expect these new arrivals not to shoot first and ask questions later. He needed a hostage.

A girl slipped on the gallery's smooth polished floor.

With one leap, he was behind her, catching hold, hauling her up, and he pressed the muzzle of his pistol to her temple. The child froze and then began to cry. A young woman gave a piercing scream, stretched out her hands but was knocked aside by others running to escape, and her husband grabbed hold of her, held her back from rushing to certain death. The next moment, uniformed figures took up position either side of the parents, calling out something in German. Xin didn't understand but he had a pretty shrewd idea of what they wanted. Without taking his eyes off them, he dragged the girl over to the tall windows and looked down to the bridge over the Spree, where by now a few gawkers had gathered.

He leaned down to the little girl.

'It'll all be all right,' he said softly into her ear. 'I promise.' She didn't understand a word of Mandarin of course, but the sibilant syllables had their effect. Her little body relaxed as though hypnotised. She became calmer, breathing in short, shallow gasps like a rabbit.

'That's good,' he whispered. 'Don't be afraid.'

'Marian!' Her mother screamed, raw misery in her voice. 'Marian!'

'Marian,' Xin repeated amiably. 'That's a very pretty name.'

He pulled the trigger.

Cries and shouts went up as the windowpane burst apart under the impact of dozens of flechette rounds. He had swung the pistol away at the last moment. Splinters of glass flew around their ears. He shielded the girl from the shrapnel with his torso, then shoved her away, crossed his arms in front of his head and chest and leapt out. While the officers were still trying to work out what had happened, he had landed cat-like among the onlookers three metres below, and he began to run.

Jericho

Muntu was closed. Hardly pausing, Jericho fired two shots into the lock and then kicked in the door. It slammed back against the wall inside. He rushed headlong into the dining area, looked behind the bar and then jumped back: but the man staring at him with puzzlement in his eyes, a light-skinned African, was clearly dead. Yesterday's chaos reigned unchallenged in the kitchen. Nobody had cleaned up since his fight with Vogelaar.

There was no sign of Nyela.

Frantically, he charged through the beaded curtain, flung open both toilet doors, then tugged uselessly at the handle of a third door – *Private*, it said, and it was locked. He shot out this lock as well. Worn stairs led down into the darkness. A smell of mould, and disinfectants. The chalky scent of damp plaster. Memories of Shenzhen, the steps leading down to Hell. He hesitated. His hand fumbled for the light-switch, found it. At the bottom of the stairs a light bulb glowed in its cage. Whitewashed plaster, a stained concrete floor, a spider scuttling away. He went down a step at a time, his Glock at the ready, his skin crawling, overcome by nausea. Kenny Xin. Animal Ma Liping. Who or what was awaiting him down below? What kind of creatures would leap out at him now, what images would burn their way into his brain?

He stepped off the last stair. He looked round. A short corridor, piled high with crates and barrels. A steel door, half open.

He went through, his gaze darting, gun ready.

Nyela!

She was squatting down on the floor with her arms behind her back, her mouth covered with tape. Her eyes glowed in the half-light. He hurried across to her, holstered his Glock, tore the tape away and put his fingers to his lips. Not yet. First he had to get her out of the cuffs. Her jailers had locked her to the pipework, and he didn't imagine that the key would be lying about somewhere as a reward for keen-eyed detectives.

'I'll be right back,' he whispered.

Back in the kitchen, he pulled open drawers, rummaged through the tools, steel, copper, chrome, looked around all the worktops and finally found what he was looking for: a cleaver. He hurried back down to the cellar.

'Lean forward,' he ordered. 'I need some room.'

Nyela nodded and turned away from him so that he had a good view of her hands. The pipe was worryingly short. Just a few centimetres from her wrists, it turned into the wall and vanished into the crumbling mortar. He took a deep breath, concentrated, and brought the blade down. The whole radiator sang like a struck bell. He frowned. There was a dent in the pipe, but otherwise nothing had changed. He struck again, and a third time, a fourth, until the pipe burst open, so that he could prise it apart with the handle of the cleaver. The chain of the cuffs scraped through the gap.

'Where—' Nyela began to ask.

'Over there.' Jericho motioned with his chin, ordering her over to a metal worktable. 'Back to the tabletop, palms down, as flat as you can. Pull the chain tight.'

Nyela's features clouded over with a premonition of the dreadful news she knew she was about to receive. She did as he said, turning her hands about.

'Don't move,' Jericho said. 'Stay still, quite still.'

She looked down at the floor. He fixed his eyes on the middle of the chain, and struck. One blow broke the chain.

'Now let's get out of here.'

'No.' She stood in his way. 'Where's Jan? What happened?'

Jericho felt his tongue go numb.

'He's dead,' he said.

Nyela looked at him. Whatever he had expected, bewilderment, shock, tears, didn't happen. Just a quiet grief, her love for the man who now lay dead in the museum, and at the same time a curious nonchalance, as though to say, there it is then, so it goes, it had to happen sometime. He hesitated, then hugged Nyela tight for a moment. She responded, a gentle embrace.

'I'll get you out of here,' he promised.

'Yes,' she said, tired, nodding. 'I hear that a lot.'

There was nobody upstairs, just the dead man staring out from behind the bar as though waiting for an explanation of what had happened to him. Jericho hurried to the closed door of the restaurant and peered outside.

'We'll have to run for it.'

'Why?'

'My car's a few streets away.'

'Mine isn't.' Nyela leaned across the bar, opened a drawer and took out a datastick. 'Jan was using it earlier today. He must have parked it in front of Muntu.'

Yoyo had spoken of a Nissan OneOne. There was just such a car parked a few steps away, its legs drawn up. The cabin was egg-shaped, its design rather like a friendly little whale. The legs on either side were thick at the base, tapering towards the wheels. When the legs were stretched out flat, the cabin hung low to the ground, but if the driver drew in his wheels, the legs drew inward and upward, lifting the cabin. The low, aerodynamic profile, like a sports car, changed to become a compact, taller car. Jericho stepped out of the door and scanned the street. Shapes and colours seemed over-exposed in the noonday sun. There was a smell of pollen, and of baking tarmac. There were hardly any pedestrians to be seen, but the traffic had picked up. He put his head back and looked up at a cigar-shaped tourist zeppelin that bumbled cheerfully into view, its engines droning.

'All clear,' he called back inside. 'Come on out.'

The car roof reflected the sky, the clouds and the buildings around, curving them into an Einsteinian space. Nyela unlocked the car, and the roof lifted like a hatch. The interior was surprisingly roomy, with a long bench right across it and extra folding seats.

'Where to?' she asked.

'The Grand Hyatt.'

'Got you.' She swung herself inside, and Jericho slid in next to her. He saw that the Nissan's steering column was adjustable. The whole thing could be swung across from the driver's side to the passenger's. The tinted glass filtered the harsher wavelengths out of the noonday light and created a cocoon-like atmosphere. The electric motor sprang to life, humming gently.

'Nyela, I—' Jericho massaged the bridge of his nose. 'I have to ask you something.'

She looked at him, the life draining from her eyes.

'What?'

'Your husband was going to give me a dossier.'

'A— My God!' She pressed her hand to her mouth. 'You don't have it? He couldn't even get the dossier to you?'

Jericho shook his head, silent.

'We could have blown the bastards' game for good and all!'

'He had it with him?'

'Not the one from the Crystal Brain, Kenny has that one, but—'

Of course he does, Jericho thought, tired.

'But the duplicate—'

'One moment!' Jericho grabbed her arm. 'There's a duplicate?'

'He wanted to give it to you.' She looked at him, pleading. 'Believe me, Jan had no choice, he had to sacrifice you and the girl! That wasn't in his nature, he wouldn't have double-crossed you. He always—'

'*Where is it*, Nyela?'

'I thought he'd have told you.'

'Told me what?' Jericho felt he was going mad. 'Nyela, damn it all, where did he have—'

'Have, have!' She shook her head furiously, spread out her fingers. 'You're asking the wrong questions. He *is* the duplicate!'

Jericho stared at her.

'What do you m—'

Her throat opened out in a red fan. Something warm sprayed out at him. He flung himself down onto Nyela's lap. Above him, the Nissan's cabin exploded, the foam seat stuffing splattered about his ears. Still bending down, he grabbed hold of the steering wheel, tugged it towards himself, revved up and sped away. A salvo stitched through the car's carbon-fibre hull with a dry staccato. Jericho raised his head just far enough to see over the dashboard, then felt Nyela slump heavily against his shoulder, and he lost control. The car careened down the street, lurched into the opposite lane and climbed the pavement, leaving the squeal of brakes and blare of horns in its wake. Pedestrians scattered. At the last moment, he wrenched the wheel to the left to come back across to his side of the street, almost colliding with a van. As the van swerved aside and rammed several parked cars, he bumped up onto the kerb on his own side and steered for the Spree.

There, tall, white-haired, he saw the angel of death.

Xin fired as he ran, coming directly towards him. Jericho nudged the wheel again. The Nissan threatened to tip over, the cabin was too high up on its legs, the wheels too close together for manoeuvres like this. He scanned the dashboard desperately. Xin had stopped to take aim. With a loud crack, part of the wrecked roof broke away. The Nissan raced towards Xin, and Jericho braced himself for an impact.

Xin leapt aside.

The car sped past him like a giant runaway pram. Xin fired after it, heard brakes squealing, dodged out of the path of a limousine by a hair's breadth and stumbled across to the other lane, forcing a motorcyclist to veer crazily. The bike skidded and slanted. Xin dodged away again, felt something brush against him, and he flew through the air; he slammed full length against the pavement, on his front. A compact car had struck him, and now the driver was roaring away. Other cars stopped, people climbed out. He rolled onto his back, moved his arms and legs, saw the motorcyclist running towards him and fumbled for his pistol.

'Good God!' The man leaned over him. 'What happened?' he asked in English. 'Are you all right?'

Xin grabbed his gun and shoved it under the man's nose.

'Couldn't be better,' he said.

The motorcyclist turned pale and scuttled backwards. Xin leapt to his feet. A few steps took him to the bike, and he swung himself into the saddle and thrashed off towards the Spree, where he drew up, tyres squealing, and looked about in all directions.

There! The Nissan. It ran a red light, vanished southwards.

Jericho looked about and saw him coming.

He had gone the wrong way. The Audi was somewhere else entirely. He could have changed cars by now, got out of this wrecked Nissan and away from the dead woman. The corpse was flung about this way and that, and kept thumping against him. He looked all over the dashboard for the control that would let the legs down. Pretty nearly everything was controlled via the touchscreen, there must be some symbol somewhere there, but he couldn't concentrate. He kept having to dodge, swerve, brake, accelerate.

Xin was catching up.

Jericho rumbled along the promenade by the river, across the cobblestones, cut up a lorry and emerged onto a majestic boulevard fringed with grand Prussian buildings. He tried to remember how to get to the hotel from here. Up on its stilts, the Nissan lurched from side to side, always threatening to tip over. All of a sudden he realised that he had no plan. Not a glimmer! He was racing through central Berlin in a wrecked compact car with a dead woman at his side, and Xin was after him, growing inexorably closer.

The traffic ground to a halt ahead. Jericho changed lanes. Another jam. Change again. A gap, a jam, a gap. Bumping from lane to lane like a pinball, he drove towards a huge equestrian statue which marked the beginning of a central island, planted with trees right down its length, a broad green lane dividing the traffic flows. He wrenched the wheel to the right, smashed into the kerb and climbed it. All of a sudden he was surrounded by pedestrians. He jammed the flat of his hand against the horn, veered about, frantically trying not to run anyone over, then the jam was past and he slalomed back down onto the road. He was going too fast, and the wheels had no grip on the road surface. The car skidded across the lanes towards the central reservation, lost contact with the tarmac. On two wheels, he was racing towards the line of trees, and he threw his weight to the side. Something slammed. The car shuddered, leapt violently, bark scraped, huge clouds of dust billowed up. The central island stretching away in front of him was almost empty of people, flanked by lime trees and by benches. To either side the traffic blurred behind the thick green foliage, an impressionist smear of cars, buses, bicycle rickshaws, colour, light, movement.

He glanced backwards.

Xin's motorcycle was thrashing on under the low-hanging branches, hunting him like a beast of prey.

Jericho accelerated. More people suddenly. A café, shady, romantic, jutting out into the tree-lined walk. Yelled curses, shaken fists, scurrying backwards. A kiosk with tall tables standing around, people playing pétanque. He was racing towards a crossroads, saw the traffic lights changing through a gap in the leaves, yellow, red, and then he was cutting under the noses of dozens of cars ready to move, and was on the next stretch of the central strip. The chorus of blaring horns died away behind him. Glance back, no sign of Xin. Jericho yelled hoarsely. Lost him! He'd shaken Xin off, at least for the moment. He'd won some time, valuable seconds, every second worth an eternity.

Suddenly he also got his bearings back.

A snack bar blocked his way, but the traffic was lighter on both sides. Jericho steered the Nissan out of the shadow of the trees, back down onto the road, and saw it on the skyline ahead of him, the Brandenburg Gate, still some way off. Not for the first time, he felt surprised at how grand it looked in photographs and how small it really was. The Prussian-era courtyards and palaces were giving way now to modern architecture, the bistros and shops were ending, there were fewer pedestrians about. Soon enough the boulevard would end at Pariser Platz, with the Academy of Arts, the French Embassy, the American, and he hoped he could turn off there. North or south, and then—

Jericho squinted.

Something was going on up ahead. To his left, the trees had ended, so that he could see the whole width of the boulevard. Horrified, he saw that he was coming to a roadblock. Whole sections of the road were barricaded off. A monstrous robot was stretching out its cantilevered arm, lowering some huge, long object down to the road surface, and he could see Xin's motorcycle tearing towards him in his only remaining rear-view mirror.

Jericho cursed. Whatever was being built up ahead had turned it into a blind alley for him. The construction robot was swinging an enormous steel girder slant-wise across the pavement and the road, while building workers waved away whatever cars had ended up here despite the road signs. There must have been announcements for the diversion, but of course he hadn't seen them because he'd been tearing down the central reservation, and now there was nowhere to turn aside to, the girder was sinking lower, Xin was coming closer, he was readying his gun—

Where was the control for the legs?

The first of the workers had turned round and spotted him, jumped aside. Shots slammed into the rear of the Nissan. If he braked now, Xin would blow his head off, and if he didn't, the girder would knock it clean off, nor could he turn around, he was going too fast, much too fast, and he couldn't find the icon on the touchscreen—

There! Not an icon at all, but a switch! A plain and simple, old-fashioned switch.

In a trice the Nissan had stretched out its wheels, becoming a low-slung, wide vehicle. The girder grew larger in front of Jericho's eyes, much too fast, dark, threatening, less than a metre and a half off the ground, a thick grey line, an end point. In a ridiculous reflex he lifted his arm up in front of his face as the cabin of his car sank further downwards, then there was a splintering, crunching sound as the edge of the steel swept away what was left of the roof. He pressed himself down into his seat. As flat as a flounder, the car shot through beneath the girder; it was briefly night, then clear blue day again. The crossroads, a bus, an inevitable collision. As though a film had jumped frames, all of a sudden the Nissan was two metres further to the right, began to turn, skated across Pariser Platz, cyclists, pedestrians, the whole world running from him. Scrabbling to get the car back under control, he screeched towards the Brandenburg Gate. A police gyrocopter came into view above the bronze statue atop the Gate, an ultralight helicopter, half open, a loud-speaker voice booming down at him. His plan to speed through the Doric columns of the Gate and get away the other side was thwarted by a row of low bollards that blocked any such attempt. He braked. The Nissan fishtailed, slid, crashed against the bollards and came to a stop. Next to him, Nyela seemed to want to say something. She straightened up, then her body was flung forward and back again into her seat, as though she had had second thoughts.

Jericho leapt clear of the wreckage.

The gyrocopter sank towards him. He ran for his life, under the Gate and through to the other side, where the boulevard continued, becoming a main road several lanes wide. Far off he could see a tall, slim column, and the road forked here just in front of the Gate. Without even looking at the traffic lights or signs, he hurried through a zebra crossing. Brakes screamed, and there was a crash as somebody shunted the car in front. Weird. Were there really cars still on the road without proximity pilots? A superannuated convertible zipped under his nose, missing running over his feet by a hair's breadth, and he heard furious yelling. He started back, then sprinted, reaching the other side by dashing past a lorry's radiator grille, and ran into a cool green passageway. This was the Tiergarten, the green park at the heart of Berlin. Sand, gravel, quiet pathways. In front of him was the statue of a lion. More trees, opening out into lawns, paths branching out in all directions. He raced down one, running, running, running until he could be sure that there was nobody following him, no Xin and no gyrocopter. He only stopped when he got to a small lake, and bent down with his hands on his knees, his sides aching, a sour taste on his tongue. He fought for breath. Gasped, spat, coughed. His heart was pounding like a battering ram. As though it wanted to break out of his ribcage.

An elderly lady looked across at him briefly, then turned her attention back to her little grandson, who was doing his best not to fall off his bike.

Xin

At last he had cleared the girder, but he had lost valuable time. He saw the Nissan racing away from him ahead, and he rode around the bus, leaning into the curve, taking aim. It looked as though the detective had lost control of the car. Good. Xin squeezed off a salvo just as a gyrocopter appeared above the Gate. To his astonishment, the police seemed to be paying more attention to his motorcycle than to Jericho, who at that moment jumped out of his car and ran away. The police dropped lower, faced the copter directly towards him; he heard shouted commands. He assessed the situation, thinking lightning-fast. The gyrocopter was still perhaps a metre above the ground. It was impossible to get past, and if he shot at the copter, the police would have no qualms about opening fire in return. He yanked his bike around and roared off along the street that crossed the boulevard.

The gyrocopter gave chase straight away. As he sped over the next crossroads, something splattered onto the tarmac in front of him, swelled up and set solid. They were firing foam cannon at him! One round of that in his spokes, and his ride would come to a sudden end. The stuff set instantly and hard as rock. Xin swerved, saw how the road in front of him led up over a bridge, turned right instead and found that he was back on the riverbank, on the Spree. If he hadn't lost his bearings, this should lead back to the Museum Island. Not a good idea to pop up there again – it must be crawling with police by now. He heard the dry clattering of the copter behind him, then above him, then ahead. The gyrocopter set down, forcing him to brake to a stop. He wheeled about, a breakneck turn, and raced off the other way, only to spot another police flyer hanging, apparently motionless, over the dome of the parliament building, the Reichstag. It raced towards him.

They had him trapped.

Xin thrashed his bike onward, headed for the Reichstag, the river to his right. Tourists were thronging up the grand stairway outside, and the promenade opened out. There was government architecture all along the river here, steel and glass dotted here and there with petite little trees, elegant topiary. Sightseeing boats chugged along the Spree, took a curve further along the river and went under a filigree bridge.

And above everything, the two copters.

Xin aimed for the bridge. A group of young people scattered in front of his eyes. He revved hard, sat up on his back wheel, gunned the engine for all it was worth and shot over the edge. For a moment the motorcycle hung above the water; the river below him was a sculpture of glass, the gyrocopters hung in the sky as though nailed there. Xin felt a pleasant breeze on his skin, an intimation of what it would be like to live a completely different life, but there was no other that he could live.

He took his hands from the handlebars.

The surface splintered into kaleidoscopes, water thumped in his ears. He tried to get away from the sinking bike as fast as he could. The front wheel caught him a blow across the hip. He ignored the pain, surfaced, pumped his lungs full of air and dived again, deep enough not to be seen from the air. With powerful strokes, he made for midstream, one of the tourist boats thrumming above him. He had been trained to stay underwater for a long while, but he would have to surface sooner or later, and he had two copters to deal with. They would split up, one of them looking for him upstream, one downstream. His reflexes racing, he saw the dark bulk of the sightseeing boat moving away above him, and kicked his way up. He surfaced with his head just by the stern of the boat, which sat low enough in the water that he could grab one of the stanchions down by the windows. He slipped, grabbed hold again, clung tight and peered up into the sky, partly obscured by the boat's deck and viewing platforms.

One of the gyrocopters was circling over the spot where he had gone under. He could hear the other one, but not see it. In the next moment it appeared, directly over the ship, and Xin slipped underwater again without letting go of the stanchion. He held his breath for as long as he could. When he risked another look, they were just passing under a bridge.

The copter was moving away.

He let the boat carry him along for a little while longer, then pushed away, swam to the bank and hauled himself up. There was a concrete embankment in front of him, with a busy road running beyond it. As far as he could see, the police were still searching on the other side of the bridge. He felt for his wig, but it was on the bottom of the Spree by now. He quickly tore off the false beard, peeled off his jacket, left everything there in the water and crept ashore, dripping wet. He had lost his gun as well, but had been able to keep hold of his phone, which was waterproof, thank God. He felt the reassuring grip of the money belt around his waist that held credit cards and the memory crystal. Xin made a point of carrying credit cards around with him, even if they were reckoned to be old-fashioned and everybody made purchases using the ID codes in their phones. He didn't like to show up on records when he went clothes shopping though.

Not far away was an express railway, up on its viaduct. He glanced up and down the street. It curved away to a building with a glass dome and gleaming blocks clustered about it, which had to be Berlin's main railway station. He rolled up his shirtsleeves, swept back his smooth, dark hair and walked along the street, quickly but without haste. Traffic streamed past him. He saw another gyrocopter a little way off, but since by now he hardly matched the description of the man the police were looking for, he felt fairly safe. He resisted the impulse to quicken his pace. In ten minutes he had reached the station concourse, and took cash from an ATM with one of his cards. He found a leisurewear store and bought jeans, trainers and a T-shirt. The salesgirl, studded with appliqués, looked at him in astonishment. He dressed in the clothes that he had bought and asked the salesgirl for a plastic bag. He paid cash, stuffed his wet clothes into the bag and then dropped it into a pavement rubbish bin outside, and went back to the Hotel Adlon by taxi.

Jericho

As far as he remembered, the Hyatt was south of the Tiergarten park, but then he lost his bearings among all the forked paths and duck-ponds, and wandered from one idyllic glade to the next. He could hear traffic sounds some indefinable way off. The sun shone down on him, unnaturally bright. He was overcome by nausea, a stitch yanked at his ribs, there was a pain spreading down from his shoulder to his left arm. The sky, the trees, the people around were all sucked into a red tunnel. Was this what a heart attack felt like? He stumbled across to a bush, his knees weak as wax, and threw up. After that he felt better, and he made it as far as the main road. At a crossroads he recognised several of the buildings, saw a Keith Haring sculpture and realised that the Grand Hyatt was just around the corner. He could have sworn that he'd been in the park for hours, but when he looked at his watch, he saw that not even fifteen minutes had passed since he had crashed at the Brandenburg Gate. It was just before half past twelve.

He called Tu.

'We're upstairs in your room. Yoyo and I—'

'Stay there. I'm coming up.'

Since Diane was in Jericho's room they had made it their command centre, so as to be able to research further and keep trying to decrypt more messages. In the lift, his thoughts shifted gear, becoming inordinately clear, self-aware. He hadn't often been so completely at a loss. So incapable of acting. Nyela had been as good as safe, and he had still lost her.

'What happened?' Tu jumped to his feet and came towards him. 'Is everything—'

'No.' Jericho reached into his jacket, fished out the packages of money and threw them onto the bed. 'Here's your money back. That's all the good news there is.'

Tu picked up one of the packages and shook his head.

'That's not good news.'

'It's not.' In curt sentences, he described how events had unfolded. Striving to remain objective, he only managed to make the whole story sound more dreadful. Yoyo grew paler with every word.

'Nyela,' she whispered. 'Whatever have we done?'

'Nothing.' He rubbed his hands over his face, tired, dispirited. 'It would have happened one way or another all the same. All we did was keep her alive a couple of minutes longer.'

'No dossier.' Her face clouded over. 'All for nothing.'

'According to Nyela, he must have been carrying it around with him!' Jericho walked over to the window and stared out, seeing nothing. 'Vogelaar had sold us out to Xin, but he was trying to turn the tables one more time. At the last moment, whatever it was that moved him to do so. He *wanted* me to have that dossier.'

'Curses and maledictions.' Tu punched a fist into the palm of his other hand. 'And Nyela's quite sure—'

'*Was* sure, Tian. She was sure.'

'—that he had it with him? She specifically said—'

'She said that Kenny had got hold of the original.'

'The memory crystal.'

'Yes. But apparently there was a duplicate.'

'Which Vogelaar was going to bring into the museum.'

'Wait a moment.' Yoyo frowned. 'That means that he still has it on him?'

'Irrelevant.' Jericho pressed two fingers against his brow. Now they really were at a dead end. 'The police will have taken it as evidence. But good, that means we have nothing more to decide. From now on, we aren't working on our own any more. I imagine we can trust the local authorities here, so that means—'

He stopped.

He heard Tu speaking as though through cotton wool, heard him saying something about surveillance cameras that would have got his picture in the museum, that they would have put his picture out on the wanted list by now, that you couldn't trust the authorities anywhere in this world. But more clearly, more meaningfully now, he heard again the last words that Nyela had ever spoken:

You're asking the wrong questions. He is *the duplicate!*

He *is* the duplicate?

'My God, how simple,' he whispered.

'What's simple?' Tu asked, baffled.

He turned around. Both of them stared at him. There it was again, his assurance, that he thought he had lost.

'I think I know where Vogelaar hid his dossier.'

Hotel Adlon

Xin took out the memory crystal, turned it between his fingers and smiled. Useless knowledge. All in all, he could rest content. Paying no attention to the grand interior, he strode across the hotel lobby, went up to his suite and tried his phone before anything else. The manufacturer's guarantee said that it was waterproof up to twenty metres, and indeed it was working as well as ever. Looking at the display, he saw that his contact had been trying to reach him, just before he had got his sights on Vogelaar.

'Hydra,' he said.

His voice was recorded, checked, ID'd.

'Orley have received a warning,' his contact announced.

'What?' Xin exploded. 'When?'

'Yesterday, late afternoon.'

'Details?'

'Someone named Tu sent across a document. It was obviously a fragment of your message.' The other man drew a deep breath. 'Kenny, they must have been able to decipher more as well! How could that happen, I thought—'

'What do you mean?' Xin began to pace up and down the room. 'What sort of fragment?'

'I don't know yet.'

'Then I'm telling you this: you'll take all of our pages down from the web.'

'If we do that, our whole email communication breaks down.'

'You've tried that argument on me before.'

'And I was right.'

'Yes, and look where it got you.' Xin tried to calm down. He opened the minibar and mechanically began to shift the bottles until they were exactly the same distance apart. 'The email idea was good for exchanging complex information and for using the global server; phones are enough for everything else. The die is cast. We can't change anything now anyway. The only thing that could still go wrong would be if my message were cracked completely, so take the pages down from the web!' He paused. 'Have you already told *him*?'

'He knows.'

'And?'

The other man sighed. 'He agrees with you. He thinks we should block the pages too, so I'll do what's needed. Your turn now. What's happening with Vogelaar?'

'He's been dealt with.'

'No more danger?'

'He had created a dossier. Memory crystal. I've got the thing now. His wife was the only one who knew all about it; she's dead too.'

'Good news there for a change, Kenny.'

'I wish I could say the same about yours,' Xin snapped. 'Why am I just hearing about this warning now?'

'Because I only learned about it myself this morning.'

'How did the company react?'

'They called Gaia.'

'What?' Xin practically dropped the telephone. 'They've told Gaia?'

'Calm down. Probably because it's in the news just now. As far as I know every-thing's running to plan, they haven't cancelled any of the trips, nobody wants to leave early.'

'And who took the call at Gaia?'

'I'm expecting more details any moment.'

Xin stared into the fridge.

'Well, fine,' he said. 'Find out something for me in the meantime, and fast. Find Yoyo and Jericho in Berlin.'

'What? They're in *Berlin*?'

'They must be staying somewhere. Hack into the hotel booking systems, the immigration databases. I don't care how you do it, but find them.'

'Dear God,' the other man groaned.

'What's up?' Xin asked threateningly. 'Are you losing your nerve?'

'No, that's no problem. Okay then. I'll do what I can.'

'No,' Xin snarled. 'You'll do more than that.'

Grand Hyatt

Just before Xin shot her, Nyela had spread her fingers as though to empha-sise what she was saying. He had thought that it was only a gesture of exasperation, but in fact she'd been doing something different. She had been pointing to her face, and at that moment, it was supposed to be Vogelaar's face. She had been pointing to her eyes.

He is the duplicate!

Vogelaar's glass eye was a memory crystal. He carried the duplicate around with him, in his eye socket.

'What a sly fox,' Yoyo said, half admiring, half disgusted.

Tu snorted with laughter. 'He could hardly have found a better place for it. An eye for the facts.'

'So that they come to light once he dies.' Yoyo had more colour in her face now. Jericho remembered last night. Not ten hours had passed since she had left his room with sunken, hollow eyes, looking dissolute, flushed, blotchy, stinking of cigarette smoke and red wine. She had gone pale again now – after all, life was playing them one dirty trick after another – but other than that, the night's excesses hadn't left a mark on her. She looked fresh, smooth-skinned and perky, practically rejuvenated. Jericho was depressed by what this said about youth and intoxicants. For himself, when he'd been drinking the night away, the enzymes only ever worked fitfully, at best, at patching him up again.

'You know this sort of thing, Owen,' Tu said. 'What happens during a forensic autopsy? Will they look at the glass eye as well?'

'They'll certainly remove it while they work.'

'And a memory crystal would stand out?'

'Anybody with medical training would certainly notice,' Yoyo said. 'Assuming that Owen's right, then the police will have our dossier in their hands in the next few hours.'

Jericho rubbed his chin. He didn't much like the idea of tangling with the German police. They'd be interrogated for hours, treated with suspicion, quite likely they'd never get a look at Vogelaar's data. Their own investigation would slow down to a crawl.

Tu handed him a printout.

'Perhaps you should have a look at what we found out while you were away. We've bolded everything that's new.'

Jan Kees Vogelaar is living in Berlin under the name Andre Donner, where he runs an African private and business address: Oranienburger Strasse 50, 10117 Berlin. What should we continues to represent a grave risk to the operation not doubt that he knows all about the payload rockets. knows at least about the but some doubt as to whether. One way or another any statement lasting Admittedly, since his Vogelaar has made no public comment about the facts behind the coup. Nevertheless Ndongo's that the Chinese government planned and implemented regime change. Vogelaar has little about the nature of Operation insight of timing Furthermore, Orley Enterprises and have no reason to suspect disruption. Nobody there suspects and by then everything is under way. I count because I know, Nevertheless urgently recommend that Donner be liquidated. There are good reasons to

'Payload rockets.' Jericho looked up. 'That's another thing that supports what Vogelaar said. That satellite launch was about more than just an experimental rocket.'

'A payload rocket has to be delivering something,' Tu said. 'How did Mayé's satellite get up into orbit?'

'Payload rocket,' Jericho suggested. 'They're called carrier rockets as well, I think.'

'But there's nothing here about a satellite.'

'No. Looks like it has nothing to do with the satellite. It's about some other payload.'

Tu nodded. 'I took the opportunity to talk to some people who my people have helped out in the past. I couldn't get any definite information, but they gave me some well-founded supposition. Apparently, the Chinese government has never launched its own space projects from foreign soil. That story about wanting to avoid the insurance treaties is as threadbare as Chairman Mao's shroud. The whole thing must have been dreamed up for Mayé's benefit; at any rate it doesn't accord with current practice to shuffle the risk onto other states like that.'

'So it could have been something that Zheng was doing on his own account?'

'There's no record of the Zheng Group having been active in Africa anywhere but in Equatorial Guinea that one time. It looks doubtful that they were acting for Beijing. My informants don't think so. So did the Chinese government have anything to do with the Equatorial Guinea space programme, or with the coup against Mayé? Yes, if you are working on the premise that people like Zheng Pang-Wang *are* the government. Not if we're talking about the government as such.'

'Which proves again that the Party is just a pretext, a phantom,' Yoyo said contemptuously. 'There's no dividing line between politics and business any longer, the State can't be trusted to act in State interests. China's oilmen putsched Mayé into power, the Zhong Chan Er Bu helped them, and the whole Party knows it. Could be that Zheng putsched him out again afterwards. He's our biggest industrialist, a power in his own right.'

'And the Party wouldn't have known about that.'

'Quite so.' Yoyo tapped the page. 'And then further down: *Nobody there suspects* – what? Something or other. The *everything* turns out to go with the next bit of the sentence. *Everything is under way.* They sit there and debate whether it's even worthwhile getting rid of Vogelaar at this stage. I don't know about you, but to me that sounds as though the balloon's about to go up.'

'Any ideas about the bit before that?'

'Vogelaar didn't know about the timing any more than the nature of the oper-ation.' Tu shrugged. 'I don't think any of it gets us anywhere.'

'Well, that's great,' Jericho said. 'We're stuck.'

Yoyo toppled backwards onto the bed, her arms spread wide. Then she sat up suddenly.

'How does that work with Vogelaar, exactly?'

'What do you mean?' Jericho blinked, confused. 'How does what work?'

'Well, right now.' She pursed her lips. 'Or let's go back an hour. Twelve o'clock. Blam. Blam! Vogelaar's shot, he's lying dead in the museum. What happens next?'

'A specialist police team arrives. The scene of the crime is secured, then forensics get to work.'

'What happens to the corpse?'

'Right now, it'll still be there. Forensics work takes time. Then it'll be on the autopsy table at, say, two o'clock at the latest, then they'll cut him open, snip snap.'

'And the eye?'

'Depends. The forensic surgeon isn't an investigating officer himself – it's a bit different from how you might have seen it at the movies. He just makes a note of everything worth handing over to the investigating team. Assuming that he notices anything odd about the eye, he'll put it in his report. Maybe he'll put it back into the socket; maybe he'll put it aside as evidence.'

'How long does an autopsy take?'

'Depends on the case. There'll be no doubt here about the cause of death. Vogelaar was shot, so it'll be quick. They'll be done in two or three hours.'

'And then?'

'The forensic surgeon will sign the corpse over.' Jericho gave a wry grin. 'You can pick it up, if you bring a hearse.'

'Good. We'll fetch it.'

'Great plan.' Tu stared at her. 'Where are you going to get a hearse?'

'No idea. Since when have we been scared of a challenge?'

'We're not, but—'

'Why do we even need a *hearse*?' Yoyo sat up straight now, all vim and vigour. 'Why not go and fetch him in an ordinary car? What if we were next of kin?'

'Well, sure,' Tu said mockingly. 'You could easily be his sister. The hair, the eyes—'

'Hold on!' Jericho raised a hand. 'First off, we wouldn't get anywhere without a hearse. Secondly, if they've taken the eye, Vogelaar's corpse will be no use to you at all.'

Yoyo's burst of energy melted away. She folded her arms and frowned despondently.

'Thirdly,' Jericho said, 'that's still a good idea you had there.'

Tu narrowed his eyes. 'What are you thinking of doing?'

'Me?' Jericho shrugged. 'Nothing. Probably I daren't even show my face any more in Berlin, they'll pick me up on the spot. My hands are tied.' He smiled grimly. 'Yours aren't though.'

Charité Hospital,
Institute of Forensic Pathology

Around three o'clock, Jan Kees Vogelaar was looking fairly good. Granted, his face was waxy and he was dead as a doornail, but he wore a proud sneer that seemed to say, *kiss my arse*. A few hours ago he had been lying in a pool of his own blood, his eyes wide open, his limbs twisted, looking more like the Ides of March. Fallen like Caesar beneath a Roman temple. A death that may sound romantic in the textbooks, but in fact it was a bloody mess. The bald man lying next to him, likewise dead, did little to make the picture any prettier.

Once he had been photographed from all angles, and the dead man next to him with the pencil jutting from his eye, they zipped him up into a plastic bag and drove him across to the Institute of Forensic Pathology at the Charité Hospital. Here he was weighed and measured, his identifying features noted down, and he was put into cold-storage. He didn't stay there for long, however, but was taken out and X-rayed several times. This showed where the flechettes had lodged or broken apart in his body, as well as revealing old bone breakages, mended now, and a titanium knee. It also showed that his left eye was artificial. He was wheeled into the autopsy theatre, along with the bald man, where they were just about to slice him open when Nyela was brought in as well. This meant that three of the five dissection tables were occupied by as yet unidentified corpses. The surgeons removed Vogelaar's organs, examined them, weighed them, drained off bodily fluids and measured the volumes, noted down all their procedures and findings. Meanwhile a case team was hastily assembled, and the investigating officers compared photographs of the corpses with pictures from the city police files. It was soon established that the female corpse had been found in a car registered in the name of Andre Donner, resident in Berlin since a year ago. He was a restaurant owner, married to Nyela Donner, and photographs from the records left no doubt as to the dead woman's identity, or that the man with the glass eye was her husband.

The bald man's name, though, was not so easily established.

Just as Donner (alias Vogelaar) was being sewn back up, the pathology lab got a phone call from the German Foreign Office, saying that Donner's murder had caught the attention of the Chinese authorities. Chinese and German police working together, so the civil servant on the phone said, had been investigating a gang of technology smugglers for some time. Perhaps the restaurant owner's death had something to do with a failed handover, and Donner might well not be Donner at all, but somebody else entirely, an alias. The Berlin government was very keen to do what they could to help the Chinese investigators, two of whom would be arriving in a few minutes to take a quick look at the body. Could the autopsy team please treat them as guests of the government?

The trainee doctor who took the call said that she would have to make enquiries. The civil servant gave his name and a telephone number, asked her to move as quickly as she could, and hung up. Next, the trainee spoke to the head of the Institute, who told her to check with the Foreign Office that it was all above board, and to bring the Chinese investigators through to theatre as soon as they arrived.

4 – 9 – 3 – 0 – she dialled—

*　　　*　　　*

—and was put through. It really was the Foreign Office number, but the extension number was a little special. It didn't actually exist. Thus she wasn't actually put through where she thought she would be when she heard a recorded voice saying:

'This is the Foreign Office. Currently all our lines are busy. You will be put through to the next free line. This is the Foreign Office. Currently—' Then a woman's voice, gentle, melodious: 'Foreign Office, good afternoon, my name is Regina Schilling.'

'Institute of Forensic Pathology, Charité. Could you put me through please to – erm—' The woman on the line paused, probably looking at her notes. 'Mr Helge Malchow.'

'One moment,' said Diane.

Jericho grinned. He had picked a first name and family name quite at random out of the Berlin telephone book, and had programmed a few sentences into Diane. The whole little show would certainly dispel any doubts the caller might have that she was speaking to the Foreign Office – and not, for instance, to a computer in a hotel room. Diane's German was perfect, of course.

'Mr Malchow's line is busy at the moment,' Diane told the trainee. 'Would you like to hold?'

'Will it take long?'

Jericho pointed to the right answer.

'Just a moment,' Diane said, and then cheerfully, 'Ah, I see that he's just hung up. I'll put you through. Have a pleasant day.'

'Thank you.'

'Helge Malchow,' Jericho said.

'Charité Hospital. You called about the Chinese police delegation.'

'That's right.' His own German wasn't bad at all. Maybe a bit rusty. 'Have they arrived yet?'

'No, but they're quite welcome. They should drive to Building O.'

'Splendid.'

'Perhaps you could tell me their names?'

'Superintendent Tu Tian is leading the investigation, Inspector Chen Yuyun will be with him. The two of them are working undercover, so perhaps you could be so good as to let them see what they need as quickly as you can, not too much red tape.' It was a ludicrous claim, but it sounded halfway plausible. 'By the way, you'll find that they only speak English.'

'That's fine. We'll keep the red tape to a mini—'

'Thank you very much indeed.' Jericho hung up, and dialled Tu's number.

'All systems go,' he said.

Tu put his phone down and looked at Yoyo. She could see it in his eyes that he absolutely loathed what they were about to do.

'I never wanted to see another corpse in my life,' he said. 'Corpses in tiled rooms. Never again.'

'Sometime or other we'll all be corpses in tiled rooms.'

'At least I won't have to see that for myself, when it's me.'

'You don't know that. They say that you see yourself when you die. See yourself lying there, and you couldn't care less.'

'I could care.'

Yoyo hesitated, then reached out and squeezed Tu's hand. Her slim white fingers against his soft, liver-spotted flesh. A child seeking to reassure a giant. She thought of the evening before and the story Tu had told her during the course of the night, of people locked away in prison for so long that in the end the prison was in them. For years now she had been carrying around her own burden of self-reproach, certain that in some obscure way she was responsible for the grown-ups' pain; and now that burden was taken from her shoulders and replaced instead with the truth, which was so much worse, so much more depressing. She had smoked, boozed, cried, and felt helpless, useless, the way children feel when they see their parents' moods, so complex, so painful, moods that they can't understand and think must be something to do with them. Every argument Tu used to make her feel better about it just deepened the pain. His story freed her from the accumulated years of self-pity, but now she felt a vast pity for Hongbing instead, and wondered if she wanted a father she had to pity. Now she was ashamed of even having had the thought, and again she felt guilty.

'Nobody wants to pity his parents,' Tu had said. 'We want them to protect us for a while, and then at some point we want to leave them alone. The most we can achieve is to understand what they do, and forgive the child we used to be.'

For all that, Tu deserved pity as well, but he seemed not to need it, unlike her father. She suspected that it had been far worse for him than it had been for Tu. But unlike the bitterness that Hongbing had eaten, Tu's fate seemed to her—

'Not so bad?' Tu had laughed. 'Of course. I'm not even your uncle. I'm an old fart with a young wife. When you look at me, you see who I am, not who I was. There's no history to chain us together.'

'But we're – friends?'

'Yes, we're friends, and if you were a bit more interested in my bank balance and had fewer scruples, we could be lovers. But you can only see Hongbing in one particular way, that's genetics for you. No place for pity there. It just doesn't feature. We each have our own genetic destiny, and when we've played that role to the full, then perhaps we can see our parents for what they really are, understand them, accept them, respect them, maybe even love them. For what they always were: just people.'

Oh God, and then dropping in on Jericho late at night. What an embarrassment! She'd been carried away by the intoxicating notion of storming his room, and then she'd crept out without achieving anything, like a silly drunk. It had been a whim, of course, and like all such whims it only made her feel stupidly ashamed. In retrospect, she didn't even know what she had wanted there.

Or did she?

'Let's get this over with,' said Tu.

They'd fetched the Audi a quarter of an hour ago from the street by the Spree, and now they were parked across from the Institute of Forensic Pathology, Charité Hospital. Tu started the engine and drove up to the barrier at the front gate. He waved his ID out of the window at the guard, told him that the Foreign Office had approved their visit and asked the way to Building O. They drove along past grand red-brick façades. Splendid green lawns beneath spreading leafy boughs called out to them to stop and linger with a loaf of bread, some cheese, a bottle of Chianti, to make the most of every minute before the die was cast and they had to enter Building O. They felt that same yearning for peace and quiet that even the liveliest extrovert feels in a graveyard.

After driving straight ahead for a long while, then turning twice, they stopped in front of a light, airy, somewhat sterile building with all the charm of a provincial clinic. There were only three police cars parked in the forecourt, with the green Berlin livery and marked *Forensics*. All this understated modesty unsettled Yoyo, gave her the odd feeling that they weren't where they needed to be, that the corpses must be somewhere else. She had imagined that in a megalopolis like Berlin, where people died every minute of every day, the Institute of Forensic Pathology had to be a vast hangar-like edifice, but this little low building hardly suggested doctors arguing, inspectors, profilers, all the scenes she knew from the movies. They went up three steps, rang the bell by a glass door and were let through by two women in white coats, one tall, young and rather pretty, the other short and wiry, in her late forties, apple-cheeked and with a no-nonsense haircut. The older woman introduced herself as Dr Marika Voss, and her young companion as Svenja Maas. Tu and Yoyo held out their IDs. Dr Voss glanced at the characters and nodded as though she dealt with Chinese documentation every working day.

'Yes, you have been announced to us,' she said, in stiffly formal English. 'Miss Chen Yuyun?'

Yoyo shook her hand. The doctor looked thoughtful for a moment. Clearly she was doing her best to reconcile Yoyo's appearance with what she imagined an undercover homicide squad must look like. She glanced across to Svenja Maas and then back again, as though remembering with an effort that there were good-looking people in all walks of life.

'And you are Mister—'

'Superintendent Tu Tian. This is very good of you,' Tu said amiably. 'We don't want to take up too much of your time. Have you already completed the autopsy?'

'You are interested in Andre Donner?'

'Yes.'

'We just finished with him a few minutes ago, but not yet with Nyela Donner. She is being examined two tables further on. Do you need to look at her as well?'

'No.'

'Or at the second dead man from the museum? We don't have his identity yet.'

Tu frowned.

'Perhaps. Yes, I think so.'

'Good. Please come.'

Dr Voss looked into a scanner. Another door opened. They entered a corridor, and here for the first time Yoyo smelled that sharp, sweet smell that the people on television always ward off with a bit of balm rubbed under their noses. It was bacterial decay; the smell thickened, from a mere hint to a miasma, as they went downstairs to the autopsy section, and from a miasma to a brackish pool as they entered the lobby to the theatre. A young man with an Arabic look about him was uploading children's portrait photos to a monitor screen. Yoyo didn't even want to think about children, here. Nor did she need to, since Dr Voss had just pressed something into her hand. She looked at the little tube, utterly at a loss, and felt her ignorance open up beneath her like a trapdoor.

'For our visitors,' the doctor said. 'You know, of course.'

No, she didn't know.

'For rubbing under your nose.' Dr Voss raised her eyebrows in surprise. 'I thought that you would—'

'This is Miss Chen's first case involving forensic pathology,' Tu said, taking the tube from Yoyo's fingers. As though he had done it all his life, he squeezed out two pea-sized blobs of the paste it contained and smeared them under his nostrils. 'She's here to get some experience.'

Dr Voss nodded understandingly.

'You've not been paying attention in theory class, Inspector,' Tu teased her in Chinese, passing Yoyo the tube. She rolled her eyes at him and rubbed a squeeze of the stuff on her upper lip, only to find out the next moment that it was, quite definitely, too much. A minty bomb exploded into her nasal passages, swept through her brain and blasted the smell of decay aside. Svenja Maas watched her with conspiratorial interest, the fellow-feeling of two beautiful people who meet in the company of the less well favoured.

'You get used to it at some point,' she declared, the voice of experience. Yoyo smiled faintly.

They followed the doctor into the theatre, tiled red and white with frosted glass windows and boxy ceiling lights. Five autopsy tables were lined up next to one another. The first two were empty, but two surgeons were bent over the table in the middle, one of them just lifting the lungs from a yawning gap in the ribcage of the black woman they were working on, while other said something into a microphone. The lungs went onto a scale. Dr Voss led the group past the fourth table, where a large corpse lay under a white sheet, and she stopped at the last. Here too the corpse was covered, but she turned the sheet back and they saw Jan Kees Vogelaar, alias Andre Donner.

Yoyo looked at him.

She hadn't particularly liked the man, but now that she saw him lying there, a Y-shaped incision freshly sewn up on his torso, she felt sorry. Just as she had felt sorry for Jack Nicholson in *One Flew Over the Cuckoo's Nest*, for Robert de Niro in *Heat*, Kevin Costner in *A Perfect World*, Chris Pine in *Neighborhood*, Emma Watson in *Pale Days*. All those who had so very nearly made it, but who always failed at the last moment no matter how often you watched the film.

'If you don't need me,' Dr Voss said, 'I'll leave you with Frau Maas. She assisted in the Donner autopsy and should be able to answer any questions you have.'

'Well, then,' said Tu, switching to Chinese. 'Let's get started, Comrade.'

They leaned down to look at his face, waxy, already tinged with blue. Yoyo tried to remember which side Vogelaar had his glass eye on. Jericho had insisted it was the right side. She wasn't so sure herself. She could readily have sworn that it was the left. It was a magnificently well-made eye, and under Vogelaar's closed lids there was no telling which it might be.

'Not sure?' Tu frowned.

'No, and that's Owen's fault.' Yoyo looked askance at Svenja Maas, who had stepped back. 'Let our friend there show you the fellow on the next table.'

'Fine, I'll keep her off your back.'

'It'll be all right.' Yoyo gave a sour smile. 'There are only two possibilities.'

She wasn't getting used to the sight of corpses, or to the idea that people she had barely got to know dropped like flies. But even as she veered between fascination and disgust, an unexpected sense of calm took hold of her, deep and clear, like a mountain lake. Tu turned to Svenja Maas and pointed to the body on table four, still under its sheet.

'Could you please uncover this man for us?'

Stupid. The trainee doctor stepped round the wrong side of the table. From where she was, she still had a good view of Yoyo. Tu shifted position to block her view.

'Great heavens above,' he cried out. 'What happened to his eye?'

'He was attacked with a pencil,' the trainee doctor said, not without some admiration in her voice. 'Straight through the bone and into the brain.'

'And how exactly did that happen?'

Yoyo put two fingers onto Vogelaar's right eyelid and lifted it. It seemed to have no particular temperature, neither cold nor warm. While Svenja Maas was explaining about angle of entry and pressure, she pressed her middle finger and thumb into the corner of the eye. The eyeball seemed to sit much too firmly in the eye socket, more like a glass marble than soft and slippery, so that for a moment she wasn't sure that Jericho hadn't been right after all, and she shoved her fingers deeper into the socket.

Resistance. Were those muscles? The eye wasn't coming out, rather it tugged backwards, leaking some kind of fluid, like a cornered animal.

That wasn't a glass eye, not on her life.

'The shaft splintered,' Maas said, walking over to the organ table between the corpse and the wash-basin, where something lay in a transparent plastic bag on a tray. Quickly, Yoyo pulled her fingers out of the socket, just before Maas happened to glance over at her. She thought she heard a squelching sound as she did so, reproachful, tell-tale. Tu hurried to block the sightlines again. Yoyo shuddered. Could the woman have heard something? Had there been anything to hear, or had she just imagined it, expecting an eye socket to squelch as you take your fingers out?

The surface of the calm lake inside her began to ruffle. There was something sticky on her fingers. Jericho had been wrong! While Tu twinkled at Svenja Maas, asking interested questions about her work, she plunged her fingers into Vogelaar's left eye socket. Straight away she could feel that this was different. The surface was harder, definitely artificial. She pushed further, flexed her middle finger and thumb. All the while, Tu was asking learned questions about the improvised use of drawing equipment as weapons. Maas pronounced that everything could be a weapon, and stepped to the left. Tu declared that she was absolutely right, and stepped to the right. The pathologists at the middle table were busy with Nyela.

Yoyo took a deep breath, high on mint rub.

Now!

The glass eye popped out, almost trustingly, and nestled into the palm of her hand. She slipped it into her jacket, closed Vogelaar's sunken eyelid as best she could and saw that she had caused lasting disfigurement. Too late. She quickly pulled the sheet back up over his face and took two steps to Tu's side.

'There is no doubt any longer about Andre Donner,' she said in English.

Tu stopped in the middle of a question.

'Oh, good,' he said. 'Very good. I think we can go.'

'When will you want my report, Superintendent?'

'What kind of question is that, Inspector! As soon as possible. The director of prosecutions is breathing down our neck.'

Curtain, applause, Yoyo thought.

'Are you done?' Svenja Maas looked from one to the other, disgruntled to be so abruptly ignored.

'Yes, we don't want to discommode you any further.'

'You are not – erm – discommoding me.'

'No, you are right of course, it was a pleasure. Goodbye, and best wishes to Dr Voss.'

Svenja Maas shrugged and led them out to the lobby, where they said goodbye. Tu marched ahead, sped up on the stairs, and practically raced along the corridor. Yoyo scurried after him. The last of her calm was gone. They didn't need any authorisation to leave. They went out into the car park and headed for the Audi, when suddenly a commanding voice rang out from the building.

'Mr Tu, Miss Chen!'

Yoyo froze. Slowly she turned, and saw Dr Marika Voss standing on the steps, her chin raised.

They've noticed, Yoyo thought. We were too slow.

'Please forgive our hasty departure.' Tu raised his arms apologetically. 'We wanted to say goodbye, but we couldn't find you.'

'Was everything as you had hoped?'

'You were extremely helpful!'

'I'm glad of that.' She smiled suddenly. 'Well, then, I hope that you make progress with your investigations.'

'Thanks to your help, we shall make great strides.'

'Good day to you.'

Dr Voss marched back inside, and Yoyo felt as though she had turned to butter in the sunshine. She slid into the Audi, and melted onto the seat.

'Do you have it?' Tu asked.

'I have it,' she replied, with the last of her strength.

Svenja Maas wasn't exactly offended, but she was rather peeved. As she went back into the autopsy theatre she felt a nagging suspicion that the Chinese policeman hadn't really been interested in her, just in keeping up some Asiatic notion of etiquette. She went to the furthest tables and noticed that his young inspector had put the sheet back up over Donner's corpse, though not very neatly. She tugged at it irritably, and found that the whole thing was crooked. She turned the sheet down.

She saw straight away that something was wrong. Vogelaar's right eye wasn't looking good, but the left eye was horrible.

With a dark presentiment, she lifted the lid.

The glass eye was missing.

For a moment she flushed hot and cold at the thought that she would be blamed. She had left the eye in its socket, but only because she wanted to take it out later and show it to a prosthetics expert. They had noticed something odd about it. It looked as though it had something inside, maybe some sort of mechanism with which Vogelaar could see, perhaps something else. They hadn't really considered it significant.

Obviously they had been wrong.

Electrified, she ran from the theatre and up the stairs. She found Dr Marika Voss in the corridor.

'Are the Chinese police still here?' she asked breathlessly.

'The Chinese?' Dr Voss raised her eyebrows. 'No, they just left. Why?'

'Shit! Shit! Shit!'

'What's up?' the older woman demanded.

'They took something with them,' Maas stammered. Bastards, landing her in it like this!

'With them?' Voss echoed.

'The eye. The glass eye.'

The doctor hadn't been in the team who had examined Donner. She knew nothing about the eye, but she understood all the same that they would be in trouble.

'I'll call the guards at the gate,' she said.

The car glided along the main road on the hospital campus, past the stern red-brick buildings, the peaceful lawns and paths, the shady trees.

'Hey,' Yoyo said, frowning. 'What's going on up ahead?'

Somebody came running out of the guards' cabin, a man in uniform. He raised his hands as though directing an aeroplane on the runway. At the same time, the barrier began to drop. Obviously the fuss was about them.

'I should imagine we've been found out.'

'Great. Now what?'

'All down to you.' Tu looked across at her. 'How do you like Berlin? Do you want to stay?'

'Not at any cost.'

'Thought not,' he said, accelerated and shot under the barrier, so close that Yoyo was surprised not to hear it scrape across the roof. Behind them, the guard's yells drifted like pollen on the summer air.

Hotel Adlon

The symbol shimmering on the display showed many twisting reptilian necks, all springing from a single body. Nine heads. The symbol of Hydra.

Xin clapped the phone to his ear.

'We've sent you data from several major Berlin hotels,' said the caller. 'No luck with the smaller ones. There's a hell of a lot of them – all Berlin seems to be nothing but hotels. The problem was that working so fast, we couldn't get into every single computer—'

'Understood. And?'

'No hits.'

'They *must* be staying somewhere,' Xin insisted.

'They're not in any of the international chains. No Chen Yuyun and no Owen Jericho. However, I can give you more details of the warning that reached London yesterday. I'll send you the text. Do you want to hear it first?'

'Spit it out.'

Xin listened to the fragmentary sentences that he already knew so well. He considered just how dangerous this fire might be that Yoyo and Jericho had started. It was hardly a fragment by now. They had decrypted almost ninety per cent of the message. All the same, the really important parts, the decisive information, was still missing. And it hadn't been Jericho, or the girl, who had called Edda Hoff, but a man called Tu. Hoff was number three in the Orley security chain of command, and Xin knew very little about her, other than that she was quite unimaginative and accordingly would never exaggerate, or downplay, a threat.

'Hoff made the decision on her own account, and she told the whole corpor-ation that there may perhaps be an attack, without pretending that she had any real information,' the caller said. 'Gaia was informed as well, just like every other link in the corporate network, but they saw no reason to change the programme up on the Moon. Hoff seems to have let all the right people know.' The caller didn't dare name names over the telephone, even though it was practically impossible that anyone might be listening in on this connection. On the other hand, they had never expected that the encrypted messages piggy-backing on harmless email attachments could be cracked.

'Tu,' said Xin thoughtfully.

'That's the name he gave. I'll send you over his mobile number. We don't know where he was calling from.'

Unlike the astonishing diversity of given names, the number of Chinese family names was limited indeed. The vast majority of Chinese people shared just a few dozen clan names, mostly monosyllables – the so-called Old Hundred Names. It was not uncommon for an entire village to be called Zheng, Wang, Han, Ma, Hu or Tu. Nevertheless Xin couldn't shake off the feeling that he had heard the name Tu quite recently, and in connection with Yoyo.

'Have you taken those pages down from the web?' he asked, since inspiration failed to strike.

'That channel of communication has been closed.'

Xin knew what the decision entailed, so he understood why his caller was so sullen. The man at the other end of the line had himself suggested the piggy-back encryption, and had written the code. It had served them well for three years. Hydra's heads had been able to exchange messages in real time, functioning as one great brain.

'We'll get over it,' he said, trying to sound friendly. 'The net served its purpose for us, and more, and it's all down to you! Everybody respects your contribution. Just as everybody will understand why we decided to break off simultaneous communication so close to our goal. The time has come when there's nothing more to say. All we can do is await developments.'

Xin hung up, stared down at his feet and shifted them to a parallel position, ankles and instep exactly the same distance apart, not touching. Slowly, he drew his knees inwards. How he hated the tangled web of accident and circumstance! As soon as he felt the hairs on his calves begin to brush against one another, he adjusted his feet, shifted his thighs, his arms, his hands, his shoulders, positioning them symmetrically along the line of an imaginary axis, until he sat there as an exact mirror image, one side of his body the perfect reflection of the other. This usually helped him to get his thoughts in order, but this time the technique failed. He felt dizzy with self-doubt, blindsided by the thought that perhaps he'd done everything wrong, that hunting Yoyo down had only made things worse.

Thoughts and afterthoughts.

Losing control.

His heart hammered like a piston. Only one last nudge, he felt, and he would burst apart into a thousand pieces. No, not him. His shell. The human cloak called Kenny Xin. He felt like a host body for his own larval self, like a cocoon, a pupa, the mid-stage of some metamorphosis, and he was horribly afraid of whatever it was that was eating him from the inside. Sometimes it grew, flexed itself and choked the breath in his throat, and he couldn't tame it, couldn't take the strain any longer; at these moments he had to give the beast something to calm it, just as he had allowed it to burn the hut where his torturers had kept him. Unredeemed, sick and poverty-stricken as they were, he had given them to the flames, and in that moment had felt himself made free, cleansed of all suffering, his mind clear and unclouded. Since then he had often wondered whether he had gone mad that day, or been cured of madness. He could hardly remember the time before. At most, he remembered his disgust at living in this world. His hatred towards his parents for having given birth to him, even if at such a tender age he knew little of just how he had been thrust into this world. He only felt certain that his family was responsible for his life, which was already enough to make him hate them, and that they were making it a living hell.

That there was no sense to his existence.

It was only after the fire that the sense of it all became clear. Could he be mad when suddenly everything made sense? How many so-called sane people spent their days in the most senseless activities? How much of accepted morality was based on ritual and dogma, with not the least shred of sense to it? The fire had broadened his horizons, so that all at once he recognised the plan, creation's twisting labyrinthine paths, its abstract beauty. There was no way back from here. He had moved up to a higher level which some might call madness, but which was simply an insight of such all-illuming power that he had to struggle to contain it. Any attempt to share it with others was mere vanity. How could he explain to others that everything he did flowed from a higher insight? It was the price that he paid, by making other people pay.

No. He hadn't made things worse.

He had had to make sure!

Xin imagined his own brain. A Rorschach universe. The purity of symmetry, predictability, control. Slowly, he felt his calm return. He stood up, plugged the phone into the room's computer console and uploaded the hotel reservation lists. He went through them one by one. Naturally he didn't expect to see Chen Yuyun or Owen Jericho turn up in the lists. Hydra's hackers had gone through the lists several times over once they had broken into the hotel systems. He didn't exactly know what he expected to find, he only knew that he felt he would find *something*.

And what a find.

It fell into place like the last piece of a puzzle, neatly explaining everything that had happened in the museum and answering half a dozen other questions besides. Three rooms in the Grand Hyatt on Marlene-Dietrich-Platz had been booked to a company called Tu Technologies, registered in Shanghai. They had been booked by the director of the company, who had signed for them in person. Tu Tian.

The outfit that Yoyo worked for.

That was where he knew the name from!

He loaded the company homepage and found a portrait of the owner. A plump man, almost bald, with a pate like a billiard ball. All in all, so ugly that he came out the other side as rather appealing. His thick lips could make a frog turn green with envy, but they were somehow sensual at the same time. His eyes, peering out from behind a tiny pair of glasses, glowed with humour and pitiless intelligence. He radiated a Buddha-like calm and iron determination, all at once. Xin could tell at first sight that Tu Tian was a streetfighter, a jackal in jester's clothing. Somebody he could ill afford to underestimate. If he was helping Yoyo and Jericho, that meant that they were mobile, that they could leave Berlin as quickly as they had shown up.

The Vogelaars were dead. Which meant that they *would* be leaving Berlin.

Very soon. Now.

Xin strapped on his gun. He chose a long red wig and a face-mask with a matching beard, then stuck appliqués to his forehead and cheekbones. He pulled on an emerald-green duster coat, put on a slim pair of mirrored holospecs and stopped in front of the mirror for a few seconds to check the effect. He looked like a pop star. Like a typical mando-progger, who had made more money than he'd ever had good taste.

He hurried from the hotel, flagged down a taxi and ordered it to the Grand Hyatt.

Grand Hyatt

Tu's face showed up on the screen. Jericho was hardly surprised to hear him say:

'Get Diane packed. We're leaving.'

'What about the glass eye?'

Yoyo's fingers appeared onscreen. Vogelaar's false eye stared at him. Denuded of its eyelids, it looked somehow surprised, even a little indignant.

'There's no doubt that it's a memory crystal,' he heard her say. 'I had a look at it, it's the usual pattern. Hurry up. The cops will be with you shortly.'

'Where are you now?'

'On our way to you,' Tu said. 'They've got the car numberplate. In other words, they know that it's a hire car, they know who rented it, they know his address, and so on and so forth. I should guess that they'll make the connection with this morning's unhappy events.'

'And with your jet,' said Jericho.

'With my—'

'*Fuck!*' said Yoyo's voice. 'He's right!'

'As soon as they find out that you rented the car at the airport, they'll twig,' said Jericho. 'They'll arrest us even before we check the car back.'

'How much time do we have?'

'Hard to say. The first thing they'll do is go through the passenger lists of all the flights that landed before you went to the rental desk. That will take a while. They won't find anything, but since you must have got here somehow or other, they'll check the private flights.'

'It'll take us at least half an hour to get to the airport in the Audi.'

'That could be too late.'

'Forget the bloody Audi,' Yoyo called out. 'If we're to have any chance at all, we need a skycab.'

'I could order one,' Jericho suggested.

'Do that,' Tu agreed. 'We'll be at the hotel in ten minutes.'

'Your wish is my command.'

Jericho hung up and ran out to the corridor. As he dashed towards the lifts, he could see with his mind's eye how the efficient German police would be unravelling the puzzle of their arrival, dauntless, dutiful and assuming the worst. He went up to the roof and found the skyport empty. A liveried hotel employee beamed at him from over the edge of his terminal. Jericho's arrival seemed to give him a new purpose in life, stranded up here as he was on the lonely expanse of the roof.

'Would you like to order an aircab?' he asked.

'Yes, that's it.'

'One moment, please.' He slid his fingers busily across the console. 'I could have one here for you in ten to fifteen minutes.'

'As quick as you can!'

'While you're waiting, would you like any help with your lugg—'

The sentence probably ended with *-age*, but Jericho was back in the lift. He hurried to his room and shoved Diane into his rucksack with all the hardware. He packed whatever clothing lay around on top, checked and holstered his Glock, ran along the corridor and left a note for Tu:

I'm on the flight deck.

Charité Hospital,
Institute of Forensic Pathology

'No, he's not,' said the voice on the telephone.

Dr Marika Voss hopped from one foot to another, while Svenja Maas stood next to her, pale and wringing her hands.

'Malchow,' she repeated stubbornly. 'Hel – ge Mal – chow.'

'As I've already said—'

'My colleague called him.'

'That may well be, but—'

'First she was held in a queue, then one of your switchboard staff put her through. To Malchow. To Hel—'

'There's no such person.'

'But—'

'Listen,' said the voice, growing audibly less patient as the conversation went round and round in circles. 'I would very much like to help you, but we have nobody of that name in the whole Foreign Office! And the extension number that you gave me doesn't exist either!'

Dr Voss pressed her lips together indignantly. She'd known as much, ever since the automated dialling system had told her that there was no such number. Despite all this, she saw no reason to back down.

'But the woman on the switchboard—'

'Ah yes, the switchboard.' A short pause, a sigh. 'And what was the woman called?'

'What was she called?' Dr Voss hissed.

'Something like Schill or Schall,' Maas whispered, hunched over, miserable.

'Schill or Schall, my colleague says.'

'No.'

'No?'

'We do have a Scholl. Miss Scholl.'

'Scholl?' asked Dr Voss.

Maas shook her head. 'It was Schill.'

'It was Schill.'

'I'm sorry. No Schill, no Schall, no Malchow. I really do advise you to call the police. Clearly you've been the butt of a very nasty joke.'

Dr Voss gave in. She thanked the civil servant in an icy tone, then called the number for the police. At her side, Svenja Maas wilted.

Within five minutes the case officers had tracked down the numberplate. Within seconds, they knew the name of the hire firm's client. They compared that information with the records from immigration, and learned that Tu Tian had touched down in Berlin early the day before, giving the Grand Hyatt on Marlene-Dietrich-Platz as his address.

Two minutes after that, a team was dispatched to the hotel.

Grand Hyatt

Thanks to Tu's dauntless driving, they reached the hotel sooner than they had expected, and with even more reason to get away again as quickly as they could – he must have chalked up dozens of traffic offences between the hospital at Turmstrasse and the hotel on Marlene-Dietrich-Platz. He got out, threw the keys to the concierge and asked him to take the car down to the underground parking.

'Shall we go to the bar?' Yoyo asked, loudly enough that the man couldn't help but overhear it. Tu winked, understanding her plan, and picked up the charade.

'To tell you the truth, I feel like something sweet.'

'There's a Starbucks in the Sony Center. Up the street.'

'Great. See you there. I'll just go tell Owen.'

It was vaudeville stuff of course, but it might buy them some time. They crossed the lobby as fast as they could without arousing suspicion, went up to the seventh floor and headed for their rooms.

'Leave everything there that you don't need,' Tu called to her. 'Bring only the bare essentials.'

'Easy enough,' Yoyo snorted. 'I don't have anything! You look after yourself, don't waste time fussing with your suitcase.'

'I don't care about fashion, me.'

'True enough, we'll have to work on that. See you on the flight deck in two minutes.'

Seven floors below, Xin jumped out of the taxi. By now he knew what floor they were on, what room numbers, the only thing he didn't know was who had which room. All the rooms were booked to Tu Technologies, and neither Yoyo nor Jericho were mentioned by name. He walked into the lobby in his full battledress. Hyatt staff and guests would certainly remember who had walked in at 15.30: a tall man, a striking figure with a flowing mane of red hair and a Genghis Khan moustache, probably some sort of artsy type. Holospecs hid the Asiatic cast of his eyes. He could easily be taken for European. The best disguise was to make yourself noticed.

He walked into a lift and pressed for the seventh floor.

Nothing happened.

Xin frowned, then spotted the thumbscan plate. Of course. The lift worked on authorisation only, as in most international hotels. He trotted obediently back into the lobby, where a contingent of his fellow-countrymen was just making their way to the reception desk. There was a sudden throng. The staff at the desk steeled themselves for the task of making sense of the new arrivals' broken English, riddling out what they meant from what they said, and adding to the rich confusion with their own small store of Chinese words. Xin headed purposefully to the only receptionist who was busy with other tasks, in this case the telephone. He drew himself up to his full height and then wondered what on earth he could ask her.

How do I get up to the seventh floor?

Would you like to check in? – No, I have some friends staying here and I wanted to drop in on them. I can authorise you and then call them for you, to let them know you're coming. Ahh, you know how it is, actually I wanted to surprise them. I understand! If you wait just a moment, I'll ride up with you. It's all a bit busy at the moment, as you see, but in a few minutes' time . . . Can't we be a bit quicker? – Well, you see, I'm not really supposed to – it's really just guests who can—

Xin turned away. The whole thing was too complicated. He didn't want to leave his thumbprint in the Hyatt's system, any more than he wanted to risk Tu, Jericho or Yoyo being warned. He mingled in with the other Chinese.

Jericho saw the skycab lift over the Tiergarten park and make for the Hyatt, a muscular-looking VTOL with four turbines. It came in fast, dipped its jets with a hissing snarl and sank slowly down onto the landing pad.

'Your taxi's here,' the hotel employee said, smiling, the joy in his voice announcing how wonderful it was that air transport was so widely available these days, and what a pleasure it was to see people use it.

In the next moment Yoyo hurried from the terminal, a crumpled shopping bag under her arm and Tu trotting in her wake. He was pulling his suitcase along behind him as though it were a recalcitrant child.

The taxi settled.

'Just what the doctor ordered,' Tu beamed.

'Just what the *detective* ordered,' Jericho reminded him amiably.

'Enough strutting and preening, you two.' Yoyo headed for the boarding hatch. 'Is your jet cleared for take-off?'

It was as though her question had slammed on the brakes in Tu's stride. He stopped, fumbled at the bare expanse of his scalp and tried to twist his fingers into the tiny short hairs there.

'What is it?'

'I forgot something,' he said.

'Say it's not so.' Yoyo stared at him.

'It is. My phone. I just now thought, all I need to do is call the airport from the taxi, and then I realised—'

'You have to go back to your room?'

'Erm – yes.' Tu left his suitcase where it was, turned around and hurried back to the lift. 'I'll be right back. Right back.'

When Xin heard that the elderly Chinese couple in front of him intended to book one of the Grand Hyatt's finest and most expensive suites, he felt a warm glow of pleasure. Not because of any sudden spasm of altruism, but because the suite was on the seventh floor. Right where he wanted to be.

The husband put his thumb on the scanplate. A young receptionist offered to show the couple up to their room, and they strolled across to the lift together. Xin fell in behind them. As they stood there waiting for the lift, the wife turned to look at him, her curiosity as strong as an elastic band tugging her head around. She looked in bemusement at the tumble of hair over his shoulders, and in bafflement at his holospecs. She eyed the toes of his snakeskin boots dubiously, visibly nervous at the thought of having to share a hotel with the likes of him. Her husband stuck to her side, short and stocky, and stared at the gap where the lift doors met until they opened. They went into the lift together. Nobody asked whether he was with the group. The young receptionist smiled warmly at him, and he smiled back, just as warmly.

'Seventh floor as well?' she asked, in English just to be on the safe side.

'Yes, please,' he said.

Next to him, the Chinese woman stiffened, horribly sure now that he was living on the same floor.

*   *   *

Tu tore back the bedclothes but his phone wasn't there, any more than it had been on the desk or on either of the night-stands. He rummaged through sheets, flung pillows aside, grabbed fistfuls of linen and damask, slid his fingers in between the mattress and the frame.

Nothing.

Who had he called last? Who had he been meaning to call?

The airport. At least, he had wanted to, but then he had decided to call later. He had even had the thing in his hand.

And he'd put it down.

He swept his eyes over the desk again, the chairs, armchair, carpeting. Incredible, he was getting old! What had he been doing just before? He saw himself standing there, his phone in his right hand, while there was something in his left hand too, something just below waist height—

Aha, of course!

Seventh floor.

The Chinese wife pushed herself brusquely past the young receptionist to get out of the lift, as though she feared that Xin might bite her at the last moment. Her husband, though, had a sudden access of Western etiquette, and took a step back to let the young woman go first, smiling broadly at her. Xin waited until the group was out of sight. The hotel corridors stretched around a sunny atrium space, four sides of a square, with the guest rooms along the front edges. He looked at the wall map. He was glad to see the receptionist and the Chinese couple had set off in the opposite direction from the rooms which Tu had taken.

He was alone.

The carpet muffled his steps. He passed a club lounge, turned into the next corridor, stopped, recalled Tu's room numbers.

712, 717, 727.

712 was to his left. He walked on quickly, counting up. 717, also locked. His coat swung out around him as he stopped still, dead in the middle of the corridor. 727 was ajar.

Tu? Jericho? Yoyo?

One of the three of them would soon regret not having locked up.

Yoyo saw the gyrocopter first.

'Where?' Jericho yelped.

'I think it's headed this way.' She ran to the edge of the skyport and stood there, hopping from one leg to the other. 'Oh, shit! The cops. It's the cops!'

Jericho had been chatting with the skycab pilot, but now he shaded his eyes with his hand. Yoyo was right. It was a police gyrocopter, coming closer, like the one he had seen above the Brandenburg Gate a few hours ago.

'They could be here for any one of a thousand reasons.'

Yoyo hared across to him. 'Tian will screw it all up.'

'Nothing's screwed up yet.' Jericho nodded towards the skycab. 'We'll get in. That way at least they won't see you leaping about up here.'

'Ha!' Tu called out.

He'd gone to have a pee, of course! And while he'd been peeing, guiding the stream with his left hand and holding the phone in his right, he'd had a momentary brainfart and had almost shaken the last drop off his phone and talked to his dick. Mankind at the mercy of communication technology. He felt outraged. A fellow should at least to be able to go to the toilet without having to communicate. There were limits. Nothing should make a man mix up his wedding tackle and his telephone.

So he had put the thing to one side – the phone that is – and had attended to the call of nature. The bathroom was inside the main suite, like a room within a room, with two doors, opposite one another. You could go into it from the bedroom and from the front lobby. Tu slid back the glass door by the bed and looked first at the toilet. The phone was lying there on top of the cistern.

Little bastard, he thought. Now to get out of here.

Xin went into the open room and looked about. A short front lobby led into a brightly lit larger room, obviously the suite. Directly to his right was a frosted glass door, closed. He could hear steps from behind it, and tuneless whistling. There was someone in the bathroom.

His hand slid under his emerald-green coat.

The gyrocopter settled down.

Yoyo squirmed back into her seat as though she wanted to melt into the upholstery. Jericho risked a glance outside. Two uniformed officers got out of the ultralight craft, went to the hotel clerk at the terminal and talked to him.

'What are they after this time?' grumbled the pilot, in German-accented English, and craned his neck inquisitively. 'Even up in the air they don't leave you alone.'

'It's good that they keep an eye on things though,' Yoyo trilled cheerfully.

Jericho looked askance at her. He expected the hotel clerk to point across at them at any moment. If the patrol had brought photos with them, then they were sunk. The man gesticulated, pointed inside the terminal to the lifts.

Jericho held his breath.

He saw the policemen exchange a few words, then one of them looked across at the skycab. For a moment it seemed that he was looking straight at Jericho. Then he glanced away, and the two officers vanished beneath the terminal roof.

'Let's just hope that Tu doesn't walk right into them,' Yoyo hissed.

The steps came closer. He heard something clatter. A silhouette appeared behind the frosted glass and stopped there, right in front of the bathroom door.

Xin readied his weapon.

He yanked the door open and grabbed the man behind it, shoving him against the wall at the back, then pulled the door closed behind him and pressed the muzzle of the gun against the man's temple.

'Don't make a sound,' he said.

'What did you say?' one of the policemen asked.

The other pointed forward. 'I think 727 is open.'

'So it is.'

'I reckon we needn't think much more about which room to start with, wouldn't you say?'

They had taken the lift down from the flight deck to the seventh floor and set out in search of the rooms which the Chinese mogul had taken. His picture had been stored in the airport databases, and was on their phones now, so they had a pretty good idea of what he looked like. On the other hand, they had no idea which of the three rooms he might be in.

'We should have shown that guy on the roof Tu's picture.'

'What makes you think so?' his colleague whispered back.

'Just because.'

The other officer gnawed at his lip. They had only asked where the rooms were.

'I don't know. What can the guy on rooftop duty tell us?'

They could see a little way through the open door of 727 and into the hallway.

'Whatever,' the other man whispered. 'It's too late anyway.'

Xin listened.

His left hand was over the fat man's mouth – he could feel sweat pearling under his fingers – and his gun was still pressed against his forehead. He would have liked the chance to ask a few questions, but now the situation had changed. Men just in front of the door to the room, at least two of them, trying to keep their voices down. They were doomed to failure there – Xin had ears like a beast of prey. As far as he was concerned, the two of them were not whispering but bellowing like drunks at a summer barbecue.

Right at this moment, they were very interested in room 727.

A muffled sound broke free from the man in front of him, a grunt from somewhere deep in the ribcage. Xin shook his head, a warning, and—

Tu held his breath. He stood there frozen like a statue, his eyes wide. The slightest mistake and things would be over for him, that much was clear.

Over and done with.

*   *   *

The police officers looked at one another. They readied their weapons, then one of them pointed to the door of the room and nodded.

In we go, he said wordlessly.

Xin ran through his options.

He could warn his victim: say one word, and you're dead! Then he'd hide in the small toilet cabin next to the shower, and hope that the man was scared enough not to betray his presence. This was risky. It would be even riskier to take him hostage. How would he get a hostage out of the Grand Hyatt? He didn't know who those men out there were. Since they were trying not to make any noise, they were probably security, maybe police.

Or maybe Jericho?

There were two doors to this bathroom. Both were drawn shut. All he could do was hope that the men would look first at the bedroom behind, and then come into the bathroom through that door. This would give him the chance to slip away unnoticed through the door to the hallway. But in order to do that—

Lightning-fast, without letting go of his gun, he placed his hands on either side of the fat man's head, and with a practised movement broke his neck. The man's body slumped. Xin caught him as he dropped, and slid him silently down to the floor.

The policemen crept along the short corridor. A mirror to their left cast their reflections back at them for company. On the right they saw a frosted glass door, which must lead to the bathroom. One of the two stopped, and looked at his colleague questioningly.

The other man hesitated, shook his head and pointed forward.

Slowly, they paced on.

Tu could breathe again.

When he had left his room and seen two uniformed officers in the corridor, his heart had sunk in his chest, right down to the threadbare seat of his trousers. Without even daring to shut the door behind himself, he had watched the policemen slow their stride at room 727, where they stopped and talked, too quiet for him to hear. They had their backs to him the whole time – although it was certainly him they were after, and there he stood, not ten metres from them, rooted to the spot as though paralysed, so that all they would have needed to do was turn round and scoop him up in their net.

But they hadn't turned round.

For some reason, all their attention was on Yoyo's room. And suddenly Tu knew why. The door was ajar. He understood it at the moment when the two policemen went inside, and he realised how outrageously lucky he had been.

Why had Yoyo left her door open? Hurry? Bad habits?

Who cared.

Quietly, he shut 717, tiptoed down the corridor past the lounge on the left and found the lifts. He pressed his thumb to the scanplate and looked up at the display.

All the lifts were downstairs.

Xin strained his senses, following the men. There were two of them, just as he had conjectured, and right now they were going into the bedroom, where their footsteps parted ways.

He glanced down at the dead body in hotel livery, its head at an unnatural angle on the broken neck. The man's right hand still held the little bottle of shampoo that he had been about to put under the mirror. At the same moment, Xin remembered that he had seen a room-service trolley in the corridor. Not making a sound, he slid open the bathroom door to the front hall, slipped out and pulled it closed behind him. He spotted a uniformed arm and shoulder in the room, hoped that they had not left another officer in front of the door, and slipped out of the room, quiet as a cat.

Tu hopped from toe to toe, snorting, peering about. He spread his fingers out, then clenched his fists.

Come along, come along, he thought. Blasted lift! Just bring me up to the damn roof.

The levels were ticking by painfully slowly on the display. Two cabins were headed up. One was stopped on five, the other on six, right below him. For a moment Tu felt murderous rage at the people getting in and out of the lifts down there. They were taking up his time. He hated them with all his heart.

Come on there, he thought. Come on!

Room 727.

The policemen approached the glass door that led straight from the double bed to the bathroom. For a moment they paused there, listening for noises from inside, but all was quiet.

At last one of them plucked up his nerve.

They must be finding the body about now.

Pacing with care, Xin approached the turn in the corridor that led on to the lifts. He stayed calm. The police had not seen him going out. He had shut the glass door behind himself, ever attentive to detail. There was nothing to show that whoever had murdered the hotel employee had been in the bathroom just a few seconds before.

No need to hurry.

Seven!

Tu could have sworn that the lift had crept up those last few metres. Finally the gleaming steel doors swept apart, letting out a horde of young folk, expensively dressed. He shoved his way brusquely through them, put his thumb to the scanplate and pressed *Skyport*. The doors slid shut.

Xin rounded the corner. Hotel guests came towards him the other way. He saw one of the lifts just closing, headed for the next one, pressed the sensor and waited.

Seconds later he was on his way down to the lobby.

*　　　*　　　*

'There you are at last!' Yoyo called.

Tu rushed from the terminal, leaning forward as he ran as though trying to outrun his own legs. He tumbled into the cabin, slumped down into the seat across from them and signalled to the pilot.

'You look as though you've seen a ghost,' Jericho observed, while the cab swung its jets downward.

'Two.' Tu held up his index and middle finger to make the point, then realised he had just made a V for victory and grinned. 'They didn't see me though.'

'Idiot,' Yoyo spat at him, softly.

'Well, do please excuse me.'

'Don't do anything like that again! Owen and I were sweating bullets.'

They lifted off. The police gyrocopter dwindled away behind them on the landing platform, then the pilot accelerated and left Potsdamer Platz behind. Tu looked out of the window, indignant.

'Feel free to keep sweating,' he said. 'We're not out of the woods yet.'

'What were the cops doing down there?'

'They went into your room. Speaking of which, you left it open.'

'I did not.'

'That's odd.' Tu shrugged. 'Well, maybe it was room service.'

'Whatever. They won't find anything there. I didn't leave anything behind.'

'Didn't forget anything?'

'Forget?' Yoyo stared at him. 'Is this really you, asking me, whether I forgot anything?'

Tu cleared his throat several times in a row, took out his phone and called the airport. Of course you forgot something, Jericho thought to himself. Same as we all forgot something. Fingerprints, hair, DNA. While his friend was on the phone, he wondered whether it might not have been smarter after all to let the local authorities know what was gong on. Tu seemed to share Yoyo's antipathy to the police, but Germany was not China. So far Germany had no obvious interests at stake in this drama that they were all living through. In the meantime, they had begun to act more and more like the outlaws. Although they weren't the ones who had committed the crimes, it must seem that they were up to their necks in guilt.

Tu snapped his phone shut and looked at Jericho for an age, while the skycab raced towards the airport.

'Forget it,' he said.

'Forget what?'

'You're wondering whether we shouldn't just give ourselves up.'

'I don't know,' Jericho sighed.

'I do, though. Until we know what's in this dossier, and we've spoken to the delightful Edda Hoff one more time, we won't trust any intelligence agency in the world.' Tu pointed to his own temple, twirling his finger meaningfully. 'Except this one.'

The massacre in the Pergamon Museum had thrown police headquarters into an uproar that made a hornets' nest look quiet. And now this as well – a dead Indonesian room-service worker, a man with no record of misbehaviour, who spoke hardly any German, whose whole job was to dole out soap, toilet paper and bedtime sweets. The risks of such a job were grumbling guests or messy rooms, not a broken neck when the body lotion began to run out.

Setting aside the two dead police from the museum for a moment, several people had some obscure connection with this new death. A murdered restaurateur from South Africa, who had taken another man with him as he died, killing the mystery man with a pencil – suggesting that he had skills mostly lacking in the restaurant business. Then his black wife, who had been shot in her car and then driven halfway across town. There was the driver to consider as well, a white man, blond, who had clearly been trying to help Donner in the museum but who had become a target in turn, drawing fire from Donner's killer, another mystery man, tall with white hair, a bristling moustache, wearing a suit and spectacles. Then there was a Chinese industrialist, head of a Shanghai technology enterprise, who had himself claimed to be a policeman and had stolen Donner's glass eye, helped by a young Chinese woman. Then last of all the Indonesian man, whose role in life had been to make sure that guests were never left lacking in the bathroom and that they always found a little treat on their pillow at bedtime.

Puzzling, all very puzzling!

Sensibly, the investigating team didn't attempt to solve all the puzzles at once, even though there were some obvious conclusions to be drawn. Whoever else he was, the white-haired man was clearly a professional killer; the glass eye held some secret around which the whole business probably revolved; and the Indonesian victim had just been at the wrong place at the wrong time. For the moment, however, the Chinese business mogul would be at the centre of the investigation – less because they wanted to understand his motives than because they simply wanted to pick him up as soon as possible. The three rooms that he had taken in the Grand Hyatt didn't look as though the guests would be returning any time soon. All that was known for sure was that Tu and the woman had driven back from the Institute of Forensic Pathology to the hotel at full tilt, had told the concierge to put the Audi down in the car park, and then had vanished into the lobby, chatting.

What had they been chatting about?

The concierge remembered quite clearly. They had been planning to meet some third person in the Sony Center, because the fat man had said that he wanted 'something sweet'. Oh, and the woman had been very, *very* pretty! The police officers pressed the concierge on whether he understood Chinese, and he said he didn't, that the two of them had been speaking English. This made the head of the enquiry team suspicious – Dr Marika Voss had reported that they had spoken Chinese to one another in the autopsy theatre. Just to be on the safe side, he had sent two men over to the Sony Center, not expecting that they would find anyone there, and set his team to digging up exactly how Tu had arrived.

The longer he thought about it, the more certain he felt that Tu and the blond man were in it together.

The skycab had needed only a trifling eight minutes to get to the airport, but it seemed like an eternity to Jericho. In his thoughts, he was imagining what the case team would be doing. What would they prioritise?

Who would their enquiries focus on? He had been at the scene of the shooting himself, and witnesses had seen him running towards the Tiergarten. They would want to know more about him. It certainly counted against him that he had been carrying a gun in the museum, although ballistics would show that he hadn't shot Nyela. As for Yoyo and Tu, they had impersonated police officers and then maltreated a corpse, on top of which Tu had driven a hole through the highway code, but the police had several leads to follow. In a way, that was good, since it meant that they would be that much slower making progress. They would have to check identities, draw up timelines, take statements, look for motives. They would get bogged down in speculation.

On the other hand, they had been notably efficient so far. They had turned up at the Grand Hyatt impressively fast, meaning that they already had Tu in their sights. It wasn't clear yet whether they knew about his jet, or indeed whether they had made the assumption that he would be leaving Berlin at short notice.

The skycab circled above the airport.

They lost height, banking about in a broad curve. They could see Tu's Aerion Supersonic from here. Its stubby wings, set far back on the fuselage, made it look like a seabird, craning its neck curiously, as eager to be gone as they were. The skycab pilot tilted the jets, let the machine sink down, and landed with a gentle rocking motion not far from the plane. Tu handed him a banknote.

'Keep the change,' he said in English.

The size of the tip made the pilot leap to attention and offer his help in loading the jet. Since they didn't even have luggage to unload from his cab, apart from Tu's small suitcase, he asked whether there was anything else he could do for them. Tu thought for a moment.

'Just wait here until we take off,' he said. 'And don't say a word to anyone until we do.'

The chief case officer was just on his way to the police skyport when his phone rang. Before he could take the call, he saw an officer running across the flight pad towards him.

'We've got Baldy,' he heard her shout.

He hesitated. The call was from one of the men he had detailed to find out more about what Tu was up to in Berlin. Meanwhile the police-woman had stopped in front of him, breathlessly holding her phone out under his nose. It showed a picture of the man who was, right now, lying on the dissection table with splinters of pencil in his frontal lobe.

'I'll call back,' he said into the telephone. 'Two minutes.'

'Mickey Reardon,' the policewoman told him. 'An old fossil from the Irish underground, a specialist in alarms systems. He's been freelancing for every Secret Service you could mention ever since the IRA decommissioned their weapons twenty years ago, and he's worked for a lot of outfits that are half political, half organised crime.'

'An Irishman? God help us all.'

He couldn't have liked it any worse if Reardon had turned out to be ex-North Korean People's Army. Whenever a regular army or a resistance movement lost its raison d'être, it would spit out creatures like Reardon, who would often make deals with international Secret Services if they weren't working for organised crime outright.

'Who did he work for?'

'We only know some names. He was with the US Secret Service a lot, then for Mossad, Zhong Chan Er Bu, our own guys. Quite the multi-talent, very clever at shutting down security systems but also at installing them. He was wanted for a number of instances of grievous bodily harm, and suspected of murder as well.'

'Reardon was armed,' said the inspector thoughtfully. 'Meaning he was on a mission. Donner gets rid of him, then he's shot. By our white-haired gentleman. Is this a Secret Service operation? Reardon and Mr White on one side, Donner and Mr Blond on the other side, Blondie tries to help Donner—'

He had almost forgotten that he was on his way to the Grand Hyatt.

'We need to get moving,' his sergeant said.

So it was only once they were in the air that he remembered he had been going to call someone back.

★   ★   ★

The jet taxied onto the runway. Tu choked back his engines and waited for permission to take off. He was far more nervous than he was letting on. Strictly speaking, Jericho was right. What they were doing here flew in the face of reason. They were picking a fight with the German police for no reason at all. Indeed, the police might even have been able to help them.

They might not have, though.

Tu had his own bitter experience of the arbitrariness of state power, which had certainly left him with scars, though he tried hard not to jump at shadows. Admittedly, his paranoia was rooted in events that lay twenty-eight years back. Here he was, though, holding the others hostage to his own mistrust, especially Yoyo, who was most receptive to such paranoid behaviours for reasons of her own. There was no doubt that he was manipulating them. He tried to persuade himself that he was doing the right thing, and perhaps he was even right about that, but it wasn't about that, hadn't been for a long time now. As he had walked the streets of Berlin at night with Yoyo, he had realised that the only difference between Hongbing's paranoia and his own was that he was more cheerful about it. His old friend wandered the vaults of his memory forlornly, while he strode through them, whistling cheerfully. Compared with Hongbing, he was fighting fit, but he couldn't fight hard enough to cope with all that life had to throw at him, not on his own.

So he had told her something of the past, and all he had achieved was to make her more confused and depressed. None of it was any help. He would have to tell her the rest as well, tell her what he had never told anybody else except Joanna, tell her the whole story. He would assume Hongbing's tacit approval, and he would cut the whole miserable tangle just as soon as the opportunity presented itself. He would have much preferred it if Hongbing himself had told Yoyo the truth, but this way was good as well. Anything was better than silence.

We have to close the door on our past, he thought. Not run away from it, not escape into success or into depression.

The voice in his earphones gave him permission.

Tu brought the jet engines up to speed and engaged thrust. The acceleration pushed him back into his seat, and they took off.

Only a few minutes later the chief case officer learned that Tu had arrived by private plane, an Aerion Supersonic. The rooms in the Hyatt were abandoned; the Chinese mogul and his companions had obviously left. Perhaps they were still in Berlin, since they hadn't checked out, and the Audi that Tu had hired at the airport was still in the Grand Hyatt's underground parking. This was the car whose registration number had set the case team onto his trail.

On the other hand, there was a corpse in one of the rooms.

The inspector ordered his team to secure the mogul's jet, just in case. Then a few minutes after that, he learned that he had lost the decisive moment by paying attention instead to Mickey Reardon's identification. He let rip with a string of curses so ripely inventive that the case officers all around him froze in their tracks, but it was no use.

Tu Tian had left Berlin.

Aerion Supersonic

'*Of course* she can read memory crystals,' Jericho yelled into the cockpit, as if Tu had asked him whether he washed every day.

'A thousand apologies,' Tu shouted back. 'I'd forgotten she was a sort of surrogate wife.'

Jericho lifted Diane's compact body from his backpack, connected it to the ports of the on-board electronics and set up the monitor on its seat bracket. The Pratt & Whitney turbines wrapped the Aerion in a cocoon of noise. The trapezoid-winged craft was still climbing. Sitting next to him, Yoyo was working on Vogelaar's glass eye, unscrewing it and taking from it a glittering structure about half the size of a sugar lump. Tu circled the plane. Berlin tilted towards them through the side windows, while at the same time the sky on the other side turned a deep, dark blue.

'Hi, Diane.'

'Hi, Owen,' said the soft, familiar voice. 'How are you?'

'Could be better.'

'What can I do to make you *well*?'

'Plenty,' Yoyo said in a quietly mocking voice. 'One day you'll have to tell me if she's a good kisser.'

Jericho grimaced. 'Open the Crystal Reader, Diane.'

A little rod slid from the front of the computer, sheathed in a transparent frame. The jet swung back to the horizontal and went on gaining height. Below them the massive scab of urban development made way for green-brown-yellow arable land, patchworked with small wooded areas, roads and villages. As if daubed on, rivers and lakes shimmered in the afternoon sunlight.

'I'll be really pissed off if that great mess in the Charité wasn't worth it,' growled Yoyo. She leaned across to Jericho and set the cube in the surround, and the tiny drawer slid shut again.

'Everyone made sacrifices,' he said wearily, while Diane uploaded the data. 'After all, Tian was prepared to chuck a hundred thousand euros to the four winds.'

'Not to mention your ear.' Yoyo looked at him. 'Or at least the snippet of your ear. The atomic layer of your—'

'The *serious* injury to my ear. There.'

The screen filled with symbols. Jericho held his breath. The dossier was much bigger than he had thought. He immediately felt that ambivalent dread that you feel just before you enter the monster's lair to see it in all its terrifying hideousness and ascertain its true nature once and for all. In a few minutes they would know the reason for the hunt that had claimed so many victims, almost including themselves, and he knew they weren't going to like what they saw. Even Yoyo seemed hesitant. She put a finger to her lips and paused.

'If I'd been him,' she said, 'I'd have provided a short version. Wouldn't you?'

'Yes,' Jericho nodded. 'But where?'

'Here.' Her finger wandered across to a symbol marked JKV *Intro*.

'JKV?' He narrowed his eyes.

'Jan Kees Vogelaar.'

'Sounds good. Let's try it. Diane?'

'Yes, Owen.'

'Open JKV Intro.'

There sat Vogelaar, in shirt and shorts, on a veranda, under a roughly hewn wooden roof, and with a drink beside him. In the background, hilly scrubland fell away to the coast. Here and there palms were sticking up from low mixed vegetation. It was plainly drizzling. A sky of indeterminate colour hung over the scene and softened the horizon of a far-off sea.

'The likelihood that I am no longer alive at this second,' Vogelaar said without preamble, 'is relatively high, so listen very carefully now, whoever you are. You won't be having any more information from me in person.'

Jericho leaned forward. It was spooky, looking Vogelaar in the eyes. More precisely, they were looking at him *through* one of his eyes. Unlike in Berlin, he was ash-blond again, with a bushy moustache, light-coloured eyebrows and eyelashes.

'There are no bugs here. You wouldn't think intimacy was a problem in a country that consists almost entirely of swamp and rainforest, but Mayé is infected with the same paranoia as almost all potentates of his stamp. I think even Ndongo would have been interested in going on listening to the parrots. But as they've appointed me head of security, the task of snooping on the good people of Equatorial Guinea, particularly the ruling family and our valued foreign guests, has fallen to me. My task is to protect Mayé. He trusts me, and I don't plan to abuse that trust.'

Vogelaar spread his arms in a gesture that took in the hinterland. 'As you see, we live in paradise. The apples drop into your mouth, and as you would expect of any decent paradise, a snake is creeping around the place, and it wants to know that everything is under control. Kenny Xin doesn't trust anyone. Not even me, although he describes himself as my friend and he was the one who got me this extremely remunerative job in the first place. Hi there, Kenny, by the way. You see, your suspicion was justified.' He laughed. 'I doubt very much that you know the guy, but he's the reason why I'm presenting this file. Some of the attached documents deal with him, so let's just say that in 2017, on the instructions of the Chinese oil companies and with the approval of Beijing, he organised the coup against Juan Aristide Ndongo and, with my help, or more precisely with the help of African Protection Services, carried it out and enthroned Mayé. The dossier records a chronicle of coups, internal information about Beijing's role in Africa and much else besides, but at its heart there lies a quite different subject.'

He crossed his legs and wearily waved away a flying insect the size of a human fist.

'Perhaps someone remembers the launch pad that Mayé had built on Bioko. International companies were involved, under the aegis of the Zheng Group, which allows us to assume that China had a hand in this as well. Personally I don't believe that. Nor is it true, even though we've repeatedly sold the idea in public, that our space programme was an initiative one hundred per cent down to Mayé. In fact it was initiated by a group of *possibly* Chinese investors which, in my opinion – and contrary to their own account – is not identical with Beijing and was represented by Kenny Xin at the time. The fact is that this organisation wanted to fire an information satellite from our soil into space, supposedly as an investigation into new kinds of rocket propulsion. Mayé was supposed to be able to use the satellite for civilian purposes, with the proviso that the whole space project was presented as his own idea. I've attached the blueprints for the launch pad, along with a list of all the companies which helped to build it.'

'He's still taking the piss out of us,' Yoyo hissed.

'Hardly.' Jericho shook his head. 'He can't take the piss out of us any more.'

'But that's exactly what he did in Muntu—'

'Wait.' Jericho raised his hand. 'Listen!'

'—the launch was scheduled for two days later. This meant that the preparations should actually have been completed, and only the satellite had still to be put on the tip of the rocket. That same night a convoy of armoured cars arrived in the grounds of the launch pad. Something was brought into the construction hangar and coupled with the satellite: a container the size of a very big suitcase or a small cupboard, fitted with landing equipment, jets and spherical tanks. The whole thing could be collapsed so that it didn't take up much room. Only close contacts of Xin dealt with the delivery and assembly of the craft, no foreign constructors were present, not even anyone from the Zheng Group. Neither Mayé nor his people knew at this point that anything but the said satellite was to be fired into space. I'm not a specialist in space travel, by the way, but I assume that the container held a small, automatic spaceship, a kind of landing unit. My people photographed the arrival of the convoy and the container; you will find the pictures in the files KON_PICS and SAT_PICS.' Vog-elaar grinned. 'Are you still watching, Kenny? While you deludedly thought you were observing me, did it never occur to you that *we* were observing *you*?'

'So.' Tu came out of the cockpit and joined them in the corridor. 'We're flying on autopilot. We're on course for London via Amsterdam, so let's have a dr—'

'Shhh!' hissed Yoyo.

'—was of course interested in what was in that container,' Vogelaar went on. 'So I had to reconstruct the route it had taken – I should perhaps mention that the people who delivered it at dead of night were almost all Chinese. Anyway, we managed to trace the route of the plane that had brought it to Africa back through a series of intermediate landings. For obvious reasons I had expected that the plane had originally started off in China, but to my surprise it came from Korea, or more precisely from a remote airport in North Korea, near the border.'

In the background it had started raining heavily. A rising rustle mingled with Vogelaar's words, a changing grey blurred the sky, scrubland and sea.

'I've built up extensive contacts over the years. Not least with southeast Asia. Someone who still owed me something set about working out what had been loaded on at the airport. You must know, the whole area is extremely unsafe. There's a lot of piracy in the surrounding waters, a high level of criminality, unemployment and frustration. The South has been paying for the North's reconstruction since 2015, but the money is disappearing in a vast bubble of speculation. Both sides feel they've been tricked, and they aren't happy about it. Corruption and black market dealings are flourishing as a result, and one of the most lucrative markets is the trade in Kim Jong Un's former arsenal of weapons, particularly the warheads. Especially popular are the mini-nukes, small atom bombs with considerable destructive power. The Soviets certainly experimented with them, in fact all the nuclear powers did. Kim had a few too, hundreds even. Except nobody knows where they ended up. After the collapse of the North Korean regime, the death of Kim and reunification they had suddenly disappeared, and since they aren't particularly big—'

The soldier measured out a length of about a metre with his hands.

'—and not much thicker than a shoe box, they won't be all that easy to find. A mini-nuke has the advantage of fitting into the smallest hiding-place, whatever infernal power it's capable of unleashing.' He smiled. 'For example a small, automatic spaceship fired into space piggy-backing on a satellite.'

Jericho stared at the monitor. Behind Vogelaar the skies had opened.

'I wanted to know if anyone had been doing any sort of shopping on the black market not long ago. My contact confirmed this. Just two years before, in the no man's land between North and South, Korean nuclear material had switched owners in a private transaction. I'm always suspicious these days, and as everybody knows you should treat hearsay with caution – but there are lots of signs that I knew the buyer very well.'

'I don't believe it,' Tu said. 'They fired an atom bomb into space?'

Vogelaar leaned forward.

'Our old friend Kenny Xin had bought the thing. And I knew already why he had hit on the idea of building the launching pad in our quiet little jungle paradise. The whole thing was illegal in the extreme! It wouldn't have been possible to plant an atom bomb unnoticed on a state space agency. Kenny's employers *had* to find a neutral country, ideally a banana republic, whose ruling clique wasn't above any kind of deal. Some unloved patch of soil where no one was watching your every move. And the ideal launching pads for rockets are distributed in the area around the equator. Which was proof for me that China's Communist Party, at least at the highest levels of government, wasn't involved in this one, or else they could simply have launched the phoney satellite from their official launch pads in Xichang, Taiyuan, Hainan or Mongolia, and not a soul would ever have guessed what it was carrying. So in my opinion we're dealing with a non-state, criminal or terrorist association. Which doesn't mean that *individual* state organisations aren't involved. Let's not forget, China's Secret Services have been developing a grotesque life of their own in the meantime, and Washington doesn't always know what the CIA's getting up to. But it could also be that there's a big company behind it. Or else good old Dr Mabuse, if anyone still remembers him.'

'And the bomb's target—' whispered Yoyo.

Vogelaar leaned back, took a swig from his drink and stroked his moustache.

'This file was actually conceived as life insurance,' he said. 'For me and for my wife, whom you may have met as Nyela. Clearly it hasn't been able to save us, so now it will serve to bring down the men behind the organisation. Kenny would definitely be of crucial importance, because he has contact with the head of the gang and might know his identity. I've attached his eye-scans, fingerprints and voice samples, under KXIN_PERS, but he definitely isn't the instigator. So who is? Certainly not Korea, they're just flogging off their Great Leader's belongings. The Communist Party, secretly arming space? As I've said, they wouldn't have needed a launch pad in Equatorial Guinea to do that. Zheng-style forces close to the government? Possibly. Perhaps the answer lies in the race to the Moon. China has made it clear more than once that it condemns America's rush into space, and Beijing is also projecting its dissatisfaction onto Orley Enterprises, Zheng's successful competitor. Or else somebody's trying to use China, because it's doing so well against the backdrop of the scramble for helium-3 and so on. With a strategically deployed atom bomb you could set the superpowers against one another, but what would be the point? They would both emerge weakened from an armed conflict. But perhaps that's exactly what they want to achieve, so who could profit from their weakness?'

The jet sped along in a straight line. UFOs could have been flying ahead of them and they wouldn't even have noticed. Their attention was focused on the monitor.

'Now we get to the question of where the bomb is at the moment. Still in the satellite? Or was it dropped as the launch vehicle was carrying it into space? There was no nuclear explosion on Earth, but okay, it needn't have exploded. On the other hand it would be idiotic to send a bomb first into orbit and from there back to Earth. Now, I think I can give a partial answer. Because even in the control room we were able to look over Kenny's people's shoulders. Under DISCONNECT_SAT you'll find film material that not only shows the satellite maintaining its position in orbit, but also something breaking away and flying off on an independent course. There's no doubt about what it is, but *where* did the mini-nuke go after decoupling? That's easy to answer too. Somewhere that an atom bomb couldn't have been sent by official channels. And what for? To destroy something that can't be easily destroyed from Earth. The target lies in space.'

Vogelaar put his fingers together.

'I'll give you one last mystery for the road. It concerns the fact that I am speaking to you in the year 2024. I don't want to bore you with personal stories, but our cute little state is bankrupt, no one is fighting over our oil any more, Mayé is starting to go round the bend, and to be honest I'd somehow imagined my government job would be more one of supporting the interests of the state. But no matter. Just bear in mind that construction of the launch pad began two years ago, and I'm sure the planning of the enterprise goes back even further than that. So the deployment of the bomb was planned a long time ago. Now it's up there. When's it going to go off? What is certain is that the target must have existed years ago, or else people knew that it *would* exist at the time of the launch of the satellite. As I said, I'm not a space expert, there are a few potential targets around the Earth and on the Moon, but to my knowledge only one has been completed and opened, probably this year. A hotel, planned for ages, location the Moon, building contractor Orley Enterprises. Does that tell us anything? Of course it does! Julian Orley, Zheng's great adversary, responsible for the permanent disadvantage of the Chinese.'

Vogelaar raised his glass in a toast to them. Behind him, Equatorial Guinea drowned in tropical torrents.

'So have fun with your investigation. I haven't been able to assemble anything more than this, you'll have to find out the rest for yourselves. And come and see me, if you know where my grave is. Nyela and I would be delighted.'

The recording ended. The only sound was the even humming of the turbines. Slowly, as if in a trance, Yoyo turned her head and looked first at Jericho and then at Tu. Her lips formed two words.

'Edda Hoff.'

'Yes.' Tu nodded grimly. 'And fast!'

30 May 2025

THE WARNING

Aristarchus Plateau, The Moon

The space shuttle Ganymede was a Hornet-model flying machine, with ion propulsion and pivotable jets to achieve thrust in any desired direction. In outward appearance it resembled a grotesquely swollen transport helicopter, Eurocopter HTH class without rotors, but sitting on short, fat legs; inside it offered the comfort of a private jet. All thirty-six seats could be turned into couches at the press of a button, each seat had its own multimedia console. There was a tiny, extravagantly equipped galley which lacked only alcohol, in line with the regulation that crews must not dull their senses in the course of the day.

At present Gaia had two Hornet shuttles, the Ganymede and the Callisto. That afternoon they were both hurtling through the vacuum, more than 1400 kilometres apart: Callisto heading towards Rupes Recta, a colossal fault in the middle of the Mare Nubium, 250 metres deep and so long that you had a sense that it circled the whole of the Moon; Ganymede flying straight towards the Aristarchus Plateau, an archipelago of craters in the middle of the Ocean of Storms. A few hours previously the Callisto, flown by Nina Hedegaard and carrying the Ögis, Nairs, Donoghues and Finn, had visited the Descartes Highlands, where the landing stage of Apollo 16 dozed in the sun and a derelict moon-car exuded a nostalgic charm, while Ganymede had borne down upon the crater of Copernicus. From the lofty heights of its outer ring, the travellers had admired its rough central range, they had penetrated its capacious interior and shuddered to think what sort of giant must have fallen from the sky here 800 million years ago.

The world was nothing but stone, and yet it was so much more.

The soft, undulating structure of its plains led you to forget that the maria were not true seas, nor the crater bottoms lakes. Curious structures suggested former habitation, as if H. G. Wells' space-travelling heroes had actually encountered insectoid selenites and herds of moon-cows here, before being abducted into the machine world of the lunar underground. They had seen a lot that day, Carl Hanna, Marc Edwards and Mimi Parker, Amber and the Locatellis, Evelyn Chambers and Oleg Rogachev, whose wife lay grimly by the moon pool, but Julian insisted that the highlight was still to come. The first spurs of the high plateau appeared in the north-west. Peter Black made the shuttle climb high above the Aristarchus Crater, which looked as if it was cast out of light.

'The Arena of the Spirits,' Julian whispered with an air of mystery, a youthful grin playing around the corners of his mouth. 'An observation point for sinister light phenomena. Some people are convinced that Aristarchus is inhabited by demons.'

'Interesting,' said Evelyn Chambers. 'Perhaps we should leave Momoka here for a while.'

'That would be the end of any sinister phenomena,' Momoka observed drily. 'After only an hour in my company the last demon would have emigrated to Mars.'

Locatelli raised his eyebrows, full of admiration at how coquettishly his wife was twisting and turning in the mirror of her own self-criticism.

'And can you tell us something about the cause?' Rogachev asked.

'Yeah, well, there are a lot of arguments about that. For decades light phenomena have been witnessed in Aristarchus and other craters, but until a few years ago ultra-orthodox astronomers refused even to acknowledge the existence of such "Lunar Transient Phenomena".'

'Perhaps volcanoes?' Hanna suggested.

'Wilhelm Herschel, an astronomer of the late eighteenth century, was convinced of that. Very popular in his day. He was one of the first to spot red dots in the lunar night, some of them around here. Herschel supposed they were glowing lava. Later his sightings were confirmed, other observers reported a violet haze, menacingly dark clouds, lightning, flames and sparks, all extremely mysterious.'

'To spit lava, the Moon would have to have a liquid core,' said Amber. 'Does it?'

'You see, that's the rub.' Julian smiled. 'It's generally assumed that it does, but so deep underground that volcanic eruptions are ruled out as an explanation.'

Momoka peered suspiciously out of the side windows into Aristarchus' gaping mouth.

'You can stop trying to make things so exciting,' Evelyn said after a while.

'Wouldn't you rather believe in demons?'

'I don't see demons as romantic,' said Parker. 'It would mean the Devil living on the Moon.'

'So?' Locatelli shrugged. 'Sooner here than in California.'

'So the Devil is someone you make jokes about.'

'Fine.' Julian raised his hands. 'There is a bit of volcanic activity up here. No lava streams, admittedly, but it's been noted that the phenomena always occur when the Moon is closest to the Earth, so when gravity is tugging at it particularly hard. The consequences are lunar quakes. When that happens, pores and cracks appear, hot gases emerge from the deeper regions to the surface, bursting out at high pressure, regolith is fired out, albedo accumulates at the exit point, and already you have a glowing cloud.'

'I get it,' said Momoka. 'It needs to fart.'

'You should stop giving away all the tricks,' Amber said with a sideways glance at Parker. 'I thought the demons were more exciting.'

'And what's that thing there?' Edwards narrowed his eyes and pointed outside. Something massive was twisting its way north-west of the crater, across the plateau with all its furrows and potholes. It looked like a huge snake, or rather like the cast for a snake, a beast of mythical proportions. The funnel-shaped head joined a twisting body that narrowed until it opened up, thin and pointed, in the next plain along. The whole thing looked as if it had once been the resting-place of Ananden, the ancient Indian world snake that carried the earth and the universe, the scaly, breathing throne of the god Vishnu.

'That,' said Julian, 'is Schröter's Valley.'

Black soared above the formation at great height, so that they could admire its vast dimensions, the whole of the great Moon valley, as Julian explained, four billion years old; and other people had in fact been struck by its serpentine nature. The head crater, six kilometres across, was called Cobra's Head, a cobra that twisted 168 kilometres to the shore of the Oceanus Procellarum. On a plateau that overlooked Cobra's Head from the north-east, a levelled area came into view, lined with hangars and collectors. A radio mast gleamed in the sunlight. Black brought the vehicle down towards the landing field and set Ganymede down gently on its beetle legs.

'Schröter space station,' he said, and grinned conspiratorially at Julian. 'Welcome to the Realm of the Spirits. The chances of us seeing any are slight, and yet, ladies and gentlemen, stay away from suspicious-looking holes and cracks. Helmets and armour on. Five in the lock at any one time, like this morning. Julian, Amber, Carl, Oleg and Evelyn first, followed by Marc, Mimi, Warren, Momoka and me. If I may ask you.'

Unlike the landing module of the Charon, in a Hornet shuttle you didn't have to suck out all the air in the cabin, but left it via a lift that doubled as an airlock. Black extended the shaft. They took their chest armour from the shelf and helped each other into their tightly fitting suits, while Julian tried to banish the shadow that stripped his mood of its usual radiant power. Lynn was starting to change, he couldn't deny it. She was showing signs of inner seclusion, had developed unattractive rings around her eyes and was treating him with growing and unprovoked aggression. In his puzzlement he had confided in Hanna – a mistake, perhaps, although he couldn't say exactly why. The Canadian was fine, in fact. And yet he had recently started feeling slightly shy around Hanna, as if he would only have to look a bit more closely, and unsettling trigonometric connections would appear between him, Lynn and the ghostly train. The longer he brooded about it, the more certain he was that the solution was right before his eyes. He saw the truth without recognising it. A detail of banal validity, but as long as his inner projectionist slept the sleep of the just, he couldn't reach it.

Along with the others, he entered the lock and put his helmet on. Through the viewing windows he could see the interior of the shuttle, while the air was being sucked out of the lock. He saw Locatelli delivering speeches, Momoka helping Parker into the survival backpack, then the lift cabin plummeted, emerged from the belly of the Ganymede and travelled down the shaft to just above the asphalt of the landing field. A ramp emerged from the floor of the cabin and they stepped outside along it. It had not been planned for shuttles to land on anything but solid surfaces, but if such a landing were necessary, any contact between the cabin and the fine dust of the regolith was to be kept to a minimum, because otherwise—

Julian hesitated.

All of a sudden it was as if the projectionist had rubbed his eyes. Yawning, he pulled himself together to climb down into the archive and look for the missing roll of film.

He had just seen it again: the truth.

And again he hadn't understood it.

He watched with irritation as the second group left the lock. Black waved them over to one of the cylindrical hangars. Three open rovers were parked in it, surprisingly like historical moon-cars, but with three axles, bigger wheels and room for six people in each. The improved design of the rover, Black explained, made it faster than in the early years of lunar car manufacture, and also fit to drive on extremely uneven ground. Each of the wheel mountings could swing if necessary to a ninety-degree vertical, which was enough to let it simply drive over large boulders.

'But not on the path that we're about to take,' he added. 'We're following the northern stretch of the valley until the first turning of the cobra's body. A rocky outcrop there, the spur of the Rupes Toscanelli scarp, runs right up to the edge of the gorge, Snake Hill. I'll tell you no more than that for the time being.'

'And how far are we going?' Locatelli wanted to know.

'Not far. Just eight kilometres, but the journey is spectacular, right along the edge of the Vallis.'

'Can I drive?' Locatelli was jumping around with excitement. 'I really want to drive that thing!'

'Of course.' Black laughed. 'The steering is easy, it's the same as the buggies. You shouldn't drive straight at the biggest obstacles, if you don't want to go flying out of your seat, but otherwise—'

'Of course not,' said Locatelli, already imagining his foot on the accelerator.

'Will we let him have his fun?' Julian said to Momoka.

'Of course. As long as you let me have the fun of driving in the other rover.'

'Good. Warren is driving rover number two, and promises to bring Carl, Mimi and Marc safely to their destination, the rest of us will take the first one. Who's the chauffeur?'

When everyone said they wanted to be the chauffeur, the choice fell on Amber. She was told how the various functions worked, took a test drive and got everything right straight away.

'I want one of these when we're back down there,' she cried.

'You don't,' Julian grinned. 'It's six times as heavy down there. It would fall to bits in the garage.'

The convoy set off. Black let Amber drive ahead to keep Locatelli from breaking speed records, so that they had been driving for ten minutes when the valley dropped away on their left in a wide curve. A narrow path led to a high ridge, from which you could enjoy an incomparable view of the Vallis Schröteri. You could see almost the whole course of it from there, but something else was holding everyone's attention. It was a crane, mounted on a platform that loomed into the gorge. As they approached they made out a winch at ground level. A steel cable ran through the cantilever and led to a capacious double seat. There was no need to explain how the crane worked. Once you had taken your seat, the cantilever swung over the gorge, and you floated, legs dangling, above the abyss.

'Brilliant! Absolutely brilliant!' Marc Edwards' extreme-sport soul was boiling over. He jumped from the parked rover, stepped to the edge of the platform and looked down. 'What's the drop here? How far could we abseil down?'

'Right to the bottom,' Peter Black explained, as if he had dug the gorge with his own hands. 'One thousand metres.'

'Bollocks to the Grand Canyon,' Locatelli observed with familiar sophistication. 'It's a trickle of piss compared to this one.'

'Does that thing work?' Edwards asked.

'Of course,' said Julian. 'Once the factory's up and running, we'll build a few more.'

'I absolutely have to try it out!'

'*We* absolutely have to try it out,' Mimi Parker corrected him.

'Me too.' Julian thought he could see Rogachev smiling. 'Perhaps Evelyn would keep me company?'

'Oh, Oleg,' laughed Evelyn. 'You want to die with me?'

'No one will die as long as I'm working the winch,' Black promised. 'Okay, Mimi and Marc will go down first—'

'I'm going with Carl,' said Amber. 'If he has the guts.'

'I do. With you I always do.'

'So then Amber with Carl after that, and then Oleg and Evelyn. Momoka?'

'No way.'

'Then Momoka will come with us,' Julian suggested. 'The rest of us will climb Snake Hill in the meantime. Oleg, Evelyn, you too. It'll take a while before Peter has lowered those four down and hoisted them back up again.'

'I've had a think,' said Amber. 'I'd rather go up the mountain with you. What's up, Carl?'

'Hey! Are you bottling out?'

'Don't get your hopes up.'

'Then see you later. Take care. I'll take a look and see what lies ahead.'

Hanna watched the others start their climb. The path led gently upwards, curved around and disappeared into a ravine. It reappeared a considerable stretch further up, ran along the flank for about a hundred metres, a steep climb now, and then vanished from view once more. Clearly you had to circle the slope to reach the high plateau. Hanna would have loved to go with them, but he was more fascinated by the gorge, a kilometre deep, with vertical walls on all sides. Perhaps he could climb the high plain later on, with Mimi and Marc. He would have preferred to take the trip on his own, but wherever he went, someone would be talking to him on his headset. At least you could turn individual participants on or off, only the guides were transmitting at all times, and had a right of access to everyone's auditory canal.

He watched with interest as Black released the winch, opened the faceplate of the console and activated the controls by pressing on one of five fist-sized buttons. Primitive lunar technology, one might have thought, built for the clumsy extremities of aliens – and wasn't that exactly what they were on this strange satellite, aliens, extraterrestrials, their fingers forced into hard shells? Black pressed a second button. The cantilever was set in motion and began to swing in. Parker and Edwards jostled each other impatiently on the edge of the platform.

'What are the other buttons for?' Hanna asked.

'The blue one swings the crane back out again,' said Black. 'The one below it turns the winch on.'

'So the black one's there to bring the lift back up again?'

'You've got it. Child's play. Like most things on the Moon, in fact, so that not everything depends on the expert.'

'If he's dead, for example.' Edwards stepped back from the edge to make room for the incoming lift.

'Don't say things like that,' Parker protested.

'Don't worry.' Black opened the safety guard of the seats. 'I'd consider it quite irresponsible of me to die while you're hanging there. If some unexpected local demons swallow me up unexpectedly, you'll still have Carl. He'll winch you back up again. Ready? Off we go!'

'Shit!' said Locatelli.

They had passed the ink-black shadow of the ravine, climbed the slope and had just reached the spot where the flank curved around, when he noticed. He looked irritably down into the valley. The gorge gaped far below them, four kilometres wide, so that the platform stuck to the edge of the rock like a toy, populated by tiny, springy figures, hopping up and down. Peter was just helping the Californian into the seat, while Hanna studied the winch.

'What's up?' Momoka turned round.

'I forgot my camera.'

'Idiot.'

'Really?' Locatelli took a sharp breath. 'And who's the other idiot? Have a think.'

'Hey, no need to fight,' Amber cut in. 'We'll just take my cam—'

'Are you talking about me?' Momoka snapped.

'Who else? You could have thought about it too.'

'Shut the hell up, Warren. What would I want to do with your stupid camera?'

'Lots, my lotus flower! Who wants to be filmed from dawn till dusk, as if the crap that you produce for the cinema wasn't enough?'

'I wouldn't pose in front of your camera if you paid me!'

'That is so funny! You really mean that? You start pissing yourself as soon as you *see* a camera.'

'Nicely put, arsehole. Go and get it, then.'

'You bet I will,' snapped Locatelli, and turned on his heel.

'Hey, Warren,' called Evelyn, quietly rapt. 'You're not going all the way back just for—'

'Yep.'

'Wait!' shouted Julian. 'Take Amber's camera, she's right. You can film Momoka with it until she pleads for mercy.'

'No! I'm going to get the damned thing!'

He stamped defiantly back in the direction of the ravine.

'I know he doesn't have an easy life with me,' he heard Momoka saying quietly to the others, as if he couldn't hear every single word, 'but Warren's only happy when something's getting on his nerves.'

'Quite honestly, you both seem to need that,' Amber remarked.

'Ah, yes.' Momoka sighed. 'I love it when he hits back. That's when I love him most.'

Julian, advancing with the pace of a natural leader, had almost reached the plateau when he heard Sophie's voice in his helmet. Parked some way off, he could just see the rovers via which he was connected to the Ganymede, and via it with Gaia.

'What is it, Sophie?'

'I'm sorry, sir, call from Earth. I've got Jennifer Shaw on the line for you. Please switch to O-SEC.'

O-SEC. Bug-proof connection. It meant that he had to sever his contact with the group. No one would be able to hear what his company's security advisor had to tell him.

'Fine.' He obliged. 'We're on our own.'

'Julian!' Jennifer's voice, urgent. 'I won't trouble you with an endless preamble. Lynn will have told you about the warning we received yesterday. We've just—'

'Lynn?' Julian interrupted her, surprised. He turned to the others and gestured to them to stop. 'No. Lynn didn't tell me anything about a warning.'

'She didn't?' Jennifer said, puzzled.

'When's that supposed to have been?'

'Last night. Edda Hoff talked to your daughter. Lynn wanted to be kept informed about the matter. Of course I assumed that she—'

'What *matter* are we talking about, Jennifer? I don't understand a word.'

Jennifer fell silent for a moment. The delay between Earth and Moon lasted only a second, but it was enough to create irritating little pauses.

'Two days ago we received a warning from a Chinese businessman,' she said. 'He happened to come into possession of a garbled text document, and since then he's been on the run. The text suggests – or seems to suggest – that one of the company's plants is threatened with attack.'

'What's that you say? Hoff said *that* to my daughter?'

'Yes.'

'Lynn? Lynn, are you there?'

'I'm here, Dad.'

'What's going on? What's all this about?'

'I – I didn't want to bother you with it.' Her voice sounded quavery and upset. 'Of course I—'

'Lynn, Julian, I'm sorry,' Jennifer cut in. 'But there's no time for all this. The Chinese guy called me again a short time ago, or one of his people did. They're coming straight to us. This morning they tried to find out more about the background to the document, and it ended in disaster. There were casualties, but they've got some new information.'

'What kind of information? Jennifer, who—'

'Wait, Julian. We're in contact with the Chinese jet. I'll put you through.'

A second passed, then a strange man's voice was heard, amidst an atmospheric hiss:

'Mr Orley? My name is Owen Jericho. I know you have a thousand questions, but I've got to ask you to listen to me now. By completing the document we've been able to discover that an information satellite was fired into the Earth's orbit from African soil. The operator was the former government of Equatorial Guinea, General Juan Mayé, who took over in a coup.'

'Yes, I know,' said Julian. 'Mayé and his satellite. He made a laughing stock of himself with that thing.'

'What you may not know is that Mayé was a straw man for Chinese lobbyists. It's possible that he was put in power at the instigation of Beijing, but it was certainly done with their connivance. By now other people are in power in Equatorial Guinea, but during his time in office the Chinese sponsored his space programme. Does the name Zheng mean anything to you?'

'The Zheng Group? Of course!'

'Zheng made lots of their technology available to him at the time, and provided know-how and hardware. But the satellite was just a pretext to fire something else into orbit from Mayé's state territory. Something that no official site would have allowed through.'

'What was that?'

'A bomb. A Korean atom bomb.'

Julian froze. He guessed, *feared* he guessed, what this man Jericho was getting at. He watched uneasily as the others scattered and gesticulated on the path.

'The Koreans?' he echoed. 'What on earth do I have to do with—'

'Not the Koreans, Mr Orley, but what Kim Jong Un's abandoned ghost train left behind. We're talking about the black market mafia. In other words, China, or somebody who's hiding behind China, has bought a handy little atom bomb from Korean stock, a so-called mini-nuke. We're sure that this bomb left the satellite just as it entered its orbit – so a year ago – then travelled on from there to an unknown destination. And in our opinion that destination is *not* on Earth.'

'Just a moment.' *Not on Earth.* 'You mean—'

'We mean it's meant to destroy one of your space installations, yes. Probably Gaia. The Moon hotel.'

'And what makes you suspect that?' Julian heard himself saying in a remarkably calm voice.

'The time delay. Of course there are a few variations. But none of them really explains why the thing has been up there for a year without being set off. Unless something got in the way.' Jericho paused for a miserably long time. 'Wasn't Gaia originally supposed to have opened in 2024? And that was postponed because of the Moon crisis?'

Julian said nothing, as something was set in motion, slowly but inexorably, inside his head. The projectionist slipped by, put in the reel of film and—

'Carl,' he whispered.

'Sorry?' asked Jericho.

'In the morning, two days ago,' cried Julian. 'My God! I saw it and didn't understand. Carl Hanna, one of our guests. I ran into him in the corridor, he said he'd been looking for the exit and hadn't found it, but he was lying! He was outside.'

'Julian.' Dana Lawrence joined in the conversation. 'I'm afraid you're wrong. You've seen the recordings. Carl definitely didn't go outside.'

'He did, Dana. He did! And idiot that I am, I even saw it. Down in the corridor, even though I didn't understand it. Someone faked the recordings, re-edited the shots. He steps onto the gangway to the Lunar Express—'

'And reappears a few seconds later.'

'No, he was outside! He steps on it wearing a very clean suit, Dana, clean as a whistle! And when he comes out again there are traces of moon dust on his legs. That was what I was looking for the whole time, that subliminal certainty that something was wrong.'

'Just a moment,' Dana said sharply. 'I'll get the recordings up on screen.'

Clever Julian, thought Hanna.

He stood there motionlessly while the cantilever swung over the gorge, Mimi and Marc hung laughing over the abyss, and Black set the winch in motion, and he heard something that he shouldn't have heard. But he was switched in. This time, once again, Ebola ensured that he was able to function, even though his room for manoeuvre was dramatically shrinking. He would never have expected to get busted, his identity was watertight. Not even when Vic Thorn had died had the operation been as precarious as it was right now. All of a sudden the planned course of action was out of the window; he had to act, carry out his mission prematurely, use the seconds, minutes at most, that Ebola had wangled for him to create the maximum possible confusion and take to his heels.

'Have the hotel searched right now,' Owen Jericho was saying. 'This guy Carl, perhaps he's been outside to hide the bomb in Gaia. Ask him—'

'I *will* ask him,' hissed Julian. 'Oh, I'll ask him!'

Yeah, right, thought Hanna.

The lift sank slowly into the gorge. Black stood by the winch, waving at the Californians. Wanted to know what it felt like being a kilometre above the ground.

'Amazing!' raved Parker. 'Better than parachute jumping. Better than anything.'

Hanna got moving, stretched his arms out.

'Can you speed the pace up a bit?' asked Edwards. 'Speed it up. Let us fly!'

'Sure, I—'

With both hands Hanna grabbed Black by the backpack, pulled him away from the console, lifted him in the air and carried him to the edge.

'Hey!' The pilot reached behind him. 'Carl, is that you?'

Hanna said nothing, walked quickly on. His captive turned, kicked his legs, tried to get a hold of his assailant.

'Carl, what's going on? Have you gone mad? – No!'

He hurled Black over the edge of the platform. For a moment the pilot seemed to find purchase in the void, then he fell, comparatively slowly at first, getting faster and faster. His shrill scream mingled with Mimi Parker's.

Nothing, not even a sixth of terrestrial gravity, could save a person falling into an abyss from a height of one thousand metres.

Gaia, Vallis Alpina

'Julian?' called Sophie. 'Miss Shaw?'

'What's going on?' snapped Dana.

'Radio silence. Both gone.' She tried in turn to re-establish connection with headquarters in London and with Julian, but all communication had been interrupted immediately after the start of the video showing the miraculous sullying of Hanna's trouser legs in the sterile surroundings of a gangway. The Canadian, small and cheerful, went for a walk on the corridor conveyor belt, unnoticed by anyone.

'Julian? Please come in!'

'Try to reach the Earth in the conventional manner,' said Dana. 'Oh, don't worry, let me do it.'

'She pushed Sophie aside, pulled up a menu, switched from LPCS on direct aerial connection to the terrestrial Tracking and Data Relay Satellite System, targeted ground stations, which was just possible within view of Earth, but Gaia seemed to have been deprived of her sensory organs. Lynn stared, her hand in front of her mouth, at the monitor wall, while Sophie shifted nervously from one leg to the other.

'I was carrying on the conversation quite normally when—'

'Don't apologise before I start blaming you,' Dana yelled at her. 'Keep on trying. Perform an analysis. I want to know where the problem lies. Lynn?'

Lynn turned her head as if in a trance.

'Can I speak to you for a minute?'

'What?'

Rigid with fury, Dana left the control centre. Lynn followed her into the hall like a robot.

'I think—'

'Sorry!' Dana flashed her inquisitorial grey-green eyes. 'You're my boss, Lynn, and that means I have to be respectful. But now I have to ask you very clearly what yesterday's warning was about.'

Lynn looked as if she had been recalled to life after a long period of unconsciousness. She raised a hand and studied its palm as if it contained something very attractive.

'It was all pretty vague.'

'What was vague?'

'Edda Hoff called and said a few people were planning some sort of attack on an Orley plant. It sounded – well, vague. Not like anything to worry about.'

'Why didn't you tell me about it straight away?'

'I didn't think it was necessary.'

'I'm the manager *and* the security officer of this hotel, and you didn't think it was necessary?'

Lynn stopped studying the palm of her hand and stared furiously back.

'As you have already observed, Dana, I am your boss and, no, I *didn't* think it was necessary to inform you. According to Hoff it was an *extremely vague* suspicion that *somewhere* in the world at *some* point an attack on *one* of our plants was planned, which was why she wanted to talk to me or Julian and not to *you*, and Julian had enough on his plate, so *I* asked to be kept informed. Does that answer your question?'

Dana took a step nearer. As if the prospect of disaster were not hovering about the hotel, Lynn found herself immersed in fascinated thoughts about the mysteries of the Dana physiognomy. How could such a sensually full mouth look so hard? Was the pallor of the face, framed by coppery red, due to the light, to a genetic predisposition or merely to

Dana's bitterness? How was it possible to seethe with rage and yet reveal such mask-like indifference?

'Maybe you missed a few things back there,' the manager said quietly. 'But there was talk of this hotel being blown up by an atom bomb. One of your guests seems to be involved in it. We've lost contact with your father and with Earth. You should at any rate have talked to me about it.'

'You know what?' said Lynn. 'You should get on with your work.'

She left Dana standing and went back to the control centre. The video of Hanna was still flickering on the monitor wall. The manager followed her slowly.

'I'd love to,' she said icily. 'Are you overworked, Lynn? Are you up to this? A moment ago you looked as if you'd been paralysed.'

Sophie looked up and away again, not liking what she saw.

'I'm afraid we've had a satellite failure,' she said. 'I can't reach Earth or Ganymede or Callisto. Shall I try the Peary Base?'

'Later. First we'll have to talk through the next few steps. If what we've just heard is true, we're threatened with catastrophe.'

'What kind of catastrophe?' asked Tim.

Aristarchus Plateau

Locatelli caught his breath.

He saw Black disappearing just as he stepped from the shadow of the ravine and back into the sunlight. He stared at the scene as if nailed to the spot. It wasn't easy to tell who had pushed whom into the gorge, and he had switched the gang down there to mute, but there was no doubt that it had been deliberate.

It had been no accident. That was murder!

Warren Locatelli was accused of lots of dubious qualities: uncouthness, recklessness, narcissism and much besides, but cowardice wasn't among them. His Italian–Algerian temperament broke through, flooded his thoughts. As he started running he saw the murderer pull something from his thigh.

And Edwards saw it too.

Below them, Black's flailing figure became smaller and smaller. He knew enough about gravitational physics to be aware that the pilot would not survive the fall, despite the reduction in gravitational pull. The rate of his fall might be slower than on Earth, twelve metres might be the equivalent of two, but there was no air resistance to counteract it. Black's body would be accelerated in a linear fashion, determined entirely by mass attraction. With each second his speed would increase by 1.63 metres until he landed at the bottom like a meteorite.

And he and Mimi would—

He was filled with fresh horror. He looked to the edge of the platform and saw the astronaut who had pushed Black into the depths, holding something long and flat in his right hand.

'Carl?' he wheezed.

The astronaut didn't reply. In the same moment Edwards worked out that they too were in extreme danger. He started tugging like mad on his safety guard, bent it to the side and rose from his seat. They had to get out of here. Climb up the rope, back over the cantilever to solid ground, their only chance.

'What are you doing?' screamed Mimi.

Edwards was about to reply, but the answer stuck in his throat. The astronaut raised the long object, aimed it at the seat contraption and fired. Instead of gunpowder the little piece of plasticene detonated in the shell. The liquid from the jelly capsule evaporated, swelled to many times its volume and produced sufficient pressure to fire the projectile at him at high speed. It pierced Parker's helmet, at which point the shower gel and shampoo combined to form what they really were, namely explosives, and the chairlift flew apart along with its occupants, flinging steel, fibreglass, electronics and body parts in all directions.

Hanna reholstered his weapon and strode towards the parked rovers.

*   *   *

Locatelli was faster. He jumped, scrabbled, slipped down the path, but he had a longer distance to travel. So he looked on as the fleeing astronaut reached the front of a rover and swung himself onto the driver's seat. Now once more within view of Julian's group, he heard a Babel of voices breaking out in his helmet, provoked by something that Amber had said. A moment later the murderer drove away at great speed.

'Shit,' wheezed Locatelli. 'Stop, you bastard!'

'Warren, what's going on?' said Momoka. 'Answer, please.'

'I'm here.'

'Amber said you'd made contact with Black and heard screams. She says—'

Locatelli stumbled. His leaps were too high, too risky. He missed the path, spread his arms out, landed on a steep bank of gravel and turned a somersault.

'Warren! For Christ's sake, what's going on?'

Up and down switched places. He hurtled downwards at great speed, towards the edge of the gorge. His body, light as a child's, took off every few metres, soared briefly before landing again, so that he could no longer see or hear; dust, nothing but dust, but his suit didn't seem to have been damaged. Otherwise I'd be dead, he thought, that doesn't take long out here, you're dead before you've even noticed.

'Warren!'

'A minute,' he yelled. 'Ow! Ouch! A minute!'

'Where are—'

The connection went dead. He slid along the plain on his belly, pushed himself up and landed on his feet, hurried to the second rover. With one spring he was behind the wheel. By now he was being yelled at from all directions, but he'd stopped paying the slightest attention. He didn't doubt for a moment what the guy was planning, namely to leave them here and clear off on Ganymede.

Was the bastard listening?

It was better to turn off all his connections. The other guy should learn as late as possible that someone was following him. He quickly pressed the central switch, silenced the voices in his head, put his foot on the accelerator and dashed after the fleeing man.

Gaia, Vallis Alpina

Tim had just appeared in the control centre when Dana gave a warning about some sort of catastrophe. The atmospheric barometer was clearly below freezing, with the hotel manager as cooling element, it seemed to him, while Sophie's features were helpless and Lynn's desolate. She looked to Tim like a drowning woman whose fear did battle with the fury of not having learned to swim in time.

'What's up?' he asked.

Dana looked at him thoughtfully. Then she delivered her report. Concise, to the point, toneless, without euphemism or down-playing of any kind. Within a minute Tim knew that someone was trying to blow Gaia to atoms, that the Chinese might be behind it, but that in all likelihood it was Carl Hanna, nice, guitar-playing Carl, in whose company Amber was currently out and about.

'For heaven's sake,' he said. 'How certain is it that there's a bomb?'

'Nothing's certain. Speculations, but as long as they haven't been refuted we should give them the status of facts.' Her eyes emitted a freezing beam towards Lynn. 'Miss Orley, any ideas, in your capacity as boss?'

Lynn gasped for air.

'There isn't the slightest reason to blow up Gaia! It must be a mistake.'

'Thanks, that's a great help to us. Give me a directive, or allow me to make some suggestions of my own. We could order an evacuation, for example.'

Lynn clenched her fists. She looked as if she wanted to tear out Dana's voice box.

'*If* there really was a bomb in the hotel, why didn't it go off ages ago? I mean, who or what was it being aimed at? The construction site? Anyone in particular?'

'We're all in danger,' said Tim. 'Who's going to bring an atom bomb to the Moon with a view to sparing human lives?'

'Exactly.' Lynn looked at them in turn. 'And so far we've all gathered together every night, so why hasn't anything happened? Perhaps because there is no bomb? Because someone's just trying to scare us?'

'Hmm,' said Sophie hesitantly. 'As this guy Jericho's already said, Hanna's task might have been to get the bomb here. If it reached the Moon a year ago—'

'Did Gaia even exist a year ago?' asked Tim.

'In its raw state.' Lynn nodded.

'That means it could have been here since then.'

'An atom bomb?' Dana's face expressed scepticism. 'Sorry, but even I don't believe *that*. I don't know much about mini-nukes, I have no idea about atomic weapons, but I think I know they give off radiation. Wouldn't this bomb do that too? How long could you ignore something like that?'

'Perhaps Hanna only brought it up here the day before yesterday,' Sophie concluded. 'On his night-time—'

'That's pure speculation!' Lynn flung her hand in the air with exasperation. 'Just because he had some dust on his trousers. And even if he did, why didn't he set it off ages ago?'

'Perhaps he was waiting for the right moment,' Tim suggested.

'And when would that be?'

'No idea.' Sophie shook her head. Her curls flew around as if having a party, in spite of the drama of the situation. 'Certainly not now. Apart from Miss Orley and Tim there are only comparatively unimportant people here.'

'Fine!' said Lynn triumphantly. 'Then that means that we don't have to evacuate after all.'

'I'm not keen on an evacuation, if that's what you mean,' Dana replied calmly. 'But I'll do it if it strikes me as advisable. For the time being I agree with Sophie. Things will probably only get critical when the shuttles come back, which should be happening at about seven o'clock. At the moment it's' – she looked at the electronic display – '16.20. More than two and a half hours to look for the thing.'

'Excuse me?' Lynn rolled her eyes. 'We're supposed to comb the hotel?'

'Yes. In teams.'

'We'd be looking for a needle in a haystack!'

'And finding it if there is one. Sophie, get the rest of them together. We'll concentrate on places where a thing like that could be hidden.'

'How big is a mini-nuke?' Sophie asked helplessly.

'The size of a briefcase?' Dana shrugged. 'Does anyone know?'

Shaking of heads. On the screen Sophie opened several windows with schemagrams and tables full of numbers.

'At any rate, we're not registering any unusual radiation levels,' she said. 'No increased radioactivity, no additional sources of heat.'

'Because there's no bomb here,' sulked Lynn.

'And the sensors cover every area?' asked Tim.

'Every accessible area, yes.'

'We should address another issue before we set off on our search,' said Dana. 'In my view we're not just dealing with a bomb.'

'What else, then?'

'With a traitor.'

'Oh Christ!' Lynn shook her head. 'I thought Carl was the bad guy.'

'Carl is *a* bad guy. But who re-edited the video? Who helped him leave Gaia on the Lunar Express?' she added with a sidelong glance at Lynn. 'Your father seems to have a very keen faculty of observation.'

'You think one of us is working for Carl?' asked Tim.

'You don't?'

'I don't know enough about it.'

'You know exactly as much as the rest of us do. How is Hanna going to cope up here all by himself? Acting and blurring his traces at the same time? Why did the satellites fail when his name was mentioned? How much can we put down to chance?'

'But who would it be?' Sophie's girlish face was filled with horror. 'Nobody on the staff. And certainly not one of the guests.'

'Hanna came here as a guest. A guest personally chosen by Julian Orley. How could he win so much trust?' Dana studied Lynn. Her gaze wandered on to Sophie, and settled on Tim. 'So, the other one, who is he? Or is it a she? Someone in this room?'

'Utter nonsense,' snapped Lynn.

'Could be. But that's one reason for us to search in teams.' Dana smiled thinly. 'So that we can keep an eye on each other.'

Aristarchus Plateau

Hanna only registered that he was being chased after quite a long time. The last thing he had heard amidst the chaos in his helmet was that there was no longer any connection between Gaia and headquarters in London, or the Chinese jet. Hydra had discussed a few possible ways of paralysing communication from the Moon or the Earth if the situation required. Clearly Ebola had been active. Now they were only connected by the radio in their suits, or by the aerials of the rovers and the shuttle, although that required visible contact. The last voice he had heard was Locatelli's, which had clearly been closer to him than the others.

Was *he* charging after him?

Hanna swerved around a small crater. The rover's top speed was eighty kilometres an hour, but that was almost impossible to reach. The vehicle was light, particularly when under-occupied, and kept lifting off the ground, leaving clouds of dust behind. Somewhere in the washed-out grey the other vehicle had suddenly appeared, and it was quickly approaching. Either the driver had underestimated the particular qualities of gravity up here, or he was working from professional experience.

Locatelli was a racing driver.

It *had* to be him!

Hanna briefly considered stopping and blowing him up, but the swirl of dust wouldn't exactly help his aim, and he would also lose time. Better to increase his distance. Once he had reached the shuttle it didn't matter what became of Locatelli and the others. It wasn't likely they'd manage to leave the Aristarchus Plateau, but even if they did, they wouldn't be able to stop him. He had more than enough time left to carry out the operation and settle in the OSS. From there he could—

The right front wheel sped up. The rover performed a leap, landed crookedly, skidded along and wrapped Hanna in grey clouds. For a moment he lost his bearings. Uncertain in which direction to turn, he set off again, found himself facing the gaping depths of the Schröter Valley, and at the very last second quickly whipped the wheel around, saved himself as best he could. Clearly the only weapon that could be used against Locatelli was speed.

Dust. The monster that swallowed everything up.

Locatelli cursed. The bastard in front of him was whirling up so much of it that he had to hold back to keep from getting too close to him and dashing blindly to his death. Then, all of a sudden, it looked as if the murderer himself were driving into the abyss. He was just short of the edge when he regained control over his vehicle and whipped it on, whirling up clouds of tiny particles that glittered in their billions in the sunlight, as if the regolith were filled with glass. Darkness fell around Locatelli, then the clouds lifted. A moment later he saw the rover right in front of him with astonishing clarity. The subfloor had changed, asphalted terrain now, only a few hundred metres still to go to the Ganymede. Dark and massive, it rested on its beetle legs—

What had the guy actually fired at him? A tiny island of pensiveness appeared in the whipped-up ocean of his fury, a place of quiet contemplation. What in hell's name was he doing here? What could he do to someone who was carrying deadly weapons and had no discernible qualms about using them? A moment later new waves of fury thundered through him, blowing away all his reservations. The murderer didn't even seem to find him worth a bullet. He hurtled like mad towards the shuttle, brought the rover to a standstill under the tail, jumped from his seat and hurried to the lock shaft that protruded from the Ganymede's abdomen like a monstrous birth canal. Only at the last second, with one leg in the cabin, did he pause and turn his reflective visor towards Locatelli.

'You miserable creep!' cried Locatelli, trying to wrest from the electric motor a performance that it had never managed before. 'Wait, just wait!'

The astronaut put his hand to his thigh and drew the long, flat thing.

He finally realised what an unfavourable position his recklessness had placed him in. He saw himself through the eyes of his enemy, the cross-hairs practically painted on his helmet, one big invitation to pull the trigger—

'Shit,' he whispered.

He let go of the wheel as if it were made of red-hot steel, jumped from the rover, turned a somersault and skidded away across the smooth asphalt, as the vehicle dashed on with no one to stop it, straight towards Ganymede and the astronaut. A bright flash outshone the cold, white sun in the sky. The rover was hurled upwards, stood upright, and spat parts of its frame, splinters of chassis, scraps of gold foil and electronic components in all directions. Locatelli instinctively threw his arms together over his helmet. Beside him, debris ploughed grooves into the asphalt. He quickly rolled onto his back, then as he sat up he saw one of the wheels wobbling wildly towards him; he catapulted himself out of the way and got to his feet.

No! *Not on my watch!*

Crouching and expecting the worst, he ran across the landing field, but his adversary had vanished. He saw the illuminated cabin climbing the lock shaft. A few minutes more. He couldn't let the murderer steal the Ganymede and leave them in the desert. Heedless of the injuries he had dealt himself in his stunt, he ran under the body of the shuttle to the lock shaft. The lift cabin was gone, but the display showed a red light, and while it was red, Black had explained to them, the shaft couldn't be retracted. The astronaut must still be in the lock, which was probably being filled with air at that very minute. Good, very good.

Locatelli panted, waited.

Green!

He struck the call button with the flat of his hand.

Hanna wasted no time taking off his helmet after leaving the lock. He hurried between the rows of seats to the cockpit. Had he killed Locatelli? Probably not. The man had jumped off, Hanna had seen his body flying through the vacuum, before the projectile had struck the rover. The wreck might have crashed on top of him, or he might have been hit by some of the flying debris. Without looking behind him, he slipped into the pilot's seat and ran an eye over the display. He knew what the devices were for, he had had an opportunity to familiarise himself with the workings of all lunar vehicles some months ago. Thanks to Hydra's perfect preparatory work he even knew enough to drive the spaceship back into orbit, and from there to the OSS, and he wasn't alone on board as long as Ebola found a way of contacting him after communication had been blocked. Something he probably didn't need to worry about. Ebola would make sure he got there, and appeared in the right place at the right time.

His fingers slid over the controls.

He hesitated.

What was that? The shaft wouldn't move. The display was red, which meant that the cabin was currently being drained, or filled with air – or on its way!

He quickly turned around.

No, it was there, the space evenly lit behind the narrow windows, and deserted. Hanna narrowed his eyes. He paused. A sudden urge impelled him to get up and check, but he couldn't afford any further delays, and the light had just switched from red to green.

Ganymede was ready to go.

'There. There!'

Amber pointed excitedly into the sky. A long way off something was climbing steeply into the sky, something long that glinted in the sun.

'The Ganymede!'

They had come hurrying down the path, mindless, breathless, in clumsy kangaroo leaps, back to the crane platform, only to discover that both rovers had disappeared. Not a soul far and wide. Black's cries still echoed in Amber's ears:

Carl, what's going on? Have you gone m— No!

Carl?

She had run anxiously out onto the platform and seen what was left of the gondola in which Mimi and Marc should have been sitting. More precisely, there was no gondola. Just the useless back of a chair, twisted steel, the contorted scrap of a safety guard and behind it, wedged in, something white, something numbingly familiar—

A single leg.

Only an extreme effort of will had kept her from throwing up in her helmet, while the others had stared down into the gorge and kept a lookout for the missing man. But large parts of the valley were in shadow, so they couldn't see anything at all.

'They're dead,' Rogachev had stated at last.

'How can you claim that they're dead?' Evelyn said excitedly.

'That *is* a corpse.' Rogachev pointed to the amputated leg in the ruined gondola.

'No, that's – that's—'

None of them had managed to speak its name. What an unbearable idea, that the fate of that shredded individual would only be fulfilled when it gave that limb an identity and thus retrospectively supplied the facts.

'We have to look for her,' said Evelyn.

'Later.' Julian stared at the place where the vehicles had just been standing. 'We have worse things to worry about right now.'

'Don't you think that's bad enough?' snapped Momoka.

'I think it's terrible. But first we have to find the rovers.'

'Warren?' Momoka resumed her mantra-like calls to her husband. 'Warren, where are you?'

'Assuming they managed it—' Evelyn tried again.

'*They're dead*,' Rogachev cut her off in a voice of ice. 'Five people are missing. At least two of those are alive, otherwise both vehicles couldn't have disappeared, but the others are down there. Do you want to abseil down there and poke about in the dark?'

'How do you know it isn't – it isn't Carl down there?'

'Because Carl's alive,' Amber had said wearily, to keep things short. 'I think he has Peter and the others on his conscience.'

'What makes you so sure about that?'

'Amber's right,' Julian had said. 'Carl's a traitor, I realised that a few minutes ago. Believe me, we do have a bigger problem than that here! We urgently have to think about how we—'

At that moment Amber saw the shuttle rising on the horizon. For a moment it seemed to stand still above Cobra Head, then it came towards them and suddenly got bigger.

It's flying this way, she thought.

The armoured body was gaining form and outline, but also, worryingly, altitude. Whoever was flying the Ganymede plainly didn't plan to land and pick them up. The machine moved silently overhead, accelerated, turned in a northerly direction, shrank to a dot and disappeared.

'Julian, call Gaia,' urged Evelyn. 'They've got to pick us up from here.'

'It's not going to happen.' Julian sighed. 'The connection's been broken.'

'Broken?' cried Momoka, horrified. 'How come it's broken?'

'No idea. I did say we had a bigger problem.'

Berlin, Germany

Xin's transformation back from a lion-maned Mando-Progger to a perfectly normal contract killer was as good as complete when his contact called.

On the way back from the Grand Hyatt he had constantly asked himself what the two policemen had been doing there. No doubt about it, they had been after Tu – Jericho and the girl as well – but to what end? Jericho wasn't mentioned by name in Berlin, so the investigators had their sights set on Tu. Why him, of all people?

On the other hand he didn't care. Admittedly he had had to disappear without having achieved anything, but his intuition told him he had arrived too late anyway. The group had cleared off. So what? What were they going to do? Vogelaar and his wife were dead, the crystal was in his possession. While he put his wigs and fake beards away, he took the call.

'Kenny, damn it, how could that happen?'

No *Hydra*, no other greeting. Just anxious whispering. Xin hesitated. His contact was beside himself.

'How could what happen?' he asked warily.

'It's all going down the tubes! This guy Tu and this Jericho guy and the girl, all the contraband is on its way to us, and they *know*! They know everything! About the parcel, about the *attack*! They've even had a chance to talk to Julian Orley. *Our cover's being blown!*'

Xin froze. The Mando-Progger's Tartar beard lay in his hand like a small, dead animal.

'That's impossible,' he whispered.

'Impossible? Well, then perhaps you could come *here*! Right now the company's being hit by a devastating earthquake.'

'But I've got the dossier.'

'So have they!'

A volley of oaths rained down on Xin, taking in, amongst other hardships, the unmasking of Hanna and the activation of the communication block. The latter had been planned as an emergency measure in case details of the attack were to seep through prematurely to the Moon. Something no one at Hydra had seriously reckoned with, but that was exactly what had happened.

'When was the net jammed?' asked Xin.

'During the linkup.' The other man breathed sharply into the receiver. 'Over the next twenty-four hours the Moon will be cut off from everything, but we can't keep the block going for ever. I just hope Hanna gets the situation under control. Not to mention Ebola.'

Ebola. Hanna's right hand was a specialist when it came to infecting supposedly independent systems and weakening them from within. That Ebola had managed to interrupt the fatal linkup could be seen as a brilliant manoeuvre, a skilful turnaround in the adverse wind of circumstances, but unfortunately on a leaking boat.

Vogelaar had outwitted him.

No! Xin forced himself to calm down. They weren't leaking yet. He had chosen Hanna and Ebola because they knew how to improvise and would keep the upper hand, regardless of how inauspicious the circumstances might be. He planned not to waste a second brooding on the possibility that the undertaking might go wrong.

'And how are you going to force this Tu and his rat-pack to see sense?' the other man raged. 'You've lost Mickey Reardon, two of your people died in Shanghai, you can't count on Gudmundsson and his team at the moment, they're otherwise engaged, so how do you think—'

'Not at all,' Xin cut in.

Puzzled, his contact fell silent.

'There's no longer any point in eliminating Tu's group,' Xin explained to him. 'The facts of the situation have become common knowledge, the dissemination of the dossier can no longer be stopped. Everything else is decided on the Moon.'

'Damn it, Kenny. We've been busted!'

'No. My task right now is to protect Hydra from being unmasked. Does *he* know about it yet?'

'I told him five minutes ago. He'd be glad of a personal call from you, otherwise I've got to sign off now, such a bloody mess! What happens if they track me down? What am I supposed to do then?'

'Nobody's going to get busted.'

'But they're bringing the dossier with them! I don't know what's in it. Perhaps it would be better—'

'Just chill.' The tearful whining at the other end was starting to make Xin feel ill. 'I'll come to London as quickly as possible. I'll be near you, and if things get tight I'll get you out.'

'My God, Kenny! How on earth could this happen?'

'Pull yourself together,' Xin snapped. 'The only risk is that you lose your nerve. Go back to the others and act as if nothing's wrong.'

'I hope Hanna knows what he's doing.'

'That's why I chose him.'

Xin finished the conversation, swapped his phone from one hand to the other and inspected the room. As might have been expected, he noticed thousands of things that weren't right, things that were asymmetrical, things that were out of proportion, strange excrescences in the design, an irritating bouquet of flowers. The florist hadn't been skilled enough to make the number of petals a multiple of the number of the flowers, thus giving the sorry effort some kind of mathematical meaning. For want of a self-contained idea, the supposedly aesthetic function failing to correspond to a structural one, the arrangement had something menacingly haphazard about it – a nightmare for Xin. The mere idea of being unable to produce a rationale for one's actions was totally horrifying! He reluctantly dialled another number, held his mobile in his left hand, while the fingers of his right gripped the flowers and tried to correct the arrangement.

'Hydra,' he said.

'How big is the dossier?' asked the voice.

'I haven't had a chance to read it yet.' Kenny pinched at a lily. 'I'm sorry about what happened. Of course I'll assume full responsibility, but we could do nothing more than threaten Vogelaar with torture and death. He must have passed on a copy of the dossier to Jericho.'

'You're not guilty,' said the voice. 'What's crucial is that the block still stands. What do you have in mind?'

'Change of tack. Take the heat off Jericho, Tu and Yoyo. Their deaths are no longer a priority, and we can't influence what's happening on the Moon. I remain convinced that the operation will be a complete success. The important thing now is to preserve Hydra's anonymity.'

'Do we agree on the weak points?'

'From my point of view there's only the one we've already discussed.'

'That's exactly how I see it.'

Xin considered the flower arrangement. Not really any better, still without any semiotic content. 'I'll take the next plane to London.'

'Are you well enough equipped there?'

'Airbike and everything. If necessary I can summon reinforcements.'

'Gudmundsson is busy, you know that.'

'My net stretches wide. I could set legions marching, but that won't be necessary. I keep myself constantly at the ready, so that should do it.'

'Tell me about the basic information in the dossier. Now that we've shelved email communication, unfortunately you can't send it to me any more.'

'But it was still right to take the pages off the net.'

'Keep me posted.'

Xin paused.

Then he threw his phone on the bed and turned his mounting rage on orchids, lilies and crocuses. He had to leave Berlin as soon as possible, but he couldn't even leave this room as long as the arrangement was subject to an unsatisfactory structure. The world was not random. Not haphazard. Everything had to yield a meaning. Where the meaning ended, madness began.

The head of a lily broke off.

Bobbing with fury, Kenny Xin tore the whole arrangement out of its bowl and shoved it in the bin.

Gaia, Vallis Alpina, The Moon

Lynn had decided to search the subterranean areas of Gaia along with Sophie. Tim sensed the reason for that. She dreaded arguments with him, because she knew very well that she would no longer be able to keep up her pretence. She was still able to lie to herself. Her attitude alternated between moments of complete clarity, subjectivity and erupting fury.

That abysmal, night-black fear dwelt once more in her every glance, the fear that might easily have killed her years before, and Tim thought he noticed something else in it, something vaguely insidious that frightened him to the core. As he poked through the casino with Axel Kokoschka, the chef, his concern swung from her to Amber, who was travelling with a suspected terrorist. Julian had received the information on a protected frequency, but how had he reacted? Peter Black was with him. Had they caught Carl?

What was happening right now on the Aristarchus Plateau?

Amber, he thought, come in! Please!

Gaia's underground floors, by Dana's estimation, deserved particular attention, because it was from there that a bomb would release its greatest destructive force. Michio Funaki and Ashwini Anand had been assigned to the staff accommodation areas, Lynn and Sophie to the underground greenhouses, aquaria and storage units. Gaia's mirror world stretched down deep – but then staff plans for 2026 allowed for one employee per guest.

'In the meantime I will try to reach the Peary Base,' Dana had said before they went off in different directions.

'How, without a satellite?' Tim had asked.

'Via the dedicated line. There's a direct laser connection between Gaia and the base. We send the data back and forth via a system of mirrors.'

'What do you mean, mirrors? Ordinary, common-or-garden mirrors?'

'The first one is on the far side of the gorge. A thin, very high mast. You can see it from your suite.'

'And how many are there?'

'Not all that many. A dozen to the Pole. Arranged in such a way that the light-beam passes around crater rims and mountains. To reach shuttles, spaceships or even the Earth, of course you need satellites, but for intralunar communication between two fixed points there's nothing better. No atmosphere to scatter the light, no rain – so I'll set out our situation to them in the hope that they aren't having any problems with their satellites there, but my optimism is muted.'

And then, after Lynn had disappeared with Sophie into the lift, Dana had taken him aside.

'Tim, this is awkward for me. You know I don't tend to beat around the bush, but in this case—'

He sighed, troubled by dark forebodings. 'Is it about Lynn?'

'Yes. What's up with her?'

Tim looked at the floor, at the walls, wherever you looked to keep from returning the other person's gaze.

'Look, Lynn and I never had personal contact,' Dana went on. 'But she supported my appointment at the time, and trained me up, in the camp, on the Moon, confidently and competently, entirely admirable. Now she strikes me as irresponsible, erratic, belligerent. She's changed completely.'

'I—' Tim hemmed and hawed for a moment. 'I'll talk to her.'

'I didn't ask you to.'

Her quizzical eyes fastened on his. Suddenly it occurred to Tim that Dana Lawrence wasn't blinking. He hadn't seen her blink for ages. He remembered a film, *Alien*, a quite old but still excellent flick that Julian loved, in which one of the crew members was unexpectedly revealed as an android.

'I don't know how I should answer that,' he said.

'No, you do, you know very well.' She lowered her voice. 'Lynn is your sister, Tim. I want to know if we can trust her. Has she got herself under control?'

The clouds began to clear in Tim's head. He looked at the manager, illuminated by the realisation of what she actually meant.

'Are you suggesting Lynn is Carl's accomplice?' he asked, almost lost for words.

'I just want to hear what you think.'

'You're crazy.'

'All of this is crazy. Come on, we're running out of time. It would be a great weight off my mind if I was wrong, but three days ago Lynn tried with all her might to persuade her father that he was imagining things. She wanted to withhold the surveillance camera videos from him, she left me in the dark about Edda Hoff's warning, although she really *should* have talked to me. All in all she's behaving as if we had dreamed up the events of the past thirty minutes, even though she herself has been involved from the very start.'

That's not true, Tim wanted to say, and in fact Dana was wrong about one thing. Lynn hadn't been there from the start. Sophie had taken the call while his sister had been sitting in the Selene with the manager and the cooks, talking about the possibility of a picnic at the bottom of the Vallis Alpina. Jennifer Shaw had wanted to talk to Lynn or her father, so Sophie had immediately sent a message to the Selene and the security advisors had immediately put it through to Julian on the Aristarchus Plateau. By the time Lynn and Dana had reached headquarters, the conversation was already well under way.

But what difference did that make?

'As you said before, Lynn is my sister.' He straightened up and shifted away a little. 'I'd walk on hot coals for her.'

'That's not enough for me.'

'Well, it'll have to be.'

'Tim.' Dana sighed. 'I just want to make sure that we're not about to face problems from somewhere we least expect it. Tell me what's up. I'll treat our conversation with complete confidentiality, no one will find out about it if you don't want them to. Not Julian, and certainly not Lynn.'

'Dana, really—'

'I've *got* to be able to do my job!'

Tim said nothing for a moment.

'She had a breakdown,' he said flatly. 'A few years ago. Exhausted, depressed. It came and went, but since then I can't stop worrying that it might repeat itself.'

'Burn-out?'

'No, more of an—' The word wouldn't leave his lips.

'Illness?' Dana completed his sentence.

'Lynn played it down, but – yes. A morbid disposition. Her – our mother was depressive. In the end she—'

He fell silent. Dana waited to see if he was going to add anything, but he thought he'd said enough.

'Thanks,' she said seriously. 'Please keep an eye on your sister.'

He nodded unhappily, joined Kokoschka, and they set off, equipped with portable detectors, while he felt like a miserable bloody collaborator. At the same time he was tormented by Dana's suspicion. Not because he saw Lynn as being exposed to unjustified suspicions, but because uncertainty was gnawing at him. Could he really walk on coals for Lynn? He would give his life for her, that much he knew, regardless of what she did.

But he just wasn't *completely sure*.

Ganymede

Locatelli lay in a foetal position, legs bent, on the floor of the lock just by the bulkheads. Almost two-thirds of the cabin was glazed, but as long as he stayed down low, shielded by the screen, no one would be able to see him from the passenger space or the cockpit. He feverishly developed and rejected one plan after another. Every time he turned his head, he could just make out the indicators on the inside wall of the lock, showing pressure, air and ambient temperature. The cabin was pressurised, but he didn't dare take off his helmet. He was too worried that the pilot might, at that precise moment, get the idea of subjecting the lock to an inspection, just as he was busying himself with his damned helmet. He had squeezed his way in between the bulkheads as soon as they had slid apart, pressed the up button, dropped to the floor, without wasting a fragment of a second. And yet it couldn't have escaped the guy that the cabin had gone back down again.

He cautiously raised himself up a little and peered around for anything that might serve as a weapon, but there was nothing inside the lock that could be used to slash or stab. The Ganymede was still accelerating. He guessed that there must be an autopilot, but as long as the shuttle hadn't reached its final speed, whoever was sitting up at the front couldn't take his eyes off the controls. Later it might be too late to shed his armour and his helmet. Perhaps he really *should* do it now.

At that moment an idea came to him.

He quickly released the catches of the helmet and took it off, set it down next to him and started frantically working away at his chest armour. The acceleration pressure eased off. He hastily fiddled around with the valves and fasteners, peeled himself out of his survival backpack and pushed everything a little way away. Now he was more mobile, and he also had something that could be used as a weapon in a surprise attack. Every muscle tensed, he lay there and waited. The shuttle flew in a curve, and went on gaining altitude. His head roared with the certainty that this was his only chance. If he didn't catch and whack Peter or Carl, whichever of them was flying the Ganymede, at the first opportunity, he might as well say goodbye to the world.

Don't complain, asshole, he thought, this was what you wanted. And strangely – or not – his inner voice, in all its condescension, and down to peculiarities of its modulation sounded exactly like Momoka's.

Gaia, Vallis Alpina

Dana walked to her desk and paused.

Depressive. That explained a few things. But how did depressive states develop? Into apathy? Aggression? Would Lynn freak out? What was Julian's daughter likely to do?

She established the laser connection with the Peary Base. After a few seconds the face of deputy commander Tommy Wachowski appeared on the screen. There wasn't much in the way of regular exchange between hotel and base, which meant that it was ages since she had last spoken to him. Wachowski looked tense and relieved at the same time, as if she had taken a weight off his mind with her call. Dana thought she knew the reason. A moment later Wachowski confirmed her suspicion.

'Am I happy to see you,' he growled. 'I thought we'd never get through to anyone ever again.'

'Have you been having problems with the satellites?' she asked.

His eyes widened. 'How do you know that?'

'Because we have too. We were in contact with Earth when the connection went down. We haven't been able to get through since then, not even to our shuttles.'

'We've been having pretty much the same thing. Completely cut off. The problem is that we're in the shadow of the libration. Alternative channels are out. We're relying on LPCS; do you have any idea what's going on?'

'No.' Dana shook her head. 'At the moment we haven't a clue. Not a clue. You?'

Aristarchus Plateau

The Moon was quite definitely more suited to route-marches than the Earth, because of its lower gravitation. Spacesuits quite definitely weren't. Even though the exosuits provided a high level of comfort and mobility, you were, regardless of the air-conditioning, in an incubator. The more energy you expended, the more you sweated, and eight kilometres, even performing leaps that would have done credit to a kangaroo, remained eight kilometres.

Assailed by questions, Julian had divulged various things: he had talked about his nocturnal observation of the Lunar Express, about Hanna's lies and dodges, and had told them something was under way against Orley Enterprises somewhere in the world. But the idea that terrorists might try to blow up his hotel with an atom bomb he kept to himself, just as he refrained from mentioning Lynn's inexcusable derelictions of duty. He was terribly worried about her, but there was a great gulf of understanding in the mountain range of his concern, in which a horrible black worm of anxiety wriggled. Who had actually re-edited the video, who had hooked up Hanna? Because there was no doubt that the Canadian had been listening in earlier: he had gone into action even while that man Jericho had been setting out his suspicions! And finally, who had deactivated the satellites in perfect synchronisation with Hanna's flight? The worm turned, glistened, quivered, and gave birth to the idea of an assistant, an accomplice in the hotel, male or female. Someone who had inexplicably refused to let him see the manipulated video, and whose attitude was becoming more mysterious with each passing hour.

'And how are we going to get out of here?' Evelyn wanted to know. 'Back to the hotel, without a shuttle or radio contact?'

'I'm just wondering where Carl's trying to get to,' Rogachev mused.

'Like that matters right now,' snorted Momoka.

'Why was he in such a rush to get away? Nothing could have been pinned on him. Well, there's the fact that he doesn't stick too closely to the truth, but okay. Why the hurry?'

'Maybe he's planning something,' said Amber. 'Something he has to get done in time, now that his cover's been blown.'

In time. That was it! How did the accomplice in the hotel manage to get away, if he existed at all? How acute was the danger of a bomb going off in Gaia within the next hour? Wouldn't Hanna's journey have had to take him back to Gaia, to set it off? Or was the bomb already ticking? In which case—

Lynn! He must have been crazy to suspect her! But even if she had some macabre, incomprehensible part in the drama, did she realise what she'd let herself in for? Did she have even the tiniest idea what was going on? Could Hanna have roped her in for his purposes, on some pretext or other? Could he have exploited her mental state, somehow hoodwinked her into doing things for him, the significance of which she completely misunderstood?

Perhaps he should have listened more closely to Tim.

Should have! The grammar of missed opportunities.

'Julian?'

'What?'

'How are we going to get out of here?' Evelyn asked again.

He hesitated. 'Peter knows – he *knew* the Schröter spaceport better than I did. I don't think there are any flying machines there, but there's definitely a third moonmobile. So we'll get away in any event.'

'But where to?' asked Rogachev. 'Crossing the Mare Imbrium in a moon car isn't exactly an encouraging prospect.'

'How far are we from the hotel, anyway?' asked Amber.

'About thirteen hundred kilometres.'

'And how long will our oxygen hold out?'

'Forget it,' wheezed Momoka. 'Certainly not long enough to get to the Vallis Alpina by car. What do you say, Julian? How long would it take to cover thirteen hundred kilometres at eighty max?'

'Sixteen hours,' said Julian. 'But realistically we'll hardly be able to go at eighty.'

'Sixty?'

'Maybe fifty.'

'Oh, brilliant!' laughed Momoka. 'Then we can take bets on who packs up first. Us or the car.'

'Stop it,' said Amber.

'My bet's on us.'

'This is pointless, Momoka. Why don't we—'

'Then the car will keep going for a while with our corpses inside, until eventually—'

'Momoka!' yelled Amber. 'Shut. The. Fuck. Up!'

'Right, that's enough!' Julian stopped and raised both hands. 'I know we have a stack of terrible things to work out. Nothing makes any sense, practically no information is confirmed. At the moment the only thing we can do is think in a straight line, *from one step to the next*, and the next step will be an examination of the Schröter spaceport. We've got enough oxygen to do that.' He paused. 'Now that Peter's dead—'

'If he really is,' said Evelyn.

'As Peter is *probably* dead, I'll take his place. Okay? Responsibility for the group lies with me now, and from this moment I only want to hear constructive comments.'

'I've got a constructive comment,' said Rogachev.

'Great stuff, Oleg,' sneered Momoka. 'Constructive comments are at a premium right now.'

Rogachev ignored her. 'Aren't the helium-3 mines a bit closer to the Aristarchus Plateau than the hotel?'

'That's right,' said Julian. 'Not half as far.'

'So if we could get there—'

'The mines are automatic,' Momoka objected. 'Peter told me. It's all robots.'

'Okay,' said Evelyn thoughtfully. 'Even so, they must have some sort of infrastructure, don't they? Accommodation for maintenance staff. Some means of transport.'

'There's definitely a survival depot,' said Julian. 'Good idea, Oleg. So let's go!'

The fact that their oxygen wouldn't get them to the mining zone he left unspoken.

Ganymede

Hanna hurried towards his goal on the hypothetical line of fifty degrees longitude, pulling the shadow of the Ganymede at a rate of 1200 kilometres an hour across the velvet monotony of the northern Oceanus Procellarum. His gaze rested on the controls. He couldn't get any more speed out of the shuttle. He still had another hour and a quarter to go, but given the pitiful possibilities at Julian's group's disposal that was hardly cause for concern. Even if they managed to leave the plateau, he still had a luxurious amount of time to finish his task and leave the Moon. But whether Ebola would get there in time, now that everything was in chaos, was anybody's guess. Admittedly he planned to wait as long as possible. But he would have to fly off sooner or later, alone if necessary. Those were the rules. Alliances served a purpose.

On his right there began a plain covered with tiny craters, which separated the northern Mare Imbrium from the Oceanus Procellarum. Behind it the helium-3 mining zone stretched into Sinus Iridum, the bay in which the Americans and the Chinese had got into such arguments the previous year. Kenny Xin had told him loads about that. Mad he might be, yet it was worth listening to him.

He looked wearily around.

The lock was bathed in a diffuse light. There was nothing to suggest that Locatelli had made it to the shuttle. And anyway, the noise of the bulkhead would give him away as soon as it opened. He turned his attention back to the controls and looked out of the window. A larger crater came into view, Mairan, as the holographic map on the console told him. The Ganymede had been travelling for a good twenty minutes now, and he was almost starting to feel something like boredom.

Okay then.

He stood up, grabbed his weapon with the non-explosive rounds and walked between the seats to the lock. The closer he got, the deeper he could see into the cabin, but at the moment it was actually empty. It was only when he was a couple of steps away that something massive and white entered his field of vision, something on the floor, and he stopped.

A survival backpack. At least that was what it looked like.

Did that mean Locatelli had actually done it?

He stepped slowly closer. Other details became visible, the shoulder of a piece of chest armour, a bent leg. It was only when he was standing so close to the glass that his breath condensed on it into a film of tiny droplets that he was also able to make out part of the face, a lifelessly staring eye, a half-open mouth. Locatelli seemed to be resting his back against the bulkhead, and he didn't look particularly well, in fact he looked a bit dead.

Hanna's fingers clutched the weapon. He rested his free hand on the sensor field, raised the bulkhead and took a step back.

Locatelli slumped out from the cabin like a sack and stared at the ceiling. His left arm weakly struck the floor, his fingers open as if he were begging for a final pittance. His right hand, still in the lock, was wrapped around the lower edge of his helmet. There was no outward sign of injury, and in any case he had been able to take off his armour before he collapsed.

Hanna frowned, leaned forward and paused.

At that moment he realised that something was wrong. The unusually healthy colour of the man's face might be just about compatible with his being a corpse – but Warren Locatelli was definitely the first dead person he'd ever seen sweating.

So, Hanna.

Locatelli cried out. With all his might he swung the helmet, hit Hanna's arm, saw the weapon flying away, leapt up.

Hanna staggered.

That the Canadian would see through his bluff and shoot him a moment later had been Locatelli's worst-case expectation. So, two seconds after the attack, what surprised him most of all was that he was still alive. Countless times during the sequence of eternities that had passed since the shuttle lifted off, he had tried to imagine the situation and calculate his chances. Now here they were, and there was no longer any time to think, not even to wonder or catch his breath. Trusting, in the Celtic manner, to the effects of a good shout, loud and inarticulate like an attacking horde, he thrashed away at his opponent with his helmet, again and again, without a pause, without giving him the slightest opportunity to retreat, saw his knees bending, aimed at the top of his shaven head, struck again, as hard as he could. The Canadian made a grab for him. Locatelli dealt him a kick to the shoulder. God knew he had fought quite enough in his life, both often and enthusiastically, but never with a professional hitman, as Hanna plainly was when you looked at things with a lucid eye, so for the sake of certainty he brought the helmet down on his head once more, even though the man hadn't moved a muscle for ages, grabbed for the curious weapon, staggered a few steps back and took aim.

Spurts of blood from the back of Hanna's head, on the floor.

Locatelli's hand was shaking.

After a while, quivering with fear, he risked stepping forward again, crouched down and held the barrel to Hanna's temple. No reaction. The Canadian's eyes were shut and his breathing was heavy. Locatelli blinked, felt his heartbeat gradually slowing down. Waited. Nothing happened. Went on waiting.

Nothing. Nothing at all.

Gradually he was starting to believe that the man really was unconscious.

Where should he put him? He thought frantically. Perhaps he should chuck him in the lock and simply get rid of him on the flight. But that would have been murder, and even at his most reckless Locatelli was no murderer. And he wanted to know why Peter, Mimi and Marc had had to die, what Hanna's crappy aims had been. He needed information, and anyway, Momoka, Julian, the others, were stuck on the Aristarchus Plateau! He had to get back and fetch them, that had absolute priority.

And how, smart-arse?

His gaze wandered to the cockpit. He knew how to drive a racing car, how to sail a yacht into the wind. But he hadn't the faintest idea about Hornets, or about where the Ganymede was headed, how high and how fast it flew. Nothing on board was designed to lift his spirits. Here the Canadian, who would eventually come round, there the unfamiliar world of the cockpit. He hadn't the first clue. He would have to learn, and fast.

No. First of all he had to put Hanna somewhere.

Nothing occurred to him even after he had gone on thinking for a few minutes longer, so he dragged the motionless body towards the cockpit, dumped it behind the co-pilot's seat and looked around for something to tie it up with.

There didn't seem to be anything like that on board either.

Right. At least no one could say things were getting boring.

London, Great Britain

One of the last works of the venerable Sir Norman Foster stood on the Isle of Dogs, a droplet-shaped peninsula in London's East End. Bent into a U at this point, the Thames flowed around an area of business districts, elegantly restored docks, exclusive apartments and preserved remainders of social housing, whose traditional inhabitants were reduced to the status of extras in this affluent architectural idyll. As early as the 1990s, well-to-do Londoners had discovered the hidden charms of the area for themselves; artists, galleries, medium-sized companies had moved here to bear down on the crumbling working-class estates like so many pest controllers. After over two decades of violent social tensions, the last stretches of estate streets had now been lovingly restored, as if by museum curators, and the families living there had been made protected species, which meant turning them, with financial support, into the kind of happy social case that stressed managers were able to envy without drawing suspicions of cynicism.

In 2025 there was no one left on the Isle of Dogs who was still really poor. Certainly not in the shadow of the Big O.

The construction of the new headquarters of Orley Enterprises had begun even in Jericho's day, the year before the fear of losing Joanna had sent him to Shanghai. In the south-east of the Isle of Dogs, in the former Island Gardens, resting on a low plinth – if you could call a twelve-storey complex low – was an O two hundred and fifty metres in diameter, circled parabolically by an artificial orange moon which contained several conference rooms and was reached via airy bridges. More than five thousand staff swarmed around the light-flooded atriums, gardens and open-plan offices of the big glass torus, busy as termites. A flight pad had been worked into the roof area so skilfully that the curve of the O was preserved from every perspective. Only as you approached it from the air did you notice that the zenith of the building was not arched but flat, a surface with two dozen helicopters and skymobiles arranged on it.

Tu's jet had landed in Heathrow at a quarter past four. While it was still on the runway, the company's security forces had welcomed them and brought them to the firm's helicopter, which flew them straight to the Isle of Dogs. Further north stretched the skyscrapers of Canary Wharf, vainly straining to be a match for the Big O, which towered over everything else in sight. Private boats, tiny and white, moved about on the waters of the renovated docks. Jericho saw two men stepping onto the landing pad. The helicopter turned in the air, settled on the pad and opened its side door. The men's steps quickened. One, with black, wiry hair and a monobrow, held his right hand out to Jericho, then reconsidered and held it out to Yoyo.

'Andrew Norrington,' he said. 'Deputy head of security. Chen Yuyun, I assume.'

'Just Yoyo.' She shook his outstretched hand. 'The honourable Tu Tian, Owen Jericho. Also *very* honourable.'

The other man coughed, wiped his palms on his trouser-legs and nodded at everyone.

'Tom Merrick, information services.'

Jericho studied him. He was young, prematurely bald, and clearly afflicted with inhibitions that kept him from looking anyone in the eye for longer than a second.

'Tom is our specialist in all kinds of communication and information transmission,' said Norrington. 'Did you bring the dossier?'

Instead of replying, Jericho held the tiny cube into the light.

'Very good!' Norrington nodded. 'Come.'

The path led them inside the roof onto a grassy track and across a bridge, beyond which there stretched a bank of glass lifts. The eye was drawn down into the open interior of the Big O, criss-crossed by further bridges. People hurried busily back and forth across them. A good hundred and fifty metres below him, Jericho saw lift-like cabins travelling along the loop of the hollow. Then they stepped into one of the high-speed lifts, plunged towards the ground and through it, and stopped on sub-level 4. Norrington marched ahead of them. Without slowing his pace, he made for a reflective wall that opened silently, and they plunged into the world of high security, dominated by computer desks and monitor walls. Men and women spoke into headsets. Video conferences were under way. Tu straightened his glasses on the bridge of his nose, made some contented noises and craned his neck, transfixed by so much technology.

'Our information centre,' Norrington explained. 'From here we stay in contact with Orley facilities everywhere in the world. We work according to the specifications of our subcontractors, which means that there are no continental heads, only security advisers to the individual subsidiaries, who report to London. All company data come together here.'

'How far under the ground are we?' asked Yoyo.

'Not *that* far. Fifteen metres. We had a lot of problems with groundwater at first, but things are sorted out now. For understandable reasons we had to protect Central Security, avoid any kind of attacks from the air, for example, and if necessary the underground of the Big O serves as a nuclear bunker.'

'That means that if England falls—'

'—Orley will still be standing.'

'The King is dead, long live the King.'

'Don't worry.' Norrington smiled. 'England isn't going to fall. Our country is changing, we had to accept the disappearance of the red telephone boxes and the red buses, but the Royal Family is non-negotiable. If it comes to the crunch, we still have room for the King down here.'

He led them into a conference room with holographic screens running all the way around it. Two women stood in hushed conversation. Jericho recognised one of them straight away. The deep black pageboy cut over the pale face belonged to Edda Hoff. The other woman was plump, with appealing if grumpy features, blue-grey eyes and short, white hair.

'Jennifer Shaw,' she said.

In charge of Central Security, Jericho completed in his head. Guard dog number one in the global Orley empire. Hands were shaken again.

'Coffee?' asked Jennifer. 'Water? Tea?'

'Something.' Tu had spotted a memory crystal reading device, and was making resolutely towards it. 'Anything.'

'Red wine,' said Yoyo.

Jennifer raised an eyebrow. 'Medium-bodied? Full-bodied? Barrel-aged?'

'Something along the lines of a narcotic, if possible.'

'Narcotic and anything,' nodded Edda Hoff, went outside for a moment and came back in as the others were taking their seats. Tu put the crystal in the reader and nodded to everyone.

'With your permission we'll let an old rascal speak first,' he said. 'It is to him that you owe your glimpse into the sick brain of your enemies, and in any case I should like to sweep away any remaining doubts about our credibility.'

'Where is the man now?' Jennifer leaned back.

'Dead,' said Jericho. 'He was murdered right in front of my eyes. They were trying to stop him passing on his knowledge.'

'Plainly without success,' said Jennifer. 'How did you come into possession of the crystal?'

'I stole his eye,' said Yoyo. 'His left one.'

Jennifer thought for a second.

'Yes, you should baulk at nothing. Let your dead friend take the floor.'

'The whole thing, erm, seems to be some sort of satellite breakdown,' said Tom Merrick, the IT Security supervisor, after Vogelaar had evoked Armageddon under West Africa's streaming sky. 'At least that's what it looks like.'

'What else could it be?' asked Jericho.

'Right, that's a bit complicated. First of all, satellites aren't things that you can click on and off as you feel like it. You have to know their codes if you want to control them.' Merrick's gaze slipped away. 'Okay, you can find out that kind of thing through espionage. You can knock out a communications satellite with directed data streams, for a few hours or a day, you can also destroy it with radiation, but what we have here is a total breakdown, you understand? We can't contact either Gaia or Peary Base.'

'Peary Base?' echoed Tu. 'The American moon base, right?'

'Exactly. For that one all you'd need to do is black the LPCS, the lunar satellites, because of the libration, but—'

'Libration?' Yoyo looked blank.

'The Moon seems to stand still,' Norrington cut in before Merrick could reply. 'But that's an illusion. It does in fact rotate. Within one Earth rotation, it turns once on its own axis, with the effect that we always see the same side. That's a thing called bound rotation, typical, by the way, of most of the moons in the solar system. However—'

'Yes, yes!' Merrick nodded impatiently. 'You have to explain to them that the angular velocity with which the Moon circles a larger body, in terms of its own rotation—'

'I think our guests would like you to keep it simpler, Tom. Basically the Moon, because of its rotation behaviour, wobbles slightly. As a result, we get to see more than half of the Moon's surface, in fact it's almost sixty per cent. Conversely, the marginal regions disappear at times.'

'And they disappear from radio range,' Merrick broke in. 'Conventional radio requires visual contact, unless you have an atmosphere that reflects radio waves, but there isn't one on the Moon. And at the moment the North Pole and Peary Base are in the libration shadow, so they can't be reached directly from the Earth via radio waves. So the Moon has been equipped with ten satellites of its own, the Lunar Positioning and Communication System, LPCS for short, which circle one another within range of the base. We're in constant contact with at least five of them, so we should be able to contact Peary, regardless of libration.'

'And what's to say that somebody hasn't taken control of precisely those ten satellites?'

'Nothing. That is to say, everything! You know how many satellites you would have to knock out to cut off the whole of the Moon from the Earth? Gaia doesn't actually have a libration problem, it's in visual range, so it can be reached at any time by TDRS satellites, even without LPCS. Except we no longer have a connection with Gaia either.'

'So someone must be blocking—'

'—terrestrial satellites too, yes, that's one hell of a lot of codes, but yes, I think so. It's just not a lot of use to them in the long term. They could attack TDRS headquarters in White Sands and paralyse all the Tracking and Data Relay Satellites at a stroke, but then we'd just switch to ground stations or civilian stations like Artemis, which are equipped with S-band transponders and pivotable antennae. How would anyone interfere with all of those?'

'That's precisely the problem,' said Edda Hoff. 'We're in touch with every available ground station in the world. There's no contact up there.'

'After the breakdown of the conference system we immediately informed NASA and Orley Space in Washington,' said Jennifer. 'And of course the Mission Control Center in Houston, our own control centres on the Isla de las Estrellas and in Perth. Nothing but radio silence.'

'And what could be the reason for that?' Jericho rubbed the tip of his chin. 'If not interference with the satellites?'

Merrick studied the lines in his right palm.

'I don't know yet.'

'Are Peary Base and Gaia cut off from one another as well?'

'Not necessarily.' Norrington shook his head. 'There's a non-satellite laser connection between them.'

'So if you got through to the base—'

'Our message could be passed on to Gaia.'

Jennifer leaned forward. 'Listen, Owen, I won't deny that until a moment ago I had some doubts about whether the evidence you have points convincingly to a threat to Gaia. You three could have been a gang of hysterical fantasists.'

'And what's your opinion now?' asked Tu.

'I'm inclined to believe you. According to your file, the bomb has been dormant up there since April of last year. The opening of Gaia was actually planned for 2024, but the Moon crisis thwarted that one. So it would make sense to detonate the bomb now that it's finished. As soon as we get a warning through to the hotel, someone sabotages our communication, another clue that it *is* going to happen, but above all that someone's got their eye on us, during these very seconds. And that's extremely worrying. On the one hand because it suggests that we have a mole in our ranks, on the other because it means that someone up there will try to get the bomb into Gaia and set it off, if they haven't done so already.'

'Listening to Vogelaar,' Norrington said, 'you'd see the Chinese everywhere.'

'Not impossible.' She paused. 'But Julian already suspected someone before the connection was severed. A guest. In fact *the* guest, the last to join the group. The perpetrator might be known to us.'

'Carl Hanna,' said Norrington.

'Carl Hanna.' Jennifer nodded. 'So please be so kind as to get hold of his papers for me. Screen the guy, I want to know what he had for breakfast! Edda, put me through to NASA and issue orders to the OSS. Our people or theirs need to send a shuttle to Gaia.'

Hoff hesitated. 'If the OSS has capacity at the moment.'

'I don't care whether they have capacity. I just care that they do it. And *straight away*.'

Aristarchus Plateau, The Moon

The rover Julian had mentioned was parked in the dugout, but the second was stranded on the runway, scorched as if it had got in the way of a shuttle jet. All that remained of the third one, however, was a pile of junk. Debris lay scattered all around the place, so Momoka immediately set off in search of Locatelli's remains. She scoured the area in grim silence. After that it was agreed that Locatelli wasn't here, and nor was any part of him.

They all knew what that meant. Locatelli must have managed to get on board the shuttle.

They listlessly trawled through the hangars. Clearly the Schröter spaceport was still in the finishing stages. Everything suggested that air-locks and pressurised habitats were planned, so that people would be able to survive here for a while, but nowhere was there a sign of a life-support system. A cold room, for the preparation of foodstuffs, lay abandoned. The section of the hangar in which the moonmobile was parked was identified by inscriptions stating that grasshoppers should have been stored there, but there was no sign of one far or wide.

'Well,' Evelyn observed caustically, after glances into steel containers that should have contained spacesuits revealed nothing but a yawning void, 'theoretically, at least, we're in safety. The whole thing should just have happened four weeks later.'

'Is the stupid moonmobile really all we've got?' groaned Momoka.

'No, we've got more than that,' said Julian's voice. He was walking through the next room with Amber and Rogachev. 'You should come over here.'

'Nothing that flies,' he went on, 'but a few things that drive. That burnt rover out there hasn't got any prettier, but it does work. So along with the one in the hangar we've got two. And look what Amber has found: charged replacement batteries for both vehicles, and in the boot of the undamaged rover enough extra oxygen for two people.'

'There are five of us,' said Momoka. 'Can we connect the tanks to our suits in alternation?'

'Yeah, that's fine. The supplies wouldn't get you to Gaia, and the rovers would be worthless in the Alps. But whatever happens, our supplies will be enough to take us to the mining station.'

'And does anyone know the way?'

Amber waved a stack of slides around. 'These guys do.'

'What, *maps*?'

'They were in the rover.'

'Oh, great!' Momoka snorted. 'Like Vasco da Gama! What sort of crap technology is that, when you can't even program in your journey?'

'The technology of a civilisation that increasingly confuses its achievements with magic,' Rogachev coolly. 'Or might it have escaped you that the satellite communication has gone down? No guidance system without LPCS.'

'It hasn't escaped me,' said Momoka sulkily. 'And incidentally, I've got a constructive remark as well.'

'Let's hear it.'

'We can't really make ourselves comfortable in this mining station, can we? I think we've got to make contact with the hotel, and that doesn't seem to be happening at the moment because of the satellite strike. So how are we going to get to the hotel under our own power?'

'What are you getting at?'

'Are there any flying machines in the mining station?'

'Maybe some grasshoppers.'

'Yeah, those'll get you around the Moon just fine, but at a snail's pace. Except, if I remember correctly, the helium tanks are taken to the Pole by magnetic rail. Right? That means there's a station there, and a train goes from there to Peary Base. And from Peary Base—'

Julian said nothing.

Of course, he thought. That might work. How obvious! Hard to believe, but just for a change Momoka really had come up with something constructive.

Ganymede

Locatelli stared at the control displays.

He had worked out by now that Hanna was taking his bearings from the holographic map, a kind of substitute LPCS. The outside cameras synched a real-time image of the visible area of the landscape with a 3D model in the computer into which you'd programmed your destination and route. That meant you could hold a steady course, practically on autopilot, because the system continually corrected itself, although that called for a high altitude. Locatelli guessed that Hanna had programmed in a destination that the controls were unable to tell him anything about. He would have bet that the Canadian was flying back to the hotel, but they were too far west for that. To get to Gaia he would have had to take a north-easterly course, and instead it looked as if he was stubbornly heading due north at fifty degrees longitude.

Was Hanna trying to get to the Pole?

Questions accumulated. Why did Hanna not use LPCS? How did you land a thing like that? How did you slow down? They were hurtling along at twelve hundred kilometres an hour, ten kilometres up, extremely worrying. How long would their fuel hold out if the jets had to constantly generate thrust in order to keep Ganymede at this altitude and accelerate at the same time?

He picked up his helmet and tried to make contact with Momoka via his suit connection. When he received no answer, he tried to get through to Julian and switched to conference reception. Nothing but atmospheric hiss. Perhaps the suit systems didn't work at such distances. After all, they had been flying northwards for half an hour. Glancing at the map, he scanned the distances and reached the conclusion that there must by now be over five hundred kilometres between the shuttle and the Aristarchus Plateau. On the right, a considerable way off, a crater stood out in the middle of a plateau: Mairan, the map told him. Another, Louville, appeared over the edge of the horizon to the north. It was time to get to know the cockpit. It must at least be possible to contact the hotel from the Ganymede.

His eye fell on a diagram above the windscreen, which he hadn't noticed until then. A simple set of instructions, but enough to get him to the main menu, and suddenly everything was much easier than he'd thought. Admittedly he still didn't know how to fly the thing, but at least he knew how to work the radio. His disappointment was all the greater, then, when he still heard nothing but silence. At first he thought the radio mustn't be working, but then at last he worked out that the satellites were out of operation.

So that was why Hanna had switched to map navigation.

At the same moment he understood why he couldn't get through to anybody on conventional channels. Traditional radio meant that the partners had to be within visible range of each other, so that there was nothing between the transmitter and the receiver to absorb the radio waves, and in the case of the Moon the strong curvature quickly absorbed all contact. That was why his connection with Momoka and the others had been severed earlier on as well, because they had been on the other side of Snake Hill when the chase was taking place. Which was how he now knew the exact time of the satellite failure.

It coincided with Hanna's escape.

Coincidence? Never in a million years! There was something bigger going on here.

Behind him, Hanna groaned quietly. Locatelli turned his head. After a long search he had finally found a few straps for lashing down cargo, and tied him to the front row of seats. You couldn't exactly have claimed that he was trussed up like a parcel, but Hanna wouldn't be able to free himself quickly enough to stop Locatelli shooting him in the leg with his own gun. He studied the murderer's pale face for a moment, but the Canadian kept his eyes closed.

He turned back to the control panel. After a while he thought he had worked out various things, such as how to regulate the altitude of Ganymede, to make it climb or descend by—

That was it. Of course!

Locatelli was suddenly very excited. The Moon had no atmosphere, so in fact flight altitude couldn't have anything to do with it, although of course it meant you were eating into your fuel supplies. It didn't alter the general conditions, a vacuum was a vacuum. But the higher he climbed, the less noticeable the curvature became, until it was entirely irrelevant. As far as he remembered, only the Rupes Toscanelli Plateau stretched north-east of the Schröter Valley, with Snake Hill. If they weren't cowering under the spurs of rock right now, but had fought their way through to the space station, he *had* to get through to them!

His fingers darted over the controls. The shuttle had a frightening number of jets, he established, some pointing stiffly downwards, others backwards, others still were on a pivot. He decided to ignore the pivotable ones, and switch thrust entirely to the vertical. He entered a value at random—

Suddenly the air was squeezed from his lungs.

Damn it! Too much, much too much! What sort of stupid bloody idiot was he! Why hadn't he started with less? The idea of a calm flight was out of the window. The Ganymede shot upwards like mad, rattled, vibrated and bucked as if trying to shake him out of its innards. He quickly reduced the thrust, worked out that not all the jets were firing evenly, hence the vibrations, corrected, regulated, balanced, and the shuttle calmed down, continued climbing, now at a more moderate speed.

Good, Warren. Very good!

'Locatelli to Orley,' he shouted. 'Momoka. Julian. Come in, please.'

All kinds of white noise emerged from the speakers, but nothing that even slightly resembled human articulation. The Ganymede was approaching the thirteen-kilometre mark. After its initial bickering, it allowed itself to be ridden like the most placid of ponies, climbing constantly higher, while Locatelli shouted Julian and Momoka's names in turn.

Fourteen kilometres.

The landscape stretched below him. Again there was rattling and trembling, as the irritable automatic controls registered deviations from the longitudinal bearings and roughly compensated for them.

'Locatelli to Orley. Julian! Momoka! Oleg, Evelyn. Can anybody hear me? Come in! Locatelli to—'

14.6 – 14.7 – 14.8

He gradually started to feel queasy, even though the rational part of his brain quickly reassured him that he could theoretically fly into outer space. All just a matter of fuel.

'Momoka! Julian!'

15.4 – 15.5 – 15.6

Nothing.

'Warren Locatelli to Orley. Come in please.'

Hiss. Crackle.

'Locatelli to Orley. Julian! Momoka!'

'Warren!'

Aristarchus Plateau

'Warren! Warren! I've got Warren on the line!'

Momoka started to do a kind of St Vitus' dance around the charred rover, whose bed they had started to load with batteries. They paused, all listening. His voice rang out with promising volume in their helmets, clear and distinct, as if he were standing right next to them.

'Warren, darling, sweetie!' cried Momoka. 'Where are you? Sweetheart, oh my sweetheart! Are you okay?'

'All fine. You?'

'A few of us are missing, we don't know exactly what happened. Peter, Mimi, Marc—'

'Dead,' said Locatelli.

Not that any confirmation was required. But the word fell like a blade and guillotined the unregenerate little optimist who had, until that moment, been tirelessly coming out with all kinds of murmured ifs and could-bes. There was a moment of hurt silence.

'Where are you now?' asked Julian, audibly chastened.

'In the shuttle. Carl, the bastard, slung Peter into the gorge and then blew up Mimi and Marc, and then he hijacked the shuttle, but I managed to get on board.'

'And where's Carl?'

'He's unconscious. I knocked him out and tied him to the seats.'

'You're a hero,' cried Momoka, delighted. 'You know that? You're a goddamn hero!'

'Of course, what else? I'm a hero in a spaceship that's going incredibly fast, with no idea of how to fly the stupid thing. That is, I'm getting the hang of it now. Turning round, getting down and landing, not so sure about.'

'Can you get through to the hotel?' asked Julian.

'Don't think so. Too far away, too many mountains. I'm over fifteen kilometres up, to be quite honest I'm starting to feel something like vertigo. And I don't know how much gas I've got left.'

'Fine, no problem. I'll help. Just stay up there for the time being, because of the radio connection.'

'The LPCS has failed, right?'

'Sabotage, if you ask me. Did Carl actually say anything to you?'

'I didn't give him much of a chance to say anything.'

'Oh, my hero!'

'Do you know your position?'

'Fifty degrees west, forty-six degrees north. On the right there's a crater plateau, with mountains attached to it.'

'Can you give me some kind of name?'

'Wait a second: Montes Jura.'

'Very good. Listen, Warren, you've got to—'

Ganymede

Locatelli listened carefully to Julian's instructions. As he did so, he found himself suspecting that his host didn't know what needed to be done down to the last detail either, but definitely had more of a notion about how to fly a Hornet shuttle than he did himself. For example, he knew how to take a bend. Locatelli would have adjusted the jets individually, and plunged to his death as a result. Whereas in fact it was relatively simple, if you bore in mind simple things like turning off the automatic course programming and switched to manual.

'Keep to the right, fly east, towards the Montes Jura, and then make a big hundred-and-eighty-degree turn and head south again.'

'I'm with you.'

'Not even nearly. Don't make any tight turns, okay? Make sure they're wide. You're going at 1200 kilometres an hour!'

Locatelli did as he was told. Perhaps he was an excessively obedient pupil, because the bend turned into an extended sightseeing tour of the landscape. When he had turned the Ganymede, he found himself to the west of forty degrees longitude, with the jagged agglomeration of the Jurassic mountains below him, arranged in a circle around a vast bay. The bay was called Sinus Iridum and adjoined the Mare Ibrium, and somehow the name struck him as familiar. Then he remembered. Sinus Iridum was the apple of discord that sparked the Moon crisis in 2024. From the windows of the cockpit he had a breathtaking view. Hardly anywhere else was the illusion of land and sea so perfect, all that was missing was a blue glow on the velvet basalt base of the Mare Ibrium. It looked particularly velvety here, most of all where it abutted the south-western foothills of the mountains.

'Where are you?' asked Julian.

'Southern half of Sinus Iridum. There's a spit of land ahead of me. Cape Heraclides. Shall I go lower? Then I won't have such a long journey down later on.'

'Do that. We'll just check how long the connection lasts.'

'Fine. As soon as it goes, I'll climb again.'

'It'll get more stable the closer you get, anyway.'

Locatelli hesitated. Going lower, fine. Perhaps it would be even better to cut back the speed a bit. Not much, just enough to take it below 1000 kilometres an hour. What he was doing wasn't even slightly comparable to a flight through the Earth's atmosphere, where you had to battle with air levels and turbulence, but hours upon hours in aeroplanes had got him used to lengthy landings, so he decelerated and began to drop.

The Ganymede plummeted like a stone towards the ground.

What had he done?

The shuttle settled at an angle. Noise flooded the interior, the tortured wails of over-extended technology.

'Julian,' he cried. 'I've fucked up!'

'What's wrong?'

'I'm crashing!'

'What have you done? Tell me what you've done!'

Locatelli's hands fluttered over the controls, uncertain about which fields they should press, which switches they should use.

'I think I've got speed and altitude regulation mixed up.'

'Okay. But don't lose your head!'

'I'm not losing my head!' yelled Locatelli, about to lose his head.

'Do the following. Just go—'

The line went dead. Shit, shit, shit! Fingers clawed, he crouched over the console. He didn't know what to do, but to do nothing would mean certain death, so he had to do *something*, but *what*?

He tried to balance out his crooked angle with a counter-thrust.

The shuttle roared like a giant wounded animal, started reeling violently and tilted to the other side. A moment later it lurched so hard that Locatelli was afraid it would break into a thousand pieces. He looked helplessly in all directions, turned his head instinctively—

Carl Hanna was staring at him.

Hanna, whose fault it all was. Under any other circumstances Locatelli would have got up, smacked him one and given him valuable advice about how to treat your holiday acquaintances, but that was out of the question right now. He saw that the Canadian was starting to tug like mad on his fetters, ignored him and bent over the console again. The shuttle was rapidly losing velocity, and tilting still further. Locatelli decided not to worry about the plunge for the time being, and instead to concentrate on stabilising his position, but the only result of his efforts was that he suddenly had no power over the controls.

'Warren, you—'

Hanna shouted something.

'—you've gone into automatic! You've got to—'

Why didn't that idiot just keep his trap shut?

'—you're out of manual! Warren, damn it to hell! Untie me.'

'Fuck off.'

'We're both going to die!'

Locatelli poked stubbornly around in the main menu. The altitude meter was counting down worryingly quickly, 5.0 – 4.8 – 4.6, they were hurtling towards the lunar ground like a meteor. A few moments before, in his excitement, he must have pressed something, he must have activated some function that had effectively disempowered him and stripped him of access to any kind of navigation. Now it looked as if he could do whatever he liked, and it would have not the slightest influence on the behaviour of the Ganymede.

'Warren!'

Who was that this time?

Try and remember, do what you did before. What worked so well under Julian's instructions. Turn off automatic pilot, switch to manual.

But how? How?

'Release me, Warren!'

Why wasn't it working this time? Bloody touchscreen! What kind of a crappy cockpit was it? Nothing but virtual fields, unfamiliar electronic landscapes, cryptic symbols instead of solid rocker switches with sensible inscriptions like HELLO, WARREN, TURN ME THE OTHER WAY AND IT'LL ALL BE FINE.

'We're going to die, Warren! That won't do anybody any good. You *can't* want that!'

'Forget it, asshole.'

'I won't hurt you, you hear me? Just set me free!'

The ground, skewed at a forty-five-degree angle, was menacingly gaining presence; the range on his right-hand side stretched its peaks over the shuttle's flight-path. As it grew closer, Sinus Iridum looked as if it were undergoing a weird and inexplicable transformation. In places the basalt plain seemed to be frozen in a process of decomposition, more mist than solid surface, with dark and mysterious phenomena in it. Little more than one kilometre separated the shuttle from the place where it was bound to crash. A vague blur turned into the line of the magnetic rail, and domes, antennae and scaffolding loomed out of it. Locatelli caught a quick glimpse of a collection of insectoid formations on an incline, and then they too were past, and they went on falling to their doom.

'Warren, you stubborn idiot!'

The worst thing was, Hanna was right.

'Fine!'

Cursing, he staggered from his seat, practically weightless, given the insane speed of their descent. Everything around him was rattling, vibrating and roaring. The floor was at such an extreme angle it was hardly possible to stand on it, except that he was floating anyway. Grabbing his gun, he made his way hand over hand towards the Canadian, crawled behind him and tugged at his bonds with his free hand.

Nothing. As if they were welded together.

Good work, Warren. Well done!

He would need both his hands. Such a bloody mess! Where should he put the gun? Wedge it under his arm, and quick! Don't panic, now. Disentangle the knots, loosen them, untie them carefully. The straps slid down. Hanna stretched his arms, leapt up, grabbed the arm of the pilot's seat and pulled himself into it. His eye fell on the console.

'Thought so,' Locatelli heard him say.

With some effort he heaved himself into the co-pilot's seat. The Canadian ignored him. He worked with great concentration, gave a series of instructions and the Ganymede righted itself. Below them drifted an endless sea of dust, blurred fingers poked from it, reaching for them, stirred up by something vast and insect-like, creeping slowly across the plain. Locatelli held his breath. In the formless grey, huge, glistening beetles seemed to be moving around, then all of a sudden he felt as if his brain were being pushed out through his ears. Hanna violently braked the shuttle. Swathes of smoke whirled in front of the glass. They thundered along blindly, far too fast! A moment ago he had been ready to smash Hanna to a pulp, now he felt a powerful desire to see him at work, as the master of the situation. Sweat ran down Hanna's face, the muscles of his jaw protruded. From the rear part of the Ganymede came a great bang that sounded like an explosion, even louder roaring, the nose of the shuttle rose—

Contact with the ground.

In a flash the landing-struts broke away. Locatelli was slung from his seat as if a giant had kicked the Ganymede in the belly. He performed a somersault and slid unimpeded to the rear. All the bones in his body seemed to want to switch places with each other. Jets hissing, the shuttle ploughed through the regolith, bounced, crashed down again, hurtled on, bucked, lurched, but the tail stayed firm. Locatelli reached desperately around for something he could hold onto. His hand closed on a stanchion. Muscles tensed, he drew himself up, lost his balance and was flying forwards when the hurtling wreck collided with something, reared up and scraped its way up a hill. Just as the machine came to rest in an avalanche of debris, he landed heavily between the seats, was carried on by his own momentum and bumped his head.

Everything around him turned red.

Then black.

Aristarchus Plateau

The brief moment of euphoria at the sound of Locatelli's voice had made way for greater anxiety. Julian was uninterruptedly trying to get through to the Ganymede, but apart from a hiss nothing issued from the speakers.

'Crashed,' Momoka whispered, over and over again.

'That needn't mean anything,' Evelyn said, trying to console her. 'Nothing at all. He must have got the thing under control, Momoka. He's done it before.'

'But he's not in contact.'

'Because he's flying too low. He *can't* get in contact.'

'We'll know in half an hour,' said Rogachev calmly. 'He should have arrived by then.'

'That's true.' Amber sat down on the floor. 'Let's wait.'

'It's not as simple as that,' said Julian. 'If we wait too long we'll use up too much oxygen. Then we won't even get to the production sites.'

'You mean we're *that* low?'

'Depends how you look at it. We could spare half an hour. But nothing must go wrong after that! And we don't know whether the rovers will get through. We may find points where they can't go on – we'll have to factor in detours.'

'Julian's right,' said Evelyn. 'It's too risky. We've just got one chance.'

'But if Warren comes and we're gone,' Momoka wailed. 'How's he supposed to find us?'

'Maybe we could leave something behind,' Rogachev said after a brief, stumped pause.

'A message?'

'A sign,' Amber suggested. 'We could form an arrow out of the debris from the wrecked rover. So that he knows in which direction we've gone.'

'Wait.' Julian was thinking. 'That's not such a bad idea. And it occurs to me that our routes should actually cross. His last position was Cape Heraclides – that was the direction he was headed. And that's exactly where we've got to get to. If we stay switched to receive, sooner or later he'll make radio contact with us.'

'You mean he—' Momoka gulped. 'He's alive?'

'Warren?' Julian laughed. 'Please! No one's going to break him, no one knows that better than you. And anyway, those things aren't that hard to fly.'

'What if he had to do a crash landing?'

'We'll meet him on the way.'

They loaded up the rovers with the spare batteries and oxygen sup-plies, carried debris, empty shelves and containers out of the shacks and arranged them all into an arrow pointing north. On the right they formed an H and a 3 out of rocks.

'Excellent,' said Evelyn contentedly.

'That's what you call a detailed location,' Amber agreed. A tiny hope was gradually forming. 'At least it'll help him find us.'

'Yes, you're right.' All the arrogance had fled from Momoka's voice. Now she only sounded terribly concerned and a tiny bit grateful. 'That's unmistakable.'

'Then we should get going,' urged Rogachev. 'Suggestions about who should take which rover?'

'Let Julian decide. He's the boss.'

'And the boss drives ahead,' said Julian. 'Along with Amber. We're polite, too, and we're going to let you guys have the nicer car.'

'Hmm, then—'

It was strange. Even though they couldn't survive here, each one of them felt the same ludicrous unease at leaving the spaceport. Perhaps because it looked like safety, even though it offered none. Now they would be heading for the desert. To no man's land.

They stared at each other, without actually being able to see anyone's face.

'Come on,' Julian decided at last. 'Let's get going.'

London, Great Britain

It was doubtless very sensible of Jennifer Shaw to have brought in people from Scotland Yard who, when the talk turned to Korean nuclear material, immediately informed the SIS. Since Orley Enterprises was based on British soil, and a non-British facility seemed to be involved, MI5 and MI6 were both let loose on the company. Jericho, on the other hand, felt as if they were running on the spot. Not because he missed Xin and the witch-hunt he had unleashed, but because all initiative seemed suddenly to have been taken out of his, Yoyo's and Tu's hands. The Big O swarmed with nothing but investigators that late afternoon. Jennifer insisted on having them there for every conversation, with the result that they droned out the same endless answers to the same endless questions, until Tu, red-faced with fury, under questioning from one of Her Majesty's agents, demanded the return of his suitcase.

'What's up?' Yoyo asked irritably.

'Didn't you hear the question?' Tu pointed a fleshy finger at the officer, who impassively wrote something down in his tiny book.

'Yes, I did,' she said cautiously.

'And?'

'He really only—'

'He's insulting me! That guy insulted me!'

'I only asked you why you dodged the German authorities,' the agent said very calmly.

'I *didn't* dodge them!' Tu snapped at him. 'I never dodge anybody! But I do know which people I can trust, and police officers are rarely among them, *very* rarely.'

'That doesn't necessarily speak in your favour.'

'It doesn't?'

Edda Hoff's waxy face showed signs of life.

'Perhaps you should bear in mind that it is to Mr Tu and his companions that we owe evidence that your authorities for a long time failed to provide,' she said in that special toneless voice of hers.

The man snapped the book shut.

'Nonetheless, it would have been better for everyone if you'd only cooperated with our German colleagues from the start,' he said. 'Or did you have reasons for not wanting to?'

Tu jumped up and brought both fists down on the table.

'What are you insinuating?'

'Nothing, just—'

'Who are you, in fact? The bloody Gestapo?'

'Hey.' Jericho took Tu by the shoulders and tried to pull him back into his chair, which was like trying to shift a parking meter. 'No one's insinuating anything. They *have* to check us out. Why don't you just tell him—'

'What, then, what?' Tu stared at him. 'That guy? Am I supposed to tell him how the police threw me about for six months of my life, so I still wake up drenched in sweat? So that I'm afraid to go to sleep because it might all start up again in my dreams?'

'No, it's just—' Jericho paused. What had his friend just said?

'Tian.' Yoyo rested a hand on Tu's fist.

'No, I've had enough.' Tu shook her off, escaped Jericho's clutches and stomped away. 'I want to go to a hotel. Right now! I want a break, I just want to be left in peace for an hour.'

'You don't need to go to a hotel,' said Edda. 'We have guest rooms in the Big O. I could have one prepared for you.'

'Do that.'

The MI6 man set the book down on the table in front of him, and twisted around towards Tu as he headed for the door. 'The questioning isn't over yet. You can't just—'

'Yes I can,' Tu said as he left. 'If you really need an asshole to put under general suspicion, use your own.'

Jericho would have liked to ask Tu, otherwise so relaxed and controlled, and to whose house the Chinese police had paid regular visits only a few days before, what had provoked his rage to such an extent, but the nature of the investigations hurled him from one conversation into the next. His friend disappeared with a remarkably solicitous Edda Hoff, the MI6 investigator went on his way. For the few seconds that elapsed before the arrival of Jennifer Shaw, he felt a festering unease, particularly since Yoyo, the guardian of dark secrets, was staring ostentatiously into the distance, joining in with Tu's misery.

'And once again you know more than I do,' he said.

She nodded mutely.

'And it's none of my business.'

'It's something I can't tell you.' Yoyo turned her head towards him. Her eyes glistened as if Tu's outburst had caused new cracks in the dam of her self-control. It was slowly starting to seem to Jericho that the whole Chen family, along with their wealthy mentor, were on the edge of a nervous breakdown, in constant danger of exploding under the pressure of traumatic bulges. Whatever it was that troubled them, it was starting to get on his nerves.

'I understand,' he growled.

And he actually did understand. The phenomenon of being tongue-tied even when you *wanted* to speak was one that he was all too familiar with. He silently looked at his fingers, which were cracked, the nails jagged, the cuticles ragged. They were not attractive. He was clean, but not well looked after. Joanna had said that. For a long time he hadn't been able to tell the difference, but at that moment he wouldn't have been able to shake hands with himself. He neglected himself. Yoyo didn't love herself, and the same went for Chen, and, to a startling extent, for Tu, the rock on which all egocentricity was founded. Were there any heads left in which the past wasn't mouldering away?

Jennifer came into the room.

'I heard you don't feel like talking any more.'

'Wrong.' Yoyo rubbed her eyes. 'We just don't like people who don't know our history sticking their great fat noses into it.'

'SIS has finished stock-taking.' Jennifer handed out thin piles of paper. 'You're credible, all three of you.'

'Oh, thanks.'

'Actually you could join your friend Tian. I'm very grateful to you, seriously!' Her blue-green eyes said precisely that, and a tiny bit more.

'But?'

'I'd be even more grateful to you if you'd go on supporting our investigation.'

'We're happy to if you'll let us,' said Jericho.

'Then I assume that's resolved to our mutual satisfaction.' Jennifer sat down. 'You're familiar with the coded message, you have been able to speculate in greater detail than we have about its missing parts, you have had contact with Kenny Xin, you know about Beijing's involvement in African coups d'état, Korean mini-nukes, a conspiracy operating past all state institutions – would you like to hear something you don't already know, for a change? Does the name Gerald Palstein mean anything to you?'

'Palstein.' Jericho scoured his memory. 'Never heard of him.'

'A chess piece. A rook, more of a queen, moved by circumstances. Palstein is the Strategic Planner for EMCO.'

'EMCO the oil giant?'

'The collapsing oil giant. Formerly number one among the companies following conservative paths that are currently perishing from an overdose of helium-3. Palstein's task was supposed to be to save EMCO, and instead he has little more to do than cancel plans for exploration, close down one subsidiary after another and consign whole tribes to unemployment. In political terms not much is happening. It's all the more remarkable that Palstein won't admit defeat. In opposition to the senior board members, he took an interest in alternative energies years ago, and particularly in us. He would have liked to join us, but at the time EMCO thought we were working on things like time travel and teleporting. They didn't take the whole business, helium-3, the space lift and so on, seriously, and when the reality of what we were doing finally kicked in no one took *them* seriously. But Palstein seems quite determined to win the battle.'

'Sounds like Don Quixote?'

'That would be to underestimate him. He isn't one to tilt at windmills. Palstein knows that helium-3 is unbeatable, so he wants into the business. The only possible way is through us, and EMCO isn't exactly broke yet. But a lot of people would rather see the remaining millions being put into protection for the workers. Palstein, on the other hand, maintains that the best protection is the continuing existence of the company, and says the money should be put into maintenance projects. Maybe that's what earned him the rifle bullet.'

'Just a moment.' Jericho paused. 'There was something about this on the web. An assassination attempt on an oil manager, that's right! Last month in Canada. Nearly got him.'

'It *did* get him, but fortunately only in the shoulder. A few days previously he and Julian negotiated EMCO participation in Orley Space. By that time it was already fixed that Palstein should go to the Moon for the unofficial opening of Gaia. He'd secured himself a place years ago, but with a gunshot wound, with your arm in a sling, you don't fly to the Moon.'

'I get it. Carl Hanna went instead. The guy that Orley suspects. The one you set Norrington on.'

Jennifer's fingers slid over the tabletop. A man's face appeared on the screen, angular, with heavy eyebrows, his beard and hair shorn almost to the skin.

'Carl Hanna. A Canadian investor. At least that's what he claims to be. Of course Norrington checked him out when they were assembling the group. Now, you don't need to put people like Mukesh Nair and Oleg Rogachev under the microscope—'

'Rogachev,' Yoyo echoed.

Jennifer Shaw looked at the stack of printed pages. 'I've put together a list for you, of the guests that Julian's travelling with. You might be more familiar with some of the others. Finn O'Keefe, for example—'

'The actor?' Yoyo's eyes sparkled. 'Of course.'

'Or Evelyn Chambers. Everybody knows America's talk-show queen. Miranda Winter, always involved in some kind of scandal, darling of the tabloids; but the real money is with the investors. Most of them are well-known figures, but Hanna seemed like a blank page. A diplomat's son, born in New Delhi, moved to Canada, studied Economics in Vancouver, Bachelor of Arts and Science. Entered the stock market and investment business, repeated stays in India. Worth an estimated fifteen billion dollars, after he inherited a lot of money and invested the money cleverly, in oil and gas, by the way, before switching to alternative energies at the right time. Remains involved in Warren Locatelli's Lightyears, Marc Edwards' Quantime Inc. and a number of other companies. By his own account he considered investing in helium-3 before, but he thought it was too much of a fly-by-night proposition at first.'

'Although that's changed, as we know.'

'As have the indicators for an investment. A year and a half ago, at a sailing tournament organised by Locatelli, he met Julian and Lynn, Julian's daughter. They liked each other, but what was crucial was that Hanna thought out loud about sponsoring India's space programme because of his old associations with the place. The bait, you might say, that landed Julian like a big fat cod. The group going to the Moon had already been decided, so Julian offered him a trip for the following year.' Jennifer paused. 'You're an experienced investigator, Owen. How much of Carl Hanna's CV could be faked?'

'All of it,' said Jericho.

'His business interests have been confirmed.'

'Since when?'

'Hanna joined Lightyears two years ago.'

'Two years is nothing. Long periods abroad, possibly born abroad, standard spy stuff. In the emerging countries all our investigations trickle away, nobody's surprised when birth certificates disappear. Sloppy work by local authorities is the order of the day. Second, investor. A disguise par excellence. Money has no personality, leaves no lasting impression. No one can prove who's really invested or since when. With a bit of preparation you could pull something out of a hat and everyone will swear it's a rabbit. Do you know him personally?'

'Yep. Pleasant enough. Attentive, friendly, not exactly chatty. Bit of a loner.'

'Hobbies? Bound to be something solitary.'

'He dives.'

'Diving. Mountain-climbing. Typical interests of private investigators and secret agents. You hardly need witnesses for either.'

'Plays guitar.'

'That fits. An instrument evokes the appearance of authenticity and creates sympathy.' Jericho rested his chin on his hands. 'And now you think Palstein had to be sacrificed to make room for Hanna.'

'I'm convinced of it.'

'I'm not,' Yoyo objected. 'Couldn't Hanna have been picked for your tour group if he'd just begged nicely? I mean, one more or less, you're not going to shoot somebody for it.'

Jennifer shook her head.

'It's different with space travel. Where you're going there are no natural resources, either to move you around or keep you alive. Every breath you take, every bite you eat, every sip of water is factored in. Every extra kilo on board a shuttle is reflected in fuel. Even the space lift is no exception. Once it's full it's full. In a vehicle that accelerates to twelve times the speed of sound, you don't really want any standing room.'

'What does Norrington have to say so far?'

'Hmm. The CV looks watertight. He's working on it.'

'And you're quite sure Hanna's our man?'

Jennifer said nothing for a while.

'Look, your late friend Vogelaar spouted a whole lot of hints. About China, the Zheng Group above all. The Russians used to be the bad guys, now it's the Chinese. Should we be bothered that Hanna's about as Chinese as a St Bernard dog? If Beijing really is behind the attack, they couldn't do anything better than send up a European, everything signed and sealed, in our lift and with an invitation from Gaia. Someone who can move about freely up there. But, Owen, I'm sure that Hanna's our man. Julian himself gave us confirmation of that before he got cut off.'

Yoyo glanced at the guest list and set it down again. 'That means, the more we know about the attack on Palstein, the better we understand what's happening on the Moon. So where is this guy based? Where is EMCO based? In America?'

'In Dallas,' said Jennifer. 'Texas.'

'Great. Seven – no, six hours behind. Our friend Palstein's having lunch. Give him a call.'

Jennifer smiled. 'That's what I was just going to do.'

Dallas, Texas, USA

Palstein's office was on the seventeenth floor of EMCO headquarters, close to several conference rooms which, like inadequately insulated basements, filled again every hour with the brackish water of bad news, every time it seemed just to have been emptied. The meeting in which he had now been stuck for over two hours was no exception. An exploratory project off the coast of Ecuador, at a depth of 3000 metres, launched as a blue-chip enterprise but now nothing but a rusting legacy. Two platforms, giving rise to the question whether they should be dragged to land or sunk, which hadn't been that easy to answer in the wake of the legendary Brent Spar debacle.

His secretary came into the room.

'Would it be possible for you to come to the phone for a moment?'

'Is it important?' Palstein asked with barely concealed gratitude at being temporarily removed from the ranks of the dead.

'Orley Enterprises.' She looked around with an encouraging smile. 'Coffee, anyone? Espresso? Doughnuts?'

'Subsidies,' said an elderly man in a croaking voice. No one laughed. Palstein got to his feet.

'Have you heard anything yet from Loreena Keowa?' he asked as he left the room.

'No.'

'Right.' He looked at his watch. 'I guess she'll be on the plane already.'

'Shall I try her mobile?'

'No, I think Loreena was going to take a later flight. She said something about getting in around twelve.'

'Where?'

'Vancouver.'

'Thanks for that. You've just reinforced my certainty that I will keep my job for another while yet.'

He stared at her.

'Twelve o'clock in Vancouver is two o'clock in Texas,' she said.

'I see!' He laughed. 'My goodness. What would I do without you?'

'Exactly. Small conference room, video link.'

A tense-looking group appeared on the wall monitor. Jennifer Shaw, the security chief of Orley Enterprises, was sitting with a fair-haired, stubbly man and a remarkably pretty Asian girl at a battered-looking table.

'Sorry to bother you, Gerald,' she said.

'Not sorry you did.' He smiled and leaned, arms folded, against the edge of the desk. 'Good to see you, Jennifer. I'm afraid I haven't got much time at the moment.'

'I know. We dragged you out of a meeting. Can I introduce you? Chen Yuyun—'

'Yoyo,' said Yoyo.

'And Owen Jericho. Unfortunately the reason for my call is anything but welcome. However, it may illuminate some questions that you may have been asking yourself every day since Calgary.'

'Calgary?' Palstein frowned. 'Let's hear it.'

Jennifer told him about the chance of a nuclear attack on Gaia, and that someone had probably wanted him out of the way to make room for a terrorist in Julian's tour group. Palstein's thoughts wandered to Loreena.

Someone wanted to stop you doing something. It seems to me it was going to the Moon with Orley.

'My God,' he whispered. 'That's terrible.'

'We need your help, Gerald.' Jennifer leaned forward, grumpy, plump, a monument of mistrust. 'We need all the picture evidence that the American and Canadian authorities hold about the attack on you, and any other information you might have, texts, state of the investigation. Of course we could take the official route, but you know the people involved in the investigation personally. It would be nice if you could speed up the process. Texas has a busy afternoon ahead, full of hard-working officials who might still be able to give us something today.'

'Have you called in the British police?'

'Special Branch, the Secret Intelligence Service. Of course we'll immediately pass on the material to the State authorities, but as you can imagine my job description doesn't just involve passing things on.'

'I'll do what I can.' Palstein shook his head, visibly agitated. 'Sorry, but this is all a big nightmare. The attempt on my life, and now this. It's less than a week since I wished Julian a pleasant journey. We were going to sign contracts as soon as he got back.'

'I know. Still no reason not to.'

'Why would anyone want to destroy Gaia?'

'That's what we're trying to find out, Gerald. And possibly, at the same time, who it was that shot you.'

'Mr Palstein.' The fair-haired man spoke for the first time. 'I know you've been asked this a thousand times, but do you suspect anyone yourself?'

'Well.' Palstein sighed and rubbed his eyes. 'Until a few days ago I would have sworn that someone was just venting his disappointment, Mr—'

'Jericho.'

'Mr Jericho.' Palstein was already standing with one foot in the adjacent conference room. 'We've had to fire an awful lot of people recently. Close down firms. You know what's going on. But there are people who assume the same as you do. That the purpose of the attack was to keep me from flying to the Moon. Except that nobody's been able to tell me why.'

'Things are clearer now.'

'Distinctly so. But these people – or one person, to be more precise – they don't rule out Chinese interests being involved.'

Jennifer, Jericho and the girl exchanged glances.

'And what leads these people to make their assumption?'

Palstein hesitated. 'Listen, Jennifer, I've got to go back in, hard as it is. First I'll make sure that you get hold of the material as quickly as possible. But there's one area in which I'll have to ask you to be patient.'

'Which is that?'

'There's a film that *possibly* shows the man who shot me.'

'What?' Chen Yuyun sat bolt upright. 'But that's exactly what—'

'And you'll get it.' Palstein raised both hands in a conciliatory manner. 'Except that I've promised the person who found the film that I'd keep it under wraps for the time being. In a few hours I will call that person and ask them to release the video, and until then I ask for your understanding.'

The pretty Chinese girl stared at him.

'We've been through quite a lot,' she said quietly.

'Me too.' Palstein pointed at his shoulder. 'But fairness dictates that sequence of events.'

'Fine.' Jennifer smiled. 'Of course we'll respect your decision.'

'One last question,' said Jericho.

'Fire away.'

'The man the person thinks is the murderer – can you make him out clearly?'

'Pretty clearly, yes.'

'And is he Chinese?'

'Asian.' Palstein fell silent for a moment. 'Possibly Chinese. Yes. He's *probably* Chinese.'

Cape Heraclides,
Montes Jura, The Moon

Locatelli was amazed. He had reached a great insight, namely that his head was the Moon, his scalp the Moon's surface, with the maria and the craters pulled over the concave bulge of the bone. From this he learned two things: one, why so much moon dust had trickled into his brain, and two, that the whole trip as he remembered it had never happened at all, but had sprung entirely from his imagination, particularly the regrettable last chapter. He would open his eyes, trusting to the comforting certainty that no one could reproach him for anything, and even the impression of constantly whirling grey would find a natural explanation. The only thing that still puzzled him was the part the universe played in the whole thing. That it was pressing against the right side of his face amazed and confused him, but since he only had to open his eyes—

It wasn't the universe. It was the ground he was lying on.

Click, click.

He raised his head and gave a start. A circular saw was running through his head. Shapes, colours – all were a blur, all bathed in a diffuse light, at once dazzling and crepuscular, so that he had to shut his eyelids tight. A constant clicking sound reached him. He tried to raise a hand, without success. It was busy somewhere with the other one, they were both off behind his back and refused to be parted.

Click, click.

His vision cleared. A little way off he saw ungainly boots and something long that swung gently back and forth and bumped with the regularity of Chinese water torture against the edge of the pilot's seat, on which the owner of the boots was crouching. Locatelli twisted his head and saw Carl Hanna, who was looking at him thoughtfully, his gun in his right hand, as if he had been sitting there for an eternity. He was rhythmically tapping the barrel against the seat.

Click, click.

Locatelli coughed.

'Did we crash?' he croaked.

Hanna went on looking at him and said nothing. Images merged to form mem-ories. No, they had landed. A crash landing. They'd gone hurtling across the regolith and collided with something. From that point onwards he could remember only that they must have switched roles in the meantime, because he was now the one who was tied up. Seething shame welled up in him. He'd messed up.

Click, click.

'Can you stop tapping that bloody thing against the chair?' he groaned. 'It's really annoying.'

To his surprise Hanna actually did stop. He set the gun aside and rubbed the point of his chin.

'And what will I do with you now?' he asked.

It didn't sound as if he really expected a constructive suggestion. Instead, there were undertones of resignation in his words, a hint of quiet regret that frightened Locatelli more than if Hanna had shouted at him.

'Why don't you just let me go?' he suggested hoarsely.

The Canadian shook his head. 'I can't do that.'

'Why not? What would be the alternative?'

'Not to let you go.'

'Shoot me down, then.'

'I don't know, Warren.' Hanna shrugged. 'Why do you have to act the hero on top of everything?'

'I understand.' Locatelli gulped. 'So why didn't you do that a long time ago? Or do you have some sort of quota? No more than three in a single day? You bastard!' All of a sudden he saw the horses galloping away, with him running after them to catch them, because it probably wasn't the best idea to annoy Hanna even more, but in the meltdown of his fury all his clear thoughts had vanished. He heaved himself up, managed to get into a seated position and glared with hatred at Hanna. 'Do you actually enjoy this? Do you get off on killing people? What sort of a perverse piece of shit are you, Carl? You revolt me! What the hell are you doing here? What do you want from us?'

'I'm doing my job.'

'Your job? Was it your fucking job to push Peter into the gorge? To blow up Marc and Mimi? Is *that* your bloody job, you stupid idiot?'

Stop, Warren!

'You fucker! You piece of shit!'

Stop it!

'You fucking douche! Wait till I get my hands free.'

Oh, Warren. Stupid, too stupid! Why had he said that? Why hadn't he just *thought* it? Hanna frowned, but it looked as if he hadn't really been listening. His gaze wandered to the airlock, then suddenly he bent forward.

'Now be careful, Warren. What I do has more to do with logging trees and drying marshes. You understand? Killing can be necessary, but my job consists not in destroying something, but in preserving or building something else. A house, an idea, a system: whatever you like.'

'So what crappy system is legitimised through killing?'

'All of them.'

'You sick fuck. And for what system did you kill Mimi, Marc and Peter?'

'Stop it, Warren. You're not seriously trying to force a guilt complex on me?'

'Are you working for some fucking government or other?'

'In the end we're all working for some fucking government or other.' Hanna sat back with a sigh of forbearance. 'Okay, I'll tell you something. You remember the global economic crisis sixteen years ago? The whole world was gnashing its teeth. Including India. But there, the crisis also provoked a spike of activity! People invested in environmental protection, high tech, education and agriculture, relaxed the caste system, exported services and innovations, halved poverty. A billion and a half predominantly young, extremely motivated architects of globalisation pushed their way to third place in the global economy.'

Locatelli nodded, puzzled. He hadn't the faintest notion why Hanna was telling him this, but it was better than being shot for want of conversational material.

'Of course Washington wondered how to respond. For example they were troubled by the idea that a stronger India, if it got closer to Beijing, might forget about good old Uncle Sam. What bloc would crystallise out of that? India and the USA? Or India, China and Russia? Washington had always seen the Indians as important allies, and would have loved to use them against China, for example, but New Delhi was insisting on autonomy, and didn't want to be talked round, let alone used, by anybody.'

'What does all this have to do with us?'

'In this phase, Warren, people like me were sent to the Subcontinent to make sure all the spin was going in the right direction. We were instructed to support the Indian miracle with all our might, but when the Chinese ambassador was blown up in 2014 by LeMGI, the League for a Muslim Greater India, Indo-Chinese relations darkened just at the right moment, favouring the finalisation of certain important Indo-American agreements.'

'You are – hang on a second!' Locatelli flashed his teeth. 'You're not trying to tell me—'

'Yep. It's thanks to some of these agreements, for example, that your solar collectors make such a huge profit on the Indian market.'

'You're a bloody CIA agent!'

Hanna gave a mildly complacent smile. 'LeMGI was my idea. One of a huge number of tricks to offset the possibility of Chinese–Indian–Russian bloc formation. Some of those tricks worked, occasionally at the cost of human lives – our own, in fact. With all due respect for your genius, Warren, people like you get rich and influential under certain conditions that had to be put in place by other people, if necessary the bloody government. Can you rule out the possibility that your market leadership on the other side of the planet might have been bought with a few human lives?'

'What?' Locatelli exploded. 'Are you off your head?'

'Can you rule it out?'

'I'm not the damned government! Of course I can—'

'But you're a beneficiary. You think I'm a bastard. But you only looked on while I did something that everybody does, and from which you profit every day without a thought. The paradigm shift in energy supply, aneutronic, clean fusion, that sounds good, really good, and the improved yield of your solar cells has revolutionised the market in solar panels. Congratulations. But when has anyone ever risen to the top without others falling? Sometimes you need a bit of help, and we're the ones who provide it.'

Locatelli looked into Hanna's eyes for the twitch that betrays the presence of lunacy, – tics, traumas and inner demons – but there was nothing but cold, dark calm.

'And what does the CIA want from us?' he asked.

'The CIA? Nothing, as far as I know. I'm no longer part of the family. Until seven years ago I was paid by the State, but one day you realise that you can get the same job from the same people for three times the pay. All you have to do is go independent on the free market, and call your boss not Mr President, but Mr CEO. Of course you've always known that you were actually working for the Vatican, the Mafia, the banks, the energy cartels, the arms producers, the environmental lobby, the Rockefellers, Warren Buffets, Zheng Pang-Wangs and Julian Orleys of this world, so from now on you're just working directly for them. It may of course happen that you go on representing the interests of some government or other. You just have to extend the concept of government appropriately: to groups like Orley Enterprises, which have accrued so much power that they *are* the government. The world is governed by companies and cartels, crossing all national boundaries. The overlaps with elected parliamentary governments are anywhere between random and complete. You never really know exactly who you're working for, so you stop asking, because it doesn't make any difference anyway.'

'I'm sorry?' Locatelli's eyes threatened to pop from his head. 'You don't even know *who* you're doing this for?'

'I couldn't tell you unequivocally, at any rate.'

'But you've killed three people!' Locatelli yelled. 'You stupid arse-hole, with your secret-agent attitude, you don't do something like that just because it's a *job*!'

Hanna opened his mouth, shut it again and ran his hand over his eyes as if to wipe away something ugly that he'd just seen.

'Okay, it was a mistake. I shouldn't have told you all that, I should be cleverer! It always ends up exactly the same, with somebody saying arsehole. Not that I'm insulted, it's just all that wasted time. Annihilated capital.'

He got to his feet, grew to menacing, primeval height, two metres of muscle encased in steel-reinforced synthetic fibre, crowned by the cold intelligence of an analyst who has just lost his patience. Locatelli feverishly wondered how this ridiculous conversation could be held in check.

'There was no need to kill Mimi and Marc,' he said hastily. 'You did *that* out of pure pleasure at least.'

Hanna shook his head thoughtfully.

'You don't understand, Warren. You know people like me from the movies, and you think we're all psychopaths. But killing isn't a pleasure or a burden. It's an act of depersonalisation. You can't see a person and a goal at the same time. Back in the Schröter Valley, those three were too close, even Mimi and Marc. Marc, for example, would have been able to climb back along the cantilever and follow me in the second rover, not to mention Peter. I couldn't take any kind of risk.'

'In that case why didn't you just kill all of—'

'Because I thought the rest of you were up on Snake Hill, and therefore too far away to be dangerous to me. Whether you believe me or not, Warren, I'm trying to *spare* lives.'

'How comforting,' Locatelli murmured.

'But I hadn't reckoned with you. Why were you suddenly there?'

'I'd gone back.'

'Why? You didn't want to see the lovely view?'

'Forgot my camera.' His voice sounded awkward to his own ears, embarrassed and hurt. Hanna smiled sympathetically.

'The most trivial things can change the course of your life,' he said. 'That's how things are.'

Locatelli pursed his lips, stared at the tips of his boots and fought down an attack of hysterical laughter. There he sat, worrying about whether his confession of forgetfulness would be posthumously weighed against his actions, reducing his heroic status. Would it? At least there would be some kind of obituary! A stirring speech. A toast, a bit of music: *Oh Danny Boy*—

He looked up.

'Why am I still alive, Carl? Aren't you in a hurry? What's all this game-playing about?'

Hanna looked at him from dark, unfathomable eyes.

'I'm not playing games, Warren. I'm not treacherous enough for that. You were unconscious for over an hour. While you were out, I analysed our situation. Doesn't look so great.'

'Mine certainly doesn't.'

'Nor mine. I couldn't understand why I wasn't able to get the thing off the ground at the last minute. We should really have been able to avoid the crash-landing with vertical counter-thrust. But the jets failed above the ground, when we were flying through those clouds of dust, perhaps they got blocked. Unfortunately, when we came down it knocked away our ground struts, so the Ganymede is lying on its belly, dug a fair way into the ground. I probably don't need to tell you what that means.'

Locatelli threw his head back and closed his eyes.

'We can't get out,' he said. 'The airlock shaft won't extend.'

'A bit of a design flaw, if you ask my opinion. Installing the only portal on the underside.'

'No emergency exit?'

'Oh, there is: the freight-room in the tail. It can be vacuumed out and flooded with air, so in principle it's an airlock too. The rear hatch can be lowered and extended into a ramp – but as I said, the Ganymede has ploughed several kilometres through the regolith, before clattering its way into a rock face over the last few metres. There are boulders lying around all over the place, as far as the eye can see. I think some of them are blocking the hatch. It won't open more than half a metre.'

Locatelli thought about it. It was funny, in fact. Really funny.

'Why are you surprised?' he laughed hoarsely. 'You're in jail, Carl. Right where you belong.'

'But so are you.'

'So? Does it make any kind of difference whether you finish me off here or out there?'

'Warren—'

'It doesn't matter. It couldn't matter less! Welcome to prison.'

'If I'd wanted to finish you off, you would never have come round. You understand? I don't plan to finish you off.'

Locatelli hesitated. His laughter died away.

'You really mean that?'

'At the moment you aren't any sort of threat to me. You're not going to dupe me again like you did in the airlock. So you have the choice of being obstructive or cooperating.'

'And what,' Locatelli said slowly, 'would my outlook be like if I chose to co-operate?'

'Your temporary survival.'

'But temporary isn't enough.'

'All I can offer. Or let's say, if you play along, at least you won't face any danger from me. I can promise you that much.'

Locatelli fell silent for a second.

'Fine, then. I'm listening.'

Rover

Over the past half-hour Amber had given up all hope of ever reaching the production plant. Seen from a high altitude, the Aristarchus Plateau looked like a softly undulating picture-book landscape for lunar drivers, particularly along the Schröter Valley, where the terrain appeared to be entirely smooth, almost as if planed. But at ground level you got an idea of the day-to-day life of an ant. Everything grew into an obstacle. As effortlessly as the rovers were able to drive over smaller bumps and boulders in their path, thanks to their flexible axles, they proved more susceptible to the tiny craters, potholes and cracks that opened up in front of them, forcing them to navigate from one hindrance to the next at between twenty and thirty kilo-metres an hour. It was only once they were past a collection of bigger craters on the way towards the Oceanus Procellarum that the ground evened out and their progress became faster.

Since then, Amber had looked into the sky more and more often, in the hope of seeing the Ganymede appearing on the horizon, while her hope made way for the horrible certainty that Locatelli hadn't made it. Momoka, who was driving the second rover, had lapsed into silence. No one was particularly talkative. Only after quite a long time did Amber speak to her father-in-law on a special frequency so that the others couldn't listen in on the conversation.

'You kept a few things to yourself back then.'

'How do you work that out?'

'Just a gut feeling.' She scanned the horizon. 'A little thing that tells women when men are lying or not telling the whole truth.'

'That's enough of your intuition.'

'No, really. It's just that women are more gifted at lying. We've perfected the repertoire of dissimulation – that's why we can see the truth gleaming as if through fine silk when you lie. You talked about the possibility of an attack. On some Orley facility somewhere or other. Carl runs amok, communication fails, and in retrospect it becomes clear that he went behind your back two days ago and took a night-time joyride on the Lunar Express.'

'And none of it makes any sense.'

'No, it does. It makes sense if Carl's the guy who's supposed to carry out the attack.'

'Here on the Moon?'

'Don't act like I'm retarded. Here on the Moon! Which would mean that it isn't just *some facility or other*, but one in particular.'

They scooted on across the dark, monotonous basalt of the Oceanus Procellarum, already within the vicinity of the Mare Imbrium. For the first time they were able to take the rover up to its top speed, albeit at the cost of a very bumpy ride, as the chassis seesawed up and down and the vehicle kept lifting off the ground. In the distance, hills became visible, the Gruithuisen region, a chain of craters, mountains and extinct volcanic domes that stretched all the way to Cape Heraclides.

'One more thing,' said Julian. 'Can I talk to you about Lynn?'

'As long as it leads to an answer to my question, whenever you like.'

'How does she seem to you?'

'She's got a problem.'

'Tim's always saying that.'

'Given that he's *always* saying it, you really don't listen to him very often.'

'Because he's always going on at me! You know that. It's impossible to say a sensible word about the girl to him!'

'Perhaps because good sense hasn't much to do with her condition.'

'Then *you* tell me what her problem is.'

'Her imagination, I would say.'

'Oh, brilliant!' snorted Julian. 'If that were the case, I'd be inundated with problems.'

'When the imagination overpowers reason, it's always a kind of madness,' Amber observed sententiously. 'You're a bit mad too, but you're a special case. You distribute your madness to everybody with both hands, you cultivate it, people applaud you for it. You love your madness, and that's why it loves you and enables you to save the world. Have you ever been troubled by the idea that you might have overstretched yourself?'

'I worry about making wrong decisions.'

'That's not the same thing. I mean, do you ever feel anything like anxiety?'

'Everyone gets frightened.'

'Hang on there. Fear. Slight difference! Fear is the result of your startled reason, my dear Julian, it's real, because it's object-related and because it's explained by concrete factors. We're afraid of dogs, drunk Arsenal fans and possible changes to tax legislation. I'm talking about anxiety. The vague fog in which anything at all might be lurking. The anxiety that you might fail, that you might fall short, you might have misjudged yourself, that you might cause some sort of disaster, paralysing anxiety, the fear of yourself, in the end. Ever have that?'

'Hmm.' Julian fell silent for a moment. 'Should I?'

'No, what would be the point? You are who you are. But Lynn isn't like that.'

'She's never said anything about anxiety.'

'Wrong. You weren't listening, because your ears were always full of adrenalin. Do you at least know what happened five years ago?'

'I know she had a huge amount to do. My fault, perhaps. But I said take a rest, didn't I? And she did. And after that she built the Stellar Island Hotel, the OSS Grand, Gaia, she was more efficient than ever. So if it's exhaustion that you're all making such a fuss about, then—'

'We're not making a fuss,' Amber said, annoyed now. 'And by the way, I was always the one who defended you to Tim, so much so that he's been asking me if I get money for it. And every time I say, "Blessed are the ignorant." Believe me, Julian, I'm on your side, I've always had a heart for slow-witted people, I can even see some lovable aspects in *your* boneheadedness; maybe that's a product of social work. So I actually love you for not understanding the slightest thing, but that doesn't mean it has to stay that way, does it? And you still haven't worked out what's going on.'

'That's enough.'

'Just to remind you, it was *you* who wanted to talk to me about Lynn rather than answering my question.'

'So explain to me what's wrong with her.'

'You want me to explain your daughter's psyche to you, here in the middle of the Oceanus Procellarum?'

'I'd be grateful for any attempt to do so.'

'Oh my good God.' She thought for a second. 'Okay, then, the headlines: do you believe Lynn was suffering from exhaustion back then?'

'Yes.'

'Would you be surprised if I told you that overwork was the least of Lynn's problems? Otherwise she could never have run Orley Travel or built your hotels. No, her problem is that as soon as she closes her eyes, mini-Lynns of every age start crowding in on her. Baby Lynns, child Lynns, teenager Lynns, daughter Lynns, Daddy's-little-girl Lynns, who think they can only earn your recognition by becoming an even tougher cookie than you are. Lynn is absolutely terrified of this army from the past, which controls her day and night. She thinks control is everything. But she's even more afraid of losing control, because she's worried that something terrible might come to light, a Lynn who can't exist, or perhaps even no Lynn at all, because the end of control would also mean the end of her existence. Do you understand?'

'I'm not entirely sure,' said Julian, like someone moving through a forest dotted with mantraps.

'For Lynn, the idea of not having herself under control is more than frightening. For her, the loss of control basically means madness. She's afraid of ending up like Crystal.'

'You mean—' He hesitated. 'She's afraid of going *mad*?'

'Tim thinks that's the case. He's spent more time with her, he's bound to know better, but I think, yes, that's it exactly. Or it was five years ago.'

'*That's* what she's afraid of?'

'Afraid of failing, afraid of losing control and losing her mind. But what frightened her most were the terrible things she might be capable of in order to stay in control. By the way, did you know that suicide is also an act of control?'

'Why are you talking about suicide now, for heaven's sake?'

'Come on, Julian.' Amber sighed. 'Because it's all part of it. It doesn't have to be physical suicide. I mean any act of self-destruction, destruction of your health, your existence, as soon as the fear of being exposed to destruction by outside forces becomes unbearable. You'd rather destroy yourself than let someone else do it. The ultimate act of control.'

'And' – Julian hesitated – 'is it true that Lynn's showing signs again, of – of this—'

'At first I thought Tim was exaggerating. Now I think he's right.'

'But why don't *I* see it? Why doesn't something like that get through *to me*? Lynn has never shown me any weakness.'

'So do you do that? Show weakness?'

'I don't know, Amber. I don't think about things like that.'

'Exactly. You don't think. But nothing does any good, Julian. She doesn't need time off to recover. She needs treatment. A long, very long course of treatment. At the end of that she may take over Orley Enterprises completely. But she might just paint flower paintings or grow hemp in Sri Lanka. Who knows who your daughter really is. She doesn't know, at all events.'

Julian slowly breathed out.

'Amber,' he said. 'There's a chance that someone's trying to blow Gaia up with an atom bomb. And that Lynn's somehow involved.'

The revelation struck her with such force that she was momentarily lost for words. Her eyes drifted hopefully towards the sky, although she knew that Ganymede wouldn't be coming.

'How certain is it?' she asked.

'Pure speculation on the part of some people I don't even know. And I don't know anything more than that, I swear. But what happened today shows that there must be something in it. You're right, Carl's task might be to carry out the attack. And I fear – okay, there's some evidence that someone on the Moon is helping him, and—'

'You think it's Lynn?'

'I don't *want* to believe that, but—'

'Why, in God's name? It's *her* hotel. Why should she be involved in an attack on her *own* hotel?'

'Perhaps she doesn't know what's really going on, but she didn't want to show me the surveillance videos from the corridor which would have proved that Hanna was outside, travelling on the Lunar Express. She has access to all the systems in the hotel, Amber, she could interfere with the communications if she wanted, and she's aggressive and strange, a mystery—'

'And Tim's in Gaia,' whispered Amber.

Cape Heraclides

'Right, listen to me. I've got to get out of here as quickly as possible.'

'Fine.'

'I've found a grasshopper in the storeroom, and a buggy. As to the hopper, I'm worried that the steering unit was damaged in the impact, but the buggy seems intact. That means we've got to get the rear hatch open.'

'What happens if we can't get out?'

'We can get out. It won't be entirely without danger, but if we put on our spacesuits and hold on tight at the right moment, I can get us out of the Ganymede. You'll help me to shift the debris and drive the buggy out, then we'll see how it goes.'

Locatelli blinked suspiciously. 'If you're trying to trick me, Carl, then you can do your shit on your own—'

'If *you're* trying to trick *me*, Warren, I *will* do my shit on my own – is that clear?'

'Yes, it is.' Locatelli nodded respectfully.

Hanna stuck the gun in a holster on his thigh, where it disappeared completely, knelt down behind him and quickly untied him. Locatelli stretched his arms. He was careful not to make any quick movements, extended his fingers, rubbed his wrists. It was only now that he noticed the slight angle of the shuttle. He still felt dazed. He hesitantly made his way to the cockpit and looked outside. Rising terrain stretched before his eyes. There was a fine haze in the air.

Air – what was he thinking of? It was dust, lousy, omnipresent moon dust, which hung like an optical illusion over the slope and settled, a dirty grey, on the glass. It wasn't being held up by air molecules, so what was keeping the stuff up there?

'Electrostatics,' he mused.

'The dust?' Hanna joined him. 'I wondered about that too. We're very close to the production site, tons of regolith are dug up here. Still, it's amazing that it doesn't sink to the ground.'

'No, I think it does,' Locatelli guessed. 'Most of it, anyway. Remember, when we were driving the buggy we stirred up loads of it. It all fell back straight away, apart from the really fine stuff, the microscopic particles.'

'Never mind. Come on.'

They put on their helmets and body armour and established radio contact. Hanna directed Warren to the rear of the vehicle behind the last row of seats, and pointed to the line of backrests.

'Set your back against them,' he said. 'To protect you. The panes in the cockpit must be made of armoured glass, so I'll aim at one of the struts. The explosive power should be enough to crack them. Otherwise, we'll have to expect a considerable amount of flying splinters. If we're successful there's going to be a hell of a draught, so stay in the lee of the seats and hold on tight.'

'What about the oxygen? Won't it go up in flames?'

'No, the concentration's the same as it is on Earth. Ready?'

Locatelli crouched behind the row of seats. In other circumstances he would have been splendidly amused, but even as it was he couldn't complain about a lack of adrenalin release.

'Ready,' he said.

Hanna pushed in beside him, brought an almost identical-looking gun out of a holster on his other thigh, leaned into the central aisle and pointed the barrel into the cockpit. Locatelli thought he heard a high-frequency hiss, and then came a detonation, so short that the explosion seemed to swallow itself just as it was produced—

Then came the suction.

Objects, splinters and shards came flying from all directions, whirled wildly around, past him and towards the cockpit. Anything that wasn't screwed or welded down was dragged outside. The escaping air pulled on his arms and legs, and pressed him against the seat-backs. Something struck his visor, indefinable things hit his shoulders and hips, a bat swarm of brochures and books came flying aggressively at them, covers flapping frantically. A volume suddenly clung to his chest armour, slid reluctantly along it, pages fluttering, broke away and disappeared down the aisle. Everything happened in complete silence.

Then it was over.

Was it really? Locatelli waited another few seconds. He slowly pulled himself up along the back of the seat and looked towards the cockpit. Where the front panes had been, a huge hole now gaped.

'My goodness.' He gasped for breath. 'What is that thing you're firing there?'

'Homemade, secret.' Hanna got up and stepped into the aisle. 'Come on, we've got to get back to the storeroom.'

The storeroom looked less chaotic than Locatelli had expected. The individual parts of a grasshopper lay strewn over the floor. He picked them up, one by one. The steering unit had been partly destroyed, but the buggy was undamaged in its mountings – a small two-seater vehicle with a flat bed for cargo. Additional mountings indicated that if need be, six such vehicles could be transported. He quickly helped Hanna unfasten the buggy. The loading hatch, which was also the back wall of the store-room, was slightly open, as if it had been dented in the impact. A hand's breadth of starry sky gleamed in at them. Hanna walked over to a rolling wall, opened it, took out batteries and two survival backpacks and stuffed everything on the bed of the buggy. They left the cargo area and helped each other out of the hole in the cockpit. The ground lay some metres below them. Locatelli jumped nimbly down, rounded the nose of the beached Ganymede and, holding his breath, looked out across the plain.

It was a ghostly sight.

As far as the eye could see, areas of swirled-up regolith stretched across the Sinus Iridum to form the swirling shape of a bell. Where the dust became more permeable, the velvety nature of the background seemed to have made way for a darker consistency. A swathe of destruc-tion led from the clouds of dust to the beach of the rising rocky terrain on which they stood, continued there as a jagged gap, described an upward curve and ended at the shuttle which, as Locatelli recognised now, had collided with an overhang and produced an avalanche. Boulders of all sizes had piled up around the tail of the Ganymede; some had rattled down the hill, but one of the biggest bits of rubble blocked the lower third of the rear hatch. The craggy ridge of the Jura Mountains ran to the north-west.

'Not all that much,' Hanna observed. 'I was afraid the rubble would reach all the way up.'

'No, it's not much,' Locatelli confirmed sourly. 'It's just that they're bloody enormous. That one there must weigh several tonnes.'

'Divided by six. Let's get to work.'

Gaia, Vallis Alpina

At half past six, Dana called the search parties back to headquarters. Lynn and Sophie had scoured most of the staff accommodation and part of the suites in the thorax, Michio Funaki and Ashwini Anand had crept like cockroaches through the greenhouses, and had turned every scrap of green and every tomato upside down before devoting themselves to the meditation centre and the multi-religious church. The third team, last of all, was able to report that the pool, the health centre and the casino were, as Kokoschka put it, clean, stressing the word like Philip Marlowe after patting down a suspect.

'And that's exactly where the problem lies,' said Dana. 'In appearance. Have we had a chance to look inside the walls and floors? In the life-support systems?'

Kokoschka waved his detector tellingly. 'Didn't even click.'

'Yes, of course, but we don't know enough about mini-nukes.'

'It was your idea to search the hotel,' Lynn said furiously. 'So don't start telling us it was pointless. And besides, Sophie and I *did* look in the life-support systems, anywhere there might be room for such a thing.'

'So?' Dana stared at her with X-ray eyes. 'How do you know how much room a mini-nuke takes up?'

'That's not fair, Dana,' said Tim quietly.

'I'm not being unfair in the slightest,' she replied, without looking at him. 'I'm concerned with minimising risks, and the search contributed to that. We've looked in the important places, I was in the head, even though I'm still of the view that there might be a bomb at some deeper, more central point.'

'Or not,' mused Anand. 'It's an atom bomb. The explosive force would be huge, so that it might not matter where you put it.'

'It might not.' Dana nodded slowly. 'At any rate what I've heard doesn't put my mind at rest. At least I was able to have a conversation with Peary Base. As I suspected, they've got the same problem, they've lost contact with the Earth and our shuttles, and they're also in the libration shadow. After I told the deputy commander a short version of—'

'What?' Lynn exploded. 'You told him what's going on here?'

'Calm down. I was—'

'You told him about the bomb?' Lynn jumped to her feet. 'You're not going to do that, do you hear me? We can't afford that!'

'—told the deputy commander—'

'Not without my authorisation!'

'—about the satellite failure,' Dana said, very slightly louder, but with a voice that sounded as if she were sawing through a bone. 'And told him we couldn't get through to our guests. That was what we agreed, correct, Miss Orley? After that I wanted to know if he'd received any unusual news from Earth before the satellites failed. But he didn't know anything.'

'So you *did* tell him—'

'No, I was just putting out feelers. And he didn't have anything to say. The base is an American facility. If Jennifer Shaw had decided to tell Houston about the bomb in the meantime, she got there too late. At least too late to tell the base crew before the satellites went down. They don't know anything about our problems over there, but I did take the opportunity to tell them of my concerns for the fate of the Ganymede. Against a background of a possible accident.'

Lynn's gaze darted around the room and fixed itself on Tim.

'We can't run the risk of this getting out.'

'If the Ganymede doesn't reply soon, it *will* get out,' said Dana. 'Then we'll have to ask the base to send a shuttle to the Aristarchus Plateau to take a look.'

'No way! We mustn't worry Julian's guests.'

Oh, Lynn! Disastrous, disastrous. Tim resisted the impulse to rest his hand on her forearm like a nurse.

'So what would you do?' he asked quickly.

'Perhaps—' She kneaded her fingers, struggled for clarity. 'First keep looking.'

'The guests will be back in half an hour,' said Funaki. 'They'll want their drinks.'

'Let Axel take care of that. No, you, Michio. You're the face of the bar. The rest of us will have to take our time. Stay calm. We'll have to plan the next few steps *calmly*.'

'I'm calm,' said Dana blankly.

'I'll take another look at the surveillance videos,' Sophie suggested. 'From the night Hanna disappeared and the ones from the day after.'

'What for?' asked Kokoschka. Only now did Tim notice that the chef was staring steadily at the freckled German girl from his hungry St Bernard's eyes, as if testing the quality of her cuts, loins, rump and breasts, and that his eyes darted furtively away every time she looked back. Aha, he thought, the cook's in love.

'Right.' Sophie shrugged. 'Whoever re-edited the recordings would have had to turn up in the control centre, right? I mean, he must have been captured on some camera or other. So if we can reconstruct—'

'Good idea!' Lynn cried exuberantly. 'Very good! Carl and this – this second person. We'll have to pump them.'

'Pump them,' echoed Dana.

'Have you got a better suggestion?' Lynn sneered.

'But Hanna isn't here.'

'So? Julian will be here soon, and he'll bring him with him. Why should we drive ourselves nuts until then? Let's ask him, and besides' – her eyes gleamed – 'nothing can happen to us here as long as we keep Carl in Gaia! He's hardly going to atomise himself.'

'Course not,' Kokoschka addressed his paunch. 'Suicide bomber. Never heard of it.'

'What do you mean?' Lynn snapped. 'Are you trying to provoke me?'

'What?' The chef recoiled and ran his hand nervously over his bald head. 'No, I – sorry, I didn't mean to—'

'Does Carl Hanna look like an Islamist or something?'

'No, sorry. Really.'

'Then stop talking such rubbish!'

'We – Our nerves are all a bit on edge.'

'Didn't you say the Chinese were behind it?' Anand asked uncertainly.

'This guy Jericho said that,' Sophie replied.

'How many Chinese Islamists are there?' Funaki pondered.

'Interesting question.'

'Oh, nonsense!' Dana raised her hands. 'Enough. Christians have taken the shortcut to heaven too. Such rubbish! In my view Lynn's just produced an argument that gives us a bit of time, as long as we can really lay our hands on this ominous second person. I think we should do as you suggested – Anand and Kokoschka will look behind the walls and floors, Sophie will watch the videos, Funaki will go down to the service section, Lynn and I—'

'Gaia, please come in!'

Dana paused. They stared at each other. The system put through a wireless message. Seven pairs of eyes were filled with hope that the call might have come via satellite. Sophie leapt to her feet and glanced at the display.

'Callisto, this is Gaia,' she replied breathlessly.

'Hungry crowd on the way!' crowed Nina. 'Do you see us? If there's nothing on the table in five minutes, we're going over to the Chinese.'

'Fuck,' whispered Dana. 'They're in range.'

Through the panorama window of the abdomen they saw the gleaming, sunlit shuttle in the sky. The Callisto had approached the hotel from behind and was flying in a final, athletic parabola. Every trip ritually ended with a fly-past above Gaia.

'You couldn't eat as much as we've cooked,' Sophie twittered with frantic exuberance. 'How was your day?'

'Great! And we didn't care *a damn* that you haven't spoken to us for hours.'

'We didn't feel like talking to you.'

'Seriously, what's up?'

'Satellite failure,' said Sophie.

'That's what I was afraid of. We couldn't get through to Julian either. Do you know what's up?'

'Not yet.'

'Weird. How could all the satellites fail at the same time?'

'You've probably rammed them accidentally. Stop chatting now, Nina, and bring your starvelings down.'

'*Oui, mon général!*'

'Then we'll have them back,' said Anand, looking around.

'Yes.' Dana watched after the Callisto until it disappeared beyond the window. 'Plus the likelihood that one of them's playing a dirty game with us. What do you think, Lynn? Shall we give them a welcome party?'

With some relief Tim registered that Dana had switched back to first names. A peace offering? Or just a tactic to lull Lynn into a false sense of security? He didn't doubt that the hotel manager still suspected his sister of conspiracy, but Lynn visibly relaxed.

'Not a word to the guests,' she said.

'Okay,' Dana nodded. 'For the time being. But once everyone's there we'll have to make a real job of it. Either Hanna and his gang give it to us straight, or we inform the base and evacuate the hotel.'

'We'll see.'

'Let's give the Ganymede another hour.'

'What makes you think the Ganymede needs another hour?'

Lynn's really lost touch with reality, thought Tim. Or else *she's* playing the dirty game.

Error! Unauthorised thought.

'Whatever,' said Dana. 'Let's go.'

Calgary to Vancouver, Canada

'Believe me, I've really scoured the net,' said the intern. 'I can't offer you anything more than I did last night.'

The Westjet Airlines Boeing 737 plummeted in an air pocket. A hundred milli-litres of orange juice sluiced from the cup as Loreena took off the tinfoil lid, spraying over her jacket and drenching her croissant.

'Shit!' she cursed.

'Gudmundsson's time at APS—'

'Shit! Fucking shit!' Juice dripped from the tray into her lap. 'Who was APS again?'

'African Protection Services.'

'Oh, right.'

'So, before Gudmundsson's time at APS, there was this period with Mamba, the other security company that was in operation in Kenya and Nigeria at the start of the millennium, which merged with a similar kind of crowd called Armed African Services to form APS in 2010. Gudmundsson led various teams—'

'You told me that yesterday,' said Loreena, trying to use her tiny paper napkin economically.

'—and was involved in operations in Gabon and Equatorial Guinea. Are you going to eat that?'

'What?'

'The croissant. It looks pretty awful, if you ask me.'

Loreena glanced at the dripping pastry. Previously it had just been floppy, now it was floppy and wet.

'No way.'

The intern lunged across and stuck half of it in his mouth.

'Here and there we find clues that APS helped some bush dictator or other to force his way into power,' he said, chewing. 'APS always denied it, but there seems to be something in it. So Gudmundsson might have been involved in a coup before he left the company to go freelance. APS was now run by a guy called Jan Kees Vogelaar, who was also a high-up in Mamba. Incidentally, Vogelaar then became a member of the government in Equatorial Guinea, that's where the coup took pl—'

'Forget it.'

'You wanted me to look into Gudmundsson's background,' the intern said, insulted.

'Yes, his, not some guy called Fogelhair or whatever his name is.' She dabbed orange juice from her trouser legs. 'Is there nothing about what he did three years ago, whether he was in Peru or somewhere? I thought they were all pretty forthcoming at Eagle Eye.'

'Patience, Pocahontas. I'm working on it.'

Loreena looked out of the window. Their flight was taking them over the Rocky Mountains. Short but turbulent. The Boeing shook. She drank the rest of the juice down and said, 'I want to give Susan as many facts as I can, you understand? She's got to work out that we can't get out of this one. We're in it up to our necks.'

'Hmyeah.' The second half of the croissant joined the first. '*Supposing* Ruiz really does have something to do with Palstein. All you've got at the moment is a suspicion.'

'I have my instinct.'

'Indian bullshit.'

'Just wait. And could you stop nattering until you've swallowed? That thing doesn't look any prettier in your oral cavity.'

'Oh, God,' sighed the intern. 'You've really got problems.'

Loreena looked outside again. The jagged ridges of the Rockies were passing far below her. The intern had meant something quite different, but what he said reminded her of Palstein's worried glance from the previous day. That she was smilingly preparing her own downfall. That she would have problems if she went on lifting up stones with creatures like Lars Gudmundsson lurking underneath them. And? Had Wood-ward and Bernstein been intimidated by the creepy-crawlies that Nixon threw at them? Palstein's anxiety was valid; Susan's worries irritated her. Was that a reason to throw away their chance to solve *their own* Watergate conspiracy?

Good intentions are useless, she thought. Courage can't be bought. Mine certainly can't.

After a while she dictated the facts of her research so far into her mobile phone, let the software turn her spoken words into writing, attached Bruford's film material and sent the dossier to both their email addresses.

Better safe than sorry.

They passed through the turbulence.

Three-quarters of an hour later the plane came down towards the foothills of the Coast Mountains and began its descent towards Vancouver International Airport. The weather was fine. Little white clouds drifted inland, sunlight glittered on the Strait of Georgia. The dark wooded body of Vancouver Island evoked Indian myths and the scent of arbor vitae and Douglas firs. As they came down, Loreena's mood lifted, because they had actually found out a hell of a lot over the previous few days. Perhaps they should settle for what they knew about Gudmundsson, and instead concentrate all their resources on researching the background to the ominous conference in Beijing. As the Boeing taxied to a standstill, she drew up a strategically sensible procedure for the imminent editorial conference, whereby she would act at first as if Palstein's name had never been mentioned. Put up a smokescreen around Susan. Enthusiastically address the topic of *Trash of the Titans*, show them her treatment, prove that they were taking their homework seriously. Then deliver their royal flush with the photograph of the fat Asian guy. Well, maybe not a royal flush. But she was perfectly willing to call what they had a full house.

'I just hope Sid's on time,' said the intern as they walked through the terminal with the woodcuts of the First Nations. 'Actually he's never on time.'

'Then we'll just wait a few minutes,' she hummed cheerfully.

'But I'm hungry. Can't we go to McDonald's first?'

'Tell your stomach—'

'Fine.'

But Sid Holland, Greenwatch's political history editor, was unusually bang on time. He had an ancient, souped-up Thunderbird, in the four-seater open-top version, and loved the car so much that he would gladly have driven half the editorial team through the district just to have a ride in it.

'Susan's looking forward to it,' he said. 'She hopes you've got something about *Trash of the Titans* in your bag.'

'Is there any breakfast?' asked the intern.

'Dude, it's half past eleven!'

'Lunch?'

Loreena looked into the azure-blue sky as the intern climbed into the back seat, and thought of her Pulitzer Prize. Sid drove the car from the airport island across the Arthur Laing Bridge and in a north-westerly direction through the neighbourhoods of Marpole, Kerrisdale and Dunbar Southlands. Past the end of the built-up areas the Pacific Spirit Regional Park began. Southwest Marine Drive, the four-lane feeder road, ran along the coast through dense vegetation towards the grounds of the university at Point Grey, far more than a classical campus, almost a small unincorporated city with a smart adjacent district of extremely Canadian-looking houses and well-tended villas. Thanks to the power of viewing figures, Greenwatch was able to live in one of the villas. Studios and editing suites were decentralised, most of the staff scattered around Canada and Alaska, so that all that remained in Point Grey were the offices of the supreme command and some stylish conference rooms. It was down to Loreena's influence that good conscience was able to unfold in elegant surroundings.

Things would go even better for Greenwatch.

The traffic was moderate, there weren't many cars about on Marine Drive. On their left the forest opened up, providing a view of a still sea and far-off, pastel-coloured mountain ranges. Hundreds of tree trunks made into rafts rested in the shallow water, evidence that the timber industry was still flourishing in spite of massive deforestation. Loreena closed her eyes and enjoyed the airstream. When she opened her eyes again, she glanced into the wing mirror.

An SUV was driving close behind them, a massive, grey off-road vehicle with darkened windows.

Suddenly she was overcome by a feeling of unease.

She wondered how often she had looked into her wing mirror over the past quarter of an hour. Probably all the time, without being aware of it. Loreena was a super-alert passenger, and her constant shouts of 'Red!' and 'When's it going to turn green?' and 'Watch where you're driving!' got on some people's nerves. Nothing escaped her. Not even who was driving behind them.

Frowning, she turned her head.

The feeling condensed into certainty. Now she was completely sure that the SUV had been tailgating them ever since the airport. The windscreen reflected the sky, so that the two occupants could only be made out very vaguely. She looked thoughtfully ahead again. The road ran evenly through luxuriant green, divided along the middle by a yellowing strip of grass on which bushes and low trees were planted at irregular intervals. Another off-road vehicle was coming towards them, equally dark, a different one.

Was she going mad? Was she developing a peculiar little paranoid fantasy? How many dark SUVs were there in Vancouver? Hundreds, certainly. Thousands. To western Canadians off-road vehicles were something like seashells to hermit crabs.

Stop thinking this stuff, she thought.

On the other hand it couldn't hurt if she jotted down the number of the car. She took out her mobile phone as the SUV suddenly switched lanes and pulled up level with them so that she couldn't see the number plate any more. Loreena knitted her brows. Fool, she thought. Couldn't you wait another few seconds? I was about to give you my—

The SUV came closer.

'Hey!' Sid honked his horn and gesticulated towards the other vehicle. 'Keep your eye on the road, you idiot!'

Still closer.

'What's up with him?' barked Sid. 'Is he drunk?'

No, thought Loreena, filled with sudden unease, no one's drunk around here. Someone knows exactly what he's doing.

Sid accelerated. So did the SUV.

'What a stupid idiot!' he raged. 'That guy ought to—'

'Careful!' yelled the intern.

Loreena saw the huge car coming, settled into her seatbelt, tried to put some distance between herself and the door, then the SUV collided with the side of the Thunderbird and forced it into the central reservation. Sid cursed and pulled the wheel round, frantically trying not to end up in the opposite lane. Veering wildly they ploughed through soil, brushed past low bushes, just missed a tree. The engine of the sports car wailed. Sid put his foot down. The SUV drew up and rammed them again, harder this time. Loreena lurched about in her seat. The metal screech of punished metal echoed in her aural passages, and suddenly they were on the opposite lane, they heard furious honking, swerved at the last moment.

'My car!' wailed Sid. 'My lovely car!'

Grim-faced, he steered the Thunderbird back onto the strip of green, but in that section someone had placed greater emphasis on bushes. They plunged noisily into a hedge. Branches flew off in all directions as the sports car crashed through several different varieties of shrub. On the right-hand side the SUV dashed along and blocked their way back onto the carriageway. Sid braked abruptly and tried to get behind the SUV, which thwarted his intention by also decelerating.

At that very moment he hurtled forward again.

This time Sid was quicker. Neatly avoiding a collision, he crossed the two opposite lanes and only just managed to dodge a motorcycle and turn into Old Marine Drive, a narrow, potholed street that led a few kilometres along the woods to the university grounds, where it opened back into the main road. There was no one to be seen for miles around; dense, dark green proliferated on both sides. Loreena registered that her seatbelt had been torn from its moorings, and clutched the edge of the windscreen.

My God, she thought. What do they want from us?

Oddly, it didn't occur to her that the attack might have anything to do with Palstein, Ruiz and the whole story. She thought instead of juvenile delinquents, carjackers or someone who did that kind of thing just for fun, who must be completely insane. She looked behind her. Potholes, woods, nothing else. For a moment she was surviving on the tender shoot of hope that Sid might have shaken off his pursuer with his manoeuvre, when he appeared behind them and came relentlessly closer.

A scraping noise emerged from the Thunderbird's engine compartment. The car stuttered.

'Faster!' she screamed.

'I'm driving as fast as I can,' Sid yelled back. Instead they were losing speed, growing steadily slower.

'You *must* be able to go faster!'

'I don't know what's going on.' Sid let go of the wheel and waved his hands around in the air. 'Something's fucked, no idea what.'

'Hands on the wheel!'

'Oh God almighty,' groaned the intern and ducked his head. The massive, dark front of the SUV roared up and crashed into them from behind. The Thunderbird gave a leap. Loreena was slung forward and bumped her head.

'Come on!' Sid pleaded with the car. 'Come on!'

Once again the SUV hammered into their rear. The Thunderbird made unhealthy noises, then their attacker was suddenly beside them, pushing them easily aside. Sid cursed, steered like crazy in the opposite direction, put his foot down, braked—

Lost control.

The moment of lift-off had the entirely curious effect that at the same moment every sound – not only that of the tyres on the gravel of the carriageway, but also the sounds of the engine, of the SUV – seemed to die away, apart from the single, bubbling call of a bird. They turned over and over in peaceful silence, the trees grew momentarily down from the sky towards them, bushy clouds sprinkled an endless blue sea of unfathomable depth, then there was a change of perspective, the wood was at an angle, a roaring and scraping, and everything was back, the whole terrifying cacophony of the crash. Loreena was hurled from her seat.

Arms flailing, she sailed through the air, while below her the Thunder-bird skidded down the embankment, undercarriage towards her, tyres spinning, an animal devouring bushes and foliage. Still flying, she became aware of the wreck abruptly reaching a standstill and coming to rest, then a piece of meadow came rushing towards her at breakneck speed.

She had no idea what exactly she broke as she landed, but judging by the pain the damage must have been considerable. Her body was slung around several times, onto her back, onto her belly, onto her side. What wasn't broken broke now. At last, after what seemed like an eternity, she lay there, limbs outstretched, blood in her eyes, blood in her mouth.

Her first thought was that she was still alive.

Her second, that her phone was flashing in the sun not very far away. It sparkled on a flat stone like an exhibition piece, right in the middle, as if lovingly placed there. Further down lay the shattered Thunderbird in the trellis of broken trees, scattered with twigs, bark and leaves, and in the car, in fact more out than in, Sid dangled, his head half torn from his shoulders, staring at her.

Tyres approached across gravel and grass.

'Loreena?'

The cry reached her, thin and plaintive. She raised her eyes and saw the intern lying in the shadow of a fir tree. He tried to prop himself up, collapsed, tried again. The SUV stopped. Someone came down the embankment with long, not particularly hurried steps. A man, tall, dark trousers, white shirt, sunglasses. He casually held a long-barrelled pistol in his right hand.

'I'll be right with you,' he said. 'Just a moment.'

Silencer, the thought ran through her head.

He smiled in a rather businesslike manner as he walked past her, stepped up to the intern and fired three shots at him, until the boy stopped moving. It went pop, pop, pop. Loreena opened her mouth because she wanted to scream, to wail, to call for help, but only an ebbing sigh escaped her chest. Every breath was torture. She struggled for-wards, propped her elbows in the grass and crawled towards the stone with the phone on it.

The man came back, picked it up and put it in his pocket.

She gave up. Rolled onto her back, blinked into the sun and thought how right Palstein had been. How close they had been, how *bloody* close! Lars Gudmundsson's head and torso entered her field of vision, the muzzle of his pistol.

'You're very clever,' he said. 'A very clever woman.'

'I know,' groaned Loreena.

'I'm sorry.'

'It's all – it's all on the net,' she murmured. 'It's all—'

'We'll check that,' he said in a friendly voice, and pulled the trigger.

Gaia, Vallis Alpina, The Moon

Nina Hedegaard tried to catch a thousand birds as she sweated away in the Finnish sauna, in a state of mounting frustration. Everywhere she saw the peacock plumage of affluence, heard a twittering exchange about nests and young, and imagined that carefree daydreaming that was only possible in Julian's world. A thousand wonderful, wildly fluttering thoughts. But Julian wasn't there, and the birds refused to be lured into the pen of her life-plans. Whenever she thought she was holding at least a sparrow, after Julian had murmured something that sounded halfway authoritative in her ear, even that little hope escaped and joined all the other ideas, enticingly close and at the same time unattainably far off, of her inflamed imagination. By now she had serious doubts about Julian's honesty. As if he didn't know *full well* that she had hopes. Why couldn't he confess openly to her? Did he have an act of adultery to conceal, social ostracism to fight against? Not a bit of it; he was single, just as she was single, good-looking and lovable single, not rich, perhaps, but then he was rich himself, so what was the problem?

Her frustration seeped like dew from every pore, collected on her forearms, breasts and belly. She furiously distributed layer after layer of warm sweat, let her hands circle around her inner thighs, her fingers working their way slowly to the middle, settling in her crotch, twitching, untameable, abject, pleasure-seeking digits. Shocking! Along with her fury, she was seized with a furious desire to make the absent figure present in her mind, and— but that was impossible, absolutely out of the question.

To cut a long story short, Julian just wanted to fuck her. That was it. He felt nothing, he didn't love. He just wanted to fuck a nice little Danish astronaut if he felt like it. Just as he fucked the whole world when he felt like it.

Stupid idiot!

She violently pulled her hands away, pressed them to the edge of the wooden bench beside her hips and looked out at the wonder of the gorge with its pastel-coloured surfaces and uncompromising shadows. Thousands upon thousands of bright, frozen stars suddenly seemed more attainable than the life that she would have liked to live by his side. She wasn't concerned with his money, or rather it wasn't *really* about the money, even though she didn't necessarily scorn it. No, she wanted a place in that vision-filled brain, capable of dreaming up space lifts, she wanted to be Julian's personal stroke of genius, his most brilliant idea, and to be seen as such by the world, as the woman he desired. She hadn't just fucked her way to that, she'd *earned* it!

Telling him things like that was the reason she was sitting here. Without wanting to put any pressure on him, of course. Just a bit of homeopathically prescribed planning for the future, allied to what she saw as the dazzlingly attractive option of an act of love in the sauna, as soon as the Ganymede landed. That was what they had agreed, and Julian had promised to join her straight away, but now it was a quarter to eight, and on demand she would have to listen to an unconvincing-sounding Lynn as she served up the fairy tale that the group, enchanted by the Schröter Valley, had forgotten time and would be an hour or two late.

How could Lynn have known that without a satellite connection?

Okay, she didn't know. Even in the morning, Julian had talked about an extended excursion into the hinterland of Snake Hill and predicted a late return. No cause for concern. Everything was bound to be fine.

Fine. Ha ha.

Nina stared dully ahead. Perhaps it was fine to fuck the guests around, but not her, thank you very much. She should never have got involved with the richest old codger in the world. It was as simple as that. High time to take an ice-cold shower and do a few lengths in the pool.

'No, there's something solemn about it,' Ögi said. 'Only if you transcend it, of course.'

'If you what?' Winter smiled.

'If you reduce the immediately perceptible to its significance, my dear,' Ögi explained. 'The most difficult exercise these days. Some people call it religion.'

'A tilted flag? An old landing module?'

'An old landing module and the essentially rather unexciting leftovers of two men in a boring-looking area of the Moon – but they were the first men who ever set foot on it! Do you understand? It gives the whole of the Mare Tranquillitatis a – a—'

Ögi struggled for words.

'Sacred dignity?' Aileen Donoghue suggested, with gleaming eyes and a churchgoing tone.

'Exactly!'

'Aha,' said Winter.

'Do you have to believe in God to feel that?' Rebecca Hsu fished a glacé cherry out of her drink, pursed her lips and sucked it into her mouth. A quiet slurp and it was gone. 'I just found it significant, but sacred—'

'Because you have no sacred tradition,' Chucky said to her. 'Your people, I mean. Your nation. The Chinese don't hold with the sacred.'

'Thanks for reminding me. At least now I know why I liked the Rupes Recta better.'

They had assembled for communicative relaxation exercises in the Mama Quilla Club, and were trying to quell their anxiety about the continued absence of the Ganymede by vociferously going through the day's events. In the western Mare Tranquillitatis they had admired the landing console of the very first lunar module, in which Armstrong and Aldrin had landed on the satellite in 1969. The area was considered a culturally protected area, along with three little craters, named after the pioneers and the third man, Collins, who had had to stay in the spaceship. Even during their approach, from a great height, the museum, as the region was generally known, had revealed the full banality of man's arrival. Small and parasitic, like a fly on the hide of an elephant, the console stuck to the regolith, and Armstrong's famous bootprint lay in splendour under a glass case. A place for pilgrims. Doubtless there were more magnificent cathedrals, and yet Ögi was right when he felt there was something in it that bestowed significance and greatness on the human race. It was the certainty that they wouldn't have been able to stand there if those men hadn't taken the journey through the airless wastes and performed the miracle of the first moon landing. So what they felt was respect, in the end. Later that afternoon, in the view of the infinite-looking wall of Rupes Recta, which looked as if the whole Moon continued on a level 200 metres higher up, they had succumbed to the sublimity of the cosmic architecture, deeply impressed, admittedly, but without feeling the curiously touching power emanated by the pitiful memorabilia of human presence in the Mare Tranquillitatis. At that moment most of them had understood that they were not pioneers. No one said hello to a pioneer. He was greeted not by shabby metal frames, not by bootprints, but only by loneliness, the unknown.

Lynn Orley and Dana Lawrence made a great effort to keep the cheerful chitchat going until Olympiada Rogacheva set down her glass and said, 'I'd like to talk to my husband now.'

The others fell silent. Clammy consternation settled on the gathering. She had just broken an unspoken covenant that they should not worry, but somehow everyone seemed happy about it, particularly Chuck, who had already had to tell three miserable jokes just to drown out the sound of his menacingly grumbling belly.

'Come on, Dana,' he blustered. 'What's going on? What are you not telling us?'

'A satellite breakdown is nothing serious, Mr Donoghue.'

'Chuck.'

'Chuck. For example a mini-meteorite the size of a grain of sand can temporarily paralyse a satellite, and the LPCS—'

'But you don't need the LPCS. Armstrong's gang didn't have an LPCS.'

'I can assure you that the technical defect will soon be repaired. That will take a while, but soon we'll be in contact with the Earth exactly as we were before.'

'It's odd, though, having no sign of them,' said Aileen.

'Not at all.' Lynn gave a strained smile. 'You know Julian. He's organised a huge schedule. He said even this morning that they'd probably be late. And by the way, have you seen the system of grooves between the Mare Tranquillitatis and the Sinus Medii? You must have done, when you flew to Rupes Recta.'

'Yes, they look like streets,' said Hsu, and the whistling in the forest resumed.

Olympiada stared straight ahead. Winter noticed her catatonia, stopped licking at the sugar rim of her strawberry daiquiri, edged closer and put a tanned arm around her narrow, drooping shoulders.

'Don't worry, sweetie. You'll have him back soon enough.'

'I feel so shabby,' Olympiada replied quietly.

'Why shabby?'

'So miserable. So useless. When you really want to talk to somebody you despise, just because there's no one else there, it's pitiful.'

'But you've got us!' Winter murmured, and kissed her on the temple, a seal of sisterhood. Only then did she seem to understand what Olympiada had just said. 'So what do you mean, despise? Not Oleg, surely?'

'Who else?'

'Hmph! You despise Oleg?'

'We despise each other.'

Winter considered those words. She tried out, one at a time, a collection of suitable-seeming facial expressions: amazement, reflection, sympathy, puzzlement; she studied the outward appearance of the Russian woman as if seeing her for the very first time. Olympiada's evening wear, a catsuit, one of Mimi Parker's, that changed colour according to the wearer's state of mind, hung on her as if it had been thrown over the back of a chair, eyeliner and jewellery competed to remove the traces of years of neglect and marital suffering. She could have looked so much better. A bit of botox in her cheeks and forehead, hyaluron to smooth the wrinkles around her mouth, a little implant here and there to firm up her confidence and her connective tissues. At that moment she decided to have the implants in her own bottom changed as soon as they got back. There was something wrong with them, if you sat on them for too long.

'Why don't you just leave him?' she asked.

'Why doesn't a doormat leave the front door that it lies outside?' Olympiada mused.

Oh, God almighty! Winter was puzzled. Of course she found herself irresistible in all her firm glory, but did you really have to look like a gym-ripped Valkyrie to be spared the sorts of thoughts that Olympiada wallowed in?

'Listen,' she said. 'I think you're making a mistake. A big fat error of reasoning.'

'Really?'

'Really. You think you're shabby because you think no one wants you, so you allow yourself to be shabbily treated, just to be treated at all.'

'Hmm.'

'But the truth is that no one wants you because you feel shabby. You understand? The other way round. Casuality, causality or whatever it's called, that thing with cause and effect, I'm not that educated, but I know that's how it works. You *think* other people think you're crap, so you feel crap and look crap, and in the end what everyone sees is crap, so it comes full circle. Am I making myself understood? A kind of inner – prejudgement. Because in fact you're your own biggest, erm . . . enemy. And because at some level you enjoy it. You *want* to suffer.'

Wow, that sounded awesome! As if she'd been to college.

'You think?' Olympiada asked, and looked at Winter from the gloomy November puddles that were her eyes.

'Of course!' She liked this, it was getting really psychological. She ought to do this kind of thing more often. 'And you know why you want to suffer? Because you're looking for confirmation! Because you think you're, as we've seen, you think you're—' Vocabulary, Miranda, vocabulary! Not just crap, what's another word? 'Shit. You think you're shit, nothing else, but being shit is still better than being nothing at all, and if someone else thinks you're shit too, you understand, then that's a crystal-clear confirmation of what you think.'

'Heavens above.'

'Misery is reliable, believe me.'

'I don't know.'

'No, it is, feeling shit gives you something to depend on. What do people say when they go to church? God, I am sinful, worthless, I've done terrible things, even before I was born, I'm a miserable piece of filth, forgive me, and if you can't that's okay too, you're right, I'm just an ant, an original ant—'

'Original ant?'

'Yes, original something or other!' She gesticulated wildly, as if intoxicated. 'There's something like that in Christian stuff, where you're the lowest of the low from the get-go. That's exactly how you feel. You think suffering is home. Wrong. Suffering is shit.'

'You never suffer?'

'Of course I do, like a dog! You know that. I was an alcoholic, I was described as the worst actress ever, I was in jail, up before the court. Wow!' She laughed, in love with the disaster of her own biography. 'That was out of order.'

'But why does none of that matter to you?'

'It does, it does! Bad luck really matters to me.'

'But you don't think that from the outset you're, erm—'

'No.' Winter shook her head. 'Just briefly, when I was drinking. Otherwise I wouldn't know what I was talking about here. But not fundamentally.'

Olympiada smiled for the first time that evening, carefully, as if she wasn't sure that her face was made for it.

'Will you tell me a secret, Miranda?'

'Anything, darling.'

'How do you become like you?'

'No idea.' Winter reflected, thought seriously about the question. 'I think you need a certain lack of . . . imagination.'

'Lack of *imagination*?'

'Yes.' She laughed a whinnying laugh. 'Just imagine, I have no imagination. Not a scrap. I can't see myself the way others do. I mean, I can see that they think I'm cool, that they undress me with their eyes, fine. But otherwise I see myself only through my own eyes, and if I don't like something I change it. I just can't imagine how other people want me to be, so I don't try to be that way.' She paused and indicated to Funaki that her glass was empty. 'And now you stop seeing yourself through Oleg's eyes, okay? You're nice, really nice! Oh, my God, you're a member of the Russian – what is it again?'

'Parliament.'

'And rich and everything! And where your appearance is concerned, okay, fine, I'll be honest with you, but give me four weeks and I'll make a femme fatale out of you! You don't need any of that, Olympiada. You certainly don't need to miss Oleg.'

'Hmm.'

'You know what?' She gripped Olympiada's upper arm and lowered her voice. 'Now I'll tell you a real secret: men only make women feel they're shit because they feel shit themselves. You get it? They try to break our confidence, they try to steal it from us because they have none themselves. Don't do that! Don't let them do that to you! You have to fly your own flag, honey. You're not what he wants you to be.' Complicated sentence structure, but it worked. She was getting better and better.

'He might never come back,' Olympiada murmured, apparently spotting a path opening up into sunnier climes.

'Exactly. Fuck him.'

Olympiada sighed. 'Okay.'

'Michio, my darling,' Winter crowed, and waved her empty glass. 'One of these for my friend!'

       ★   ★   ★

Sophie Thiel was stumbling around in betrayal and deception when Tim came into the control centre. A dozen windows on the big multimedia wall reanimated the past.

'Totally fake,' said Sophie listlessly.

He watched people crossing the lobby, entering the control centre, going about their work, leaving it. Then the rooms lay there again, gloomy and desperate, lit only by the harsh reflection of the sunlight on the edge of the gorge and the controls of the tireless machinery that kept the hotel alive. Sophie pointed to one of the shots. The camera angle was arranged in such a way that you could make out the far side of the Vallis Alpina, with mountains and monorail through the panoramic window.

'The control centre, deserted. That night when Hanna went out on the Lunar Express.'

Tim narrowed his eyes and leaned forward.

'Don't try just yet, you won't get to see him. Your sister would say it's because no one went anywhere. In fact, someone's hoodwinking us with the oldest trick in the book. You see that thing blinking on the right-hand edge of the video wall?'

'Yes.'

'At almost exactly the same time something lights up down here, and there, a bit further on, an indicator light comes on. You see? Trivial things that no one would normally notice, but I've taken the trouble to look for matches. Take a look at the timecode.'

05.53, Tim read.

'You'll find exactly the same sequence at ten past five.'

'Coincidence?'

'Not if close analysis reveals a tiny jump in the shadow on the Moon's surface. The sequence was copied and added to hide an event that lasted just two minutes.'

'The arrival of the Lunar Express,' whispered Tim.

'Yes, and that's exactly how it goes on. Hanna in the corridor, edited out, just like your father said. The control centre, apparently empty. But there was someone there. Someone who sat here and changed these videos; he's just cut himself out. Perfectly done, the whole thing. The lobby, a different perspective that would show you Mr X coming into the control centre, but also faked, unfortunately.'

'Someone must have spent an endless amount of time over it,' Tim said, amazed.

'No, it's pretty fast if you know what needs to be done.'

'Astounding!'

'Frustrating above all, because it doesn't get us anywhere. Now we know *that* it was done. But not *who* did it.'

Tim pursed his lips. Suddenly he had an idea.

'Sophie, if we can trace back *when* the work on the videos was done – if we could take a look at the records – I mean, can you manipulate the records as well?'

She frowned. 'Only if you take a lot of trouble.'

'But it could be done?'

'Basically it couldn't. The intervention would be recorded as well. Hmm. I see.'

'If we knew the exact times of the interventions, we could match them with the presence and absence of the guests and the staff. Who was where at the time in question? Who saw who? Our mystery person can't possibly have changed *all* the data in the hotel system in the time available to him. So as soon as we see the records—'

'We'll have him.' Sophie nodded. 'But to do that we'd need an authorisation program.'

'I've got one.'

'What?' She looked at him in surprise. 'An authorisation program for this system?'

'No, a common or garden little mole that I downloaded from the net last winter to look at a colleague's data. With his permission,' he added quickly. 'His system did a screen shot every sixty seconds, and I had to get at those shots, but I didn't have authorisation. So I resorted to the knowledge of some of my students. One of them recommended Gravedigger, an, erm, a not entirely legal reconstruction program, but one that's quite easy to get hold of and compatible with almost every system. I kept it. It's on my computer, and my computer—'

'—is here in Gaia.'

'Bingo.' Tim grinned. 'In my room.'

Sophie smiled broadly. 'Right, Mr Orley, so if you don't mind—'

'I'm on my way.'

It was only when he was on the way to the suite that it occurred to him that there might be another reason why Sophie found nothing but manipulated videos:

She herself had recut the material.

Mukesh Nair pulled himself snorting out of the crater pool. A little further off Sushma was towelling herself dry, in conversation with Eva Borelius and Karla Kramp, while Heidrun Ögi and Finn O'Keefe played childish competitions, to see who could stay underwater longest. The Earth shone in through the panoramic window, like a reliable old friend. Nair picked a towel off the pile and rubbed the water out of his hair.

'Do you feel like this?' he said. 'When I see our home, it's curious: it looks entirely unimpressed.'

'Unimpressed by what?' asked Karla, and disappeared into her dressing gown.

'By us.' Mukesh Nair lowered the towel and looked up to the sky. 'By the consequences of our actions. It's got hotter everywhere. Previously inhabited areas are underwater, others are turning into deserts. Whole tribes of people are on the move, hungry, thirsty, unemployed, homeless, we're seeing the biggest migrations in centuries, but there's no sign of it at all. Not from this distance.'

'Looking at the old lady from this distance, you wouldn't know if we were bombing each other flat,' said Karla. 'Means nothing.'

Nair shook his head, fascinated.

'The deserts must have got bigger, don't you think? Whole coastlines have changed. But if you're far enough away – it doesn't change her beauty in the slightest.'

'If you're far enough away,' Sushma smiled, 'even I'm beautiful.'

'Oh, Sushma!' Her husband tilted his head and laughed, showing perfectly restored teeth. 'You will always be the most beautiful woman in the world to me, near or far. You're my most beautiful vegetable of all!'

'There's a compliment,' said Heidrun to Finn, water in one ear, Nair's flattering baritone in the other. 'Why do I never get to hear things like that?'

'Because I'm not Walo.'

'Lousy explanation.'

'Comparing people to foodstuffs is his department.'

'Is it just me, or have you stopped making much of an effort lately?'

'Vegetables don't spring to mind when I look at you. Asparagus, perhaps.'

'Finn, I really have to say, that's going to get you nowhere.' She hurried to the edge of the pool, straightened and sent a great spray of water in Nair's direction. 'Hey! What are you talking about?'

'The beauty of the Earth,' smiled Sushma Nair. 'And a bit about the beauty of women.'

'Same thing,' said Heidrun. 'The Earth is female.'

Eva tied the belt of her kimono. 'You see beauty out there?'

'Of course.' Nair nodded enthusiastically. 'Beauty and simplicity.'

'Shall I tell you what I see?' Eva Borelius said after thinking for a moment. 'A misunderstanding.'

'How so?'

'Complete disproportion. The Earth out there has nothing to do with our familiar perception of it.'

'That's true,' said Heidrun. 'For example, Switzerland normally seems the size of Africa to a Swiss person. On the other hand, in the emotional reality of a Swiss person, Africa shrinks to a hot, damp island full of poor people, mosquitoes, snakes and diseases.'

'That's exactly what I'm talking about.' Eva nodded. 'I see a beautiful planet, but not one that we share. A world which, in terms of what some have and others don't, should look completely different.'

'Bravo.' Finn O'Keefe bobbed over and applauded.

'Enough, Finn,' hissed Heidrun. 'Do you even know what we're talking about?'

'Of course,' he yawned. 'About how Eva Borelius had to fly to the Moon to discover the bleedin' obvious.'

'No.' Eva laughed drily and started picking up her swimming things. 'I've always known what the planet looks like, Finn, but it's still different seeing it like this. It reminds me who we're actually researching for.'

'You're researching for the guy who's paying you. Have you only just realised?'

'That free research is going down the toilet? No.'

'Not that you personally have any reason to complain,' Karla joined in maliciously.

'Hey, hang on.' Eva, caught in a pincer movement, raised her eyebrows. 'Am I complaining?'

Karla looked innocently back. 'I just wanted to say.'

'Of course, stem cell research brings in money, so she gets some too. It cost a lot of money to take the isolation and investigation of adult cells and develop it into the production of artificial tissue. Now we've decoded the protein blueprints of our body cells, we work successfully with molecular prosthetics, we have replacements for destroyed nerves and burnt skin, we can produce new cardiac muscle cells, we can cure cancer, because not even the wealthiest people in the world are spared heart attacks, cancer and burn injuries.' She paused. 'But they are spared malaria. And cholera. Those are diseases for poor people. If we were to apportion budgets purely on the quantitative occurrence of such diseases, the greatest amount of research money would flow to the Third World. Instead, the majority of all malaria patents, even the most promising, are put on ice, because you can't earn any money with them.'

Nair went on looking at the far-away Earth, still smiling, but more thoughtfully.

'I come from an unimaginably big country,' he said. 'And at the same time from a graspable cosmos. I've never had the impression that there's just one world, not least because we see it from all perspectives at the same time. No one sees it as a whole, no one sees the whole truth. But if we see the world as a multiplicity of small, interlocking worlds, each determined by its own rules, you can try to improve some of them. And that helps you to understand the whole. If my job had been to improve *the* world, I would definitely have failed.'

'So what have you improved?' asked Karla.

'A few of those little worlds.' He beamed at them. 'At least I hope so.'

'You've carpeted India with air-conditioned shopping centres, connected whole villages to the internet, provided God knows how many thousands of Indian farmers with a basic living. But haven't you also opened the door to multinational companies, by offering them the chance to get involved?'

'Of course.'

'And haven't some of them gratefully taken up your model, rented Indian land and replaced the farmers with machines and cheap labourers?'

Nair's smile froze on his face. 'Any idea can be corrupted.'

'I'd just like to understand.'

'Certainly, such things happen. We can't allow that.'

'Look, I don't entirely agree with your romanticisation of inequality. Small, autonomous worlds. You do a lot of good things, Mukesh, but you're globalisation personified. Which I think is fine, as long as the tiny little worlds aren't swallowed up by the big companies—'

'Shouldn't we be getting back to our rooms?' said Eva.

'Yes, of course.' Karla shrugged. 'Let's go. Typical of you, always going on about how annoyed you are, and then getting all ashamed when I mention some concrete examples.'

'Where have the others got to, by the way?' Sushma shook her head uneasily. 'They should have been back ages ago.'

'When we came down here they were still on their way.'

'And they still are, by the look of it,' said Nair. Then he rested a friendly hand on Karla's shoulder. 'And you're completely right, Karla. We should talk about this kind of thing more often. And not spare each other's feelings.'

'Shall I tell you how I see it?' asked Finn.

They all looked at him.

'I see two dozen of the richest people on this much-discussed planet Earth feeling trapped between malaria and champagne and, in line with the disproportion that you mentioned, Eva, escaping to the Moon, where they reach remarkable insights in the most expensive hotel in the solar system. You know what? I'm going for another couple of lengths.'

Sophie had installed Tim's program and asked him casually whether it hadn't occurred to him that she might be the traitor. He had looked baffled for a moment, before exploding with laughter.

'Is it that obvious?'

'You bet.'

'Well—'

'I'm not,' she said. 'Happy now?'

He laughed again. 'If people got out of jail by saying that, we could convert our prisons into hen houses.'

'You're a teacher, right?'

'Yes.'

'How many times do you hear that every day?'

'What? "It's not me, it wasn't me"?' He shrugged. 'No idea. I usually lose track at about midday. But okay, it wasn't you. Do you suspect anybody?'

She lowered her head over the keyboard, so that her blonde curls hid her facial expression.

'Not directly.'

'You're thinking about my sister, aren't you?' He sighed. 'Come on, Sophie, it's not a problem, I'm not cross with you. You're not the only person who feels that way. Dana has completely homed in on Lynn.'

'I know.' Sophie looked up. 'But I don't believe for a second that your sister has anything to do with it. Lynn built this hotel. It would be completely idiotic. And what's more, it's only just now occurred to me, but when she refused to let your father see the corridor video – why would she have done that? I mean, why, if she had actually recut it herself? In her place I'd have proudly rubbed his nose in it.'

Tim looked grateful and curiously glum at the same time. It was immediately clear to her that he was more inclined towards Dana's opinion than her own, and that he was bothered by the fact.

'Quite honestly,' she smiled shyly, 'I was wondering before whether you yourself mightn't—'

'Ah!' he grinned. 'No, it wasn't me.'

'More hen houses.' She smiled back. 'Would you like to keep me company while I reconstruct the records?'

'No, I'd just like to see where Lynn's got to. But call me if you think of anything.' He smiled. 'You're very brave, Sophie. Will you manage?'

'Somehow.'

'Not a bit scared?'

She shrugged. 'Oddly, the thing I'm least worried about is the idea of being blown up. It's too unreal. If it does happen, we'll all go in a flash, but we're not going to know all that much about it.'

'I feel the same.'

'So what are *you* afraid of?'

'Right now? I'm worried about Amber. Very worried. About my wife, about my father—'

'About your sister—'

'Yes. About Lynn too. See you later, Sophie.'

'That wasn't nice,' Heidrun mocked, after the others had fled the pool area. Only she and Finn were still drifting in the black water of the crater, somewhere between idyll and apocalypse.

'But true,' said Finn, launching into a crawl away from her.

She pushed her wet hair behind her ears. Below the surface of the water her body was compressed into a bony caricature of itself, as if the waves were starting to dissolve her. Finn cut a swathe through the water like a motorboat, sending watery chaos in all directions, great surges that a swimmer could never have produced in terrestrial waters. An amusement factor reserved only for moon travellers. You could catapult yourself out of the water like a dolphin and, when you splashed back in again, set small tsunamis on their way. You were operating in arrogant opposition to the laws of gravity, but Finn's mood was closer to the grey of the surrounding landscape. Heidrun stretched, dived, slipped after him and past him and burst through the surface. Finn saw that the way to the opposite edge of the crater was blocked, and balanced himself in the water.

'What's up?' she asked. 'Bad mood?'

'No idea.' He shrugged. 'Aren't you supposed to be going up?'

'And what about you?'

'I haven't made any dates with anybody.'

Heidrun thought for a moment. Had she made any dates? With Walo, of course, but could you really describe the day-to-day magnetism of marriage as a date?

'So you've no idea what your mood is.'

'I don't know.'

It was true, she guessed, Finn probably just had no idea why his mood had so suddenly soured. He had been in great form all day, making her laugh with his laconic sarcasm, a gift that Heidrun valued above all others. She liked men whose wit sprang from easy understatement, which gave them the ultimate accolade of cool. In her opinion there was hardly anything more erotic than laughter, sadly an attitude fraught with difficulties, because the majority of the male sex tended to try to produce it intellectually. The result was usually tiresome and discouraging. In their constant bid to score points with hilarious thigh-slappers, these suitors lost what remained of their natural machismo, and there was much worse to come. For her part, Heidrun derived intense and noisy pleasure from sex, and had ended up in paroxysms of laughter during so many orgasms that the gentlemen in question, convinced that they were the object of her laughter, were thrown spontaneously off their stroke. The drop in pleasure pressure was always followed by the same embarrassment, she always felt guilty, but what was she supposed to do? She loved laughing. Ögi was the first to understand. Heidrun's natural responses neither inhibited his erections nor slowed him down in any way. Walo Ögi with his chiselled Zürich physiognomy, which could break out into ringing laughter at any time, took sex no more seriously than she did, with the result that they both enjoyed it a great deal.

Finn, on the other hand. Viewed objectively, in so far as the objectification of beauty was ever justified, he was far better looking than Walo, in terms of classical proportion at any rate: he was perfectly built and a good sixteen years younger. Apart from that, he had the appearance of an uncommunicative and sometimes sulky melancholic. He concealed his stroppiness behind insecurity, his shyness behind indifference, but he was enough of an actor to flirt professionally with all of these qualities. As a result he was surrounded by the aura of mystery that turned millions of emancipated female individuals into spineless mush. Supposedly shy, he cultivated the pose of the eternal outsider in a world whose cofounder and original inhabitant he was; he acted the part of the lout, as if Marlon Brando, James Dean and Johnny Depp hadn't already taken the idea to ludicrous extremes, and exuded a sweaty rebellious appeal. He couldn't, with the best will in the world, ever have been described as the life and soul. And yet behind the forbidding façade Heidrun sensed an inclination to excess, to anarchic fun, to wild parties, as long as the right people were invited. She had no doubt that one could fool about with him, and have laughing sex until libido and diaphragm both gave in, after hours.

'They're getting on your nerves, aren't they?' she surmised. 'Our lovely fellow travellers.'

Finn rubbed water out of his eyes.

'I get on my own nerves,' he said. 'Because I think it's my problem.'

'What is?'

'Not rising like a spiritual soufflé up here. It seems almost unavoidable. Everyone is constantly coming out with the loveliest philosophical observations. There isn't anyone who hasn't a clever thing to say. Some of them burst into tears at the very sight of the Earth, others wallow in self-mortification at the thought of their earthly striving. Eva sees injustice and Mukesh Nair sees miracles and wonder in every grain of moon dust. A complete social elite seem determined to relativise their previous lives, just because they're sitting on a lump of stone so far from the Earth that you can see the whole thing. And what occurs to me? Just a stupid old saying from the Pre-Cambrian era of space travel.'

'Let's hear it.'

'Astronauts are men who don't have to bring their wives anything back from their travels.'

'Pretty dumb.'

'You see? Everyone seems to *find himself* up here. And I don't even know what I'm supposed to be *looking* for.'

'So? Let them.'

'I did say it isn't their problem. It's mine.'

'You're complaining on quite a high level, my dearest Finn.'

'No, I'm not.' He glared at her angrily. 'It hasn't the slightest thing to do with self-pity. I just feel *empty*, crippled. I'd love to feel that same powerful emotion, vaporise with reverence and get back to Earth inside out, to preach the word of enlightenment, but I don't feel any of it. I can't think of anything to say about this trip except that it's nice, it's a bit different. But it is, and remains, the bloody Moon, damn it all! No higher level of existence, no understanding or comprehension of anything at all. It doesn't spiritualise me, it stirs nothing in me, and that's *got* to be my problem! *There must be more!* I feel as if I've withered away.'

Doggy-paddling, they drifted towards one another. And while Heidrun was still wondering what she could reply to this outburst without sounding like a maiden aunt, she was suddenly close to him. His lines and wrinkles revealed a life of clueless carousal. She recognised Finn's inability to make his brilliant talent chime with the banal realisation that in spite of his special gift he was not a special person, simply alive and, like everyone else, damned, on the highway that they were all hurtling along, one day to crash into the wall without ever having come close to the meaning of everything. Not a trace of apotheosis. Just someone who had had too much of everything without ever feeling sated by it, and who now, in his total cluelessness, reacted more honestly to the impressions of the journey than the rest of the group put together.

A moment later she sensed him.

She felt his hands on her hips, her backside. She felt them exploring her waist and back, his lips strangely cool on hers, wrapped both legs around him and pulled him so tightly to her that his sex pressed against hers, ambushed by the brazenness of his approach and even more by her own simmering readiness for a fling. She knew she was about to do something incredibly stupid that she would bitterly regret afterwards, but the whole catechism of marital fidelity was consumed in the heat of that moment, and if men thought with their dicks, as was so often rightly said, then her will and intelligence had just irrevocably faded away in her cunt, and that too was something so terrifyingly banal that all she could do was erupt with laughter.

Finn joined in.

It was the worst thing he could have done. Even an irritated twitch of his eyebrows would have saved her, a hint of incomprehension, but he just laughed and started rubbing her between the legs until she was terrified, even as her fingers clawed at the hem of his trunks and pulled them down, to liberate the engorged beast within.

Water monkeys, she thought. We're water monkeys!

Uh! Uh!

'I'd leave it if I were you,' she heard Nina Hedegaard saying, just before the water started splashing. 'He'll bring you nothing but frustration and a whole host of problems.'

As if struck by lightning they parted. Finn reached irritably for his trunks. Heidrun dipped her head beneath the surface, breathed in crater water, came back up and coughed her lungs up. Scooping water like a paddle-steamer, Nina passed them on her back.

'Sorry, I didn't want to spoil your fun. But you should really think about it.'

And that was that.

Heidrun lacked the genetic prerequisites for blushing, but at that moment she could have sworn she turned *beetroot*, a beacon of embarrassment. She stared at Finn. To her infinite relief nothing in his expression suggested that the past few minutes had been embarrassing to him, only regret and a vague understanding that it was over. He plainly still wanted her, and she wanted him a bit less, but at the same time she felt an urgent longing for Walo, and the desire to kiss Nina for her intervention.

'Yeah, we' – Finn grinned crookedly – 'were just about to go upstairs.'

'So I saw,' Nina said sullenly. She swam powerfully over to them and stood up in the water. 'I'll keep my mouth shut, don't worry. The rest is your business. They're starting to get worried up there. Julian's group still isn't back, and neither are the satellites.'

'Didn't Julian say anything?' Heidrun asked, her whole body still one big heartbeat. 'This morning, I mean.'

'No, he said they'd be showing up later. Too busy a schedule, says Lynn.'

'Then that's how it is.'

'Seems odd to me.'

'Julian would definitely have tried to get through, to you first of all,' said O'Keefe.

'Yeah, great, and what would you do, Finn, if you didn't get through? You'd be on time! So as not to worry the others. And I'm not stupid, there's more to it than that. There's something they aren't telling me.'

'Who's they?'

'Dana Lawrence, the cold fish. Lynn. Who knows? Dinner's now been arranged for nine, by the way.'

Heidrun could tell by the tip of Finn's nose that he was thinking exactly the same as she was, whether they shouldn't make use of that time in his suite. But it was a pale, threadbare thought, less than a thought, in fact, since it came not from the head, not from the heart, but from the abdomen, whose coup had just been permanently thwarted. Finn slipped over and gave her a quick kiss. There was something conciliatory, something final about it.

'Come on,' he said. 'Let's go up and join the others.'

London, Great Britain

After the conversation with Palstein, Jericho had taken a trip around the highly armed information centre and introduced Jennifer to the contents of his rucksack.

'Diane,' he said. 'The fourth member of the alliance.'

'Diane?' An eyebrow rose in her grumpy face.

'Mm-hm. Diane.'

'I see. Your daughter or your wife?'

Since then Diane had been alternately connected to the public internet and the internal, hacker-protected intranet of the Big O, a system locked against the outside world, with no way in, but no way out either. Jennifer had summarily authorised him to access parts of the company's own database, equipped with a password that allowed him to trace the global network of the company, its history and its staff structure. At the same time, thanks to Diane, he was working on familiar ground. Without the company of Tu or Yoyo, who had wanted to visit the fat guy for a few minutes and had been overdue since then, he felt miserably alone, just a messenger, good enough to lay his head on the line for others, but not to be taken into anybody's friendly confidence.

Pah, friends! Let the two of them wallow in misery. At last he was warmed again by Diane's soft, dark computer voice, untroubled by any kind of sensitivity.

He asked her to go through the net for arrangements of terms, *Palstein*, *attempted murder*, *assassination*, *assassin*, *Orley*, *China*, *investigations*, *discoveries*, *results*, etc. On the oil manager's initiative, the Canadian authorities had sent a large supply of pictures and film material which he, Edda Hoff, a member of the IT security department and a woman from MI6 were now assessing together. If only Palstein had been willing to hand over the video that supposedly showed his attacker, they could presumably have spared themselves all that wretched work. Diane brought him things she'd found about the Calgary shooting the way a cat brings in half-dead mice, but where the rest of the decoding of the text fragment was concerned she was poking around in the dark. Clearly the hurricane murmur of the dark network had fallen silent. In contrast, pictures, reports, assessments and conspiracy theories about Calgary were flooding in, but without shedding light on anything.

He went to see Jennifer Shaw.

'Good to see you.' Jennifer was in a video conference with representatives of MI6, and waved him in. 'If you've got anything new—'

'When was Gaia originally supposed to open?' Jericho asked, pulling up a chair.

'You know that. Last year.'

'When exactly?'

'Okay, it had been planned for late summer, but projects like that are never as ready as you hope they're going to be. It could have been autumn or winter.'

'And because of the Moon crisis—'

'No, not just because of that.' Norrington came into the room. 'You're in the temple of truth here, Owen. We're happy to admit that there were technical delays. The unofficial opening was scheduled for August 2024, but even without a crisis we'd hardly have managed it before 2025.'

'So the completion date wasn't foreseeable at the time?'

'Why do you ask?' one of the MI6 people wanted to know.

'Because I'm wondering whether the mini-nuke was put up there only in order to destroy Gaia. Something people knew *would* be finished, but didn't know *when*. But when the satellite was started, it wasn't finished.'

'You're right,' the MI6 man said thoughtfully. 'They could have waited for the launch, in fact they should have done.'

'Why should they?' asked another one.

'Because every atom bomb gives off radiation. You can't store a thing like that on the Moon indefinitely, where there's no convection to carry away the heat. There's a danger of the bomb overheating and going off prematurely.'

'So it was definitely supposed to detonate in 2024,' Jennifer surmised.

'That's exactly what I mean,' said Jericho. 'Was it or is it meant only for Gaia? How much explosive do you need to blow up a hotel?'

'Lots,' said Norrington.

'But not an atom bomb?'

'Not unless you want to contaminate the whole site, the wider surroundings,' said the MI6 man.

Jericho nodded. 'So what's up with it?'

'With the Vallis Alpina?' Jennifer thought for a minute. 'Nothing, as far as I know. But that needn't mean anything.'

'What are you getting at?' asked Norrington.

'Very simple,' Jericho said. 'If we agree that the bomb was to be detonated in 2024, regardless of whether Gaia had been completed or not, the question arises as to why it didn't happen.'

'Because something got in the way,' Jennifer reflected.

Jericho smiled. 'Because something got in *someone's* way. Because *someone* was prevented from setting the thing off, one way or another. That means we should stop wondering about the where and the when, and concentrate on that person who *possibly*, in fact *probably* isn't called Carl Hanna. So who was on the Moon or on the way to the Moon last year who could have detonated the bomb? What happened to make sure that it didn't go off?'

And meanwhile he was thinking: who am I telling all this to? Jennifer had mentioned the possibility of a mole, a traitor who drew his information from the inner security circle. Who was the mole? Edda Hoff, opaque and brittle? One of the divisional directors? Tom Merrick, that bundle of nerves responsible for communication security – could he have been responsible for the block that he was pretending to investigate? And apart from Andrew Norrington, was there someone listening to his hypotheses who shouldn't have known about them? Always allowing that Jennifer hadn't mentioned moles to distract attention from herself.

How safe were they really in the Big O?

Gaia, Vallis Alpina, The Moon

The chronological recording was swiftly reconstructed. True to its name, the Gravedigger burrowed its way into the depths of the system and drew up a complete list, but because this encompassed activities carried out over several days, it looked like something that would keep you occupied for three rainy weekends.

'Shit,' whispered Sophie.

But if you cut down the periods of time in question, the work went faster than you might have expected. And the faker's trail ran like a pattern through the recordings, because after every action he erased his traces. The video of Hanna's night-time trip, for example, had been recut while the Canadian had been exploring Gaia's surroundings with Julian, or more precisely between a quarter past six and half past on the morning in question. Unambiguous proof that Hanna himself hadn't set about erasing his traces.

Where had *she* been at that point? In bed. Hadn't got up till seven. Until then the lobby and the control centre had been populated only by machines. In a simultaneous projection, she screened all the recordings of the period during which the phantom had done his work, but no one left his room, no one crouched in a hidden corner operating the system from somewhere else.

Impossible!

Someone must surely have been wandering about the hotel at that time.

Had these videos been manipulated too?

She studied the recordings more precisely, and had the computer examine all the films for subsequently introduced cuts.

Sure enough.

Sophie stared at the monitor wall. This thing was getting increasingly weird. Everything she saw here, or rather didn't see, was evidence of unsettling professionalism and strength of nerve. If it went on like this, in the end she would have to go through every single order in the vague hope that the faker might give himself away by some tiny blunder. Just as it had soared a moment before, her mood now plummeted. It was pointless. The stranger had used his time and opportunities to the full, he was ahead of her.

Maybe she should approach the business the other way round, she thought. Start with the *last* significant event, the satellite failure.

Perhaps the phantom hadn't had time to clean up after himself when that happened.

She isolated the passage from the conference call until it suddenly broke off, and had the computer play through the whole sequence again. Her own actions were visible in the reconstruction: her taking the call, informing Dana and Lynn in the Selene and putting it through to Julian Orley. After that—

A shadow settled over her. She gave a start, threw her head back and sat bolt upright.

'Erm – thought you might be hungry.'

'Axel!'

Kokoschka's monolithic appearance darkened her desktop. He held a plate in his right hand. The bony claw of a rack of lamb protruded from it, a nutty smell of courgettes wafted towards her.

'God, Axel!' she panted. 'You frightened the life out of me!'

'I'm sorry, I—'

'Don't worry. Phew! Shouldn't you be tearing up walls and floors?'

'Cerberus took us off the job,' he grinned. 'Hungry? East Friesian saltmarsh lamb.'

He looked at her, to the side, at the floor, then dared to make eye contact again. Christ, no. She'd guessed it. German boy loves German girl. Kokoschka had fallen for her.

'That's really sweet of you,' she said, glancing at the plate.

His grin widened and he set the dish down on a free corner of the desktop, next to her, along with a napkin and cutlery. Suddenly she realised that over the course of the past hour hunger had crept up on her and was devouring her from within. She greedily inhaled the aromas. Kokoschka had separated out the cutlets for her. She took one of the fragile ribs between her fingers and gnawed the butter-soft flesh from the bone, as she turned once again to the screens.

'Whatcha doin'?' asked Kokoschka.

'Checking the recordings from the afternoon,' she said with her mouth full. 'To see if I can find something out about the satellite failure.'

'Do you think we've really got a bomb?'

'Not the faintest, Axel.'

'Hmm. Weird. Doesn't really bother me, to be honest.' His forehead was covered with sweat. In visible contradiction to his words, he seemed nervous and twitchy, stepped from one leg to the other, sniffed. 'So you're trying to find out where the bomb is?'

'No, I want to know who Hanna's accomplice—'

She stared at him.

Kokoschka held her eye for a few seconds, then his eyes drifted down to the video wall. He was perspiring more heavily now. His bald head was drenched, a vein throbbed in his temple. Sophie stopped chewing, and paused with her chin thrust out and her cheek bulging.

'Okay, you've probably known for ages,' Kokoschka said wearily into the room.

She gulped, and recoiled. 'What?'

He looked at her.

'Could we have a quick chat?' Dana nodded to Lynn to follow her to the stairs that led from the Mama Quilla Club to the Luna Bar below it, and from there to the Selene and Chang'e. At that moment everyone's attention was focused on Chuck, who stood there with a sly grin on his face, holding both hands, palms up and all ten fingers pointing upwards, stretched out in front of him.

'What does the Pope mean when he does this?'

'No idea,' said Olympiada gloomily. Winter, unfamiliar with the habits of the Pontifex and clerical matters in general, shook her head in hopeful expectation that she might possibly get the punchline, while a chill gust of outrage blew all the benevolence from Aileen's features. Rebecca Hsu sat next to her like a circus lion on a bar stool, and spoke into her hand computer in a hushed voice. Walo Ögi had absconded to his suite to read.

'Chuck, please don't.'

'Oh, come on, Aileen.'

'Don't tell this one!'

'What does the Pope mean?' Winter giggled.

'Chuck, no!'

'Very simple.' Donoghue snapped nine fingers closed, so that only the middle finger of his right hand was still pointing upwards. 'The same as *this*, but in ten languages.'

Winter went on giggling, Hsu laughed, Olympiada pulled a face. Aileen looked around at everyone, hoping for forgiveness, with a tortured, powerless smile on her face. Lynn processed none of this as she would usually have done. Whatever she saw and heard looked like a sequence of rattling, stroboscopic flashes. Aileen accused Chuck of violating a joke-free zone called the Church, about which *everyone had agreed*, mercilessly wielding her falsetto scalpel, while Winter tee-heed inanely, a source of relentless torment.

'We must assume that something has happened on the Aristarchus Plateau,' Dana Lawrence said abruptly. 'Something unpleasant.'

Lynn's fingers bent and stretched.

'Okay, we'll send Nina out in the shuttle.'

'We should do that,' Dana nodded. 'And evacuate Gaia.'

'Hang on! We said we were going to wait.'

'What for?'

'For Julian.'

Dana glanced quickly at the seated group. Miranda Winter was chortling, 'That's great. Why in ten languages?' while Chuck eyed them suspiciously.

'Don't you listen?' she hissed. 'I mentioned that Julian's team might be in difficulties. We have no idea whether they're going to turn up here, and we have a bomb threat. There are guests in the hotel now. We *have* to evacuate.'

'But we've laid nine places for dinner.'

'That doesn't matter now.'

'It does.'

'It doesn't, Lynn. I've had enough. I'll call everyone together. Meet at half past eight in the Mama Quilla Club, give it to them straight. Then we'll send out a radio flare for Julian, Nina will go in search of them, the rest of us will take the Lunar Express to—'

'Nonsense. You're talking nonsense!'

'*I'm* talking nonsense?'

Chuck got to his feet and smoothed his trouser legs.

'I really thought you knew,' Kokoschka said, embarrassed.

Sophie shook her head in mute horror.

'Hmm.' He wiped the sweat from his brow. 'Doesn't really matter anyway. Bad moment, I guess.'

'What for?'

'I've fallen – I've sort of fallen – oh, forget it. I just wanted to say that I really . . . erm—'

Sophie melted with relief. Her hand strayed to the plate, but her belly hadn't yet accepted the fact that Kokoschka had only wanted to declare his love, and it categorically refused to take in any more food.

'I like you too,' she said, trying to make sure that the *like* really meant *like* and nothing more.

Kokoschka rubbed his fingers over his spanking clean chef's jacket.

'I can't wait to see if you find something,' he said, looking at the display.

'Me too, you can be sure of that.' Switch of topic, thank heavens. She looked at the picture details, the list of recordings, the data flow. 'The whole thing is very mysterious. We—'

She took a closer look.

'What's *that*?' she whispered.

Kokoschka pushed in closer. 'What?'

Sophie paused the reconstruction program. There was something. Something weird that she couldn't quite place. A kind of menu, but a sort she'd never seen before. Simple, compact, connected to a rat's tail of data, bundles of commands that had been sent only seconds before the breakdown of communication from Gaia. She understood a bit of computer language. She could read a lot of it, but this cryptic sequence of commands would have been meaningless in her eyes, if some of the codes hadn't seemed familiar.

Codes for satellites.

The command to freeze communications had come from Gaia. She could see when and from where it had happened.

She knew *who* had done it.

'Oh, my Christ,' she whispered.

Fear, terrible, long-suppressed fear flooded all her cells, all her thoughts. Her fingers started trembling. Kokoschka leaned down to her.

'What's up?' he asked

All sign of shyness had fled. The German's eyes peered from his angular head. She spun round in her chair, opened a drawer, reached for a piece of paper, a pen, as she now no longer trusted the computer system. She hastily scribbled a few words on the paper, folded it together and pressed the little paper packet into his hand.

'Take this to Tim Orley,' she whispered. 'Straight away.'

'What is it?'

She hesitated. Should she tell him what she had found? Why not? But Kokoschka, with his childish temperament, was unpredictable, strong as a bear, capable of running off and thumping the person in question, which might prove to be a mistake.

'Just take it to Tim,' she said quietly. 'Wherever he is. Tell him to come here straight away. Please, Axel, be quick. Don't waste any time.'

Kokoschka turned the packet over in his fingers and stared at it for a second. Then he nodded, turned round and disappeared without another word.

'We *can't* evacuate,' Lynn insisted feverishly. Her fingers became claws, her perfectly filed nails pressed into the flesh of her palms. 'We can't gamble with the trust of our guests.'

'With the greatest respect, have you gone mad?' whispered Dana. 'This place could go up at any minute, and you're talking about abusing the trust of your guests?'

Lynn stared at her and shook her head. Chuck strode resolutely forward.

'Enough of this nonsense,' he said. 'I demand to know right now what's actually going on here.'

'Nothing,' said Dana. 'We're just considering sending Nina Hedegaard to the Artistarchus Plateau on the Callisto, in case there really is something—'

'Listen, girly, I may be old, but I'm not stupid.' Chuck leaned down to Dana and brought his great leonine head level with her eyes. 'So don't underestimate me, okay? I run the best hotels in the world, I've built more of the things than you will ever set foot in, so stop trying to bullshit me.'

'No one's bullshitting you, Chuck, we've just—'

'Lynn.' Donoghue spread his arms in a conciliatory gesture. 'Please tell her to drop it! I know this conniving expression, this whispering. Obviously there's a crisis, but can you please *tell me what's happening here?*'

Chuck had stopped being Chuck. He'd turned into a battering ram, he was trying to get inside her, to overwhelm her, but she wouldn't let him in, wouldn't let anyone in, she had to resist! Julian. Where was Julian? Far away! Just as he always had been, throughout her life. When she was born. When she needed him. When Crystal died. When, when, when. Julian? Far away! All the responsibility rested on her shoulders.

'Lynn?'

Don't lose control. Not now. Hold off the breakdown that was clearly coming with the inevitability of a supernova, long enough to act. Hold off Dana, her enemy. And everyone else who knew. Each one of them was her enemy. She was completely alone. She could only rely on herself.

'Please excuse me.'

She had to act. Bumble, hum, buzz, bzzzz. A swarm of hornets, she ran down the stairs to the lift.

Chuck watched her open-mouthed.

'What's up with her?'

'No idea,' said Dana.

'I didn't mean to insult her,' he stammered. 'I really didn't. I just wanted to—'

'Do me a favour, okay? Go and join the others.'

Chuck rubbed his chin.

'Please, Chuck,' she said. 'It's all okay. I'll keep you posted, I promise.'

She left him standing there and went after Lynn.

*   *   *

It wasn't that Axel Kokoschka thought he was overweight, or not *really*. On the other hand his art represented the compatibility of genuine gourmet cuisine with the requirements of a fitness society fixated on the burning of calories. And in those terms he *was* overweight. Firmly resolved to reduce the fifteen kilos that he weighed up here at least to fourteen, he hardly ever used the lifts. Here again he leapt from bridge to bridge, forcing his burly body up one floor after another, and then took the flight of stairs to the neck. The area between Gaia's shoulders and head was little more than a mezzanine where the passenger lifts stopped, and only the freight elevators and the staff lift continued to the kitchen. Where the side neck muscles would have been in a human being, stairs led to the suite wing below, swinging into the head with its restaurants and bars. The neck was also a storage area for spherical tanks of liquid oxygen to make up for any leakage. The tanks were hidden behind the walls and took up a considerable amount of room, so that only Gaia's throat was glazed. A number of oxygen candles hung in wall holders.

Kokoschka snorted. Without resorting to the scales, he knew he had in fact put on some weight over the past few days. No wonder Sophie had been a bit stand-offish with him. He would have to work out more often, go to the gym, on the treadmill, or else his fleshly contact would be restricted to fillets, schnitzels and mince.

There was no one in Chang'e. Selene, a floor up, was also contenting itself with its own company, and so was the Luna Bar. To judge by the voices, the gang was right up at the top. Strangely, Kokoschka barely felt frightened, in spite of the possible risk of death. He couldn't imagine an atom bomb, or an atom bomb exploding. And besides, they hadn't found anything, and wouldn't such a thing give off radiation? He was far more concerned about Sophie. Something had startled her. All of a sudden she had seemed absolutely terrified, and then there was that scribbled note that she had given him to give to Tim.

But Tim Orley wasn't there. Only the Donoghues, Rebecca Hsu, Miranda Winter, and the Russian's sad wife sat hunched over their drinks, looking dazed. Funaki said Tim had been there just before he arrived, and had asked after Lynn, while as for her, she had lost her head a few moments before.

'And I hadn't done anything,' Donoghue mumbled to nobody in particular. 'I really hadn't.'

'Yeah.' Aileen looked sagely around. 'She's looked stressed lately, don't you think?'

'Lynn's okay.'

'Well that's how it seemed to me. Not you? Even in the space station.'

'Lynn's okay,' Chuck repeated. 'It's this hotel manager I can't stand.'

'Why not?' Rebecca raised her eyebrows. 'She's just doing her job.'

'She's hiding something.'

'Yes, then—' Kokoschka made as if to leave the Mama Quilla Club. 'Then—'

'My experience tells me so!' Chuck slammed his hand down on the table. 'And my prostate. Where experience fails, my prostate knows. I'm telling you, she's shitting the lot of us. I wouldn't be surprised if we found out that she was pulling the wool over all our eyes.'

'Then I need to—'

'And what are you going to surprise us with this evening, young man?' Aileen asked in a saccharine voice.

Kokoschka ran his hand over his bald head. Amazing, just a few millimetres of scalp. How it kept producing more sweat. Layer after layer, as if he were sweating out his brain.

'Ossobucco with risotto milanese,' he murmured.

'Ooooh!' said Winter. 'I love risotto!'

'I make it the Venetian way,' Aileen told Kokoschka. 'You know you constantly have to keep stirring? Never stop stirring.'

'He's a chef, darling,' said Chuck.

'I know that. May I ask where you learned your craft?'

'Erm . . .' Kokoschka squirmed, like a bug on flypaper. 'Sylt – among other places.'

'Oh, Sylt, wait, that's, that's, don't tell me, it's that city in northern Norway, right? Up at the top.'

'No.'

'It isn't?'

'No.' He had to get away, find Tim. 'An island.'

'And *who* did you learn from, Alex?' Aileen twinkled intimately at him. 'I can say Alex, can't I?'

'Axel. From Johannes King. Sorry, I've really got to—'

'Do you use beef marrow in your risotto?'

Kokoschka looked nervously at the stairs, a fox in a trap, a fish in a net.

'Come on, tell us your secrets.' Aileen smiled. 'Sit down, Alex, Axel, sit down.'

The deeper Sophie Thiel dug into the recordings, the stranger it all seemed. Via cleverly disguised cross-connections, you reached lists of unofficial hot keys, some of them cryptic, others designed to control the hotel's communication system. Among other things, they also blocked the laser connection between Gaia and the moon base, or more precisely they directed the signal to a mobile phone connection. By now she also thought she knew what the mysterious menu was for. It wasn't the LPCS itself that was coming under attack, it was more that an impulse was sent to the Earth, and as far as she could tell that impulse had prompted a block that didn't just affect lunar satellites. A lot of work had been done here; the Moon had been completely cut off from the Earth.

And suddenly she doubted that all that effort had been devoted only to the purpose of destroying the hotel.

Who *were* they?

Tim! She desperately hoped Tim would appear at last. Hadn't Axel found him? She didn't know enough to lift the block, particularly since she didn't know what it had actually unleashed. On the other hand she was confident that she could undo the interference with the laser connection to Peary Base. She would make contact with the astronauts there and ask for help, even if it might put her life in danger, because somebody might be listening in on her, but in that case she would just lock herself away somewhere.

Lock herself away, what nonsense! Childish idea. Where are you going to lock yourself away when the bomb goes off?

She had to get out of here! They all had to get out of here!

Her fingers darted over the touchscreen, barely touching the smooth, cool surface. After a few seconds she heard footsteps, and the familiar shadow settled on her again. The lamb cutlets were going cold beside her, in silent reproach.

'Did you find him?' she asked, without looking up, as she corrected a command. She had to rewrite that one sequence, but perhaps it wasn't even Axel, it was Tim.

No reply.

Sophie looked up.

As she leapt up and recoiled, sending her chair flying, she realised that she had made a crucial blunder. She should have stayed calm. She shouldn't have turned a hair. Instead her eyes were wide with horror, revealing all her deadly knowledge.

'You,' Sophie whispered. 'It's you.'

Again, no answer. At least not in words.

Heidrun felt a little awkward as she stepped into the suite, in dressing gown and flipflops. Unusually, but in pointed contrast to Finn, she had opted against the familiar rock-climbing match up the bridges, and instead primly pressed the lift button, as if it was the last thing that the pitiful remains of her arrogance could still manage. Aghast at what she had just surrendered, when Walo had never been unsatisfactory in that regard, she had the lift cabin carry her up to Gaia's ribcage, away from the pool of temptation, stiff as a board, no false moves, just carefully sniffing her fingers for traces of lust. She felt as if her whole body exuded betrayal. The air in the lift struck her as heavy with clues, thick with vaginal aromas and the ozone stench of alien sperm, even though nothing had happened, at least not *really*, and yet –

Walo, her heart thumped. Walo, oh Walo!

She found him reading, gave him a kiss, that familiar, scratchy moustachioed kiss. He smiled.

'Have fun?'

'Lots,' she said and fled to the bathroom. 'And you? Not in the bar?'

'I was, darling. It was only moderately bearable. Chuck's jokes are starting to offend Aileen's Christian sensibilities. A while ago he asked what a healthy dog and a short-sighted gynaecologist have in common.'

'Let me guess. A wet nose?'

'So I thought I might as well read.'

She looked at herself in the mirror, her white, violet-eyed elfin face, just as she had seen Finn's face down below, in the merciless light of the realisation that people aged, they aged inexorably, that their once immaculate skin began to wrinkle, that she was a depressing forty-six, and had something in common with many men who tried to recapture their lost youth, something that women generally said they would never undergo: a proper midlife crisis.

If you want to grow old with someone, she thought, you shouldn't need anyone else to make you feel younger.

And she loved Walo, she loved him so much!

Naked, she walked back into the living room, lay down on the carpet in front of him, folded her hands behind her head, stretched out a foot and tapped his left knee.

'What are you reading there?'

He lowered the book and studied her outstretched body with a smile.

'Whatever it was,' he said, 'I've just forgotten it.'

Tim pressed the door buzzer again.

'Lynn? Please let me in. Let's talk.'

No reaction. What if he was mistaken? He'd just missed her in the Mama Quilla Club, and had assumed that she had gone to her suite. But perhaps she was doing other things. What frightened him more than any bomb was the idea that she might actually be losing her mind, that she had already lost it. Crystal, too, hadn't just been depressive, she'd increasingly lost touch with reality.

'Lynn? If you're there, open up.'

After a while he gave in and jumped down the bridges to the lobby, deeply concerned. He wondered what Sophie was up to. Whether the Gravedigger had uncovered the footage. At the same time his thoughts revolved around himself: Amber, Julian, bomb, Lynn, Hanna, accomplices, satellite failure, bomb, Amber, Lynn, worries that devoured one another, a madhouse.

The control centre was empty. Sophie was nowhere to be seen.

'Sophie?'

He looked helplessly around. A bulkhead led to a back room, but when he put his finger on the sensor field, he found it was locked. He saw Dana running towards him through the lobby. She entered the control centre and looked around with a frown.

'Have you seen Sophie?'

'No.'

'Is everything spiralling out of control?' Her face darkened. 'She was supposed to be here. Someone has to be in the control centre. I guess you haven't bumped into Kokoschka?'

'No.' Tim scratched the back of his head. 'Weird. Sophie was working on something very interesting.'

'Which was?'

He told Dana about the authorisation program and what they'd hoped to find with it. The manager's face was expressionless. When he had finished, she did what he too had done when he came in, and studied the monitor wall.

'Forget it,' said Tim. 'There's nothing there.'

'No, she doesn't seem to have got very far. Did she even install the program?'

'I was here when she did.'

Dana walked in silence to the touchscreen, keyed in the call-codes of Ashwini Anand, Axel Kokoschka, Michio Funaki and Sophie Thiel and put all of them on a single channel. Only Ashwini and Michio replied.

'Can anyone tell me where Sophie and Axel are?'

'Not here,' said Michio. Chuck's booming bass voice could be heard in the background.

'Not with me either,' said Ashwini. 'Isn't Sophie in the control centre?'

'No. Tell them to check in as soon as possible if you meet them. Point number two – we're evacuating.'

'What?' cried Tim.

She told him to keep his voice down.

'In five minutes I'm going to put out a message and ask our guests to make their way to the Mama Quilla Club at half past eight. You are to be there too. We'll tell them exactly what's going on, and then leave the hotel together.'

'What's happening to the Ganymede?' Anand asked.

'I don't know.' She glanced at the time. 'We're going to put out a radio flare for it Ganymede, which will reach it as soon as it's within range of Gaia. They aren't to land, but to fly on immediately to Peary Base. Not a word to the guests before eight thirty.'

'Got it.'

'Okay,' said Funaki.

'I'm not surprised about Axel Kokoschka,' said Dana, and rang off. 'You can never get hold of him; he's always forgetting his phone. A great chef, a hopeless knucklehead in every other respect. If he and Sophie haven't appeared by eight thirty, put out a call for them.'

'Are we really going to clear this place?' asked Tim.

'What would you do in my place?'

'I don't know.'

'You see? I do, though. Let's not fool ourselves – our father's been overdue for an hour and a half now, and even though we haven't found a bomb, it doesn't necessarily mean that it isn't ticking away somewhere even so.' She put a finger to her lips. 'Hmm. Do atom bombs tick?'

'No idea.'

'No matter. We'll send Nina Hedegaard to the Aristarchus Plateau and take the Lunar Express to the base.'

'End of a pleasure trip,' said Tim, and suddenly he became aware that his bottom lip was beginning to tremble. Amber! He fought against it and stared at his shoes. Dana let a smile play around her lips.

'We will find Ganymede,' she said. 'Hey, Tim, chin up.'

'It's okay.'

'I need you with a clear head right now. Go back to the bar, tell a joke, lighten the mood a bit.'

Tim gulped. 'Chuck's the guy in charge of jokes.'

'Tell *better ones*.'

'Mr Orley? Er – Tim?'

The fitness area was huge. Quite how huge, you discovered when you set about trying to find someone there, and Kokoschka looked conscientiously. After escaping Aileen's suffocating curiosity, he had to face fatherly advice from Chuck. He should look for Julian's son where men who valued high life expectation and firm abdominal muscles tended to go, and where Tim had been going every evening.

But the gyms were deserted, the tennis courts abandoned. In the steam bath, a mist of droplets mixed with tinkling Far Eastern music. Tim wasn't in the Finnish sauna, he wasn't pounding along a treadmill or punishing an exercise bike, in fact he seemed instead to have put all his energy into running away from Kokoschka. A moment of optimism when he heard sounds from the pool, but it made for disappointment when he discovered that only Nina Hedegaard was there, swimming lonely lengths in the crater. Tim wasn't there, and he hadn't been there, and what was going on, where was the Ganymede and were the satellites still sleeping?

Kokoschka concluded that Nina knew nothing about the bomb. Perhaps because in all the excitement they'd forgotten to tell her. He was tempted for a moment to put her in the picture, but tough girl Dana might have reasons for restricting the number of initiates. He was a chef, not a corrector of higher decisions, so he mumbled a word of thanks and decided to give Sophie Thiel at least an interim report.

As soon as Tim appeared in Gaia's forehead again, the announcement came through:

'As you will already have established, ladies and gentlemen, our schedule is rather disrupted, not least because Ganymede is late and we are unfortunately having problems with satellite communication.' Dana's voice sounded apathetic and toneless. 'There is no need to worry, but I ask all of Gaia's guests and staff members to make their way to the Mama

Quilla Club at 8.30 p.m., where we will inform you about the latest state of development. Please be on time.'

'That's in ten minutes,' Rebecca said in a thick voice.

'Doesn't sound good,' muttered Chuck.

'How come?' Unimpressed, Miranda emptied down a bowl of cheese puffs. 'She said there was no need to worry.'

'Sure, that's her job.' Chuck rocked angrily back and forth, fists clenched, drumming arhythmically on the seat of his chair. 'I'm telling you, she's messing with us. I've been saying that all along!'

'At least we're going to be informed now,' Aileen reassured him.

'No, Chuck's right,' Olympiada observed listlessly. 'The most reliable clue for an impending catastrophe is when higher authorities deny them.'

'Rubbish,' said Miranda.

'No, we've got to assume the worst,' Donoghue said to Olympiada.

Miranda plundered another bowl. 'You guys are all so negative. Bad karma.'

'Remember my words.'

'Silly nonsense.'

'I know this from my parliamentary work,' Olympiada explained to her half-empty glass. 'For example when we say we aren't going to raise taxes, it means we are. And when—'

'But we're not in parliament,' Tim replied, more sharply than he had meant to. 'So far everything in this hotel has been organised very professionally, hasn't it?'

She looked at him. 'My husband is on Ganymede.'

'So's my wife.'

'Okay, you lot can wait.' Chuck jumped up and hurried to the stairs. 'I'm going down there!'

'Where's Sophie?'

'*Mister* Kokoschka!' Dana glared at him. 'How about being contactable for a change?'

Kokoschka flinched. He rubbed his big paws on his jacket and glanced around the control centre.

'Sorry. I know we're supposed to be meeting in the Mama Quilla—'

'Get used to carrying your phone around with you. The question comes back to you. Where is Sophie?'

'Sophie?' Kokoschka started poking around in his left ear. 'I thought she was here. Don't know. Shall I start on the dinner? I've got to—' He hesitated. The note seemed to be burning a hole in his jacket pocket. 'You wouldn't happen to know where Tim Orley is?'

'What is this?' A wrinkle appeared between Dana's eyebrows. 'A quiz show? Are we playing hide-and-seek?'

'I'm just asking.'

'Tim Orley should be in the bar. He went up there a few minutes ago.'

'Okay, then—' Kokoschka took a step back.

'Stay where you are,' Dana said severely. 'Tell me again exactly where you looked this afternoon. Did you check the sauna too?'

'Yep.' He fidgeted around in the doorway, suddenly very worried about Sophie. What was going on?

'Calm down,' said Dana. 'We'll go up there together in a few minutes.'

The bar was filling up. Karla Kramp and Eva Borelius appeared on the stairs, followed by the Nairs and Finn, and blocked Chuck's way as he came charging down as if pursued by the four horsemen of the Apocalypse.

'Do you know anything?' He flashed his eyes at them.

'No more than you do, I should think.' Eva shrugged. 'They want to tell us something.'

'I hope it's nothing bad,' said Sushma anxiously.

'It'll be more than the time of day, I can promise you that,' blustered Donoghue. 'Something's happened.'

'You think?'

'Friends, why all this speculation?' Nair smiled. 'In a few minutes we will know more.'

'In a few minutes we'll hear a load of prepared blarney,' Chuck bellowed. 'I could tell by looking at Lynn and all those plaster saints. You can't fool Chucky.'

'Who says they're trying to fool you?' asked Finn.

'My experience,' snapped Donoghue. 'My prostate!'

'Have you had the golden finger?'

'Now listen, young man—'

'What are you getting worked up about? That they're hiding something from us? They aren't, you know.'

'They aren't?' Chuck narrowed his eyes. 'And how do you know that?'

'*My* prostate!' Finn grinned. 'Claptrap, Chucky. If they wanted to keep something from us, they'd hardly have called a meeting.'

'But I don't want to know what just *anyone* gets to hear.' Chuck struck his chest with his fist. 'I want the *whole* truth, you understand?' He pushed past them. 'And first, I'm telling you now, I'm not letting that stupid skank of a hotel manager go up there, just so as you know!'

'Tsk, tsk.' Karla watched after him. 'For a hotelier, he really sounds like a grumpy guest.'

'We've got to get up there,' said Heidrun.

She was half lying on top of Ögi, half beside him, with his hairy arm under her back. As if infected by the virus of infidelity, she had forced him to make love, to receive the antidote to her own lust, and it was at the sound of Dana's voice that she had experienced an exorbitant neuronal firework, as if it had been sparked by the hotel manager's monotonous voice. Whatever the reason for the disturbance, Heidrun was so furious with Dana that she chose to ignore the announcement, and proceeded to do just that for a whole six minutes, with Ögi's fingers stroking the back of her neck.

'What time is it?' he asked.

She rolled reluctantly onto her back and glanced at the digital display above the door.

'Four minutes before half past eight. We *could* still try to be on time.'

'What, are you crazy?'

'It's what people generally expect of the Swiss.'

'Time to demolish some clichés, perhaps?' Ögi picked up a strand of her hair. Unpigmented keratin, but in it he saw white moonlight melting between his fingers. 'Okay, maybe you're right, we shouldn't dawdle. People will be getting worried.'

'About Ganymede?'

'About whatever. It isn't very comforting to be invited to this kind of meeting.'

'Motormouth told us not to worry.'

'And you couldn't really say we had, could you?' He grinned and sat up. 'Come on, *mein Schatz*. Let's get into social contract mode.'

With silent, sweating Kokoschka by her side, Dana was going up. The lift stopped at the fifteenth floor. Lynn joined them. She looked dreadful, as if she'd aged several years, hardly able to focus, her eyes darting unsteadily around. A curiously distant, sly-looking smile played around the corners of her mouth.

'What's all this?' she said to Dana without looking at her. She ignored Kokoschka completely.

'What's all what?'

'What's the meeting for?'

The lift doors closed.

'We're evacuating,' Dana said bluntly. 'Where have you been, Lynn? Have you seen Sophie?'

'Sophie?' Lynn looked at her as if she'd never heard the name before but thought it was very interesting.

'Yes. You remember Sophie Thiel.'

'We can't evacuate,' Lynn said, almost cheerfully. 'Julian wouldn't want that.'

'Your father isn't here.'

'Call it off.'

'Excuse me, but I think it's exactly what he would want.'

'No! No, no, no, no, no.'

'Yes, Lynn.'

'You're messing up the whole trip.'

Kokoschka hunched his shoulders and stuck his hand in his

pocket. Dana noticed and gave a start. Was he holding something in his hand?

'You stupid bitch,' Lynn said brightly, and the lift doors opened again.

Chuck Donoghue was waiting in the neck. He was quivering with rage. Aileen came hurrying down the stairs wearing a concerned expression. Dana came out of the lift, with Lynn and Kokoschka hot on her heels.

'What can I do for you, Chuck?'

'You're taking us for idiots, aren't you?'

'I'm here to inform you about the state of developments.' Dana faked a smile. 'So could we go upstairs, please?'

'No, we couldn't.'

'Please, Chucky.' Aileen fiddled with Donoghue's sleeve. The lift doors slid shut. 'Listen to what she has to say.'

'I'll listen to it *here*.'

'There's nothing to say,' Lynn twittered. 'Everything's hunky-dory. Shall we go and eat?'

'I want to know what's going on right now!' snapped Donoghue. He came closer, entered her personal space. 'Where's Julian? Where are the others? You've known what's happening for ages, why can't we talk to anybody? You've known all along.'

'Are you threatening me, Chuck?'

'Come on. Say it.'

Dana Lawrence didn't budge from the spot. She stared calmly into the big man's eyes. To do so, she had to throw her head back, but inside it was as if she was looking down at Donoghue.

'*When* I've told you, shall we go up?'

Donoghue clearly hadn't expected her to give in so easily. He took a step back.

'Of course,' Aileen hurried to reassure her in his place.

'Yes, of course,' Donoghue repeated lamely.

'No!' screamed Lynn.

*　　　*　　　*

Tim heard her in the Mama Quilla Club, even though the Chang'e, the Selene and the Luna Bar were in between. He heard her fear, her rage, her madness. All at once he leapt to his feet and dived down the stairs taking four at a time. Dana's authoritarian alto joined in, counterpointed by arpeggios of high, frightened, Aileen wails, over Donoghue's rumbling bass. He plunged down into Gaia's throat.

Strange. His sister had pulled one of the oxygen candles from its mounting and was swinging the steel cylinder like a club, while Dana, Chuck, Aileen and Kokoschka circled her like a pack of wolves.

Tim pushed his way between the Donoghues, saw Lynn stepping back and roared, 'What's going on? What are you doing to her?'

'Why don't you ask *her* what she's doing to us,' growled Chuck.

'Lynn—'

'Leave me alone! Don't get too close!'

Tim held his hand out to her. She recoiled still further, raised the candle and stared at him, eyes darting from side to side.

'Tell me what's going on.'

'She wants to evacuate Gaia,' Lynn panted. 'That's what's going on. The bitch wants to evacuate Gaia.'

Kokoschka was so confused that he didn't even try to understand what was going on. Clearly the business manager of Orley Travel was going mad. His thoughts had turned entirely to Tim and the end of his personal odyssey. He drew Sophie's note from his pocket. 'Mr Orley, I've got—'

Tim ignored him. 'Lynn, come to your senses.'

'She wants to evacuate the hotel.' The woman's voice was reduced to a whisper. 'But I won't let her, under any circumstances.'

'Of course, we've got to talk about it. But first give me the candle.'

'Evacuate?' Chuck echoed, eyes rolling.

'You should listen to your brother.' Dana pointed at Lynn's makeshift club. 'You're putting us all in danger.'

Tim knew what she meant. The cylinder contained large quantities of compressed oxygen, and Lynn's fingers were dangerously close to the detonator. As soon as she set the exothermic reaction in motion, the contents would spread slowly into the environment, a pointless waste, along with the danger that the partial pressure of the oxygen would exceed permitted levels. The cartridges were meant for emergencies, when breathable air was in short supply.

'Mr Orley!' Kokoschka was waving a piece of paper.

'*What do you mean, evacuate?*' Donoghue snapped.

'Dana's right,' said Tim. 'Please, Lynn. Give me the candle.'

'Julian doesn't want us to evacuate,' Lynn explained dreamily to an imaginary audience. For a second she seemed completely absent. Then her gaze settled on her brother. 'You know that, don't you? We mustn't frighten Daddy's guests, so we'll all stay here like good boys and girls.'

'That would suit you, wouldn't it?' Dana snorted.

Lynn's dreamy expression made way for seething fury. She swung the cartridge again.

'Tim, tell her to shut up!'

'Oh, so I'm supposed to shut up, am I?' Dana took a step forward. 'What about, Lynn? Everybody here has known for ages.'

Tim looked at her in confusion. 'What are you talking about?'

'About how your sister manipulated the tapes. That she's been used by Hanna. That she's losing her marbles. Isn't that true, Miss Orley?'

Lynn ducked down. A sly spark appeared in her eyes, then she suddenly jumped forwards and swung a blow at Dana, who effortlessly dodged it.

'*You* were the one who let Hanna take his trip on the Lunar Express. Why, Lynn? Was he supposed to bring something back? To us in the hotel?'

'Stop!'

'You blocked the satellites. You're paranoid, Lynn. You're in cahoots with a criminal.'

'*What do you mean, evacuate?*' roared Chuck. He gripped Dana roughly by the shoulder. '*I said, what do you mean, evacuate?*'

The manager whirled around and knocked his hand away.

'You shut your mouth!'

Donoghue's massive head turned crimson. 'You – you jumped-up chambermaid, I'll—'

'Chuck, no!' pleaded Aileen.

'*Miss Orley*—' Dana repeated.

With a tormented expression on her face, Lynn shook her head. Tears were collecting on her eyelids.

'What have you done with Sophie Thiel, Lynn?' Dana insisted. '*You* were in the control centre not long ago.'

'That's not true. I've been—'

'Of course you were there!'

'Dana, that's enough,' hissed Tim.

'You bet.' Dana glared at him. '*I've* had enough. I've had enough of this circus. Give up, Lynn. Tell us the truth about this bomb.'

'*Bomb?*' roared Chuck. He charged forwards like a water buffalo, pushed Lynn against the wall, stretched out his big hands and pulled the cartridge from her fingers. 'Has everybody here gone mad?'

Lynn's fingers bent into claws. She lashed out, drawing a bloody trail across Donoghue's cheek. Before Chuck could recover from his amazement, she was at the stairs, jumped down and disappeared into the floor below.

'Lynn!' cried Tim.

'No, wait! Please wait!'

Kokoschka watched in horror as young Orley dashed after his crazed sister. Stay here, he thought. Not again, I've got to give you—

'Sophie told me to give you . . .'

Too late. Run after him? But the general madness required its tribute, so that he had to look on helplessly as Chuck raged at the hotel manager and stormed after her, holding the oxygen candle menacingly aloft. Storms raged inside his head, downdraughts, plunging temperatures, tornadoes, accumulated fear. Something terrible would happen. His thoughts danced around like faded leaves, blown in all directions by gusts of confusion. Every time he tried to catch them, they whirled away, while he impotently turned and turned. What was he to do? At last he caught one of those leaves, it flapped and fluttered, trying desperately to escape: that whatever Sophie had written on that piece of paper would explain the escalation that was going on in front of his eyes, that the piece of paper would tell him what he needed to do, that perhaps, seeing as how he hadn't managed to carry out his mission, he ought to read it.

Fingers trembling, he unfolded the piece of paper.

At that moment, Dana sensed the change. Her whole body reacted. All the hairs on her forearms registered the disaster. Voices reached her from the restaurant. The tumult must have reached the upper floors, and some people were coming down to see what had happened, while Axel's statue-like face sent out waves of disbelief and fury.

Dana slowly turned her head towards him.

The chef stared at her, a piece of paper in his left hand. His right hand slowly rose, an index finger raised in accusation. Dana took the paper from him and glanced at the words scribbled on it.

'Rubbish,' she said.

'No.' Kokoschka came closer. 'No, not rubbish. She found out. *She found out!*'

'Who found out what?' barked Donoghue.

'Sophie.' Kokoschka's finger twitched; an eyeless, sniffing creature, it swung around and rested on Dana. '*She's the one.* Not Lynn. It's her!'

'You've been spending too much time at the oven.' Dana stepped back. 'Your brain's overcooked, you great idiot.'

'No.' Kokoschka's massive form started moving, a Frankenstein's monster taking its first steps. 'She paralysed the communications. She wants to blow us all up! *She's the one! Dana Lawrence!*'

'You're mad!'

'Oh, really?' Donoghue's eyes narrowed to slits. 'I think we can find that one out pretty quickly.' He picked up the oxygen cartridge and approached her from the other side. 'I remember this great joke where—'

Dana reached into her hip pocket, drew a gun and pointed it at Donoghue's head.

'Here comes the punchline,' she said, and squeezed the trigger.

Donoghue stopped dead. Brain matter spilled from the hole in his forehead, a trickle of blood ran between his eyebrows and along the bridge of his nose. The candle slipped from his hands. Aileen's mouth gaped, and an unearthly wail issued from it. Dana was just swinging the gun around, when the doors of E2 opened and Ashwini Anand stepped out, impelled into the lion's den by her fear of being late. The bullet struck the Indian woman before she had a chance to grasp the situation. She slumped to the ground, blocking the lift door, but her unexpected arrival had lost Dana valuable seconds, which Kokoschka exploited to go on the attack. She took aim at him and at the same moment she was attacked by Aileen, who leapt at her, grabbed her hair and pulled her head back. Aileen was still uninterruptedly wailing, a ghostly funeral lament. Dana reached behind her, trying to shake Aileen off and Kokoschka grabbed her wrist and she managed to knee him in the testicles, before firing off two shots. The chef bent double, but he managed to knock the gun from Dana's fingers. She struck him in the throat with the edge of her hand, and shook the Fury from her back with a roll of her shoulders. Almost gracefully, Aileen sailed against her husband, who was still standing, and dragged him down with her. Kokoschka was crawling along the floor on all fours. Dana kicked him in the chest, just as she heard a metallic hiss that didn't bode well.

The bulkheads were closing.

She stared at the holes in the wall, where the two stray bullets had struck.

The tanks! They must have hit one of the hidden tanks. Compressed oxygen was bursting out, raising the partial pressure and causing the sensors to close off access to the levels above and below. It wasn't impossible that the external cooling pipe had been hit, releasing toxic, inflammable ammonia.

She was in a bomb.

She had to get out of here!

The invisible gas settled on the wildly flailing Aileen, on Chuck's corpse, streamed into the open lift, whose doors were blocked by Anand's dead body. Kokoschka's eyes widened. Gurgling, he got to his feet and stretched out both arms towards Dana. She paid him no attention and ran off. The doors were closing at worrying speed. With one bound she reached the entrance to the suites, jumped and just managed to get past the bulkhead from Gaia's neck, somersaulted down the stairs and landed on her back.

Kokoschka came after her. Properly trained, he knew the potentially disastrous effect of an uncontrolled release of oxygen. Desperate to get out in time, he followed Dana to the bulkhead, but didn't get all the way through. He was trapped.

'No, no, no, no, no . . .' he whimpered.

Now he could hear the faint hiss of the escaping oxygen. Terrified, he tried to brace himself against the approaching metal plate. His breath was forced out of him, his organs crushed. He heard one of his lower ribs breaking, saw Aileen kneeling over Chuck's corpse and burying her face in the crook of his neck. A metallic taste spread through his mouth, and his eyes bulged. He tried to shout, but all he managed was a dying croak.

'Chuck,' Aileen whimpered.

There was a not especially loud puffing sound as the oxygen went up. Two glowing spears of fire suddenly thrust from the wall where the bullets had hit, striking Aileen, Chuck's corpse and Ashwini Anand's bent body, the walls and the floor. The flames quickly swept along the lift doors, forced their way into the open cabin of the staff lift, like living creatures, fire spirits in orgiastic exuberance. A moment later half of the mezzanine was alight. Kokoschka had never seen a fire raging like that. People said that fires spread more slowly in reduced gravity, but this—

He spewed a stream of blood. The bulkhead pressed relentlessly against his tortured body, and as if the fire had only just noticed him, it reared up to new heights and seemed to pause uncertainly for a moment.

Then it leapt at him hungrily.

Miranda Winter had, with Sushma Nair, set off for the lower floors, once it could no longer be ignored that there were noisy arguments going on

down there. On the stairs from Selene to Chang'e, they heard two muffled bangs in quick succession, which anyone who had ever been to the
movies would have recognised as pistol shots from a silenced weapon,
followed by Aileen's bloodcurdling howl, then some bell-like chimes,
as if a hammer were being struck against metal. Sushma's expression
turned to one of naked fear; Winter, however, was made of sterner
stuff, so she beckoned Sushma to wait and approached the passageway
through the neck.

What the—?

'The bulkhead is closing,' she cried. 'Hey, they're locking us in!'

Baffled, she stepped closer to get a glimpse through the crack of
what lay below.

A figure of flame came flying at her. The demon hissed and roared at
her, reached for her with sparks flying from its finger, singed her eyelids,
brows and hair. She stumbled, fell and pushed herself up as she tried to
get away from the raging flames.

'Oh, shit!' she cried. 'Get out, Sushma, get out!'

The demon tumbled and licked its way around, multiplied, giving
birth to new, twitching creatures that darted around gleefully setting
ablaze anything that stood in their way. With uncanny speed they covered
the glass façade, found little of interest there and concentrated their campaign on the floor, the pillars and the furniture. Miranda leapt to her feet,
hurried up the stairs, driving the distraught Sushma ahead of her with a
series of loud shrieks. The bulkheads to Selene were closing right above
them. A wall of heat was surging at them from behind. Sushma stumbled. Miranda slapped her on the backside, and Sushma pushed her way
past the bulkhead to the next floor up.

Close! Christ, that was close!

Like a gymnast, she grabbed the edge of the bulkhead and pulled herself up on it. For a moment she was afraid her ankle would get stuck in
the lock, but then, by a hair, she got into Selene, and the bulkhead closed
with a dull thud and saved them from the wave of fire.

'The others,' she panted. 'God alive! The others!'

*　　　*　　　*

Dana was lying on her back, Kokoschka's legs pedalling wildly above her, hammering the steps of the spiral staircase. The roar of the fire reached her from the neck, followed by the flames themselves, greedily creeping up Kokoschka's jacket and trousers. They looked as if they were feeling, searching for something. They flowed in waves over the ceiling, the structure and its coverings in its quest for food.

Dana leapt to her feet.

She had to dislodge Kokoschka's body so that the bulkhead could close. Oxygen fires were uncontrollable, hotter and more destructive than any conventional kind. Even though the gas as such didn't burn, it fatally encouraged the destruction of all kinds of material, and it was heavier than air. The blaze would spill like lava from Gaia's throat and engulf the entire suite section. One leap and she was at the manual control panel, crouched down to get as far as she could from the heat, and activated the mechanism that operated the bulkhead. It opened, and Kokoschka was free. He dashed down the steps and leapt onto the gallery, kicking instinctively around. Tentacles of flame shot from the gap, as if to drag back the prey that had just been snatched from them. But the bulkhead closed on them, cutting off the blaze and isolating Gaia's neck from its shoulders.

The chef was a human torch. A fog of chemical extinguishing agents forced its way out of the ventilation system, but it wasn't nearly enough. In a few moments, the plants, the walls, the floor would all be ablaze. Dana pulled a portable CO_2 fire extinguisher from the wall, emptied it on the body now lying motionless and then pointed what was left at the ceiling. In the inferno above her, the extinguisher system had probably given up long ago. By now the temperatures up there must be unimaginable. Sooty smoke entered her airways and blinded her eyes. Her chest began to hurt. If she didn't get fresh air in a minute, she would die of smoke poisoning. Kokoschka and the stairs and parts of the ceiling were still smouldering away, little fires still flared here and there, but instead of trying to quell them, she staggered along the gallery, eyes streaming, unable to breathe, the creak and clatter of the bulkhead in her ears, now sealing off Gaia's shoulder. Where the gallery ended in the figure's right arm, there was an emergency storeroom which contained, alongside the inev-itable candles, some oxygen masks. She quickly put one of the masks on, greedily sucked in the oxygen and watched as access to the arm was sealed off.

She hadn't been fast enough.

She was trapped.

Tim managed to catch up with his sister in the hall. She'd been trying to escape across the glass bridges, leaping like a satyr but with her knees trembling, so that he was terrified he was about to watch her slip to her doom, but nothing could stop her attempt to escape. It was only at the last jump that she faltered, fell and crept away on all fours. Tim jumped down immediately behind her and grabbed her ankle. Lynn's elbows bent. She slipped away on her belly, trying to escape him. He held her firmly, turned her on her back and received a smack in the face. Lynn panted, grunted, tried to scratch him. He gripped her wrists and forced her down.

'No!' he cried. 'Stop! It's me!'

She raged and snapped at him. It was like fighting a rabid animal. Now that her hands had been immobilised, she struck out with her legs, threw herself back and forth, then suddenly rolled her eyes and lay slack. Her breathing was fitful. For a moment he was afraid he was going to lose her to unconsciousness, then he saw her eyelids flutter. Her eyes cleared. 'It's fine,' he said. 'I'm with you.'

'I'm sorry,' she whimpered. 'I'm so sorry!'

She started sobbing. He let go of her wrists, took her in his arms and started rocking her like a baby.

'Help me, Tim. Please help me.'

'I'm here. It's fine. Everything's fine.'

'No, it isn't.' She pressed herself against him, clawed her fingers into the fabric of his jacket. 'I'm going mad. I'm losing my mind. I—'

The rest was drowned by fresh sobbing, and Tim felt as unprepared as a schoolboy, even though it was the terrifying spectre of this situation that had prompted him to come on Julian's idiotic pleasure trip in the first place. But now his brain threatened to go on strike on grounds of continuous overload and abandon him to naked terror. He threw back his head and looked at the phantom of smoke in the dome of the atrium, menacingly spreading its wings. Something grew from the balconies, metal plates, enormous bulkheads, and he started to sense that something terrible was going on up there.

Cape Heraclides, Montes Jura

For the first few minutes they had made quick progress, until it turned out that the bigger boulders supported one another, and developed a curious dynamism of their own as soon as you removed one of them. Several times he and Hanna were nearly crushed by a rolling rock. Whenever Locatelli jumped out of the way at the last second, his mind came up with bold scenarios of cause and effect in which debris – guided in precise trajectories – would crush Hanna as flat as a pancake. The Achilles heel of all these plans was that nothing in the field of debris around Ganymede lent itself to precise calculation, so he resigned himself to cooperation. They carried the rubble down, alert, watching out for each other's safety, they pushed, pulled, dragged and lifted, and after two hours of backbreaking work they reached their physical limits. Several of the colossal boulders showed some movement, to be sure, but refused to be shifted. Breathless, Locatelli leaned against one of the rocks and was amazed not to hear Hanna panting like a dog as well.

Clearly the Canadian was in better shape.

'What now?' he asked.

'What indeed. We've got to get the hatch open.'

'Oh really, Cleverdick? Shame it's impossible.'

Hanna leaned down and studied the blockage. Locatelli could hear the gears whirring in his head.

'Why don't you chuck one of your bombs in?' he suggested. 'Let's blow these bloody things up.'

'No, the energy would disperse outside. Although—' Hanna hesitated, stepped over and crouched down to a spot where two of the rocks touched. His hand dug into the crack in the ground and brought out some gravel. 'Perhaps you're right.'

'Of course I'm right,' panted Locatelli. 'I'm generally right. The bane and blessing of my existence. The deeper your blasted shot goes in, the more it can do.'

'Even so, I'm not sure the explosive will be enough. The stones are enormous.'

'But porous! This stuff's basalt, volcanic rock. With a bit of luck bits of it will come flying off, and you'll destabilise the whole pile.'

'Fine,' Hanna agreed. 'Let's try that.'

They began deepening and widening the channel. After an interval the Canadian disappeared inside the ship, brought out the console struts of the grasshopper, and they went on digging with that makeshift tool; they scraped and scrabbled until Hanna thought the channel was deep enough. At an appropriate distance from the Ganymede, at a slightly elevated position, they piled the smaller stones from the surroundings into a wall, lay down flat behind it, and Hanna took aim.

'Heads down!'

Like a newborn cosmos, a grey cloud expanded among the rocks. Warren Locatelli crouched lower. Bits of rock were hitting the basalt to right and left of the wall. When he raised his head above the parapet, it looked at first as if nothing had happened. Then he saw the huge boulder at the front shifting incredibly slowly and then spinning on its own axis. The one next to it dislodged as well, pushed its neighbour aside, and immediately collapsed, sending fragments scattering down the slope.

'Yeah!' cried Locatelli. 'My idea. My idea!'

The big boulder was still spinning, and when it was jostled by a third that toppled into the gap, it finally leaned over, rolled heavily a few more metres and produced a chain reaction of tumbling debris that rattled cheerfully down the hill.

'Yeah! Yeah!'

He jumped to his feet. They leapt from their improvised trench, and shoved the remaining rubble aside. Drunk on dopamine and thrilled by their joint success, Locatelli forgot the circumstances of their enmity, as if the disputes of the past few hours had been based on a script error, in which Hanna, the good mate, had been unjustly demonised, but was now, once again, someone with whom you could run races and blow up moon mountains. They freed the hatch of the Ganymede, and Hanna gave him a friendly slap on the shoulder.

'Well done, Warren. Very good!'

That contact, even though he barely felt it through his thick armour, brought Warren to his senses with a start. He couldn't get so drunk on his body's stimulants that he would actually let Hanna touch him. He had always liked the Canadian, with his moderate machismo, his monosyllabic manner, and now he thought he could discern something vaguely friendly about him, which made things even worse.

'Let's get it over with,' he said roughly. 'You open the hatch, I drive the buggy out and—'

'No, you can take a break,' Hanna said equably. 'I'll drive it out myself.'

'Why? Do you think I'll try and get away?'

'Yes, that's exactly what I think.'

And you're right, you fucker, thought Locatelli. He had flirted with the idea. Now he had conflicted feelings. He watched Hanna as he ran up the slope, climbed the nose of the Ganymede and disappeared from view. Suddenly he was aware that the hitman didn't need him any more. Feeling uneasy, he took a step back, as the hatch swung open and started to lower. He could see the inside of the freight space. A ramp emerged from the tipping hatch, and there was Hanna, already standing next to the buggy. He sat down in the driver's seat, checked the controls and started. The ramp came down towards the ground, and Locatelli spotted that its rim wasn't going to make contact. The furrow that the shuttle had made had piled the debris up too far. It stopped a good metre above the regolith. For a moment the little vehicle looked like an animal about to spring, then it came to a standstill just beyond the edge of the ramp.

Locatelli hesitated. He didn't really know what to hope for, or what to fear. For a moment he had been worried that Hanna might simply drive on and leave him here, in the shadow of a broken-down spaceship that could no longer even be flooded with breathable air. Now, when he saw the Canadian climbing out, the source of his unease shifted to the possibility that the Canadian would proceed to make short work of him before driving off. Nervously, he took a step towards the ramp.

'What's up?' asked Hanna. 'Aren't you coming?'

'Coming?' echoed Locatelli.

'You can still be useful to me.'

Useful. Aha.

'And for how long,' Locatelli asked, 'will I be useful?'

'Until we've reached the American extraction station.' Hanna pointed outside at the dusty plain. 'When you were unconscious, I did a rough calculation of our position. What I see from here tells me that we're stranded precisely at the tip of Cape Heraclides. That means that the station is to the north-east, in the middle of the basalt lake, where the Sinus Iridum and the Mare Imbrium meet. About a hundred kilometres from here.'

'And why do you want to go there?'

'The station's automated,' said Hanna. 'But inspectors are always going there. A terminal was set up for them. Pressurised. A proper little base, where you could live for several months. We'll have to rely on our own sense of direction to get there, since all the satellites are out.'

'Turn them back on, then.'

'What makes you think I can do that?'

'What makes you think I've got shit for brains?' barked Locatelli. 'They all failed when you set off on your crazy little journey. Are you trying to tell me that was coincidence?'

Hanna said nothing for a few moments.

'Of course not,' he said. 'But it's not in my power to correct that. We had to interrupt communication after I'd been busted, and now stop bugging me, okay? Help me to navigate and I'll leave you at the extraction station. If you want to live—'

Hanna went on talking, but Locatelli wasn't listening. He stared past the ramp. Something to the side of the Ganymede had attracted his attention.

'—rid of me,' Hanna was saying. 'You've just got to—'

Why was dust swirling up where the body of the shuttle was in the regolith? Little clouds puffing up along its flank, like an approaching steam train. What was happening? The outlines of the spaceship blurred, its steel fuselage quivered. The edge of the ramp barely rose above the debris, but more dust was pouring out. The ground was trembling too.

'—then we'll—'

'The shuttle's slipping!' yelled Locatelli.

Hanna jerked around. The Ganymede reared up, no longer stabilised by the boulders that they had blown away. A moment later it started moving again and slipped backwards, spraying up sand and gravel. Locatelli saw Hanna dash up and jump onto the ramp that was now hurtling towards them, which swept the buggy up and away; he tried to leap to safety, stumbled and fell. He was back on his feet in a moment, pushed himself away, dived to the side—

Another half-metre and he would have done it.

The moment the rim cut into his belly, he saw with crystal clarity the image of Carl Hanna who, a universe further off, had done the right thing and sought refuge in altitude. Then a searing pain erased all other thoughts. He instinctively gripped the steel, a torero impaled on the bull's horns, shaken to the core by the downhill race of the Ganymede, which dropped one last time, pitched and slung him away in a high arc. He landed on his back several metres away, became aware that the shuttle had stopped sliding just as suddenly as it had started, wedged on a ledge of rock, saw the buggy somersaulting and Hanna leaping along the loading bed and jumping into the rubble.

He pressed both hands to his belly, as hard as he could.

Hanna came running across and bent over him. Locatelli tried to say something, but all that came out was groaning and retching. He didn't need to look down at himself – which he couldn't have done anyway – to know that his suit had a tiny tear in it. If he was still alive, it was only because bio-suits didn't immediately burst like balloons, losing all their air at once.

Perhaps if he kept his hands pressed against the wound—

'You're bleeding,' said Hanna.

'Sh-shit,' he managed to gasp. 'Can you—?'

'Idiot!' How strange. The Canadian seemed to be angry. 'What were you doing? I spared you, for God's sake! I could have brought you to safety!'

'I'm – I'm s—'

What? Sorry? Was he apologising to Hanna for allowing himself to be rammed in the body by the Ganymede? Whose fault was that, then, damn it? But right now he felt terribly cold, and he understood that apart from Hanna he had no one now.

'Please – don't – let – me—'

'You're going to die,' Hanna said soberly.

'N-no.'

'There's nothing to be done, Warren. The vacuum will suck you empty as soon as you take your hands away.'

Locatelli's lips moved. Connect me to something, he wanted to say, repair the suit, but all that came out was gurgles and coughing.

'Every second that we drag things out, you will suffer.'

Suffer? He shook his head weakly. Stupid idea, he thought as he did so. No one can see you anyway. Each saw himself reflected in the helmet of the other. Searing hooks tore at his guts. He groaned.

'Warren?' Hanna's hands approached his helmet. 'Do you hear me?'

'Shhhh—'

'Look at the stars. Look at the starry sky.'

'Carl—' he whispered. The pain was almost unbearable.

'I'm with you. Look at the stars.'

The stars. They circled above Locatelli, sending out messages that he didn't understand. Not yet. Oh, Christ, he thought, as Hanna busied himself with his helmet, who ever died with such an image before his eyes? How fantastic, in fact.

'Sh – it,' he gasped once more, still his favourite word.

His helmet was taken off.

Gaia, Vallis Alpina

However many heads Hydra had, at that moment they all had cause for the greatest concern.

And there had been problems on the horizon. The disaster of 2024 cast its long shadow, since Vic Thorn, the bacillus that they had been cultivating at such expense, had vanished into the expanses of interstellar space. More than a year of dread, month by month, during which the package frayed her nerves, as no one was able to say whether it would be able to survive that long in the lonely bleakness of the crater. Admittedly mini-nukes were almost impossible to find, as Dana Lawrence knew very well, although of course she hadn't told the assiduous afternoon search party. The little nuclear weapons got their energy from uranium-235. They didn't give off gamma rays like their beloved cousins, but instead produced alpha waves; even a sheet of paper was enough to dupe detectors. Nonetheless, in a stored state they gave off thermal energy that had to be dispersed somewhere or other, a process performed on Earth by the atmosphere. On the Moon, on the other hand, there were no busily circulating molecules to pick up the little packets of heat and carry them off. To counteract the overheating of an atom bomb in an airless space, you needed big radiators, which the little bomb did not possess, because it was designed to be hidden for three months after the landing of Thorn, who would have been just around the corner from it on the moon base. If everything had gone to plan, Thorn would have positioned the bomb, set the timer, headed for Earth on the pretext of sudden illness, and the rest would have been available to read in the chronicles of noteworthy disasters.

Dana looked with revulsion at Kokoschka's charred and smoking body. At last she had managed to put out the remaining fires. She couldn't imagine what kind of inferno was currently raging in Gaia's sealed-off neck, but there too the flames must already have consumed much of the oxygen that had been there at the outset. The life-saving mask filled her lungs with oxygen, and a visual barrier protected her eyes against the stinging smoke, but the real problem was that she wasn't going to get out of here very quickly.

And all because of Julian's crazy daughter!

What the hell was up with Lynn? Never, not during her interviews for the job, and not afterwards, either, had she ever given the impression of being mad. Controlling, certainly. Almost pathological in her striving for perfection, but she also *seemed* to be more or less perfect. Even until a few days previously, Dana wouldn't have been able to say anything else about Lynn Orley, except that she was the legitimate architect of three extraordinary hotels, and completely capable of running a global company.

Then, as a complete surprise, the first symptoms of paranoia had appeared and, initially uneasy, Dana had seen a certain potential in them, because the change in Lynn's nature predestined Lynn for the role of scapegoat. She hadn't let an opportunity pass to discredit Julian's daughter and feed suspicions of her dishonesty. But back in the Mama Quilla Club, with Donoghue bellowing in her ear, she had suddenly been filled with the worry that Lynn might spoil everything. For the sake of caution she had followed her, but Lynn had only withdrawn to her suite, so she had gone on to the control centre, to find Sophie Thiel, incapable of any kind of dissemblance, eating from the Tree of Knowledge. Weak nerves, that one, although she deserved to be admired for her meticulous detective work. Dana's only mistake had promptly become an albatross – not immediately manipulating the recordings after she'd sent the search parties off on their wild goose chase. With a single glance Sophie had worked out that her boss had started the communications block during the conference call between Earth and Moon, on the pretext of loading the video of the corridor. Clever, Sophie, really clever. Aware that digital messengers were terribly indiscreet, Sophie had relied on pen, paper and Kokoschka, and given the infatuated lunkhead the task of looking for Tim, to tell him who the real enemy was. It was only chance that she had ended up in the control centre at the right time; otherwise she might have been unmasked even sooner.

Now the recordings had been corrected, although that probably didn't matter any more. The opportunity to lock both guests and staff away in Gaia's head on the pretext of a meeting, and turn their air off, so that she could head for Peary Base, had been irrevocably missed. She was trapped.

Dana breathed deeply into her mask.

The circulators hummed around her. They did battle with the sooty remains of the flames, sucked up the toxic components and pumped fresh oxygen into the wing. More in a spirit of sportsmanship than anything else, Dana got to work on the bulkhead beyond which escalators led down Gaia's arm into the lower levels, turned on the automatic settings, tried muscle power, with no success. And how could it have worked? In the hermetically sealed area, the partial destruction of the oxygen had produced a slight but serious reduction in pressure. Until it was resolved, the armour plating wasn't going to budge an inch. She could safely ignore the bulkhead opposite, behind which lay Gaia's uncontaminated half. It would take at least two hours until pressure was restored. Time enough to wonder about how that bloody detective had managed to penetrate Hydra's data banks. Any other setbacks could have been coped with, for example the bomb sustaining damage when it fell into the crater, or Julian's unexpected appearance in the corridor when Hanna had come back from his night-time excursion. Dana had manipulated the data, and skilfully blurred all the traces. No reason for panic.

But then everything had spun out of control.

At the same time, Hydra seemed to have emerged strengthened from its setback with Thorn, and they had agreed to give it a second try, with a team this time. No one was being recruited from NASA now. Thorn had been a happy chance: a generally popular bastard, yet in spite of his ostentatious joviality he was nobody's mate, and was free of any moral principles whatsoever. Years ago, Hydra had sensed his corruptibility; when he had still been training in simulators on Earth, they had observed him and finally made him an offer that he, by now elevated to the rank of moon base commander, had turned down without a flicker of an eyelash, but also with a request for double the money. When this turned out not to be a problem, everything else had gone like clockwork.

In the jungle of Equatorial Guinea, work was coming to an end, Hydra's buyers had been successful in the black market of international terrorism. A masterpiece of criminal logistics was taking shape, conceived by a phantom that Dana had never met, but whose master of ceremonies she knew very well.

Kenny Xin, the crazed prince of darkness.

Even though he was the very model of a psychopath, and she found him in many respects unappealing, Dana could not conceal a certain admiration for him. For the architecture of the conspiracy of which she had been a part for years, crossing continental and cosmic bridges, Hydra couldn't have wished for a better stress analyst. Immediately after Thorn's death, Xin, more familiar than anyone else with the pandemonium of freelance spies, ex-Secret Service men and contract killers, had engaged in a conversation with Dana – a former Mossad agent, specialising in the infiltration of luxury hotels, which meant that she was particularly qualified for Gaia – and had also come up with the ideal cover of a Canadian investor to win Julian's trust.

But judging by events, the prince of darkness had lost control of the situation.

Dana wondered if there was anyone still alive in the hotel. The area that she was trapped in looked deserted, but she didn't know who had been in Gaia's head when the oxygen had gone up. If luck had been on her side, they would all have been there. Not that she had any particular predilection for mass murder, but the group's fate had been sealed the minute Carl Hanna's cover had been blown. Dana was sure that the man would reach the moon base, but she couldn't know when and whether she would be able to contact him. By blocking communications, she had tried to allow him a little time; however, if Jennifer Shaw and that detective managed to contact Peary Base via NASA, it would be a real disaster. Hanna had a better chance of carrying out his mission if there was no one waiting at the North Pole to stop him.

The idea of the communications block had also been a well-aimed and timely arrow from Kenny Xin's inexhaustible quiver of far-sighted ideas. Sending the staff off in search of the bomb had been a doddle.

Like listening in on Tommy Wachowski, the deputy commander of the base, although of course not asking him for help in the search for the Ganymede. To her great relief, they had known nothing at the Pole about a planned attack, a clear indication that neither Jennifer Shaw nor NASA had been able to get a warning to them before communications had broken down. Then she had manipulated the laser connection so that calls from the base were received only on her phone. Now she just had to wait until Hanna called, and leave the hotel for good.

But first she would have to get rid of the guests. With the best will in the world, she couldn't send that crowd to the Pole and risk them getting there before Hanna and telling stories about atom bombs. No one from the group must reach the base.

Who had survived?

Lynn, she thought. And Tim. Those two at least. They were somewhere in the hotel, possibly in the control centre.

Time to make contact.

Cape Heraclides, Montes Jura

The behaviour of bodies in a vacuum has always inspired vivid speculation. Some of these stories correspond to fact. Objects of soft consistency with air pockets, for example, stretch apart like dough as the gas forces its way out. This isn't caused by the vacuum sucking it out, but by the atmosphere exerting pressure. Some things deform, others explode. Frothy, chocolate-coated marshmallows balloon up to four times their volume. If the original ambient pressure were then to be reinstated, they would transform into shapeless grease, indicating profound structural dilapidation. A knotted condom, however, would regain its original form after a temporary existence as a balloon. Of course, it certainly wouldn't be advisable to use it for its originally intended purpose. A cow's lung would collapse into shreds, while holey cheese and aubergines would show no visible change, and nor would chickens' eggs. Beer foams up like crazy, pommes frites secrete fat and solidify, and ketchup sachets buckle.

When it comes to human beings, the rumour stubbornly persists that we would explode if exposed to a vacuum. After all, we're more like marshmallows than condoms in consistency: soft, porous, and interwoven with gases and fluids. And yet, something much more complex happened when Warren Locatelli's helmet came off. Pressurised water in deep-sea trenches on Earth doesn't start to boil until it reaches 200 to 300 degrees Celsius, whereas in the rarefied air of Mount Everest it would start to boil at 70 degrees; on the same principle, the liquid components in Locatelli's skull boiled within a fraction of a second of being exposed to a complete lack of pressure, then immediately cooled again due to the induced loss of energy. Anything that vaporises in a vacuum creates evaporative cooling, so the now liquefied Locatelli froze as soon as he had boiled. His skull didn't explode, but his physiognomy went through rapid changes and left behind a mask-like grimace, coated with a thin layer of ice. As he was in the shadow of a rock overhang, the ice would stay until the beams of light stretched across and evaporated it. Lastly, Locatelli would suffer terrible sunburn, but luckily he wouldn't feel a thing. He died so suddenly that the last thing he noticed was the beauty of the starlit sky.

Hanna sat up straight.

It was just as he had said. The act of killing was neither a burden nor a source of pleasure. His victims never came back to haunt him in his sleep. If he had been convinced that Locatelli posed a danger to him, he would have shot him. But at some point in the course of the last two hours, he had become convinced that he didn't need to. Locatelli's bravery had won his respect, and even though the guy had been a pompous, arrogant jerk, Hanna had developed something akin to a fondness for him, accompanied by the desire to protect him. The prospect of saving Locatelli's life had, in some indefinable way, done him good.

At least he had saved him from suffering.

He turned away and erased the dead man from his memory. He had to finish the job.

The buggy lay on its side, having been pushed against the rock face by the Ganymede. Hanna heaved the vehicle back upright and inspected it. He immediately noticed that one of the axles had been so badly damaged that the question was not *whether* it would break, but *when*. He could only hope that the buggy would hold out until he reached the mining station.

Without giving Locatelli or the shuttle another glance, he drove off.

Gaia, Vallis Alpina

It was unbelievable, thought Finn O'Keefe, how deathly pale Mukesh suddenly looked. Incomprehensible that someone whose natural pigmentation resembled that of Italian espresso could ever look so pale. His blood-drained face was as empty as the words he used in a vain attempt to raise their morale.

'They'll come for us, Sushma, don't worry.'

'Who's "they"?'

'You know, our friend Funaki—'

'No, Mukesh, there's no one left, he can't get hold of anyone!' Sushma began to sob. 'No one's answering at the control centre, and it's on fire, everything's in flames down there!'

How strange. O'Keefe couldn't stop staring at Mukesh. Particularly his nose. It was as though it had gone numb, a pale radish stuck onto Mr Tomato's face. The subject of his interest laid his arm protectively around Sushma's shoulders.

'He'll get in touch with someone, my love. I'm sure of it.'

'Has it got a little warmer already?' Rebecca Hsu's brow was wrinkled with alarm. 'By a few degrees?'

'No,' said Eva Borelius.

'Well, I think it has.'

'*You've* probably got warmer, Rebecca.' Karla Kramp went over to the landing and looked down. 'A side effect of stress hormones, increased blood pressure. It's completely normal at your age.'

O'Keefe followed her. Two storeys below, the spiral staircase ended at a steel barrier.

'Perhaps we should try to open the bulkheads,' he suggested.

Funaki looked over at them and shook his head.

'As long as the indicators on the control panel are still lit red, we'd better leave it alone. There's a risk of fatality.'

'But why?' Miranda fished a strawberry out of her daiquiri and sucked the fruit pulp from its little green star. 'The automatic system has shut down, so it should be okay for us to take a look, shouldn't it?' Her skin was reminiscent of cooked lobster; her face and cleavage glowing. Her chemical-saturated hair had been badly singed above the forehead, and even her eyebrows were damaged. Regardless of all that, she exuded the kind of confidence found only in people who are either especially superior or especially simple.

'It's not that easy,' said Funaki.

'Nonsense.' She licked strawberry juices from the corner of her mouth. 'Just a quick look. If it's still burning, we'll close up again quickly.'

'You wouldn't even be able to get the bulkheads open.'

'Finn has strong muscles, and Mukesh—'

'It has nothing to do with body strength. Not when the partial pressure of the oxygen has dropped.'

'I see.' Miranda raised what remained of her eyebrows in interest. 'Wasn't he one of the Arthurian knights?'

'Sorry?'

'Partial.'

'Percival,' said Olympiada Rogacheva wearily.

'Oh, that's right. So what does he have to do with our oxygen?'

'Michio, you old Samurai,' O'Keefe turned round. 'Please be so kind as to talk in a way that the billionairess can understand you. I think you meant to say that there's now a vacuum on the other side, right? Which means we need to think of another way of getting out of here.'

'But how?' Eva looked at him helplessly. 'Without the elevator.'

They had climbed down to Selene in order to inspect the staff elevator, the only one of the three lifts that went through into the restaurant area, but Funaki had energetically intervened:

'Not until the system or control centre signal that it's safe! We don't know what's happening in the elevator shaft. If you don't want to be hit by a wall of flames, then don't even think about opening those doors.'

But the control centre still hadn't been in touch.

'If we need to we can climb down through the ventilation shaft,' he had added. 'It's not the most comfortable of methods, but it's safe.'

A while had passed since then. Karla looked back down into the worm casing of the spiral staircase.

'Well, I'm certainly not going to let myself get roasted up here,' she decided.

'Roasted?' Hsu's eyes widened in horror. 'Why? Do you mean that—'

'Karla,' whispered Eva. 'Do you have to?'

'What?' Karla whispered back in German. 'There's nothing but stars above us. We can't get to the viewing platform without space-suits, and everything's burning down below. Fire has a tendency to rise, you know. If Funaki doesn't make contact with the control centre soon, we'll all meet our maker up here, mark my words. I want to get out of here.'

'We all want to get out of here, but—'

'Michio!' A distorted voice came out of the intercom in the bar. 'Michio, can you hear me? It's Tim. Tim Orley!'

Maybe he'd got his priorities wrong. He should have ignored Lynn's misery and made contact with the others without delay, but in the face of her suffering that had seemed an unbearable prospect. The level of her sobbing seemed to indicate that the medication she had taken was helping a little. He had fetched the elevator at once, calling it down from the very top in order to go to her suite on the thirteenth floor with her. At first, only his subconscious registered the fact that it was unusually warm in the cabin. It was only once they reached the glass bridge that he had remembered the worrying noises from the neck of Gaia, the phantom of smoke in the dome of the atrium and how the architecture seemed, bizarrely, to be in motion. Then he had looked up at the ceiling.

A massive armour shield was stretched out above him.

Perplexed, he wondered where the steel panels and bulkheads had come from all of a sudden. They must have been stored between the floors, hidden from view.

What on earth had happened up there?

By the time they got to the bathroom, Lynn was shaking so much that he had to lay the green tablets and white capsules she asked for on her tongue, one after another, and hold the glass for her as she drank, panting, like a little child. The resulting coughing fit gave reason to fear that she might bring up the cocktail of medicine again in a projectile arc, but then it had begun to take effect. A quarter of an hour later, she had got a grip of herself; at least enough to allow them to leave the suite. They immediately ran into Heidrun and Walo Ögi.

'What's wrong?' asked the Swiss man in a concerned voice as he looked around. 'Where are the others?'

'Up there,' whispered Lynn. Based on the colour of her skin, she could have passed for Heidrun's sister.

'We've been up there,' said Ögi. 'We wanted to go to the meeting, but everything's locked up and barricaded.'

'Barricaded?'

'I think you'd better come with us,' said Heidrun.

It was only as they went further up that Tim realised just how extensive the armour plating really was. A solid steel wall without even the slightest hint of a gap had descended diagonally over the gallery. The doors of E2, one of the two guest elevators, had disappeared behind it, as had the left-hand side entrance to the neck. The one accessible spiral staircase ended in a closed bulkhead. It was only now that he realised his vision was imperceptibly impaired, as if some wafer-thin film had been pulled over his retina. Here and there, black bits of fluff were spinning through the air. He reached out to catch some and they crumbled into grease between his fingers.

'Soot,' he said.

'Do you smell that?' Ögi was snuffling all around, his moustache twitching. 'Like something's burnt.'

Horror crept over him. If the bulkheads were closed, then that could only mean it was *still* burning! Filled with dread, they rode down and could already hear Funaki's urgent calls by the time they reached the lobby. Lynn shuffled over to the controls, activated the speech function, waved her brother over wearily and sank down into one of the rolling chairs.

'Michio!' called Tim breathlessly. 'Michio, can you hear me? Tim here! Tim Orley!'

'Mr Orley!' Funaki's relief was palpable. 'We thought no one would ever answer. I've been trying to reach someone for half an hour.'

'I'm sorry, we had to – we had a few problems to solve.'

'Where's Miss Dana?'

'Not here.'

'Sophie?'

'She's not here either, none of the staff are. Just the Ögis, my sister and I.'

Funaki fell silent for a moment. 'Then I fear you'll have even more problems to solve, Tim. We're stuck up here.'

'What happened—'

'Control centre!' Dana's voice. 'Please respond.'

'Excuse me a moment, Michio.' Wrinkling his brow, he tried to orientate between the two flashing indicators. 'I'll be back in just a moment – I have Dana Lawrence – just a moment, for God's sake, how do I switch over?'

His sister heaved herself up from the chair with a blank expression, pushed him aside and tapped a flashing section of the controls.

'Dana? It's Lynn here.'

'Lynn! Finally. I've been trying for half an hour—'

'You can save the speech, Funaki already did it. Where are you?'

'Locked in. In the right shoulder.'

'Fine, we'll be in touch. Stand by.'

'But I have to—'

'Shut your mouth, Dana. Just wait until someone's ready to play with you.'

'What did you say?' Dana exploded.

'Oh yes, and you're fired. Michio?' Lynn put the enraged hotel director on hold. 'This is Lynn Orley. Can you tell me your location?'

'Okay, yes. The Mama Quilla Club, the Luna Bar and the Selene are accessible, but the Chang'e is sealed off. According to the computer the conditions beneath are life-threatening. A fire in the neck of the automatic system must have caused the area to be sealed off. Miss Miranda saw a jet of flame—'

'*Saw* one?' They heard Miranda's penetrating voice in the background. 'I was practically barbecued by it.'

'—and only just managed to get away.'

Lynn leaned heavily against the control console. To Tim, she looked like a zombie trying to do something its body was no longer capable of.

'Who was in the neck when the fire broke out?' she asked, her voice flat.

'We're not entirely sure. It seems like there was an argument there. The Donoghues left the bar to find out, and we heard Miss Dana's voice, and—' He hesitated. 'And yours, Miss Orley. *Sumimasen*, but you probably know better yourself who was there.'

Lynn fell silent for a few seconds.

'Yes, I know,' she said softly. 'At least for the time before I – left. Your observations are correct. Just after Tim and I left, it must have—' She cleared her throat. 'Who's with you right now?'

Funaki said nine names and assured her that, apart from Miranda's minor burns, they were all uninjured. Tim shuddered at the thought of the neck, now completely sealed off. He didn't dare imagine what fate had befallen Chuck, Aileen and the chef.

'Thanks, Michio.' Lynn's fingers wandered over the touchscreen, altering controls, changing parameters.

'What are you doing?' asked Tim.

'I'm stopping the convection in the elevator section and in the ventilation shafts.'

'Convection?' echoed Ögi.

'The air circulation. There could be massive amounts of smoke forming up there. We have to stop the ventilators from distributing it and encouraging the fire to spread. Dana?'

'Lynn, damn it! You can't do this to me, I—'

'Are you alone?'

'Yes.'

'What happened?'

'I – listen, I'm sorry if I accused you of being in the wrong, but *everything* indicated that *you* were the one we were looking for. I'm responsible for the safety of the hotel, so that's why—'

'You *were*.'

'I had no other choice. And you have to admit that your recent behaviour hasn't exactly been normal.' Dana hesitated. As she continued, her voice suddenly sounded sympathetic, as if there should be a leather psychologist's chair and a diploma on the wall. 'No one is angry with you. Anyone can stumble now and then, but maybe you're ill, Lynn. Maybe you need help. Are you sure you still have things under control? Would *you* have trusted you?'

For a moment, the incapacitating tone seemed to be taking effect. Lynn sank her head and breathed deeply. Then she stiffened and jutted her chin out.

'The only thing I need to know is that I have you under control, you scheming little bitch.'

'No, Lynn, you don't understand, I—'

'You won't do this to me twice, do you hear?'

'I just want to—'

'Shut it. What happened in the neck?'

'But that's what I've been trying to tell you the whole time.'

'What then?'

'Kokoschka. He betrayed you! It was him.'

'Ko-Kokoschka?'

'Yes! He was Hanna's accomplice.'

'Dana!' Tim walked over. 'It's me. Are you sure about that? I think he wanted to give me something.'

'No idea what, but that's right, yes. He got really angry when you didn't pay attention to him, it seemed things didn't go as he had imagined. Then – right after you and Lyn left the neck, Anand appeared. I don't know exactly what she had found out and how, but she said straight to Kokoschka's face that he was the agent, and Kokoschka, my God . . . he just snapped. He pulled out a gun and shot her, then Chuck and Aileen too, everything happened so horribly quickly. I tried to knock the gun out of his hand, and it went off, then one of the oxygen tanks suddenly started spitting out fire and – I just ran, just got out, before the bulkheads closed. He came after me, but he didn't make it. He burned. The gallery burned, everything. I—' Dana's voice ebbed away. As she continued, her attempt to control her emotions was audible. 'I managed to get him out and close the bulkhead, to extinguish the flames, but—'

'What is it? Are *you* okay?'

'Yes, thank you, Tim.' There was a muffled cough. 'I've probably inhaled a little too much CO_2 into my lungs, but I'm okay. I'll keep myself going with oxygen masks until the pressure comes back and the bulkheads open.'

'And – Kokoschka?'

'Dead. I couldn't get anything else out of him. Unfortunately.'

Silent horror and complete incomprehension descended over Heidrun and Walo's faces. Lynn stepped away from the console, swayed a little, staggered and then crashed down into the chair.

'It's my fault,' she whispered. 'All of this is my fault.'

Nina Hedegaard had long suspected that Julian might be a reincarnation of the Comte de Saint-Germain: the alchemist and adventurer regarded as 'immortal and all-knowing', as Voltaire once wrote to Frederick the Great, and whose mysterious elixirs and essences he had wanted to use in order to unleash the lasting strength and stamina of a thirty-year-old. During her two semesters of studying history – which she passed inadvertently due to the blossoming of a brief liaison with a historian – the mysterious count had been Nina's favourite figure. An ingenious gambler, companion to Casanova and teacher to Cagliostro, even the pompadours hung on his every word, because he claimed to be in possession of an *acqua benedetta*, a potion which stopped the ageing process. Born sometime in the early eighteenth century, official date of death 1784; biographers swore blind that they still found traces of him in the nineteenth century. Rich, eloquent, charming and – behind the façade of wanting to make the world a better place – thoroughly unscrupulous, it could only be Julian! The twenty-first-century Comte de Saint-Germain had created a space station and hotel on the Moon, making gold out of earth just as he had since time began, this time by transforming his alchemical genius helium-3 into energy, creating carbon tubes instead of diamonds, making a fool of the world and breaking the heart of a petite Danish pilot.

Exhausted from self-pity and six consecutive nights of sex, unproductive conversations about a future together, more sex, brooding wakefulness and a mere three hours of sleep, she felt so close to fainting that she had finally been tempted away from the pool and into the chill-out room. She didn't feel the slightest desire to have another opulent dinner in Selene, play-acting the sweet travel guide. She'd had enough. Either Julian went public about their relationship while they were still on the Moon, or he could rot alone on the Aristarchus Plateau. Her bad mood swelled into a reservoir of rage. So they couldn't make contact? There was no response from Ganymede? The last sighting of the count was in 2025? Well, so what! It wasn't her responsibility to keep checking up and searching. She was completely worn out, and now she didn't even want Julian to find her – if he ever turned up again. In reality, she wanted nothing more than for him to find her, but just not right now. She wanted him to go out of his mind with worry first. To beat his fists into the empty pillow beside him. Miss her. Simmer in his guilt. Yes, that's what he should do!

Similar to the design of the pool, the chill-out area was modelled on the surface of the Moon, full of little craters and secluded corners. Her bathrobe slung around her, she selected a discreetly located lounger, perfectly suited to not being found, stretched out on it and fell into a deep, dreamless sleep in just a matter of minutes. Breathing evenly, away from the gaze of possible search parties, she rested at the very base of all consciousness. Removed from time and reality, lured into the waiting room of death, she snored softly and felt nothing but heavenly peace, and then not even that.

Four storeys above her, hell was bubbling away.

Even though Gaia in its intact state resembled a youthful, perfectly functioning organism, whose life-support systems predestined it for heroic acts, gold medals and immortality, a few stray projectiles from a handgun had been enough to turn all the advantages of its systems and sub-systems against it in the blink of an eye. The hidden tanks, designed to offset shortages in the bio-regenerative circulation by pumping the most accurately gauged quantities of oxygen into the atmosphere, had revealed themselves to be a fatal weakness. Twenty minutes after the catastrophe had struck, the affected tank was already burnt out, while other systems, originally intended to be life-saving, gave the hellfire new nourishment. By this point, the sealed-off area had temperatures of over 1000 degrees Celsius. The casing on the oxygen candles had melted and liberated their contents, burning coolants had caused the pipelines to explode, and supposedly non-flammable wall casings were flowing down like glowing slurry. Unlike in the Earth's gravitational pull, the blaze didn't flare up high, but instead drifted curiously around, creeping into every corner, including the cabin of E2, the guest elevator, the doors of which hadn't managed to shut in time because Anand's collapsed body was blocking them. Only tarry clumps and bones remained of the three corpses; everything else had been swallowed up by the flame monster. Human tissue, synthetic materials, plants, and still its hunger was far from sated. While the prisoners in the Mama Quilla Club were planning their escape with Lynn and Tim, while Dana Lawrence was foaming with rage, hammering against the closed bulkhead, and while Nina Hedegaard was sleeping through the destruction, the flames raged against a second tank, until eventually its sealing couldn't hold out any more and a further twenty litres of compressed oxygen unleashed the next phase of the inferno. In the absence of other materials, the monster began to gnaw at the security glass of the window and at the steel brace which held Gaia's neck upright, weakening its structural solidarity.

At a quarter past nine, the first load-bearing constructions slowly began to give way.

'No, it was absolutely right not to use the elevator,' they heard Lynn say through the intercom system. She sounded tired and drained, robbed of all her strength. 'The problem is that we can only make assumptions from down here. The sensors in the neck have failed; it's possible that it's still burning down there. The fire-extinguishing system was clearly able to make some progress in Chang'e, but there's still contamination and considerable vacuum pressure. Almost all the oxygen has gone to blazes. I imagine the ventilators will balance that out in the course of the next two hours, just like in the shoulder area.'

'But we can't wait two hours,' said Funaki, with a sideways glance at Rebecca Hsu. 'And it's getting hotter in here too.'

'Okay, then—'

'What about the ventilator shafts? We could climb down over the staircase.'

'The data for that is contradictory. There seems to have been a slight loss of pressure in the eastern shaft, but that might just be because a little bit of smoke forced its way in. The western shaft looks okay. As far as the guest elevators are concerned, E2 has broken down, its cabin is stuck in the neck, and the staff elevator is in the cellar. E1 is in the lobby, near us. We've used it several times without any problems.'

'E1 won't be of much help to us,' said Funaki. 'It stops in the neck. If we're going to use anything it can only be the staff elevator – that's the only one that goes through to Selene.'

'Just a moment.'

Muffled voices could be heard in the control centre. First Tim's, then Walo Ögi's.

'I'd like to remind you that E1 and E2 are a good distance apart,' Funaki added. 'If E2 has been compromised, that doesn't affect E1. The staff elevator, on the other hand, travels between the two, and would get very close to E2.'

'Lynn?' O'Keefe leaned over the intercom. 'Could the fire spread to the other elevator shafts?'

'In principle, no.' She hesitated. 'The likelihood is very slim. The shaft system is connected via passageways, but structured in such a way that flames and smoke can't spread that quickly. And besides, the shaft itself is inflammable.'

'What does "that quickly" mean exactly?' asked Eva Borelius.

'It means that we should test it,' said Lynn with a steady voice. 'We'll send the staff elevator up to you. If the system considers it to be safe, its doors would open in Selene. After that we'll call it back, look inside, and if there's nothing to suggest otherwise, we'll send it up again. Then you should be able to actually use it.'

O'Keefe exchanged glances with Funaki and tried to make eye contact with the others. Sushma was frozen in a state of fear, Olympiada was gnawing at her lower lip, and Karla and Eva were signalling their agreement.

'Sounds sensible,' said Mukesh.

'Yes.' A nervous laugh escaped from Karla. 'Better than smoke-filled ventilation shafts.'

'Okay,' decided Funaki. 'So let's do it.'

'Nothing can shock me now anyway,' warbled Miranda.

The re-enlivening effect of having a plan seeped into the bloodstream of the small group and motivated them to climb down to Selene, where the temperatures were significantly higher. Funaki threw a precautionary glance at the bulkheads on the floor. There was nothing to suggest that smoke or flames were making their way upwards.

They waited. After a short while they heard the elevator approaching. For what felt like an eternity, the doors remained closed, then finally glided silently apart.

The cabin looked the same as it always did.

Funaki took a step inside and looked around.

'It looks good. Very good even.'

'Mukesh.' Sushma grabbed her husband's upper arm and looked at him pleadingly. 'Did you hear what he said? We could go now—'

'No, no.' Funaki, with one leg still in the cabin, turned around hurriedly and shook his head. 'We're supposed to send it down empty. Just like Miss Orley said.'

'But it's fine.' Sushma's shoulders were quivering with tension. 'It's intact, isn't it? Every time we send it back and forth, it could only get more dangerous. I want to go down now, *please*, Mukesh.'

'Oh, honey, I don't know.' Mukesh looked at Funaki uncertainly. 'If Michio says—'

'It's *my* decision!'

The Japanese man pulled a face and scratched himself behind the ear.

'I'm in,' said Karla. 'I agree.'

'What, you want to go down now?' asked Eva. 'Do you think that's a good idea?'

'What is there to debate? The cabin made it up, so it will make it back down again too. Sushma's right.'

'I'm coming in any case,' said Hsu. 'Finn?'

O'Keefe shook his head.

'I'm staying here.'

'Me too,' said Olympiada.

Funaki looked helplessly at Miranda Winter. She ran her hands through the singed tips of her hair and pinched her nose.

'So, the thing is, I believe in voices,' she said, rolling her eyes towards the ceiling. 'Voices from the universe, you know – sometimes you have to listen really closely, then the universe speaks to you and tells you what you have to do.'

'Uh-huh,' said Karla.

'You have to listen with your whole body of course.'

O'Keefe gave her a friendly nod. 'And what does it say, the cosmos?'

'To wait. I mean, that *I* should wait!' she hurried to confirm. 'It can only speak for me after all.'

'Of course.'

'We're losing time,' urged Funaki. 'They've already called the elevator back down again. The light's flashing.'

Mukesh grasped Sushma's hand.

'Come on' he said.

They walked past Funaki into the cabin, followed by Hsu, Karla and Eva, who peered in sceptically.

'You're coming too?' asked Karla, surprised.

'Do you think I'm going to let you go down by yourselves?'

'It's best if you stay in Selene.' Mukesh called out to those staying behind. 'We'll send the elevator back right away.'

The doors closed.

Am I too cautious? wondered O'Keefe. When all is said and done, am I just a coward?

Suddenly the disquieting feeling crept over him that he'd just thrown away his last chance of getting out of here alive.

'It's awful,' said Eva softly. 'When I think of how Aileen and Chuck—'

'Don't think about it then,' said Karla, staring straight ahead.

The cabin set itself in motion.

'It's moving,' commented Hsu.

'I just hope it will a second time too,' said Sushma, concerned. 'The others should have come with us.'

'Don't worry,' Mukesh reassured her. 'It *will*.'

The familiar feeling of weight loss set in. The elevator sped up, past—

—the cabin of E2, the interior of which was shimmering with red-yellow embers as the oxygen tank incessantly spat flames out into the wasteland of the neck. Inside the lift it was getting hotter and hotter. In spite of their density, the panes of the glazed section at the front were straining to brace themselves against the fire, but in vain, as the pressure began to shift to the inside and forced the components of the cabin slowly but steadily apart. The elevator shafts were separated from one another by thin, longitudinal walls, that were pierced by passageways a metre square.

Contrary to their outer appearance, they were incredibly robust, made of mooncrete and designed to stand up to even heavy loads.

Not as heavy as this, though, admittedly.

For over three-quarters of an hour, ferrostatic tension had been building up inside the cabin. Now that the tolerable maximum had been exceeded, it exploded with such destructive force that one of the side casings split off with a deafening noise, smashed the shaft wall into pieces and spread out like shrapnel into the neighbouring shaft, making the staff elevator come to a jolting standstill.

It stopped so abruptly that its passengers were torn off their feet, shot up weightlessly, banged their heads together and tumbled down wildly. In the next moment, something crashed down onto the roof, making the cabin shake heftily.

'What was that?' Sushma sat up and looked around, her eyes wide. 'What happened?'

'We're stuck!'

'Mukesh?' Panic rippled through her voice. 'I want to get out. I want to get out *immediately*.'

'Calm down, my love, I'm sure everything is—'

'I want to get out. *I want to get out!*'

He took her arm and spoke to her insistently, quickly and under his breath. One after another, they clambered to their feet, their faces pale and anxious.

'Did you hear that crash?' Hsu stared up at the roof of the cabin.

'But we were already past it,' Karla said to herself, as if wanting to make the obvious impossible. 'We were already below the gallery.'

'Something stopped us.' Eva glanced at the controls. The lights had gone out. She pressed the button for the intercom system. 'Hello? Can anyone hear us?'

No answer.

'What a mess,' cursed Hsu.

'I want to get out,' pleaded Sushma. 'Please, I want—'

'Don't start!' Hsu barked at her. 'You were the one that talked us into getting in this thing. It's because of you that we're stuck.'

'You didn't have to come too!' Mukesh replied furiously. 'Leave her be.'

'Oh, shut it, Mukesh.'

'Hey!' Eva interrupted. 'Don't argue, we—'

Something made a crunching noise above them. A hollow, grinding noise joined it, followed by deathly silence.

The cabin jolted.

Then it fell.

'You did what?'

Lynn stared at the monitor and Funaki's baffled face.

'They wanted to get in at all costs, Miss Orley,' the Japanese man groaned. He gazed downwards. His head jerked forwards and backwards in quick succession, gestures of submission. 'What was I supposed to do? I'm not an army general – people have their own free will.'

'But it didn't work! And we can't make contact with them any more.'

'Did they – get stuck?'

Lynn glanced at the controls. They had seen the cabin stop suddenly under the gallery, but after that the icon had disappeared.

No one said a word. Walo Ögi was pacing through the room, while Heidrun and Tim stared at the controls as if they could conjure up the icon again just by gazing at it.

There was a state of emergency in Lynn's mind.

The drugs had unleashed their narcotic effect while the acute drama lashed away at her, pushing her beyond her limits. She felt confused, drunk almost, but at the same time acutely aware of every detail of her surroundings, a strange, unsettling clarity. There was no before and after, no more primary and secondary perception. Everything bombarded her at once, while less and less was making its way out. Different levels of reality layered on top of one another, broke apart, forced their way back together again, splintered, and created surreal backing scenery for the performance of incomprehensible plays. The blood rushed in her ears. For the hundredth, thousandth, zillionth time, she asked herself how on earth she could have let herself in for this, building space stations and moon hotels, instead of finally standing up to Julian and making it clear to him that she wasn't perfect, wasn't a superhuman, wasn't even a healthy human for that matter. She should have told him that the task would destroy her, that you may well need a lunatic to create something brilliant and crazy, but certainly not to maintain it or even promote it. Because that, *precisely that*, was a task for the healthy ones, the mentally clear and stable, those who flirted with lunacy, flirted with it without a care in the world, not having the slightest idea what it really felt like.

How long would she be able to keep going?

Her head was ringing. She closed her eyes, pressing the tips of her fingers against her temples. She had to stay upright. She couldn't allow the dam holding the flood of blackness to break. She was the only one that knew the hotel like the back of her hand. She had built it.

It was all down to her.

Filled with fear, she opened her eyes.

The symbol was back.

'Help! Help! Can anyone hear us?'

Eva hammered furiously on the intercom button, shouting and shouting, while Sushma threw herself against the closed internal doors and tried to force them apart with her bare hands. Mukesh pulled her back by her shoulders and held her close to him.

'I want to get out of here,' she whimpered. 'Please.'

The elevator had only dropped a metre, but the blood had rushed from all five faces and collected in their feet. As white as chalk, they looked at one another, like a group of ghosts suddenly realising they have already been dead for a long time.

'Okay.' Eva abandoned the intercom, raised her hand and tried to sound practical, which she was remarkably successful in doing. 'The most important thing now is that we stay calm. That means you too, Sushma. Sushma? Okay?'

Sushma nodded, her lower lip trembling, her face wet with tears.

'Good. We don't know what's wrong, and we can't get through to anyone, so we have to find out.'

'It can't be all that bad,' said Hsu. 'I mean, there's only a sixth of the—'

'Twelve metres on the Moon are like two on Earth, you know that,' retorted Karla. 'And I guess we're about a hundred and twenty metres up.'

'Sshh! Listen.'

A rising and falling roaring sound filled their ears. A tormented howling mixed in with it, like a material under intense strain. Eva looked up to the ceiling. There was a bulkhead in clear view in the middle. She saw the operator control next to the display. She hesitated for a moment, then activated the mechanism. For a number of seconds, nothing happened, giving rise to the fear that this function had been damaged too. How were they supposed to get outside if the bulkhead had failed? But even while she was still pondering the alternatives, it stirred into motion and slowly rose. A flickering orange-red glow made its way in, the roaring intensified. She crouched down, pushing off from her knees, got a grip on the edge of the hatch, pulled herself up with a powerful swinging movement and clambered onto the roof.

'My God,' she whispered.

On the right-hand side, a large section of the dividing wall had been torn away, which meant she could see through to the neighbouring shaft. Five, perhaps six metres above her, was the smouldering, half-destroyed cabin of E2. The side casing was completely gone, exposing its inside, the source of the roaring sound, which was now even louder. Red apparitions darted across the floor of the burning elevator, streaks of rust were collecting further up in the shaft. There was debris wherever she looked. A bizarrely distorted, glowing and pulsing piece of metal was directly in front of her feet. She took a step back. At first she thought the brake shoes of the staff elevator had gripped and surrounded the guide rails, but on closer inspection two of them seemed to be blocked by splinters or possibly damaged. The heat was making thick beads of sweat build up over her forehead and upper lip.

Then, suddenly, the floor collapsed from under her feet.

A collective scream forced its way up to her as the cabin dropped another metre. Eva staggered, caught her balance, and saw that one of the brake shoes had opened up. No, worse than that, it had broken! In panic, she looked for a way out. Right in front of her eyes was the lower edge of the doors which led to the gallery. She wedged her finger between the gap, making a useless attempt to open them, but of course they didn't move a single millimetre. Why would they? These weren't normal elevator doors, but completely sealed-off bulkheads. As long as the system didn't decide to open them, or unless someone activated them from the outside, she was only making a fool of herself and wasting valuable time.

'Eva!' She heard Sushma snivelling. 'What's happening?'

It was hard for her to ignore the poor woman, but she didn't have time to tend to the others' sensitivities as well. Feverishly, she searched for a solution. The still-intact wall, she now noticed, revealed a passage through to the E1 shaft, around a square metre in size. Several metres above, she spotted another passage, too high to reach, and the glowing and smoky fragments of the blasted-away cabin casing were splayed out in it. Feeling an unpleasant pressure on her chest, Eva turned to the other side to get a look at the E2 shaft. The entire upper section of the dividing wall had disappeared, replaced by a huge, gaping hole, the jagged edge of which was level with her forehead. She had to hoist herself up a bit to look over it. Vertical guide rails stretched down into the depths of the unknown. There were crossbars positioned at intervals in between, wide enough to be able to get a grip and a foothold on them, and on the other side of the shaft she saw—

A passageway.

A rectangular hole leading into a short, horizontal tunnel. It lay there buried in the wall, dark and mysterious, but Eva was pretty sure she knew where it led, and it was big enough for two people to crawl along it at once. With a little dexterity, they'd be able to get across to it.

The cabin creaked in its rails beneath her, metal scraping over metal. Mukesh Nair hoisted himself up through the hatch, raised his head and stared, aghast, at the glowing wreckage of E2.

'Good God! What happened here—?'

'Everyone out,' said Eva. She pushed past him and called down to the others. 'Out, quickly! And be careful, there's burning debris everywhere.'

'What's the plan?' asked Mukesh.

'Help me.'

The elevator groaned and dropped a little more, while sparks rained down on her from above. In pain, Eva felt the dot-sized burns on her hands and upper arms. She had picked out a simple, sleeveless top for the evening, and now she was cursing herself for it. Hurrying, she helped Karla, Sushma and the alarmingly stiff Rebecca Hsu clamber out, until they were all standing on the roof.

'Take your clothes off,' said Eva, untucking her top from her trousers and pulling it over her head. 'T-shirts, blouses, shirts, anything you can wrap around your hands.'

Sushma's head jerked back and forth.

'Why?'

'Because we'll burn our mitts if we don't protect them.' She gestured her head towards the gaping opening. 'We need to get over there. Once you get to the other side, stay right up against the wall. There's strutting between the elevator rails that you can grip onto to make your way along. Don't look down, or up, just keep going. There's a passageway on the other side, and I suspect it leads into the ventilator shaft.'

'I'll never make it,' said Sushma in an anxious whisper.

'Yes, you will,' said Hsu decisively. 'We'll all make it, including you. And I'm sorry about before.'

Sushma smiled, her lips twitching. Without hesitation, Eva ripped the thin fabric of her top. It had been sinfully expensive, but that was irrelevant now. She wrapped the scraps around her hands and wrists and helped Karla deconstruct her own T-shirt while Mukesh assisted his wife. Hsu cursed as she stripped down to her underwear, despairing at the misappropriation of her cocktail dress. Mukesh handed her strips of his shirt.

'Good' said Eva. 'I'll go first.'

The cabin of the staff elevator shook. Eva clasped the edge of the destroyed dividing wall, pulled herself up and swung a leg onto the other side.

Not look down?

Eva, Eva. It was easier said than done. She suddenly felt queasy, and her courage disintegrated. The distant bottom of the shaft disappeared into the ominous darkness, and even the bars suddenly seemed disconcertingly narrow. Forcing herself not to look up at the demolished remains of cabin E2, she reached out, grabbed one of the bars and felt the heat penetrate the material wrapped around her hand. With her teeth clenched, she clambered right over to the other side and rested her feet on the hot steel.

Well, it wasn't exactly a boulevard. But she was standing.

Resolved, she dared to take a step sideways and groped her way forwards until she reached the front-facing shaft wall. She bridged the corner with her leg and sent the tip of her foot searching for something to grip on to. Her upper body leaned backwards, the material of her improvised bandage slipped off against the steel of the brace. For a moment she feared losing her grip and clung on with her heart beating wildly. She couldn't stop herself from craning her head back and staring at the underside of the glowing cabin. E2 was now directly above her, black and threatening, its edges fiery.

If the thing falls now, she thought to herself, at least I won't have to worry about whether they still have the blouse at Louis Vuitton. Then she remembered that Rebecca Hsu had bought Louis Vuitton, years ago even.

Rebecca will just have to sort something out for me then, she thought grimly.

She tightened her grip. With one more courageous step, she reached the bars on the front wall. Quickly now! The heat was starting to get painful through the bandages, burn blisters were inevitable. They wouldn't be able to last all that long in here, and to top it all off she had a sneaking suspicion that the smoke was making its way downwards now too. Arching her feet like a ballerina, she pushed her way past the lower edge of the elevator doors, then conquered the second corner as well. The opening was to her right, barely a metre away. Cautiously, she turned her head and saw Karla at the height of the doors, closely followed by Sushma, who had her face turned towards the wall and was obediently refusing to look up or down. Mukesh, who had just made it to the other side, secured himself with his right hand and helped Hsu heave her ample body across the ledge.

'Take care of Sushma,' said Hsu, ignoring Mukesh's outstretched hand. 'I can make it by myse—'

Her words were drowned out by metallic screeching. She hurriedly swung herself over the ledge. A crash and clatter sounded out, disappearing quickly into the depths as the staff elevator fell.

'Everything okay?' Mukesh's voice echoed off the walls and was swallowed by the abyss.

Hsu nodded, trembling on one of the bars. 'God that's hot!'

'Wait, I'm coming.'

'No, I'm fine. Go. Go!'

Eva took a deep breath and pushed herself forward to just below the passageway. It was higher up than she had thought and she could only just peer over the ledge, but there were two narrow rungs built into the wall. With a chin-up, she managed to get inside. She crawled forwards and, almost immediately, her hands came up against a metal plate which sealed off the back of the passageway. To the side of it was a small control panel. Taking a chance, she pressed her finger on it, and at the same moment icy horror rushed through her.

Vacuum pressure! What if the fire and smoke had already annihilated too much of the oxygen in the elevator shaft?

To her incredible relief, the panel glided to the side and revealed an evenly lit, two-metre-square shaft. There was a ladder on the left-hand side. She contorted herself to turn around, crept back and stretched both hands out towards Karla.

'In here,' she called, her voice reverberating. 'The ventilation shaft is behind here.'

Karla slithered into the passage next to her.

'Climb down the ladder,' said Eva. 'At some point there should be a way of getting out.'

'What about you?'

'I'm helping the others.'

'Okay.'

Sushma turned her face towards her. In it, hope and deathly fear were grappling for supremacy.

'Everything's okay, Sushma.' Eva smiled. 'Everything's fine now.'

There was a loud creak above her, then a metallic crash, and sparks rained down in dense showers.

Eva looked up. A fiery glow was gleaming through a crack in the cabin. Had that been there before? It looked as though the floor of the burning cabin was beginning to break away from the rest of it.

No, she thought. Not yet. Please!

Hsu looked towards the ceiling in alarm as she battled to overcome the second corner. Her knees were shaking violently.

Sushma started to cry. Hastily, Eva pulled the Indian woman into the shaft, helped by Mukesh, who pushed from below and then hesitated, unsure as to whether he should follow his wife or help Hsu, who was edging her way along centimetre by centimetre.

'Get in!' ordered Eva. 'I'll take care of Rebecca. Come on!'

Mukesh obeyed, squeezed past her and disappeared into the ventilation shaft. Another creak came from above. The glowing rain became denser. Hsu screamed as sparks landed on her naked shoulders. She pressed herself against the wall, unable to carry on, frozen with fear.

'Rebecca!' Eva stretched her upper body out.

'I can't,' groaned Hsu.

'You're almost there.' She stretched her long arms out to the Chinese woman, trying to get a hold on her.

'My legs aren't doing what I tell them.'

'Just a little further! Hold on to me.'

Volley-like blows droned through the shaft. The cabin floor of E2 bulged out, then exploded into pieces.

No, pleaded Eva. Not now. Not yet. Please not yet!

She reached out as far as she could. Fiery reflections darted over the walls of the shaft. The Chinese woman overcame both her rigidity and the corner, managed to take an utterly fearless step, came closer, made her way to right beneath her, grasped her outstretched right hand, lifted her gaze to Eva—

And then up to the ceiling.

Time stood still.

With a crash, the floor plate broke free. Hsu's features contorted, reflecting the realisation that she had lost, and froze. For the duration of a heartbeat, her gaze rested on Eva.

'No!' screamed Eva. 'No!'

The Chinese woman pulled her hands away. As if wanting to welcome her end with open arms, she spread them out, let herself fall and tipped backwards into the shaft. Eva reacted instinctively. In a flash, she pulled back, protected her head and buried her face in her elbows. Centimetres away from her, the cabin floor thundered past, spitting out fountains of embers. It singed her lower arms, hands and hair, but she didn't feel a thing. The elevator shaft filled with the sounds of crashing and banging. In distraught disbelief, she pulled herself over the edge and watched as the fiery cloud became smaller and paler, until it seemed to implode into the depths as the cabin floor fell deeper and deeper.

Rebecca's coffin lid.

'No,' she whispered.

Tongues of fire lashed down from above. Eva pulled herself back into the ventilation shaft. Her feet found the ladder of their own accord. There was an identical control panel to the one in the passageway. On autopilot now, she touched it and the trapdoor glided shut without a sound. Below her, she heard voices, the echo of feet on metallic ladder rungs. She had lost all concept of an imaginable future. Listlessly, she hung there in the heat of the shaft. The heat was unbearable here too, but she was shaking all over, freezing, as if her heart were pumping icy water, and couldn't get a grip of her thoughts, not even when the tears began to stream down her bony cheeks.

'Eva?' It was Karla, from deep below her. 'Eva, are you there?'

Silently, she made her way down. To wherever that might be.

*   *   *

'Hey!' Heidrun pointed at the wall monitor showing the plan of the elevators. Through a channel to the left of E2, glowing dots were moving, disappearing for a short while, then appearing again, constantly changing their position. 'What's that?'

'The ventilation shaft!' Lynn pushed her sweat-soaked hair off her forehead. 'They're in the ventilation shaft.'

By now, the staff elevator had disappeared from the screen. The computer reported it as having fallen, but had no information about E2 at all.

'Can they get out of there by themselves?' asked Ögi.

'It depends. If the fire has spread to the elevator shaft, then the loss of pressure could mean the exits are blocked.'

'If there were a fire in the ventilation shaft they would be dead by now.'

'The E2 shaft is on fire too, but they still made it through and across to the other side.' Lynn massaged her temples. 'Someone has to go to the lobby, quickly!'

'I'll go,' said Heidrun.

'Good. To the left of E2 there's a wall casing made of bamboo—'

'I know it.'

'The trough is on rails; just push it to the side. Behind it, you'll see a bulkhead with a control panel.'

Heidrun nodded and set off.

'It leads into a short passageway,' Lynn called after her. 'Very short, not even two metres long, then there's another bulkhead. From there—'

'—it leads into the ventilation shaft. I've got it.'

In long, bouncing strides, she hurried through the lobby, under the circulating model of the solar system and through to the elevators, of which only one was still usable at most. She turned her attention to the bamboo trough, rolled it aside, then hesitated. Mid-motion, she suddenly felt paralysed. Millimetres above the sensor, the tips of her fingers froze, while a chill crept down her spine at the thought of what might lie behind the bulkhead. Would flames lash out at her? Was this her last conscious moment, would it be her last memory of a life of physical freedom, free from injury?

The fear subsided. Resolute now, she tapped the field. The bulkhead swung open and cool air came out. She walked into the passageway, opened the second bulkhead, put her head through and looked up. It was a surreal sight. Walls, ladders and emergency lights stretched out towards a murky vanishing point. High above her, she caught sight of people on the rungs.

'Down here!' she cried. 'Here!'

Miranda Winter had lost her composure.

'Rebecca?' she sobbed.

Feeling distanced from the situation for a moment, O'Keefe reflected that she was one of the few people who still looked attractive while they were in tears. Many with well-formed physiognomy took on frog-like features in a state of tormented suffering, while others looked as if they actually wanted to laugh and weren't really sure how. Eyebrows slid up to the hairline, usually pretty noses swelled up to become oozing boils. He had seen every conceivable deformation in his time, but Miranda's despair harboured erotic charm, accentuated by her streaky, running black make-up.

Why was something like that going through his mind? He was tired of his thoughts. They were all just diversionary tactics to prevent him from feeling. And for what? Because grief created intimacy with others who were grieving, and because he took care to keep his distance from all kinds of intimacy? Was it really so much better to stumble out of Madigan's Pub on Talbot Street, utterly alone and completely pissed, all just to keep his distance?

'So we'll use the ventilation shafts,' resumed Funaki, struggling to stay composed.

'Not the western shaft,' said Lynn's image on the monitor. 'It's too close to E2, and besides, the sensors there are reporting increasing smoke development. Try the other side – everything seems to be okay there.'

'And what—' Funaki swallowed. 'What about the others? Are they at least—'

Lynn fell silent. She looked away. O'Keefe noticed how awful she looked, just a Lynn-like shell with something staring out from it. Something he had no desire to get to know.

'They're fine,' she said tonelessly.

Funaki nodded in self-reproach. 'Then we'll open up the eastern shaft now.'

'See you in the lobby, Michio. You know the way out.'

As it happened, there was nothing left that could be burned.

The second oxygen tank had been drained to the last dregs, and all that remained of the three corpses was caked ashes. Whatever could have gone up in flames was already consumed, but it still continued to flicker and glow. After the partial fall of E2, the smoke in the shaft of the staff elevator had risen and become trapped, prevented from circulating by the shutdown of the ventilators, which would have distributed it everywhere. The temperature difference had created its own circulation system, however, and more and more clouds of smoke were emerging from the deformed materials. This meant that the elevator shaft which Eva and the others had crossed through barely fifteen minutes before now didn't even offer a breath of air or a centimetre of vision. At the height of the cabin's smouldering remains, the sealed trapdoors had melted to the west ventilation shaft, and this too was now full of smoke, although the shields of the east shaft were holding out for the time being. In the neck of Gaia, the temperature still resembled that of a solar furnace, dramatically increasing the viscosity of the steel beam which was supporting the head of the figure. Once again, Gaia's chin tilted a little, and this time—

—it was noticeable.

'The floor just moved,' whispered Olympiada Rogacheva, grabbing on to Miranda, whose flood of tears ran dry at that very moment.

'I'm sure it's built to be elastic,' she sniffed, patting Olympiada's hand. 'Don't worry, sweetheart. Skyscrapers on Earth shake too, you know, when there's an earthquake.'

'*You* may well be built elastically.' O'Keefe stared outside, his mouth dry. 'But Gaia certainly isn't.'

'How would you know? Hey, Michio, what—'

'There's no time!' Funaki stood on the landing, waving wildly with both arms. 'Come on. Quickly!'

'Maybe we're just suffering from mass hysteria,' said Miranda to the distraught Olympiada as she followed Funaki into the Luna Bar and from there down into Selene. Again, the floor gave way beneath them.

'*Chikusho!*' hissed Funaki.

O'Keefe's knowledge of Japanese was practically nonexistent, but after several days in the company of Momoka Omura he had become sufficiently familiar with swearwords.

'That bad?' he asked.

'Very. We can't afford to lose a single second.' Funaki opened a cabinet, took out four oxygen masks and hurried to one of the two free-standing columns, which O'Keefe had until now assumed to be decorative, clad with holographs of constellations. Now, as the Japanese man pushed one of their surfaces to the side, a man-size bulkhead came into view behind it.

'The ventilation shaft!'

'Yes.' Funaki nodded. 'It starts up here. Let's all cross our fingers. The control centre said it's smoke-free inside, no loss of pressure.' He handed out the masks. 'But regardless. Let's put them on until we know for sure. Just slip them on so they're snug and the eyes are protected behind the visor. No, the other way around, Miss Olympiada, the other way around!' His hands flapped. 'Miss Miranda, could you help her? Thank you. Mr O'Keefe, may I see? Yes, just like that. Very good.'

In no time at all, he had pulled his own mask on, checked it and carried on talking, his voice muffled now. 'As soon as the bulkhead is open, I'll go in. Wait until I give you the signal, then follow me one after the other, first Miss Olympiada, then Miss Miranda, then Mr O'Keefe bringing up the rear. The ladder leads directly into the lobby. Stay close to me. Any questions?'

The women shook their heads.

'No,' said Finn.

Funaki tapped the sensor, stepped back and waited. The bulkhead swung open and warm air came out. O'Keefe stepped next to the

Japanese man and looked down. They peered into a dimly lit shaft which dropped down into the depths.

'Visibility seems clear.'

Funaki nodded. 'Wait until I give the green light.'

He climbed in, put both feet on the rungs, put his hands on the side struts and began to clamber down. His chest, shoulders and head disappeared beneath the ledge. O'Keefe peered in after him. Funaki looked around and gazed appraisingly down below. After about five metres, he stopped his descent and tipped his face up towards them.

'Everything's okay so far. Come on.'

'Olympiada, darling!' Miranda took the Russian woman in her arms, held her close and kissed her on the forehead. 'We're almost there, my sweet.' She sank her voice to a whisper: 'And after that you leave him. Do you hear me? You have to. Leave him. No woman has to put up with that.'

The molecular bonds were starting to break.

It would have taken higher temperatures to melt the steel like butter, but the heat was still enough to transform some of the braces into a kind of glutinous rubber, which slowly deformed under the pressure of the tonnes of weight they bore. Gaia's head visibly compacted the weakened materials together and, in the process, created tensions which the stressed glass façade and mooncrete plates weren't able to withstand. The water between the panes of the double glazing, evaporating, forced the structures apart – and, suddenly, one of the concrete modules simply broke right across, the full width of it.

Gaia's lower jaw dropped heavily onto the glass façade.

One after another, the inner and outer panes shattered. Splinters and water vapour swirled into the vacuum; rendered unstable, structural elements, tattered components of the life-support systems and ashes were carried away in a chain reaction. The artificial atmosphere spread out around Gaia's neck like a cloud and evaporated in the heat of the sun's rays. But the major part was in the shade, with the result that the air crystallised as the coldness of outer space forced its way inside, extinguishing all flames in a second and cooling down the glowing steel so quickly that it wasn't able to solidify slowly, but instead froze in brittle fragility.

The support beams held out for a few more seconds.

Then they gave way.

This time, Gaia's head sank forward much more, held only by the main cord of the massive steel spine, which so far had not been so badly affected. The last remains of the neck front splintered, the chin tilted further, the layers of insulation above the shoulders cracked, the concrete modules ruptured and a gaping hole opened up in the ventilation shaft.

O'Keefe stumbled backwards over a table. Olympiada, who was just about to clamber into the shaft, was hurled against Miranda, knocking her down to the floor.

We're falling, he thought. The head is falling!

Filled with horror, he pulled himself up, trying to get a grip on something. His right hand grasped hold of the edge of the airlock.

'Into the shaft,' he cried out. 'Quickly!'

He looked inside.

Into the shaft?

Maybe not! Funaki was staring up at him with his eyes wide, trying to climb back up again, but something was stopping him, pulling at him with all its might. He screamed something and stretched out his arm. O'Keefe leaned over to grasp his outstretched hand, when he suddenly had the eerie sensation that he was looking into the gullet of a living thing. His hair, his clothes, everything began to flap wildly. A powerful suction seized him, and in a flash he realised what was happening.

The air was being sucked out of Gaia's head. There must be a leak somewhere in the shaft.

The vacuum was threatening to swallow them up.

He braced himself against the frame, trying to reach Funaki's hand. The Japanese man tried with all his might to reach the next rung of the ladder. Out of the corner of his eye, O'Keefe saw the bulkhead starting to move, making its way up, the goddamn automatic mechanism, but it was just doing its job; the shaft had to close so they wouldn't all be sucked into it, but Funaki, he couldn't leave Funaki! Hands clung to his clothing; Miranda and Olympiada were screaming, preventing him from being sucked in. The bulkhead came closer. He stretched out his arm as far as he could, felt his fingertips touch the other man's for a second – then Funaki was torn from the rungs and disappeared into the abyss with a shrill scream.

The women pulled Finn away. The bulkhead slammed shut in front of his eyes. Breathless, they helped one another up, struggling to balance on the uneven floor of the restaurant. Eerie creaks and groans forced their way up to them from Gaia's depths, harbingers of even worse disaster.

Dana heard the same noises directly above her. A powerful blow had ripped her off her feet, followed by an immense roar, which had died away as abruptly as it came. But the gallery still seemed to be echoing from the explosion-like crash which had come before the roar. The entire building had swung like a tuning fork, then finally settled, and all at once there was deathly silence. Apart from the wails and squeaks in the roof, which sounded like cats roaming through the night in search of mates.

She ran to the bulkhead and hit her hands against the mechanism. It stayed shut.

'Lynn,' she screamed.

'No answer.

'Lynn! What's going on? Lynn!'

No one in the control centre responded.

'Come on, talk to me! Something huge has broken up there. I don't want to die in here.'

She looked around. By now, visibility in the gallery was pretty much clear again; the ventilators had done a good job. The pressure would soon be restored, but if what had happened up there was what she feared, then this area was in danger of being buried under the weight of the head sooner or later too.

She had to get out of here! She had to take control again.

'Lynn!'

'Dana.' Lynn sounded like a robot. 'There have been a number of incidents. Wait your turn.'

Dana sank down with her back to the wall, exhausted. That damn bitch! She couldn't blame her of course, she had every reason to be angry, but pure hatred for Julian's daughter was burning up within Dana. In a way that was completely contrary to her nature, she began to take it personally. Lynn had brought this disaster on her. Just you wait, she thought.

Cape Heraclides, Montes Jura

At about eleven o'clock, Momoka suddenly stopped.

'If he fell anywhere, then it would have been here,' she said.

Julian, who was driving ahead of her, stopped too. They parked behind one another on the sunlit expanse of the Mare Imbrium. To their left, Cape Heraclides and the southern foothills of the Montes Jura towered out from the basalt sea, the steep outposts of the Sinus Iridum, the Rainbow Bay. It wasn't difficult to imagine that, instead of sitting in rovers, they were in expedition boats, looking at the land across the calm sea; the only thing missing was perhaps a little colour and a picturesque lighthouse on the rocky cliffs. As if to complete the illusion, satellite images were displaying the widely dispersed, flat waves in which the frozen flood of the mare fell into the Rainbow Bay. They were, however, old images, as the weather conditions over Sinus Iridum had changed since the beginning of helium-3 mining. A broad bank of fog had now swallowed the waves and seemed to be drawing in landwards. From where they had stopped, they could just make out the clouds in the distance, a shapeless grey weighing down on the stony sea.

'Could he have flown another route?' asked Evelyn.

'It's possible.' Julian looked up at the sky, as if Locatelli had left some sign behind for them in it.

'Probable even,' said Rogachev. 'He had problems regaining control of the shuttle. If he succeeded, he could have drifted off course a fair bit.'

'Where exactly is the mining station again?' asked Amber.

'In the mining zone.' Julian pointed his outstretched arm towards the dust barrier. 'Just a hundred kilometres from here on the axis between Cape Heraclides and Cape Laplace in the north.'

'By the way, how's our oxygen looking?'

'Good, considering the circumstances. The problem is that we can't rely on the maps any more.'

Amber lowered her map. Until now, she had had the advantage of clear visibility. Every crater, every hill marked on the lunar maps had reliably appeared on the horizon at some point, clarifying their position precisely, but in the sea of dust their sense of orientation would be incredibly reduced.

'So we should try our best not to get lost,' Evelyn put in with matter-of-fact firmness.

'And Warren?' asked Momoka insistently. 'What about Warren?'

'Well . . .' Julian hesitated. 'If only we knew that.'

'What a helpful response, thank you!' She snorted. 'Why don't we look for him?'

'We can't risk that, Momoka.'

'Why not? We have to go to the foot of the Cape anyway.'

'And from there directly on to the station.'

'We don't even know if he really fell,' Evelyn reflected. 'Maybe—'

'Of course he did!' exploded Momoka. 'Don't kid yourself! Do you really want to drive happily on while he's stuck in a wreck together with that arsehole Carl?'

'There's no question of us doing it happily,' protested Evelyn. 'But the zone is huge. He could be anywhere.'

'But—'

'We're not looking for him,' said Julian decisively. 'I can't be responsible for that.'

'You really are unbelievable!'

'No, but it would be unbelievable to not get to the mining station because of you,' said Evelyn, her tone audibly cooler. 'It's not that we don't care about Warren, but we can't search the entire Mare Imbrium until we run out of oxygen.'

'I have a suggestion.' Oleg cleared his throat. 'In a way, Momoka is right. We have to go over to the Cape anyway, so why don't we just drive along a little and keep our eyes open? Not an organised search, just three, four kilometres and then on towards the mining station.'

'Sounds sensible,' said Evelyn.

Julian pondered the suggestion for a moment. So far they hadn't needed to touch the oxygen reserves.

'Okay, I think we can do that,' he said reluctantly.

They veered off, headed for the landmass and steered into the bay a little, the ascending mountain range to their left. A few minutes later, they reached a shallow ditch which stretched out diagonally across the ground, seeming to emerge right out of the fog.

Julian slowed down the rover.

'That's not a ditch,' said Oleg.

They were staring at a broadly carved-out path. It had been torn into the regolith like a wound, its edges forced up.

'It's fresh,' said Amber.

Momoka stood up from her seat and stared into the distant cloud, then turned to the other side.

'There,' she whispered.

Something was lying at an angle on the slope where the strand of the Cape swung up to the mountain range. It was reflecting the sunlight: a small, elongated and alarmingly familiar shape.

It also marked the end of the path.

Without saying a word, Julian accelerated. He drove at top speed, and yet Momoka still managed to overtake him. The terrain was only gently inclined, bearable for the rovers, which thanks to the flexible wheel suspension were able to work their way swiftly up the path. By now there was no longer any doubt that they were looking at the wreck of the Ganymede. Its legs gone, it rested in the middle of the rockfall on the slope, wedged tightly between larger chunks of rock. Its rear hatch was wide open. Not far from the ramp lay a body, its head and shoulders in the shadow of the rock. While Julian was still figuring out how he could hold Momoka back, she had already jumped down from the driver's seat and was rushing up the hill. He heard her wheezing on the speakers in his helmet, saw her fall to her knees. Her upper body was swallowed by the shadow, then a short, ghostly cry resounded.

'Evelyn,' said Julian on a separate frequency. 'I think you would be the best one to . . .'

'Okay,' said Evelyn unhappily. 'I'll look after her.'

Sinus Iridum

Considering all the setbacks he had faced so far, Hanna had been amazed to make it to the mining station without problem. He was all too familiar with the nature of escalation. The damaged axle of the buggy was *bound* to break apart prematurely, and that's exactly what it did, the dramaturgy of failure obliging fifteen kilometres too soon. It wasn't a pothole or geological fault that finished it off, however. It broke in two with banal finality on even ground, bringing the vehicle to an abrupt halt, forcing it into a spin, and that was that.

Hanna sprang down into the debris. The basic rule of survival was to think positive. The fact that the old banger had even made it that far, for example. And the fact that he had an extraordinary sense of orientation, which had enabled him to find his way without fail so far. Regardless of the miserable visibility, he had held his course, of that he was certain. As long as he just kept going in a straight line, he should reach the mining station within about an hour. But he would have to really watch out from now on. The dust concealed dangers that weren't so easy to get away from on foot as in the buggy. He would have to keep his distance. Admittedly the beetles were quite slow, but the filigree, nimble spiders had a tendency to make unpleasant surprise appearances.

Hanna let his gaze wander. Some distance away, he saw a ghostly silhouette hurrying along towards him. He walked over to the buggy's cargo bed, grabbed a survival pack in each hand and marched off.

Cape Heraclides, Montes Jura

While Evelyn attended to her emotional support duties, Julian, Amber and Oleg feverishly searched the inside of the wreck and the nearby area, but there was nothing to suggest that Hanna was still around.

'How did he get away?' Amber wondered.

'The Ganymede had a buggy on board,' said Julian, as he trudged around the nose of the shuttle. 'And it's disappeared.'

'Yes, and I know where,' Oleg's voice rang out from the opposite end of the ship. 'Maybe you should come over here.'

Seconds later, they were all standing in the path. So far they had only noticed the devastation the shuttle had inflicted on the regolith when making its emergency landing, the brutality with which it had dug into the surface, but something different now captured their attention: a story about someone who had set off into the far-away dust, a story told by—

'Tyre tracks,' said Julian.

'Your buggy,' confirmed Oleg. 'Hanna has driven down along the path and out onto the plain. I don't know how well he knows the area, but what else could he be interested in other than the place we also want to get to?'

'So the bastard just fucked off!' Momoka came over with Evelyn, down from the hill where Warren Locatelli lay.

'Momoka,' began Julian, 'I'm so terribly—'

'There's no need. No outpourings of sympathy, please. The only thing I'm interested in is killing him.'

'We'll give Warren a proper burial.'

'There's no time for that.' Her voice had lost all modulation. Autopilot driven by rage. 'I looked at Warren's face, Julian. And do you know what? He spoke to me. Not some jabbering from the other side, not that old shit. He would speak to you too, if you took the effort to go over there to him. You just have to look him in the face. He doesn't look the same as he did before, but you can hear him say loudly and clearly that humans have no business being up here. None at all! Not us, and not you either,' she added in a hostile tone.

'Momoka, I—'

'He said we should never have accepted your invitation!'

But you did, thought Julian, though he didn't say a word.

'Carl has driven to the mining zone,' said Amber.

'Very well.' Momoka marched over to the rovers. 'We have to go there anyway, right?'

'No, wait,' said Julian.

'For what?' She stopped. 'You seemed to be in a hurry just now.'

'I've found some additional oxygen reserves in the storage space of the shuttle. Really, Momoka, we have time to give him a decent—'

'That's very sensitive of you, but Warren is already buried. Carl slit open his stomach and took off his helmet. I don't see any reason to stone him too.'

There was icy silence for a second.

'So?' she asked. 'Shall we go?'

'I'll drive,' said Evelyn.

'I'm happy to as well—' Oleg offered.

'None of you will drive,' decided Momoka. 'If any of us has reason to drive, then it's me. To follow him.'

'Are you sure?' asked Amber cautiously.

'I've never been so sure,' said Momoka, and her voice made her visor steam up.

'Fine.' Julian looked out over the plain. 'Seeing as we don't have any satellite connection, I'll link the four of us on one frequency. From now on, no one will be able to hear us, not even Carl, should we get close to him. It might help.'

Gaia, Vallis Alpina

'There must be a way!'

Tim had lost all sense of time. Seconds seemed to drag out endlessly, but at the same time an hour dwindled into a disheartening nothing, brief enough to feel useless. Although the deaths had had the relative advantage of distracting them from the bomb, it took on a new, tyrannical presence now that they had alerted the prisoners to the threatening cataclysm. Strangely, Lynn seemed to gain more strength the more confused the situation became. It wasn't that she was really doing any better, but catastrophes, *real* catastrophes, seemed to have an exorcising effect on the demons in her head – even her perception of Tim was gradually becoming closer to his true nature. They were nothing other than the monsters of hypothesis, creatures from the family of what-ifs, the genus of could-bes, all equipped with the torture devices of paths left untaken.

He felt deeply sorry for his sister.

The fear that her work could turn out to be vulnerable and faulty must have cost her every last rational thought. Tim was now convinced that his uneasiness, fed by Dana Lawrence's suspicions, had proved to be a tragic misunderstanding. Lynn wasn't the one trying to cause damage to her own creation and its occupants. Her mind might be struggling against disintegration, but for the moment there was probably nothing better than for her to be forced to react by her nightmares being realised. After all, she was even explaining the latest developments to Dana, her newly elected arch enemy, and taking a huge, humbling leap by asking the fired director for her advice.

'We've looked at the images from the external camera,' she said. 'The flames have clearly led to a partial breakdown in the steel skeleton within Gaia's neck. So the fire should have been extinguished, but now the structure is damaged. There are a number of gaping leaks up there.'

Dana was silent. She seemed to be thinking.

'Come on, Dana,' pressed Lynn. 'I need your assessment of the situation.'

'Well, what's yours?'

'That there's only one way out for Miranda, Olympiada and Finn, and it's not downwards.'

'Over the viewing terrace, you mean?'

'Yes. Out through the airlock in the Mama Quilla Club.'

'We'd have to overcome two problems with that,' said Dana. 'First, you can't climb up over the outside of the head.'

'Yes, you can. We planned for a roll-out ladder in case of emergency.'

'But it wasn't installed.'

'Why not? According to the safety regulations—'

'For optical reasons. On your instructions, by the way,' added Dana, with audible satisfaction. 'We could carry out the installation of course, but it would be dreadfully complicated under the prevailing conditions and it would also take a considerable amount of time.'

'The second problem is harder to solve,' interjected O'Keefe, who was switched on to their frequency. So the fibre-optic connection still seemed to be intact at least. 'We don't have any spacesuits up here. So the terrace won't be much help to us.'

'Couldn't we bring some up?' asked Ögi. He was relentlessly pacing the room, taking equally long, precisely measured steps, or so it seemed to Tim. He was the only one who had stayed behind in the control centre. The others were seated in the lobby, trying to get a grip on things with Heidrun's help. 'E1 still seems to be functioning.'

'But E1 only goes to the neck,' said Tim.

'Forget it.' Lynn shook her head. 'The shaft is completely sealed off to protect us from the vacuum. After the structural changes up there the doors wouldn't open up again anyway. There's only one option.'

'Through the airlock,' said Dana.

'Yes.' Lynn dug her teeth into her lower lip. 'From the outside. We have to get the suits inside through the airlock of the viewing platform.'

'But for that you'll have to bring them *up* first,' said Finn. 'And it won't stop creaking up here so it has to be quick! I don't know how much longer the head will hold.'

'Callisto,' said Dana. 'Bring them up on the Callisto.'

'Where is Nina anyway?' asked Tim.

Lynn looked at him in surprise. In the heat of the moment she had completely forgotten the Danish pilot.

'Wasn't she with you in the bar?' asked Lynn.

'Who – Nina?' O'Keefe shook his head. 'No.'

'And has someone down here—' Lynn paused. 'Oh, shit! In order to bring up the Callisto, we need someone who can carry out precision manoeuvres in a large craft.' The last trace of colour drained from her face. 'We have to find Nina!'

'We can't wait that long,' urged Finn.

'Then—' She tried to catch her breath in an effort to fight off a panic attack. 'We could – we have ten grasshoppers in the garage! Almost all of you have already flown a craft like that.'

'Sure, close to the ground,' said Dana. 'But do you think you could manage this? Climb up more than a hundred and fifty metres with a grasshopper and carry out a precision landing on the terrace?'

'The precision landing isn't a problem,' said Tim. 'But the height—'

'Technically speaking the height is the least of our worries; theoretically they can be used to fly in open space.' Lynn brushed her hands over her eyes. 'But Dana's right. I don't trust myself. Not in my condition. I'd lose my nerve.'

It was the first time she had publicly dropped her guard. Tim had never known her to do that. He took it as a good sign.

'Okay, fine,' he said. 'How many of the things do we need? Each hopper can take one additional person, so three all together, right? Three pilots. I'll do it. Walo?'

'I've never been up that high with one, but if Lynn thinks it will work—'

Tim ran into the lobby and clapped his hands.

'Someone!' he called. 'We need one person for the third hopper.'

'Me' said Heidrun, without knowing what it was even about.

'Are you sure? You have to land the thing on Gaia's head. Do you think you can do it?'

'Generally speaking, I think I'm capable of doing anything . . .'

'No fear of heights?'

'. . . but whether I manage it or not is a different matter.'

'No, it's not.' Tim shook his head. 'You *have* to manage it. You have to know *now* whether you can or not, otherwise—'

She stood up and brushed her white hair behind her ears.

'No, no "otherwise". I'll manage it.'

There were spares of all the spacesuits concealed behind a wall in the lobby, which meant they didn't have to go up over the bridges to the lockers. They helped each other into the suits, put the gear for Olympiada Rogacheva, Miranda and Finn together and packed it into boxes.

'Are there problems in the corridor?' asked Tim.

'No, the sensors are registering steady values.' Lynn went ahead of them, led them to a passageway the other side of the elevators and opened a large bulkhead. Behind it was a spacious stairway with steep steps.

'You'll get down below this way. I'll open the garage from the control centre.'

Tim reflected that she should perhaps have built a route like this upstairs too, but bit back the observation.

'Good luck,' said Lynn.

Tim hesitated. Then he put both arms around his sister and pulled her close. 'I know what you're going through,' he said softly, 'and I'm unbelievably proud of you. I have no idea how you're coping with all this.'

'Nor do I,' she whispered.

'Everything's going to be fine,' he said.

'What's left?' She pulled away from his embrace and grasped his hands. 'Tim, you have to believe me, I have nothing to do with Carl, no matter what Dana says. It's myself I'm destroying, not anything else.'

'This isn't *your* fault, Lynn. There's nothing you can do!'

'Now go.' The corner of her mouth twitched. 'Quickly!'

*　　　*　　　*

There was something inherently calming about the empty, coolly lit corridor, designed to reinstate and strengthen trust in technological advancement. Its rationality made it seem immune to corruption from recklessly caused catastrophes, but Tim reminded himself that, in a way, it had all started here, with the appearance of Carl Hanna rousing Julian's mistrust. He wondered whether the bomb was hidden below them. A few hours hadn't been enough to search every nook and cranny. How small was a mini-nuke? Was it under the conveyor belt that stretched out alongside them? Under one of the floor tiles? Behind the wall, in the ceiling?

They had suggested that Sushma, Mukesh, Eva and Karla take the Lunar Express to the foot of the Montes Alpes and wait there at a safe distance until they had either freed the prisoners or been blown to smithereens with the hotel. But they had all insisted on staying, even Sushma, who had bravely tried to suppress her fear. In order to give their battered morale a boost, Lynn had ended up sending the women to look for Nina Hedegaard, since this would at least keep them occupied. Tim hoped fervently that his sister wouldn't crack up back at the control centre, but was re-assured to a certain extent by the fact that Mukesh had stayed with her. They reached the garage and saw the rafters of the retractable roof disappear into their cases. The starry sky was twinkling above them. A dozen buggies stood there waiting for a party that would never take place.

The shapeless Callisto rested opposite them with clumsy assertiveness, as if suggesting it was capable of flying to Mars. *Ugly but reliable*, as poor Chuck had joked just the day before. Compared with the shuttle, the laughable grasshoppers looked like toys.

'Who's flying in front?' asked Heidrun.

'Tim,' said Ögi decisively as he stowed the box containing Olympiada's suit into the small cargo hold. 'Then you, then me, to make sure I don't lose you.'

'Lynn,' said Tim over his helmet radio, 'we're setting off.'

He still couldn't get used to the lack of engine noise. The hopper rose without a sound, exited the garage and started its ascent. From behind, Gaia looked just the same as it always had: superior and indestructible.

The camera in his helmet sent images back to the control centre. He flew in an arc, as agreed with Lynn beforehand, so she could get an idea of how the front section looked. He intensified the thrust, let the force carry him towards the shoulder of the huge figure, then held his breath.

'Good God.' Walo's voice piped up in his helmet.

It had been obvious even from the side view that something wasn't right. Parts of the façade were missing or lay in ruins, and in places the naked steel of the support framework was exposed. Now, as they flew directly towards it, the full extent of the destruction was revealed. The contourless face was no longer focused on the Earth, but just beneath it. Where the neck had once been, there was now a gaping, black, collapsed hole. The complete front section was broken away, and Gaia's chin was sunk so far that only the lower half of the elevator doors was still peeping out.

Tim steered the hopper closer. The colossal skull seemed to be hanging by a thread at the neck. E2 stood open, its insides just a gullet corroded by flames. Steel columns, grotesquely deformed, faced towards him. His stomach filled with dread as he dared to look down one more time. There was debris distributed all over the figure's upper thigh, albeit not much. And it looked as if Gaia were nodding to him. Finn was right: they had come not a moment too soon.

On the ascent, he saw the sealed-off Chang'e, and was convinced he could make out smoke and rust inside it, burnt furnishings, but the dark windows with their gold filtering concealed what lay beyond, leaving any detail to the imagination. Out of the blue, he was overcome by an attack of vertigo. The hopper's platform had no railings, and any flying carpet would have seemed like a spacious dance floor in comparison. Quickly reassuring himself that Heidrun and Walo were behind him, he passed Selene and the Luna Bar and followed the arch of the forehead round to the viewing platform. Figures started to move beneath him: O'Keefe, Olympiada and Miranda were making their way towards the airlock. He swivelled the jets, reduced his speed, overshot the terrace a little, turned and came to a standstill right next to the railing. Not the most elegant of landings. Alongside him, at an appropriate distance, Heidrun landed as if she had been flying hoppers her whole life. Meanwhile, Ögi flew a lap of honour amidst a great deal of cursing, then finally forced the hopper down, clattering one of the telescopic legs along the railing in the process.

'I'm actually a gliding and ballooning enthusiast,' he said apologetically, before unloading his box and carrying it to the airlock, a double bulkhead in the floor which measured several metres in diameter, 'but Switzerland is a little more spacious.'

Tim jumped off his hopper.

'Finn, we're above you,' he said. Lynn had connected their helmet radios with Gaia's internal network so that everyone could communicate at once. A few seconds passed, then O'Keefe chimed in:

'Okay, Tim. What should we do?'

'Nothing just yet. We'll call up the airlock elevator, send the boxes with the spacesuits down to you and—'

He stopped.

Was it his imagination, or had the floor begun to shake under his feet?

'Hurry up!' called O'Keefe. 'It's starting again!'

Where was the control console for the airlock? There. His fingers darted as he entered the command, and the air was sucked out at an agonisingly slow speed. The shaking intensified and became like an earthquake. Then the whole thing stopped as abruptly as it had begun.

'The elevator's on its way up,' Ögi gasped breathlessly.

The airlock doors opened in the floor beneath them. A glass cabin pushed its way out, spacious enough to hold a dozen people, and opened at the front. They quickly piled the boxes inside.

'I'll go down with them,' said Heidrun.

'What?' Ögi looked alarmed. 'Why?'

'To help them. With the suits, so it's quicker.' Before he could protest, she had disappeared into the cabin and pressed the down switch. The elevator closed.

'My darling,' whispered Ögi.

'Don't worry, commander. We'll all be back in five minutes.'

         *   *   *

Finn O'Keefe saw the elevator approaching, with someone in it whose slim legs were familiar to him even through centimetre-thick, steel-strengthened artificial fibres. He waited impatiently until the internal pressure was restored and the front bulkhead had glided to the side.

'Here we go!' said Heidrun, throwing the first of the boxes towards him.

Olympiada, as white as chalk, handed the second box on to Miranda, then began to empty her own.

'Thank you,' she said earnestly. 'I'll never forget this.'

In immense hurry, they slipped into their gear: helping one another, closing hinges, fastening clamps, heaving packs onto their backs and putting their helmets on.

'Would it be asking too much to want to get out of the hotel right away?' asked Miranda. 'It's just, you know, I don't want to get blown into the sky, and I've emptied the minibar already, so—'

'You can count on it,' said Lynn's voice.

'Oh, don't get me wrong,' Miranda hurried to assure her. 'There's nothing wrong with your hotel.'

'Yes, there is. It's a piece of shit,' said Lynn coldly.

Miranda giggled.

At that very moment, the floor gave way.

For one strange moment, Tim thought the entire opposite side of the ravine was being lifted up by elemental forces. Then, as he watched the grasshoppers hopping across the terrace and Ögi whooshing towards the railings with his arms flailing about, he lost his balance, landed on his stomach and slid behind the flying machines.

Gaia was bowing her head in face of the inevitable.

Chaos roared in his helmet. Anyone who had a voice was screaming in competition with all the others. He rolled over, got back on his feet and stretched out, which was a mistake, because he lost his balance again right away. He was pulled forcefully against the railing, tumbled right over it and smacked down onto the smooth, sloping glass surface.

And slid down.

No, he thought. No!

In fear and panic, he tried to get a grip on the reflective surface, but there was nothing there to get hold of. He slipped further, away from the protective enclosure of the terrace. One of the hoppers sailed down behind him and crashed onto the glass. Tim reached out for it and grasped the steering handle just as he saw another flying device disappear into the depths. It suddenly felt as if he were hovering in the air; he couldn't get a grip any more and hung over the abyss, his legs flailing around. With his hand clamped onto the machine's handle, he screamed 'Stop!' – and as if his plea, his wretched wish to survive, had been acknowledged somewhere out there amongst the cold gaze of the myriad stars, the movement of the huge skull came to an abrupt halt.

'Tim! Tim!'

'Everything's okay, Lynn,' he panted. 'Everything's—'

Okay? Nothing was okay. With both arms – thank God he wasn't heavy – he pulled himself up on the flying device, noticing with relief that one of its telescopic legs had got wedged in the railings, then realising, with horror, that it was slowly slipping out.

A jolt went through the hopper.

Dismayed, Tim dangled in open air, unable to decide whether he should resume his ascent and thereby rip the hopper out of its anchorage once and for all, or not move at all, which would only delay his death by a few seconds. At the next moment, a figure appeared behind the terrace railing, climbed over it and slid carefully downwards, both hands bent around the rails.

'Climb up onto me,' panted Ögi. 'Come on!'

Ögi's feet were now level with Tim's helmet, right next to him. Tim gasped for air, reached his arm out—

The hopper came loose.

Swinging back and forth, he hung on to Ögi's ankles, grasped his shin guards, clung to his knees, climbed up him like a ladder and over the railing, then helped his rescuer to get back to safety. In front of them, tilted to about forty-five degrees, the floor of the terrace rose up into the heights like a smooth slide.

He had survived.

But they'd now lost all three grasshoppers.

'No! I'm flying up there.'

Lynn pushed herself away from the control panel, crumpled over and fell against Mukesh. Horrified, the Indian stared at the wall monitor, watching the terrible images being transmitted by Tim's camera and the external cameras on the opposite side of the ravine. The fibre-optic connection to the Mama Quilla Club had been broken, but they could now hear the voices of those trapped via the helmet radio.

'It's stopped.' Miranda, out of breath. 'What do we do now?'

'Olympiada?' O'Keefe.

'I'm here.' Olympiada spoke, sounding haggard.

'Where?'

'Behind the bar, I'm . . . behind the bar.'

'My darling?' Ögi, distraught. 'Where on earth—'

'I don't know.' Heidrun, sucking in air through her teeth. 'Somewhere. Hit my head.'

'Everyone out!' Tim. 'You can't stay there. See whether the airlock is working.'

Lynn's temples were throbbing with hypnotic rhythm. Colourful smog began to whirl around. Having to watch Gaia's skull tilt so suddenly that the chin was now almost resting on the chest had made her heart stop, and now it was pumping all the harder to make up for it. Gaia looked as though she were sleeping. Her head must truly now be hanging on to the shoulders by a thread.

'Everything's at an angle,' said O'Keefe. 'We're tumbling all over each other like skittles. I don't know if we'll even get into the airlock.'

Head. Head. Head. How much longer would *her* head stay on her shoulders?

'We'll come and get you,' she said. 'We still have seven grasshoppers. I'll fly.'

'Me too,' said Mukesh.

'We need a third. Quickly! Fetch Karla – she's in the best state out of all of us.'

Mukesh hurried out. Lynn followed him and plundered the depot with the substitute spacesuits. Several were missing, including hers. Suddenly remembering that not all the suits were stored in the lobby, she ran back into the control centre and to the closed bulkhead on the rear wall. Behind it lay a small storeroom for spare equipment, including fire extinguishers, suits and air masks. She waited until the steel door had glided to the side, walked in, and was surprised to find the light on. Her gaze fell on the locker with the equipment, on the piles of boxes, on the dead faces of the air masks neatly lined up in their cabinets, and on the dead face of Sophie Thiel, who was leaning upright against the wall. Her eyes were open, and her pretty face had been divided in two by a streak of dried blood originating from a hole in her forehead.

Lynn didn't move.

She just stood there, gawping at the corpse. Strangely – and thankfully, in the face of everything – it didn't unleash any emotions in her. None at all. Maybe it was just the fact that its appearance was too much and too late, or the pushiness with which it demanded its moment in the lime-light amidst an inferno of Dante-like proportions, as if they didn't have other problems. So after a few seconds she ignored Sophie and started carrying out the boxes containing the bio-suits.

'Hello, Lynn.'

She looked up, confused.

Dana Lawrence was standing in the doorway.

Heidrun and O'Keefe made their way hand over hand over table and chair legs, supporting, pulling and pushing Olympiada up towards the airlock. Contrary to what she had thought, the Russian woman had not fallen behind the bar but behind the DJ booth. Meanwhile, Miranda hung on to the side of the airlock like a monkey on a pole, her hand lying across the sensor field to keep it open.

'Can you guys make it? Shall I help?'

'I can get up there by myself,' groaned Olympiada defiantly.

'No, you can't,' said Heidrun. 'Your leg is injured; you can hardly stand on it.'

The main problem resulting from the change to their spatial surroundings was not so much the tilting of the floor, as that of the airlock. The front section was now turned towards Gaia's glass face and pointing downwards. And it wasn't just that it was incredibly difficult to get into it in this way; if they didn't watch out up there, they would fall outside faster than they intended.

'You'll have to try to get behind the elevator as soon as you get to the terrace,' said Tim. 'It will give you something to grip. Oh, and bring something long and sharp with you, like a knife.'

'What for?' groaned O'Keefe, as he steered Olympiada towards Miranda Winter's outstretched hand.

'To block the cabin so it doesn't go down again.'

'I said I could manage.' Olympiada wrapped her hands around the cabin railing and pulled herself into the elevator with a grimly determined expression. 'Go and look for your knife, Finn.'

They grasped the railing tightly and waited. O'Keefe was only gone for a minute. When he came back, carrying an ice pick, he had a wad of material flung over his shoulder. Miranda let the bulkheads close and pump the air out.

The cabin shuddered.

'Not again,' groaned Olympiada.

'Don't worry,' Miranda reassured her. 'It'll stop in a second.'

'What are you planning to do?' asked Dana.

The bulkheads had finally opened and the armoured plating had crept back into the hidden cavities. Freed from her prison, Dana had jumped down from the gallery over the bridge into the lobby, all the while thinking through her next steps: to break off the rescue mission, capture the Callisto, and get the hell out of here. In the course of the past hour and a half, she had been forced to win back trust by making out she sympathised with Lynn, but that was over now. Julian's hated daughter was alone in the control centre. She was no serious opponent; the loss of Dana's weapon wouldn't make the task easy, but she could make do with her hands.

'I'm flying up there,' said Lynn, her face devoid of any expression, then went back into the room and hauled out two large boxes containing spacesuits. Dana cocked her head. Had she not seen Sophie? No, there was no way she hadn't seen her, but why did she seem so unaffected? Surely such a sight would have thrown her off track, but Lynn looked indifferent, as if she were on autopilot. Her gaze empty, she took off her jacket and began to unbutton her blouse.

'Come on, Dana, get yourself a suit too.'

'What for?'

'You're flying one of the hoppers. The more of us there are, the quicker—' Suddenly she stopped and stared at Dana with her red-rimmed eyes. 'Hey, you've piloted the Callisto before, right?'

Dana came slowly closer, bent over and readied her own bodily murder weapons.

'Yes,' she said slowly.

'Good, then we'll do it like that. No hoppers.'

Incoherent conversation came out of the loudspeakers, hastily uttered sentences. Silently, Dana walked around the console.

'Hey, Dana!' Lynn wrinkled her forehead. 'Are you listening to me?'

She moved faster. Lynn craned her head back, looked her up and down from beneath her half-closed eyelids and took a step back. Her expression came back to life. A hardly perceptible flicker betrayed her suspicion.

'You'll fly the Callisto, do you hear me?'

Sure, thought Dana, but without you.

'No, that won't be necessary!'

As if she'd been hit by lightning, Dana stopped and turned round. Nina had come into the control centre, accompanied by Karla. She was dressed in her spacesuit, carrying her helmet under her arm, and looked thoroughly contrite.

'I'm sorry, Lynn, Miss Lawrence, I'm very sorry indeed: I wasn't at my post. I fell asleep in the rest area. Karla walked past me three times, but then she managed to find me after all and told me everything. I'll fly the shuttle.'

Dana forced a smile. She would have been confident enough of taking on Lynn and Karla, but Nina Hedegaard was incredibly fit and had quick reflexes. At that moment, Mukesh Nair stormed in, bathed in sweat, and the bubble of Dana's quick getaway burst.

'Karla,' he called, exhausted. 'There you are. And Nina! Miss Lawrence, thank heavens.'

'Our plan has changed,' said Lynn. 'Nina's flying up with the shuttle.' She walked over to the console and spoke into the microphone: 'Sushma, Eva, back to the control centre. Right away!'

Dana folded her arms behind her back. Nina was by far the better pilot; any objections on her part would have been futile.

'You have a lot to make up for,' she said strictly. 'I'm sure you realise that.'

'I'm sorry, really I am!' Nina lowered her gaze. 'I'll get them out of there.'

'I'll come too. You'll need help.'

Without waiting for an answer, Dana walked across the control centre, went into the room containing Sophie's corpse and jumped back. Feigning rage and horror, she spun round towards Lynn.

'Damn it! Why didn't you tell me about *that*?'

'Because it's not important,' answered Lynn calmly.

'Not important? Again something that's not important? Are you completely insa—'

In a flash, Lynn stormed over, grabbed Dana by the neck and threw her against the doorframe, making her head jerk back and crash against it painfully.

'Just you dare,' she hissed.

'You *are* insane.'

'If you suggest one more time that I'm insane, you'll get a very tangible impression of what insanity really is. Mukesh, put your suit on, the box with the XL label! Karla, box S!'

Dana stared at her with unconcealed rage. Her entire body was trembling. She could have killed Julian's daughter with a few unspectacular hand movements, right this very second. Without breaking eye contact, she put one finger after another around Lynn's wrist and wrenched it from her throat.

'Now, now, Lynn,' she whispered. 'Not in front of the guests! How would that look?'

After Gaia's last nod, the airlock was jutting out from the viewing platform at such an angle that it was now pointing at the far-away Earth like a cannon. They held on to the railing, and each other, as the cabin bulkheads glided to the side.

'Oh, wonderful,' said Miranda sarcastically. The view over the terrace couldn't have been more worrying.

The world had tipped by forty-five degrees; millions of tonnes of rock seemed to be eager to topple towards them from the ravine opposite. Where the terrace ended, Tim and Ögi were huddled against the railing to prevent whichever one of them might lose their grip from falling into the depths. Miranda reached out for the frame of the open airlock, grasped hold of it and pulled herself outside. The boots of her bio-suit were equipped with powerful treads to prevent them from slipping. Her fingers found a grip in an indentation. With her legs spread and the unrolled wad of material – several tablecloths from Selene knotted together – slung around her hips, she worked her way up the slope. The makeshift rope had been O'Keefe's brilliant idea; the other end of it was fastened to Olympiada's chest guard.

'Okay. Pass her towards me.'

Heidrun steered the Russian woman out of the airlock, waited until she had a firm grasp on the railing, then let her go. Olympiada immediately crumpled over and slipped down the slope, but instead of falling she hung on the end of Miranda's umbilical cord. Miranda climbed further up along the shaft of the cabin until she was able to crawl under it. With her feet wedged against the wall of the shaft, she heaved Olympiada up, unknotted the cloth and let it back down. Heidrun then hurried swiftly upwards, followed by O'Keefe, who had rammed the ice pick into the airlock door to prevent it from shutting and sending the shaft back down.

'Everything okay there?' called Ögi.

'More than okay!' said Heidrun.

'Good. We're coming up to you.'

It was relatively easy to pull themselves up over the railing, but once they got there it was still a fair distance to the airlock. Miranda threw the rope to them. After two attempts, Tim finally got hold of it, knotted it around the bars of the railing, and they made their way across hand over hand. It was incredibly tight behind the cabin with six of them, but at least they had a stable wall at their backs to prevent them from sliding down. They clung on alongside one another, hardly daring to move through fear that too much movement could tip Gaia's head clean off.

'Lynn, everyone's outside now,' said Tim.

The glass wall shook. Heidrun reached for Ögi's hand.

'Lynn?'

No answer.

'Strange,' sighed Miranda. 'I never thought I'd end up regretting it.'

'Regretting what?' asked Olympiada hoarsely.

'The swimming accident.'

'Before Miami?' She cleared her throat. 'The one you went to court for?'

'Yes, exactly. My poor Louis.'

'What exactly do you regret?' asked O'Keefe, tired. 'The fact that he died, or that you helped?'

'I was found innocent,' said Miranda, in an almost cheerful tone. 'They couldn't prove anything.'

A new quake ran through Gaia's skull and refused to let up. Olympiada groaned and fastened her grip to O'Keefe's thigh.

'Lynn!' screamed Tim. 'What's going on there?'

'Tim?' It was Lynn. Finally! 'Hold on, I'm on my way. We're coming to get you.'

Lynn had insisted on their all leaving the Gaia together. In the maelstrom of her disintegrating sanity, the realisation still won through that Dana was playing dirty somehow, and that it wouldn't have been a good idea to let her fly alone with Nina. Resolving both evacuation and rescue at the same time seemed to be the most efficient plan, and had a sense of well-ordered finality. She graciously acknowledged Dana's laboriously concealed rage and ferocious hate and felt herself become strangely calm. Yet at the same time she was overwhelmed by the desire to roar with laughter. It was just that, if she started, she probably wouldn't ever be able to stop.

They went into the sweltering body of the Callisto. Nina opened the rear hatch and ignited the jets. They rose vertically up into the star-sprinkled circus dome, below which they had once had the best seats in the house for viewing magic tricks and clownery, and where they now had to pull off the murderous acrobatics of saving lives.

'Hey, you guys,' said Nina. 'Are you still there?'

'Not for much longer,' prophesied Heidrun.

'We can forget the shuttle airlock. It's too near to the engines, and I have to maintain the counter-thrust in order not to slip. I'll approach in reverse with the rear hatch open, okay? I'll have to avoid touching the head, so get ready to do some chin-ups.'

'Chin-ups, somersaults, we'll do whatever you want.'

They ascended further. First Gaia's back was visible from the cockpit of the shuttle, then the neck with its exposed steel backbone came into full view. Lynn couldn't help thinking about what Gaia embodied in Julian's eyes: her own image, to excess. And they really were becoming more and more alike. Two queens about to lose their heads.

The Callisto rose up slowly over the curve of the skull.

O'Keefe helped the others onto their feet. Pressed between the airlock wall and the terrace floor, they gripped to one another and waved at the helmeted silhouette behind the cockpit window. The shuttle began to turn on its axis, first turning its side towards them, then the open rear with the lowered tailboard.

'Nearer!' shouted Tim.

A jolt went through the head. Ögi lost his grip and was caught by Heidrun. The Callisto swivelled two of its jets. With absolute precision, Nina Hedegaard steered the huge craft backwards. The tailboard came closer, closer still, too close—

'Stop!'

The shuttle stopped, motionless in open space.

'Can you make it?' asked Nina.

O'Keefe raised both hands, grabbed the edge and pulled himself up onto the tailboard with a powerful swinging motion. He turned round right away, lay down on his stomach and stretched his arms out below.

'Nina? Can you lower the machine a little further?'

'I'll try.'

His right hand brushed Heidrun's fingertips. The Callisto sank another metre, now hovering at helmet-height across from the others.

'That's as far as I can go,' said Nina. 'I'm afraid of touching the head.'

'That'll do.' Heidrun clambered up to O'Keefe on the hatch. To the right of her, Ögi pulled himself up, crouched down and grasped Olympiada, who was handed up to him from below, steadying herself on his shoulder. Hands stretched out towards Miranda and Tim, helping them up.

'We made it,' whispered Olympiada, then crumpled over, as the damaged bone in her shin finally broke. With a scream, she rolled over the edge of the hatch and tumbled back into the tiny gap between the terrace and the airlock.

'Olympiada!'

Miranda, who was almost all the way up, dropped back down next to the Russian woman and grabbed her under the arms.

'No – don't—'

'Are you crazy? Up you go – as if I would leave you lying here.'

'I'm useless,' whimpered Olympiada.

'No, you're wonderful, you just don't know it yet.'

Miranda effortlessly lifted the petite woman up and towards O'Keefe, who pulled her back onto the tailboard and handed her over to Tim.

'Yeah!' called Miranda. 'See, there was nothing to it!'

She laughed and stretched her arms out. O'Keefe went to grab her, but her hands were suddenly out of reach. Confused, he leaned his upper body further forward. She was moving away from him at an ever greater speed, and for a moment he thought Nina had flown away without her. Then he realised the shuttle hadn't moved an inch.

Gaia's head was breaking off!

'Miranda!' he screamed.

He could hear her choking gasps in his helmet as if she were right there next to him, while her tottering form dwindled before his eyes. She was waving her arms wildly, which in some gruesome way could have been mistaken for a gesture of exuberance, the way they knew her to be, always in a good mood, always pushing herself to the very limit, but as she called O'Keefe's name, her voice expressed the absolute despair of a person who knew that nothing and no one would be able to save them.

'Finn! Finn! – Finn!'

'Miranda!'

Then she fell.

Her body tipped over the cabin shaft, flashed in the sunlight and then disappeared behind the head of Gaia, which did a half-turn, seemed to stand still for a moment, then fell completely from the shoulders, crashing into the immense Romanesque window of the abdominal wall.

'Inside, everyone inside!' shouted O'Keefe, his voice cracking. 'Nina!'

'What's wrong, Finn, we—'

'She fell!' He jumped into the cargo hold. 'Miranda fell overboard; you have to go round to the front section.'

'Is everyone else in?'

His eyes darted around. Next to him, Tim stumbled across, a groaning Olympiada in his arms, and collapsed down to the floor of the hold.

'Yes! Quickly, for heaven's sake, go quickly!'

Not waiting until the hatch was closed, he ran like crazy to the connecting bulkhead and pushed himself through while there was still barely a crack's width open. Stumbling along the central gangway, he was hurled against a seat, the revving of the engines in his ears as Nina steered the Callisto backwards over the figure's tattered stump of a neck. Then he struggled to his feet again and rushed into the cockpit.

And looked down.

The abdominal cavity was destroyed. Fireballs appeared which extinguished as soon as they were ignited. Rubble rained down as the rib-cage containing the suites collapsed floor by floor. Then, Gaia's immense, regal skull, the glazing on the face surprisingly still intact, rolled over the gentle inclination of the upper thigh towards the valley, passed the knee almost hesitantly and shattered on the plateau two hundred metres below.

'Go down! Down!'

The shuttle sank, but Miranda was nowhere to be seen, neither on the upper surface of the thigh, now covered in debris, nor on the moon surface around it.

'To the plateau! She was torn down with it! You have to—'

'Finn—'

'No! Look! Look for her!'

Without arguing, Nina turned the shuttle around, descended further and flew in a curve directly over and around the widely scattered remains of the head. By now, the others were gathering together in the space behind the cockpit.

'She can't have disappeared!' screamed O'Keefe.

'Finn.'

He felt the soft pressure of a hand on his upper arm and turned round. Heidrun had taken her helmet off and was looking at him with red eyes.

'She can't have just disappeared,' he repeated softly.

'She's dead, Finn. Miranda's dead.'

He stared at her.

Then he started to cry. Blinded by tears, he sank to the floor in front of Heidrun. He couldn't remember ever having cried.

Lynn sat in the first row of seats, distancing herself from the group, completely expressionless. She had beamed her former light for the last time, had unified the group in the glow of the dying star that she was, had illuminated them, blinded and driven back Dana, her enemy, but the fuel of her life's energy was used up now, her collapse unavoidable. Everything inside her skull was rushing around with maximum kinetic energy: impressions, facts, probability of occurrences. Dependable knowledge was pulverised into hypotheses. The unending condensing of impressions caused them to be fractured into the smallest, the very smallest thought particles, to which no time, no perceptual level, no history could be assigned. Increasingly brief thought phases, thought particles whirling at the speed of light, a collapsing spirit, unceasingly crashing without the opposing pressure of will, falling short of the event horizon, no transmission, only reception now, ongoing compromise, the end of all processes, of all contour, all form, just situation, and even the pitiful remains of what had once been Lynn Orley would corrode and evaporate under their own pressure, leaving nothing behind but an abandoned, imaginary space.

Someone had died. So many had died.

Her memory was empty.

London, Great Britain

Yoyo, presumed missing, had arrived at the stroke of 22.00 just as Diane was carrying out the electronic exhumation of a person presumed dead. Presumed, because no one had been able to get even a fleeting glance of the corpse. Because it was still undiscovered, as all objects moving in unknown or unpredictable orbits tend to be.

'Victor Thorn, known as Vic,' Jericho said, without deigning to ask Yoyo why five minutes had turned into three hours and what Tu was up to in his state of rage.

'I'm sorry, I . . .' Yoyo fidgeted hesitantly. She had a frog in her throat and it had to come out. 'I know I was planning to be back much sooner—'

'Commander of the first moon base occupation. A NASA man. In 2021, he ran the show for six months.'

'—Tian isn't really like that. I mean, you know him.'

'It seems that Thorn did a good job. So good, that in 2024 they entrusted him with another six-month mission.'

'To be honest, we haven't spoken that much,' said Yoyo, a little shrilly. The frog was croaking on her tongue. 'He was just terribly angry. We ended up watching a film, pretending everything was normal, you know. It was probably the worst conceivable moment, but you shouldn't believe—'

'Yoyo.' Jericho sighed and shrugged his shoulders. 'It's your business. It has nothing to do with me.'

'Of course it has something to do with you!'

The frog was on the move.

'No, it doesn't.' To his amazement, he meant it. The old, unconquered hurt which had lingered on him so long, like a bad odour on clothes, gave way to the insight that neither Tu nor Yoyo was responsible for his bad mood. However well they were getting on, it really had nothing to do with him. 'It's your lives, your story. You don't have to tell me anything.'

Yoyo stared at the monitor unhappily. Their surroundings left a little to be desired in terms of intimacy. The space in the information centre had been screened in a makeshift way; people were working all around them, like microorganisms in the abdominal cavity of the Big O, digesting and processing information, then expelling it.

'And if I *want* to tell you something?'

'Then now is definitely not a good time.'

'Fine.' She sighed. 'So what's this about Thorn?'

'Well, assuming that the explosion of the mini-nuke was planned for 2024 *without fail* – then someone must have been up there at the time: to hide, position and ignite the bomb. Either that or someone else was supposed to travel on after it and do that.'

'Sounds logical.'

'But no explosion was registered, and the people from MI6 think that storing a mini-nuke in a vacuum for too long could pose the risk of a premature decay. So why wasn't it ignited?'

Yoyo looked at him, a small, steep line of thoughtfulness between her eyes.

'Because the person in question wasn't able to carry out the ignition as planned. Because something happened.'

'Correct. So I sent Diane on the hunt. There's information on the internet about all the space missions in the last year, and I stumbled across Thorn. A fatal accident during an external mission on the OSS, on 2 August 2024. It was completely unexpected and happened before he could take up his position on the Peary Base, but the most significant thing is that it was almost three months to the day after Mayé's satellite was launched.'

Yoyo gnawed at her lower lip.

'And the Chinese? Have you checked?'

'You can't "check" the Chinese,' said Jericho. 'The best you can find is their own statements, and according to them there was no loss of personnel in 2024.'

'Apart from the Moon crisis. The commander of the Chinese base was imprisoned by the Americans.'

'Oh, come on! First they shoot an atomic bomb up to the Moon as part of some unbelievably elaborate and sophisticated camouflage manoeuvre, then a few taiko-nauts stumble into American mining territory like a couple of idiots and get themselves caught?'

'Hmm.' Yoyo wrinkled her forehead. 'So someone took the elevator. But to do that they would either have had to plant someone in an authorised team—'

'Or bribe someone who was already in it.'

'And Thorn *was* in the team.'

'On his mission to the Moon, all official and above board.' Jericho nodded. 'In the role of a commander, with almost unlimited access. And above all, he knew his way around up there like the back of his hand. He'd been there before.'

'Have you told Shaw and Norrington about this?' Yoyo's eyes were gleaming. Suddenly she was a Guardian again, infected by curiosity.

'No.' Jericho stood up. 'But I think we should remedy that right away.'

Shaw and Norrington were wandering around somewhere in the Big O with delegates from MI5, but Edda Hoff gobbled up the fillet steak of their investigations hungrily. She knew about Thorn's case of course, but so far no one had come up with the idea that the respected two-time commander of the Peary Base might have been the chosen one for blowing Gaia to smithereens. She promised to put together some information about Thorn and fill her superiors in on Jericho's theory. Then Tu Tian reappeared, looking perfectly composed, as if nothing had happened. He told a joke and listened to the latest news before retreating into the guest area.

'Business,' he said, with an apologetic gesture. 'The day's just getting started in China. Armies of hard-working competitors are sharpening their knives; I can't act as if I don't have a company to run. So if you don't need me to save the world—'

'No, not right this moment, Tian.'

'Excellent. *Fenshou!*'

Shaw and Norrington came back in, but Hoff was tied up in a video conversation with NASA. Jericho was just about to speak to Shaw about Vic Thorn when Tom Merrick announced that, in all probability, he had found the reason for the communication blockade but was unable to lift it.

'Knowing why it doesn't work is still progress,' said Shaw as they gathered in the large conference room.

'As I already mentioned' – Merrick's gaze flitted from one face to the next – 'to be able to cut the Moon off from all communication, you'd need to interfere with so many satellites and ground control stations that it would be practically impossible. So my guess is that it's something else: IOF.'

'IO what?' said Shaw.

Merrick looked at her as if he found it incomprehensible that people didn't talk exclusively in abbreviations.

'Information Overflow.'

'Paralysis of the terminal device by botnet mass mails,' said Yoyo. 'Data congestion.'

One of the MI6 people present looked confused.

'Imagine there's someone sitting in a room, and you want to silence them,' she explained. 'And you don't want them to be able to hear either.

Assuming that you succeed in getting your hands on all the keys, you'll try to bolt all the doors in order to cut them off from the world. The doors are the satellites and ground control stations, but you can't stop more and more doors being built in, not to mention the fact that you won't be able to get all the keys anyway. The alternative is incredibly simple. You just go into the room, put a gag in their mouth and cotton wool in their ears.'

'So, as far as I understand it, that man is Gaia's computer.'

'Two men,' said Merrick. 'Gaia's computer and the Peary Base system.'

'Don't they have any mirror systems?' asked Jericho.

'Okay, four men then.' Merrick waved his hand impatiently. 'Or even more, as it's possible the shuttles' satellite receivers were gagged too. In any case, the procedure is much more efficient because you only interfere with the terminal device, that is the IP addresses of the people you want to target. Everything is fine with the satellites –, you can have a million of them flying around and it won't change anything, quite the contrary. Nowadays, satellites and ground control stations function increasingly as knots in an IP network, like an internet in space! The botnet can jump from one knot to another in order to fight its way through.'

Jericho realised immediately that Merrick was right. In essence, botnets were old hat. Hackers gained control over as many computers as possible by implanting special software. Generally speaking, the users didn't know that it would make their computers turn into bots, soldiers of an automated army. Theoretically, the illegal software could lie dormant in the infiltrated computers indefinitely, until it awakened at a pre-programmed time and prompted its host computer to ceaselessly send emails to a defined target: totally legal enquiries, but in torrential proportions. On the black market for cyberterrorism, networks with up to 100,000 bots had been exposed. When the botnet struck, it simultaneously fired billions of emails and flooded the target with data, until the attacked computer was no longer able to cope with the volume and perished under IOF, Information Overload.

'What are your thoughts, Tom?' asked Shaw. 'How long can they keep their attacks up for?'

'It's difficult to say. Botnets are usually unstoppable. You tell the software in advance how long it should keep at it for, then smuggle it in. After that, there's no way of getting to it.'

'So you can also program into the software when it should stop?'

'Sure, you can do anything. But my suspicion is that the one we're dealing with is a little different. The attack came as a direct reaction to our attempt to warn Julian and the Gaia, so someone *must* have started the bots individually.'

'Which means they must have directed a query at this someone after the software was installed,' said Yoyo. 'And that question was: Shall I attack? So the person in question must have said yes at some stage.'

'And while they were attacking the Gaia and the Peary Base, they directed another query at Mister Unknown,' nodded Merrick. 'This time: Shall I stop?'

'So if we only knew who started it—' said the MI6 man.

'Then we could make him stop it.'

'Where could the person be?' asked Shaw.

Merrick stared at her. 'How should I know? There could be a number of people involved. The person who set the attacks in motion could be on the Moon. If he smuggled control software into the Gaia's computer, then it would have been no problem for him to start the bots from there, although admittedly he would have crippled himself in the process. So I suspect the jerk who can stop all this madness is somewhere on Earth. For heaven's sake, Jennifer!' His arms flailed around wildly. 'He could be anywhere. He could be *here*. In the Big O. In this very room!'

Not long after, they heard from Gerald Palstein. The face staring at them through the monitor window from Texas looked dejected, and Jericho couldn't help being reminded of Shaw's words, about the unpleasant decisions EMCO's chief strategist was responsible for on a daily basis.

Then he looked closer.

No, it was something else. Palstein looked like someone who had just been given devastating news.

'I can supply you with the film now,' he said wearily.

'You were able to speak to your contact?' Shaw's voice sneaked up, cautious and tentative.

'No.' Palstein rubbed his eyes. 'Something happened.'

For a moment his forehead appeared in disproportion to the rest of his body as he leaned forward and pressed something underneath the transmission camera. Then the image changed, and they saw a news report from CNN.

'An incomprehensible tragedy took place today in Vancouver in Canada,' said Christine Roberts, the smartly dressed frontwoman of *Breaking News*. 'In an act of unprecedented violence, practically the entire leadership of the internet portal Greenwatch has been wiped out. The ecologically orientated station, known for its engaged and critical reportage, has contributed again and again to the resolution of environmental scandals in recent years, as well as bringing multiple suits against companies and politicians. They were known to be balanced and fair. Our corres-pondent in Vancouver can now speak to us. Rick Lester, are there any indications yet as to who could be behind the bloodbath which may mean the end of Greenwatch?'

The picture changed. Early evening light. A man in front of a Canadian villa-style property, crime-scene tape fluttering all around him, along with police vehicles and uniformed officers.

'No, Christine, and that's exactly what makes the whole thing so eerie: so far there are no clues at all as to who is responsible for these murders, or rather executions, and above all, why.' Rick Lester spoke in an emphasised staccato, pausing after every half-sentence. 'Greenwatch were working, as we now know, on an extensive report about the destruction of the boreal forest in Canada and other parts of the world, so that would make the oil industry a prime suspect, but the report was more looking back at what damage has been caused over the years, that can't be undone, and at first glance there's nothing there which could serve as an explanation for a massacre like this.'

'There's now talk of ten fatalities, Rick. What exactly happened, and what names are amongst the victims?'

'So, I should add that this is probably a concerted action, because it not only affected the headquarters of Greenwatch, where seven people have been found dead' – he turned slightly to indicate the scene behind him – 'but a quarter of an hour before there was also a wild pursuit on Marine Drive, a coastal road that leads out to Point Grey, and witnesses claim to have seen a large four-by-four repeatedly ram into a Thunderbird containing three Greenwatch staff, and then intentionally cause an accident. It seems that two of the people in the car initially survived the crash, but were then immediately shot. One of the victims is, incidentally, the chief reporter of Greenwatch, Loreena Keowa. So the murderers may have driven on to the Greenwatch headquarters, here at Point Grey, gained access and created this bloodbath within a matter of minutes.'

'A bloodbath which – according to the latest reports – also cost the director, Susan Hudsucker, her life?'

'Yes, that has been confirmed.'

'It's terrible, Rick, really unbelievable, but it's not just the murders which are giving the investigators clues, but some things which seem to have disappeared—'

'That's right, Christine, and this shines a particular light on the incident. Because there is not one single computer to be found in the whole building; all of Greenwatch's data has been stolen, as well as handwritten notes, so pretty much the station's entire memory.'

'Rick, doesn't that imply that someone here was trying to prevent the publication of potentially controversial information?'

Lester nodded. 'Someone was undoubtedly trying to *delay* its publication, and we've just heard that contact has been made with freelance workers to find out more about the current projects, but Greenwatch always took great pains to keep hot information and stories within the inner circle right up to the last moment, so it could mean those final projects will never be reconstructed.'

'An immense tragedy indeed. So, that's all from Vancouver for now, thank you, Rick Lester. And now—'

The recording came to an end. Palstein reappeared, alone in front of the polished mahogany table in his conference room in Dallas.

'Was that your contact person?' asked Shaw. 'The woman in the car?'

'Yes.' Palstein nodded. 'Loreena Keowa.'

'And you think the events are directly connected to the assassination attempt in Calgary?'

'I don't know.' Palstein sighed. 'A film clip turned up showing a man. He could be the assassin, but does that justify a massacre like this? I mean, I'm in possession of the pictures too, and Loreena said she showed them to a number of people. We were planning to talk on the phone right after her landing in Vancouver, I asked her to call me without fail—'

'Because you were worried.'

'Yes, of course.' Palstein shook his head. 'It was like she was obsessed with the case. I was very worried.'

'Mr Palstein,' said Jericho, 'how quickly could we get hold of the film? Every second—'

'No problem. I can show you the extract right away.'

The picture changed once again. This time they saw the entrance hall of a building. Jericho thought he recognised the run-down façade: the empty business complex opposite the Imperial Oil HQ in Calgary, from which the shot at Palstein was alleged to have been fired. People were walking around aimlessly. Two men and a woman came out of the building into the sunlight. The men joined a policeman and engaged him in conversation, while the woman positioned herself to the side. A figure crept up from the left, a fat, bulky man with long black hair.

Jericho leaned forwards. A still image appeared on the monitor, just a head and shoulders. He was clearly an Asian man. A corpulent, unkempt appearance, greasy hair, his beard thin and dishevelled; but what couldn't be accomplished with a bit of latex, foam and make-up?

Even Yoyo was staring at the Asian man.

'Almost unrecognisable,' she whispered.

Shaw looked at her keenly. 'You know him?'

'Absolutely.' Jericho nodded. He couldn't help but laugh. 'Unbelievable, but it's him!'

The disguise was worthy of an Oscar, but the circumstances under which they had met him meant they couldn't be misled. Jericho had already fallen for it once, but wouldn't let it happen again, even if the bastard covered himself in fur and went down on all fours.

'That,' he said, 'is without a doubt the Calgary assassin.'

Shaw raised her eyebrows. 'And do you have a name?'

'Yes, but it won't help you much. The guy is as volatile as gas. His name is Xin. Kenny Xin.'

Sinus Iridum, The Moon

The Land of Mist.

It was only after getting to the Moon that Evelyn had learned the astronauts' name for the mining zone, and to her the term seemed corny and inapplicable. According to her school education, mist was a meteorological phenomenon, an aerosol, and there was certainly no droplet formation on the Moon. She had asked around as to whether the name resulted from some pretentious need to pay homage to Riccioli and his historical misinterpretations, but didn't receive any adequate answers. In general, the zone was hardly ever discussed. Julian had scheduled in a presentation of a documentary for the last day of their stay; so there were no plans to visit the mining zone at all.

But now that she had ended up here after all, one glance was enough to make her see why prosaic minds had named the stretch of land between Sinus Iridum and Mare Imbrium the Land of Mist. A flat, iridescent barrier stretched out from horizon to horizon, over a kilometre high and not in the slightest bit suited to lifting Chambers' mood. It weighed down on the land desolately, hopelessness which had turned into dust. No one in their right mind would feel the desire to cross it.

But Hanna's wheel tracks led right into it.

He had driven down the path for several hundred metres, then veered off in a north-easterly direction. According to Julian, he was travelling along the imaginary line that linked Cape Heraclides to Cape Laplace.

Giving in to the conflicting hope that their opponent might be a survival expert, and possibly the better pathfinder, they followed in his tracks. Amber continued to study her maps, but as good as their services had been so far, here they proved to be useless. Everywhere they looked, visibility was cut short by mist, sometimes after a hundred metres, but mostly after just ten. There was no horizon now, no hills, no mountain ranges, only Hanna's solitary tracks on his way into the unknown. Something that fed on life itself crept up out of the dust, weighed heavily on Chambers' ribcage and unleashed in her the childlike longing to cry. The Moon was dead matter, and yet until now she had seen it as strangely alive, like an old and wise human being, a wonderful Methuselah, whose wrinkles preserved the history of creation. Here, though, history seemed to have been erased. The familiar powdery consistency of the regolith, its gentle slopes and miniature craters, had given way to crumbly uniformity, as if something had glided over and subjected it to an eerie transformation. For a moment, she thought she could make out the edge of a small crater, but it vanished into dust before her eyes, mere hallucination.

'There's nothing left here to get your bearings from,' said Julian to Amber. 'The beetles have changed the landscape permanently.'

Beetles? Evelyn stopped. She couldn't recall ever having heard of beetles being on the Moon. But whatever they were up to, in her eyes it amounted to desecration. All around them, it looked as though someone had inflicted grievous bodily harm on the satellite. This crumbly stuff was the ashes of the dead. It was racked up in parallel, shallow ramparts, like powerful furrows, as if something had been ploughing the ground.

'Julian, it looks awful here,' she said.

'I know. Not exactly the dream destination for tourists. People only ever come here if there are problems the maintenance robots can't cope with.'

'And what in God's name are the beetles?'

'Look over there.' Julian raised his arm and pointed ahead. 'That's one.'

She squinted. At first she just saw the sunlight flickering on the dust particles. Then, amidst enigmatic grey tones, a silhouette came into view at an indefinable distance from them, a thing of primeval appearance. It slowly pushed its hunched, strangely weightless-looking body forwards, making bizarre details visible: a rotating jaw system beneath a low, oblate head, which rummaged industriously through the regolith, insectoid legs spread out wide. Unrelentingly, it kept adding to the dust across the plateau, causing it to whirl around as it continued to eat and move forwards. The microscopic suspended matter enshrouded its bulky body, surrounding its legs like a cocoon. By now, Evelyn was pretty sure she knew what she was looking at, except all her perceptions were stunted by the impression of just how inconceivably powerful the beetle was. The nearer they got to it, the more monstrous it looked, stretching out its humpback, which was covered in enormous, glinting, shell-like mirrors, a mythical monster, as tall as a high-rise building.

Julian bore down on it. 'Momoka, stay behind me,' he ordered. 'We have to stick together. If we want to stay on course, we can't avoid getting close to these machines. They're sluggish, but sluggishness is relative when you consider their size.'

The visibility got worse. By the time the velvety regolith was under their wheels again, just before they reached the beetle, its torso was outlined, dark and threatening, against the clouded sky. For its enormous height, it was astonishingly narrow.

It disappeared behind plumes of whirling dust. As the giant lifted one of its powerful, many-jointed legs and took a step forwards, it seemed to Evelyn as if it was ever so slowly swivelling its stooped skull around to look at them. The rover juddered softly. She put it down to Momoka driving over a bump on the ground, but an inner certainty told her it had happened at the very moment when the beetle rammed its foot into the regolith.

'A mining machine!' Rogachev turned round to stare at the vanishing silhouette. 'Fantastic! How could you have kept that from me for so long?'

'We call them beetles,' said Julian. 'On account of their shape and the way they move. And yes, they are fantastic. But there are far too few of them.'

'Do they turn the regolith into this – stuff?' asked Evelyn, thinking of the crumbly wasteland.

Julian hesitated. 'As I said, they transform the landscape.'

'I was just wondering, I mean, I wasn't really sure how the mining takes place. I thought, I mean, I expected to see something along the lines of drilling rigs.'

As soon as the words had left her mouth, she felt ashamed for discussing mining techniques with Julian so casually, as if forgetting that Momoka had been confronted with Locatelli's deformed corpse just half an hour before. Since their departure from the Cape, the Japanese woman had not uttered a single word, but she was certainly driving the rover with care. She had retreated within herself, in an eerie, ghostly way. The creature behind the reflective visor pane steering the vehicle could easily have been mistaken for a robot.

'Helium-3 can't be produced in the same way as oil, gas or coal,' said Julian. 'The isotope is atomically bound into the moon dust. Around three nanograms per gram of regolith, evenly distributed.'

'Nanogram, wait a moment,' pondered Evelyn. 'That's a billionth of a gram, right?'

'So little?' Rogachev was stunned.

'Not *that* little,' said Julian. 'Just think, the stuff was stored up over billions of years by solar wind. Far over half a billion tonnes in total, ten times as much as all the coal, oil and gas reserves on Earth! That's a hell of a lot! It's just that, in order to get to it, you have to process the moon surface too.'

So that's what you call it, thought Evelyn. Processing. And out of that comes a wasteland of crumb-like debris. Feeling uneasy, she stared off into the glistening distance. Far behind them, a second beetle was creeping through the dust, and suddenly the terrain became ugly and crumbly again.

'And yet it's an astonishingly low concentration,' Rogachev persisted. 'It sounds to me as though *vast* amounts of lunar soil would need to be processed. How deep do those things burrow down into the ground?'

'Two to three metres. Helium-3 can still be found even five metres down, but they get most of it from above that.'

'And that's enough?'

'It depends what for.'

'I mean, is it enough to supply the world with helium-3?'

'Well, it was enough to make the fossil energy market collapse on Earth.'

'It collapsed prematurely. How many machines are in use at the moment?'

'Thirty. Believe me, Oleg, helium-3 represents a lasting solution to our energy problems, and the Moon can provide it. But you're right of course. We need a lot more machines to be able to graze all the terrain.'

'Graze,' echoed Amber. 'That sounds more like a cow than a beetle.'

'Yes.' Julian's laughter was a little forced. 'They really do move across the land like herds. Like a herd of cows.'

'Impressive,' said Rogachev, but Evelyn thought she could detect a hint of scepticism. The silhouette of a third beetle came into sight in the hazy distance. It seemed to be standing still. Evelyn's attention was drawn to something agile, something smaller, that was approaching the machine from behind, at first glance a flying machine, until the suspicion took hold that the thing was hurrying over on high, intricate legs, and she couldn't help thinking of a spider. The apparition paused underneath the monstrous abdomen, ducked down, and seemed to temporarily merge with the beetle. Evelyn stared at it curiously. She wanted to ask Julian, but Momoka's silence weighed heavily over the group like a stormy sky, so she held her tongue, deeply unsettled. This insectarium was not at all to her liking. Not that she had anything against technology: she conscientiously drove her environmentally friendly electric car, had converted her home to Locatelli's solar technology and always separated her trash – though she certainly couldn't claim a devoutly green mindset. Phenomena like robotics, nanotechnology and space travel were just as interesting to her as waterfalls, giant sequoia trees and the endangered tufted-ear marmosets, whose continued existence couldn't necessarily be regarded as essential to the Earth's ecological foundations.

New technologies fascinated her, but something about this realm of the dead exuded a horror that even Rogachev's less than squeamish industrial nature seemed to be developing antibodies against.

Hanna's tracks veered off in a wide arc. The huge imprints suggested that he had been forced to dodge one of the mining machines. The crater-like tracks were joined by some of lesser diameter, and less deep too. Evelyn looked behind and saw a beetle shimmering in its cocoon of dust like a mirage. She couldn't make out the spider-like creature any more. She closed her eyes, and the image of the colossal machine left a ghostly afterglow on her retinas.

The beetle was eating.

It worked its way unceasingly through the undergrowth with its shovel-like jaw, loosening the rocks, sieving out the indigestible fragments and guiding the fine-grained matter that remained into its glowing insides. Meanwhile, huge reflectors atop its hunchback followed the course of the sun, bundled photons and sent them off to smaller parabolic reflectors. From there, the light made its way into the cybernetic organism and created a burning hell of 1000 degrees Celsius, not enough to melt the regolith, but enough to divest it of its bound elements. Hydrogen, carbon and nitrogen and minute quantities of helium-3 rose in gas form into the solar oven, and from there made their way into the highly compressed counter-world of its abdomen. At minus 260 degrees Celsius and under enormous pressure, the obtained gases condensed into liquid and were then transmitted to batteries of spherical tanks, separated according to their elementary affiliation: minute amounts of helium-3, every drop a carefully protected treasure, and everything else in huge quantities. Despite the potential value of the hydrogen for fuel production, the nitrogen for the enrichment of air supplies and the carbon for building materials, vast as the beetle was, it still had to release most of these liquefied elements back into the vacuum, where they instantly evaporated, forming a fleeting, cyclically renewed atmosphere around the machine. In this way the beetles altered everything surrounding them: the lunar soil, which they regurgitated in the form of baked crumbs, and the vacuum, which was constantly enriched with the noble gases that the machine constantly expelled.

As a result of the gas emissions, the dust around the machine became even denser. Strictly speaking, given that there were no air molecules to hold the floating pieces of rock in suspension, they should have been incapable of forming the kilometre-high barrier. But it was the very lack of atmospheric pressure, as well as the scant gravity and electrostatic phenomena, that caused their extremely long and high flight-paths, from which they sank down, as if reluctantly, hours later. So, over time, a permanent haze had descended over the mining zone. The clouds produced by the beetle under high pressure formed additional dust in such large quantities that the chewing apparatus and insect legs completely disappeared behind it at times. In addition to this, there was an iridescent gleam on the crystalline structure of the suspended matter, almost like aurora, which made it even harder to see.

This was exactly what happened to Hanna on his solitary trek; the reason why he only became aware of the proximity of one of the mining machines crossing his path once its shovel had practically swallowed him up and passed him through the sieve – only a jump of possibly record-breaking proportions had saved him from being industrially processed. He hastily put some distance between himself and the beetle, aghast that he'd overlooked something so colossal that it could make the ground shake. The machine had towered above him, but it was a well-known fact that small creatures tended to be blinded when they got too close to large ones. He aligned his course to the path of the machine and carried on. From the inexhaustible information provided as part of the conspiracy, he knew that the beetles ploughed the regolith in rectangular paths on the imaginary line between Cape Heraclides and Cape Laplace, and that you couldn't miss the station as long as you kept at a ninety-degree angle to the pasture routes – the only orientation device in a world where, due to the lack of a magnetic field, even compasses didn't work. He had been on the go for well over an hour now since the buggy had served its last, and his long, springing steps had necessitated his breaking into his first oxygen reserves. But he still didn't feel any sign of fatigue. As long as nothing unexpected happened, the mining station should appear before him in the next fifteen to twenty minutes. If not, he would be in serious difficulties, and there would be plenty of time to worry then.

Totally unexpectedly, they met a spider.

It emerged from the shadow of a beetle and crossed their path with such speed that Julian had to whip the steering wheel around to stop them from colliding with it. For a moment, Evelyn was reminded of H. G. Wells' tripods, the machines from Mars in *War of the Worlds* which attacked entire cities using heat rays, burning them to cinders. But this thing had eight legs instead of three, daddy-long-legs-thin and several metres long, making it look as if its body were hovering in space. There were dozens of spherical tanks lined up right behind its pincers. Another thing that set the spider apart from its Martian colleagues was its complete lack of interest in human presence. Without Julian's quick-wittedness, Evelyn suspected it would simply have run right over the vehicle.

'What in God's name was that brute of a thing?' shrieked Momoka.

She was communicating again now, although admittedly in a way which was provoking wistful memories of her silence. Any trace of grief seemed to have been transformed into rage. Evelyn suddenly wondered whether Momoka's joyless personality was less shaped by arrogance than by pent-up aggression, hoarded over many years, and she became less and less happy about her driving the rover. Her heart racing, she stared after the robot as it hurried away. In front of them, Julian slowly began to drive forwards again.

'A spider,' he said, as if there had been any doubt on the matter. 'Loading and unloading robots. They receive the full tanks from the beetles, exchange them for empty ones, bring the loot to the station and load them up to be transported on.'

'I don't exactly feel welcome here,' observed Rogachev.

'They won't hurt you,' murmured Amber. 'They just want to play.'

'Is the area under surveillance?'

'Yes and no.'

'Which means?'

'The CCTV only switches on if there's an error message. As I said, the mining is automated. Distributed intelligence in a real-time network. The robots only react to each other; we don't exist in their internal image.'

'Pieces of shit!' snarled Momoka. 'Your goddamn Moon is starting to really get on my tits.'

'Maybe it would be worth enriching their internal image with some additional data,' Evelyn suggested. 'I mean, if a spider has room in its reality cosmos for something as space-consuming as a beetle, surely it can't be that complicated to squeeze in *Homo sapiens* too.'

'Humans aren't supposed be in the mining zone,' said Julian, a little on edge. 'The zone is a self-enclosed technosphere.'

'And how big is this technosphere?'

'At the moment, one hundred square kilometres. On the American side. The Chinese occupy a smaller zone.'

'And you're sure that those are American machines?'

'The Chinese use caterpillar tracks.'

'Well' said Evelyn, 'at least we won't get trampled by the enemy.'

From that point on, they paid even more attention to what was lurking in the shadows, and – because it was impossible to hear anything in a vacuum – also strained their eyes until they hurt. That's how Amber noticed the buggy, even from a distance.

'What's going on?' asked Momoka as she saw Julian stop.

'Carl might be up ahead.'

'Oh, that's good.' She laughed drily. 'Very good! For me, not for him.' She tried to overtake Julian but Rogachev put his hand on her forearm.

'Wait.'

'What for, for God's sake?'

'I said, wait.'

His unusually authoritative tone made Momoka stop. Rogachev pulled himself up. There were no spiders nor beetles as far as the eye could see. The baked regolith was the only indication that the mining machines had already processed this part of the Sinus Iridum. Amidst the bleak landscape, Hanna's buggy looked like the remains of a long-lost battle.

'I can't see him anywhere,' said Amber after a while.

'No.' Rogachev turned his upper body round and back. 'It really doesn't look like he's there.'

'How could you tell in all this fucking dust?' growled Momoka. 'He could be anywhere.'

'I don't know, Momoka. All I know is that – so far – we haven't been shot at.'

There was expectant silence for a while.

'Okay,' Julian decided. 'Let's go over there.'

Within a few minutes it became clear that Hanna wasn't lying in wait for them somewhere. His buggy had succumbed to an axle fracture. Bootprints led off in a straight line away from it.

'He set off on foot,' commented Amber.

'Will he be able to make it?' asked Evelyn.

'Sure, as long as he has enough air.' Julian bent over the cargo area. 'He hasn't left anything behind in any case, and I know for sure that he took oxygen reserves from the Ganymede with him.'

'Shouldn't we be there soon?' Evelyn stared into the distance. 'I mean, we've been on the go for over an hour now.'

'According to the rover it's another fifteen kilometres to the station.'

'A piece of cake then, really.'

'For us, but not so much for him.' Julian straightened up. 'He'll need one to two hours from here. That means he's still out there somewhere. There's no way he's already reached the station.'

'So we'll run into him.'

'And soon, I think.'

'And what will we do with him when we do?'

'The question's more what he'll do with us,' snorted Amber.

'Well, I know what *I'm* going to do with him,' hissed Momoka. 'I'm going to—'

'No, you won't,' Julian interrupted her. 'Don't get me wrong, Momoka. We're grieving with you, but—'

'Oh, spare me that shit!'

'But we have to find out what Carl is planning. I want to know what this is all about. We need him alive!'

'That won't be easy,' said Rogachev. 'He's armed.'

'Do you have any ideas?'

'Well.' Rogachev was silent for a moment. 'We've got the advantage in some ways. We have the rovers. And we're approaching him from behind. If he doesn't happen to turn round right at the decisive moment, then we could drive right up without him even realising.'

'And do you want to risk him shooting at us as soon as he does realise?' Amber turned round. 'Driving right up close is all well and good. But what then?'

'We could surround him,' Julian mused. 'Approach from both sides.'

'Then he'd definitely see us,' said Rogachev.

'How about a friendly ramming?' Evelyn suggested.

'Hmm, not bad.' Julian thought for a moment. 'Let's say we drive next to one another, nice and slow. Then one of us can run him down from behind, and then, before he has time to react, the ones in the other rover can jump down and grab his weapons, and so on.'

'And so on. So who's doing the ramming?'

'Julian,' said Rogachev. 'And we'll form the attack commando.'

'And who's driving?'

'Well . . .' Rogachev turned to Momoka, who was standing there motionless as if waiting for someone to activate her vital functions. 'Momoka is very emotionally charged right now.'

'Don't you worry about me,' said Momoka tonelessly.

'But I do,' said Rogachev coolly. 'I don't know whether we can let you drive. You'll mess things up.'

'And?' Momoka broke out of her frozen state and climbed back into the driver's seat. 'What's the alternative, Oleg? If you let me jump on him you'll be risking much more. For example, the fact that I'll smash in his visor with the nearest available rock.'

'We need him alive,' Julian repeated insistently. 'Under no circumstances will we—'

'I got it!' she snapped.

'No vigilantes, Momoka!'

'I'll play by the rules. We'll do it the way you just said.'

'Sure?'

Momoka sighed. When she spoke, her voice trembled as if she was holding back tears. 'Yes, I'm sure. I promise.'

'I don't trust you,' said Rogachev after a while.

'You don't?'

'No. I think you'll put us all in danger. But it's your decision, Julian. If you want to let her drive – then go ahead.'

Hanna saw the mining machine approaching from the left. Dust billowed out around its legs and shovel wheels, while freezing clouds forced their way out of its sides and mixed with the suspended matter to form a hazy camouflage. He tried to estimate whether he could safely cross in front of it. It was pretty close already, but if he stepped up his pace he should be able to manage it.

On Earth, he thought to himself, that thing would create a hell of a racket. Here, it approached with malicious silence. The only thing he could hear was the whoosh of the air-conditioning system in his suit and his own disciplined breathing. He knew that silence nourished foolishness, and that – especially in the glistening haze – correct estimations of distance were hardly possible, but on the other hand he didn't feel the slightest inclination to wait until the monstrous thing had crawled by. The mining station had to be really close by now. He'd had enough now, he just wanted to get there.

Clasping the last of the survival backpacks tightly under his arm, he sprinted off.

'I see him!'

The Canadian's blurred silhouette had appeared on the horizon. He was sprinting over the plain with long springing jumps, while the colossal body of a mining machine was approaching from the left. Julian waved Momoka's rover over next to his and waited until they were alongside each other.

'He's taking quite a risk there,' whispered Amber.

'And rather an inconvenient one, for us,' grumbled Rogachev. 'The beetle is already quite close. Should we really risk it?'

'I don't know.' Julian hesitated. 'If we let the machine pass it could take ages.'

'We could drive around it,' suggested Evelyn.

'And then what?'

'Approach him from the other side.'

'No, then he'll see us. Our only chance of taking him by surprise is if we stay behind.'

'Then let's go,' hissed Momoka. 'If *he* can get through ahead of the beetle, then so can *we*.'

'The machine really is very close, Momoka,' said Rogachev insistently. 'Shouldn't we wait? I mean, it's not like Carl can give us the slip.'

'Unless he's seen us,' Evelyn pondered.

'Then he would have shot at us.'

'Perhaps he's trying to throw us off.'

'Not Carl. He's a professional. I know people like him – none of them would think twice about shooting in his situation.' Rogachev paused. 'Nor would I, for that matter.'

The rovers were approaching the fleeing figure at a steady speed. At the same time, the beetle was getting closer and closer to Hanna, who was now running even faster. The stomping choreography of the six powerful insect legs was only vaguely outlined in the dust. The Canadian looked like vermin in front of the monstrosity, but he seemed to have estimated his chances accurately.

'He's going to get through,' whispered Momoka.

'And then some,' said Amber. 'Oleg's right, he can't slip through our fingers. We should wait.'

'Nonsense! We'll make it.'

'But why would we take a risk, and especially now? We have his footprints.'

'The beetle will erase them.'

'So far we've found them again every time.'

'Momoka,' said Rogachev in a dangerously quiet tone, 'you promised—'

'End of discussion,' decided Julian. 'We'll wait.'

'No!'

Momoka's rover jerked as she pressed down on the pedal. Regolith sprayed up on all sides. Rogachev, who had almost straightened himself up, lost his grip, was hurled out of the vehicle and landed in the dust. The vehicle swerved for a moment, then thrashed forwards.

'You piece of shit!' she screamed. 'You miserable—'

'Momoka, no!'

'Come back!'

Paying no attention to their cries, Momoka sped the rover forwards after the running figure. Evelyn held tightly to the back seat but was thrown backwards, hearing Rogachev utter a string of sonorous Russian swearwords. They shot off towards Hanna at top speed. In a matter of seconds he would be killed by the force of the collision.

'Momoka, stop! We need him—'

At that moment, the Canadian turned round.

Hanna believed neither in intuition nor in some higher inspiration. As far as he remembered, none of his colleagues who had trusted their gut, so to speak, had survived very long. The regulatory authority of the intellect commanded the use of careful thought to compensate for the lack of eyes in the back of one's head; anything else was pure chance, although looking behind him at that one, decisive moment turned out to be pretty useful too.

He saw the rover shooting towards him.

Assessment of the situation: a design he was familiar with from the Schröter space station, so they had clearly made it from Aristarchus to here. He and the vehicle, tangential to the marching direction of the beetle. Time until the mining machine arrives: unknown. Time until the collision with the rover: three seconds. Pulling out weapon and firing: pointless. Two seconds. One second—

He threw himself to the side.

Rolling away, he got back onto his feet and found himself danger-ously close to the beetle. Tonnes of regolith were spraying up high in front of his eyes. Behind it gaped the cloud-covered, jagged mouth of a gigantic shovel, filled to the brim and rising up from the ground, fol-lowed by another, another, another. The mining wheel was turning at an incredible speed, hovering from left to right in the process, transporting more and more masses of lunar rock into the sieve and onto the con-veyor belt. The beetle took a step forward, stomping powerfully, making the ground shake.

Where was the rover?

Hanna whipped around. He saw his spare backpack lying on the ground a short distance away; it had slipped from him when he fell. He needed the oxygen reserves, but the vehicle had already turned in a fountain of dust and was speeding over to him again, and now there was a second rover too, approaching from the opposite side. His hand moved up to his thigh, tearing the weapon with the explosive bullets from its case.

'I knew it!' cursed Rogachev. 'I knew it!'

He had clambered onto the seat behind Julian as Hanna flew through the air, had seen him thud down and get back up again. The Canadian produced a long and thin object, clearly undecided as to which of the two vehicles he should target. The second of hesitation sealed his fate. Momoka's rover caught him on the shoulder with one of its man-size wheels. He flew a considerable distance, landed on his side and rolled over towards the walking factory, directly towards the rotating shovel, which was approaching at a worryingly fast pace.

'Enough, Momoka,' screamed Julian. 'Let *us* get the bastard.'

But it seemed the Japanese woman was suffering from sudden deaf-ness. Even while Hanna was still pulling himself up, visibly dazed, she jerked the steering wheel around once again, forced the vehicle into too sharp a turn and lost control. This time, everything went wrong. The vehicle became airborne, overturned several times in a row and ploughed through the spraying rocks towards the beetle. Momoka was hurled out and slid through the rubble with her arms and legs spreadeagled, screaming like a banshee. She jumped up and rushed on, seemingly uninjured, and went straight for Hanna. Horrified, Amber watched as the rover came to a halt with its wheels still in the air, a blanket of dust sinking down on it.

'My God, Evelyn,' she groaned. 'Evelyn!'

Evelyn's only thought was to grip on to the strutting of the seat as tightly as she could. Unable to scream, she tried to picture the vehicle as a beetle, within which she would be protected as long as she managed not to lose her grip. Momoka had disappeared. There was no up or down any more, only bumps and dust and more bumps, smashing the chassis to pieces. Finally, she did let go. She fell to the ground and stared up at a wheel wobbling above her.

The rover had come to a halt, and she was alive. So far.

She immediately tried to free herself from the wreck, but she was stuck. But where? Her arms were free. She kicked her legs forcefully, and she could move them too, but the pile of junk still didn't want to let her go. The ground shuddered as something colossal rammed into the regolith, right next to her, and with icy clarity she realised what it was.

'Evelyn!' Amber. 'Evelyn!'

'I'm stuck,' she screamed. 'I'm stuck!'

The ground trembled again.

The robots only react to one another; we're not present in their internal image.

She had to get out of here! As fast as she could!

She began to pull wildly at the frame, scared out of her wits, but it was as if she were rooted to it, as if her back were soldered to the rover. She began to howl like a wolf in a trap, because she knew she would die.

Julian brought his rover to a standstill right next to the wreckage. He didn't care in the slightest what Hanna and Momoka were doing. The two of them had disappeared on the other side of the mining machine, away from the gluttonous shovelling.

They had to get Evelyn out of there.

Rogachev and Amber jumped from their seats and hurried over to the wrecked vehicle. Evelyn stretched her arm out towards them. It wasn't hard to see that her backpack had wedged itself into the grotesquely twisted strutting and was alarmingly stuck. Julian, overcome with worry, dared to glance up. The colossal body of the machine was making its way unrelentingly forward, darkening the sky, bathing the plain, people and vehicles in its ravine-like shadow. The strutting of its armoured plates was visible only in silhouette: rivets, seams and bolts, the trichina mechanism of the pipes. The insectoid curve of the skull with its chewing apparatus, sieves and mining belts swayed slowly back and forth, as if the thing were picking up their scent. Conically formed hip joints sprang out from angled legs, each around ten metres high, multiple-jointed and as thick as the crossbeams of a building crane.

The crashed rover lay directly in its path.

At that moment, in a way that was more perceptible than it was visible, the leg right at the front of its body lethargically began to rise.

Hanna struggled to get his bearings.

He had hit the back of his head on the inner casing of his helmet, something which should have been practically impossible, because the head covering was supposed to be large enough to prevent such accidents. His skull and neck hurt, and his shoulder too had seen better days, but at least the armour seemed to have absorbed some of the collision. He could move his arms still, but the weapon with the explosive bullets had fallen from his hand.

He couldn't lose his weapon!

Red and yellow circles were rotating in front of his eyes, trying to suck away his consciousness. Half blinded, he stumbled a few steps forwards, fell on his knees, then shook his head and fought against a strong wave of nausea.

Momoka was just a few steps behind him.

She rushed along, fuelled by hate. Like Medea, Electra, Nemesis, she was the incarnation of vengeance, unchecked by reason, without fear, without any plan. All thought processes were brought to a standstill; her thoughts were ruled purely by the idea of killing Hanna, and she didn't care how.

Something on the ground caught her gaze.

Something long and light in colour. It reminded her of a gun, but there was no trigger, just some buttons.

It *was* a gun.

Hanna's gun!

'Try to push the strap down.'

'Which strap, dammit?'

'There, that one! Strap, bar, whatever it is!'

Whatever it *was*, thought Amber, before the rover had been transformed into a pile of debris. A piece of the shaft? The mount from a radio receiver? She pushed against it with all her might while Rogachev pulled at the back of Chambers' seat. A part of it had wedged itself between the backpack and her suit and was refusing to budge.

'Hurry!' shouted Julian.

Rogachev kicked against the backrest with his boot. It gave a little, but the real problem was the twisted bar. Amber looked up and saw the mining machine's foot rising higher and higher, like something out of a nightmare.

'Again, Oleg,' she pleaded. 'Kick it again.'

The foot was now hovering above their heads. Wheelbarrow-sized loads of dust and small stones hailed down on them. Rogachev cursed again in Russian, which Amber interpreted as a bad sign. She pushed herself against the strap once more, burrowing the tips of her boots into the ground, tensing her muscles, and suddenly the entire thing broke right through the middle. Rogachev grabbed it, pulled the released backrest out from under the backpack and hurled it away.

'I'll make it by myself from here!'

In a flash, Evelyn pulled herself out of the rubble and jumped up. They ran away just as the beetle's leg was making its descent, throwing themselves onto the back seat of Julian's rover. At the very moment when he drove away, the monstrous foot crashed down onto the wreck and crunched it with such force that their getaway car was jolted into the air for a second.

'Where to now?' called Julian.

Amber pointed into the dust. 'The other side. They must be on the other side of the machine!'

What a discovery! Momoka bent over, clasped the unexpected instrument of her vengeance and went after Hanna, who had pulled himself to his feet and was staggering away like a drunkard. It had become significantly darker and a hazy shadow had descended on them, but Momoka paid no attention to it. She made a leap and kicked out at the Canadian, knocking him off his feet once again.

Hanna rolled onto his stomach.

No, don't shoot yet, she told herself. She wanted him to be watching her as she did it. To look at her as he died! Breathless, she waited until he had rolled over, then pointed the weapon at his helmet.

'You piece of shit!'

She pressed one of the buttons. Then another.

'Do you see this? Do you see it, you piece of shit?'

Nothing. How did you shoot this thing? Oh, it must be here, a safety measure: the detonator was protected by a shield, so she just had to push it up with her thumb, and then—

Hanna crawled backwards, staring at the armoured, faceless figure in disbelief. It could only be her. He would have credited Rogachev with the same fighting spirit, but this person was small and petite, unmistakably Momoka Omura, and she was ready to make him pay for Warren Locatelli's death. She had discovered the safety shield. She was pushing it up. He had no chance of grabbing the weapon in time. He had to get away, put distance between himself and the Japanese woman. Was she screaming at him? Momoka was locked on to a different frequency, but he was certain she was screaming at him, and suddenly he felt unfairly treated. I didn't kill your husband, he wanted to say, as if that would have changed anything, but he *hadn't* killed him, instead he had wanted to spare him and make his death less painful, and now he was going to be punished for that?

His gaze wandered to a point high above her.

Oh God!

Distance! He had to get away!

'Through the legs,' called Amber.

'Are you crazy?' Julian was driving alongside the mining machine at high speed. 'Was that not enough for you just then?'

She leaned back and stared up at the giant. Julian was right. It was too dangerous. It was only now, right next to it, that she appreciated how huge the beetle really was. A walking mountain. Each one of its six legs could end her existence with just one blow. The highest concentration of dust was beneath the torso, visibility was nonexistent, and to top it all off, extensive white clouds were breaking out of openings along the torso seam and spreading out rapidly. They made it past the machine and drove around its rear end, from which avalanches of baked regolith were hailing out. They dodged the rain of debris and drove back along the other side.

Back to the monster's head.

Momoka wanted to relish the moment as long as she could, so she didn't press immediately, but instead watched as Hanna crawled away, as if there were still the ghost of a chance he could get away from her. Ha! As if there were even the slightest cause to hope that she would change her mind.

'Scared?' she hissed.

He should be scared. Just like Warren had been scared. We need him alive, she heard Julian bleating in her mind, that shitty, stupid arsehole who had lured them here, to the bloody Moon, her and Warren. Alive? Fuck you, Julian! *She needed him dead!* And she would kill him, now, as he pulled himself to his feet. *Sayonara*, Carl Hanna. A good moment.

She could barely see.

It was darkening rapidly. What was happening? She leaned back and looked up. Unbelievable! Fucking Moon! This Moon was really starting to get on her—

'Tits,' she whispered.

A huge black stomper of a foot hung in the air above her.

Then it came down.

The beetle ended Momoka's life without giving her the opportunity for inner reflection, something that wouldn't have suited her character anyway. Instead, in honour of her temperament and her belief that people should die as they lived, she exploded one last time: in the course of her physical compression, Hanna's weapon smashed against the breastplate of her spacesuit and one of the bullets broke in half. A chemical union occurred between shower gel and shampoo. The projectile flew apart, and the nine remaining ones blew up with it, blasting the beetle's foot clean away.

This time, an error message was sent to the control centre of the moon base. It informed the crew about material damage to the front left walking apparatus of BUG-24, signifying that the machine was in danger of failure and had to shut itself down, which it did that very moment. It stopped all activity directly after the explosion, but that was of no help. The beetle's amputation was complete. Overloaded by the loss of the front leg, the middle one buckled too, and the colossal machine began to tilt.

Tits. That was the last word they had heard from Momoka.

'I can't see her,' said Amber.

And how could we, in all this dust? thought Evelyn. Her entire body was still shaking. She was reliving the moment in her mind again and again, the moment when she had almost been trampled, a true groundhog day of a thought, splintering off into an eerie alternate reality crowned by the notion that she would wake up the next moment and find she had only dreamed her escape, and the steel foot would—

Steel foot?

Evelyn looked more closely. Something about the beetle was nagging at her. Was she hallucinating? Had they got closer to the machine, or had the machine got closer to them?

Then she saw that one of the beetle's legs was breaking away.

'It's tipping over,' she stammered.

'What?'

'It's tipping over!' Evelyn began to shout. 'It's tipping over! The machine's tipping over. It's tipping over!'

In a second, they were all shouting over one another. The powerful body had unmistakably lost its balance and was indeed beginning to tip over. Fatally, it was tipping in the wrong direction.

In their direction.

Julian changed course, trying to get power out of the rover that it just didn't possess. On their way from Aristarchus, eighty kilometres per hour had often seemed unreasonably fast to them, when the vehicle, despite being restricted by its weight and lack of traction, had completed the most adventurous leaps and jumps. Now Evelyn felt they were crawling along at a snail's pace. She looked behind them and saw the machine struggling to balance. For one blessed moment it seemed as if the giant had stabilised again, but it was beyond hope. Although the rear leg held up to the weight at first, it soon started to sway back and forth.

Then it collapsed.

The monster's torso crashed down into the regolith in a spring tide of dust, and the immense abdomen tipped towards them.

'What's *that*?' screamed Amber at the same moment.

It took Evelyn a moment to realise that her agitation wasn't caused by the machine, but by something else that was rushing towards them from the opposite direction.

'Swerve! Swerve!'

'I can't swerve!'

While the beetle continued to fall at an ever greater speed, they found themselves confronted with a spider that had appeared out of nowhere, whose internal world clearly failed to recognise not only humans, but falling mining machines too. The loading robot hurried purposefully towards the collapsing giant, seemingly intent on cutting off their path. Julian jerked the steering wheel to the left, and the robot changed its course too.

'Right! Right!'

The ground shook. A shock-wave gripped the rover and submerged the world in cold grey. The vehicle skidded, then began to turn on its own axis, knocking one of the spider's filigree legs off. The spider began to stagger. Travelling backwards, Evelyn saw the mining machine go down, a collapsing mountain in a hurricane of whirling regolith. The rover took a hit, came to an abrupt halt and tipped over. High above them, the spider went into a frenzy, teetering around aimlessly on its long legs.

'Get out!' screamed Rogachev.

They jumped out of their seats, fell, stumbled, and ran for their lives. New clouds shot over and wrapped around them, carrying them off. A huge parabolic reflector spun towards Evelyn, rotating like the blade of an oversized buzz saw. It hacked into the ground not even an arm's length away from her and disappeared, rolling into the pyroclastic greyness. The beetle had gone down completely, missing her by a hair's breadth and catching the injured spider instead. With its pincers flailing wildly, it went into an arabesque, lost its grip and collapsed feebly, directly above the rover. Its torso crashed into the steering wheel and seats, then bounced up one more time, rotated and released helium-3 tanks in all directions, aggressive, hopping spherical things which began to hunt down the fleeing people.

Evelyn ran.

And so did Hanna.

At the moment when the beetle's leg came down on Momoka, he knew what catastrophe was about to unfold. The mining machine's motion apparatus looked incredibly stable, but ten simultaneously fired detonating caps were designed to rip even the most stable of structures to shreds. Hanna had no intention of waiting to see whether the remaining legs would compensate for the loss. He hadn't gone far by the time the collision shook the ground and gave him his answer. All around him, a layer of the finest powder flew up. He ran on without stopping. It was only after a while that he forced himself to pause, wheezing, with a painful head and throbbing shoulder. He gave himself a shake and looked back at the scene of the disaster. Grey clouds were forming some distance away. He should have still been able to see the bold silhouette of the machine from here. He took its disappearance as an indication that it really had crashed down. With any luck it had caused havoc amongst his pursuers – a vague prospect, he had to admit.

What else could go wrong? What in God's name was he doing wrong?

He wasn't doing anything wrong. The circumstances were what they were. He had learned a long time ago how it felt to be in the pinball machine of circumstance. To be relentlessly pinged around in it, however clever one saw oneself to be. It was so much harder to gain control over oneself than it was to take it away from others. Plans were constructs, well thought out straight lines. On the drawing board, they functioned excellently. In practice, though, it was about not going off course along the winding road of chance. He knew all of that, so why was he getting worked up?

Fine, so the worst possible scenario was that, apart from Momoka, they had all made it through. He thought he remembered having seen her rover in a crash, but supposing they had managed to heave it onto its wheels again, they still had two vehicles. He, on the other hand, was on foot and robbed of his explosives. Status: critical!

He moved his arm cautiously, stretching it out and bending it. Nothing was broken, nothing dislocated. It was possible that he was concussed. Apart from that, though, he was fine, and he still had the two pistols with conventional bullets, which admittedly made smaller holes, but were just as deadly.

Which direction had he run in? His head-over-heels flight had brought him into uncharted territory. That was bad. Without the beetle tracks, he could end up missing the station. His own tracks were sure to be visible over the not-yet-processed ground, but then the rover hadn't turned up yet. They might be looking for Momoka, but could they risk letting him get away for her sake? If they really did still have both the rovers, then wouldn't one of them have started hunting him down by now?

Maybe things weren't that bad after all. Strengthened by confidence, he turned his attention to working out where he was.

They struggled up one by one, clumsy, dazed, their white spacesuits dirty, as though they were clambering out of their own graves. All around them, it looked like the scene after a bomb attack or a natural catastrophe. The hunchback of the mining machine, still towering up into the skies, now a massif in the regolith. The snapped spider limbs of the loading robot. Their smashed rover. And over everything, a ghost of swirling dust.

'Momoka?'

They called her name unrelentingly, wandering around in search, but received no answer, nor did they find any trace of her. Momoka seemed to have been swallowed up by the dust, and suddenly Evelyn couldn't even see the others any more. She stopped. Shuddered as something cold touched her deep within. The dust around her billowed out, forming a kind of tunnel. On the other side it seemed different in nature, darker, more threatening, and at the same time more inviting, and all of a sudden it seemed to Evelyn that she was seeing herself disappear in the tunnel, and with every step that she took away from herself, her silhouette swirled beyond recognition, until she lost herself. An indefinable amount of time later, she found the others on the other side.

'Where were you?' asked Julian, concerned. 'We were calling you the whole time.'

Where had she been? At a border, a border to forgetting. She had glanced momentarily into the shadows; that's how it had seemed to her at least, as if something were tugging and sucking at her, using its dark temptations to try to make her surrender. She knew about the irrationality of perception. Borderline experiences had been the subject of esoteric debate on her programmes more than once, without she herself having any perception of the other side, but in the moment when

Amber, Oleg and Julian turned up by her side again, she had known that Momoka Omura was dead. The silence that met their calls was the silence of death. The only thing they found was tracks, which led away from the head of the beetle and which could only be Hanna's.

But Momoka had disappeared without a trace.

In the moments that followed, Evelyn didn't say a word about her unusual experi-ence. After a short time they gave up the search and went back to the rover. It was no longer functional, but at least they managed to salvage their oxygen supplies. For the first time since they had been on Hanna's trail, it looked as though his tracks were going to lead them the wrong way.

They weighed up their options.

In the end, they decided to keep following him.

31 May 2025

MINI-NUKE

Callisto, The Moon

Finn O'Keefe closed his eyes. He was no coward. And the absence of other human beings certainly didn't scare him. He had discovered years ago how calm and agreeable his own company could be, and had experienced many wonderful moments of solitude with nothing above him but the sky and the cries of seagulls riding the salty west winds, scanning the sea for tell-tale signs of glistening backs. The only time he ever experienced loneliness, solitude's desperate sister, was in crowded places. For this reason, the Moon was completely to his taste, despite having so far failed to have any spiritual effect on him. It was easy to be alone here: all you had to do was go behind a hill, switch yourself off from the radio-wave chatter and pretend the others didn't even exist.

Now, on the flight to the Peary Base, his self-deception was revealed. It was laughable to think that you could turn your back on the world in the certainty that it was still there, to assume that you could opt back into its incredibly noisy civilisation at any moment. Even in the expanse of the Mojave Desert, in the mountain range of the Himalayas, or in the perpetual ice, you would still be sharing the planet with thinking beings, a thought which gave solitude a comfortable foundation.

But the Moon was *lonely*.

Banished from Gaia's protective body, cut off from all communication and from the whole of humanity, it had become clear to him during the two hours they had been en route that Luna placed no value on *Homo sapiens*. Never before had he felt so ignored and devoid of importance. The hotel, gone to ruin. Peary Base, no longer a certainty. The plateaux and mountain ranges all around them suddenly seemed hostile – no, not even that, because hostility would mean they were acknowledged here. But in the context of what religious people defined as Creation, the human race clearly had less significance than a microbe under a skirting board. If one took Luna to be exemplary of the trillions of galaxies in the visible cosmos, it became clear that all of this had *not* been made for humans – if it had been *made* at all.

He suddenly found comfort in the group and was thankful for every word that was spoken. And even though he hadn't known Miranda Winter that well, her death felt like a personal tragedy, because just a few centimetres would have been enough to prevent it. She might have driven her beloved Louis around the bend, named her breasts, and believed any old nonsense that dried-up old Hollywood divas like Olinda Brannigan deduced from tarot cards and tea leaves; but the way she saw herself, her resolutely cheerful determination not to let anything or anyone destroy her good mood, the sublime in the ridiculous, he had admired all of that about her, and possibly even loved it a little too. He wondered whether he had ever been as honest in his arrogance as Miranda Winter had been in her simplicity.

His gaze wandered over to Lynn Orley.

What had happened to *her*?

The living dead. It was as though she had been erased. Nina had mentioned some kind of shock to Deputy Commander Wachowski, but she seemed to be working her way through self-destruction programme; she hadn't spoken a single word since Miranda's death. There was hardly anything to indicate that she was even aware of her surroundings. Everything—

—had vanished into the event horizon; nothing could make its way out.

She had become a black hole.

And yet, sitting in the depths of the black hole, she found herself capable of following the echoes of her thoughts. This was unusual for a Hawking-like black hole. Something wasn't right. If she really had fallen into her collapsed core and ended up as a singularity, this would also have meant the end of all cognition. Instead, she had made her way to *somewhere*. There was certainly no other way to explain the fact that she was still thinking and making speculations, although she had to admit she would probably be doing better if certain green tablets hadn't been burned when—

—with the destruction of the hotel, any hope of a message from Hanna had been erased. If he was still able to send out messages, that was.

By now, with the chaotic evening on her mind, Dana was having doubts about this. Was a little pessimism advisable? After all, anything could have happened on Aristarchus. Maybe – although of course without writing Hanna off right away – she should confront the possibility of taking things into her own hands. Her cover hadn't been blown yet, and her avowed opponent didn't seem aware of anything, not even herself. All the others trusted her. Even Tim, who—

—was in increasing despair about how to fairly distribute his worries. Worries for Amber, for Julian (more than he would like to admit), for Lynn and all the rest in the shuttle, and the others wherever they were at that moment; worries as to the limit of his own capacity for suffering, one endless round of anxiety. After flying for more than two hours they had to be nearing the base by now, but they still hadn't been able to establish contact. Dana had put it down to the tiresome satellite problem, and said they would have a connection as soon as they came into the transmission area. Tim's worry-list expanded to include the horror of a deserted and somehow destroyed base. The time crept by, or was it racing? The Moon offered no reference points for human perceptions of the passing of time; his species' timekeeping had absurd continuance only within the enclave of the Callisto, while all around them there was no time, and they would never arrive anywhere ever again.

And as the horror of the vision, fed by his torturously brooding imagination, threatened to overpower him—

—four words and a yawn provided the solution.

'Tommy Wachowski. Peary Base.'

'Peary Base, this is Callisto. We're coming in for landing. Request permission to land in around ten minutes.'

'A social visit?' Wachowski asked sleepily. 'Heavens. Do you know how late it is? I just hope we've cleaned up and cleared away the bottles.'

'This is no time for jokes,' said Nina.

'Just a moment.' Wachowski's tone changed in a flash. 'Landing field 7. Do you need assistance?'

'We're okay. One injured, not life-threatening, and one person in shock.'

'Why aren't you flying to Gaia?'

'We've come from there. There was a fire. Gaia has been destroyed, but there are other reasons why we can't go back to Vallis Alpina.'

'God! What's happened?'

'Tommy.' Dana tuned in. 'We'll tell you the details later, okay? We have a lot to report and a great deal more to process. But right now we're just happy to be able to land.'

Wachowski fell silent for a moment.

'Okay,' he said. 'We'll get everything ready here. See you soon.'

American Mining Station, Sinus Iridum

The dust cleared after just a quarter of an hour, restoring the views over to the distant Mare Imbrium, to the mountain range of Montes Jura – and to the mining station.

Hanna allowed himself a moment of rest, stretching out and tilting his head back. Despite veering too far north-west, he had nearly made it. As long as he kept up the pace he would be there very soon. His hunch that the others were either dead or severely limited in their transport capabilities had turned into a certainty. They could have caught him up in no time with a rover, but no one had appeared.

His head felt as though it were stuffed with cotton wool, and he was struggling against light dizziness and nausea. He started to walk again. Within a quarter of an hour, he reached the station. Unlike Peary Base, its design was entirely celestial: a large, regolith-covered igloo, connected to cylindrical, pressurised insectoids, a U-formation of spherical tank depots and hangars framing a landing field, bordered by the railhead with its main and siding tracks. Steps and elevators led up to the tracks, freight trains – basic flatbed wagons coupled together – dozed ahead of their next journey. To the side of the landing field, two dozen spiders, frozen and motionless, waited for the command to deployment. Two more had taken up position right next to the rail track and were loading one of the trains with spherical tanks, while a third, fully laden, was on the approach. The plant seemed to be undergoing some development, and Hanna noticed that the hangars, depots and the igloo-shaped habitat were resting on caterpillar tracks. As soon as the zone had been fully processed, the entire station would move on. The visibility was much better here, even though a thin veil of dust hung over everything. Harsh, bright sunlight was reflected back by the crystalline facets of the suspended particles, creating an oppressive, post-nuclear-disaster mood. A world of machines.

Hanna searched through the hangars and, alongside various maintenance robots, managed to find four robust grasshoppers with larger cargo holds and higher stilts than the ones used in Gaia. There was no trace of anything quicker, like a shuttle. There were no conventionally driven vehicles here at all; in the mining zone everything was on legs, thereby reducing the amount of dust stirred up and providing better protection for the mechanical components. The beetles' maintenance interfaces were located in the head and the hunchback, which made the design of the grasshoppers logical. They could get above the blanket of dust and, from there, execute precision landings on the vast bodies; the robots took care of the rest. Hanna had no doubt that one of the hoppers would get him to his destination – they hardly used any fuel – but they were terribly slow. He would be en route for almost two days with one of those things, the cargo hold filled up with oxygen reserves – always supposing he found something of the kind in the station. His suit would provide him with drinking water, but he wouldn't be able to have a bite to eat. He was prepared to put up with that, but not with the time delay.

He *had* to act within the next two hours.

He paced through the airlock of the habitat and went into a disinfection room, where cleaning fluids were sprayed on him at high pressure to cleanse his suit of moon dust. Then he was finally able to take his helmet off and search the quarters. It was spacious and comfortable enough that you could tolerate several days here, with sanitary facilities, a kitchen, a generous amount of food supplies, working and sleeping quarters, a communal room, even a small fitness centre. Hanna paid a visit to the toilet, ate two wholegrain bars covered in chocolate, drank as much water as he could manage, washed his face and looked for headache tablets. The station pharmacy was excellently equipped. After that, he inspected one of the insectoid transporters connected to the station, but that too proved to be unsuitable for his needs, because it was even slower than the hoppers. He at least managed to find additional oxygen which would assure his survival out there for some days. But on the question of how to finish the job in the near future, he was still at a loss.

He put his helmet back on and hauled all the oxygen reserves he could find out to the landing field.

His gaze wandered over to the spiders. The last one in the row was just heaving its tanks onto the freight train, which was loaded almost to capacity, then securing them in place with the rib-like clamps that extended from the sides. From the looks of things, the train would soon be setting off towards the moon base.

At 700 kilometres an hour!

His thoughts came tumbling thick and fast. There were still around a dozen tanks to be loaded. He had maybe ten minutes. Too little to destroy the hoppers as he had planned, but he could still take the oxygen reserves with him. Running now, he brought them to the elevator and threw them in. The barred cabin set off at an annoyingly slow pace. He could see the spider's legs through the crossbars, its body, the industrious pincers. Three tanks to go. He rushed out onto the railway platform and squeezed the reserves between the piled-up globes on a freight wagon. The penultimate tank was passed over by the praying-mantis-like extremities and stowed away. Where would be the best place to sit? Nonsense, there was no ideal location; this wasn't the Lunar Express, it was a cargo train. Certainly one whose acceleration a human could survive without harm. Beyond that, it didn't matter how quickly the train went. In the moon vacuum it was no different to being in free fall, where you could leave the vessel at 40,000 kilometres an hour and take a casual look around.

The last tank was just being secured.

In front of the tanks! That was the best place.

He pulled himself up onto the wagon bed, then went hand over hand along the metal globes and under the spider's pincers to the front, until he found a place which seemed good to him, an empty passage between two traction elements. He squeezed himself in, crouched down, wedged in his feet and leaned his back against the tanks.

And waited.

Minutes passed by, and he started to have doubts. Had he been wrong? The fact that the train was fully loaded didn't necessarily mean it was setting off now. But while he was still brooding over it, there was a slight jolt. Turning his head, he saw the spider disappear from his field of vision. Then the pressure of acceleration followed as the train got faster and faster. The plain flew past him, the dust-saturation around him gradually gave way. For the first time since his cover had been blown, Hanna didn't feel trapped in a nightmare of someone else's making.

'Lousy grasshoppers!' cursed Julian.

They had made it to the mining station with the very last of their strength. Oleg Rogachev, trained to stay standing for so long that his opponent would fall over from exhaustion, was the only one to show no signs of fatigue. He had rediscovered his gentle, controlled way of speaking and was emitting the freshness of an air-conditioned room. Amber, however, could have sworn that her spacesuit had developed a life of its own, maliciously intent on obstructing her movements and exposing her to the unfamiliar experience of claustrophobia. Soaking wet, she slumped in her gear, bathed in bad odours. Evelyn was faring similarly, traumatised from almost being trampled to death and still a little unsure on her feet. Even Julian seemed to be discovering, with surprise, that he really was sixty years old. Never before had they heard Peter Pan snort so loudly.

It didn't take them long to discover that there wasn't a single oxygen reserve in the entire station.

'We could get some air from the life-support systems,' Evelyn suggested.

'We could, but it's not that easy.' They were sitting in the living quarters, helmets off, drinking tea. Julian's face was flushed and his beard unkempt, as if he'd been burrowing around in it for hours on end on the hunt for solutions. 'We need *compressed* oxygen. For that we'd need to make various conversions, and to be honest—'

'Don't beat around the bush, Julian. Just come out with it.'

'—at the moment I'm not sure how that works. I mean, I know roughly. But that won't solve our problem. We would only be able fill up our own tanks. All the reserve tanks have disappeared.'

'Carl,' said Rogachev tonelessly.

Amber stared straight ahead. Of course. Hanna had been in the living quarters. They had searched the station in constant expectation of being attacked by him, but he had disappeared without a trace. Which raised the question of how, as it seemed no hoppers were missing – until Julian discovered the transport and oper-ation schedules and found out that a helium-3 transport had set off to Peary Base immediately before they had arrived.

'So he's on his way there.'

'Yes. And from the Pole back to the hotel.'

'Right, let's follow him then! When does the next train leave?'

'Hmm, let me see . . . oh, the day after tomorrow.'

'*The day after tomorrow?*'

'Guys, the Americans aren't pumping streams of helium-3 on an hourly basis here! It's just small quantities. At some stage in the future there'll be more trains, but right now—'

'The day after tomorrow. Dammit! That's two days of sitting around.'

Even the satellites were still refusing to offer them any concessions. Amber crouched in front of her now cold cup of tea, as if by pulling her shoulders up she could stop her head falling down to her feet. Some governing authority seemed to have taken up residence inside her skull. She was afraid of cracking up over her fear for Tim, Lynn and the others. But at the same time she felt as though she were looking at the mountainous skyline of a desk weighed down with the demands of her own survival. No one came to help. Applications for grief and sadness lay around unprocessed, the empathy department had all gone for a coffee break, and the answer phone was on in the Department of Examination for Post-traumatic Syndrome, announcing only the hours of business. Every other service desk had closed due to dismissals. She wanted to cry, or at least whimper a little, but tears required a request form that couldn't be located, and the Dissociation Department was putting in overtime. Escape plans were checked, considered and discarded as her shocked self sat there in the company of five dead people, waiting for one of the neurotransmitters hurrying by to declare themselves responsible.

'And how far will we get with the grasshoppers?' she asked.

'Theoretically, to the hotel.' Julian gnawed at his lower lip. 'But that would take two days. And we don't have enough oxygen for that.'

'Could we perhaps reprogram the control system for the trains?' asked Oleg Rogachev. 'There are some parked outside after all. If we could manage to start one of them—'

'I certainly can't do anything like that. Can you?'

'Okay, let's take a different approach,' said Evelyn. 'How much longer will our reserves last?'

'Three to four hours each, I guess.'

'Right, so that means we can forget all forms of transport that take longer than that.'

'Well we won't get to the hotel with that much, that's for sure. Here, on the other hand, our ability to survive is practically unlimited.'

'So you want to rot in here while everything else gets destroyed?' cried

Amber angrily. 'What about the insectoids? Those strange crawling vehicles. They're equipped with life-support systems, right?'

'Yes, but they're even slower than the hoppers. With them it would take three or four days to get even to the foot of the Alps. And climbing after that would take longer than our reserves will last.'

'The oxygen again,' said Evelyn bitterly.

'It's not just that, Evelyn. Even if we had enough of it, we're still running out of time.'

Oleg looked at Julian intently. 'What do you mean by that?'

'What?'

'That we're running out of time.'

Julian held the Russian's gaze. He tried to get the words out several times, then turned his head towards Amber in a silent plea for help. She nodded imperceptibly. Julian opened up the dungeons of discretion and finally told Evelyn and Rogachev the whole truth.

Rogachev's face was expressionless. Evelyn was looking at the tips of her fingers, stupefied. Her lips moved as if she were uttering inaudible prayers.

'And that's everything?' she said finally.

'Far from it.' Julian shook his head gloomily. 'But that's all I know. Honestly! I would never have brought you all here if I had had the slightest suspicion that—'

'No one is accusing you of thoughtlessness,' said Oleg coolly. 'On the other hand, it is your hotel. So, *think*. Do you have any idea why someone would blow up Gaia, and with an atomic bomb at that?'

'I've been racking my brains for hours trying to work that one out.'

'And?'

'I don't have a clue.'

'Exactly.' Oleg nodded. 'It doesn't make any sense. Unless there's something about the hotel that you yourself don't know.'

Or about its *architect*, thought Amber. Julian's suspicion came to her mind. She dismissed the thought as nonsense, but the uneasy feeling remained.

'Why the Gaia?' brooded Oleg. 'Why a nuclear bomb? I mean, that's completely over the top.'

'Unless it's not just about the hotel.'

'Don't mini-nukes have less explosive force than normal nuclear bombs?' asked Amber.

'Yes, that's true.' Oleg nodded. 'On the scale of the largest possible disaster. Which means you could contaminate half of the Vallis Alpina even with a mini-nuke. So what's there? What's the deal with the alpine valley, Julian?'

'Again: not the faintest idea!'

'Maybe it's nothing,' said Evelyn. 'I mean, all we have to go on is this detective's theory.'

'You're wrong.' Julian shook his head. 'We have five dead people and a killer flushed out of hiding. Everything that Carl's done in the last hours amounts to an admission of guilt.'

Oleg put his fingertips together.

'Maybe we should stop wishing for the impossible.'

'Well, there's an idea.'

'Patience.' Oleg uttered a humourless laugh. 'If we can't get to the hotel via the direct route, then we should think about making a detour. Do you know what?' He looked at them each in turn. 'I'm going to tell you a joke.'

'A joke.' Evelyn stared at him distrustfully. 'Should I be worried?'

'The joke of my life. My father often told it. A little story he believed led people towards ideas—'

'Well, given that Chucky's not here—'

Julian propped his chin in his hands. 'Go on then.'

'So, two Chukchi are walking through the Serengeti when a lion suddenly jumps out at them from behind the bushes. Both of them are scared out of their wits. The lion growls and is clearly very hungry, so one of the Chukchi runs away as quickly as he can. But the other one pulls his rucksack from his shoulder, opens it in a leis-urely fashion, takes a pair of running shoes out and puts them on. Are you crazy? shouts the fleeing Chukchi. Do you seriously think those shoes will make you faster than the lion? No, says his friend, they won't.' Oleg smiled broadly. 'But they'll make me faster than you.'

Julian looked at the Russian. His shoulders shook, then he started to giggle. Evelyn joined in, a little hesitantly. Amber inspected the contents in a bureaucratic manner then decided to laugh too.

'So we need running shoes,' she said. 'Great, Oleg. Let's just run home.'

Julian's expression froze. 'Hang on!'

'What is it?'

'We *have* running shoes!'

'What?'

'I'm such an idiot.' He looked at them, his eyes wide in amazement that he hadn't thought of it sooner. 'The Chinese are our running shoes.'

'The Chinese?'

'The Chinese mining station. Of course! It's inhabited. We could get there within an hour with the grasshoppers, without our oxygen reserves running out, there are shuttles there, they have their own satellites—'

'And they could be behind the attack!' cried Amber. 'Isn't that what that Jericho guy suspected?'

'Yes, but the people we have to thank for warning us are Chinese too.' Suddenly, decisiveness was shining in Julian's gaze again. 'I mean, what do we have to lose? If there really is a Chinese conspiracy against Orley Enterprises, then bad luck. We can hardly make things any worse. But if not, or if these Chinese people in particular aren't behind it – then all we can do is win.'

They looked at one another, letting the thought sink in.

'You should tell jokes more often,' said Evelyn to Oleg.

The Russian shrugged. 'Do I look like I know any more?'

'No.' Julian laughed. 'Come on. Let's pack our stuff.'

London, Great Britain

The China theory.

Ever since they had recognised Kenny Xin in the fat Asian from Calgary, the term had been in frequent use in the Big O and at SIS. The never entirely believed and yet most logical of all explanations, that a Chinese causative agent was causing havoc in Orley's bloodstream, was experiencing a renaissance. And why? Because of a Chinese assassination attempt.

Jericho was more at a loss than ever.

After the initial moment of triumph at having exposed Kenny Xin, joining the small streams of realisation into a river, he had begun to doubt the paradox of the obvious more and more. At first glance, the China theory made sense. Xin had turned out to be the nucleus of atrocious activity all over the world, and all of his actions served the implementation of the planned attack. Admittedly, he could hardly be held responsible for the massacre in Vancouver: although a jet could have taken him from Berlin to Canada in time to murder ten people there, Jericho doubted he had left Europe. It was more likely that he had followed them to London and was observing the goings-on from somewhere close by, like a fly on the wall. He could have delegated Vancouver, and it was obvious he had helpers, Chinese, for sure. Mayé's launching pad, the purchase and installation of the mini-nuke, all of it was in Chinese hands. China was said to be the provocateur of the Moon crisis, Beijing resented the USA, Zheng was trying to both fight Orley *and* get on his side. In short, the China theory conformed perfectly to Secret Service thought processes. In Jericho's view there was only one thing to say against it: when it came down to it, it just didn't add up.

'Crikey, you're good.' Norrington sounded appalled. 'It was Xin who shot at Palstein – that must give you food for thought.'

'It does,' said Jericho.

'The guy isn't just someone's weapon, but I don't need to tell you that! He's right at the top of the organisation, and he's a *goddamn Chinese Secret Service man*. It would be negligent to rule out China being behind all this.'

Yoyo indicated she'd had enough of sitting around in a cellar, however nicely furnished it might be.

'I asked Jennifer. She said the atomic obliteration of London wouldn't take place before tomorrow morning, so we might as well go to one of the large offices up in the roof with Diane.'

In its simplicity, it was the best idea for a long while.

The two of them went up. London at two o' clock in the morning was a sea of lights, and it was London: perhaps not the most modern, but for Jericho the most beautiful and charming city in the world. The O_2 Arena was gleaming on the opposite bank of the Thames, and the Hungerford Bridge lay to the west, held up by glistening spider's webs and towered over by the wheel of the London Eye. The orange luminescent moon circled mysteriously in the gravitational field of the Big O. Yoyo leaned back on the floor-to-ceiling window, unleashing in Jericho the spontaneous impulse to grab her in his arms and hold her tight.

'Doesn't the thing in Vancouver remind you of Quyu?'

The paleness of defeat had retreated from their features. Red wine and fighting spirit were conjuring up fresh sparkle in their eyes.

'I don't think that was Xin,' he said.

'But the process is similar. The Guardians, Greenwatch, and in both cases information was spread virulently through the net. Containing that spread is practically impossible. So you don't attempt a surgically precise operation, but instead immediately destroy the entire infrastructure and kill everyone that comes into question as a knowledge carrier. And even that doesn't give you any guarantees, but you can delay the spread. That's exactly what Kenny's doing. I'm telling you, he'd blow up this very building if he could be sure that it would buy him some time.'

'Because the operation is about to take place.'

'And we can't do a damn thing about it.' Yoyo slammed her fist into the palm of her other hand. 'Time's working against us. He's going to win, Owen, that piece of shit is going to win.'

Jericho walked up next to her and looked out into the London night.

'We have to find out who's pulling the strings. *Before* they can carry out the attack.'

'But how?' snorted Yoyo. 'We only ever find Xin.'

'And MI6 have homed in on the Chinese. The MI5, Norrington, Shaw—'

'Well.' She shrugged. 'We thought it was them almost the whole time too, right?'

Jericho sighed. She was right, of course. They were the ones who had ignited the China theory smoke bomb.

'On the other hand, as you've already said: the Moon crisis doesn't fit. Why would China unleash an argument over mining zones at a time when the last thing it needs is international attention?'

'Norrington thinks it's a distraction tactic.'

'Great distraction tactic. It led to Beijing being accused of putting weapons on the Moon! Not exactly trust-inspiring if a bomb does end up going off. And besides, Owen, why didn't they just send a Chinese assassin up in a Chinese rocket?'

'Because, according to Norrington, a member of the tour group had better access to the Gaia.'

'Nonsense, what kind of access? To set off an atomic bomb? You don't need access for that, you just chuck it down outside the door, make a run for it and blow the thing sky high. Remember what Vogelaar said. It was Zheng he didn't trust, not Beijing.'

'And what would Zheng get from killing Orley and destroying his hotel? Would that help him to build better space elevators? Better fusion reactors?'

'Hmm.' Yoyo sucked on her index finger. 'Unless Orley's death would turn the balance of power in the company upside down to Zheng's advantage.'

'Vogelaar had another theory.'

'That someone's trying to turn the Moon powers against one another?'

'Well, it wouldn't have to go to extremes right away. They wouldn't unleash world war that quickly. But a few things would change.'

'One of them would be weakened—'

'And the third party strengthened, secretly laughing all the while.' Jericho hit the palm of his hand against the windowpane. 'Do you see, that's what strikes me about the whole thing. It's all so obvious! It seems so – staged!'

'Okay, fine, let's leave China aside for a moment. Who else would benefit from Orley's downfall?'

'A bullet would be enough for just him. You don't need a nuclear bomb for that.' Jericho turned away. 'You know what, before we drive ourselves crazy going over it all, we should ask Aunt Jennifer.'

'MI6 loves the China theory,' said Shaw a few minutes later, 'and so does MI5. Andrew Norrington even wants to call in the Chinese ambassador.'

'And you?'

'I'm torn. The theory doesn't seem to make sense to me, but then it doesn't necessarily make much sense to a dog when his master puts the dog food on the top shelf. We *have* to put China as the focus of our mistrust. And as far as Julian is concerned, there are whole armies who would rather see him dead than alive.'

'There's a rumour that he wants to make his patent accessible to the world.'

'That's possible,' Shaw conceded.

'Could that be in Zheng's interest?'

'It definitely wouldn't be in America's. A change at the top of our organisation would be very useful to Washington right now. The chemistry is a little off at the moment, as you know.'

Jericho hesitated. The branch of a new thought was appearing in his mind and developing lively side shoots.

'Are there individuals in the Orley enterprise who don't agree with Julian?' he asked. 'Who represent Washington's position?'

Shaw smiled grimly.

'What do you think? That we hold hands? Just the fact that Julian is *considering* freeing himself from American monogamy is considered by many to be tantamount to sacrilege. Except, as long as the boss has the say, they just grumble over their beers and keep their traps shut. You would like Julian, Owen, he's the kind of man you can have fun with. Meanwhile you quickly forget that he'll fight to get what he wants with despotic energy, if that's what it takes. Creatives and strategists have all the freedom they want with him, as long as they sing from his hymn sheet. Palace revolutionaries should just be happy that the guillotine was done away with.'

'Isn't his daughter the second in command in the company? What does she think about the patent thing?'

'Exactly the same as her father. I know what you're getting at. You can't corrode Orley Enterprises from the inside.'

'Unless—'

'Over Julian's dead body.'

'There you go,' said Yoyo, unmoved. 'There may be forces in the company that want him dead, but can't do anything by themselves. Who would they collaborate with?'

'The CIA,' said Shaw, without hesitation.

'Oh.'

'I know that for a fact. The CIA are developing scenarios of what form a partnership without Julian might take. They're thinking about everything. The Americans are worried about their national security.'

'It's a known fact that the State can withdraw patents if national security is at risk' said Jericho.

'Yes, but Julian is British, not American. And the Brits have no issues with him, quite the opposite in fact. With the taxes he pays, the prime minister himself would personally take a bullet for him. And besides, it's about economy, not war. Julian isn't endangering anyone's national security, just their profits.'

'The only way of controlling the company from the outside would be to get rid of him.'

'Correct.'

'Could Zheng Pang-Wang—?'

'No. After all, Zheng's hopes rest entirely on Julian, and the possibility that he may at least talk him into a joint venture one day. As soon as other people are running Orley, Zheng would be completely out of the picture. That reminds me, Edda put together the data you asked for.'

'Yes, it's about—'

'Vic Thorn, I know. Interesting idea. Excuse me, Owen, I'm just getting a call from our control centre in the Isla de las Estrellas. We'll put the data on your computer.'

'The CIA,' ruminated Yoyo. 'That's a new one.'

'Yet another theory.' Jericho rested his head in his hands. It suddenly felt as heavy as lead. 'Getting rid of their own business partner and putting the blame on the Chinese.'

'Plausible?'

'Of course it is!'

They sat there silently for a while. An icon had appeared on Diane's monitor, VICTHORN, but Jericho was overcome by the paralysis of mental overload. He needed a jump start to get going. Some insignificant little victory.

'Listen,' he said. 'We're going to do something now that we should have done a lot sooner.'

He pulled the icon of the intertwined snake bodies onto the screen and named it UNKNOWN.

'Diane.'

'Yes, Owen?'

'Look in the net for equivalents of UNKNOWN. What is it about? Show me the corresponding data and deliver contextual background.'

'One moment, Owen.'

Yoyo came and sat next to him, crossed her arms on the table and laid her chin in the crook of an elbow. 'Her voice is very lovely, I grant you,' she said. 'If she looked as—'

The screen filled with images.

'Would you like to hear a summary, Owen?'

'Yes, please, Diane.'

'It's very likely that the graphics show a Hydra. A nine-headed, snake-like monster from Greek mythology, which lived in the swamps of the

Argolid and prowled through the surrounding lands, killing cattle and humans and destroying harvests. Even though the Hydra's middle head was immortal, she was defeated by Heracles, a son of Zeus. Would you like to hear more about Heracles?'

'Tell me how Heracles defeated the Hydra.'

'The snake's distinguishing characteristic was that it grew two new heads for every one that was chopped off, with the result that it became increasingly dangerous as the fight went on. It was only when Heracles began to *burn* off the neck stumps with the help of his nephew Ioalaus that the new heads were no longer able to grow. Eventually, Heracles succeeded in striking off Hydra's immortal head too. He dismembered the body and immersed a stake in its blood, which from then on could create incurable wounds. Would you like to hear more details?'

'Not right now, Diane, thank you.'

'A Greek monster,' said Yoyo, her eyes wide. 'In the picture it looks more Asian.'

'An organisation with lots of heads.'

'That grow back when you knock them off.'

'But would Chinese conspirators really make a creature from Greek mythology into their symbol?'

Yoyo stared at the monitor. Diane had found around two dozen images of the Hydra, various depictions, in artefacts spread across two millennia, all of which showed a scaly snake body with nine tongued heads.

'No, not a chance in hell,' she said.

Peary Base, North Pole, The Moon

They felt a little like the survivors from a wagon-train of white settlers, the ones who had made it to the fort in the nick of time, even though there were no equivalents of Indians to be seen anywhere. But at the moment when the Callisto descended over the base's space station, O'Keefe couldn't help but picture US cavalry stationed at the Pole, a troop of riders who came tearing over the plateau to protect them, hats and flashing epaulettes, fanfares, shots fired in the air, the familiar tropes: *Are you safe, Sergeant? – Aye, sir! A hell of a journey. I didn't think we'd make it. I see the Donoghues aren't here. Dead, sir. Blast! And the staff? – Dead, sir, all dead. My God! And Winter? – Didn't make it, sir. We lost Hsu too. Terrible! – Yes, sir, horrible.*

How strange. Even something as exotic as space travel only seemed to function through the cultivation of earthly myths, by imposing elements of the familiar onto the unfamiliar. Something designed to expand the mind ended up being subjected to musty familiarity and forced into narrow spectrums of association. Perhaps people couldn't help it. Perhaps making the unusual seem banal prevented them from perishing of their own banality, even if it meant their subconscious calling on the services of the western, a genre whose task had been to put a chaotic world back to order with the assistance of sharp ammunition and sublime landscapes. *A lot of bad things have happened, Sergeant. Aye, sir. So many have died. Aye. But look at the land, Sergeant! Is it not worth every man lost? – I wouldn't miss it, sir! – What a wonderful country! Our hearts beat for it, our blood flows for it. We may die, but the land remains. I love this country. By God, me too! Let's ride!*

My arse!

As soon as Nina landed the Callisto at the Pole, all eyes were directed towards the Charon. To the southern end of the landing field, surrounded by the base's spaceships, the landing module rested like a small, impregnable castle on stilt legs. O'Keefe recalled their first leaps and steps, filled with that conquistador-like feeling of having conquered something, unsuspecting that they would come back just a few days later, depleted and demoralised. The monochrome landscape and mother-of-pearl sea of stars had lost none of their beauty, even after the disaster in Gaia, but their gazes had now turned inwards. The adventure was over. The desire to escape had extinguished the pioneering spirit.

'Well, I don't know.' Leland Palmer, a small, Irish-looking man and commander of the base, looked around at them sceptically. 'None of it seems to make sense to me.'

'Well, then a lot of people had to die for something that makes no sense,' said O'Keefe.

A robot bus had brought them from the landing field to Igloo 2, one of the two domed living quarters which formed the centre of the base. Igloo 1 contained the headquarters and scientific working area, while its neighbouring counterpart was for leisure activities and medical care. In a lounge which oscillated between comfort and functionality, they had told the residents their story, while Karla, Eva and the Nairs were examined for signs of smoke poisoning and Olympiada Rogacheva, in a state of self-reproach, had her leg put in splints. Lynn had sat amongst them silently for a while, until Tim, his face contorted with worry, had taken her hand and told her she should lie down, sleep and forget, a suggestion that she had followed apathetically.

'I mean there's no sense to the *expense*,' said Palmer. 'I mean, just look at what a simple oxygen fire can do! What would someone need a *nuclear bomb* for?'

'Unless you factor in the location,' Dana suggested.

'You mean you think the bomb isn't for the Gaia at all?'

'Not exclusively, I would say.'

'That's true,' said Ögi. 'A few hand grenades, correctly positioned, would have done the job, no problem. I happen to know a thing or two about mini-nukes—'

'You do?' said Heidrun, amazed.

'From the television, my dear. And one thing I know is that you shouldn't let yourself be fooled by the cute terminology, you know, Mini Rock, Mini Mouse, Mini Nuke. Every one of the mini-nukes which disappeared from the holdings of the former Soviet Union in the early nineties was capable of obliterating Manhattan.'

'So what are they trying to destroy, then?' asked Wachowski.

'Gaia is at the edge of a basin,' said Tim, his head resting in his hands. 'Where the Vallis Alpina rounds out.'

'What would happen if someone set off a nuclear bomb in a basin like that?' asked O'Keefe.

'Well.' Wachowski shrugged. 'It would contaminate it.'

'More than that,' said Palmer. 'There's no air here to spread radioactive material, no atmospheric fallout. But on the other hand nor is there anything to slow down the explosion's energy. The direct destruction itself would be enormous, a bit like the impact of a meteorite. The pressure would blast away the edges of the basin, the heat would turn its walls to glass, vast quantities of rock would be catapulted into the air, but above all, the detonation would be tunnelled.'

'Which means?' asked Heidrun.

'That there's only one direction, apart from upwards, that the pressure can be released.'

'Into the valley.'

'Yes. The waves of pressure would graze along the entire Vallis Alpina, accelerated by the steep walls. I'd estimate that the whole area would be lost.'

'But to what purpose? What's so special about the valley, apart from the fact that it's beautiful?'

Tim crossed his fingers and shook his head. 'I'm more concerned with wondering why the bomb hasn't gone off yet.'

'Well, up to three and a half hours ago it hadn't gone off yet,' O'Keefe corrected him. 'By now it could have blown sky high.'

'And we wouldn't have a clue here!' growled Wachowski. 'What a mess! What the hell is wrong with the satellites?'

I could tell you all a thing or two, thought Dana. 'Either way,' she said, 'we won't solve the problem here and now, and to be honest I'm not interested right at this moment. I want to know what has happened on Aristarchus.'

'The shuttles should be fuelled up soon,' promised Wachowski.

'Hmm, Carl.' Heidrun wrinkled her forehead. 'I wonder what he'll do?'

'That depends. Is he alive, are the others alive? Was he able to flee? My bet is that he still has something he needs to do in the hotel.'

'And what would that be?' asked Tim.

'Priming the bomb.' She looked at him. 'What else?'

'He needs to prime it?'

'Possibly.' Wachowski nodded. 'How else would you ignite the thing?'

'Remote control.'

'In order to ignite it via remote control you'd need a very large antenna, which you would have seen when you were searching the Gaia. Otherwise, he'll need to do the ignition himself.'

'Which explains why we're still alive,' said Ögi. 'Carl didn't have a chance to set up a timed fuse. His plans were turned upside down.'

'Do we care about that?' O'Keefe looked around at them all. 'I wouldn't waste a minute looking for him. Let's concentrate on the Ganymede.'

'I totally agree with you,' said Dana. 'But it could come down to the same thing. If we find the Ganymede, we may stumble upon Hanna.'

'That's fine by me,' growled O'Keefe. 'More than fine.'

Nina came into the lounge.

'We're ready!'

'Good.' Dana and Palmer had agreed to send two search teams off right away. Nina was to fly the Callisto to the Plato crater, follow the Montes Jura along the mining zones and then head for Aristarchus. The Io, a shuttle belonging to the Peary Base, would set off fifteen minutes later, keep a southerly course by Plato, and then, 500 kilometres on, swing over the plain of the Mare Imbrium towards Callisto. Dana got up. 'Let's put the teams together.'

'You can fly with me.'

'Thank you, but I think my presence is more needed here. Someone has to look after the others. How many people can you spare, Leland?'

Palmer rubbed his chin. 'Kyra Gore is our head pilot. She can fly the Io with Annie Jagellovsk, our astronomer—'

'My apologies,' Dana cut him off mid-sentence. 'I didn't express myself correctly. How many people have to stay in the base in order to ensure everything can function?'

'One. Well, let's say two.'

'I want you to be clear about how dangerous this man is. It's possible that the search teams will be forced to attack Hanna. They may have to free the group from under his control. Each shuttle should be occupied by four, or preferably five people.'

'But there're only eight of us.'

'I'll come too,' said O'Keefe.

'Me too,' said Tim.

'Heidrun and I—' Ögi started to say.

'I'm sorry, Walo, but you're not the ideal person.' Dana made the effort to smile. 'You're certainly courageous enough, but we need younger, fitter people. So, Tim and Finn will fly with Nina, plus two more people from the base. The Io will fly with five men from the base—'

'Just a minute.' Palmer was trying to rein in the galloping horse. 'That would be an extraordinary mission.'

'Well, we have an extraordinary problem,' replied Dana ungraciously. 'In case you haven't noticed.'

'Six out of eight people. I'd need to consult—'

'Consult who?'

'Well—'

'You won't reach anyone.'

'Okay, but – it's not that simple, Dana. That's three-quarters of my team. And the shuttles will have no contact to base for most of the time.'

'View *me* as a reinforcement here,' said Dana. 'My responsibility is the safety of Julian Orley and his guests. And, to be honest, Leland, I would be less than understanding if the rescue mission were to fail due to lack of—'

'Fine.' Palmer exchanged a look with Wachowski. 'I think it's doable. Tommy, you stay here and – hmm, Minnie DeLucas.'

'Who's that?' asked Dana.

'Our specialist for life-support systems.'

'Wouldn't it be better if Jan stayed?' wondered Wachowski.

'And who's *that*?'

'Jan Crippen. Our technical director.'

'Not necessarily,' said Palmer. 'Minnie can take on his duties, and besides, we won't be gone for all that long.'

'I don't care how long you're gone,' said Dana. 'As long as you find Julian Orley.'

More importantly, as long as you're all out of the picture for the next few hours, she thought. Carl and I can handle Wachowski and this woman DeLucas.

If Hanna was still coming, that was.

At around 02.40 that morning, the shuttle bus finally took the search teams over to the landing field.

O'Keefe sat on the bench of the open vehicle and let his gaze wander. On their second evening on the Moon, in an effort not to expose himself to too much conversation, he had retreated to the Gaia's multimedia centre before the meal was over, and had watched a film about the Peary Base. So he knew that it covered over ten square kilometres and that the landing field alone took up three times the space of a football field. The silo-like towers on the western wall were spaceships left behind by the teams who had first ventured to the North Pole. Originally converted into living quarters, they now served as emergency accommodation, themselves dwarfed by a telescope currently under construction, while the domes in the centre, Igloos 1 and 2, formed the heart of the base. Both had been brought to the Pole as collapsible structures, and had then been blown up to house size and coated with a layer of regolith several metres thick, in order to protect the inhabitants from solar storms and meteorites. Airlocks had been cut into the walls, the ground levelled off all around them, and vehicles and equipment had been stored in hangars, those halved tubes which Momoka had referred to in her usual defeatist manner as junk, and which were actually burnt-out fuel tanks from the Space Shuttle era.

Over the years, the station had grown, expanding to include streets, annexe buildings and a vast open-cast mine. In the distance, against a backdrop of automated factories in which the regolith was processed into building components, the framework of huge, open assembly facilities towered up. Manipulators ran on rails along the bodies of mining machines in the making: welding, riveting and adjusting parts, while humanoid robots carried out precise mechanical work. Cable cars and railway trucks were carrying material from the factories to the building yards. Wherever you looked, machines were hard at work. Lifelessness in its most vivid form.

O'Keefe looked towards the east as the bus made its way towards the landing field, two kilometres away from the main site. Fields of solar collectors, their panels directed at the wandering, never-setting sun, covered low, undulating hills. The craters were interspersed with canals of lava. Thanks to them, the Peary Base had a widely ramified system of natural catacombs, the majority of which hadn't yet been explored. Just one feature betrayed what the ground was concealing: a crack, or rather a chasm. It gaped at its full width in the high plateau, spread out to the west and opened into a steeply descending valley, the bottom of which wasn't touched by a single ray of sunlight. Bridges crossed over what seemed like the remains of a severe earthquake, although it was actually a caved-in lava canal, through which liquid stone had flowed billions of years ago. As O'Keefe knew from the documentary, some of the cave branches led into the chasm, which made him wonder whether the underground of the base was accessible from there.

They drove through the gate in the screens surrounding the landing field. There was moderate activity taking place all around them. One of the grasshopper-like forklifts was corresponding soundlessly with a manipulator, whose segmented arm rose in their direction like a final greeting, then froze. So far as could be seen, the tracks on the rail station gallery lay there abandoned. Beneath the harsh, uneven light, the lonely route wound off into the valley. The activity of the machines had a ritualistic quality to it; one could even say post-apocalyptic mindlessness, an image of strange self-contentment.

What would they find at Aristarchus? Suddenly, he was overcome by the desire to go to sleep and wake up in the timelessness of a Dublin pub of somewhat ill repute, where the customers were more concerned with the accurate proportion of foam to black stout than all the wonders of the Milky Way put together, and often sighed in remembrance of allegedly better times as they raised the glasses to their lips.

London, Great Britain

The night crawled by.

Yoyo was off somewhere on the phone to Chen Hongbing, Tu was discussing the possibility of a joint venture with Dao IT, his still-furious, abhorrent competitor, and Jericho was struggling to keep his eyes open. Three hundred metres above London, his brain had turned into a swamp, gurgling and mumbling with decaying theories, all paths either reaching a dead end or getting lost in the unknown. He was finding it harder and harder to concentrate. Vic Thorn on his journey into eternity. Kenny Xin, slinking towards Palstein's planned assassination. The nine heads of Hydra. Carl Hanna, on whom Norrington hadn't yet managed to find even the smallest blemish. Diane with her ever increasing messages about Calgary and the massacre in Vancouver. Sinister representatives of the CIA, living up to the cliché. From a great height, he could see himself running around in a circle so big it felt like he was going in a straight line, but he always ended up back in the same place.

He was absolutely shattered.

Yoyo came back from her phone conversation just as he was about to stretch out on the floor and close his eyes for a moment. But then he might have gone to sleep, and his overtaxed brain would have conjured up dreams of hunting and being hunted. He was actually pleased that Yoyo was keeping him awake, even though her mercurial vitality was increasingly getting on his nerves. Since their arrival in the Big O, she had single-handedly polished off a bottle of Brunello di Montalcino, had the ruby-red tones of Sangiovese Grosso in her cheeks and the never-tiring look of youth, and all without showing any sign of drunkenness. For every cigarette she smoked, two new ones seemed to grow out of her fingers. She was even more unpredictable than the Welsh weather: gloomy and glowering one moment, bright the next.

'How's your father doing?' he yawned.

'As can be expected.' Yoyo sank down into a swivel chair then jumped right up again. 'Really well actually. I didn't tell him everything, of course. Like what happened at the Pergamon Museum, he doesn't need to know that, right? Just so you know, in case you speak to him.'

'I can't see any reason why I should.'

'Hongbing is your client.' She went over to the coffee machine. 'Have you forgotten that already?'

Jericho blinked. He suspected that, if he looked in the mirror, he would find his eyes had been replaced by computer monitors. He forced himself to look up from the screen.

'I brought you back to him,' he said. 'So the honourable Chen is no longer my client.'

'Oh great.' Yoyo studied the selection on the machine. 'There's a thousand varieties of coffee, but no tea.'

'Look more closely. The English are tea-drinkers.'

'Where is it then?'

'Bottom right. Hot water. The box of teabags is next to it. So what did you tell him?'

'Hongbing?' Yoyo rummaged through the box. 'I told him that we had a heartfelt conversation with Vogelaar and that he filled us in on what was going on, and that Donner turned out to be a cover.' She put her cup under the nozzle, dropped in a bag of Oolong and ran boiling water over it.

'So in other words you said we were having a lovely holiday,' mocked Jericho. 'And have we been to Madame Tussaud's and shopping on the King's Road?'

'So should I have told him about the experience of pressing the eyeballs out of a dead man?'

'Fine, enough said. A mocha, please.'

'A what?'

'Coffee with chocolate. Left row, third button from the top. So how far did you get with Thorn?'

They had divided up their tasks, which meant that Yoyo was evaluating the data relayed by Edda Hoff and completing it with information she found online.

'I'll be finished in a few minutes,' she said, watching as the machine spat out a mixture of cappuccino and chocolate. 'Would I be correct in assuming that you're tired?'

Jericho was just about to answer when he realised that Diane was simultaneously uploading 112 new reports about Calgary and Vancouver. He sank into a depressed silence. Yoyo put the steaming cup in front of him and began to slurp down her tea in front of her monitor. He listlessly decided to have one final look at the message that had set everything off, then to go and sleep.

Just as the text appeared on his screen, Yoyo whistled lightly through her teeth.

'Do you want to know who was project leader for the Peary Missions from 2020 to the end of 2024?'

'From the way you say it I take it that I do want to know.'

'Andrew Norrington.'

'Norrington?' Jericho's slumped shoulders tightened up. 'Shaw's deputy?'

'Wait.' She wrinkled her brow. 'There were a number of project leaders, but Norrington was definitely in the team. It doesn't say to what extent or how direct his contact with Thorn was.'

'And you're sure it's the same Norrington?'

'Andrew Norrington,' she read. 'Responsible for personnel and security, transferred in November 2024 to Orley Enterprises as deputy head of security.'

'Strange.' Jericho wrinkled his forehead. 'So it should have rung a bell with Hoff when I spoke to her about Thorn.'

'She's Norrington's subordinate. Why would she be concerned with the details of his past career?'

'But Norrington didn't say anything either.'

'Did you speak to him about Thorn?'

'Not directly. Shaw and he were in a meeting. I came over and said that some unexpected event must have stopped the mini-nuke being ignited the year before.'

'Mind you, Shaw already knew about your Vic Thorn theory.'

'That's true, probably from Hoff. Hmm. She must have clocked that Norrington was with NASA at the same time as Thorn. Sure, she had a hell of a lot on her plate – but Norrington—'

'You mean, he should have thought of Thorn himself?'

'Maybe that's asking too much.' Jericho rested his chin in his hands. 'But do you know what? I'm going to go and ask him.'

'Victor Thorn—'

Norrington was sitting in his surprisingly small office, one of the few rooms that weren't open-plan. Jericho had turned up unannounced, as if he were just passing.

'Yes, Thorn,' he nodded. 'He could be our man, don't you think?'

Norrington gazed at an imaginary point in the room.

'Hmm,' he said distinctly, very distinctly. A clearly audible *H*, followed by a time-winning *mmm*. 'Interesting thought.'

'He died three months after the launch of the satellite. It would fit time-wise.'

'You're right. Why didn't I think of that myself?'

'People often overlook the things that are right in front of them.' Jericho smiled. 'Did you have close contact with him?'

'No.' Norrington shook his head slowly. 'I'm sure I wouldn't have been so slow on the uptake if I had.'

'No contact at all?'

'My role was related to the general project security. Sure, we crossed each other's path now and then, but other people were responsible for personnel issues.'

'And what was Thorn like?'

'As I said, we had nothing to do with one another. Rumour was that he was a playboy, which may have been an exaggeration. I think he just enjoyed life, but on the other hand he was enormously disciplined. A good – a *very* good astronaut. People don't normally get put forward for a second Peary Mission that quickly.'

'Think back, Andrew,' asked Jericho. 'Any information would be helpful.'

'Of course. Although I fear that I won't be able to offer anything that enlightening. Is Jennifer already in the picture on this?'

'Hoff seems to have mentioned it to her. She knew about my suspicion.'

'She didn't tell *me*.' Norrington sighed. 'But you can see what it's like here: we rush from one meeting to the next; everything's so chaotic. Hanna is driving me insane. I can't find anything dodgy in his background, and God knows it's not the first time I've looked.'

'You were responsible for the tour group?'

'Yes. We didn't know much about Hanna, but Julian was adamant about taking him along. Believe you me, I X-rayed the guy thoroughly. And nothing: he was clean.'

'Anything new from Merrick?'

'No. He's trying to make contact. His botnet theory is probably correct.' Norrington hesitated. 'Owen, I don't mean to suggest I don't trust your instincts, but we have to look at other Orley organisations too. We can't be certain that we're not dealing with a concerted action. Give me a bit of time with Thorn. I'll be in touch as soon as I can.'

'He's lying,' said Yoyo, when Jericho came back and filled her in on the conversation. 'Norrington knew Thorn.'

'He didn't say he didn't *know* him.'

'No, I mean he *really* knew him.' Yoyo pointed at her monitor. 'Thorn attracted a lot of interest from the media, because of Peary, but also because he was good-looking and talkative. There are dozens of interviews with him, but I found the best one while you were away. A special report about the Peary crew of 2024, plus a human-interest piece. Vic Thorn, sought-after bachelor, on the Moon for the second time, blah blah blah. They took a film crew to his house and were given access while he threw a birthday party, and guess who was on the guest list?'

She started the video. An open-plan kitchen, a relaxed atmosphere. About two dozen people gathered around platters of finger food. Light jazz breezing over a sea of chatter, classics from the Rat Pack era. People dancing in the background, and a lot of dedicated drinking. Thorn laughs into the camera and says something about how wonderful friendship is, then can be seen in animated discussion with a man who slaps him familiarly on the shoulder a few frames later.

'Is that what people who don't have any contact with one another look like?'

Jericho shook his head.

'Most definitely not.'

'That some of these men will soon spend six months on another celestial body,' said the female commentator, 'seems strangely unreal on an evening like this, where—'

'It could be coincidence,' Yoyo conceded. 'We can't necessarily assume that Norrington is our mole, or even that Thorn had something to do with it. It's pure speculation.'

'Nonetheless, I want to know more about his time with NASA. What exactly he was responsible for, how close the contact really was. We know one thing for sure: he lied when he denied knowing Thorn well.'

'—already his second mission in the Mountains of Eternal Light,' the commentator was saying. 'So called because the sun never sets at the lunar Pole. Originally, this played a decisive role for the energy supply to the Peary Base, but since then the construction of a fusion reactor has—'

'Mountains of Eternal Light,' whispered Jericho.

Yoyo looked up at him, confused.

'Yes, that's what the Polar regions are called. You know that.'

The cogs were turning in Jericho's mind. As if in a trance, he went over to his desk and stared at the text of the fragmentary message:

Jan Kees Vogelaar is living in Berlin under the name Andre Donner, where he runs an African private and business address: Oranienburger Strasse 50, 10117 Berlin. What should we continues to represent a grave risk to the operation not doubt that he knows all about the payload rockets. knows at least about the but some doubt as to whether. One way or another any statement lasting Admittedly, since his Vogelaar has made no public comment about the facts behind the coup. Nevertheless Ndongo's that the Chinese government planned and implemented regime change.

Vogelaar has little about the nature of Operation MoonLight of timing Furthermore, Orley Enterprises and have no reason to suspect disruption. Nobody there suspects and by then everything is under way. I count because I know, Nevertheless urgently recommend that Donner be liquidated. There are good reasons to

There was very little of the text that still puzzled him. In essence, just one single word, added before the dark network went silent, and only because it occupied the space between *Operation* and *of timing* in such an odd way, as if it didn't belong there.

MoonLight

That's what he'd assumed it said, at any rate.

'Diane. Fragment analysis. Attribute the origin data to the text building stones.'

'Colour recognition?'

'Yes, please.'

A moment later, words like *payload rocket* and *Enterprises* were transformed into colourful chains of alphabet letters. *Ent erpr ises* was, for example, assembled from three sections of data and other terms like *Operation* and *implemented*, came from a single data section.

Four fragments created *Mo o n light*.

'Oh, God,' whispered Jericho.

'What's wrong?' Yoyo jumped up, came over and leaned over his shoulder.

'I think we've made a mistake.'

'A mistake?'

'A huge mistake.' How could he have missed it? It was right in front of him. 'We may have put them on the wrong track. The bomb isn't supposed to go off in Gaia—'

'Not in Gaia? But—'

'There would be no point if it did, and we knew that the whole time. Idiot! I'm such a stupid, blind idiot!'

Operation Mo o n Light

Operation Mountains of Eternal Light.

Chinese Mining Station, Sinus Iridum, The Moon

Jia Keqiang was no politician. He was a taikonaut, a geologist and a major, in that order, or possibly the other way around depending on his mood, but he was no politician, that was for sure. In his experience, the only difference between Chinese and American spacemen, or indeed Russian, Indian, German and French, was the ideology behind them, and whether they were called astronauts, cosmonauts or taikonauts. What they all had in common though was a way of looking at the big picture which politicians, in his experience, never had, except of course for those few statesmen who had been in space themselves. Hua Liwei, his predecessor up on the Moon, had been an American captive for a while and still took every official appearance as an opportunity to accuse the Americans of hair-raising breaches of the lunar peace, but this couldn't shake Jia's opinion that spacemen were easygoing, unpolitical people. It was just that each and every one of them followed their script faithfully. Even Hua Liwei, once he had a drink or two inside him, in private, would happily admit that he liked the Yanks, that they had treated him very well and that, as it happened, they had some excellent Scotch tucked away in the catacombs at Peary Base.

Mind you, Hua also reckoned that the Americans were to blame for the whole farcical episode, and Jia agreed with him there. Nevertheless, he had done his best during the Moon crisis to argue for de-escalation and understanding all round, using what influence he had. The Party held him in high esteem as a bright young hope of the Chinese space programme; he was a highly decorated officer in the Air Force and had trained as a taikonaut under the watchful eye of the legendary Zhai Zhigang. On top of all this, he also had a doctorate in geology, specialising in exo-geology, qualifying him to work on the helium-3 mining operation. Zhai had passed on to Jia his love of ballroom dancing, and he was also inordinately fond of naval history, spending hours on end researching the brief flowering of Chinese seamanship in the fifteenth century and the fabled nine-masted ships of the time; he had painstakingly built a three-metre-long scale model of Admiral Zhang He's flagship. When he wasn't up in space, he loved to sail with his wife and sons, to read books on maritime history and to cook, which he did as a sort of meditation. He was proud that his country had become the first after the USA to make it to the Moon, he was irked that Zheng Pang-Wang hadn't made any progress on the space elevator, he was worried about America's dominance in space and he was slow to make predictions about the future. He was a perfect public face for China, friendly, media-savvy, patriotic, and always careful to keep to himself his own personal opinion that politicians both sides of the Great Wall were not the brightest bulbs in the shop. 'Frankly', as the Americans would say, he thought that politicians were idiots.

But right now he had to think about politics, if he didn't want to lose control of the story he'd suddenly found himself caught up in.

Julian Orley was sitting across from him.

The very fact that he was here was remarkable enough, but what Orley had to tell him was even more startling. Twenty minutes ago he had appeared from the dustbowl of the mining camp, along with his daughter-in-law, the American talk-show queen Evelyn Chambers and some Russian Jia knew nothing at all about, all riding on grasshoppers like a squad of defeated Jedi fleeing the field, and they had asked for shelter and for help. Everyone in the base had been asleep, of course, since it was half past three in the morning, though Orley seemed surprised when Jia pointed this out to him. They had hurried to take care of their unexpected guests, fussed around them and made hot tea, but even so the commander found himself in a tricky situation, since—

'—without wishing to offend, Mr Orley, last time the Americans entered our territory, there was some trouble.'

They had tried talking Chinese for a while, but Orley's laborious, broken Mandarin was no match for Jia's fluent English. Jia's crew, Zhou

Jinping and Na Mou, were in the next room, looking after the others. Evelyn Chambers in particular was in a bad state, showing signs of an imminent nervous breakdown.

'Your territory?' Orley raised an eyebrow. 'Wasn't it the other way about?'

'We are of course aware that America takes, let us say, a different view of the matter,' Jia said. 'That is, regarding who intruded into whose territory. Perception is such a subjective thing.'

'It certainly is.' The Englishman nodded. 'But you see, Commander, I couldn't give two hoots about any of that. I'm not answerable for the local mining operation, or for Washington's territorial issues. I've built an elevator, a space station and a hotel.'

'If you will permit me an observation, that list is not quite complete. You benefit from the mining, because you're the one who can build the reactors.'

'Still, I do it as a private businessman.'

'NASA's technologies would be inconceivable without Orley Enterprises, and vice versa. In China's view, that makes you more than just a private businessman.'

Orley smiled. 'So why does Zheng Pang-Wang constantly remind me that that's just what I am?'

'Perhaps to reassure you that you have a free choice in the matter?' Jia smiled back. 'Please don't misunderstand me. I would not presume to question the honourable Zheng's motives, but he is no more a private businessman than you are. You have more influence over world politics than many a politician. More tea?'

'Please.'

'You see, I am concerned that you should understand my situation, Mr Orley—'

'Julian.'

Jia was silent for a moment, uncomfortable, then poured the tea. He had never understood what made the English and the Americans so keen to get onto first-name terms at every conceivable opportunity.

'The extended agreements signed in November 2024 commit us to helping one another here on the Moon,' he said. 'We are taikonauts, you are astronauts, we are all of us humanity's ambassadors to the stars. We should stand shoulder to shoulder. Speaking personally, I would allow you to use our shuttle the moment you ask for it, but the very fact that it is *you* asking gives the whole thing a very political aspect. On top of all which, there might be nuclear bombs involved.'

'It wouldn't be the first time we've had Chinese help in the matter. Without that, we'd probably know nothing at all about the bomb, and we'd be hiking happily around the lunar hills with Hanna until the whole place blew up.'

'Hmm, well—'

'On the other hand—' Orley steepled his fingers. 'I'll put my cards on the table. The people who warned us can't rule out that China might actually have a hand in the planned attack—'

'Preposterous!' Jia snorted. 'What interest would my country have in destroying your hotel?'

'You think it's ridiculous?'

'Quite ridiculous!'

Julian looked thoughtfully at the man sitting across from him. Jia was a pleasant enough chap, but he was a Beijing company man through and through. If the plot against Orley Enterprises really had been hatched in China, then Jia might well have some part in it. In which case, he was speaking to his enemy right now, which was one more reason to speak openly; he would have to make the man understand that the puppet-masters were about to be unmasked, and that it might be a good move to spill the beans. If Jericho and his friends were wrong, then every secret and suspicion he aired was just one step closer to winning Jia's trust. He leaned forward.

'The bomb was put into orbit in 2024,' he said.

'Okay, so?'

'That was when we had that crisis you mentioned.'

'We did everything that we could to ensure a peaceful resolution.'

'There's no arguing, though, that at the time, Beijing wasn't very well inclined towards Washington. This being so, you may be interested to learn that the bomb was bought from Korean stockpiles, on the black market, and that the buyers were Chinese.'

Jia looked at him in astonishment. Then he passed his hand over his eyes, as though he had just walked head-on into a cobweb.

'We're a nuclear power,' he said. 'Why would the Party buy nuclear weapons on the black market?'

'I never said that it was the Party who bought it.'

'Hmm. Go on.'

'It's also worth noting that although the bomb was launched from African soil, the president of Equatorial Guinea at the time was just a puppet, and one that *your* government had installed. From what I understand, the technology for the Equator-ial Guinea space programme all came from Zheng—'

'Hold on!' Jia expostulated. 'What are you saying? That Zheng wanted to destroy your hotel, with an atom bomb?'

'Please persuade me otherwise.'

'Why would he do that?'

'I have no idea. Because we're commercial rivals?'

'But you're not! You're not competing for the same markets. You're competing for know-how. So you spy on one another, pay bribes, argue your corner, try to form alliances – but you don't start hurling nuclear bombs about.'

'The gloves are off now.'

'But an attack like that would be of absolutely no benefit to Zheng, or to my country! What would destroying your hotel do to change the balance of power, even if you died as well?'

'Quite so. What?'

For a long moment Jia said nothing at all, but kneaded at the bridge of his nose and kept his lids shut tight. When he opened them again, the question in his eyes was easy to read.

'No,' Julian answered.

'No?'

'My visit here isn't part of some double-cross, honourable Jia, it's not a plan or an operation. I truly have no wish to harm you or your country. There's a lot I could have left unmentioned if I had wanted to steer your decision-making.'

'And what do you expect me to do now?'

'I can tell you what I need.'

'You want me to take you and your friends back to the hotel with our shuttle?'

'As fast as you can! My son and daughter are in Gaia, as well as the guests and staff. We have reason to fear that Hanna is making his own way back there. I also need the use of your satellites.'

'My satellites?'

'Yes. Have you had any trouble with them in the last few hours?'

'Not that I know of.'

'Ours have failed completely, as I told you at the beginning. Yours seem to be working. I need two connections. One to my headquarters in London, and another to Gaia.' Julian paused. 'I have put my trust in you completely, Commander, even at the risk of your refusing my request. I can do no more. The rest is up to you.'

The taikonaut fell silent again, then said slowly, 'You would of course be in China's debt if I were to help you.'

'Of course.'

Julian could see the wheels going round in Jia's head. Right at this moment, the commander was worrying about whether his visitor might actually be right, and his government had plotted some dirty trick that he knew nothing about. And whether, perhaps, he was in danger of committing high treason if he offered unconditional help to the man who had put America where it was today.

Julian cleared his throat.

'Perhaps you might bear in mind that somebody is trying to make a cat's paw of your country,' he said. 'I wouldn't take too kindly to that, if I were you.'

Jia glowered at him.

'Entry-level Psychology.'

'Ah, well.' Julian shrugged and smiled. 'Something of the sort.'

'Go next door and join your friends,' Jia said. 'Wait.'

Chambers couldn't stop the loop from playing. Over and over again she saw the beetle's foot coming down to crush her, and suddenly she began to twitch epileptically. She slid down the wall of the hab module like a wet rag. Amber and Oleg were in there with her. It was cramped in the station, horribly cramped, quite unlike the American living quarters. Na Mou, one of the taikonauts, was fussing over them with tea and spicy crab cakes. While Julian was softening up the commander, Chambers had been telling the Chinese woman about the events of the last few hours. Perhaps Na understood more English than she spoke, but Chambers herself was so horrified by her own story that the words stuck in her throat.

'You lie down,' Na said, kindly. She was a Mongolian-looking woman with broad cheekbones and strongly slanted eyes, with something of the past about her, a suggestion of marching parades and collective farms.

'It keeps on coming,' Chambers whispered. 'It keeps on and on.'

'Yes. Legs up.'

'Whether I shut my eyes or keep them open, it never stops.' She grabbed Na's wrist, and felt ice-cold sweat start up on her own upper lip and forehead. 'I'll squashed any moment. By a beetle. Isn't that crazy? People squash beetles, not the other way around. But I can't stop seeing it.'

'You *can* stop.' Amber turned away from Zhou Jinping, the third crew member at the base, who had been questioning her eagerly. She sat down next to Chambers. 'You've had a shock, that's all.'

'No, I—'

'It's okay, Evy. I'm pretty close to collapsing myself.'

'No, there was something there.' Chambers rolled her eyes, rather like a voodoo priestess in a trance, a mambo. 'Death was there.'

'I know.'

'No, I was over on the other side, do you understand? I was really there. And Momoka was there, and – I mean, I knew that she was dead, but—'

Two dams broke, grief and shock, and tears spilled down over

Chambers' beautiful Latin features. She gesticulated as though trying to ward off some spell, then let her hands drop, exhausted, and began to cry. Amber put an arm around her shoulder and drew her in close, gently.

'Too much,' Na Mou said, nodding wisely.

'It'll all be all right, Evy.'

'I wanted to ask her what happens to us next,' Chambers sobbed. 'It was so cold in her world. I think she laid a curse on me, she makes me see this terrible sight over and over, she must have seen something just as awful before she died, and—'

'Evy,' Amber said quietly but firmly. 'You're not clairvoyant. Your nerves are shot, that's all.'

'I didn't even like her very much.'

'None of us liked her very much.' Amber sighed. 'Apart from Warren, I suppose.'

'But that's awful!' Chambers clung tightly to her, racked by sobs. 'And now she's gone, we couldn't even – couldn't even say something nice—'

Do we have to? Amber thought. Do you have to say nice things to someone who's clearly a bitch, just on the off-chance that she'll kick the bucket in the near future?

'I don't think she really saw it like that,' she said.

'Really?'

'Really. Momoka had her own ideas about what's nice or not.'

Chambers buried her face in Amber's shoulder. The most powerful woman in American media, the voice who made presidents, cried for a few more minutes until she fell asleep from sheer exhaustion. Na Mou and Zhou Jinping had fallen quiet, respecting her sorrow. Rogachev was lying on one of the narrow beds, his legs crossed, and scribbling away on a piece of paper they had found for him.

'What are you doing there?' Amber asked, tired.

The Russian twiddled the pen in his fingers without looking at her.

'I'm doing my sums.'

Jia Keqiang was wrestling with himself. It was a tough fight.

Plentiful experience told him what a long and stony path lay ahead if he took the matter through official channels, just as he knew that the Chinese space agency was largely staffed by paranoiacs. On the other hand, all he needed to do was make one telephone call, and he'd be free of all responsibility. He'd be out of danger of making any mistake, whereas if he spoke up for Orley on his own initiative he would be doomed to mistakes. All he had to do was pass the buck to one of the Party paper-shufflers, and if Orley's hotel actually was destroyed, it would be no fault of his. Then Beijing would have to face accusations of failing to live up to their treaty obligations and provide adequate help, while he could make loud noises about how he had wanted to help and hadn't been allowed. He could sleep easy in his bed, and not worry about his career.

If he *could* sleep easy.

On the other hand – what if Orley was right, and Beijing really was pulling the strings?

He turned his teacup thoughtfully between his fingers, staring down into the green tea. What then? He would dutifully call his superiors and tell them of Orley's suspicions, only to find himself up to the neck in state secrets. *Real* state secrets, which were no concern at all of his, because nobody had brought him into the circle. Obviously, he'd be classed as a national security risk straight away. Flying Julian Orley over to Gaia in the shuttle was the least of his problems. It was hostile territory up here, and in case of doubt, they just didn't fly. Similarly, it would need permission and approvals in triplicate to let the Englishman use Chinese satellites to communicate. Before the Moon crisis, Jia would have been able to make a decision like that on his own, but that option was off the table now.

He would *have* to call.

So what would he tell them?

He pushed his teacup from right to left, left to right.

And all of a sudden he knew.

There was still a risk, but it could work. He stood up, went to the control panel, put a call through to Earth and had two short conversations.

'I'll sum it up,' Jia said, after he had asked Julian back into the narrow control room to join him. 'You invite some friends for a private trip. Quite unexpectedly, one of your guests turns out to be a killer, he mows down five people and leaves you stranded on the Aristarchus Plateau.'

'That's right.'

'All this in response to his overhearing a conversation between yourself, Gaia and company headquarters in London, which was about how terrorists may have smuggled a nuclear bomb onto the Moon to destroy an American or Chinese moon base.'

'A Chi—' Julian blinked, bewildered. Then he understood. 'Yes. That's right. That's just how it was.'

'And you have no idea who might be behind it.'

'Now that you put it that way, Commander, I haven't the foggiest idea. All I know is that Chinese or American citizens may be in danger.'

'Mm-hm.' Jia nodded earnestly. 'I understand. That makes it all very clear. By which I mean to say that it is in the interests of our national security to look into the matter together with you. I have explained precisely these facts to my superiors, and I have been given permission to prepare the satellite for your use, and then to fly you on to Vallis Alpina afterwards.'

Julian looked at the taikonaut.

'Thank you,' he said softly.

'I'm pleased to be able to help.'

'You do know, however, that the conversation I am about to conduct may lead to some unjustifiable accusations against China.'

Jia shrugged.

'All that matters is that I don't know right now.'

Shaw stood by the table of the conference room. She looked unkempt, as though she had been running about the whole day. Andrew Norrington and Edda Hoff were with her. Behind them, a rather rumpled-looking blond man leaned in the doorway.

'Julian!' she called aloud. 'My God, are you all right? We've been trying to reach you for hours.'

'Have you been able to make contact with Gaia?'

'No.'

'Why not? You should be able to reach Gaia by the normal radio chann—'

'We've tried that. Nobody is responding.'

Julian felt his heart skip a beat.

'Before you ask, there hasn't been an explosion at Vallis Alpina,' Shaw said hurriedly. 'At least that much is good news.'

'And the base? Have you been able to talk to the moon base?'

'No response.'

'Erm, Julian,' Norrington broke in. 'Our theory is that somebody is using the satellites to disrupt communication by unleashing a huge botnet on the Moon. The comms equipment up there is completely clogged up, so to speak. The truth is, we're half blind and completely deaf, we need information from you.'

'How could anybody clog up our comms?' Julian snapped.

'Quite simple. You need an inside man.'

Inside man. Inside woman. Great God, why couldn't he shake the idea that Lynn had something to do with it.

'We're just going over Hanna's background,' Hoff said. 'There's not a great deal we can say about him for sure, though his whole life story turns out not to be worth the paper it's printed on. We are however agreed that he can't be operating on his own up there.'

'Once again, *where are you?*' Norrington urged him.

Julian sighed. He gave a brief account of what had happened in the hours since communications had collapsed. Shaw's face turned paler with every death he recounted.

'Jia Keqiang has been kind enough to agree to fly us to the hotel,' he finished up. 'We'll try to reach Gaia through the Chinese satellite first, to—'

'Mr Orley.' The blond man straightened up from the doorway and took a step forward. 'You shouldn't fly back to Gaia.'

Julian looked at the man, frowning in confusion. Then all of a sudden he realised.

'You're Owen Jericho.'

'Yes.'

'I beg your pardon.' He spread his hands. 'I should have thanked you long ago, but—'

'Some other time. Does the name Hydra mean anything to you?'

Julian gawped. 'Greek mythology,' he ventured. 'Monster with nine heads.'

'Nothing else spring to mind?'

'No.'

'It looks as though an organisation called Hydra is responsible for all this. Heads that grow back when you cut them off. A great many heads. Invincible, worldwide. For a while we thought that the people pulling the strings were in Chinese high finance or politics, but whichever way you look at it, that doesn't make any sense. By the way, a friend of yours was on Hydra's hit list.'

'What? Who was that, for heaven's sake?'

'Gerald Palstein.'

'What? Why would they want to get Gerald?'

'That's the easiest question to answer,' Norrington chipped in. 'When Palstein was shot, that meant that he had to pull out of the moon trip at short notice and make room for Hanna.'

'But how—'

'Later.' Jericho came closer. 'The most important thing for you to know right now is that the attack isn't aimed at Gaia.'

'It's not?' Julian asked. 'But you said—'

'I know. It looks like we made a mistake. In the meantime we've been able to decode more of the message, and it seems that the bomb isn't there to destroy your hotel.'

'But what, then?'

There was silence for a moment, as though everyone in the room was waiting for someone else to spill the beans.

'Peary Base,' Shaw said.

Julian stared at her, his mouth open. Jia looked as though the ground had opened up under his feet.

'Beijing would never plan—' he began.

'We're not certain that Beijing's behind it,' Shaw interrupted. 'At least, not Chinese government circles. But that's irrelevant right now. Hydra want to contaminate Peary Crater, the Mountains of Eternal Light, the whole region! They don't want anything from us, they just used us to get up to the Moon. Contact the base straight away, however you do it! They've got to search the place with a fine-toothed comb, and evacuate if need be.'

'Good God,' Julian whispered. 'Who are Hydra?'

'No idea. But whoever they are – they want to wipe America off the face of the Moon.'

'And Carl's headed there right now.' In an instant, it all became clear. He leapt to his feet and stared at Jia. 'He's going to arm the bomb. He'll arm it, and then clear out!'

They couldn't reach Peary Base with the Chinese satellite either, which made Orley even more frantic. They tried to reach Gaia, with no luck. Then the base again. Then Gaia again. Shortly after four o'clock, they gave up.

'It can't be anything to do with our satellite,' Jia argued. 'We could talk to London no problem.'

Orley looked at him. 'Are you thinking what I'm thinking?'

'That the bomb has already exploded, and that's why we can't reach anybody?' Jia rubbed his eyes. 'I'll admit, I had considered it.'

'It's horrific,' Orley whispered.

'But we heard that the satellites aren't the problem. It's the communications equipment. Peary Base and Gaia have been attacked; we haven't. Which means that we can communicate, just not with the hotel, and not with the Pole. Besides, a nuclear explosion—' Jia hesitated. 'Don't you think we'd have been told? My country keeps a very close eye on the Moon. I think your hotel must still be in one piece.'

'But the base is in the libration shadow, which means that your country can watch until they go blue in the face, they won't see anything!'

'Please be assured that China has nothing to do with it.'

'I don't understand.' Orley paced around the small control room. 'I simply don't understand. What's all this in aid of?'

Jia turned his head. 'When do you want to set off?'

'Now. I'll tell the others.' Orley paused. 'I am really very grateful, Commander. Very.'

'Keqiang,' Jia heard himself say.

Really? For a moment, he felt an urge to withdraw the offer, but he liked this easygoing, long-haired Englishman. Had he been too harsh in judging the relaxed Western ways? Maybe being on first-name terms was a step towards harmony among the nations.

'One thing's for sure, Keqiang,' Orley said with a sour grimace. 'There'd have been no Moon crisis if it had been down to us two.'

At that moment, they heard his name.

It droned from the loudspeakers, part of a looped message, an automatic broadcast signal.

'Callisto to Ganymede. Callisto to Julian Orley. Please come in. Julian Orley, Ganymede, please come in. Callisto to—'

Jia leapt up and raced to the console.

'Callisto? This is Jia Keqiang, commander of the Chinese mining operations. Where are you?'

For a second there was only crackling from the loudspeakers, then Nina Hedegaard's face appeared on the screen.

'We're flying over the Montes Jura,' she said. 'How come—'

'We're keeping our ears open. Are you looking for Julian Orley?'

'Yes.' She nodded emphatically. 'Yes!'

Julian shoved into view. 'Nina! Where are you?'

'Julian!' Suddenly Tim's face appeared next to hers. 'At last! Is everybody all right?'

'I'm afraid not.'

'But—' Tim was visibly distraught.

'That's to say, Amber's fine,' Julian reassured him hurriedly. 'What happened to Lynn? And Gaia? Tim, what's going on here?'

'We don't know. Lynn's – we're alive.'

'You're *alive*?'

'Gaia was destroyed.'

Julian stared at the screen, lost for words.

'There was a fire, several people died. We had to evacuate anyway, because of the bomb.'

The bomb—

'No, Tim.' He shook his head, and clenched his fists.

'Don't worry, we're safe. At the moon base. That's where we just flew from. There are two search parties out to—'

'Are you in touch with the base?'

'No, they're cut off from the outside world.'

'Tim—'

'Julian, I'm coming in to land,' Nina said. 'We'll be back at the Pole in an hour. Then we can—'

'Too late, that's too late!' he yelled. 'The bomb's not in Gaia. Do you hear? Gaia has nothing to do with all that. The bomb's stored at the Pole, it's meant for the moon base. Where's Lynn, Tim? *Where's Lynn?*'

Tim froze. His lips formed three silent words:

At the Pole.

'Don't tell me that!' Julian wrung his hands and looked about frantically. 'You have to get her out some—'

'Julian,' Nina said, 'the second search party set out after us, they're circling over the Mare Imbrium. As soon as we've picked you up, we'll climb until we can make contact and we'll send them straight back to the base. They're closer than we are.'

'Hurry! Carl's on his way to Peary. He's going to arm it!'

'We're on our way.'

Peary Base, North Pole

Dana Lawrence sat in the half-dark of the command centre in Igloo 1, breathing in pure oxygen through a mask, staring dead ahead. She'd had enough oxygen back in Gaia to see to the smoke inhalation, but a couple more breaths couldn't hurt.

'Don't you want to go get some sleep?' Wachowski asked sympathetically. The lights from the control panels and screens bathed his face in an anaemic blue-white glow. 'I'll wake you if anything happens.'

'Thanks, I'm fine.'

In fact she didn't feel tired at all. For as long as she could remember, all her strength had been focused on not falling asleep. In the sickbay, Kramp, Eva and the Nairs were lying comatose, exhausted. They were all under sedation, and tended by DeLucas, the station medic and life-support specialist. Even DeLucas, though, had no idea what Lynn needed. A young geologist called Jean-Jacques Laurie had suggested leaving her in the care of ISLAND-I, an older model than ISLAND-II. The programmed psychologist had diagnosed shock, to nobody's astonishment, along with a possible case of late-onset psychosomatic mutism. Since then, Julian's daughter had been either lying wide-eyed in the dark, or wandering about like a zombie, a prisoner in her own body. The Ögis were the only ones who were healthy and in full possession of their wits, and they had taken a room in one of the western towers. The base was short-staffed, all the survivors were out of action, the search parties had set off on their fool's errand, and Hanna would be trying to get back to the hotel. God knows she had done everything she could to make things easy for him, but Hanna wasn't coming. By now it was past four o'clock, and any confidence she had had that he would turn up was gone. The plan had been that they would carry out the operation together, but in this trade, you fought side by side with your comrade until circumstances demanded you sacrifice him. In two to three hours, the search parties would be back. By then, one of them *had* to have done the deed.

She got up.

'I'm going to stretch my legs. It'll help me stay awake.'

'We brew a pretty good coffee up here as well,' Wachowski said.

'I know. I've had four cups already.'

'I'll put on some more.'

'I've had enough smoke inside me to poison my system, thanks, I won't risk a caffeine overdose. I'll be next door in the fitness room if anything happens.'

'Dana?' Wachowski smiled, embarrassed.

'Yes?'

'I can call you Dana, can't I?'

Dana raised an eyebrow. 'Of course – Tommy.'

'Respect.'

'Oh.' She smiled again. 'Thank you.'

'I really mean it. You're keeping it all together! After everything that happened, Orley can be glad he has you. You're keeping a cool head.'

'Well, I try to.'

'His daughter's pretty much in a world of her own.'

'Hmm. ISLAND-I says she's suffering from shock.'

'Pretty severe shock. What's up with her? You know her better, Dana, what's her problem?'

Dana was silent for a moment.

'The same problem we all have,' she said as she left the room. 'She has her demons.'

Hanna

The freight train with the helium-3 tanks shot up the valley bed to Peary launch field at more than 700 kilometres per hour, but Hanna's thoughts were moving faster.

He had to arm the bomb, but before he did that, it would be best to make contact with Dana. He hadn't the first idea what might have happened at the hotel. All he knew for sure was that with his cover blown, they had a lot less room for manoeuvre. If he waited for her at the Pole, they could escape together, but he'd find himself an officially wanted man, by the time they boarded the OSS at the latest, and he could forget taking the elevator back down to Earth. The whole screw-up called for quick action. Set the fuse timer, then get out of there on the Charon. Xin's finely crafted plan could still work. Not exactly in all details, perhaps, but with the same results. It would be best if Dana were still safely tucked away in the Vallis Alpina, putting on a show of concern, and hoping that the Chinese could put her through to Earth under their treaty obligations for mutual assistance.

The high plain drew closer. He could see the blast walls around the spaceport, the hangars, antennae, the neat lines of human presence. He was pressed against the tank in front of him as the maglev slowed, much more sharply than the Lunar Express. For a moment he was afraid that he had misjudged things, that he would be crushed in the murderous deceleration, then the train slid round the last curve as gently as a Sunday excursion and drew to a halt at the station. Hanna jumped onto the platform before a manipulator arm could mistake him for a helium-3 tank, taking care to stay out of sight of the surveillance cameras. All around him the machinery awoke to life, forklifts rolled up, the arms began to unload. He scurried to the further edge of the platform and leapt the fifteen metres to the ground in a single bound. Two kilometres of rough ground stretched away ahead of him, broken only by the road from the spaceport to the igloos. They showed starkly against the hills beyond and the factory buildings around, flanked on either side by the towers of the residential quarters and, in amongst them, a seemingly random assortment of warehouses and huts. Some distance away, a vast structure reared out of the stony surge of a hillside, the shell of the helium-3 power station, under construction.

Hanna loped away at an even, unhurried pace, keeping off the road and in the shelter of the slopes for as long as he could see the base to his right. Soon enough there'd be another sun shining here, only briefly but so blazing bright, and it would change everything. The landscape around. The course of history.

Lawrence

She went up to the top level of Igloo 1 in the lift, then took the connecting walkway between the two domes. Beneath her the road ran off to the factories behind. There were a few small windows here, with views out to the edge of the crater, the industrial plant and the spaceport. The sun cast a panorama of shadow like a painting by Giorgio de Chirico, but Dana had no eyes for the surreal beauty of the landscape under the billions of stars. Intent on her task, she crossed to Igloo 2 and took the lift down to the lounge, where she put on the armoured plates and backpack of her spacesuit. She picked up her helmet and then took the lift on down, past the fitness studios and the sickbay, through a layer of rock into the winding labyrinthine caves and pathways of the underground level. She had memorised every detail of Peary Base from Thorn's maps and descriptions, so that without ever having been here before, she knew what lay ahead of her, knew which way to turn once the lift doors glided apart.

She stepped out onto a seabed.

At least that was how it looked. The glass walls of fishtanks stretched up, metres high, all around her. Flickering pools of light chased one another like will-o-the-wisps across the floor, reflected from the water when the ruffled surface was stirred up by salmon and trout and perch as they darted about, by the schools of fish flitting back and forth. A little while later the cave divided, most branches leading off into the darkness, only a few passages shimmering with blue-green or white light, and beyond them the greenhouses, the genetic laboratories and production facilities which kept the moon base stocked with fruit and vegetables. She crossed a passageway, walked along a short corridor and emerged into a vast, almost round stone hall. She could have taken a lift down here directly from Igloo 1, but Wachowski had to believe that she was in the fitness studio. Her eyes swept around the place, looking for cameras.

There hadn't been any here back in Thorn's day, nor could she see any now. Even if there was any such thing down here, Wachowski would have enough on his hands – short-staffed as the moon base was – watching the external cameras. The fishtanks and kitchen gardens were the last thing that he would be looking at.

Several passageways led off from the hall, leading to the laboratories, storehouses and residential blocks. Only one passage had an airlock, that gave onto hundreds of kilometres of unexplored caves, unused, branching endlessly in the vacuum. Most of the lava tubes petered out in the cliff-like rim of Peary Crater, while others burrowed downward, some of them opening out into the canyon fault that ran through the whole site. She put on her helmet, stepped into the airlock and pumped out the air. After a minute, the outer door opened. She switched on her helmet lamp and went into an unhewn rocky passageway which led her onward into the darkness, black as night. The torchbeam skittered nervously over vitrified basalt. After about a hundred metres, she saw a gap open up in the wall to her left, just as Hanna had said. It was narrow, unnervingly so. She squirmed through, pulled her shoulders in, got down on all fours when the roof suddenly dipped down towards her, and crawled through the last part of the cleft on her belly. It had almost become too narrow to bear when the walls suddenly swept apart and she could see a pile of rubble that had obviously been heaped up by the hand of man; she stretched out both hands and moved the rocks aside.

She could see something low, flat and shimmering. Something with a blinking display, and an arming panel.

Hanna had positioned it neatly, she had to admit.

All of a sudden she realised that her cloud had a silver lining here. If all had gone according to plan, the package would have reached the base of the canyon under its own power, and lain there undisturbed until the last day of the trip. Only then, during the official visit to the base just before they all returned to the OSS, would Hanna have left the group, retrieved the contents and taken the bomb up into the caves. Charon would have left the Moon that same evening, and then the payload would have blown twenty-four hours later. But the package's mechanisms had failed, so Hanna had had to take the contents up to the base ahead of schedule, to hide the mini-nuke here in the bowels of the caves. In hindsight, since his cover had been blown and everything thrown into disarray, it was a blessing that he had been forced to do that.

She opened the catch, lifted the cover to the keypad, and hesitated.

When should she set the detonator for? By now everybody knew that there was an attack planned. They still believed that it was aimed at Gaia, and she had done all she could to encourage that. But perhaps the search parties up on Aristarchus might realise what was going on. What if they came back, knowing that the base itself was in danger, and then started to search here at the Pole?

She mustn't give them enough time to find the bomb.

A short fuse, then.

Dana shivered. Better if she wasn't vaporised by the nuclear blast herself. Right now, her fingers were hovering over the control panel of a miracle of destructive technology which could turn Peary Crater into one of the circles of hell, sweeping away every trace of human presence as though it had never been. A good idea then to be as far away as possible, but when would the search parties return, when would the Charon set off? The safe option to make sure that she survived would be to set the detonator at twenty-four hours. But what if the communications jam failed prematurely, and they learned that the mini-nuke really was here at the Pole?

There was no way they could find that out.

But they could. The very fact that they knew that the bomb existed at all proved that they could find out anything. Callisto must have reached the Aristarchus Plateau by now. If they had found any survivors, then she could expect them back soon. If not, then they would keep searching for who knew how long. She couldn't decide based on what she thought the shuttles might do. She had to arm this bomb, hijack the Charon and then fly to OSS. She'd have a lot of explaining to do once she got there; why she had flown off without the others, why she had flown off at all, how she could have known about the bomb. Especially if there were any survivors, who could bring all her carefully placed lies tumbling down.

But she would have to deal with that when it happened. She had been trained to deal with that sort of thing.

Her fingers twitched, indecisive.

Then she punched in a timecode, piled the rocks up in front of the bomb again and squirmed hastily backwards. The inferno was set. Time to get out of here.

Igloo 1

Wachowski was visibly startled.

'What are you doing here?'

Lynn looked down at him, mildly surprised to see herself in his eyes as he so clearly saw her, a pale phantom with wild hair, looming up silently as though driven into the room by a gust of wind, an apparition: Lady Madeline Usher, Elsa Lanchester as the Bride of Frankenstein, the very image of a B-movie. Quite astonishing, how clearly she could see all these pictures shining out in the darkness of her thoughts, now that her sanity had fled the scene – although it had obviously left a breadcrumb trail to guide the little girl lost back into the waking world.

Follow your thoughts, astral voices whispered to her. Go into the light, into the light, star-child, they muttered, higher intelligences without need of physical bodies but with a twisted sense of humour, who lured unsuspecting astronauts into monoliths, dumping them into bad copies of Louis XIV bedrooms, just as had happened to poor Bowman, who—

Bowman? Lady Madeline?

This is my mind, she screamed. My mind, Julian!

And her scream, that brave little scream, set out, bold little fellow, dragged itself the whole long way out to the event horizon, then lost its strength, lost its courage, tottered over backwards and died.

'Are you all right?'

Wachowski cocked his head. Interesting. The way the snaking arteries at his temples busily pumped blood showed he was on edge, alert. Lynn could see the tiny submarines sailing through the flow.

'I didn't hear you come in.'

Submarines in the blood. Dennis Quaid in *Innerspace*. No. Raquel Welch and Donald Pleasence, *Fantastic Voyage*. The o-o-o-o-riginal!

Oh, yes. Sorry, Daddy.

She was contaminated ground. Poisoned by Julian. No mistake, there he was, teasing her, making a fool of her with his movie mania. Whenever she thought she had reached her real self, there she was in one of *his* worlds, Alice in Orley-Land, eternal heroine in *his* invention, *his* original creation.

You're mad, Lynn, she thought. You've ended up like Crystal. First depressive, then mad.

Or had Julian written *this* role for her as well?

His flashing eyes, his floating hands, whenever he took her and Tim into his private cinema, where they had to watch every metre of celluloid or digital drama that ever a science-fiction author or director had dreamed up: Georges Méliès' *Le voyage dans la lune*, Fritz Lang's *Girl in the Moon*, Nathan Juran's *First Men in the Moon*, *This Island Earth* with Jeff Morrow and Faith Domergue and the mutant – oh my word, that mutant! – *Star Trek*, *The Man Who Fell to Earth*, *2001: A Space Odyssey*, *Star Wars*, *Alien*, *Independence Day*, *War of the Worlds*, *Perry Rhodan* with Finn O'Keefe, hey, Finn O'Keefe, wasn't he somewhere hereabouts, and always – fanfare! – Lynn Orley, the lead role in—

'You really gave me a shock.'

Wachowski. All alone in the twilit control room, surrounded by screens and consoles. Shouldn't make such a fuss, the bastard. He looked a fright himself.

'That's good,' Lynn whispered.

She leaned down to him, put her hand to the back of his neck and pressed her lips to his. Mm-hm, warm, that was good. She was Grace Kelly. Wasn't she? And he—

'Miss Orley, Lynn—' Cary Grant stiffened.

Sorry, is this the right set for *To Catch a Thief*?

Funny. That wasn't even a science-fiction film. Julian liked it, though.

Click, hssss, verify.

You lost the hotel.

Another of those lit-up signposts. What was she doing here? What the hell was she doing in the control room, with her nose full of Wachowski's greasy smell? She pushed him away, started back and wiped her lips in disgust.

'Are you okay?' he whispered, in fascinated horror.

'Never better!' she snarled at him. 'Do you have anything to drink?'

He jumped to his feet, nodding.

Glug, glug, and her thoughts were draining away once more, whirled down the plug. When he put the glass of water in her hand, she couldn't even remember having asked for it.

Hanna

He had given the residential towers a wide berth, trudging past them in an arc along the edge of the chasm. The canyon was a collapsed lava channel, and not all of its walls were sheer drops; rather they formed staircases and steps, so that Hanna could make his way down easily. To the west, the canyon opened out into a steep valley that cut through Peary Crater's flank, while to his right, towards the base, the chasm grew narrower. Standing on its floor, Hanna could just about see the tops of two residential towers, shining in the sunlight, and two bridges, not far apart, that spanned the canyon above. It was dark down here, and the canyon floor was strewn with rubble. He picked his way through under the first bridge, following a groove in the rock that led him like a path over the gently sloping ground, as far as the second bridge. Then he twisted to look upwards.

About ten metres above him, a hole yawned in the cliff-face.

Several such holes dotted the rock where lava tubes opened up into the canyon, but this one in particular interested him. He clambered up, reached the opening, then switched on his helmet lamp and made his way into the twisting cave. The cave mouth was steep for a moment, and then levelled off. His headlamp caught the ragged gap through to where the bomb lay slumbering. For a moment he considered skipping the visit to the control room and programming the thing straight away, but he had to speak to Dana first. A lot could have happened in the past few hours that would force them to make a whole new plan, and on top of that he urgently needed information to help him see where he stood personally. If all was going according to plan, the laser link between the base and Gaia would be functioning, but Dana would have fixed it so that all signals went straight through to her mobile phone.

He ignored the crack and went to the airlock instead, stepped into it. There was light coming through the tiny viewport. On the other side of the airlock was the room they called the Great Hall, a large natural cave leading off to the laboratories, greenhouses and fishtanks. A lift from the Hall up to Igloo 1 led straight to the control room. Hanna glanced at his watch. Almost half past four. Could be that the control room wasn't even occupied. Nevertheless he drew his gun as he went into the Hall, scanned all around for threats and then tapped the sensor that would bring the lift down.

Lawrence

She was determined not to spend a second longer in the base than she had to. She'd glanced through the sickbay door in Igloo 2, heard the roomful of snoring sleepers like an orchestra playing softly, with Mukesh Nair taking the solo lead as far as she could tell. Minnie DeLucas, an African-American woman with dreadlocks, was working at a computer.

'How are they?' Dana asked, concern in her voice.

'They're as well as they can be.' The medic put a finger to her lips and glanced over to the beds. 'The smoke inhalation isn't so bad, but the tall German lady seems pretty traumatised, I'd say. She was telling me what happened in the lift-shafts at the hotel. How she couldn't save that woman.'

'Yes,' Dana whispered. 'We saw some dreadful things. How is Miss Orley, though?'

'I would have had to strap her down to keep her here.'

'She's gone then?'

'Wandering around somewhere. She can't sleep, or doesn't want to. I think she went over to Tommy in the control room. And you? Are you coping?'

'Oh yes. I've breathed in so much oxygen these past few hours that I don't think the smoke inhalation can touch me.'

'I mean mentally.'

'I cope.' She shrugged her shoulders. 'I try my best to do without mental traumas, I find they're something of a luxury.'

'You should see a psychologist, in any case,' DeLucas advised.

'Of course.'

'I'm serious, Dana. Don't try burying it. There's no shame in asking for help.'

'What makes you think I might be ashamed?'

'You just give the impression that you—' DeLucas hesitated. 'That you're very hard on yourself. Yourself, and others.'

'Oh.' Dana raised her eyebrows, interested. 'Do I?'

'There's nothing wrong with putting yourself on the couch,' DeLucas smiled.

'Oh, there are some people who reckon I belong on the couch.' She winked confidingly. 'See you later. I'm going to run for a bit.'

Igloo 1

In a lucid interval, Lynn had sought out the control room's coffee nook to put down her empty glass. It was a small space, half screened off from the rest of the room by a sheet of sand-blasted glass. Something inside her said that it was important to put things back where they belonged, after she'd spent weeks and months torturing herself with wild terrors, visions of destruction. Gaia was in ruins. She had wrecked it so often in her dreams that she felt a gnawing suspicion that she truly had destroyed it herself, but she wasn't really sure.

At the very moment that she put the glass down, suddenly all the pieces fell into place, and she remembered.

The rescue mission up on the crown of Gaia's head. Miranda's death.

She tried to cry. Turned down the corners of her mouth. Made a tearful face. But her tear ducts wouldn't do their job, and until she could cry she would wander onward through the maze of her own soul, without hope of redemption. Undecided, she was staring dumbly at the glass when she heard the lift humming.

Somebody was coming up here.

Her face twisted into a mask of rage. She didn't want anybody up here. She didn't want Tommy Wachowski anywhere near her. He'd kissed her, the pig! Hadn't he? How could he do a thing like that? As though she were some cheap tart! A slut in a spacesuit. There for anyone to fuck, a toy, an avatar, a plaything for other people's fantasies!

You can all go fuck yourselves, she thought.

Fuck you, Julian!

She leaned back a little, so that she could see past the edge of the frosted glass – and into the control room. The lift-shaft passed through the middle of the igloo like an axis. Somebody in a spacesuit came out of the lift, helmet in one hand, gun in the other. It was quite obviously a gun, since he was pointing it at Wachowski, who jumped up and scurried backwards in surprise.

'Who else is here?' the new arrival asked in a low voice.

'Nobody.'

'Are you sure?'

Wachowski somehow managed not to glance towards the coffee nook.

'Just me,' he said hoarsely.

'Anybody who might turn up anytime soon?'

Wachowski hesitated. He had been left as base commander. He hunched a little. He seemed to be considering whether to attack the other man, who was much bigger than him. Lynn was staring, paralysed, at the shaven back of the big man's head, unable to move even a finger or turn away her gaze.

Carl Hanna!

'You never know who may just turn up,' Wachowski said, playing for time. 'It wouldn't be too smart to—'

There was a soft pop. The base commander dropped to the ground and didn't move.

Hanna turned round.

Nothing. Just the big, softly lit space of the control room. Deserted, save for the dead man at his feet.

Hanna put his helmet down on the console, kept his gun at the ready and walked once around the lift-shaft. None of the other workstations was occupied. Faint light glowed from behind a frosted-glass screen, where he could see part of a shelf, full of packs of coffee, filters and mugs.

He stopped dead, moved closer.

He heard a faint shuffling sound from where he had shot the other man. He spun around in an instant, trained the gun on the motionless body and then dropped the muzzle at the same moment when he realised that the man was dead as dead could be. It had just been his arm, slipping down to the side. He holstered his weapon and leaned over the console, studying its controls. His fingers scurried over the touchscreen, called up a connection with Gaia – or what ought to have been a connection, but there was no answer.

He tried again. The channel was dead.

What was happening over there?

'Dana, dammit,' he hissed. 'Pick up.'

After he had tried one more time, it slowly dawned on him that it couldn't be Dana's fault. The computer was telling him that no connection could be made. In other words, there was no connection through to the hotel, even by laser link.

Gaia wasn't answering.

Lynn huddled against the sink, clenched like a fist, making herself smaller and smaller, pressing her face between her knees. She had overcome her paralysis at the last moment and pulled her head back in a flash – oh, the things you can do, thought little girl lost jubilantly, following the glowing trail of crumbs, amazed at her own miraculous reflexes, while the grown-up woman, the body she lived in, cramped up with tension and her lungs began to ache from holding her breath.

Another chasm yawned in her thoughts. That was Carl Hanna, the guy who would rather have been a pop star. Hanna, maybe a little stand-offish, but pleasant enough for all that, popular with all, the man she'd chatted to one late evening in Gaia, the man whose muscular body she'd imagined – just for a moment – on hers, his strong hands passing skilfully across her, if only she could work up the nerve to drag him off to her suite. That hideous suite, oh hell, where the mirror held a hysteric, a notorious madwoman who gulped down green tablets, that was why she didn't like to spend time in that suite. Hanna had been cool and collected, and she had reined herself in, and after that there were a few chapters missing in the chronology, things were mixed up. Somebody had said that Hanna was a bad guy, that he wanted to blow up her hotel. Just a few words had turned her world topsyturvy, and now the same nice guy she'd been flirting with in the Mama Quilla Club had shot poor Tommy Wachowski, and all of a sudden she felt a horror of his muscular body and his skilled hands. Fear bathed her brain in ice-water, so that for a moment she could think clearly again, at least enough to know that she mustn't move a muscle, mustn't surrender to the urge to whimper helplessly and whistle the songs of a little girl lost, because if she did, the man who'd been calling himself Carl Hanna would kill her too.

She held her breath and listened, heard him curse, heard every word he spoke, heard his secrets.

Hanna

Change of plan. Dana was no longer a factor. Whatever had happened to her, he had to go on without her.

Those were the rules.

Hanna swung the dead man over his shoulders like a sack of Christmas toys and went back down to the Great Hall, dragged him out into the airlock and watched his face distend in the vacuum. Then he pulled Wachowski into the cave beyond and didn't spare him another thought. He ran to the cleft, squirmed in, got down on his hands and knees and slithered along like a snake until the passage opened out again and the familiar pile of rubble appeared in the torchlight. He shovelled the stones aside with both hands, opened up the control panel on the mini-nuke, lifted the cover—

And froze.

The detonator had been programmed.

For a moment, there was a vacuum in his mind. He refused to believe what he saw, but there was no doubt, somebody had activated the bomb. And that somebody could only be—

Dana Lawrence.

She was here! No, she was gone. As good as gone. If Dana Lawrence didn't want to risk being vaporised on the slopes of Peary Crater, she had to be leaving the base on board the Charon, probably at this very moment. Which meant—

He scrambled hastily backwards out of the tunnel, stood up too soon, bashed his helmet on the roof, found his way out, and then ran along to the rift, following the bobbing light from his headlamp. He leapt down to the canyon floor, stumbled along the grooved path, climbed the cliff wall by the first bridge and heaved himself over the edge. He loped along the road in long strides, past the residential towers, hurrying over the dusty regolith.

Igloo 2

Minnie DeLucas glided her fingers over the touchscreen and completed a set of four bases.

She had always argued that it would be possible to raise moon calves in the catacombs of Peary Base. Chickens could barely survive in the extremes of zero-g, but they did well enough in one-sixth of Earth gravity, laying eggs that dropped neatly to the floor of their hutches. They also made a pretty good lunar chicken burger. So why shouldn't calves and lambs thrive at the Pole? Maybe even pigs, although the whole problem with the smell meant opening up some of the more distant caves. As a scientist, DeLucas was used to tackling problems from the practical and the theoretical side, and since there was no livestock to be had, she was busy experimenting with the genomes. Watching other people sleep wasn't exactly a challenge. As long as none of them fell out of bed, she could work undisturbed. Right now she had loaded data from some experiments with Galloway cattle embryos to the sickbay computer, and was so busy with the results that at first she didn't realise someone was talking to her.

'Peary, please come in. Io to Peary. This is Kyra Gore. Wachowski, why aren't you picking up?'

DeLucas looked at the clock: ten to five. Io was back within radio range. They'd got back surprisingly quickly, but why were they calling her?

'Minnie here,' she said.

'Hey, what's up?' Gore asked urgently. 'Where's Tommy kicking his heels?'

'No idea. Perhaps he's gone to the little boys' room.'

'Tommy wouldn't go pee without taking his radio with him.'

'He's not been by to talk to me. Where are—'

'We'll be with you in five minutes! Listen, Minnie, you've got to get the people out of there! Get out of the base! Bring them all to the landing field.'

'What? Why?'

'The bomb's *in the base*.'

'In the base?'

'It's been hidden somewhere under our noses! The guy who's going to prime it is on his way to you. Get everybody into their spacesuits and bring them outside. And go look for Tommy.'

The Landing Field

Dana had switched her transceiver to pick up all frequencies, so that she heard Io's call as she went through the gate to the spaceport.

She stopped dead. What the hell were they doing back here already? At the very most, she'd have expected Tommy Wachowski to radio her to ask what she was up to, since she'd made no effort to stay out of sight as she dashed to the landing field, but now Io was coming in to land. And to make it even worse:

They knew about the bomb!

Now she really did have just a matter of minutes.

Dana began to run.

DeLucas

Fighting to remain calm, Minnie ran next door and shook the German women awake, then the Indian couple. Which wasn't so easy, as she found out. Certainly Mukesh Nair started up from his sleep with one last trumpeting blast of snores, and Karla Kramp sat up straight, blinking curiously, but Eva Borelius and Sushma Nair both lay there as though in an enchanted slumber.

'What's going on?' asked Kramp.

'You'll have to get dressed,' DeLucas said, her eyes skittering about. 'Everyone into their spacesuits. We're leaving the base.'

'Aha,' said Kramp. 'And why are we doing that?'

'It's a – precaution.'

'Against?'

'Sushma?' Mukesh Nair was struggling visibly against the sedatives, and it looked as if he was losing. 'Sushma, my love! Get up.'

'I just want to know what's going on,' Kramp said, but she was obediently gathering her belongings as she spoke.

'So do I,' DeLucas said as she hurried out. 'You just make sure that everyone here is ready to leave in five minutes.'

Instead of taking the lift, she ran up the stairs to the top floor, looked in the lounge, then sprang back down the steps and checked the fitness studio. Hadn't Dana said that she would be running? And where was Tommy lurking? Where was Lynn Orley? Her uneventful vigil had suddenly turned into herding cats. DeLucas dashed back up to the top floor, hurried along the passageway to Igloo 1, and went into the control room. It was lit only by the dim glow of computer screens, and seemed deserted.

'Tommy?' she called.

There was nobody here. The only noise in the room was the machines chattering away to one another, a faint humming of transistors and ventilation, whirring, clicking, beeping. She walked quickly around the room, looking at every screen in the hope that she might spot Wachowski, but he was nowhere to be seen. As she left she heard a new sound, a noise she couldn't quite recognise, a soft, high squeak. She paused on the threshold, hesitant, filled with dread, then turned around.

What was that?

Now she couldn't hear it.

Just as she was about to turn away again, she heard it once more. Not a squeak, more like a whimper. It was coming from somewhere towards the far end of the room, and it was creepy. Her heart beat faster as she went back into the control room and circled the lift-shaft. Halfway round, it was closer, much closer, a thin, unhappy sound coming from the small recessed space of the coffee nook.

DeLucas drew a deep breath and looked inside.

Lynn Orley was squatting in front of the sink, her arms wrapped tightly around herself, making those forlorn sounds.

DeLucas squatted level with her.

'Miss Orley.'

No reaction. The woman simply looked straight through her as though she wasn't there. DeLucas hesitated, put out her hand and touched her shoulder gently.

She might just as well have pulled the ring on a hand grenade.

The Landing Field

Dana cursed. Why did the landing module have to be right at the other end of the spaceport? Every second that passed lessened her chances of being able to clear out of here.

She had to think of some alternatives.

What if she—

'Wait.'

Someone grabbed her upper arm.

Dana leapt to one side, turning. She saw a tall, well-built astronaut, barely recognisable behind his mirrored faceplate, but his height and voice left her in no doubt. She immediately switched to a secure channel.

'Where were you?' she hissed.

'You set the timer,' Hanna stated, without answering her question. 'Did you want to leave without me?'

'You weren't there.'

'Now I'm here. Come along.'

He started moving. Dana followed, just as the bulky shape of the Io came into sight on the other side of the blast walls. The next moment the shuttle was hanging over the landing field, dropping, its engines pumping, blocking their way.

Hanna stopped dead, reached for his thigh, drew his gun.

'Forget it,' Dana whispered.

Io settled down, bouncing slightly, and the lift-shaft extended from its belly. There were two of them, facing Leland Palmer's troupe of five astronauts in peak physical condition and with excellent reflexes, admittedly unarmed but fast and with close-combat training. It might just be possible to take them down in a skirmish, but whatever happened, Dana's cover would be blown, and she couldn't allow that at any cost.

That made up her mind.

She switched back to the general-broadcast channel, and unclipped the little pick-axe from its place on her suit. Everyone had one for emergencies. Hanna had spread his legs, taking up position, aiming. The airlock cabin travelled down the shaft to the landing pad. The doors opened. Astronauts emerged. She saw the pistol muzzle track upwards, and she lifted the pick-axe over her head—

And brought it smashing down.

The point of the pick stabbed through the tough material of the suit and into the back of Hanna's hand, deep in between the bones and sinews. The Canadian groaned in pain. He spun about and struck out at Dana, knocking her off her feet.

'Help!' she yelled. 'Help!'

There was a hubbub of voices. Incomprehensibly, Hanna was still holding his gun, the fingers of his left hand clenched over the hole in his spacesuit, and was aiming at Dana. She rolled, kicked out at his knee and made him stagger. The next moment, she had sprung to her feet and swung the pick again. This time the needle-sharp end hit Hanna's face-plate and made a tiny hole in the armoured glass. He leapt backwards and kicked her in the belly. The pick-axe was torn from her grasp and stayed where it was, lodged in his visor. She flew away and landed a few metres off, scrambling to her feet. Part of her chestplate splintered off, and she knew he had shot at her. The crew of Io were running towards them across the landing field in huge lunar leaps.

She had to finish this. Whatever happened, the astronauts mustn't take Hanna alive. She hurled herself at him with a great jump, knocked him to the ground and grabbed hold of the pick-handle that jutted from his faceplate.

For a ghastly moment she thought that she could see his eyes, despite the mirrored glass.

'Dana,' he whispered.

She wrenched at the pick and tore it free. Shards broke loose from the visor. Hanna dropped his gun and lifted both hands, but the air left his suit far faster than he could put his hands to his helmet. He lay there with his arms raised as though embracing a woman she could not see. Dana felt for his gun and slipped it into a pocket on her thigh – nobody could have seen her do it – then toppled ostentatiously to one side and called for help.

People hurried towards her. They helped her up. Gabbled at her.

'Hanna,' she gasped. 'It's Hanna. He – I think he was planning to escape with the Charon.'

'Did he say anything?' Palmer asked urgently. 'Did he say anything about the bomb?'

'He—' Whatever you do, don't seem too unruffled, Dana! Best to make a drama of the situation, so she staggered exaggeratedly, letting the others catch her. 'I was outside. I saw him running from the base towards the spaceport. First I thought it was Wachowski, but from his size it could – it could only be Hanna—' She shook off the hands supporting her, took several deep breaths. 'Then I ran after him, called him on the radio. He ran out onto the landing field—'

'Did he say anything?'

'Yes, when – when I caught up with him. I was trying to stop him, and he shouted that this whole place was about to blow up, and – that's when he attacked me. He just jumped at me, he was going to kill me, what could I have done?'

'Shit!' Palmer cursed.

'I had to defend myself,' Dana wailed, putting a note of hysteria into her voice. Kyra Gore took her by the shoulders.

'You did good, Miss Lawrence, what you did was incredibly brave.'

'Yes, it was,' Palmer said, pacing back and forth for a moment, then he stopped dead and clenched his fists. 'Crap! Damn the guy! He's dead now, the bastard. What are we going to do? *What are we going to do?*'

Igloo 1

DeLucas felt carefully at her face. Glistening crimson liquid slicked her fingertips. Blood. Her blood.

The woman was mad!

Lynn Orley had unfolded like a flick-knife and launched herself at her, swiping her fingernails across DeLucas' face and slicing her cheek open, then tried to run out of the control room. She had chased after the fleeing woman, grabbed hold of her and shoved her up against the lift-shaft.

'Miss Orley, stop it! It's me. Minnie!'

Then all of a sudden shouts for help were coming over the loudspeakers, snatches of words, Dana Lawrence, Palmer's voice.

Lynn tore free, swung an arm and hit DeLucas on the nose so hard that for a moment all she saw was a red haze. When she could see clearly again, Lynn was just leaving the control room. Her head pounding, DeLucas ran after her, caught hold again and clutched her tight, doing what she could to dodge the rain of blows from her fists. Lynn stumbled against Wachowski's empty chair, looked at the lift-shaft and started backwards, her eyes wide.

'Everything's okay,' DeLucas said, coughing. 'Everything's okay.'

Lynn's lips opened. Her eyes darted from her to the lift-shaft, and back again.

'Can you understand me? Miss Orley? We have to get out of here.'

Cautiously, she stretched out her right hand.

Lynn scurried backwards.

'You have to come with me,' DeLucas said firmly, even as she felt a thick trickle of something warm running down her upper lip. She put her tongue out, automatically, and licked at it. 'Come next door. Put on your spacesuit.'

All at once, there was sanity and comprehension in Lynn's eyes. She moved her lips again and put out a trembling finger.

'That's where he came from,' she rasped.

DeLucas followed her gesture. The woman was obviously acutely frightened of the lift-shaft, or more exactly of someone who had come out of it.

'Who?' she asked. 'Wachowski?'

Lynn shook her head. DeLucas felt a cold fear grip her.

'Who, Lynn? Who came out?'

'He just shot him,' Lynn whispered. 'Just like that. He could have shot me too.' She began to hum a tune.

'Who, Lynn? Who shot who?'

'Minnie? Tommy!' Palmer's voice from the loudspeakers. 'Please come in, we have a problem.'

Lynn stopped humming and stared at DeLucas.

'What do you want from me anyway, you silly cow?' she snapped.

The Landing Field

'Leland, I'm having trouble with Lynn Orley.'

'Oh great, that too! What about the rest of them?'

'They must be ready by now.'

'Then get them out of there, Minnie!' Palmer paced up and down impatiently, with Hanna's corpse at his feet. 'What are you waiting for?'

'Something seems to have happened to Tommy,' DeLucas said. 'Lynn claims that somebody appeared in the control room and shot some other person, she's scared out of her wits and—'

'Hanna,' Palmer snarled.

'I think she's been trying to tell me that Tommy's been shot. But he's not here, nor is anybody else.'

'Crap,' murmured Gore.

'We have to make a decision,' Palmer said. 'Dana's managed to stop Hanna from escaping. She had to kill him to do it, but before that he said—'

'I caught what he said,' DeLucas interrupted. 'That this place is about to blow.'

'So stop jabbering,' Dana spat at her. 'Will you kindly ensure that my guests are evacuated!'

'I can't be everywhere at once,' DeLucas snapped back. 'Tell her—'

'Listen, Minnie, I'm not going to give up the base as easily as that, but she's right, you have to get those people out of there.'

Palmer stopped dead and gazed upwards at the shimmering oceans of stars, fading out over to the east where the sun glowed low on the horizon. He simply couldn't imagine that all this might end.

'Could be we still have time,' he said. 'Hanna must have given himself long enough to get away.'

'He was in a hell of a hurry,' Dana remarked.

'Whatever. We'll search the area while Kyra flies the guests to a safe distance on the Io.'

'And where should I fly them to?' Gore asked.

'Take them to meet Callisto. Tell her to turn round right away. You should be in radio contact as soon as you're up there. Then go back to the Chinese base.'

'That's madness,' Dana said. 'Forget it. How do you expect to find a bomb on a huge installation like this?'

'We'll look for it.'

'Sheer idiocy! All you're doing is putting your people in danger.'

'You'll be flying with the Io anyway.' Palmer paid her no further attention, and turned to his crew. 'Does anybody else want to fly with them? You have a free choice – we're not the army here. I'm going to look for the thing. The bastard must have given himself at least half an hour!'

Dana spread her arms to concede defeat.

'Leland?' Minnie DeLucas. 'If what Lynn was telling me is true, maybe Hanna came up from underground. From the Great Hall.'

'Good.' Palmer nodded grimly. 'Let's start there.'

London, Great Britain

Had his suspicion been right, or did *MoonLight* really just mean 'Moon-Light'? There was uproar and disagreement in the Big O. The Moon was still besieged by the bot army, with no end in sight. No contact with Peary Base or Gaia. Merrick was hurrying, burrowing, scurrying from satellites to ground stations, but getting nowhere.

Meanwhile the MI6 delegation were in a feeding frenzy over the theory that China might be behind the attack. It was a beautiful theory, it fit everything so neatly, temptingly. Gaia, well indeed, why would China have Gaia in their sights, but Peary Base – if that were destroyed, a substantial part of America's lunar infrastructure would be knocked out. Not an attack on Orley, but on Washington's supremacy. Knock the enemy off his feet. Weaken the American helium-3 industry. It *had* to be China! Beijing, or Zheng, or both of them.

The CIA had barely joined the list of potential suspects than it was off again.

'Whatever the truth of it,' Shaw said, 'we've reached a whole new level of helplessness.'

'Oh, great,' said Yoyo.

Security departments at Orley subsidiaries worldwide were reporting back to the London situation room, but there were no concrete leads on further attacks. Norrington insisted that the corporation had to take every conceivable precaution. He hadn't come up with any more information on Thorn. A photograph of Kenny Xin had been distributed which his own mother wouldn't have recognised. A shuttle had set out from the OSS to the Moon, but it would take more than two days to reach Peary Base.

'Norrington looks nervous to me,' Jericho said. 'Don't you think so?'

'Yes, he's fighting on too many fronts, opening up one campaign after another.' Yoyo got to her feet. 'If he carries on like this, he'll bring the whole operation to a grinding halt.'

Just a few minutes ago, another crisis meeting with MI5 had broken up, since the agencies now reckoned that domestic security was threatened. There wasn't even a pause to draw breath. One discussion led straight into the next. The air twanged with the buzz of ideas, urgent purpose and determination. But there was an undertone too, a feeling that all this to-do was deluded, based on the belief that being there and acting busy would lead to answers.

'So why's he doing that?' Jericho mused, following Yoyo outside. 'Is he so worried?'

'You don't even believe that yourself. Norrington's not an idiot.'

'Of course I don't believe it. He wants to put a spanner in the works.' Jericho looked around. Nobody was paying any attention to them. Norrington was making phone calls in his room, and Shaw was doing the same in hers. 'I just haven't the first idea who we should trust to talk to about him.'

'You mean that they could all be in it together?'

'How would we know?'

'Hmm.' Yoyo looked across at Shaw's open office door, dubious. 'She doesn't exactly look like a mole.'

'Nobody looks like a mole, apart from moles.'

'Also true.' She fell silent for a while. 'Good. Let's break in.'

'Break in? Where?'

'The central computer. The drives we aren't authorised for. Norrington's patch.'

Jericho stared at her. Somebody scurried past them, talking urgently into a phone. Yoyo waited until he was out of earshot, and dropped her voice in a conspiratorial fashion. 'Simple enough, isn't it? If you know your enemies and know yourself, you will not be imperilled in a hundred battles; if you know yourself but do not know your enemy, then for every victory you gain you will suffer a defeat.'

'Is that yours?'

'Sun Tzu, *Art of War*. Written two and a half thousand years ago, and every word is as true as the day it was written. You want to know who's pulling the strings? I'll tell you what we'll do, then. Your charming friend Diane will fish for Norrington's password, and we'll have a look around his parlour.'

'You're pulling my leg! How is she going to do that?'

'Why are you asking me?' Yoyo raised her eyebrows, all innocence. 'I thought you were the cyber-detective.'

'And you're the cyber-dissident.'

'True,' she said, unruffled. 'I'm better than you.'

'How's that?' he asked, stung.

'Aren't I? Stop moaning, then, and give me some ideas.'

Jericho glanced around. There was still no one paying them any attention. He might just as well have gone off to sleep somewhere, popping up every couple of hours with more ominous news to set them all scurrying.

'Right then,' he hissed. 'We only have one chance, if that.'

'We'll do it, whatever it is.'

Twelve minutes later Norrington left his glassed-in cubicle and joined one of the working groups, which was busy making telescopic observations of the Moon. He talked to them about this and that, and then went to fetch a coffee. Then he went to see Shaw in her office, briefly, and went back to work at his own desk.

Access denied, said the computer.

Baffled, he clicked on the file again, with the same result. It was only then that he realised he wasn't logged on.

But he hadn't logged out when he left the room.

Or had he?

He glanced around the control room. Everybody was looking busy, except for the Chinese girl, who was standing not far from one of the workstations as though she didn't know where to go.

Norrington felt a gnawing doubt. Uneasy, he restarted the system to log himself in.

Yoyo watched him out of the corner of her eye. Nobody had noticed her slip into his office and log him out – it had only taken a few seconds. She pretended to be absorbed by one of the wall monitors, and pressed a button on her phone to send a signal up to the roof.

Jericho gave Diane the command to start recording.

Data coursed through the processors in the Big O. Nobody in the whole building had their own computer in the sense of an autonomous unit. All employees had a standardised hardware kit, a portable version of the boxy lavobots that Tu Technologies used. Everybody could access the Big O central computer from any jack or port, simply by logging in with name, eight-character password and a thumbprint. But not everybody had access to all the drives. Even the powerful sysadmins who managed the superbrain and issued passwords couldn't access the whole machine. The ebb and flow of data in the Big O was like the roar and hum of traffic in a big city, and of course, the roar was loudest during normal working hours.

If you knew how, you could listen to the roar. Not by listening to every part of it at once. The information that coursed through the network was encoded of course, in bits and bytes. But if you knew the precise moment when a piece of information would be sent from A to B, you could record that transmission and then set to work painstakingly filtering out individual data packets, then you could apply powerful decoder programs to unlock the words and images inside. At the moment the system was fairly quiet, so that it was easy enough to isolate Norrington's data packet right at the moment when he logged on. And Diane began her calculations.

Six minutes later, she had the eight-character password. It took her another three minutes to crack the software that had carried Norrington's thumbscan to the central processors, and now she had his print as well.

Jericho stared at the prize. Now there was only one more hurdle to clear. Once logged on, nobody could log in again using the same personal data without raising a flag – no more than you could ring your own front doorbell while you were already inside in the living room.

They had to lock Norrington out again.

The chance came a little while later. Norrington was called to a pow-wow, but he spent a long time lingering near the workstations which gave him a view of his office. Edda Hoff chivvied him along. He hemmed and hawed, but finally gave up his watchpost and went into the room, not without casting one last, mistrustful look behind himself.

Jericho smiled at him.

He and Yoyo had switched places. One of the basic rules of surveillance was not to let the target see the same face the whole time. Now she was upstairs, waiting for *his* signal. The door to the conference room clicked shut. Unhurriedly, Jericho was on his way across to Norrington's office when the conference-room door opened again, and Shaw emerged.

'Owen,' she called.

He stopped. He was ten, perhaps twelve steps from Norrington's office. He could be going anywhere.

'I think perhaps you should join the discussion. We've sifted some more data from Vogelaar's dossier, material which has to do with your friend Xin, and the Zheng Group.' She glanced about. 'By the way, where are your colleagues?'

Jericho went over to join her.

'Yoyo's on Vic Thorn's trail.'

Her habitual scowl softened to a smile. 'Could be that you'll be quicker about it than MI6 with your enquiries. And Tu Tian?'

'We've given him the day off. He has a business to run.'

'Splendid. God forbid that the Chinese economy should falter. The American crash was quite enough. Are you coming?'

'Right away. Give me a minute.'

Shaw went back inside without quite closing the door. Jericho strolled casually back to Norrington's office. Somebody at one of the workstations looked up at him, then back at the screen. Without stopping, Jericho stepped into the little room, logged Norrington out and then walked purposefully across to the other side, and to the conference rooms. Just before he joined the others, he sent Yoyo the agreed signal.

Straight away, she typed Norrington's name. The system asked for authorisations. She entered the eight-character password, squirted Norrington's thumbprint and waited.

The screen filled with icons.

'There you go,' Yoyo whispered, and told Diane to download Norrington's personal data.

'As you wish, Yoyo.'

Yoyo? How nice. Owen must have stored her voiceprint. She watched eagerly as Diane's hard drive gulped down one data packet after another, holding her breath for the *Download complete* message.

Jericho was just as impatient, waiting for the signal that would tell him that the transfer had worked and that the false Norrington was now logged out. Once that happened, there was one more thing for him to do: leave the conference, go across to the office and log the deputy head of security back in, so that Norrington would not notice the theft later.

At that moment, Norrington stood up.

'Excuse me,' he said, smiled at the assembled talking heads, and left.

Jericho stared at his empty chair. Yoyo, he thought, what's going on? Why's it taking so long?

Should he leave too, and catch up with Norrington? Stop him from going into his office? What would that look like? Norrington was already on edge at the idea that the central computer had simply shut him out, and if Jericho took any action, he would certainly suspect trickery. Ill at ease, he resisted the urge. He sat there hoping for the all-important signal, and tried to look interested.

Ever since he could remember, Norrington had suffered gut-ache and stomach cramps whenever he was scared. He made for the toilet, sank down, grunting, and then left with a lighter step. He was at the door of the conference room, holding the handle in his hand, when all of a sudden he had the feeling that someone was staring at the back of his head. Not someone, something, some grinning, goggle-eyed bogeyman. He stopped dead, and whipped round towards his office.

Nobody there.

For a second he hesitated, but the whatever-it-was was still staring at him. Slowly he crossed the space, walked into his office and around his desk. Everything seemed to be in order. He tapped the touchscreen and tried to open one of his files.

Access denied.

Norrington stumbled backwards, looked around in a panic. What was happening here? A system error? Not on your life! He felt a trickle of ice creep up his spine as he remembered how Jericho had niggled at the matter of Vic Thorn, and what a stupid mistake he'd made in replying. Why hadn't he just admitted that they'd been friends, good friends at that? What the hell would that prove, that he'd known Thorn, even if the guy turned out to be a terrorist a thousand times over?

He opened a login window and typed in his name.

The system told him that he was already logged in.

*   *   *

Download complete.

'At last,' Yoyo said, logged Norrington out and sent the message to Jericho's phone.

Norrington stared at his screen.

Somebody was helping themselves to his data.

His fingers trembling, he tried again. This time the system accepted his codes and let him in, but he knew all the same that they had been through his files. They had got hold of his access data and they'd been spying on him.

They were onto him.

Norrington steepled his index fingers, and put them to his lips. He was fairly sure that he knew who 'they' were, but what could he do to stop them? Demand that Jericho's computer be searched? Then the detective would cast his loyalty in doubt. Norrington would have to agree to a search of his own data if he didn't want to arouse suspicion, and that would be the beginning of the end. Once they started to piece together his deleted emails—

One moment though. Jericho was sitting in the conference room. It might have been Jericho who had logged him out, but he could hardly have anything to do with what had just happened. One of the others, either Tu Tian or Chen Yuyun, was sitting in front of Jericho's computer right now – what kind of stupid name had he given it? Diane? It was probably the girl. Hadn't she been roaming through the control room just a while back, looking as though she had nothing better to do?

Yoyo. He had to get rid of her.

'Andrew?'

He jumped. Edda Hoff. Pale and expressionless under her lacquered black pageboy cut. Expressionless? Really? Or wasn't there rather a gleam in her eye, the sly look of someone watching a trap to see who will walk into it?

'Jennifer rather urgently needs you to come back for the rest of the meeting.' She drew her eyebrows together, infinitesimally. 'Is everything all right? Are you not feeling well?'

'The tummy.' Norrington got to his feet. 'I'm fine.'

The way he came back to the conference table set alarm bells ringing for Jericho. The man's face was a jaundiced yellow colour, and his fore-head was creased and lined with worry. There was no mistaking that Norrington knew exactly what was going on, but instead of pointing the finger at him and demanding an explanation, he sat down to suffer in silence. If any further proof of his perfidy were needed, Norrington had just supplied it.

'Possibly I should recap on the—' he began, when all of a sudden more faces appeared on the video wall, and the Xin working group broke in to have their say.

'Miss Shaw, Andrew, Tom—' One of the new arrivals held up a thin file. 'You'll want to hear this.'

'What have you got?' Shaw asked.

'It's about Julian Orley's good friend Carl Hanna. He's a Canadian investor, and he's worth fifteen billion, isn't that right?'

'That was his story,' Norrington said, nodding.

'And you checked him out.'

'You know that I did.'

'Well, everybody makes mistakes. We asked around a little. In the end the CIA dug up his family tree.'

Expectant silence.

'Hey.' The man smiled at each of them in turn. 'Anybody want to get to know the guy a little better? After all, this is somebody you people decided you could trust to go on a trip with Julian Orley.'

'This is quite a build-up.' Shaw gave them a razor-thin smile. 'Is there going to be another advertisement break, or will you get to the point?'

The agent put the file down in front of him.

'From now on, you can call him Neil Gabriel. He's American, born in 1981 in Baltimore, Maryland. High school and US Navy, then after that he was with the police as an undercover detective. The CIA noticed him, recruited him and sent him off to New Delhi for an operation. He did such good work there that they let him stay several years. He became something of an expert on the region, but also a bit of a lone wolf. So he was telling the truth about India, although that's about the only truth he did tell. In 2016 he left the good guys and signed up with African Protection Services.'

'Hanna was with APS?' Jericho blurted out.

The man leafed through his pages. 'Vogelaar mentions pretty nearly everybody in his dossier who was connected with the Mayé coup in 2017. There's a Neil Gabriel in that list, although he was only with the outfit for a little while and then went independent. It looks as though he did jobs for the Zhong Chan Er Bu as well, at least Vogelaar says that Xin liked his work. So now that we've talked to our American friends, we know who Neil Gabriel is. Clearly APS must have split at the time. One part stuck with Vogelaar, while the others became Kenny Xin's creatures.'

Jericho listened, fascinated, and kept an eye on Norrington at the same time. The security number two was visibly distressed by the barrage of facts.

'Right now we're busy trying to unravel Hanna's fake CV, pardon me, I mean Gabriel's. We hope to find out who set him up with shares in Lightyears and Quantime. People with serious money. This won't be anywhere near as easy as it was to crack who he really is.'

'You know one of them already,' Jericho said. 'Xin.'

The agent turned towards him. 'We don't hold out much hope of getting a glimpse of him. He seems to just melt away into thin air whenever you think you have him in your sights.'

'Was it easy to crack Hanna's identity?' Shaw asked.

'Well, easy would be overstating the case. We have good contacts with our friends across the pond, and we couldn't have done it without them. But the bottom line is' – he paused, and looked at Norrington – 'a quiet chat with the Central Intelligence Agency would have done the trick back at the start.'

Norrington leaned forward.

'Do you really think we didn't talk to them?'

'I have absolutely no wish to question your competence,' the agent said, cheerily. 'I leave that to others.'

Jericho's phone rang. He glanced at the screen, excused himself and went outside, shutting the door behind him.

'Norrington knows,' he said quietly.

'Crap.' Yoyo was silent for a moment. 'I thought—'

'Didn't work out as we expected. Were you able to download everything, at least?'

'I've been hard at work already! The search program can't find anything about Thorn in Norrington's data, but there's some stuff about Hanna. He was a long way from being the only one who could have taken Palstein's place. There was a regular queue of candidates: Orley's business partners, it looks like, or people he wanted to do business with. Multi-billionaires, the lot of them, but Norrington always managed to find something to cavil at. Heart condition, high blood pressure, this one's been in therapy, that one might be flirting with the competition, the other's got close links with the Chinese government and he doesn't like the look of it, et cetera, et cetera. You can't help but think that he was being paid money to find reasons to rule them all out of going along.'

'Maybe he *was* paid.'

'And after all that, Hanna's just smiles and sunshine. The perfect travelling companion for Julian Orley.'

'And nobody double-checked?'

'Norrington's not just a line manager, Owen. He's deputy head of security. If somebody like him recommends Hanna, then Hanna flies. Orley must have trusted him – after all he pays him a lot of money for his expertise.'

'All right, I'll talk to Shaw. Enough hide-and-seek.'

She hesitated. 'Are you sure that you can trust her?'

'Sure enough to take the risk. If the whole thing turns out to be flim-flam, she'll throw us out on our ear, but we'll chance it.'

'Good. I'll spend some more time going through Norrington's sock drawers.'

The door to the conference room opened. Norrington hurried over to his office. Shaw, Merrick and the others got ready to go their separate ways.

'Jennifer.' Jericho moved to intercept her. 'Can I talk to you for a moment?'

She looked at him, her face expressionless.

Peary Base, North Pole, The Moon

In the end DeLucas had given up caring and had marched Lynn up to the top floor by main force, then along to Igloo 2, where she threw her a spacesuit, backpack and helmet, and threatened to beat her up if she didn't pull herself together. She'd run out of patience, whether or not this was Julian Orley's beloved daughter. The woman was clearly two sandwiches short of a picnic. Sometimes she seemed to be perfectly lucid, then at the next moment DeLucas wouldn't have been surprised to see her crawling around on all fours, or stepping gaily into the airlock without putting her helmet on. She turfed the Ögis out of bed, who were mercifully cooperative and quick to understand the situation, but by the time she had got the whole crowd of them into one of the robot buses and over to the landing field, Palmer and his crew had already arrived and begun to search the caves. They turned the laboratories upside down as though carrying out a drugs raid, tore the mattresses from the bunks in all the bedrooms, looked into all the lockers and behind the wall panels, in the aquaria and the vegetable patches. Finally DeLucas, already in her spacesuit, her helmet under her arm, went into the Great Hall to join them. She hadn't the first idea what a mini-nuke looked like. All she knew was that it was small, and could be anywhere.

Where would *she* hide something like that? In the jungle of the greenhouses? In among the trout and the salmon?

In the ceiling?

She looked up at the Great Hall's basalt dome. She felt a feverish desire to get out of there, to go with the guests. What they were doing here was crazy! The fact that Hanna had showed up in the control room didn't remotely mean that the bomb had to be here in the underground. It could be anywhere in the whole vast complex.

She peered indecisively into the corridors.

What would make sense?

What did people do when nuclear attack threatened? They built bunkers, underground bases for protection. That was because an atom bomb exploding up on the surface would destroy everything for miles around, but there was some chance of survival if you were in a reinforced bunker. Did that mean that the underground would survive at Peary Base?

Hardly.

She looked at her watch. Twenty to five.

Think, Minnie! An atom bomb was an inferno, devouring everything in its path, but even a doomsday device could be deployed more or less optimally. Towns and cities were built on the surface, never mind all the tunnels, cellars and sewers below ground. If you wanted to destroy New York with an atom bomb, your best bet was to drop it from above, but life on the Moon demanded a mole's-eye perspective once you'd lived there for a few months. If you wanted to destroy the base, *really* destroy it, it had to be done from inside. The bomb would have to tear apart the bowels of the plateau, and only then blaze up over the crater.

It *had* to be down in the catacombs. Between the aquaria, the greenhouses, the residential quarters and the laboratories.

She glanced across at the airlock.

Hmm. She didn't need to search beyond the airlock. There was nothing there.

Wrong! That was where the unused part of the labyrinth began, and some of the passages led into the canyon.

How had Hanna even managed to get into the igloo? Through the surface-level airlocks? It was possible. But if he had, wouldn't Wachowski have seen him on the screens? Well, maybe he had. Maybe Hanna had just strolled in, all above board and official, but if so, why hadn't he gone from the ground floor to the control room on foot? It was only a couple of metres. Why had he taken the lift?

Because he had come from underground.

'Nothing here,' said a tense voice over her helmet link.

'Here neither,' Palmer answered.

And how had he got into the catacombs unnoticed?

She walked towards the airlock. Hardly anybody ever went into the caves beyond. From here, the labyrinth burrowed endlessly into the massif and the crater wall beyond. It would have taken a whole army of astronauts weeks or months to search the labyrinth's full extent, but DeLucas knew that the only logical place to look for the bomb was nearby, somewhere central, below the habs, and that meant the Great Hall and its immediate surroundings.

She went into the airlock, put on her helmet and pushed the button that would pump the air out. When the airlock door on the further side opened, she switched on her helmet lamp and stepped out into the forgotten corridor beyond.

Almost immediately, she stumbled across Tommy Wachowski's corpse.

'Tommy,' she gasped. 'Oh my God!'

Her knees trembling, she squatted down and played the cone of light over the body. His limbs were twisted as he lay there, his face deformed.

'Leland!' she called out. 'Leland, Tommy's here, and—'

Then she realised that the interior radio network didn't work this side of the bulkheads. She was in no man's land, cut off from the world.

She felt sick.

Gasping, she fell to all fours. Cold sweat broke out all over her body. It was only by a mighty effort of will that she succeeded in not throwing up inside her helmet. She crawled away from the dead man on all fours like an animal, into the corridor, where she closed her eyes and quickly took in a few deep breaths. Once she dared open her eyes again, she saw a shadow in the light from her helmet. It was just a few paces away.

For a second, her heart skipped a beat.

Then she realised that there was nobody standing there, that this was just a narrow gap in the cave wall. She squinted, her eyes still watering from retching, then pulled herself together and stamped on her fear. She climbed to her feet like a puppet, walked across to the gap and looked inside. She saw that it was more like a crack than a corridor. Not very inviting. Nowhere you would choose to go of your own accord.

And that, she thought, is exactly why you'll go in.

She drew in her shoulders and pushed her way in until the roof dipped sharply down and she had to crawl. Her breath caught and choked in her throat as the fear fought back. Then there wasn't even room to crawl. She had to lie flat on her belly, feeling her heart hammering against the rock below her like a jackhammer. She considered turning back. This was going nowhere. Dead end. She would go one more metre. Gasping, she pushed herself on, following the scurrying disc of light, imagining what it would be like to be buried alive here, and then all of a sudden the passage opened wide and her fingers were scrabbling in a heap of rubble.

That was it. End of the line.

Or was it? She hesitated. The rubble looked odd. Not a natural pile. DeLucas stooped, and the light scurried over the stones and reflected off something buried in among them. She began to clear the rocks away with one hand, and then saw the surface of something bulky and metallic, smooth, machine-tooled, sleek.

It couldn't be anything else but—

She shovelled the rubble aside madly, uncovering the thing. It was the size of a briefcase. She tugged it towards herself. There could be no doubt, now she saw the blinking display and the timecode running backwards from—

'Oh no,' she whispered.

So little time. So little time.

Frantic, clinging on to the bomb with both hands, she began to wriggle out. She had to get out of here, but the next moment her backpack was wedged against the low roof and she couldn't move another inch. She was stuck fast.

Waves of panic came crashing together over her head.

London, Great Britain

'You are crazy,' said Shaw.

Her workspace was an identical copy of Norrington's office, modest and functional, the only difference being a few hints that she had a life beyond the Big O. Photographs showed that Shaw had a husband and grown-up children, that little kids somewhere called her granny. Jericho thought of the exile of his own existence, and had a hard time imagining this flinty-featured security chief as someone with wants and needs, hormones, a woman who had whispered and moaned and cried out with pleasure, limbs entangled. Jennifer Shaw was in charge of the safety of the world's largest technology corporation. He wondered what her pet name was. At home, within her own four walls, between the TV set and the dental floss, was she Bunnikins or Mummy Bear? He glanced outside quickly, but Norrington's office was out of sight from here.

'Doesn't all that give you pause for thought?' he asked.

'What makes me pause is the thought that you've been abusing my trust,' said Bunnikins, or Mother Bear, sternly.

'No, you're not looking at it right. We're trying to *stop* someone from abusing your trust.' He drew up a chair and sat down. 'Jennifer, I know we're on very thin ice here, but Norrington lied about his relationship to Vic Thorn. He obviously knew him better than he's letting on. Why would he do that if he had nothing to hide? He may have had perfectly understandable reasons to take Hanna under his wing, but given all the resources he has at his disposal, how come he couldn't identify an ex-CIA man? *Before* the moon trip! And once he noticed that we'd cracked his passcodes, well – what would *you* have done, in his place?'

She looked levelly at him with her grey-blue eyes.

'I would have nailed you to the wall.'

'Quite!' Jericho slapped his hand down on the desk. 'And what does he do? Comes slinking in, lets the MI6 fellows haul him over the coals and then rushes off again. Now, you told me that it was Edda Hoff who passed on my theory that Thorn had been supposed to arrange the attack, and that she told the security services too. Shouldn't we suppose that she told Norrington as well?'

'She's certain to have done so. Edda is extremely conscientious.'

'But when I went into his office to talk to him about it, he acted as though it were a complete surprise! Even though, by that point, he must have known we were thinking along those lines. And don't you get the feeling that all his activity is actually slowing down the Big O's attempts to find anything out, rather than helping?'

'I have told him that we're fighting on too many fronts at once.' Shaw gave him a level look. 'And what should I do about that, in your opinion? Relieve him of his duties because of one or two odd bits of behaviour? Have his data searched?'

'I think you know quite well what you should do.'

Shaw was silent.

Two doors down, Norrington was dialling a number on his phone, his fingers trembling.

He had made mistakes. He'd reacted without stopping to think. The noose was tightening, since they would find proof, and once they decided to put him through the wringer he would lose his nerve, he'd break down, he'd spill the beans. He was an idiot to have got involved in the whole thing to begin with, from the moment they offered him money to suggest Thorn for a second mission. But it had been so much money, so incredibly much, and there was the promise of much more once Operation Mountains of Eternal Light was done with, once the course of history had been changed. He had been a quick learner in the school of corruption, and had risen to be one of Hydra's chief planners, had fed the many-headed monster with information about the OSS, about Gaia and Peary Base. He had even come up with the shadow network which the conspirators used to communicate their murderous plans. A white-hot inferno, disguised as mere white noise. He had met Hydra's immortal head, the brains behind the whole scheme, the criminal mastermind whose identity only six other people knew. It had been seven, but one of them had got cold feet. That was when Norrington had learned that if need be Hydra would sooner cut off one of its own heads than let it turn blabbermouth.

He *mustn't* end up in Secret Service hands.

Xin picked up.

'We've been found out, Kenny! Just like I told you we would be.'

'And I told you to keep your nerve.'

'You go to hell with your know-it-all remarks! MI6 blew Gabriel's identity. Jeri-cho and the girl hacked into my data. I don't know when Shaw's going to shut the trap on me – it could be that I already wouldn't be allowed out of the building. Get me out of here.'

Xin was silent for a moment.

'What about Ebola?' he asked. 'Do they know about her, too?'

Norrington hesitated. For some reason, he just couldn't get used to Dana's code-name.

'They don't know anything about her, nor about the rest of it. They just know that the bomb's at Peary. But of course the next thing they'll do is make use of all my data, and then they'll take another look at everybody whose appointment I approved.'

'Are you sure that Jericho's been talking to Shaw about you?'

'No idea,' he groaned. 'I hope he hasn't yet. Under the circumstances, nothing's certain.'

Xin thought.

'Good. I'll be on the flight deck in five minutes. Maybe you should try getting Jericho's computer out of the building.'

'Maybe we should try painting the Moon yellow and putting a smiley face on it,' Norrington snapped. 'They mustn't get their hands on me, Kenny, don't you understand? *I have to get out of here!*'

'Everything's all right.' Suddenly Xin's voice took on that soft, sibilant note. 'Nobody's going to get their hands on you, Andrew. I promised to be there, and I keep my promises.'

'You hurry up, damn you!'

⋆   ⋆   ⋆

While the street lights of London faded away under a magnificent dawn sky, Yoyo decided to call Jericho again. During the night, she and Diane had become fast friends. She'd never worked with such excellent search programs or selection parameters.

'I have some news,' she said. 'Where are you?'

'In Jennifer's office. We can speak openly. Wait a moment.' He listened to a soft voice in the background, then said, 'Look, the best thing to do is call again, direct to her number, okay?'

'You can tell her straight away that—'

'Tell her yourself.'

He hung up. Yoyo squirmed around impatiently on her chair. She was burning to tell him about the dossiers Norrington had put together on the guests and staff at Gaia. Diane had done a lightning search, comparing Norrington's supposed findings with publicly available biographies on the net and found no significant discrepancies, except perhaps for the fact that Evelyn Chambers was telling some whopping lies about her age. As for the staff at Gaia, two Germans, an Indian and a Japanese, they had been chosen by the director of the hotel, Dana Lawrence, who in turn had got the job on the strength of a report from Norrington, knocking four other highly qualified candidates out of the running. Norrington hadn't actually turned any of these other four down flat, quite the opposite, it was rather that Lawrence's track record put all the others in the shade. Lynn Orley had made the final appointment, and she would have had to have been insane to refuse Lawrence the job, given such excellent references. It was only when you looked closer that you realised that Lawrence's official CV on the net was strangely different. Certain jobs that she had supposedly held made her just the right woman for the job in Gaia, but online they were missing, or didn't quite match up. It was certainly the career of a dedicated professional, but if you wanted to assume the worst, you could easily say that Norrington had massaged the facts to help Lynn make her decision. Yoyo saw nothing at all wrong in assuming the worst.

Eager to know what the others would make of her findings, she typed in Shaw's name and was just about to let the computer make the call when she heard a noise.

A lift had stopped outside on the gallery. She heard the doors slide apart.

Yoyo froze. Nobody was supposed to be in the Big O right now except for the security patrols and the tireless crew down in the situation room. She strained her ears, becoming aware of her surroundings for the first time. She was sitting at somebody's workplace, an entirely interchangeable, uniform cell; employees kept their personal possessions in the mobile units that let them log in anywhere needed, throughout the building. Diane lay to her left, beneath the holographic display, a slim, shimmering machine, while on her right was a wheeled set of drawers, probably containing all the clutter that a computer still couldn't replace, even in 2025.

She opened the top drawer, peered into it, opened the next one down.

She glanced at the panoramic windows. London's night was slowly giving way to early morning light, but over in the west it was stubbornly dark. She could see the office interior reflected in outline in the window-pane, the workstations, the door in the wall behind her that led through to the hallway and the gallery.

She could see a silhouette in the hallway.

Yoyo ducked. Whoever it was hesitated. A man, judging by the height. He was just standing there, staring.

He had to take her by surprise. It could be that Shaw still didn't know about the hacking. It would be one thing to overpower Yoyo and get hold of the computer, but then there would be Jericho to deal with. Perhaps there would be a way to lure him upstairs. Assuming that the two of them hadn't told Tu Tian what they were up to, it might be enough to get rid of them and then the computer as well, then it would be as if none of this had ever happened, nobody would ever suspect that—

Rubbish! This was wishful thinking from start to finish. How would he explain it once they were both dead? The surveillance system would show everything. Why grab Jericho's computer, when it didn't hold anything that wasn't also stored in the Big O mainframes? Shaw could get at his data any time she liked, which is what she *would* do if he killed two people up here – not to mention the fact that he'd never manage that, since in stark contrast to people like Xin, Hanna, Lawrence and Gudmundsson, he wasn't a killer. It wasn't game over for Hydra yet, but for him it certainly was. Even making a break for it was as good as a confession of guilt, but if he stayed, he might just as well put the cuffs on himself. There wasn't any point cleaning up his trail now. He had to get out of here, drop out of sight!

He had enough money for a new life, quite a comfortable one at that.

The open-plan office lay in twilight.

How much had she learned? Had Jericho's computer been able to retrieve his deleted emails and reconstruct them?

Where was the girl?

He was torn between the urge to find out more and the need to get away. He looked across the room, then his feet carried him forward as though of their own accord. He stepped into the office. It looked empty. The overhead lights were dimmed. Two workstations away, monitor screens glowed, and he saw the modest little box that Yoyo had left there, the one they called Diane. He should search the office. The workstations offered various hiding-places. Indecisive, he walked a little way into the room, paced this way and that, looked at the clock. Xin must be here by now, he should get out, but the monitors glowed like the lights of some safe refuge.

He hurried across to the workstation, bent down and had his hands on the little computer when the room burst into life behind him.

Petite though she might have been, Yoyo was also muscular and in good shape, so she had no trouble in picking up a fairly heavy office chair and taking a swing. As Norrington spun round to face her, the back of the chair caught him full-on, slamming into his head and his chest and knocking him backwards onto the desk. He grunted, and scrabbled for a handhold. Yoyo swung at him again, from the side this time, and he fell to the floor. Even as he landed there on his back next to Diane, she flung the chair aside and drew from her belt the scissors she had found in the drawer. She landed hard on his chest with both knees.

There was an audible crack. Norrington made a choking, hacking sound. His eyes bulged. Yoyo clamped the fingers of her left hand around his throat, leaned down low and shoved the point of the scissors so hard against his balls that he could feel it poised there.

'One false move,' she hissed, 'and the Westminster Abbey Boys' Choir will be glad to make your acquaintance.'

Norrington stared at her. Suddenly, he swung at her. She saw his clenched fist flying at her, ducked aside and drove the scissors deeper into his crotch. He flinched with his whole body and then froze completely, simply staring at her again.

'What do you want from me, you madwoman?' he gasped.

'I want a little talk.'

'You're crazy. I came up here to see whether everything's okay, whether you need anything, and you—'

'Andrew, hey, Andrew!' she interrupted. 'That's crap. I don't want to hear any crap.'

'I just wanted—'

'You wanted to swipe the computer. I saw that, thanks. I don't need any more proof, so get talking. Who are you working with, and what do they want? Were we right about Peary? Who's pulling the strings?'

'With the best will in the world, I don't know what you're—'

'Andrew, you're being foolish.'

'– talking about.'

Dark red swamped her vision, glowing and all-consuming. Utterly forgotten was any chance that the man beneath her might have had nothing to do with the deaths of her friends, with the agonies that Chen Hongbing had gone through while Xin had him trapped in front of the automatic rifle. Forgotten any idea that she might be wrong about him, that Norrington might have had nothing to do with any of this. Every cell of her body burned with hatred. She wanted, she *needed* a culprit, here, now, at last, anyone to blame before she lost her mind, a bad guy to stand in for the monsters who had tortured the people she loved, the people whose love she needed. Her loved ones, who had seen things that they couldn't talk about, things that clamped a mask over their faces. She jerked back her arm and rammed the scissors into Norrington's thigh, stabbing so hard that skin and flesh parted like butter before the blades, and the point scraped hard against the bone. Norrington screamed like a stuck pig. He raised both hands and tried to shove her away. Still wrapped in her red rage, she yanked the improvised weapon from the wound and set the point against Norrington's genitals again.

'It hurts, wherever I aim,' she whispered. 'But next time the consequences may be rather more permanent. Were we right about Peary?'

'Yes,' he screamed.

'When? When's the bomb due to go off?'

'I don't know.' He twisted and turned, his eyes stark with pain. 'Sometime. Now. Soon. We're out of contact.'

'You started the botnet.'

'Yes.'

'Can you stop it?'

'Yes, let me go, you're insane!'

'Is your organisation called Hydra? Who's behind it all?'

Without warning Norrington's head jerked up, and Yoyo realised that it had been a mistake to crouch so low above him. There was a noise like two blocks of wood being slammed together as his forehead met hers. She was flung back. By reflex, she stabbed and heard him howl, then felt him grab hold of her and fling her aside. There were spots dancing in front of her eyes. Her head roared and her nose seemed to have swollen to several times its original size. She rolled swiftly out of Norrington's reach, holding the scissors out in front of her, but instead of launching himself at her, he hobbled away.

'You stay here,' she gasped.

Norrington began to run, as much as his wounded leg would allow. Yoyo clambered to her feet, then fell down again straight away and felt at her face. Blood was pouring from her nose. She felt sickeningly dizzy, but finally managed to stand up, staggered from the office out to the gallery and saw Norrington climbing some stairs on the other side of the glass bridge between the Big O's western and eastern wings.

The shithead was making for the flight deck.

A quiet voice inside her warned her not to give way to her hatred, to consider that it might be dangerous up there. She didn't listen. Just as she could not doubt Norrington's guilt, right at this moment she couldn't think of anything but stopping him from getting away. She ran after him, glanced down at the dark glass canyon that yawned below the bridge and felt a wave of nausea climb her throat. She fought it down.

Norrington was fighting his way up the last steps.

He was lost to sight.

She shook herself. She resumed the chase, crossed the bridge at last, hurried up the steps two at a time, in constant danger of losing her balance. She made it to the top and saw one of the glass doors out to the roof gliding shut.

Norrington was outside.

Holding the scissors tightly, she went after him, and the glass doors slid open again. The flight deck stretched away before her eyes, with its helicopters and skycars. Norrington hobbled towards something without looking round, waving.

'Over here!' he called.

She quickened her pace. She was puzzled to note that there were airbikes up here as well, more exactly, *one* airbike. She hadn't noticed it the previous morning, and all of a sudden she knew why.

Because it hadn't been there.

She stopped. Her eyes skittered around the flight deck, and she saw two guards lying on the floor, their limbs outflung. A figure dismounted. Norrington staggered, recovered and then dragged himself on towards the bike. The figure pointed a gun at him and he stopped, his hand pressed to his thigh.

'Kenny, what is this?' he asked, his voice wavering.

'We've classed you as a risk,' Xin said. 'You're stupid enough to get caught, and then you'll tell them what you mustn't tell anyone.'

'No!' Norrington screamed. 'No, I promise—'

He was flung upward a little into the air, and his body hung there for a moment like a puppet before he flew backwards, his arms spread, and thudded at Yoyo's feet.

There was a only a mass of red where his face had been.

She froze. Sank to her knees, and dropped the scissors. Xin walked towards her and pressed the muzzle of the gun against her forehead.

'How nice,' he whispered. 'I had already given up all hope.'

Yoyo stared dead ahead. She thought that if she ignored him perhaps he might just vanish, but he didn't, and her eyes filled slowly with tears, because it was over. Finally over. This time nobody would ride to her rescue. There was nobody who could turn up and take Xin by surprise.

Very softly, her voice hoarse, so that she could barely understand the word she spoke, she said, 'Please.'

Xin squatted down in front of her. Yoyo raised her eyes to the handsome, symmetrical mask of his face.

'You're pleading with me?'

She nodded. The gun's mouth pressed harder against her brow, as though boring a hole.

'For what? For your life?'

'For everyone's lives.'

'How very exorbitant of you.'

'I know.' Fat tears rolled down her cheeks, and her lower lip began to tremble. And suddenly, curiously, she felt fear washed away with her tears, the fear that had been her constant companion for so long, leaving only a deep, painful sorrow behind. Sorrow that she would never learn now what had happened to Hongbing, why her life had been the way it was, why their lives hadn't been different. Xin couldn't scare her now, nor any of his kind. It wouldn't have taken much for her to fling her arms around his neck to sob on his shoulders. Why not?

'Yoyo?'

Someone was calling her name in the distance.

'Yoyo! Where are you?'

Jericho! Was that Owen?

Xin smiled. 'Brave little Yoyo. Admirable. It's a shame, I would have liked the chance for a longer chat with you, but as you see, there's no rest for the wicked. They're looking for you, I'm afraid, so now I shall have to leave you.'

He stood up, the gun still pointing straight at her forehead. Yoyo turned her face towards him. The dawn breeze was pleasant as it dried the tears on her cheeks. Caressing. Forgiving.

She heard Jericho shout, 'Yoyo!'

Xin shook his head.

'I'm sorry about this, Yoyo.'

Peary Base, North Pole, The Moon

The evacuated guests took their seats in the Io and buckled themselves in. Kyra Gore was on her way to the cockpit when a call came through from Callisto. Nina Hedegaard's face appeared on the screen.

'Where are you?' Gore asked as she warmed up her engines.

'On our way to land soon.'

'Turn around, right now! Orders from Palmer.'

'What about our group?'

'They're all on board here with me.' She modified thrust, aimed her jets and lifted the shuttle slowly. 'Here on Io.'

'All of them?'

'The only ones left in the base are Palmer and some of our crew. We had a visit from Carl Hanna. The whole place might blow up any moment now, so turn round and cover some ground away out of here!'

'What about Carl?' Julian Orley broke in. 'Where is he?'

'Dead.'

She cast her eyes over the control panel, from sheer force of habit. The landing field was dwindling away below the Io, and the whole scattered assembly, factories, pipelines, igloos and corridors, were only toys, a bucket-and-spade set for scientists to muck about in the lunar sand. The roads ran across the regolith like grooves on a toybox lid. In the tiny hangars, little machines assembled other machines, not quite so little. The sunlight gleamed blindingly from the solar panels. Gore curved her flight-path, climbed again and steered Io across the crater wall to the west.

'Dead?' Orley snapped.

'Miss Lawrence killed him. She's with me, along with your daughter and your guests. They're all right.'

'And the bomb? What are Palmer and his crew doing?'

'They're looking for it.'

'We can't just leave them to—'

'Yes, we can. Turn around. We're flying back to the Chinese.'

DeLucas

Had only seconds passed? Or hours? DeLucas couldn't have said, but when she saw the timecode ticking backwards on the bomb, she knew that the worst experience of her life had not even taken a minute. Kicking and screaming, she had finally managed to break free. After a few metres, the bomb wedged against the rock. She had had enough of being afraid, so this time she simply yelled at the mini-nuke as though it were a snot-nosed kid who only heeded harsh words. Wonder of wonders, it actually listened to her, and the low box came free of the wall. A surge of adrenalin carried her along the corridor and past Tommy Wachowski's body into the airlock, where she hopped from one leg to the other as though the floor were electrified. As the air pumped slowly in, she saw through the viewport Palmer and Jagellovsk coming into the Great Hall, and she slammed her fists against the pane. Palmer spotted her and stopped dead in his tracks. The door glided open. DeLucas stumbled over the threshold and fell full-length on the floor, and the bomb skittered across to stop at the commander's feet.

'Six o'clock,' she panted. 'We have thirty-five minutes.'

Palmer grabbed the box with both hands and stared at it.

'Let's get it out of here,' he said.

They went up with the lift, left the igloo and ran outside onto the bulldozed plain, out amongst the hangars. The Io was just disappearing off past the crater wall.

'What do we do with it now?'

'Disarm it!'

'Thanks, wise guy! Do you know how to do that?'

'Oh, man, I must have seen it a thousand times in the movies. We just have to—'

'Red wire or green wire? Movies are movies. Are you out of your mind?'

'Twenty-nine minutes!'

The mini-nuke lay there between them on the asphalt, a squat, malevolent box. The timecode ticked down mercilessly, a countdown to the end of creation, bringing a new Big Bang.

'Stop!' Palmer shouted, holding up both hands. 'Everybody just shut up! Nobody's disarming a damn thing round here. Get it over to the landing field. We have to get rid of it.'

'We'll never manage it,' DeLucas said. 'How do you intend to—'

Palmer switched over to the shuttle frequency.

'Io? Callisto? Leland Palmer here, can you hear me?'

'Kyra here. What's up, Leland?'

'We found the darn thing! It's going to blow in twenty-eight minutes, excuse me, twenty-seven. I need one of you back here, right now!'

'All right,' Gore said. 'We're turning round.'

'We're nearer,' Nina said.

'What? But you have to—'

'There!' called Jagellovsk.

DeLucas held her breath. Callisto broke free against the backdrop of the stars, curved about and dropped down towards the base.

'I'm coming in to land,' said Nina.

'Over to Igloo 1!' Palmer shouted. He leapt and danced like a dervish, waving his arms. 'Igloo 1, you hear me? We're outside! Get the bomb on board and then dump it as far away as you can, in some goddam crater!'

Callisto

'I see them,' Nina said.

Julian bent down. 'Once we've got the thing on board—'

'Once *I've* got the thing on board.' She turned her head and looked at him. 'You're getting out.'

'What? Out of the question!'

'You are.'

'We're flying together—'

'You're all getting out,' she said, with an air of quiet command. 'You too, Julian.'

And then there it was.

For one deeply satisfying moment she saw fear in Julian's eyes. For just an instant, but an instant that would be with her for ever, she saw at last what she knew she had earned, knew that she deserved from him, that she'd never asked for, in all the time by his side. He wasn't afraid for his guests, or his precious daughter, or for his hotel. He was afraid only for her, afraid that she might be hurt. Fearful of the hole she would leave in his life if she died, the hole in his heart.

She slowed, and let the shuttle sink down.

Down below, the astronauts were scurrying about and waving to her. She choked back on the thrust. The bulldozed patch down here was relatively small, full of vehicles and machinery. Carefully, she guided Callisto over to a spot near the igloo that offered just enough room for her to land, then settled with a bump, extended the airlock and turned around to her passengers.

'Everybody out!' she shouted, clapping her hands. 'Then bring the damn bomb in here. Quick!'

She looked at Julian. He hesitated. The storm-clouds cleared on his face and she saw a beam of honest-to-goodness affection break through like the sun, and all of a sudden he was hugging her to himself, and gave her a scratchy kiss.

'Take care of yourself,' he whispered.

'You won't get rid of me that easily.' She smiled. 'Watch out for the engines when you get out. Don't let them wander about under the thrusters.'

He nodded, slid from his chair and hurried to catch up with the others. Nina turned back to the controls. The lift control showed her that the group was going down to the ground. She watched through the cockpit window as an astronaut hurried across carrying something about the size of a suitcase in both hands. The figure disappeared under Callisto's belly, and then she heard Palmer's voice.

'It's in!'

'Got you.'

'Get going then! Twenty minutes to go! Get the thing away from us!'

'You can say that again,' she murmured, revving. She brought the shuttle up a few metres even as the airlock was retracting, and turned. A shudder ran through Callisto.

'What happened?' she called.

'You struck the lock against one of the hangars here,' Julian said. 'Just brushed the roof.'

Nina cursed, and lifted higher. She glanced around for any error message.

'Is it still retracting?'

'Yes! Seems fine.'

The controls showed that the lock was fully inside Callisto. Nina climbed to three hundred metres, then accelerated faster than she would ever have dared with passengers on board. The thrust pushed her back into her seat as Callisto shot off at more than twelve hundred kilometres per hour. The base dropped away out of sight. Cliffs, chasms and plateaux flew past below like a time-lapse landscape. She would have to make for lower ground as soon as she could, but the stark mountains below seemed to climb and climb for ever where the edges of Peary Crater fused into Hermite to the west. Range reared up after range, ridges and plateaux marched on endlessly, but then at last she saw a ragged abyss yawn wide.

The bowl of Hermite Crater.

Still too close.

Even if the mountain ranges protected the base from the blast itself, there was no telling where the debris would rain down. Nina called up a polar map on her holographic display and looked for a suitable spot. The question was how far she could make the time left to her stretch out. If she waited too long to chuck the mini-nuke overboard, she was in danger of being caught in the nuclear furnace herself, but she didn't want to dump it out of the airlock too soon. The shadows of a sunlit plain rushed past below her, sown with impact craters from smaller meteorites. Flying as low as she was, she had lost radio contact with everyone. According to the dashboard clock she had been flying for eight minutes, and she still wasn't past the whole of Hermite. She could see the crater's western wall looming in the distance, a vast, curving cliff, growing fast, growing closer.

Twelve minutes left.

She looked back at her map. Further to the south-west was a smaller crater, in deep shadow, which suggested that it must be fairly deep. She asked the computer for more information, and a text field unrolled on top of the hologram.

Sylvester Crater, she read. 58 kilometres in diameter.

Depth: unknown.

She liked the look òf it. It looked almost tailor-made to swallow the energy of a nuclear bomb, and all of a sudden she had to smile. Sylvester, how appropriate. A crater named for the father of industrial explosives, and it would see the biggest damn explosion the Moon had known for thousands of years. Grinning, she changed course a few degrees south-west, and Callisto tore over Hermit's western rim.

Eleven minutes.

The crater wall fell away beneath her, rugged, pocked by lesser impacts, and gave way to a broad, flat valley. The other side of the valley had to be Sylvester's outer wall. Nina leapt from the pilot's seat and ran to the airlock, suddenly scared that Palmer might have misread the timecode, but when she peered through the pane she saw the mini-nuke sitting on the cabin floor, its counter just ticking down from the ten-minute mark.

The sight of the bomb made her suddenly queasy.

09.57

09.56

09.55

Time to throw in her hand; she'd pushed her luck as far as she could. There was enough distance now between the bomb and the base. She ran back to the cockpit and gave the command to extend the airlock.

The computer gave her an error report.

Incredulous, she stared at the console. Suddenly the lift symbol was blinking, fiery red. She tried again to extend the shaft, but without success.

Impossible. Just impossible!

She demanded a report.

Airlock not fully drawn up, it said. *Please draw up lock before attempting to extend.*

Her legs trembled wildly. Hastily she ordered the shaft to draw up, even though it was already drawn up – at least, it had seemed that way, but perhaps there was a centimetre or so still to go. But the display didn't stop blinking.

Airlock cannot be drawn up.

Cannot be drawn up?

Nine minutes.

Less than nine.

'Are you crazy?' she shouted at the control system. 'Draw up, extend! How the hell am I supposed to—'

She stopped. You had to be completely crazy yourself to try arguing with a computer. The airlock wouldn't open, and that was that. Which meant that she couldn't just spit the bomb out that way, and she couldn't fetch it from the lock to throw it out of the rear hatch.

The rear hatch!

Her heart pounding, she raced to the stern, opened the bulkhead to the cargo hold, charged inside and looked around. There were a few grasshoppers here, hanging in their brackets and ready to roam. It had hardly been eighteen hours since they had been using them to tour the legendary Apollo landing site. She loosened the clips on one of them, stood it up on its telescopic legs and checked the fuel tank. Enough. All right then, back to the bridge, but as she drew level with the airlock she couldn't resist glancing inside. She hesitated, then looked in at the infernal device, saw the timecode running down—

06.44

06.43

– she tore herself away. Dashed into the cockpit.

Looked out.

Sylvester's crater wall, still a good way off but growing larger every moment. She had to make sure that the bomb would explode on the crater floor, deep inside. Otherwise she would be dead for sure. Her fingers leapt across the instrument panel like a virtuoso at the keyboard as she calculated the angle of approach she would need for a controlled crash, and the shuttle's nose dipped – no, that was too much, less! – there, that was it. A steady descent.

And now, out of here. Helmet on.

Her hands were trembling. Why were her hands trembling, now of all times?

05.59

The helmet wouldn't fit.

05.58

She had left it too late.

05.57

05.56

Now!

Cargo hold. Manual controls.

The loading hatch sank down, infuriatingly slowly, to reveal the stars and, far off, the Peary–Hermite range. Nina climbed up onto the grasshopper platform and kicked the thing up into the air, just a little. The hatch yawned wider. A hair's breadth was all she needed. Without waiting for it to open entirely, she steered the hopper along the cargo hold and through the shuttle's rear hatch as it tore down towards the ground.

It would be an illusion to think that she was safe now. The shuttle seemed to be standing still relative to her speed, which meant that she was still hurtling towards Sylvester at 1200 kilometres per hour on her tiny craft, just as fast as Callisto itself. Realistically, her chances were just about as bad as could be, though she still had five minutes to achieve the impossible, maybe four. Somewhere between 250 and 300 seconds, at any rate. All her hopes hung on having calculated the proper angle of impact for the shuttle. She swung her nozzles to the horizontal and opened the throttle for as much thrust as the little machine could muster.

The hopper bucked and tried to throw her off.

Then it rushed for all its engines were worth away from Callisto, bravely doing its best against the murderous acceleration, and losing height all the while. The shuttle dwindled away rapidly in front of Nina's eyes. She swung the nozzles around a little further and went down to the ground, too close to the ground, as she established the next moment, since she was still going much too fast. She was in danger of being smashed to pieces, and she steered the hopper up again, wringing the last drop of thrust out of its jets, and saw Callisto speeding towards Sylvester's sunlit slopes. The dusty lunar surface was not racing past quite so fast beneath her now, the hopper was battling against its own momentum and winning. It was slowing down, but would there be time to slow it to a safe landing speed?

And if she could? How much time did she still have?

Two minutes?

One?

A small crater rushed towards her, zipped by below and then was lost to sight. An ideal spot to take shelter. Somehow she had to make her way back to the crater, but she was still travelling at considerable speed. Over on the horizon, Callisto hung above the sweeping wall of mountains, a gleaming point, so close to the rim that for a moment she was afraid that she had miscalculated and the shuttle would smash into the crater wall, that the bomb would explode there on the slopes, and that nothing would protect her from the fury of the blast.

Then the shining dot disappeared inside Sylvester, and she gave a victory whoop, since she'd won this point at least in the deadly game. Still whooping, she steered the hopper down, fought against her own headlong hurtle, and gradually, little by little, the contraption seemed to be bleeding off the speed that the shuttle had given it, even if it was still going too fast to land. She could forget about that little crater by now, it was already much too far behind her, but something about the same size sped towards her, maybe a little smaller. The ring wall was two, perhaps three kilometres across but it was astonishingly high, so that all of a sudden she was afraid that the hopper wouldn't make it over the peaks, would crash. Just before impact, she yanked the machine upwards, scraping over the rim, and then looked down. The crater wall cast a threatening shadow into the cauldron, a curve of blackness like a scythe. She slowed further, flew over the opposite wall, then she could see the plain again and Sylvester, its peaks terrifyingly near, unsoftened by atmospheric haze.

There was something happening there.

Hildegaard narrowed her eyes.

The sky above Sylvester blazed.

She held her breath.

From one moment to the next, the stars were swallowed up by a smear of blazing light as though a second sun were being born inside the crater. Instantly, she turned her eyes away, flew a 180-degree curve and realised that she now had full control of speed and direction. Her second little crater was some distance off by now, but the ground below was no longer hurtling past. She had won the battle against her acceleration and now she had to find shelter. All around, the slopes and cliffs, even the distant polar massif, were glowing in the light of the nuclear explosion, but that died away so suddenly that she couldn't resist her curiosity. She turned the hopper.

The light had vanished.

For a moment she thought that Sylvester had absorbed the energy of an entire nuclear explosion, but something was different now. At first she couldn't understand what she was seeing, but then the shock of recognition hit.

The ridge of the crater wall had vanished.

No, not vanished. It was hidden by a screen of dust that shrouded the upper slopes and fountained skywards, swallowing the stars, a plume many kilometres high, growing higher and higher, unreal, bizarre, a nightmare image—

Crawling down the slopes.

Crawling?

'Oh shit,' whispered Nina.

All of a sudden, the wall of dust had become a huge wave, spilling over the crater wall in all directions and racing down towards the plain. Nina had no idea just how fast it was travelling, but it was certainly coming ten times faster than her little hopper could fly, twenty times, thirty. For a moment she was paralysed, not able even to tear her eyes away, then she yanked the machine around and thrashed it back towards the nameless little crater. After the breakneck ride out of Callisto, it was as though the hopper was just creeping along. She risked another look. Sylvester had vanished completely. There was only the dust racing towards her, swallowing the sky and devouring all before it.

Faster. Faster!

The crater wall, her only hope of shelter!

Desperately, she yanked the grasshopper upwards, and it hauled itself up the slope as though worn out by the excitement of the past few minutes. Its telescopic legs scrabbled across the rocks and it tottered from side to side, then with one leap it was over the ridge. Nina spread her arms and leapt from the platform. Her body slammed into the steep regolith and then she was rolling down, over a sudden edge. She fell in a long arc and landed quite a way further off, in the shadow of a sheer cliff-face. From the corner of her eyes she could see the grasshopper tumbling end over end. She braced her feet in the scree slope and managed to stop her downward slide. She crawled into the shelter of an overhang and curled up into a ball.

Above her, the sky grew dark.

In the next moment, everything was grey. A hail of pebbles, tiny stones, pattered down into the crater's bowl. Nina cowered as small as she could, protected against the pressure wave and the rubble by her overhang, but the rocks falling in front of her sent up a spray of regolith in turn. She crossed her arms in front of her helmet for protection and hoped that the suit would hold up to the onslaught. She could see nothing at all, merely a thick grey cloud on a grey ground, and she shut her eyes.

The wall raced past her.

She had no idea how long she had been lying there. When she finally dared take her arms from her faceplate, the impacts had stopped and a hazy, shifting cloud of dust hung everywhere.

She clambered to her feet and stretched her limbs. She could hardly believe that she was still alive. That nothing had broken. Apparently, she was totally unharmed.

She had survived an atom bomb.

On the other hand, she was now stuck in a nameless crater miles from Peary with no means of getting away. Her own little crater, that had saved her life. She had an intact spacesuit, her radio and enough oxygen for the next few hours until Io found her. At least, she hoped that they'd be looking for her and hadn't simply assumed that her death was inevitable.

First of all, she decided, she had to get out of this crater. Better for the radio reception once Io turned up.

Resigned, she set out on the long climb.

London, Great Britain

I'm sorry about this, Yoyo—

Whatever else Xin said after that reached her as mere wordsound, a voiceprint only, since at that moment her overloaded nerves gave way.

The nervus vagus, that had survived so many lesser crises before now, simply stopped all regulatory function and left the organs under its command to their own devices, plunging them into chaos. Without higher functions to command them, arteries let the blood rush unhindered to her legs, her heart found nothing to pump, her brain waited in vain for the oxygen to arrive and Xin's next words were nothing more than a half-heard electrochemical impulse. 'You lose.' Maybe he said them, maybe he didn't. At that moment, all systems shut down. Her eyes turned up, and she slumped. Shot down by a bullet that never hit her.

That was how Jericho found her. As part of a collection of bodies scattered over the flight deck: two dead guards, the dead traitor, and Yoyo lying there as though dead, without a pulse, unbreathing, drenched in cold sweat. She hadn't picked up when Shaw called from her extension, nor when he tried his own phone. One look into Norrington's office told them that he wasn't there. This was enough to send him up to the sixty-eighth floor, worried, where he found Diane lying pitifully, her cables wrenched out, and clear signs of a fight. No sign at all of Yoyo but a trail of blood on the floor, on the gallery, the bridge, the steps up to the deck.

The rest was intuition.

He had burst out onto the roof just in time to see the airbike vanishing into the sky, and for a dreadful moment he thought that Yoyo was dead. He sank to his knees beside her, broken by his failure, seeing clearly the grief that would seize Tu and Hongbing when he brought them the news. But then he heard a barely perceptible heartbeat, his ear pressed to her ribcage. Another followed. A slow, faltering rhythm that picked up speed and grew stronger, and then the blood flowed back to her brain and consciousness returned. When he propped her legs up she came to, groggy, confused, just about able to see and speak. Who am I? Headache, tired, sleep.

Xin had let her live.

Why?

Meanwhile Shaw was growing apoplectic. Norrington's guilt still had to be proved, even if she no longer doubted it. She was prey to a whole swarm of suspicions about what the deputy head of security could have done to damage Orley, and she ordered his data combed, his body searched. They found a datastick disguised as a house key, containing only a single program which uploaded as the image of a nine-headed snake, a shimmering, pulsing sign of his treachery.

That was the point when Jericho decided to give up.

They could fix their own problems. He couldn't do any more, didn't want to. It was as though he and Xin had some tacit agreement now that the killer had spared Yoyo's life and vanished, leaving a curt but unambiguous message: Mind your own business. Maybe Xin had simply recognised that by now Yoyo's death was unnecessary, since so many other people knew her secret. It would have been pointless to kill her now, and somehow or other pointless actions simply didn't fit into Xin's . . . philosophy, if that was what it was.

Never mind.

He was a detective, and he had kept his promise. He had brought Yoyo back to his two clients, to Tu and Chen. Everything else was for Shaw and the British Secret Services to bother about, none of his business, and he was also horribly tired. At the same time, he knew that he wouldn't be able to sleep a wink, no matter how hard he was yawning now.

Tu on the other hand hardly appeared to sleep at all, and the shock seemed to have jolted him into a state of unceasing wakefulness, driven by the guilt of not having been there at Yoyo's side. She had been asleep in her bed for two hours now – all the guest suites in the Big O had several rooms, and spectacular views – while he sat with Jericho in the living room, drinking tea and gobbling down the nuts and nibbles like a maniac.

'I have to eat,' he said half apologetically, belching loudly. 'Food and sex are man's essential desires.'

'Says who?' muttered Jericho.

'Confucius, since you ask, and he meant by it that we should be sure to eat well so that we can protect our women. Which means I have some catching up to do.' A handful of Brazil nuts and jelly babies together. 'And if I ever get my hands on that swine—'

'You won't.'

Tu slapped the table. 'We've got this far, *xiongdi*. Do you really think that I'll knuckle under and let the bastard get clean away? Think of what he did to Yoyo's friends, to Hongbing. The tortures he put him through!'

'Not so loud.' Jericho glanced at the half-closed bedroom door. 'No question that you're right to be angry, but perhaps you should just be grateful that you're not dead.'

'All right, I'm grateful. What next?'

'Nothing next.' Jericho spread his hands and rolled his eyes. 'Live. Life goes on.'

'It's not like you to take this attitude,' Tu chided him. 'The woodworm doesn't just sit about making comments on the carpentry.'

'Thanks for the comparison.'

'So why did we get involved in the first place?' Tu asked between gritted teeth. 'So that the bastards could get away with it?'

'You listen to me.' Jericho put down his teacup and leaned forward. 'Maybe you're right, and maybe next week I'll see it all differently, but where has all this got us? Following leads in ever-widening circles, all these killers, mercenary armies, Secret Services, coups in West Africa, government ploys and corporation plots, yesterday Equatorial Guinea, today the Moon, the day after tomorrow who knows, maybe Venus? Where has it got us? Corrupt oil cartels, Korean atom bombs, hotels on the Moon, rogue astronauts, oil managers getting shot at, Greenwatch wiped out, theories about China and the CIA, nine-headed monsters? Where? To a baking hot day and a man scared for his daughter. The furniture still in its packing and he's worried that she's disappeared, but first of all he has to help me get two chairs out of the bubble-wrap so that we have something to sit on. To be blunt, I couldn't give a shit about Xin and his Hydra. With the best will in the world, I have no idea what we have to do with Orley Enterprises. There's a girl in the next room, still breathing, we didn't have to lay her out in a shroud, and to me that's worth all the global conspiracies you could pile up together, since it looks as though we're well out of this game, however the whole thing plays out. We've got those sods on the run, Tian, so much so that they can't see any point in killing us. The story will fizzle out of its own accord. It begins and ends on the Shanghai Pudong golf course when you asked me to bring your friend his daughter back, alive and in one piece. That's what I did. Thank you, next please.'

Tian looked at him appraisingly, a handful of nuts raised halfway to his mouth.

'I'm very grate—'

'No, you're not following me.' Jericho shook his head. 'We're all grateful, all of us, to one another, but now we're going to fly off home, you can take care of your joint venture with Dao IT, Yoyo will carry on her studies, Hongbing will sell that silver Rolls that he was telling me about and enjoy his commission, and I'll wipe Xin's fingerprints from my furniture and try to fall in love with some woman who's not called Diane or Joanna. And won't it just be wonderful to be able to do all that? To lead a perfectly ordinary, boring life. We'll wake up from this hideous dream, we'll rub our eyes and that will be that, because *this* isn't our life, Tian! These are other people's problems.'

Tu scratched his belly. Jericho sank back into the depths of the sofa and wished he could believe what he'd just said.

'A perfectly ordinary, boring life,' Tu echoed.

'Yes, Tian,' he said. 'Ordinary, boring. And if I can give you some advice, as a friend: talk to Yoyo. Both of you. Talking helps.'

It was rude to talk this way in Chinese culture, even with a friend. But perhaps after all the last two days had brought – how much closer did you need to be before you allowed such trust? He looked out at London as the day began, and wondered whether he should leave Shanghai and come back here. Actually, he didn't much care either way.

'I'm sorry,' he sighed. 'I know it's nothing to do with me.'

Tu let the nuts he was holding rattle back down into the bowl, and stirred them with his finger. For a while, neither of them said anything.

'Do you know what an ankang is?' he asked at last.

Jericho turned his head. 'Yes.'

'Would you like to hear a story about an ankang?' Tu smiled. 'Of course you wouldn't. Nobody wants to hear a story about an ankang, but you've brought it upon yourself. This is a story which begins on 12 January 1968 in Zhejiang province, when a child is born, an only child. Nothing to do with the one-child policy, by the way, that was only proclaimed years later, though of course you know that, since you're practically Chinese yourself.'

12 January—

'Not your own birthday,' Jericho said.

'No, besides which I was born in Shanghai, and this happened in a small town. The child's father was a teacher, meaning that he was under serious suspicion of harbouring such heinous aims as wanting to educate people, or using his brain to develop an intellectual position. In other words, suspected of thought. Back in those days even knowing the rudiments of your own country's history was enough to have you beaten in the streets, but when Beijing's creatures began to destroy our culture in the name of revolutionising it, this teacher of ours adapted to the new circumstances. At first. After all, the capital was a vipers' nest of Red Guards, but out in the provinces the local Party leaders were fighting the Guards. The peasants and workers out there were doing quite well from the policies of Deng Xiaoping and Liu Shaoqi. So our teacher worked in a tractor factory to avoid the suspicion of intellectualism, and he did what little he could to stop Deng and Liu from being toppled by the Maoists. There was a Red Guard faction established in his town that was openly sympathetic to Deng, the Coordinated Work Committee, and this teacher thought it would be a good idea to join them. Which it was. Until '68, when the committee broke up under pressure from the hard-liners, who didn't need to know more than that he had once *been* a teacher. The day that he began to fear for his life was the day his son was born.'

Jericho sipped at his tea, and a suspicion stole over him.

'What was this teacher called, Tian?'

'Chen De.' Tu tapped at a peanut with his finger, sending it skittering over the table. 'You can probably guess his son's name for yourself.'

'A name meant to show how faithful the father was. Red Soldier.'

'Hongbing. A clever enough tactic, but it didn't help much. At the end of '68 they came to arrest Hongbing's mother for reactionary statements supposedly, though it was actually because quite a few Guards had been practising Cultural Revolution between her legs, and she wouldn't accept that it helped the poor peasants one jot if people like them dragged her into bed. They took her off to a re-education camp, where they, well, re-educated her. She came back home very ill, and broken, not the same person as she had been. Chen De started teaching again, sporadically, taking enormous risks to do so, but mostly he worked in the factory and did his best to teach his boy as much as he could, in secret, for instance telling him how to live an ethical life and why – highly dangerous propaganda, I can tell you! Then in the mid-seventies they noticed his links to the old committee. By now Mao liked to spend most of his time with the daughters of the Revolution, making sure that none of them were virgins. Chen De was accused of counter-revolutionary tendencies, seven years late, very quick trial, then prison. Hongbing was left behind, a child alone, looking after his sick mother, so he took over the job in the tractor factory.'

Tu paused, pouring himself more tea.

'Well, various things changed, some for the better, some for the worse. His mother died, and then Mao soon after, Deng was rehabilitated from having been in disgrace, and Hongbing's father could teach again – as long as he stuck to the Party line, of course. The boy grows up caught between ideology and despair. Since he has no role-models around him, he falls in love with cars, which were very rare indeed at the time. You can't make a living from something like that out in the country, so when he's seventeen he moves to Shanghai, which is as fun-loving as Beijing is scler-otic. He takes a string of odd jobs and falls in with a group of students who are tending the delicate shoots of democratic thought in post-revolutionary China, and they introduce him to books by Wei Jingsheng and Fang Lizhi – the Fifth Modernisation, opening of society, all those enticing, forbidden thoughts.'

'Hongbing was a democracy activist?'

'Oh, yes!' Tu nodded enthusiastically. 'He was up there in the front line, Owen my friend. A fighter! 20 December 1986, seventy thousand people took to the streets in Shanghai to protest against the way the Party had manipulated appointments to the People's Congress, and Hongbing was at their head. It's a miracle that they didn't fling him behind bars right then. Meanwhile he'd also got a job at a repairs garage, fixing up cadre cars, making influential friends. This was where he lost the last of his illusions, since the new brand of Chinese managers could have invented corruption. Well, never mind that. Tell me, does 15 April 1989 mean anything to you?'

'4 June does.'

'Yes, but it all began earlier. Hu Yaobang died, a politician the students had always seen as their friend, especially after the Party made him their own internal scapegoat for the disturbances of '86. Thousands of people march in Beijing to remember him and pay their respects on Tiananmen Square, and the old demands come up again: democracy, freedom, all the stuff that enrages the old men in power. Then criticism of the regime spreads to other cities, Shanghai as well, of course, and Hongbing raises a clenched fist once more and organises protests. Deng refuses dialogue with the students, the demonstrators go on hunger strike, Tiananmen becomes the centre of something like a huge carnival, there's something in the air, a mood of change, a happening, and Hongbing wants to see it for himself. By now there are a million people on the square. Journalists from all over the world, and the last straw comes when Mikhail Gorbachev arrives with his ideas of perestroika and glasnost. The Party is in a tight corner indeed.'

'And Hongbing's in the thick of it.'

'For all that, it could have ended peacefully. By the end of May most of the Beijing students want to wind the movement up, happy to have humiliated Deng, but the new arrivals like Hongbing insist that all demands must be met, and that escalates things. The rest is well known – I don't have to tell you about the Tiananmen Massacre. And once again, Hongbing has the most incredible luck. Nothing happens to him because his name's not on any of the blacklists. He went back to Shanghai, with the last of his illusions in shreds, decided to concentrate on his job instead and made it to deputy foreman. It's grown up to be a lovely big garage over all these years, the nouveaux riches have turned their backs on bicycles and nobody knows cars like Hongbing does. Every now and again he gets a trip to the brothel as a gift from a customer, the upper cadre invite him for meals, he's a good-looking lad, some fat cat functionaries wouldn't much mind if he got their daughters pregnant.'

'So he's adapted to the times.'

'Up until winter of '92, which is when Chen De hangs himself. He's spent all those years keeping his head down, and then he strings himself up. Depression. His wife had died, you see, and the Revolution had destroyed his family. Hongbing explodes with self-loathing. He hates his own name, he hates it when his drinking buddies boast and blather and yell *ganbei*, profiteers who used to be interested in the democracy movement but have sold out. He wants to make his voice heard. The year before, the dissident Wang Wanxing had been arrested for unfurling a banner on the anniversary of the Tiananmen Massacre, right in the middle of the square. It called for the rehabilitation of the demonstrators who had been killed. So the Tiananmen anniversary comes round again, 4 June 1993, and Hongbing demonstrates for Wang's release along with a couple of like-minded souls. He reckons that this is a small thing to ask, modest enough, that it might have better chances of success than always pissing up the same tree and shouting that the whole system should change. And lo and behold, someone takes notice of him. The wrong kind, unfortunately.'

'He's arrested.'

'On the spot. And this is where things get really despicable, although you might say that it's all been quite despicable enough. You'd be wrong. So far, it's just been brutal.'

Tu paused, while the sun climbed higher and flooded the Thames with light.

'For many years there was a pretty little Buddhist temple a few kilometres outside Hangzhou, in an idyllic spot between rice fields and tea plantations. Until they tore it down to build something in its place that was deemed more useful to Chinese society.'

'An ankang.'

Jericho felt his tiredness vanish. He had heard about the ankangs, though he had never seen one. The literal meaning of ankang was *safety, peace and health*, but in fact these were the police psychiatric prisons.

'The ankang at Hangzhou was the first psychiatric clinic of its kind in China,' Tu said. 'Based on the belief that there is one perfect ideology, and that anybody who questions it must be suffering from some sort of mental illness, either acute or chronic. Just like you'd have to be mentally ill to believe that the Earth is a cube, or that your spouse is really a dog in disguise. Taking the Soviet Union as their example, China had always made a habit of declaring that its dissidents were crazy, but the Party only gave the psychiatric clinics that cute little name – *ankang* – at the end of the eighties. Up till then, they had operated in secret.'

'Tell me, that dissident whom Hongbing was trying to get freed from prison, Wang Wanxing – wasn't he in an ankang as well?'

'For thirteen years, and then in the end he was deported in 2005. Up until then, there had only ever been rumours about the ankangs, dark mutterings that they had less to do with caring for the mentally ill than humiliating people who were of sound mind. That was when a debate began, very tentative at first, and it didn't stop the Party from opening more of these so-called clinics. There's a constant supply of people with paranoid delusions of human rights or schizophrenic beliefs about free elections. The world is full of lunatics, Owen, you just have to pay close attention: trade unionists, democrats, religious believers, people presenting petitions and lodging complaints about the demolitions and urban planning policy in Shanghai, for instance, and demanding outlandish things like citizen consultation. Not to mention the real crazies, the ones who think that our perfect society could harbour corruption.'

Jericho kept quiet. Tu slurped at his tea, as though to wash the taste of the word ankang from his mouth.

'Well, anyway, since Wanxing was deported in 2005 the victims have begun to speak up for themselves. Early 2005 the People's Congress even passed a law forbidding police torture, though this was a farce of course. It's still standard operating practice to work suspects over until they sign some kind of confession as proof of mental illness, then you can torture merrily away and call it medical treatment. There are about a hundred ankangs in China, and these days there's a lot of public debate and international pressure because of them, but back when Hongbing was admitted to the Hangzhou clinic it was still 1993 and there was no such thing as a right of appeal. There was a red banner hanging in the plane trees in the grounds, a very pretty thing to look at, saying *A healthy mind in a healthy body means lifelong happiness*, the usual cynical vocabulary of the gulag. Hongbing gets a diagnosis: he's suffering from paranoid psychosis and political monomania. You won't find a doctor outside China who's heard of either of these conditions, they're not on any international list, but that's just more proof of how stupid foreigners are. The clinical assessment is all couched in the most harmless terms, it says that Hongbing makes a good impression, his mental condition is stable, he does as he's told, he listens to the radio, he likes reading, he's keen to help, it's just that – and I'm quoting word for word here – he displays *massive impairment in logical thought* as soon as talk turns to politics. He's quite obviously mentally disturbed and his thought processes display clear signs of megalomania, affective aggression and a pathologically overdeveloped will. The doctors prescribe a course of pharmaceutical treatment and close supervision to bring poor Hongbing back to his wits, and with a stroke of their pen, he has no more rights.'

'Couldn't he talk to a lawyer, at least?' Jericho asked, nonplussed. 'There must have been some way to get his case heard.'

'But, Owen.' – Tu had started eating the nibbles again, scooping up another handful just as soon as he'd swallowed the first – 'that would have been a nonsense. I mean, how can a madman contest the fact that he's mad? After all, everybody knows that loonies always think they're the only sane ones. There's no way to appeal against a police finding that you're mad; the only people who decide how long you're detained are the police psychiatrists and functionaries. That's what makes it so unbearable for the victims. In a prison or a work camp, at least you know how long they've sent you down for, but when you're in an ankang it's entirely up to your tormentors. But do you know what's truly despicable here?'

Jericho shook his head.

'That most of the inmates really are mentally ill. That's cruel, eh? Just imagine how a healthy person suffers when he's surrounded by others who are seriously disturbed, criminals, threatening him the whole time. Not even half a year after admission, Hongbing sees two inmates murdered, and the staff stand by and watch. Night after night he forces himself to stay awake, for fear he could be next. Then there are other prisoners, pardon me, patients, who are perfectly sane, just like he is. Doesn't matter. They all have to go through the same hell. They're given regular therapy, the chemical cosh, insulin shock, electroshock therapy. You'd never believe all the cures they have for a sick mind! They stub their cigarettes out on your skin, genitals preferably, they torture you with hot wires. Extreme heat, sleep deprivation, dunking in ice-cold water, and beatings, always the beatings. Troublemakers get chained to the bed and tortured till they pass out, for instance by sticking a needle into their upper lip and then passing a current through – they vary the voltage, switching from high to low so that you can't get used to the pain. Sometimes, if the doctors and nurses feel in the mood, all the inmates in a section have to submit to punishment, whether or not they've done anything wrong. Given this level of expert care, many patients die of heart attacks. One that Hongbing had befriended was so desperate that he went on hunger strike. So they chained him to the bed as well, and then the mentally ill inmates were told to force-feed him, under staff supervision. But how do you go about that? Since nobody actually taught them what to do, they just force the poor guy's jaws open and tip the liquid food into him until he suffocates, but at least he's eaten. The death certificate called it a heart attack. Nobody was charged. Hongbing was lucky, if you want to call it that: they didn't use the worst tortures on him. There are some car-crazy cadre members in Shanghai who put in a word on his behalf, discreetly, so that they wouldn't draw reprisals onto themselves, but it was enough to make sure he got relatively privileged treatment. He gets a cell to himself, he's allowed to read and watch television. Three times a day he gets a dose of narcoleptics, with very pronounced side-effects, and all the while many of the doctors are quietly letting him know that they think he's entirely healthy. Hongbing hides the pills under his upper lip and then gets rid of them down the loo, then he gets insulin shock therapy as punishment and lies in a coma for days. Another time he's strapped down, the doctor puts on a pair of gloves with metal plates on them and puts his hand on his forehead, boom, there's an almighty bang and he can't see or hear. Electroshock therapy, this time as a punishment for being Hongbing. It's always booming and banging in the ankang – you can't get a wink of sleep for all the screams of pain. The patients hide under the beds, in the toilet, under the wash-basin, no use any of it. If you've been chosen, they'll find you. Oh, we're out of nibbles.'

It took Jericho a moment to react. In a trance, he stood up, went to the bar and came back with a couple of bags of crisps.

'Cheese and onion,' he read out. 'Or would you like bacon?'

'All the same to me. In the second year, Hongbing tries to escape. He's almost out and then they catch him. He still dreams about that today, more than about all the rest of it. As a reward for showing so much initiative they dose him with scopol-amine, which makes you listless, so that you don't spend your time thinking about silly things like escape. I hardly need mention that the stuff causes serious physical and psychological injury. In the third year of his stay, summer of '96, a young worker is admitted to the clinic who had reported her factory manager's son for taking bribes. The son beat her senseless, and she reported that as well, so the factory manager decided that anyone who could act with such a lack of decorum must be insane. The chief of police and the director of the ankang agreed. She's whisked away to the clinic without any medical diagnosis, without standing trial or being sentenced, while the ankang director's son-in-law is named a section manager in the factory. Coincidences do happen. Oh, and Hongbing? Falls in love with the lady, and looks after her until six months after her admission, when she dies under insulin shock therapy. Which breaks the last of his resistance. On the day he lost that woman, Hongbing lost the last of his strength.'

'That's dreadful, Tian,' Jericho said softly.

Tu shrugged. 'It's the story of a wrong turn, as so many of us have taken in life. A story of might-have-been and had-I-only. Then, spring '97, our merry band of madmen get a new member in their ranks, a well-to-do sort, pragmatic, self-assured. As you might expect, the first thing the doctors do is take care of that self-assurance. He's not exactly an unknown quantity in dissident circles, this chap, he's something of a local hero for fighting against corruption. He was section head in an electronic components factory and led thousands of employees in a protest against the management getting rich on the backs of the workers. Went to Beijing with proof, and was arrested and sectioned for his pains. In the ankang they give him all kinds of muck, he gets ill, his hair falls out, he has fits, can't sleep, his nerves are shot and his memory's full of holes but they can't break his will to live. His only goal is to get out of there as quick as he can, and he has powerful friends in Shanghai, for instance his brother-in-law plays golf with the chief of police. This man likes Hongbing. He spends a lot of time with him, listens to what he has to say, slowly puts him back together again. Six months later he's back outside, gets a senior job at a software company and makes plans to get rich and powerful. The year after that, when Hongbing's finally free, he's thirty years old and he's spent five of those years in the clinic; his friend from the ankang fixes him a job with a car dealer and takes it upon himself to take care of him whenever and however he can.'

The sun had climbed higher. Soft, rosy dawn light touched all the rooftops.

'You're the friend from the ankang,' Jericho said softly.

'Yes.' Tu took his glasses off and began to clean them on a corner of his shirt. 'I'm the friend. That's the link between Hongbing and me.'

Jericho was silent for a while.

'And Hongbing has never talked to Yoyo about this time?'

'Never.' Tu held the glasses up to the light and looked thoughtfully at the lenses. 'Have a look at your own life, Owen. You know it yourself, there are some experiences that just lock your vocal cords tight. You're tongue-tied by the shame, and also, you think that if you don't talk about it, it will fade with the years, but its power over you simply grows. After he was freed, Hongbing considered going to court. I told him, build your own life up first before you take any more steps. He had such a knack with cars! Whenever a new model came onto the market, he would know all there was to know about it within days. He listened to me, and worked up to being a salesman. In 1999 he got to know a girl from Ningbo and married her, in a great rush. They didn't suit one another, not one tiny bit, but he wanted to catch up on his five lost years, fast-forward and start a family as soon as possible. Yoyo was born, the marriage broke up just as predicted, since Hongbing suddenly decided he wasn't able to love any more. Truth was it was only himself he couldn't love, and he still can't today. The girl went back to Ningbo, Hongbing was given custody and tried to give Yoyo what he didn't have.'

'Kindness.'

'Hongbing's problem is that he thinks he doesn't deserve kindness. But Yoyo has got the wrong idea. She thinks that she's done something wrong. By saying nothing he's given her an enormous guilt complex, which is exactly the opposite of what he intended, but you've met him, you know what he's like by now. He's walled himself up in his own silence.' Tu sighed. 'The night before last, in Berlin, when I was out on the tiles with Yoyo and you were sulking in the hotel, I finally got round to telling her my story. She's clever, Yoyo, and straight away she asked whether something like that had happened to Hongbing.'

'What did you say?'

'Nothing.'

'He'll have to talk to her.'

'Yes.' Tu nodded. 'Once he can break out of his shell. I have to tell you that in secret, without her having the least idea, he's still fighting to be rehabilitated.'

'And you? Were you ever rehabilitated?'

'In 2002, when I became manager at the software company, I decided to lodge an appeal. It was rejected nine times. Then, totally out of the blue, I heard that it was all a dreadful mistake and that I had been the victim of misdiagnosis, even of a criminal conspiracy! My reputation was restored and that smoothed the path for my career. I put in a word for Hongbing and got him made technical director of a Mercedes dealership, which gave him enough of a livelihood that he could go to court at last, and he's been making his case ever since. He's gathered whole crates full of evidence, medical affidavits showing that he was never mentally ill, but so far his sentence has only ever been partially revised. I picked my fight with corrupt managers, but they'd broken the law after all. He took on the Party. And the Party's an elephant, Owen. He's a marked man, he's scarred for life. I think that if he were fully rehabilitated, he might even be able to confide in Yoyo, but as it is—'

Jericho turned his teacup around between his fingers.

'Yoyo has to learn the truth, Tian,' he said. 'If Hongbing won't talk to her, you'll have to.'

'Ah well.' Tu perched his glasses back on his nose and gave a wry grin. 'After this morning, at least I have some practice.'

'Thank you for telling me.'

Tu gazed at the empty crisp packets, lost in thought. Then he looked Jericho in the eyes.

'You're my friend, Owen. Our friend. You're one of us. You're part of it.'

2 June 2025

LYNN

London, Great Britain

The address 85 Vauxhall Cross, in the south-west of the city, on Albert Embankment near Vauxhall Bridge, looked as if King Nebuchadnezzar II had tried to build a Babylonian ziggurat with Lego bricks. In fact, the sand-coloured hulk with the green armoured glass surfaces contained the beating heart of British security, the Secret Intelligence Service, also known as SIS or MI6. In spite of its playful appearance, it was a genuine bulwark against the enemies of the United Kingdom, last attacked by an IRA unit twenty-five years ago, when a missile had been fired at it from the opposite bank, although without doing much more than shake the cups and saucers in the Secret Service coffee lounge.

Jennifer Shaw was on her way to her son's birthday dinner when she received a call from a very senior authority. She switched to receive, and C's voice filled the leather-scented interior of her freshly restored Jaguar Mark 2. In most people's eyes, the head of the British Foreign Secret Service was, after thirty-one James Bond films, called M, which was quite close to the reality, except that Sir Mansfield Smith-Cumming, the legendary first director, had introduced the letter C, and since then all directors had been called C – not least because it happened to stand for 'control'.

'Hello, Bernard,' said Shaw, in the certain knowledge that her evening was stuffed.

'Jennifer. I hope I'm not disturbing you.'

A set phrase. Bernard Lee, the current director, couldn't have cared less if he was disturbing her, or how. The only disturbance that he would have acknowledged was the disturbance to national security.

'I'm on my way to Bibendum,' she said truthfully.

'Oh, always excellent. Especially the skate wing. I haven't been there for ages. Could you call in on me for a moment beforehand?'

'How long's a moment?'

'Only if you have time. On the other hand—'

'The traffic's not too bad. Give me ten minutes.'

'Thanks.'

She called her son from her mobile and told him to go ahead and order a starter without her, but to get her a double portion of the iced lime soufflé.

'Which means that I won't see you before pudding,' her son complained.

'I'll aim to be there for the main.'

'Has this got anything to do with Orley's moon trip?'

'No idea, darling.'

'I thought the bomb went off and didn't do any harm, and they were all coming home safe and sound.'

'I don't really know.'

'Oh, well. I guess the Prime Minister's kids see their mother even more rarely.'

'How nice to have brought positive-thinking people into the world. Don't be cross with me, sweetie, I'll call as soon as I can.'

At Wellington Arch she turned from Piccadilly into Grosvenor Place and followed Vauxhall Bridge Road over the Thames. Soon she was sitting in full evening dress in Lee's office, with a glass of water in front of her.

'We've reconstructed Norrington's deleted emails,' the director said without any preamble.

'And?' she asked excitedly.

'Well.' Lee pursed his lips. 'You know, all the clues pointed to him, but we didn't have any real evidence—'

'The fact that Kenny Xin shot him full in the face seems pretty convincing to me. Have you found any trace of Xin, by the way?'

'Not the slightest. But we have come across something alarming. Our American colleagues are worried too. Norrington's mails didn't make any sense at all at first, he had deleted nothing but white noise, so we tried it with the Hydra program. And suddenly we had a complex correspondence in front of our eyes. Unfortunately there's nothing to tell us who Hydra is, and it isn't clear who else received the messages. What is certain is that Norrington must have had access to a secret router, to which he sent encrypted emails.'

'All from the central computer of the Big O?'

'Definitely. Without the mask, that snake-headed icon, we can't do a thing with the emails. It wouldn't have occurred to anybody that they are encoded, and he was too clever to install the decoding program on his work computer, and instead carried it around with him on a memory stick. However, we're getting some insights into the planning and construction of the launching pad in Equatorial Guinea, and learning some amazing things about the black market in Korean atom bombs, things that even we weren't aware of. Okay, the bomb went off, as we know, without doing any damage.'

'Indirectly it caused a lot of damage,' said Jennifer. 'But okay, Julian, Lynn and most of the guests are on the way home. They should be at OSS in a few hours.'

'You see; and now it's imperative that you talk to Julian.'

'Will do.'

'As soon as possible, I mean. Within the next hour. I need his assessment.'

Shaw raised an eyebrow. 'About what?'

'According to Norrington's correspondence, the whole business isn't quite over yet.'

'Tell me quite clearly. I have to know that it's worth leaving my son to celebrate his thirtieth birthday without his mummy.'

Lee nodded. 'I think it's worth it, Jennifer. Last year, there wasn't just one mini-nuke sent to the Moon.' He paused, sipped on his water and set the glass down carefully in front of him. 'There were two.'

'Two,' echoed Jennifer.

'Yes. Kenny Xin bought two, and both were put on Mayé's rocket. And now we're asking ourselves: where's the second one?'

Shaw stared at him. Lee was right, this *was* alarming. This meant *no* lime soufflé. What it did mean, she didn't want to think about.

Charon, Outer Space

Evelyn Chambers saw Olympiada Rogacheva floating from the sleeping area into the lounge with an expression of grim contentment. The spookily unreal aspect of her appearance had vanished. For the first time, the Russian seemed to see herself as the chief indicator of her own presence, as someone who didn't only exist thanks to her association with other people, but who would continue to be there even if her life's coordinators took their eyes off her.

'I told him to kiss my ass,' she announced, and settled next to Heidrun.

'And how did he take that?'

'He said he wouldn't do that, exactly, but he wished me luck.'

'Seriously,' said Heidrun, amazed. 'You told him you were leaving him?'

Olympiada Rogacheva looked down at herself with the shy sensuality of a teenager exploring the new territory of her body.

'Do you think I'm too old to—'

'Nonsense,' Heidrun said stoutly.

Olympiada smiled, looked up and floated away. An imaginary Miranda Winter somersaulted weightlessly, shrieked and squeaked. Finn O'Keefe read his book, to keep from seeing her red lips forming a blossom of promise, or uttering words of breathtaking banality. They were hurrying through space in the constant presence of Rebecca Hsu, they heard Momoka Omura making her acid comments, and Warren Locatelli boasting, Chucky telling bad jokes even more badly than they deserved, Aileen making bouquets of brightly coloured flowers of wisdom, Mimi Parker and Marc Edwards finding fulfilment in togetherness and Peter Black telling the latest news from time and space. They even heard Carl Hanna playing guitar, the other Carl, who wasn't a terrorist, just a nice guy. Walo Ögi played chess under the ceiling and lost his third game against Karla Kramp, Eva Borelius was trapped in the hamster-wheel of her self-reproach, and Dana Lawrence, the self-declared heroine, was writing a report.

Evelyn Chambers said nothing, glad of the emptiness in her head. For the first time since leaving the Moon, she felt distinctly better. Looking back, that strange experience in the mining area had been too embarrassing for her to mention, but she would have to find words for it sooner or later. She felt a vague sense of dread, as if a monstrous presence in that sea of mist had become aware of her, and had been watching her since then, but even that she would deal with. She gently pushed herself away, left Olympiada to her own devices and floated over to the bistro.

'How are you?' she asked.

'Fine.' Rogachev, strapped into a harness, looked up from his computer. 'You?'

'Better.' She rubbed her temples with her index fingers. 'The pressure is easing.'

'Glad to hear it.'

'But what if I yield to my professional curiosity?'

'You can ask anything you like.' Rogachev's smile melted the ice between his blond eyelashes a little. 'As long as you don't expect to get an answer to everything.'

'What are you doing on that computer all the time?'

'Julian deserves a response. We had a fantastic week thanks to him. However it may have ended, we were given a lot. And now we've got to give something in return.'

'You want to invest?' asked Mukesh Nair, floating over.

'Why not?'

'After this disaster?'

'So?' Oleg Rogachev shrugged. 'Did people stop building ships just because the *Titanic* went down?'

'I'll admit, I'm uneasy.'

'You know how failure works, Mukesh. It's always sparked by a fear of crisis. It starts with a soluble problem, but it drags a psychosis along behind it. A shark psychosis. It only takes one shark to paralyse the tourism of a whole region, because no one will go into the water even though the likelihood of being eaten tends to zero. The collapse of the economy, of the financial markets, has always involved psychoses. Not the individual terrorist attack, not the bankruptcy of an individual bank, the threat comes from the general paralysis that follows. Should I make my decision to invest in Julian's project, in the breakthrough of the global energy supply, dependent on a shark?'

'The shark was an *atom bomb*, Oleg!' Nair opened his eyes wide. 'Possibly the start of a global conflict.'

'Or not.'

'At any rate, there was nothing Julian could have done about it,' Evelyn confirmed. 'We were the victim of an attack meant for somebody else. We were simply in the wrong place at the wrong time.'

'But someone must know who was behind it!'

'And what are you going to do if they don't?' Rogachev asked ironically. 'Suspend all space travel?'

'You know very well that's not what I think,' Mukesh grumbled. 'I just wonder if an investment would be *sensible*.'

'I do too.'

'And?'

Rogachev pointed at the computer screen. 'I've worked it out. There's about six hundred thousand tonnes of helium-3 stored on the Moon, ten times the potential energy yield of all the oil, gas and coal supplies on Earth. Perhaps even more, because the concentration of the isotope on the back of the Moon might be even higher than it is in the Earth's shadow. That's five metres of saturated regolith; the most interesting part is the first two to three metres, or exactly the depth ploughed by the beetles.' Rogachev typed on his computer. 'Leaving out transport to Earth, the energy balance is as follows: one gram of regolith equals seventeen hundred and fifty Joules. Some of this is lost in heating and processing, leaving us with, let's say, fifteen hundred Joules. That's an area of ten thousand square kilometres that needs to be ploughed and processed to cover the current energy needs of Earth. One thousandth of the Moon's surface. Where productivity is concerned, beetles work with sunlight, which means that they spend half the year without energy, meaning that we would need twice as many of the things as we have at present.'

'And how many is that?'

'A few thousand.'

'A few *thousand*?' cried Mukesh.

'Yes, of course,' said Oleg, unmoved. 'Assuming we're deploying that many, then supplies would last for around four thousand years, always assuming that the world population stagnates and the Third World's energy needs remain lower than those of the developed countries. Neither of these two things will be the case. Realistically, we can expect a global population of twenty-five billion by the end of the century, and an overall increase in electricity usage. In that case the Moon will supply us with energy for seven hundred years at most.'

'And then?' asked Evelyn Chambers.

'We'll have used up another fossil resource, and we'll be standing right where we are today. The Moon will have been levelled, uninteresting to hotels and pleasure trips, but may have been able to preserve a few conservation areas. Whether we'll be able to see them for dust is a whole other question.'

'Thousands of mining machines.' Nair shook his head. 'That's crazy! We'll never be able to pay for them.'

'We will.' Rogachev snapped the computer shut. 'We had a deficit problem with space travel, too. The lift changed everything, and building a few thousand machines like that isn't such big news. Thousands of tanks will be built too, and a levelled moon is just a levelled moon.'

'Shit,' Chambers said to herself.

'Yes, shit. I know what you're thinking. Yet again we've destroyed a natural wonder for the sake of a short-term effect.'

'But it's going to be worth it?'

'It'll be worth it for seven hundred years, and from a distance the Moon won't look much different from what it looks like today.' Oleg pursed his lips. 'So I think I'm going to invest part of the originally planned sum in Orley Space.'

'Congratulations.'

'Not least on *your* advice.' He raised his eyebrows. 'Have you forgotten? Isla de las Estrellas?'

'I hadn't been to the mining zone then.'

'I understand. Shark psychosis.'

'No, not at all. You've just expressed in words what I'd already worked out in the land of mists. The idiocy of the whole thing. When we talk about moon mining, most people think about a few lonely bulldozers lost in the vastness of the Moon. Instead, we're losing the Moon to the bulldozers.' She shook her head. 'Of course it's better to destroy the Moon than the Earth, aneutronic fusion is clean, and if it lasts seven hundred years, then fine. But I'm still allowed to think it's crap.'

'I thought I'd put the other half of the money into buying up Warren Locatelli's Lightyears.'

'What?' Mukesh Nair rolled his eyes. 'You want to—'

'I don't want to look ruthless.' Rogachev raised both hands. 'Warren's dead, but holding back won't bring him back to life. He was a little god, and like all gods he left a vacuum. In my view, Lightyears is the best imaginable candidate for a buyout. Warren Locatelli did amazing things in solar technology, there's still much to come and the best brains in the sector are working for his company. So let's be under no illusions: solar technology's going to be the only way of solving our energy problems in the long term!' He smiled. 'So we may not even have to level the Moon.'

'And you're sure that Lightyears will simply allow itself to be swallowed up?' the Indian asked suspiciously.

'Hostile takeover.'

'You'll have to offer a huge amount of money.'

'I know. Are you in?'

'God almighty, you ask some questions!' Nair rubbed his fleshy nose. 'This isn't really my area. I'm just a simple—'

'Farmer's son, I know.'

'I'll have to think about it, Oleg.'

'Do that. I've already talked to Julian. He's with me. Walo too.'

'One of them gets a leg, the other an arm,' hummed Evelyn, as Nair floated off with solar cells in his eyes. Rogachev smiled his vulpine smile and remained silent for a moment.

'And you?' he asked. 'What are you going to do?'

She looked at him. 'About Julian?'

'You do administer the capital of public opinion, as you put it so nicely.'

'Don't worry.' Evelyn pulled a face. 'I won't hurt him.'

'A good friend,' Rogachev chuckled.

'Friendship hasn't got much to do with it, Oleg. I was well disposed towards his projects *before* I went to the Moon, and I still am, regardless of what I think about the plundering that's going on up there. He's a pioneer, an innovator. No criminal gang is going to blow my sympathies for him out of my head just like that.'

'So are you going to make a programme about what happened?'

'Of course. Will you be on it?'

'If you like.'

'In that case can I take the opportunity to ask you some questions about your private life?'

'No, you can only do that here.' He winked at her. 'As a *friend*.'

'At the moment the word is that you're being abandoned.'

'Ah, right.' He glanced away. 'Yes, I think Olympiada mentioned something along those lines.'

'Christ, Oleg!'

He shrugged. 'What do you expect? Since we got married she's left me every two weeks or so.'

'She seems to mean it this time.'

'I'd be glad if she would turn her thoughts into actions. Admittedly this is the first time she's left me without being falling-down drunk.'

'You don't care?'

'No! It's way overdue.'

'I'm sorry, but I don't get this at all. Why don't *you* just leave *her*, in that case?'

'I did, ages ago.'

'Officially, I mean.'

'Because I promised her father I wouldn't.'

'I see. All that macho crap.'

'What? Keeping your promises?' Rogachev studied her. 'Shall I tell you the biggest reproach she levels at me, Evelyn? Do you want to know? What do you think?'

'No idea.' She shrugged. 'Infidelity? Cynicism?'

'No. That I've never taken the trouble to lie to her. Can you imagine that? *The trouble?*'

Confused, Evelyn said nothing.

'But I don't lie,' said Rogachev. 'You can accuse me of all sorts of things, probably rightly, but if there's something that I've never done and never will do, it's lying or breaking promises. Can you imagine that? Someone ignoring all your bad qualities and telling you off for your good one?'

'Perhaps she means it's more bearable—'

'For whom? For her? She could have gone, at any time. She should never have married me. She knew me, she knew exactly who I am, and that Ginsburg and I were just trying to marry our *fortunes* together. But Olympiada agreed because she couldn't think of anything better to do, and even today she can't think of anything to do but suffer.' Rogachev shook his head. 'Believe me, I'll never stop her. I'll never *force* her to leave me. She may think I've degraded her, but she's got to regain her own dignity. Olympiada says she's dying by my side. That's tough. But I can't save her life, she has to save her own life, by *going.*'

Evelyn stared at her fingertips. Suddenly she saw the foot of the beetle coming down again, felt the creature's pale eye settling on her from the realm of the dead. I see you, it said. I'll watch you every day as you prepare yourself for death.

'You've saved *my* life,' she said quietly. 'Did I ever thank you for that?'

'I think you're trying to right now,' said Rogachev.

She hesitated. Then she leaned across and kissed him on the cheek.

'I think you've got a few more positive characteristics,' she said. 'Even if you're pretty ignorant otherwise.'

Rogachev nodded.

'I should have started sooner,' he said. 'My father was a brave man, braver than the lot of us put together, but I couldn't save his life. I try again every day, by piling up money for him, buying companies for him, submitting people to my will and thus to his, but still he is shot over and over again. He will never come back to life, and I don't know how to deal with it. There's no middle way, Evelyn. Either you're too far away, or you're too close to it.'

'You're not that far apart,' hissed Amber. She was angry, because Julian and Tim could do nothing but bicker, and even angrier about the immovable persistence with which each clung to his resentment, while Lynn slept her time away as if under chloroform. 'Both of you suspected her of being in a pact with Carl.'

'Because that's how she behaved,' said Tim.

'Ludicrous! As if Lynn would seriously have been capable of destroying her own hotel!'

'You saw her yourself,' bellowed Julian. 'It may seem weird to us in retrospect, but Lynn is mentally disturbed.'

'Not much gets past you, does it?' sneered Tim.

'That's enough,' Amber snapped at him. 'This is kindergarten stuff. Either you learn to talk to each other sensibly, or it'll be me you're dealing with. Both of you!'

They had withdrawn into the landing module so as not to let the others see the spectacle of their rancour. Neither of them was any good at holding things back. The mouldering corpse of their family life lay naked and repulsive before them, ready for the autopsy. After the Io had rescued Nina Hedegaard from a hell of dust, and the surviving members of the group had climbed aboard the landing module to get back to the mother ship, Lynn had collapsed in tears. Immediately after the coupling manoeuvre, she had regained consciousness, without recognising anybody, faded away again and set off on a horrific twenty-four-hour journey. Since then she had looked more or less composed, except that she couldn't remember most of what had happened on the Moon. Now she was asleep again.

'Just to clear up a few things—' Tim began.

'Stop.' Amber shook her head.

'Why?'

'I said, stop!'

'You don't know what I—'

'I do. You want to attack your father! How long is this going to go on for? What are you actually accusing him of? Of making space travel economically viable? Of giving zillions of people jobs?'

'No.'

'Of making people's dreams come true? Of fighting for clean energy, for a better world?'

'Of course not.'

'Then what?' she yelled. 'Oh, Christ, I'm so fed up with this wretched trench warfare. So fed up!'

'Amber.' Tim crouched down. 'He didn't care. When we—'

'Care about what?' she interrupted him. 'Maybe he wasn't there for you very often. As I see it, he cares day in, day out, for a weird cosmic phenomenon called humanity, which does all kinds of terrible, stupid things. Sorry, Tim, but I can't stand the peevish way young people talk about their parents, even if they produce miracles, all that in-an-ideal-world claptrap – I don't buy it, I'm afraid.'

'It isn't just that he wasn't around,' Tim defended himself, 'but that on the few occasions when he should have been there, he wasn't! That Crystal lost her m—'

'You're completely unfair, you little shit,' Julian snorted. 'Your mother had a genetic predisposition.'

'Crap!'

'She did! *Capito, hombre?* She'd have lost her mind even if I'd been there for her every hour of every day.'

'You know very well that—'

'No, she was sick! It was in her genes, and before I married her she'd fried half of her brain on coke anyway. And where Lynn's concerned—'

'Where Lynn's concerned, you listen to me,' Amber interrupted. 'Because as a matter of fact, and Tim's completely right here, you can't look into anyone else's head. You think life's a film and you're directing it, and everyone acts and thinks according to the script. I don't know whether you really love Lynn, or only the part that she's supposed to play for you—'

'Of course I love her!'

'Okay, you've done everything for her, you've made sure she had the best possible career, but have you ever been *interested* in her? Are you sure you've ever really been interested in anyone?'

'Christ alive, why have I organised all this, in that case?'

'No, no.' She raised a finger. 'Listen, little Julian, to what your aunt says! You make films and you cast people in them. With ten billion extras and Lynn in the main part.'

'That's not true!'

'Yes, it is. You can't see that your daughter is manic-depressive, and that she threatens to suffer the same fate as her mother.'

'Exactly,' cried Tim. 'Because you—'

'Shut it, Tim! Look, Julian, it's not that you don't want to see it, you just *don't* see it! Come down to earth. Lynn's unusually talented, she has brilliant qualities, just like you do, but unlike you she hasn't got power flowing through her veins, she's not a natural mover and shaker, and she doesn't have a buffalo hide. So stop selling her as perfect and beating up on her because she'll never dare to contradict you. Ease off on the pressure. Say after me: Lynn – is – not – like – me!'

'Erm – Julian?'

Amber looked up. Nina Hedegaard, visibly troubled, was hovering in the airlock leading to the habitation units. Julian turned his head and forced himself to assume a relaxed expression.

'Come in, come in. We were just swapping funny family stories and discussing our next Christmas party.'

'I don't mean to bother you.' She smiled shyly. 'Hello, Amber. Hi, Tim.'

Since the Charon had set off on its long trip back to the OSS, Julian had stopped trying to hide his relationship with the pilot. Amber liked Nina and felt sorry for her, particularly for the way she believed Julian when he hinted at their future together.

'What's up?' asked Julian.

'I've got Jennifer Shaw on the line.'

'I'll be right there.' He strolled to the airlock, all too willingly, it seemed to Amber.

'And then you come right back,' she added. 'I haven't finished with you yet.'

'Yes,' sighed Julian. 'I was afraid of that.'

Tim opened his mouth to make a disagreeable remark. Amber flashed a glance at him that made him think better of it.

Lynn was sharpening the blade of her suspicions.

What had happened on the Moon seemed like a single, painful dream sequence, and in fact she had difficulty remembering the last few hours in Gaia. But when Dana Lawrence floated past in her sleeping bag at the same moment as she opened her eyes, cast her a glance and asked her how she was, a synaptic firework exploded in her brain, and she couldn't help it. She said:

'Piss off to hell, you two-faced snake.'

Dana paused, with her head thrown back, her eyelids heavy with arrogance. The voices of the others could be heard from the next sector along. Then she came closer.

'What's your problem with me, Lynn? I haven't done anything to you.'

'You've questioned my authority.'

'No, I was loyal. Do you think it was fun watching Kokoschka burn, even if he was in cahoots with Hanna? I had to order the evacuation.'

The stupid thing was that she was right. By now Lynn knew that she had behaved in an extremely paranoid way, even though she wondered in what context it might have been. For example she hadn't understood why she hadn't wanted to show Julian certain films. And she couldn't remember her wild escape across the glass bridges, seconds before the fire had broken out, but she could remember Hanna's betrayal, the bomb and the operation to rescue the people trapped in Gaia's head. For a moment she had regained her leadership qualities, before her mind had given in once and for all. That it was now working again seemed at first like a miracle, although she wasn't particularly pleased, since the generator of her emotions had clearly suffered some damage. Listless and depressed, she couldn't even remember what it was like to feel joy. On the other hand she knew what she definitely *hadn't* dreamed about in all that confusion. It was clearly in front of her eyes, it echoed in her ears, a matter in which Lawrence played an inglorious part.

'Leave me alone,' she said.

'I did my job, Lynn,' Dana said, insulted. 'If shortcomings in the planning and construction of Gaia led to disaster, you can't blame me.'

'There were no shortcomings. When will we actually get there?'

'In about three hours.'.

Lynn started unbuckling herself. She was thirsty. And for something specific, grapefruit juice. So she wasn't just thirsty, she'd got an appetite. An emotional reaction, almost.

'They should have put in more emergency exits,' Dana Lawrence said, trickling acid into the wounds. 'The throat was a bottleneck.'

'Didn't I sack you?'

'You did.'

'Then shut up.'

Lynn pushed Lawrence aside and slipped over to the hatch leading to the next area. As always, everyone would be very nice and caring, Embarrassing, embarrassing, it should have been her task to ask Julian's guests what they would like. But she was ill. Gradually, in manageable portions, Tim had told her the full extent of the disaster, so by now she knew who had died and under what circumstances. And again she had struggled to feel anything, grief, or at the very least rage, and had come up with nothing but dull despair.

'What did she want?'

'What?' Julian took off his headphones.

'I said, what did she want?'

Tim tried not to sound unfriendly. Julian turned his head. The command panel of the Charon was in the back part of the sleeping area. Through the open bulkhead they could see into the adjacent lounge, where Heidrun, Sushma and Olympiada were in conversation with Finn O'Keefe, while Walo Ögi was despairing over one of Karla Kramp's castling manoeuvres.

'Something really strange,' Julian said quietly. 'She was asking how many bombs we found at the moon base.'

'How *many*?'

'Apparently there were *two* mini-nukes aboard that rocket from Equatorial Guinea. There's another one of those things up there.'

He said it in such a calm and matter-of-fact way that it took Tim a moment to understand the full import of the news.

'Shit,' he whispered. 'Does Palmer know about this?'

'They informed him straight away. Panic must have broken out at the base. They want to inspect the caves again.'

'You mean, in case a bomb is found—'

'Hanna may have hidden a second one.'

'Pah.'

'Mm-hm.' Julian rested a hand on Tim's shoulder. 'Whatever, we don't want to tell the world about it.'

'I don't know, Julian.' Tim frowned. 'Do you seriously think he put the second bomb in the caves as well?'

'You don't?'

'When there was already one in there? I'd find a different place for a second one.'

'That's true too.' Julian rubbed his beard. 'And what if the second mini-nuke isn't meant for the base?'

'Who else would it be meant for?'

'I've just got this idea. A bit crude, perhaps. But just imagine that someone's trying to stir the Chinese and Americans up against each other. Not hard, given that they mixed it up last year. So what if the second bomb—'

'Was meant for the Chinese?' Tim slowly exhaled. 'You should write novels. But okay. There's a third possibility.'

'Which is?'

'The mining zone.'

'Yeah.' Julian gnawed on his lower lip. 'And there's nothing we can do about it.'

'But how about I tell Amber?'

'Okay, but no one else. I'll have a talk to Jennifer and tell her what we think.'

Orley Space Station (OSS), Geostationary Orbit

They approached the space station at an angle, so that the massive 280-metre mushroom-shaped structure hung at a diagonal. By now they were all wearing their spacesuits again. Even though the Earth was still 36,000 kilometres away, seeing the OSS getting bigger on the screens was a bit like coming home: its five tori, the wide circle of its wharf, the extravagant modules of the Kirk and the Picard, the ring-shaped space harbour with its mobile airlocks, manipulators, freight shuttles and pha-lanxes of stumpy-winged evacuation pods. At 23.45 a hollow chime rang through the spaceship, along with a faint vibration as Hedegaard docked on the ring.

'Please keep your suits on,' said Nina. 'The full kit. Your luggage—'

She fell silent. She had clearly realised that no one had any luggage. It had all been left in Gaia.

'From the Charon we go straight to the Picard, where a snack bar has already been set up. We haven't got much time – the lift will be there at about a quarter past twelve, and will leave the OSS straight away. We thought it – ahem, in your interest to get back to Earth as quickly as possible. You can store your helmets and backpacks in Torus-2.'

No one said anything. Gloomily they left the spaceship by the airlock, said farewell to their cramped flying hotel and, in a sense, belatedly to the Moon, which couldn't in the end do anything about what had happened. They floated one after the other down the corridor to Torus-2, the distributor ring that accommodated the lobby and hotel reception. From there, connecting tunnels branched out, leading down to the suites and up through the levels to the part of the station used by the research teams with its labs, observatories and workshops. The two extendable airlocks on the inside of the torus which led to lift cabins were locked. Three astronauts were working on the consoles, checking the lift systems, overseeing the unloading of a freighter and repair work on a manipulator.

O'Keefe thought of the disc of the wharf, where spaceships were being built for bolder missions, of machines dashing through the silence of the universe and solar panels sparkling in the cold, white sun. Heidrun had pushed him out of the airlock up there, she had made fun of him, and Warren Locatelli had puked in his helmet.

How long ago was that? A decade? A century?

He wouldn't be coming back, he knew that, as he set his helmet down on its shelf. Making brash science-fiction films, saving the universe, any time! Whatever the script called for. But no going back.

'No,' he said to himself.

'No?'

Heidrun set her helmet down next to his. He turned his head and looked into her violet eyes. He studied her elfin face, saw her hair forming a flowing white fan in zero gravity. Felt his heart like a lump in his chest.

'Would you come back?' he asked. 'Here? To the Moon?'

She thought for a moment.

'Yes. I think I would.'

'So you found something up here.'

'A few things, Finn.' She smiled. 'Quite a lot, in fact. And you?'

Nothing, he wanted to say. I've just lost something. Before I had it.

'Don't know.'

He would never see her again either. He would stay out of everyone's way. The world was full of lonely places, it *was* a lonely place. You didn't have to go to the Moon to find one of those. Heidrun opened her lips and raised a hand as if to touch him.

'In our next life,' she said quietly.

'But there's only this one here,' he answered roughly.

She nodded, lowered her head and slipped past him. A strand of her hair passed across his face and tickled his nose.

'*Mein Schatz*,' he heard Walo say. 'Are you coming?'

'Coming, sweetie!'

The lump was starting to hurt. Finn O'Keefe stared at his helmet, turned round and drifted after the others, his mind a blank.

Midnight had just gone. It had been such an effort to quell the excitement of the last few days that no one felt much like reviving it with caffeine, so everyone pounced on fruit juice and tea in the Picard. Julian would have liked to have some soup, but because eating soup in micro-gravity was pretty much a no-no, there was lasagne. He sawed a piece of it off and disappeared into the tunnel that led down to the suites, to phone the Earth from there.

Dana Lawrence joined him.

'Not hungry?' he asked.

'No, I am. I just left my report in the Charon.'

He stopped outside his cabin, balancing his lasagne. Did this woman make any sense at all? In Gaia, she had proved her mettle, she had challenged the traitor Kokoschka and finished off Carl Hanna. Lynn couldn't have made a better choice, and yet, thinking about it, it was the fact that any other choice was rationally unthinkable that unsettled him. Perhaps it was because of the image he had of women, of people in general, that he couldn't make head or tail of her. He couldn't imagine her bursting into tears or bursting out laughing. Her Madonna face with its heart-shaped mouth and piercing eyes made him think of a replicant, of Brooke Adams' postpod character in *Invasion of the Body Snatchers*, in the scene in which she opens her mouth and emits the hollow, unearthly scream of an alien. Clearly very intelligent and passably attractive, Dana Lawrence was miles away from any kind of passion.

'I must thank you,' he said. 'I know Lynn wasn't always – always quite up to it during the crisis.'

'She fought remarkably well.'

'But I also know that Lynn's initial enthusiasm for you turned into rejection. Don't blame her. Lynn's judgement was clouded during this trip. You were far-sighted and brave.'

'I did my job.' She mimicked a smile, making her features softer but no more sensual. 'Will you excuse me?'

'Of course.' She floated past him and disappeared down the next side corridor.

Julian immediately forgot about her. He hungrily sniffed his lasagne, looked into the scanner and slipped into his cabin.

Dana reached Torus-1, with its bars, libraries and common rooms – then continued on and slipped into the long tunnel which led towards the upper level and connected the OSS Grand with Torus-2. Only two astronauts were still on duty at the terminal.

'I have to go to Charon for a minute,' she said to them. 'For some documents.'

One of the men nodded. 'Fine.'

She turned away, disappeared into the corridor that linked Torus-2 with the outer ring of the space harbour and drifted towards the airlock behind which the spaceship lay at anchor. Everything was still going to plan. Hydra still hadn't lost, quite the contrary. It was only Lynn's suspicion that unsettled her, as she couldn't work out how it had come about. But even that wasn't particularly important. Dana opened the bulkhead leading to the Charon and looked behind her, but no one had followed her down the corridor. In the Picard they were indulging in lasagne and homesickness. She sped into the landing unit and on into the habitation module, crossed the bistro, the lounge and started working away at the wall covering.

Hanna had told her exactly where to do it.

And there she was.

The lightning flash of memory. Amazing how it appeared in the middle of heavy cloud cover. She couldn't remember exactly what she'd done in the igloo, but she could see Carl Hanna very clearly, before she had sunk to the floor by the coffee machine, frozen with terror. She saw him murdering Tommy Wachowski, heard his quiet, traitorous cursing:

Dana, for fuck's sake. Come on!

Dana.

Her suspicions had already been aroused a few hours ago, when Dana Lawrence had hypocritically asked her how she was, but now it was certain. Hanna had tried to make contact with the bitch, in a way that revealed that the contact had been prearranged. Why? Drawing the necessary conclusions would have taken a considerable amount of energy, too much to put Julian in the picture as well, particularly since she didn't talk much to her father any more. It had dawned on her that she felt a lot better as soon as she banished him from the centre of her thoughts. At the same time she missed him, as a puppet misses the hand that moves it, and she was already aware, at least on an intellectual level, that she actually idolised him. Maybe she no longer *felt* what she felt, but at least she still *knew* what she felt.

Something had gone wrong in her life, and Dana Lawrence had played an inglorious part in that.

Lynn peered down the corridor.

Determined not to let her enemy out of her sight, she had followed Dana Lawrence when she had left the Picard with Julian. The cunning of madness, she thought, *almost* with amusement, but the madness had fled. A few seconds passed, then she slipped after Lawrence. At the end of the corridor she saw that the Charon's bulkhead was open, and knew that Lawrence was in the spaceship.

I'll get you, she thought. I will prove you're a snake, and the seething hatred that I know you feel for me will be your downfall. You shouldn't have allowed yourself to be dragged into all this, unapproachable, unassailable, controlled Dana, but you aren't unassailable after all. You didn't try to shatter the others' confidence in me for nothing. You will pay.

She floated silently over the rim of the bulkhead, crossed the landing module, the bistro, the lounge. She glimpsed Dana in the sleeping area bent over something angular, the size of a briefcase, that she had taken from the opened wall. Saw her fingers darting over a keyboard and entering some data:

*   *   *

Nine hours: 09.00

The plan was so simple, so efficient at its core. Launching a rocket to the Moon and detonating it above Peary Base might have worked, but its trajectory would be immediately traceable, and the risk of missing the base was great as well. To fire another missile at the OSS, whether from Earth or a satellite, was practically impossible. The rocket would have been intercepted, and here too the reconstruction of its flight-path would have led straight to its originator.

But Hydra had come up with the perfect solution. Two mini-nukes, disguised in a communication satellite, from which they could travel unnoticed to the Moon and land some distance from the base, to stay there until someone came to take them out of the capsule and put them in the right places. One in the base, the second in the spaceship that would bring the bomb and the killers back to the OSS. Immediately before leaving the base, set bomb 1, then hide bomb 2 in the OSS, program that too and travel quite officially back to Earth in the lift before the timers set off both explosions, destroying both Peary Base and the OSS. The perfect double whammy.

A trajectory that couldn't be reconstructed.

Okay, they'd messed up Peary. They wouldn't mess up the OSS. At half past nine, when they had all long-since arrived on Isla de las Estrellas, or were back on the way to their own countries, the space station would vaporise, leaving only a few thousand kilometres of feather-light carbon rope to fall into the Pacific. They probably didn't even need to get the bomb out of the spaceship. The Charon was supposed to be at anchor for at least two days, as she had learned in the terminal. It didn't really make any difference whether she hid the mini-nuke in the ceiling cover of the airlock or just left it where it was.

08.59

08.58

She looked contentedly at the blinking box. And as she was savouring her triumph, the hairs on the back of her neck stood up.

There was someone there.

Right behind her.

Dana swung round.

That moment she felt a kick in the chest that threw her against the wall of the cabin. The mini-nuke slipped from her hands and sailed away. Lynn reached out for it, missed it, ended up at an angle and started rotating on her own axis. Dana dashed after the spinning bomb, felt a hand gripping her ankle and was pulled back. In front of her eyes Julian's daughter darted upwards, grabbed the box and fled, carried on her own momentum, to the lounge and from there to the landing module.

She must not leave the Charon.

Dana hurried after her. Just before the airlock she caught up with Lynn, grabbed her by the collar and dragged her back inside the unit. Lynn somersaulted, tightly gripping the bomb, and wedged herself, legs spread, in the passageway to the habitation module. Lawrence risked a glance over her shoulder. Through the open bulkhead she could see into the airlock and glimpse the connecting corridor. There was still no one to be seen, but she knew the airlock was under surveillance. She couldn't afford to let the silent struggle continue outside the Charon.

Julian's daughter stared at her, gripping the ticking atom bomb like a cherished object from which she never wanted to be parted.

'Indecisive?' she grinned.

'Give me that thing, Lynn.' Dana was breathing heavily, less out of exertion than out of rage. 'Right now.'

'No.'

'It's an expensive scientific device. I don't know what's got into you, but you're about to ruin a very high-level experiment. Your father will be furious.'

'Oh, really?' Lynn rolled her eyes spookily. 'Will he?'

'Lynn, please!'

'I know what this is, you bitch. It's a bomb, exactly like the one you and Carl hid in the base.'

'You're confused, Lynn. You—'

'Don't you dare!' yelled Lynn. 'I'm completely fine.'

'Okay.' Dana raised conciliatory hands. 'You're completely fine. But that isn't a bomb.'

'Then you won't have a problem letting me out!'

Dana clenched her fists and didn't move, as her thoughts did somersaults. She had to get hold of the mini-nuke, but what was she to do with the madwoman who clearly wasn't as crazy as all that? If she let Lynn live and go back to the others, she might just as well hand over the bomb and admit everything.

'Problems?' Lynn giggled. 'Without me the lift won't return to Earth, will it? They'll spend hours looking for me, and you'll have to join in. There's nothing you can do.'

'Give me the box,' Dana said, struggling to control herself, and floated closer.

Lynn lowered the bomb. For a moment it looked as if she was wondering whether she could comply with Dana's demand, then she suddenly threw herself back into the habitation module.

'And now?' she asked.

Dana bared her teeth.

And suddenly she lost her head, reached for the disguised pocket on her thigh and brought out Carl Hanna's gun. Lynn's eyes widened. She leapt after the bomb. Her hand hit the sensor that controlled the bulkhead between the module and the habitation unit. Dana cursed, but the connecting door closed too quickly, no chance of getting through it, at best she'd be trapped. Through the narrowing gap she saw Lynn's torso, her flying, ash-blonde hair half covering her face, took aim and shot.

The bulkhead thumped shut. She went straight to the control panel and tried to open it again, but it didn't budge. Lynn must have activated the emergency lock.

She hammered furiously against the steel door.

Too late.

Her body drifted somersaulting through the lounge.

Spirals turned before her eyes. With a great effort, Lynn focused her ideas on the command panel in the rear zone, straightened out, gripped the edge of the next passageway and impelled herself forwards to the control console.

The terminal. She had to call the terminal.

'Lynn Orley,' she gasped. 'Can anyone hear me?' Oops! Something wrong with her voice? Why did she sound so feeble, so crushed?

'Miss Orley, yes, I can hear you.'

'Put me through to my father. He's in his – his suite. Quickly, get a move on!'

'Straight away, Miss Orley.'

Something had found its way through the crack. Something that hurt and dulled her senses. Everything went dark.

'Julian,' she whispered. 'Daddy?'

Dana was beside herself. She'd been duped. She'd let her feelings take control, rather than diplomacy. Flight was the only option now. It didn't matter whether she'd killed Lynn, wounded her, or even missed her entirely, she had to get out of the OSS before the lift arrived. She furiously catapulted herself out of the landing module, pelted down the corridor and into the torus, took aim and shot one of the astronauts in the head.

The man tipped sideways and drifted slowly away. With her legs outstretched she braked herself and aimed the barrel of her gun at the other one. He stared at her in silent horror, his hands over the touchscreen.

'Get one of the evacuation pods!' she yelled. 'Quickly!'

The man trembled.

'Go, now! Get it!'

Inflamed with rage, she whacked him in the face. He gripped the console to stay upright.

'I can't,' he panted.

'Are you mad?' Of course he could, why couldn't he? 'Do you want to die?'

'No – please—'

Stupid jerk! Trying to hold her up! All the docking ports could be relocated along the ring, she knew that. He would just park the Charon somewhere else, and instead take one of the pods to the airlock and anchor it there.

'Just do it,' she hissed.

'I can't, I really can't.' The astronaut gulped and licked his lips. 'Not during the launching process.'

'Why the launching process?'

'Wh-when a ship launches, I can't relocate the docking port, I have to wait till—'

'Launches?' she yelled at him. 'What's launching?'

'The—' He closed his eyes. The movement of his lips was oddly out of time with what he said, as if he were praying at the same time. Spittle glistened at the corners of his mouth, and he was losing control of his bladder.

'Open your mouth, damn it!'

'The Charon. It's the Charon. It's – it's launching.'

'Daddy?'

Julian gave a start. He had just been talking to Jennifer Shaw, when a second window had appeared in the holowall.

'Lynn,' he said with surprise. 'Sorry, Jennifer.'

'Daddy, you've got to stop her.'

Her face was right up against the camera, sunken and waxy, as if she were about to lose consciousness. He immediately switched Shaw to standby.

'Lynn, is everything okay?'

She shook her head feebly.

'Where are you?'

'In the spaceship. I've launched Charon.'

'What's going on?'

'I'm flying away – I'm taking – the bomb away from here.' Julian saw her eyelids fluttering and her head tipping over. 'She's smuggled a second bomb on board, she or – Carl, I don't know—'

'Lynn!'

His hands gripped the console. Slow as snake venom the realisation of what was happening seeped into his consciousness. Of course! It made horrible sense. This wasn't just a blow against the Americans, it was an attack on space travel!

'Lynn, don't do it!' he urged. 'Bring Charon back! You can't do this!'

'You've got to stop her,' she whispered. 'Dana – it's Dana Lawrence. She's the – she's Hanna's—'

'Lynn! No!'

'I'm – I'm sorry, Daddy.' Her words were barely audible, a breath. She closed her eyes. 'So sorry.'

The spaceship decoupled. The massive steel claws that connected it to the airlock opened to reveal the Charon.

It drifted slowly out into open space.

Julian's voice reached her ear. He called her name, over and over again, as if he had lost his mind.

Lynn lay down on her back.

Nonsense, of course, she was weightless. Just a matter of perspective whether she was lying on her back or her belly. She might even have been lying on her side, of course she was lying on her side, all at the same time, but from here she could see the bomb that floated above her, spinning listlessly.

The display blurred in front of her eyes.

08.47

No, not 8. Wasn't that two zeros? 00.47?

00.46

46 minutes? Minutes, of course, what else. Or seconds?

Not enough time. She needed thrust.

Thrust!

Before her eyes, little red spheres wobbled through space, some tiny, others as big as marbles. She reached for them, rubbed one to goo between her fingers, and suddenly she realised that the red bead curtain was coming out of her chest. There was something annoying there, eating away at her strength and restricting her movements, and she was terribly tired, but she couldn't lapse into unconsciousness. She had to pick up speed to put some distance between herself and the OSS. Then, once she was far enough away, get rid of the bomb. Somehow. Throw it overboard. Or escape into the landing module and decouple the habitation unit with the mini-nuke. And get back.

Something like that.

Her jaws opened and closed like a fish. She painfully pumped air into her lungs and rolled around.

'Haskin,' yelled Julian. He'd tried to call the terminal, but there had been no answer. Now he was talking to the technical department. In fact, Haskin hadn't been on duty that night, but in the circumstances he'd been willing to assume charge of the standby team. Unfortunately he was in Torus-5, in the roof of OSS, far from the space harbour.

'My God, Julian, what—'

'Comb the station! Look for Dana Lawrence, arrest the woman. Possibly she's in the terminal!'

'Just a moment. I don't understand—'

'I don't care whether you understand it or not! Look for Dana Lawrence – the woman's a terrorist. No one's answering in the terminal. And stop the Charon. Stop it!'

He left Haskin's helpless, startled face on the screen and whirled around to the cabin bulkhead.

'Open up!'

Dana stared at the controls, with the barrel of the gun pressed against the astronaut's temple, and listened to the radio traffic. She'd heard every word. The touching conversation between Lynn and her father, Julian's patriarchal bellow. Lynn sounded injured, she'd managed to hit the miserable spoilsport. Small consolation, but Haskin's men would be here soon.

'Block access to the torus,' she ordered.

'I can't,' panted the astronaut.

'You can! I know you can.'

'You don't know shit. I can close the entryways, but I can't lock them. They're going to get in, whether it suits you or not.'

'What about the pod?'

'The Charon's too close. I swear that's the truth!'

Then she would have to do something else. She didn't need the external airlock. There were emergency entrances to the pods themselves, wherever they happened to be parked, she just somehow had to get to the outer ring and grab one of them. That jabbering piece of humanity there couldn't help her, but she might still need the guy. Lawrence whacked him over the head again and left the toppling body to its own devices as she headed for the shelves of helmets.

Julian was consumed with anxiety. He bumped his shoulders and his head as he dashed through Torus-1 towards the corridor that led up to the terminal, tried to regain control of himself, and that wasn't good. He'd never found any of the distances in the station particularly great, but now he felt as if he were floating on the spot, and he kept crashing into things.

He was terribly worried.

She had looked as if the life was flowing out of her. Her voice had been getting more and more halting and thin – she must have been injured, seriously injured. But the worst thing was that Haskin had hardly any chance of getting the Charon back. It wasn't a drifting astronaut this time, it was a massive spaceship, and if Lynn—

Oh, no, he thought. Please not. Don't start the engine.

Lynn! Please don't—

—start the engine.

Again and again she had to fight the descending darkness, while her fingers groped around, but as long as she couldn't see anything it wasn't much use. She knew she was still too close to the OSS. For safety's sake she needed to get a lot further away, because otherwise there was a danger that the burning gases would damage parts of the construction. With the best will in the world she couldn't remember the time span on the display of the mini-nuke, just that it was tight, bloody tight!

She coughed. All around her, weird and beautiful, drifted the sparkling red beads of her blood. Weightlessness had the advantage that you couldn't really collapse, you didn't need any energy to stay on your feet, so that her physical systems were able to mobilise one last, impossible reserve of energy. Her vision cleared. Her fingers, determined, albeit hesitant and straying, went travelling: stretched and bent. Indicators lit up, a soft, automatic voice began to speak. She forced her body into the pilot's seat, but she hadn't the strength to buckle herself in. Just to start the acceleration process.

Lynn stretched out her right arm. The tip of her index finger landed gently on the smooth surface of the touchscreen, and the jets ignited, developing maximum thrust. She was pressed into the padding and lost consciousness.

The Charon fired away.

Leave the torus. Via one of the internal gangways. Get to one of the massive lattice masts that formed the spine of the OSS, climb along the struts to the space harbour, prepare one of the pods, decouple, set course for Earth. The things worked a bit like old-fashioned space shuttles, which they also superficially resembled, except that unlike their predecessors they had generous fuel supplies, so that once the stolen vehicle had entered the Earth's atmosphere she could land anywhere in the world, where no one would find her.

That was the plan.

Lawrence floated to one of the two gangways, as her suit checked the life-support systems and made sure her helmet was on correctly. Behind the closed bulkhead lay a short tunnel, a mobile airlock whose segments were still telescoped together. When the space-lift reached the inside of the torus, they would stretch out to their full length and connect the torus with the cabin, so that the guests could transfer from there to the station, just as they had done on her arrival. She quickly opened the bulkhead. The opposite end of the airlock was sealed, with a porthole in the middle through which the external lights of the lift cables shimmered.

She had been faster than Haskin. She no longer needed the unconscious astronaut. Just to pump the air out of the lock, open it and get out, without any of those idiots stopping her. With her gun ready in its holster, she slipped into the tunnel.

*　　*　　*

Julian flew out of the corridor, bumped against the ceiling, ignored the pain, looked wildly in all directions. Someone drifted below him. Open eyes staring vacantly, liquid pearling from a small hole in his forehead. Where the bagel-shaped body of the torus curved away, a second body circulated slowly, impossible to say whether it was dead or unconscious. Julian pushed himself off, slid along just below the ceiling and saw that a bulkhead was open on the inward-facing side, immediately below him.

One of the gangways branched off from it.

Dana?

Fury, hatred, fear, they all came together. He did a handstand, darted into the airlock, bumped against a person in a spacesuit who was about to operate the closing mechanism, pulled them away from the controls and deeper inside the airlock. He clearly recognised Dana Lawrence's surprised Madonna face, as her UV visor was still raised, then their bodies struck the outer portal, rebounded and spun somersaulting back towards the torus. Dana fumbled for purchase, collided with the wall of the tunnel, pushed away and threw herself against him. Julian saw her fist flying at him, tried in vain to dodge it. A galaxy exploded in his head. He was slung around, flailed with his arms, fought for control. Dana came flying after him. The second blow broke his nose. He should have put on a helmet, bloody idiot, too late. Red and black mist floated in front of his eyes. He just managed to grab on to one of the hand-grips along the walls and kicked at random, hit Dana's helmet and sent her flying round in circles.

'What have you done with Lynn?' he shouted. 'What have you done with my daughter?'

His hatred exploded. Again he kicked, his hand gripping the butt of his gun. Dana was whirled around, turned upside down, caught herself, launched at him and grabbed him by the shoulders. A moment later he flew off. Like a pinball he touched one side of the tunnel, then the other, and was carried out of the airlock.

Where was Haskin? Where was the dozy standby crew?

Lawrence was reaching for the control panel. She wanted to seal the airlock, to lock him out. What was her plan? Did she want to get out? What for? What did she want to do out there?

Clear off?

The blood was clotting in his nose, his head was swinging like a bell when he dashed back into the airlock at the last minute and managed to grab her arm. Lawrence's fingers couldn't reach the closing mechanism. Without letting go of her, and with blows drumming down on him from her free hand, he pushed her back. They started spinning and collided against the outside portal. For a moment, through the porthole, Julian saw the brightly lit opposite side of the enormous ring module, the cables ending in the middle, only minutes to go till the cabin arrived – and then Lawrence rammed her knee into his stomach.

He felt a wave of nausea, he couldn't breathe. He let go of her arm and she hurled him against the wall, where he managed to grab onto a strut. Lawrence was floating upright by the outer portal, turned round and faced him. Her right hand wandered to her thigh and took something out of a sheath, a flat thing that looked like a pistol.

He had lost.

As in a stupor, Julian leaned his head to one side. It couldn't, mustn't end like this! His glance fell on a flap in the wall beside him. It took him a second to remember what it did, or more precisely what lay behind it, and then it came to him.

OSS handbook, Letter B:

Bulkhead emergency detonation.

In emergencies it may be necessary to blast open the outer portal of an airlock, regardless of whether or not a vacuum has been created inside it. This measure may be necessary if the bulkhead or airlock casing is caught or wedged in the rump of the lift cabin or a docking spaceship and launch or departure are impeded, particularly when human lives are at stake. In the event of a detonation, care should be taken that the side of the airlock channel facing the habitation sector is closed and the person undertaking the detonation is wearing a spacesuit and is securely fastened to the wall of the airlock.

He wasn't securely fastened. He was just holding on with sheer muscle power, and the bulkhead to the torus was open. He wasn't even wearing a helmet.

To hell with it!

Holding tightly on to the bar, he pulled up the flap. A bright red handle became visible. Dana's eyes behind the visor widened as she worked out what he was planning. The barrel of her gun came flying up, but not fast enough. He pulled hard on the handle and brought it straight down.

Held his breath.

With a deafening crash the charges in the fixing pins went up and blew the bulkhead from its mooring. Tumbling over and over it whirled into open space, and at the same moment the suction began, a wailing, murderous storm, as the air flowed out, pulling Dana out of the airlock with it. Julian clung to the metal pole with both hands. More air streamed out of the torus, a hurricane now. That moment he realised all passageways to the adjacent corridors would close automatically, and he was unprotected, not even wearing a helmet. If he didn't make it out of the tunnel in the next few seconds and close the internal bulkhead, he would die in the vacuum, so he gritted his teeth, tensed his muscles and tried to crawl his way back inside.

His fingers started sliding from the rail.

He panicked. He couldn't let go, but the hurricane was pulling at him, and most particularly it was pulling his leg. He turned his head and saw Dana Lawrence gripping onto one of his boots. The suction intensified, but she wouldn't let go, she hung horizontal in the roaring inferno, tried to aim her gun.

She pointed it at him.

Tiny muzzle, black.

Death.

And suddenly he'd just had enough of the bloody woman. His rage, his fear, everything turned into pure strength.

'This is *my* space station,' he yelled. 'Now get *out!*'

And he kicked.

His boot crashed against her helmet. Lawrence's fingers slipped away,

In a split second she had been swept outside, into the centre of the torus, and even then she kept her gun pointed at him, took aim, and Julian waited for the end.

Her body passed the cable.

For a moment he didn't understand what he was seeing. Lawrence was flying in two directions at once. More precisely, her shoulder, part of her torso and the right arm holding the gun had separated themselves from the rest.

Because direct contact with the cable can cost you a body-part in a fraction of a second. You must bear in mind that it's thinner than a razor-blade, but incredibly hard.

His own words, down on the Isla de las Estrellas.

The storm raged around him. With an extreme effort of strength he pulled his way further along the rail, without any illusions of his own survival. He wasn't going to make it. He *couldn't* make it. His lungs hurt, his eyes watered, his head thumped like a jackhammer.

Lynn, he thought. My God, Lynn.

A figure appeared in his field of vision, wearing a helmet, secured with a safetyline. Someone else. Hands grabbed him and pulled him back into the shelter of the torus. Gripped him tightly. The interior bulkhead slid shut.

Haskin.

Stars. Like dust.

Lynn is far away, far, far away. The spaceship silently ploughs the time-less, glittering night, an enclave of peace and refuge. When she briefly regains consciousness, she merely wonders why the bomb hasn't gone off, but perhaps she just hasn't been travelling for long enough. She vaguely remembers a plan she had to leave the mini-nuke in the habitation module and return to the OSS in the landing unit, to save herself.

Landing unit. Uning landit.

Mini-nuke. Nuki-Duke. Muki-Nuki-Duki, Mini-Something-Something. Bruce Dern in *Silent Running.*

Great film. And at the end: *Boooooommmmmm!*

No, she'll stay here. And anyway, she's out of strength. So many things have gone wrong. Sorry, Julian. Didn't we want to go to the Moon? How is work going at the Stellar Island Hotel? What? Oh, shit, it's not finished, that's it, she knew it, she always knew, it's not finished! It will *never* be finished. Never, never, never!

Cold.

The little robot watering the flowers with Bruce Dern. He's sweet. On that platform in space, the last plants are on it before Dern blows himself up, and then there's a song by that eco-trollop, Joan Baez, Julian says that every time he hears her he has the feeling somebody's chiselling his head open, and she messes up the whole great finale with her hysterical soprano.

'Lynn?'

There he is.

'Please answer! Lynn! Lynn!'

Oh! Is he crying? Why? Her fault? Did she do something wrong?

Don't cry, Julian. Come on, let's look at another one of those ropy old movies. *Armageddon*. No, he doesn't like that one, everything about it's wrong, he says, there's too much wrong, so how about Ed Wood, *Plan 9 from Outer Space*, or how about *It Came from Outer Space*? Come on, that one's cool! Jack Arnold, the old fairy-tale uncle. Always good for a joke or a horror story. The extraterrestrials with the big brains. That's what they really look like.

Really? Nonsense. They don't!

Do so too!

Daddy! Tim doesn't think they look like that.

'Lynn!'

Coming. I'm coming, Daddy.

I'm there.

3–8 June 2025

LIMIT

Xintiandi, Shanghai, China

A perfectly normal life—

Hanging pictures, taking a step back, adjusting the angle. Sorting out books, arranging furniture, stepping back, rearranging. Making small changes, stepping back again, approaching things while remaining detached from them, establishing harmony, the universal Confucian formula against the powers of chaos.

If that was what constituted a normal life, Jericho had fitted himself back into normality without the slightest transition. Xin hadn't burned down his loft, everything was in its place or waiting to be assigned one. The television was on, a kaleidoscope of soundless world events, because he was less concerned with the content of information than with its decorative properties. He had an urgent need not to have to know anything any more. He didn't want to understand any more connections, only to roll out the little carpet, which was to lie like *that* – or was it better like *that*? Jericho pulled it into a diagonal, took a step back, studied his work and found it lacked balance, because it put a standard lamp in difficulties. Not harmonious, said Confucius, stressing the rights of lamps.

How was Yoyo?

At noon on the day of her rebirth thanks to Xin's mercy she had woken up, plagued by severe headaches, doubtless partly due to the encounter with Norrington's skull, also to an unaccustomed excess of Brunello di Montalcino, but finally also to the experience of having been practically shot. The resulting emotional hangover meant that she didn't talk much on the flight home. At around midday Tu had started the Aerion Supersonic. Four hours later the jet had landed at Pudong Airport, and they had been home again. Of course, in the days that followed there was no escaping the news coverage. Once the Charon had come within range of terrestrial broadcasting, measurements had been confirmed corroborating that there had been a nuclear explosion in the no man's land of the lunar North Pole, and the outing of the tour group had ended in disaster, with some prominent fatalities. And although the Secret Services tried to spread a cloak of silence over the events, there were rumours of a conspiracy aimed at destroying the American lunar base, with China as a possible source – totally unconsidered assertions that buzzed cheerfully around the net.

Downwinds of suspicion blew anti-Chinese ideas all around the world. In fact there wasn't the slightest concrete evidence concerning the real masterminds behind it. Orley himself had taken the sting from the suspicions on the way back to OSS, announcing that it was only with the help of the taikonaut Jia Keqiang and the Chinese space authorities that it had been possible to prevent the attack at all. Regardless of this, British, American and Chinese media used the vocabulary of aggression. Not for the first time, China had attacked foreign networks, and it was common knowledge that Beijing administered Kim Jong Un's military legacy. Voices warning that the space-travelling nations should finally pull together mingled with fears about the armament of space. Zheng Pang-Wang found himself in a public relations crisis when details emerged about the role of the Zheng Group in the construction of the launching pad in Equatorial Guinea. Rushing ahead, the Zhong Chan Er Bu made clear that nothing was known about anyone called Kenny Xin or an organisation called Yü Shen, which supposedly drew its recruits from psychiatric institutions and mental hospitals and trained them up as killers. But if this man Xin did exist, he was operating unambiguously against the interests of the Party. And why were Mr Orley and the Americans really surprised, when they withheld important technologies from the world and snubbed the international community with continued violations of the treaty concerning the Moon and space? This all sounded so familiar in terms of the lunar crisis that serious considerations about what the Chinese actually stood to gain from the destruction of Peary Base (nothing at all, according to seasoned analysts) faded into the background.

Standard lamp and carpet. Harmony refused to establish itself between the two.

Although her shared flat had gained an extra room after Grand Cherokee Wang's demise, Yoyo had moved in with Tu. Temporarily, she stressed. Perhaps she wanted to stand by Hongbing, who was also staying in the villa until his own apartment had been refurbished, but Jericho suspected she was hoping for something like a confession after the openness of the last few days. She was preparing to resume her studies. Daxiong was working on his bike, disregarding medical advice, as if he didn't have a freshly stitched wound in his back and an even bigger one in his heart, Tu devoted himself to the steam-train rhythm of his businesses, and pleasantly boring cases of web espionage awaited Jericho. After Operation Mountains of Eternal Light had come to such a bloody end, they had agreed that Hydra no longer posed a threat. They still faced questioning by the Chinese police, but did not feel obliged to reveal the circumstances under which Yoyo had come across the message fragment, particularly since the Secret Services had every reason to be grateful to them: in the end, what was more likely to exonerate Beijing from the accusations that were flying around than that the attack had been scuppered by the feisty actions of two Chinese and an Englishman living in China? The first three days of June had passed uneventfully, and Patrice Ho, Jericho's high-ranking policeman friend from Shanghai, had called to announce his promotion and his move to Beijing.

'Of course I know that your investigations gave a great boost to my career,' he said. 'So if you have any idea of how I can pay you back—'

'Let's just see it as a credit,' said Jericho.

'Hmm.' Ho paused. 'Perhaps I can come up with a way of increasing that credit.'

'Aha.'

'As you know, our investigations in Lanzhou were highly successful. We were able to take out a nest of paedophiles, and came across evidence that suggests—'

'Hang on a second! You want me to go on poking around in the paedophile scene?'

'Your experience might be very useful to us. Beijing places a lot of hope in me. After the double success in Shenzhen and Lanzhou, it might provoke irritation if our series of triumphs suddenly came to an end—'

'I understand,' sighed Jericho. 'At the risk of squandering my credit, I've decided not to take on any more jobs of that kind. A few days ago I moved into a larger flat, and it's already too small for all the ghosts I have lodging with me.'

'You won't have to go to the front line,' Ho hurried to reassure him.

'You know one *always* ends up on the front line.'

'Of course. Sorry if I've put you under extra pressure.'

'You haven't. Can I think about it?'

'Of course! When are we going to go for a beer?'

'What about this week?'

'Wonderful.'

Nothing was wonderful. The carpet and the standard lamp understood one another marvellously well. The point was that neither of them was in harmony with *him*. There was no harmony anywhere, and certainly no normality. As if by way of confirmation, Julian Orley's face appeared larger than life-size on the holowall, against the open sky and surrounded by people. He was saying something as he pushed his way through the crowd, followed by the actor Finn O'Keefe and a thrillingly weird-looking woman with snow-white hair. Clearly the tour group had come back to Earth. Jericho turned up the sound and heard the commentator say:

'—the explosion of the second mini-nuke at nine o'clock Central European time at a distance of 45,000 kilometres from the OSS, which it was clearly designed to destroy. Meanwhile fears are being raised that the series of nuclear attacks might resume. Julian Orley, who plans to leave Quito in the next few minutes, has so far refused—'

Jericho gave a start and turned the sound up again, but he seemed to have missed the most important bit. A news-ticker along the bottom of the screen carried the message of an attempted nuclear attack on the OSS, and said that the number of victims was as yet unknown. Jericho zapped through the channels. Clearly there had been a second atom bomb hidden on the shuttle that had carried the survivors from the Peary Base to the space station, but this had been discovered in time and detonated at a considerable distance from the OSS. Orley himself said that he didn't plan to comment in any way. Jericho thought he had aged several years.

Yoyo called. 'Did you hear that? The stuff about the second bomb?'

He switched from CNN to a Chinese news channel, but it was running a story about university reform. Another one was trying to talk down new Uyghur revolts in Xinjiang.

'Very strange,' he said. 'Vogelaar didn't mention a second bomb in his dossier.'

'That means he only knew about one.'

'Probably.' The BBC was showing a special report on the events. 'Luckily it's nothing to do with us any more.'

'Yeah, you're right. God, I'm glad we're out of that! And that they're leaving us in peace – On the other hand, it's awesome, isn't it? It's *really* awesome!'

Jericho stared at the red strip of the news-ticker.

'Mm-hm,' he said. 'Everything else okay with you?'

'Yep, fine.' She hesitated. 'By the way, I'm sorry I haven't called, but there's so much happening at the moment, I'm – I'm just trying to get back in step. It's not that easy. I've got funerals of friends to go to, Daxiong is acting the hero, and my father – okay, we had a long talk, I think you know what about—'

These topics were always awkward. 'And?' he asked cautiously.

'It's all right, Owen, we can talk openly about it. You can't tell me anything I haven't found out already. What can I say? I'm glad he told me.'

She sounded oddly terse. She had suffered from Hongbing's silence all her life, and now all she could find to say was that she was *glad* that he was suddenly communicating openly with her.

'Hey!' she said suddenly. 'You do understand that *we* prevented those attacks? Without us there would be no moon base, and no OSS.'

A German channel. The same wobbly pictures of Orley and his group flickered across the holowall. A journalist with a microphone in his hand

and the Pacific in the background claimed to have heard that a bomb had gone off on a spaceship, a moon shuttle, and that contrary to the initial reports there *had* been fatalities, at least one.

'Just think about it – that would have set American space travel back by decades,' Yoyo observed. 'Wouldn't it? What do you think? No space lift, no helium-3. Orley could have mothballed his fusion reactors.'

'It almost looks as if we're heroes,' he said sourly.

'Yeah. So we can cautiously start being proud of ourselves, can we? What are your plans for this evening?'

'Shifting furniture. Sleeping.' Jericho glanced at his watch. Half past ten. 'Hopefully. I've been exhausted for three days and can't get to sleep. Only towards the morning, for two or three hours.'

'I'm the same. Take a pill.'

'Don't want to.'

'Then it's your own fault. See you later.'

After the call he no longer felt able to think in categories of Confucian interior design. Everything around him seemed to have lost its meaning, he could imagine any arrangement of furniture and none. A glass wall had appeared between him and the objects, harmony and normality became purely academic categories, as if a blind man were talking about colours. He turned off the television and found his jaws stretching into an endless, leonine yawn. According to Schopenhauer, the hero of his youth: *Yawning is one of the reflex movements. I suspect that its more distant cause may be a momentary depotentiation of the brain caused by boredom, mental slackness or somnolence.*

Was he bored? Was his brain growing slack? Was he depotentiated? Not at all. He was unsettlingly wide awake. He lay down fully dressed on the couch, turned out the light and tentatively closed his eyes. Perhaps if he avoided official actions like getting undressed or going to bed, he might trick his body and mind, which seemed to think that they had to resist sleep the more clearly he attempted to achieve it.

Half an hour later he knew better.

It wasn't over. Hydra still held him in its embrace, its poison would rage in him until he had finally understood its nature. He couldn't pretend that none of it concerned him any longer just because no one was trying to kill him. You couldn't *decide* on normality; things didn't come to an end just because you'd buried them in the past. The nightmare continued.

Who was Hydra?

He turned the lights back on. Yoyo was right. They'd found out a hell of a lot of things, they'd thwarted the plans of the conspirators, they had good reason to be proud. At the same time he felt as if they'd been looking through the wrong end of a telescope all along. The closest things had drifted into the distance, into supposed insignificance, but in fact all you had to do was turn the telescope around and the truth would move into the foreground. He opened a bottle of Shiraz, poured himself a glass and systematically crossed all previous suspects off the list: Beijing, Zheng Pang-Wang, the CIA. On closer inspection all of these trails had turned in a circle, but there might have been one that he hadn't properly understood, one that carried straight on.

The Greenwatch massacre.

The complete leadership of the environmental broadcaster, all wiped out. Why? No one was able to say what Greenwatch had been working on most recently, even though there were several suggestions that there had been a report on environmental damage by oil companies. Loreena's ambition to clear up the Calgary attack had finally focused attention on the film that supposedly showed Gerald Palstein's attacker. But given how quickly these pictures had spread, the massacre could hardly have taken place in order to prevent their further dissemination.

He had Diane play through the film sequence once more. Towards the end, as the camera swung round towards the stage, you could see that the square was full of people with mobile phones, and surrounded by television crews. A miracle, in fact, that Xin hadn't been captured more often, fat suit and all, at any rate Hydra should have predicted that and factored it in, but equally that might have been the first error of reasoning.

Perhaps they'd been *banking* on it!

The longer Jericho thought about the sequence, the more Xin's weird disguise and his stately way of creeping around seemed to be part of an act designed to present investigators with an Asian assassin just in case he was caught on camera – just as Zheng's visible presence in Equatorial Guinea had left an elephant track in the Middle Kingdom. There was a glimpse of Lars Gudmundsson with his double game; Palstein was still alive by happy chance, leaving the way open for Carl Hanna; Loreena Keowa got to the bottom of that, costing ten people their lives and Greenwatch its memory.

Did that make sense? Not really.

Unless she'd found out things at Greenwatch that *really* put the pressure on Hydra.

Loreena had travelled in from Calgary. Possibly in possession of explosive information. She had immediately gone to the editorial conference, a meeting that Hydra had been able to prevent at the last minute, although this meant that the conspirators still didn't know how much of the unwelcome research was already stored on the channel's hard drives, because Loreena might have sent emails in the run-up!

That was it.

Jericho got to work. While it was approaching midnight in Shanghai, the noon-day sun was shining on the other side of the Pacific. He had Diane draw up a list of all the relevant internet service providers and started phoning them, one after the other, always on the same pretext: he was calling on behalf of Loreena, because it was impossible to send or receive emails from her web address, and would they please be so kind as to take a look and see why that wasn't working. Eleven times he was told that no Loreena Keowa was stored as a customer, three of the people he spoke to knew Loreena from the net, had learned of her death and expressed their dismay, for which Jericho thanked them in his best funeral-director voice. He only struck gold with the twelfth call. He was asked to give a password, which meant that she was registered there. Jericho promised to call back. Then he hacked his way into the provider's system and put Diane to decoding Loreena's password. Every data transfer had been recorded, so that within a few minutes he received information about Loreena's mail provider. He rang back, gave the password, and asked if any emails sent over the last fourteen days were still stored in the system. They were stored for up to six weeks, he was told, and which ones did he wish to see?

All of them, he said.

Half an hour later he had viewed all the documents concerning the environmental scandal, which, under the title *Trash of the Titans*, had been supposed to form the core of that broadcast. It named a lot of names, but Jericho didn't believe in a connection for a second. The massacre had occurred as a reaction to the last email sent. It contained the answers to all the questions.

Hydra's identity.

Gerald Palstein

  Director, Strategic Management, EMCO (USA), victim of an assassination attempt in Calgary on 21.4.2025, probable aim to prevent him from flying to the Moon (there are data on Palstein).

  Assassin Asian, possibly Chinese.

  (Chinese interests in EMCO? Oil-sand business?)

  Alejandro Ruiz

  Strategy manager (since July 2022) of Repsol YPF (Spanish-Argentinian). Nickname Ruiz El Verde, married, two children, conventional lifestyle, debt-free.

  Disappeared in Lima, 2022, during an inspection tour (crime?). Previously several days at conference in Beijing, incl. joint venture with Sinopec. Last meeting outside of Beijing on 1.9.2022: subject and participants unknown (Repsol wants to look through documents, I'm waiting to be called back). 2.9. flew on to Lima, phone calls to his wife. Ruiz depressed and anxious. Cause probably previous day's meeting.

  Common factors Palstein, Ruiz:

  Both men have tried to expand their companies' areas of business in new directions, e.g. solar power, Orley Enterprises. Ethical standpoints. Against oil-sand mining. Opponents in their own camp.

  Appointed strategy managers when the threatened bankruptcy of their companies leaves them with hardly any room to negotiate.

However: hardly any points of contact between EMCO and Repsol. According to Palstein, no personal contact between him and Ruiz.

Lars Gudmundsson

Palstein's bodyguard, freelance operative for Texan security company Eagle Eye.

Career: Navy Seal, sniper training, moved to Africa to join Mamba private army, from there to APS (African Protection Services), possible involvement in coup d'état in West Africa, since 2000 back in the USA.

Playing false game: with his people, ensured that Palstein's attacker was able to enter the building opposite Imperial Oil unimpeded (have informed Palstein of Gudmundsson's betrayal and asked Eagle Eye about G. G. and his team have since gone missing).

Gudmundsson—

The name sparked something in Jericho's mind. Following an intuition, he took out Vogelaar's dossier again, and there it was: Lars Gudmundsson had belonged to the special unit that had brought Mayé to power – along with Neil Gabriel, aka Carl Hanna. They both seemed to have got on particularly well with Kenny Xin, so well, in fact, that they had worked for him in various ways and finally quit APS. Loreena's email also included the film from the crime scene, a direct line to Repsol and the private number of the presumably widowed Señora Ruiz. He had Diane assemble further facts about the Spaniard, but didn't come up with much more than the journalist had already put together. In film sequences and pictures the man looked sympathetic, positive and energetic.

But after the meeting in Beijing he'd been worried.

And then he'd disappeared.

Why had that sudden change occurred? Because he'd experienced or learned something at the meeting that stressed him? Right, but more likely because he could no longer be sure of his life. If Alejandro Ruiz had actually fallen victim to a crime, it was because someone had wanted to keep the contents of that meeting from becoming public.

Had Hydra killed Ruiz because he knew about Operation Mountains of Eternal Light? But in that case how was Palstein involved? Loreena found striking factors in common between the two. Might Palstein have been informed about Hydra's plans?

Jericho took a sip of Shiraz.

Nonsense. These were ludicrous hypotheses. Ruiz had disappeared *immediately* after the meeting. Before he could open his mouth. Why would they have given Palstein three years to bring his knowledge to the people? Calgary had clearly served the purpose of slipping an agent into Orley's tour group, and also Palstein was *alive*, even if it was only by chance. Since then there had been no more attempts on his life, even though opportunities had arisen. Gudmundsson, for example, constantly near him for professional reasons, could have killed him with a close-range bullet at any time.

And why hadn't he done it?

And why hadn't he done it *before*? Before Calgary?

Hydra had managed to infiltrate Palstein's inner circle, his security men. Why go to all that effort? A public event. Agents distracting the police. Kenny Xin, firing from an empty building? Why so *laborious*?

Because it was supposed to look like something that it wasn't.

No doubt about it: the connection between Lima and Calgary, between Ruiz and Palstein, existed. Loreena's research led directly to Hydra, otherwise the butchers of Vancouver wouldn't have murdered ten people and got rid of their computers. So what had *really* happened on 21 April in Canada?

The meeting in Beijing provided the key.

He was about to phone Repsol in Madrid when the doorbell rang. Startled, he looked at his watch. Twenty past one. Drunks? The bell rang again. For a moment he toyed with the idea of ignoring it, then he went to the intercom and looked at the screen.

Yoyo.

'What are you doing here?' he asked in a puzzled voice.

'How about you press the button?' she snapped at him. 'Or do I have to announce my visits in writing first?'

'It's not exactly the time of day when you expect visitors,' he said as she stepped into his loft, her motorbike helmet under her arm. Yoyo shrugged. She set the helmet down on the central kitchen counter, ambled into the living area and glanced curiously around in all directions. He followed her.

'Pretty.'

'Not quite finished.'

'Still.' She pointed at the open bottle of Shiraz. 'Is there another glass?'

Jericho scratched himself irritably behind the ear as she slipped out of her leather jacket and threw herself on his sofa.

'Of course,' he said. 'Wait.'

He looked across to her and brought out a second glass. In the gloom of the lounge a reddish glimmer indicated that she had lit a cigarette. After he had filled her glass, they sat there for a few minutes, drinking in silence, and Yoyo sent smoke signals issuing from the corners of her mouth, encoded explanations for her presence. She stared into the void. From time to time the heavy curtains of her eyelashes seemed to want to wipe away what they had seen, but whenever she looked up her gaze was as lost as before. More than ever she reminded him of the girl in the video film that Chen Hongbing had shown him a week and a half before.

A week and a half?

It could just as easily have been a year.

'And what are you up to at the moment?' she asked, glancing at Diane.

'Wondering what's brought you here.'

'Didn't you want to go to bed? Get some sleep at last?'

'I've tried.'

She nodded. 'Me too. I thought it would be easier.'

'Sleeping?'

'Carrying on from where you've left off. But it's like reaching into the void. A lot of things no longer exist. The control centre at the steelworks. The Guardians. And I've seen Grand Cherokee's room with all his stuff in it, as if he were about to come back. Spooky. On the other hand, college is college. The same professors, the same lecture theatres. The same administration that makes sure you don't start thinking too independently. The same chicken coop, the same battles and trivia. I listen to music, I go out, watch television, remind myself that everyone else is even worse off than me, that I could be dead, and that the banality of everyday life has its good side. I try to convince myself that I should be feeling relieved.'

Jericho crossed his legs. He sat in silence on the floor in front of her, his back resting against a chair.

'And then the thing I've been waiting for all my life happens. Hongbing takes me in his arms, tells me how much he loves me and showers me with tragedies. The whole terrible story. And I know I should be letting off fireworks for this moment, I should die of pity, go mad with joy, throw my arms around his neck, the bastards have no power over us now, it's all going to be okay, we can talk to each other at last, we're a family! Instead' – she blew smoke-snakes in the air – 'my head feels like a chest of a thousand drawers, everyone stuffs whatever he feels like into it, and now my father's joining in! I think, Yoyo, you miserable little cripple, why don't you feel anything? Come on, now, you've got to *feel* something, after all, you wished—' She reached for her glass, downed the contents and sucked the remaining life from her cigarette. 'You so wished he would talk to you! Even when Kenny held his bloody gun to my head, I thought, no! I don't want to die without finding out what threw *his* life so far off the rails. But now I know, I just feel . . . full.'

Jericho turned his glass around in his hand.

'And at the same time hollowed out,' she went on. 'That's crazy, isn't it? Nothing moves me! As if this isn't the world as I used to know it, but a mere copy of it. Everything looks as if it's made of cardboard.'

'And you think it'll never be normal again.'

'It scares me, Owen. Maybe everything's all right with the world, and *I'm* the copy. Maybe the real Yoyo was shot by Xin after all.'

Jericho stared at his feet.

'In a sense she was.'

'Xin stole something that night.' She looked at him. 'Took something. Took me away. I can no longer feel what I should be feeling. I'm no longer able to give my father the respect I should. Not even to burst dramatically into floods of tears.'

'Because it isn't over yet.'

'I want it back. I want to be me again.'

She lit another cigarette. Again they were silent for a while, lost in smoke and thoughts.

'We haven't yet woken up, Yoyo.' He threw his head back and looked at the ceiling. 'That's our problem. For three days I've been trying to tell myself that I don't want to have anything more to do with Hydra. Or with Xin and all the freaks that frolic in my head when everyone else is asleep. I furnish my life with knick-knacks, I try and make it look as normal and unspectacular as possible, but it feels wrong. As if I'd ended up on a stage—'

'Yes, exactly!'

'And a little while ago, after we spoke on the phone, I understood. We're still trapped in this nightmare, Yoyo. It pretends we're awake, but we aren't. We're watching an illusion. It's far from over.' He sighed. 'I'm actually obsessed by Hydra! I have to go on working on this case. Clearing out the cellar in which I've been burying people alive for years. Hydra is turning into the model of my life and the question of how it's going to go on from here. I have to face up to these ghosts to get rid of them, even if it costs me my courage or my reason. I can't, won't, go on like this. I can't bear living like this, do you understand? I want to wake up at last.'

Otherwise we will be trapped for ever in an imaginary world, he thought. Then we won't be proper people, we'll only ever be the echoes of our unresolved past.

'And – have you kept on working on the case? On our case?'

'Yes.' Jericho nodded. 'Over the past two hours. When you arrived, I was about to phone Madrid.'

'Madrid?'

'An oil company called Repsol.'

He saw her face light up, so he told her about his research, familiarised her with Loreena's last email and introduced her to his theories. With every word Hydra slithered further into that dark loft, stretched her necks, fixed her pale yellow eyes on them. In their effort to shake the monster off, they had conjured it up, but something had changed. The monster didn't come to ambush and chase them, but because they had lured it, and for the first time Jericho felt stronger than the snake. Finally he dialled the number of the Spanish company.

'Of course!' a man's voice said in English. 'Loreena Keowa! I tried to get through to her a number of times. Why does she never answer?'

'She had an accident,' said Jericho. 'A fatal accident.'

'How terrible.' The man paused. When he went on speaking, there was an undertone of suspicion. 'And you are—'

'A private detective. I'm trying to continue Miss Keowa's work and shed some light on the circumstances of her death.'

'I see.'

'She'd asked you for information, right?'

'Erm – that's right.'

'About a meeting in Beijing that Alejandro Ruiz took part in before he disappeared?'

'Yes. Yes, exactly.'

'I'm pursuing that trail. It might be the same people that have Ruiz and Loreena on their conscience. You would be doing me a great favour if you would let me have the information.'

'Well—' The other man hesitated. Then he sighed. 'Sure, why not. Will you keep us up to date? We'd very much like to know what happened to Ruiz.'

'Of course.'

'So, we've gone through the documents here. In 2022 Ruiz had just been appointed head of the strategy department. He was moving heaven and earth to open up new areas of business. Some of the oil multinationals were increasingly looking into joint ventures, so there were discussions in Beijing, for a whole week—'

'Why there?'

'No real reason. They could equally well have met in Texas or Spain. Perhaps because the most important was a project between Repsol, EMCO and the Chinese oil company Sinopec, so they agreed on Beijing. The initiator of the joint venture suggested that it should be turned into a business summit. Almost all the big companies agreed to take part, which meant that discussions went on all week without interruption. Ruiz was happy about that. He thought something might change.'

'Do you have any idea what he might have meant by that?'

'Not really, to be quite honest.'

'And where did the summit meet?'

'At the Sinopec Congress Centre on the edge of Chaoyang, a district to the north-east of Beijing.'

'And Ruiz was in good spirits?'

'Most of the time, yes, although it turned out that the train had already pulled out. On the other hand, it could hardly have got worse. On the last day of the summit he called and said that at least the week hadn't been wasted, and there was one last session that evening, more of an unofficial meeting. A few of them wanted to get together and discuss a few ideas.'

'And the meeting was also held in the Congress Centre?'

'No, further out. In the district of Shunyi, he said, at a private house. The next day he looked depressed and unwell. I asked him how the meeting had gone. He reacted oddly. He said nothing had come out of it, and he'd left early.'

'Do you know who took part in it?'

'Not explicitly. Ruiz had hinted that representatives of the big companies had come together – I guess we were the smallest fish in the pond. Russians, Americans, Chinese, British, South Americans, Arabs. A proper summit. Not much seems to have come out of it.'

I wouldn't be so sure of that, thought Jericho.

'I'd need a list of official participants at the summit,' he said, 'if such a thing still exists.'

'I'll send it to you. Give me an email address.'

Jericho passed on his details and thanked the man. He promised to get in touch as soon as anything new came in, signed off and looked at Yoyo.

'What do you think?'

'A meeting in which senior oil company representatives take part,' she mused. 'An unofficial one. Ruiz doesn't wait for the end. Why does he leave?'

'He might have felt unwell. That's the harmless explanation.'

'That we don't believe.'

'Of course not. He left because he'd come to the conclusion that the whole thing was going nowhere, because there was an argument, or because he didn't want to go along with whatever they decided.'

'If he'd just been angry, he'd have told his people or his wife the reasons. Instead he said nothing.'

'He felt threatened.'

'He was afraid they might hush him up because he didn't want to play.'

'As they did, by the look of it.'

'And who are *they*?'

'Hmm.' Jericho pursed his lips. 'We're thinking along the same lines, aren't we?'

Yoyo stayed with him that night. Nothing happened except that they emptied another bottle of wine together and he held her in his arms, faintly surprised that he only wanted to console her: a girl overtaxed by adulthood, intelligent, talented and beautiful who, at the age of only twenty-five, had already driven wedges of insecurity into the armour of the Party and at the same time preserved the attitude of a teenager, a punishing, immature stroppiness that was every bit as unerotic as her efforts to defy biology and keep from growing up. It seemed to him that Yoyo wanted to stay in adolescence for ever, or until circumstances calmed down enough to grant her a more peaceful youth than the one she had already had. He, on the other hand, wanted only to wipe out this phase of his life, those said transitional years. Small wonder, then, that neither of them felt what they should have felt, as Yoyo had put it.

He thought about this, and suddenly, quite unexpectedly, he felt lighter.

There was someone else with them in the room. He looked up, and that shy boy who had been hurt so often was sitting in the gloom of the loft, watching his fingers glide through Yoyo's hair. Numbed with red wine and worry, he stared straight ahead, while the boy's eyes filled with tears of disappointment that girls like Yoyo only ever used boys like him to talk to. His nose, disproportionately swollen by the beginnings of puberty, was still too big for his otherwise childish face. His hair needed washing, and of course he was wearing the stuff he always wore, a human being who loved everyone and everything more than he loved himself. How Jericho had hated the little bastard who couldn't understand why that adult man with the girl in his arms, the girl he could have had there and then, wasn't declaring his love – why he suddenly didn't desire her, when he had desired her, hadn't he?

Had he?

Jericho saw the boy sitting there, felt his paralysing, nagging fear of being inadequate, failing, being rejected. And suddenly he didn't hate him any more. Instead he drew him into the embrace, he granted him absolution and assured him that he wasn't to blame for anything, anything at all. He expressed his sympathy. Explained the necessity of finally disappearing from his life, since he had vanished from it in a purely physical sense long ago, and promised him that they would both find peace sooner or later.

The boy turned pale.

He would come back, that much was certain, but for that night at least they were reconciled. The world became more tangible, more colourful. Towards morning, when Yoyo lay snoring quietly on his belly, he still hadn't slept a wink, and yet he wasn't tired in the slightest. He carefully lifted her shoulders, slipped from the sofa and let her drop back. She murmured, turned on her side and rolled into a ball. Jericho looked at her. He wondered excitedly who would appear once she had shed the foolish costume of the eternal teenager. Someone very thrilling, he suspected. And she *would* be happy and adult. She just didn't know it yet. She would be able to feel everything, not what she was supposed to feel, not what she wanted to feel, but just what she actually felt.

Just before nine. He picked up his phone, went into the kitchen area and put on a strong pot of coffee. He knew what he had to do, and how they could nail those bastards.

Time to make a call.

'I've been thinking about your offer,' he said.

'Oh.' Patrice Ho seemed surprised. 'I hadn't expected to hear from you so soon.'

'Some decisions are quick to make.'

'Owen, before you say something—' Ho hemmed and hawed. 'I'm sorry if I behaved badly in any way. I didn't mean to put any pressure on you – you must think I'm never satisfied.'

'I hope you aren't,' said Jericho. 'Not in terms of the results, anyway. So I will go on supporting you in this paedophile case.'

'You will?' Short pause. 'You're a friend! A true friend. I'm more obliged to you than ever.'

'Good. Then I'd like to call in some of my credit.'

'And I'll be happy to help you!'

'Just wait. It's possible that you're not going to like it.'

'That's what I'm assuming,' Ho said drily.

'Right, listen. In the last week of August 2022, in Beijing, or more precisely in the Sinopec Congress Centre in the district of Chaoyang, there was a meeting of international oil companies. I'll send you the list of participants. On the last day of the summit, on the evening of 1 September, some of these people met up unofficially in the district of Shunyi. I don't know who took part in that meeting, but it seems to have been an illustrious circle. And I don't know where the meeting took place.'

'And that's what I'm to find out. I get it.' Ho paused. 'This sounds like a routine investigation. What wouldn't I like about it?'

'The second part of my request.'

'Which would be?'

'I can only tell you once I've got the answer to part one.'

'Fine. I'll sort it out.'

Jericho felt the life flowing back into his veins. The prey had become the hunter! In tense expectation he viewed his emails and saw that the Repsol man had sent the whole schedule of the summit, and sure enough, everybody had met in Beijing, representatives of almost every company that was involved or ever had been involved in the oil and gas business, strategists almost to a man.

He went through the list and gave a start.

Of course! That was only to be expected. And yet—

He quickly passed on the details to Ho, looked in on Yoyo, who was fast asleep, sat back down at the kitchen counter and started coming up with theories.

And all of a sudden everything fell into place.

Late that afternoon – Yoyo had groggily gone on her way, not without asking to be updated on the latest developments – Patrice Ho called him back.

'Three years is a long time,' he said, trying to make it sound exciting, 'but I may have found something. I can't tell you exactly who took part in the meeting, but I can tell you with some certainty where it took place and who the host was.'

'A private house?'

'Correct. There are no Sinopec facilities in Shunyi, but the strategy manager of the company lives there. Big property. We looked into him just for a laugh, and found out that he lives notoriously beyond his means, but yes, lots of people do that. His name is Joe Song. He represented Sinopec during the summit. Can you do anything with that?'

'I think so, yeah.' A name, another name! Now it would all depend on whether he was right. 'Thanks! That's all fine.'

'I get it. Now comes the bit I'm not going to like.'

'Yes. You have to hack into Song's computer.'

'Hmm.'

'It could be that I'm mistaken and the guy has nothing to hide. But if—'

'Owen, listen. A promise is a promise, okay? But before I do that, I need more information. I've got to know where your investigations are leading.'

Jericho hesitated. 'Possibly to the retrieval of the Chinese government's honour.'

'Aha.'

'You promise to help me anyway?'

'As I said—'

'Okay, listen up. I'll give you the background. Then I'll tell you what you need to look for.'

Twenty minutes later, when he could be certain that the Repsol man had drunk his first café con leche, he called Madrid again.

'Can I bother you again?'

'Of course.'

'You mentioned that the joint venture planned between Sinopec, Repsol and EMCO was based on an initiative. Can you remember who the initiator was?'

'Sure.' The man told him the name. 'By the way, he was the one who blew the whole thing up into a summit and suggested holding it in Beijing. Sinopec liked that. The Chinese like the world being negotiated on their territory.'

'Thanks. You've been a great help.'

The initiator—

Jericho smiled grimly. He saw the Hydra stretching its necks, darting its heads forwards, baring its fangs. It hissed at him, but its mighty serpentine body bent and started slowly retreating.

That night he slept a deep and dreamless sleep.

The next day, radio silence till lunchtime. Then Ho rang, and he sounded just as excited as he had two and a half weeks previously, when Jericho had passed on the news of the capture of Animal Ma Liping.

'Incredible,' he said. 'You were right.'

Jericho's heartbeat did a drumroll.

'What exactly did you find?'

'The icon. That snaky thing, what's the creature called again?'

'Hydra.'

'On Song's company computer! Hidden among other programs. To make his deleted emails visible again. However, we'll have to get at his hard disk.'

'No problem. You have sufficient grounds to arrest him officially.'

'Owen, that could—' Ho caught his breath. 'That could make my promotion to Beijing—'

'I know.' Jericho smiled. 'Bust the guy. You'll find data that look like white noise, but using that icon you'll be able to get a message out of it without too much difficulty.'

'I'll call you. I'll call you!'

'Wait!' Jericho started to pace back and forth, kept in motion by adrenalin. 'We need the other participants in the meeting. It only looks like a plot by a business sector, it's really a conspiracy by a small number of people. We've got to get to them. Focused and fast, so that none of them has a chance to get away. Perhaps you'll manage to wring a confession from our friend by pointing out the mitigating circumstances.'

'Like him being able to keep his head attached to his neck,' sniffed Ho.

'Oh, come on. I thought the death penalty was abolished in 2021.'

'So it was. But I can always threaten to bring it back specially for him. Soon we'll know who the other participants were, you can be sure of that!'

'Fine. If he doesn't talk, we'll have to check out every single alibi. I know that's going to be a big job.'

'Not really. I'd say the companies will be very interested in getting the truth into the open. In times like these, they don't want to cock up their reputations.'

'Whatever. It will have to be a concerted action. That means you'll have to bring in MI6 and the American Secret Service, as well as the Secret Services of all the countries affected. Then I'm going to phone Orley Enterprises, so promise me that the Chinese police won't stonewall. You're going to be bathed in glory.'

'The glory will be yours, Owen!'

Jericho said nothing.

Did he want that? Did he want to be bathed in glory? A little bit proud, perhaps, as Yoyo had suggested. They'd earned that, Yoyo, Tian and he. And apart from that, he just needed one more good night's sleep.

Early in the afternoon, Joe Song, the oil strategist, was arrested in his office, looked completely dumbfounded, and the investigators went to work. Just as restorers work their way through layers of paint to reveal much older art, they brought to light Song's deleted emails, supposed white noise which, with the expert use of the decoding program, was shaped into a document whose contents were enough to put Song in jail for the rest of his life.

And yet he denied everything. For an evening and a night he denied having anything to do with the attacks, and nor did he know anything about an organisation called Hydra, or how the icon and the message had found their way onto the Sinopec computer. Meanwhile a police unit was raging around his house before the eyes of his terrified wife, and found another gleaming, pulsing Hydra on Song's private computer, and the manager still claimed not to know anything. It took a night in jail and two consultations with his lawyers, before Patrice Ho, on the afternoon of 6 June – in a soundproofed room – vividly presented him with the bleakness of the rest of his life, but not without suggesting a possible way out in the event that he admitted everything.

After that Joe Song couldn't stop talking.

Jericho listened ecstatically to what Ho went on to tell him. Immediately afterwards he dialled Jennifer Shaw's number. It was nine in the morning in London, and he was almost pleased to be seeing her again.

'Owen! You keeping okay?'

'Pretty good now, thanks. You?'

'The Big O makes an ants' nest look like a Zen monastery. All the investigations get concentrated here so that you can't take so much as a step without getting hopelessly entangled.'

'Doesn't necessarily sound as if you've achieved clarity.'

'Still, by now we know that Gaia's hotel manager was a former Mossad agent. Good that you called, though. Julian seems to have triplicated himself. He's working round the clock, but I know he wanted to call you at the next possible opportunity.'

'So is he there?'

'He's buzzing around the place. Shall I try to put you through?'

'I've got a much better suggestion, Jennifer. Bring him here.'

Shaw raised a Mr Spock eyebrow.

'I assume you have more on your mind than just saying hello.'

He smiled. 'You're going to like it.'

A short time later they were all gathered in Jericho's loft, projected vivid and life-sized on Tu's holowall, and Jericho played his cards. Orley didn't interrupt him once, while his eyebrows drew together until they stood like craggy mountain ranges above his clear blue eyes, but when he finally turned his head towards Shaw, his voice sounded calm and relaxed.

'Prepare a helicopter to the airport,' he said. 'From there we'll take the jet. We'll pay him a visit.'

'Now?' asked Shaw.

'When else do you suggest?'

'To be quite honest I haven't the faintest idea where he is right now. But okay, of course we can—'

'You don't need to.' Orley smiled fiercely. 'I know where he is. He told me, right after we got back. When he called to express his dismay.'

'Of course,' said Shaw devotedly. 'When do you want to fly?'

'Give me an hour for hand luggage. Inform Interpol, MI6, but they're not to steal the show. Owen?' Orley stood up. 'Do you want to come?'

Jericho hesitated. 'Where to?'

Orley told him the name of the city. It really wasn't terribly far – for a well-motorised Englishman.

Suddenly he burst out laughing.

'I'm in Shanghai, Julian.'

'So?' Orley looked around, as if to prove that there were no problems in view. 'This is *your* moment, Owen! Who cares about distances? I don't. Take the next highspeed jet, I'll book you a ticket.'

'Very kind of you, but—'

'Kind?' Orley tilted his head. 'Do you have any idea what I owe you? I'll carry you on my shoulders if I have to! No, here's what we'll do, have we got one of our Mach 4 jets anywhere in his vicinity? Find that out for me, Jennifer, I think there's one in Tokyo, isn't there? We'll collect you, Owen. And bring Tu Tian with you, and that wonderful girl—'

'Julian, wait.'

'It's not a problem, it really isn't.'

Jericho shook his head. I've got more important things to do, he was about to say. I have to marry a standard lamp and a carpet in a Confucian ceremony, that's *my* life, but he didn't want to insult Orley, particularly since, as Shaw had predicted, he actually liked him. The Englishman radiated something that made you unreservedly willing to plunge into the next adventure with him.

'I can't get away from here right now,' he said. 'I have clients, and you know how it is – you shouldn't leave anyone in the lurch.'

'No, you're right.' Orley stroked his beard, clearly displeased by the situation. Then he turned his sea-blue eyes back towards Jericho. 'But perhaps there's a possibility of staying in Shanghai and still being in on it – but honestly, Owen, can you sleep peacefully without having brought all this to its conclusion?'

'No,' said Jericho wearily. 'But it's no longer my—' He paused, searching for the right word.

'Campaign?' Orley nodded. 'Okay, my friend. I know. You have to finish off your own story, not mine. Still, listen to my suggestion. It involves putting in a brief appearance, but you shouldn't miss out on that, Owen. You really shouldn't!'

Venice, Italy

The record for the biggest man-made mirror in the world was disputed by the Large Binocular Telescope Observatory in Arizona on the top of Mount Graham – two individual mirrors, to be precise, each one eight and a half metres in diameter and sixteen tonnes in weight – and the Hobby Eberle Telescope in Texas, consisting of reflecting cells over a surface of eleven metres by ten. On the other hand, there was no disputing the most beautiful mirror in the world. In times of global flooding, the

Piazza San Marco in Venice surpassed anything that had ever been seen before.

Gerald Palstein sat outside the Caffè Florian, buffeted by the unceasing stream of tourists that repelled him just as much as the flooded Piazza San Marco magically attracted him. For some years now the square had been continuously underwater. For the sake of it, he accepted the invasive spectacle, particularly since something was slowly changing in the behaviour of the visitors. Even in Japanese tour groups, you could now detect a certain reluctance to cross the square on sunny days like this and disturb the peace of the ankle-high standing water that perfectly reflected the Basilica di San Marco, the Campanile in front of it and the surrounding Procuratie, a world based on water and at the same time commemorated in it, a symbolic glimpse of the future. As inexorably as the lagoon rose, the city was sinking into the sea, like lovers seeking to unite even if it means that they merge together.

Apart from that, nothing in the city had changed. As ever, the clock tower diagonally opposite, with its passageway to the Mercerie, showed the phases of the sun and moon and the star signs on a background of lapis lazuli, and sent out bronze guardians to segment the earth and the universe into hours with its booming chimes, while faint breezes drifted across the one-and-a-half-square-kilometre mirror and rippled the architecture without dissolving it, as if the ghosts of Dalí and Hundertwasser were frolicking in the square.

Palstein scraped the sticky and delicious crust of sugar from the bottom of his espresso cup. His wife hadn't wanted to come and was preparing to leave for an Indian ashram, which she had been visiting at increasingly close intervals ever since an exhibition opening where she had met a guru who had a knack of luring what he wanted from people's souls and bank balances. In point of fact Palstein preferred it that way. Alone, he didn't have to talk, or pretend to be interested, or see things that he would rather block out. He could live in the pleasant stillness of Venice reflected in the water, just as Alice had passed through her mirror to visit the world that lay on the other side.

Noise. Shouts. Laughter.

A moment later the illusion passed, as a group of teenagers splashed their way through the surface of the water and everything turned into a wild, splashing daub.

Idiots, destroying a masterpiece!

The illusion of a masterpiece.

Palstein watched after them, too tired to get angry. Wasn't that always the way? You took such trouble building something, brought it to a state of perfection, and then a few hooligans came along and destroyed it all. He paid the exorbitant cost of the espresso and chamber music, strolled through the arcades of the piazzetta to the Bacino di San Marco, where the Doge's Palace lay along the deeper water, and followed the footbridges to the Biennale gardens. Near there, by a quiet canal in the tranquil sestiere of Castello, he had an early dinner at the Hostaria da Franz, which experts held to be the best fish restaurant in Venice, had a chat with Gianfranco, the old proprietor, a man whose life was a Humboldt-style exploration of the world along paths both straight and winding, who would stir himself for nothing except perhaps the sight of a few empty glasses, hugged both him and Maurizio, his son, as he left, and boarded a water taxi that brought him to the Grand Canal and the Palazzo Loredan. EMCO had bought the magnificent early Renaissance building in better days, and had forgotten, during the insanity of its systematic decline, to get rid of it. The building still stood open to the company executives, though it had not been used for ages. But because Palstein loved Venice, and thought nothing was more appropriate to his position than the symbol of everything transient, he had come here for a week.

By now the sun was low over the canal. The rattle and chug of the vaporetti and the barges mingled with the hum of elegant motorboats, the sound of accordions and the tenor voices of the gondolieri, to form an aural backdrop unlike anything anywhere else in the world. Now that the ground floor was underwater, he entered the palazzo via a higher entrance, and climbed the wooden staircase to the piano nobile, the first floor. Where the late sunlight came in through the windows, sofas and armchairs were gathered around a low glass table.

In one of the chairs sat Julian Orley.

Palstein gave a start. Then he quickened his pace, hurried the cathedral-like width of the room and spread out his arms.

'Julian,' he exclaimed. 'What a surprise!'

'Gerald.' Orley got to his feet. 'You weren't expecting me, were you?'

'No, absolutely not.' Palstein hugged the Englishman, who returned the embrace, a bit firmly, it seemed to him.

'How long have you been in Venice?'

'Got here an hour ago. Your concierge was kind enough to let me in, once I'd persuaded him I wasn't about to steal the Murano chandeliers.'

'Why didn't you call? We could have gone for dinner. As it was I had to make do with the best turbot I've ever eaten, all by myself.' Palstein walked over to a little bar, took out two glasses and a bottle and turned round. 'Grappa? *Prime uve*, soft in the mouth, and drinkable in large quantities.'

'Bring it over.' Julian sat back down. 'We must clink glasses, my old friend. We have something to celebrate.'

'Yes, your return.' Palstein thoughtfully considered the label, half filled the glasses and sat down opposite Julian. 'Let's drink to survival,' he smiled. 'To *your* survival.'

'Good idea.' The Englishman raised his glass, took a good swig and set the drink back down. Then he opened a bag, took out a laptop, flipped it open and turned it on. 'Because drinking to yours would be like drinking to the future of a hanged man. If you catch my meaning.'

Palstein blinked, still smiling.

'Quite honestly, no.'

The screen lit up. A camera showed the picture of a man who looked familiar to Palstein. A moment later he remembered. Jericho! Of course! That damned detective.

'Good evening, Gerald,' Jericho said in a friendly voice.

Palstein hesitated.

'Hello, Owen. What can I do for you?'

'The same thing you once did in the Big O. Help us. You helped us a lot back then, you remember?'

'Of course. I'd have been happy to do even more.'

'Fine. Now's your chance. Julian would like to know a lot of things, but first there's something I'd like to tell you. You'll be pleased to hear that we've solved the mystery of the Calgary shooting.'

Palstein said nothing.

'Even though I was worried I would have a tough time of it.' Jericho smiled, as if remembering a hurdle overcome. 'Because you see, Gerald, if someone had wanted you out of the way – someone who had managed to infiltrate Lars Gudmundsson into your security men – why would he have needed a spectacle like Calgary? Why didn't Gudmundsson just quietly get on with it and shoot you? Even in the Big O it seemed to me that the whole assassination attempt was a staged event, but who was it for? Eventually it occurred to me that Hydra – an organisation I don't need to tell you anything more about – had decided to present the world with a Chinese assassin, if Xin was captured on camera in Calgary. And that was certainly one of the reasons, just as Hydra went on leaving trails back to China – on the one hand because the Chinese were the ideal scapegoat, but probably also because open conflict would have further held up the lunar projects of the space powers after the success of Operation Mountains of Eternal Light. But even seen in this perspective, the attack made no sense. Anyone as intimately acquainted with Kenny Xin as we are knows, for example, that he is infatuated with flechettes. In Quyu, in Berlin, on the roof of the Big O, it's the ammunition he's always used. But in Calgary he settled for decidedly smaller projectiles. Your injury will have been painful, but entirely harmless, as a conversation with your doctors should confirm.'

Palstein stared into his glass.

'Take this from someone who's managed to escape Xin several times. He was ahead of us in London and Berlin, and he cost us a lot of lives. He's a phenomenal marksman! Definitely not somebody who's going to miss a target just because he trips, especially when he's got an unobstructed view. But even if we were willing to accept that stumbling drew the first shot to your shoulder rather than your head, the second would have got you before you reached the ground.' Jericho paused. 'You were hit, nevertheless, Gerald. But certainly, however much you've risked and invested, it can't have been in your interest to come away with a *serious* injury. And I know very few marksmen who could pull off such a precision shot as the one in Calgary: hitting a man while he pretends to slip, without giving him anything more than a completely harmless flesh wound that will heal very quickly. A masterpiece, after which with the best will in the world, no one could suspect that you'd cleared the way for Gabriel – or shall we call him Hanna? – to join Julian's group. Even in the unlikely event that someone discovered details about the operation, you'd covered your tracks. Against this background, Loreena's discovery of the video can hardly have troubled you that much, can it? It too was factored in.'

'I admired Loreena for her sharpness of mind,' said Palstein. He was listening with great interest to the lecture.

'Of course you did,' said the detective. 'Except that you wouldn't have predicted in a million years that she would dig out Ruiz and establish a connection with a very particular meeting in Beijing three years ago. At that point things got tight, very tight.'

'I warned Loreena,' sighed Palstein. 'Several times. You may not believe it, but I was very keen to spare her that death. I liked her.'

'And Lynn?' Julian said, quietly severe. 'What about Lynn? Didn't you like her?'

'I was prepared to make sacrifices.'

'My daughter.'

Palstein thoughtfully slipped his finger along the edge of his glass.

'Seven people in Quyu,' Jericho went on. 'Ten in Vancouver, Vogelaar, Nyela. Even Norrington couldn't have imagined that working with you would be quite like that. And purely out of interest, who took care of Greenwatch?'

'Gudmundsson.' Palstein stiffened. 'We had to make sure that there was no editorial conference. I told him to disappear immediately after the operation.'

'Which wonderfully confirmed your victim status once again. Gerald Palstein, betrayed by everybody. Might I also take the opportunity to ask you what happened to Alejandro Ruiz?'

'We had to disassociate ourselves from him.'

Should he tell them how Xin and Gudmundsson had put the Spaniard on a boat while the city of Lima slept, and introduced him to the world of marine life? What sharks, crabs and bacteria had left of him rested in the silent darkness of the Peruvian ocean trench. No, too many details. They'd never get out of here.

'He was a weakling,' he said. 'He was more than happy to do something about helium-3, convinced as he was that we were merely going to blow up a few digging machines. When Hydra met at Song's house on the evening of 1 September, it turned out that I'd misjudged him. Unlike everyone else, by the way. I selected the heads of Hydra very carefully over a period of months. They had to have influence, and the power to divert large sums into fake projects without anyone asking any questions. But above all they had to be willing to do anything. As expected, when Xin and I presented Operation Mountains of Eternal Light, it only came as a surprise to Ruiz. He was completely horrified. Turned white as a sheet. Stormed out.'

'He threatened to blow Hydra's cover?'

'His next step was predictable.'

'Which meant that his fate was too.'

Palstein ran his hands over his eyes. He was tired. Shockingly tired.

'And how are you going to prove all this?' he asked.

'It's been proved already, Gerald. Joe Song's confessed. We know the heads of Hydra, and right at this very minute they're all getting visits from representatives of their national authorities. They will find snake icons and white noise on the computers of some of the world's biggest oil companies. Really titanic stuff, Gerald. Regardless of borders and ideologies. You were the initiator of the joint venture between Sinopec, Repsol and EMCO, you turned the meeting in Beijing into a summit, but it's Hydra that'll make you go down in history.' Jericho paused. 'Except that your name will not be mentioned in very flattering contexts. By the way, how did you get hold of guys like Xin?'

'I wouldn't put it quite like that, Owen.' Julian, who had until then been sitting with legs crossed, sat forward. 'It should be: how did Xin get hold of people like Gerald.'

'In Africa,' Palstein said calmly. 'In Equatorial Guinea, 2020, when Mayé was still of interest to EMCO.'

'Why all this, Gerald?' Julian shook his head. 'Why?'

'Why what?'

'Why did you go so far?'

'You're seriously asking me that?' Palstein stared at him listlessly. 'To defend my interests. Just as you defend yours. The interests of my sector.'

'With atom bombs?'

'Do you seriously imagine I wouldn't have done absolutely anything to solve the problems in a peaceful manner? Everybody knows how much I fought to steer the dinosaur in a different direction to the one it was cheerfully heading in, towards the hurtling meteorite that would seal its extinction. In most alternative sectors we could have held our own. But we missed all opportunities, we neglected to buy Lightyears, to get Locatelli on our side, even though it was already clear that helium-3 would mean the end for us. And I even tried to get a foothold in the helium-3 business, as you know, except that I wasn't given permission to draw up an agreement with you.'

'Which you were on the point of doing.'

'In the event of failure, yes. Not if two atom bombs had just destroyed the helium-3 mining infrastructure and set things back by decades.'

And suddenly, enraged by the wasted potential of his plan, he jumped to his feet, fists clenched.

'I'd calculated everything, Julian! The consequences if we'd destroyed either the space lift or Peary Base, but it was only the double whammy that produced the best results. Like China, the Americans would have had to deploy conventional rockets to carry helium-3 to Earth, which would never have happened! Everyone knows that China's extraction is running at a loss. But even if they'd taken such a step, the extracted quantities would have remained pitiful. You would have had to build a new space lift, a new space station, and that would have taken at least twenty years. You wouldn't have had it financed as quickly as you did the first time. And only if shuttle transports had been possible from the orbit to the Moon would you have been able to rebuild the infrastructure up there, and even that would have taken years, maybe decades.'

'But in forty or fifty years it'll all be over anyway. Then you'll be finished, *because there'll be nothing left!*'

'Forty years, yes!' snorted Palstein. 'Forty years of business left to us. Four decades of survival, in the course of which we could have made up for the mess made by all those idiots, my predecessors included. We could have reorganised. As long ago as 2020 I commissioned an analysis of all the possible scenarios of what would happen if helium-3 extraction were carried out successfully within a precise time frame. It meant our annihilation. We *had* to stand up to you!'

'We?' whispered Julian. 'You and your gang of lunatics dare to speak for the whole sector? For thousands of decent people?'

'Thousands of people who would have lost their jobs,' yelled Palstein. 'A damaged global economy! Look around you! Wake up! How many countries, how many people who depend on oil will be damaged by your helium-3? Have you thought about that?'

'And you were once called the green conscience of the energy sector.'

'Because I *am*!' Palstein cried. 'But sometimes you have to go against your convictions. Do you think four more decades of oil economy would do more damage to the planet than it's done already? We might be a gang of lunatics, but—'

'No,' said Jericho's voice from the laptop. 'You're not insane, Gerald. You are calculating, and that's the worst thing about you. Like any other halfwit, you find a reason to blame your crimes on circumstances. You're not special.'

Palstein said nothing. He slowly dropped back into his chair and stared at his feet.

'Why the flight to the Moon?' Julian asked quietly.

'Because something got in the way in 2024.' Palstein shrugged. 'An astronaut called Thorn was supposed to have—'

'I don't mean that. Why that one and not the next one? Why the one my children and I were on, people like Warren Locatelli, the Donoghues, Miranda Winter—'

'I didn't care about your guests, Julian,' sighed Palstein. 'It was the first opportunity that offered itself since Thorn's failure. When would the next trip have taken place? Only after the official opening. This year? Next year? How long would we have had to wait?'

'Perhaps you also factored in the possibility of Julian's death,' said Jericho.

'Nonsense.'

'His death would have strengthened the conservative forces at Orley. The people opposed to the idea of selling off technologies. The smaller the number of countries that can build a space lift, the smaller the chance that a second—'

'You're fantasising, Jericho. If you hadn't spoiled everything, Julian would have been back on Earth ages before the explosions took place. And his son and daughter too.'

The muffled chugging and thudding of the boats reached them from outside. Right below their window someone was singing 'O Sole Mio' with businesslike ardour.

'But we weren't on Earth,' said Julian.

'That wasn't the plan.'

'Fuck your plan. You went beyond the limit, Gerald. In every respect.'

Palstein looked up.

'And you? You and your American friends? How is what you're doing any different from what we've been doing for decades? You extract something from the ground until it's all gone and you find you've destroyed a planet in the process. What limit do you lot go beyond? What limit do you in particular go beyond when you run your company like a state that dictates the rules of play to real states? Do you think you're being public-spirited? At least the oil companies served their countries. Who are you serving, apart from your own vanity? There are no social states without state organisations, but you're behaving like a modern Captain Nemo and spitting on the world as it happens to work. We merely played the game that the circumstances required. Only look at mankind, their clean, just wars, the cyclical collapse of their financial systems, the cynicism of their profiteers, the unscrupulousness and stupidity of their politicians, the perversion of their religious leaders, and don't talk to me about limits.'

Julian stroked his beard.

'You could be right, Gerald.' He nodded and got to his feet. 'But it doesn't change anything. Owen, thanks for giving up your time. We're going.'

'Take care, Gerald,' said Jericho. 'Or not.'

The picture on the screen went out. Julian snapped the laptop shut and put it back in its bag.

'A little while ago,' he said, 'when I was stepping inside your lovely residence, I noticed a little plaque: in the mezzanine of a building across the courtyard from this palazzo, Richard Wagner died. You know what? I liked that. I like the idea of great men dying in great houses.' He reached into his jacket, took out a pistol and set it down on the table in front of Palstein. His clear blue eyes had a penetrating expression, almost friendly and encouraging. 'It's loaded. One shot is generally enough, but you're a big man, Gerald. A very big man. You might take two.'

He turned round and crossed the room at a leisurely pace. Palstein watched after him, until Julian's grey-blond ponytail had disappeared beyond the landing. As if of their own accord, his fingers found their way to his phone and keyed in a number.

'Hydra,' he said mechanically.

'What can I do?'

'Get me out of here. I've been unmasked.'

'Unma—' Xin fell silent for a moment. 'You know, Gerald, I think my contract's just run out.'

'You're walking out on me?'

'I wouldn't put it like that. You know me, I'm loyal and I'm not afraid to take risks, but in hopeless cases – and your case is unfortunately *completely* hopeless . . .'

'What—' Palstein gulped. 'What are you going to do?'

'Hmm.' Xin seemed to think for a moment. 'Quite honestly, it's been rather tiring lately. I think I need a bit of a holiday. You take care.'

Take care. The second person who'd said that to him.

Palstein froze. He slowly lowered his phone. Voices rose to him from below.

His eyes wandered to the gun.

The people from Interpol and MI6 were waiting for him in the stairwell. Shaw looked at him quizzically.

'Give him a minute,' said Julian.

'Well, I'm not sure.' One of the agents frowned. 'He could do something to himself.'

'Yes, exactly.' Julian pushed past him. 'Jennifer, let's go. I have to look after my daughter.'

London, Great Britain

Stars like dust.

She had been lost in sleep, and the dream had put her back into the stillness of the spaceship dashing through the sparkling night, carrying her and the bomb. She had lived through everything all over again. Again she had come up with the plan to stow the mini-nuke in the living module, uncouple it and come back to the OSS with the landing unit. Back to Tim and Amber and Julian, who had cried so hard when he called her name. In her mind she had promised him never to leave him alone again, but her thoughts had been all that she was able to mobilise, and that wasn't much.

Then the moment when the spinning bomb, lit by the flickering of her dying consciousness, had revealed the truth, that there were still *hours* to go until detonation, not minutes or seconds as she had thought. That she would have had a chance.

She had gone to sleep in the pearly rain of her blood.

I'm coming. I'm coming, Daddy.

I'm there.

Clunk!

One of those noises that feel like a nuisance, even if they mean the salvation of *really* having made your peace. In the absence of choice, of course. But she *had* made her peace before the shuttle on which Julian, Nina, Tim and Amber had followed her docked to the Charon – her lonely spaceship that had not had the chance of filling its tanks on the OSS, which was why it had finally run out of fuel. Even before it reached its top speed.

But she hadn't known anything about any of that.

Voices around her. People in spacesuits.

'Lynn? Lynn!'

Impotence. Scraps of words. As if through cotton wool.

'How long now?'

'Just over five hours. Enough time to bring both shuttles back.'

'I think Lynn's stable.' Nina. 'She's lost a lot of blood, but it seems to me—'

Silence again. Then a voice on an endless loop:

'And now get the thing out of here!'

Thing out of here, thing out of here, thing out of here, thingoutofhere, thingoutofherething-out—

'Lynn.'

She blinked. The hospital room. Back in the present. Hang on, wasn't there a film called—

Doesn't matter, what a film!

'How are you?' said Julian.

'Been dreaming.' She sat up. Her left side hurt, but she was feeling better every day. Lawrence, the bitch, had missed taking her life by inches. 'We were back in the spaceship.' Christ, she was hungry. Incredibly hungry! She could have eaten the bed. 'A nightmare, to be honest. Always the same nightmare.'

'It's over.'

'Hey, no big deal. It wasn't all that bad, either.' She yawned. 'Hopefully I'll dream something else eventually.'

'No. It's *over*, Lynn.' Julian took her hand and smiled, very much the magician of her childhood. 'The nightmare is over.'

Xintiandi, Shanghai, China

'Yoyo could really give us a call,' Jericho complained.

Tu pulled a sticky strand of noodle from the cardboard box that stood in for his lunch plate.

'And you could *drop by* again,' he said, chewing. 'Instead of only ever phoning. Burying yourself away in your stupid loft.'

'I'm busy. Honestly.'

Tu gave him a disapproving look over the rim of his glasses. The bridge looked as if it was about to snap in two over his nose.

'You have friends to cultivate,' he chided him. 'What about this evening? A bunch of us are going out to eat. And drink, more importantly.'

'Who's we?'

'Everyone you can think of. Yoyo too, once she's stopped crying. She's been sobbing away constantly, I'm thinking of installing a dam in the guest room. Terrible. Nothing but tears. A great big crybaby.'

'And Hongbing?'

'He's crying too. They're closer than they've ever been.'

'Sounds good.'

'Yeah, great,' growled Tu. 'You just don't have to put up with it. What about tonight?'

'Fine.'

'Good. I wouldn't have let you get away with anything else, *xiongdi!*'

Jericho sat there for a while.

Then he went across to the kitchen area to magic a cappuccino from the coffee machine. His journey took him past the ensemble that he had now got used to calling 'the odd couple', Jack Lemmon and Walter Matthau embodied by a standard lamp and a carpet, which failed, failed, failed to accomplish the ideal of Confucian harmony, in any imaginable arrangement.

He studied them for a moment.

Then he moved them aside, put them in the cellar and looked at the corner. And finally, flooded only by light, clear and tidy, he liked it.

That had been important!

Principal Characters

Anand, Ashwini   Staff member at the Gaia moon hotel, responsible for accommodation, technology and logistics.

Black, Peter   Tour guide at the Gaia moon hotel, pilot of the moon shuttle Charon. Knows all the moon craters by name.

Borelius, Eva   Scientist and CEO of the German research company Borelius Pharmaceuticals. Northern German, dry character. Likes classical music, horses and chess. Married to the surgeon Karla Kramp. Member of the moon tour group.

Bruford, Sid   Former oil worker at EMCO Imperial Oil, Canada, unemployed. Dreams of a career as an actor.

Chambers, Evelyn   Most prominent and influential talk-show host in the USA, presenter of the show *Chambers*. Latina, whose bisexuality has turned her into a hate figure. Brilliant analyst, perceptive and curious. Member of the moon tour group.

Chen Hongbing   Car salesman, Yoyo's father. Polite, but reserved, with a murky past. Commissions Owen Jericho to find his missing daughter.

Chen 'Yoyo' Yuyun   Student, daughter of Chen Hongbing, founder of the internet dissident group 'the Guardians', member of the motorcycle club City Demons. Sings in a neo-prog band, loves parties and the excessive lifestyle. Beautiful and quite exhausting.

Crippen, Jan   Technical director of the American Peary Base, lunar North Pole.

'Daxiong' Guan Guo   Founder member and vice head of the internet dissident group 'the Guardians', head of the motorcycle club City Demons and owner of the Demon Point motorbike workshop. Giant with bear-like strength and French-style spleen.

DeLucas, Minnie   Doctor and specialist in life-support systems at the

American Peary Base, lunar North Pole. Investigating the possibility of raising livestock on the Moon.

Diane   Owen Jericho's computer.

Donner, Andre   Owner of the Muntu African restaurant in Berlin. Murky past in Equatorial Guinea.

Donner, Nyela   West African, co-owner of the Muntu African restaurant in Berlin, Andre Donner's wife.

Donoghue, Aileen   CEO and artistic manager of the Xanadu hotel and casino company. Wife of Chuck Donoghue. Dominant-mother type. Member of the moon tour group.

Donoghue, Chuck   Hotel mogul, founder and CEO of the Xanadu hotel and casino company. Amateur boxer and hard-line Republican. Loud and jovial. Cheerfully tells the world's worst jokes. Member of the moon tour group.

Edwards, Marc   Founder and CEO of the microchip company Quantime Inc., extreme sports fanatic and diver, creationist view of the world. Husband of Mimi Parker. Member of the moon tour group.

Funaki, Michio   Sous-chef and barman in the Gaia moon hotel, sushi specialist.

Gore, Kyra   Shuttle pilot at the American Peary Base, lunar North Pole.

Gudmundsson, Lars   Bodyguard, employed with his team by the Eagle Eye security company to protect the oil manager Gerald Palstein.

Hanna, Carl   Canadian large-scale investor, main area alternative energies. Solitary type, macho, but likeable. Always has his guitar in his luggage. Member of the moon tour group.

Haskin, Ed   Chief technician, Orley Space Station (OSS).

Hedegaard, Nina   Tour guide at the Gaia moon hotel, moon shuttle pilot. Capable and romantic. Involved in relationship with Julian Orley.

Ho, Patrice   Senior Shanghai police officer and careerist, friend of Owen Jericho. Jericho has supported Ho in several investigations and is therefore owed a favour.

Hoff, Edda   Project manager, central security division, Orley Enterprises. Pale, expressionless and extremely reliable.

Holland, Sid   Political history editor at environmental broadcaster

Greenwatch. Likes driving his friends and colleagues around in his old Thunderbird.

Hsu, Rebecca   Founder and CEO of the Taiwanese luxury company Rebecca Hsu, workaholic, incapable of being on her own. Fights a hopeless war with her obesity. Member of the moon tour group.

Hudsucker, Susan   Director of the environmental broadcaster Greenwatch and immediate superior of Loreena Keowa. Prudent, sometimes hesitant.

Hui Xiao-Tong   Member of the City Demons motorcycle club.

Intern   Colleague of Loreena Keowa at environmental broadcaster Greenwatch. Glutton and tireless researcher.

ISLAND-II   Psychotherapeutic aid program.

Jagellovsk, Annie   Astronomer and pilot at the American Peary Base, lunar North Pole.

Jericho, Owen   Cyber-detective from Great Britain, brought to Shanghai by an unhappy love affair. Outstanding investigator, lone wolf and linguistic genius. Suffers from loneliness and nightmares. Hired by his friend Tu Tian to find Yoyo.

Jia Keqiang   Commander of the Chinese helium-3 mining station, Sinus Iridum, Moon. Both a patriot and a supporter of international understanding.

Jin Jia Wei   Student, member of the internet dissident group 'the Guardians' and of the City Demons motorcycle club.

Keowa, Loreena   Reporter for the environmental broadcaster Greenwatch, native American of the Tlingit tribe. Green views, elegant appearance. Determined to solve the assassination attempt on Gerald Palstein.

Kokoschka, Axel   Head chef, Gaia moon hotel. Genius at the stove, in the company of others shy, uncommunicative and awkward.

Kramp, Karla   German surgeon, critical and analytic. Asks tough questions. Wife of Eva Borelius, member of moon tour group..

Laurie, Jean-Jacques   Geologist at the American Peary Base, lunar North Pole.

Lau Ye   Daxiong's right-hand man, mechanic at Demon Point motorbike workshop and member of City Demons motorcycle club. Small, slight, but intrepid and loyal.

Lawrence, Dana   Manager and head of security, Gaia moon hotel. Cool, unapproachable and thorough.

Lee, Bernard, 'C'   Head of MI6, London.

Leto   Former mercenary, friend of Jan Kees Vogelaar, Berlin.

Liu, Naomi   Senior secretary at Tu Technologies; stylish appearance, with liking for strawberry tea.

Locatelli, Warren   Founder and CEO of photovoltaic manufacturer Lightyears. American of Algerian–Italian descent, irascible and ego-centric, although not without charm. Likes cursing, car-racing and sailing regattas. Winner of the America's Cup. Married to Momoka Omura. Member of moon tour group.

Lurkin, Laura   Fitness trainer, Orley Space Station (OSS).

Maas, Svenja   Attractive postgraduate at the Charité Hospital, Berlin.

Ma 'Animal' Liping   Violent paedophile, initiator of the child porn ring Paradise of the Little Emperors. In spite of hip and eye problems, extremely dangerous.

Ma Mak   Member of City Demons motorcycle club.

Mayé, Juan Alfonso Nguema   West African general and sometime leader of Equatorial Guinea. Successor to Teodoro Obiang, came to power in a coup in 2017. Corrupt and megalomaniac.

Merrick, Tom   Specialist in information and communication, central security division, Orley Enterprises. Introvert.

Moto, Severo   Opposition politician in Equatorial Guinea, during Teodoro Obiang's time in office.

Nair, Mukesh   Founder and CEO of the Tomato food company. Wealthy son of a farmer, with a liking for the simple life, sees the beautiful and the good in every-thing. Member of moon tour group.

Nair, Sushma   Paediatrician, wife of Mukesh Nair, warm-hearted, sometimes a little fearful. Member of moon tour group.

Na Mou   Crew member, Chinese helium-3 extraction station, Sinus Iridum, Moon.

Ndongo, Juan Aristide Ruler of Equatorial Guinea after the fall of General Mayé. Trying to rebuild the country in a decent way.

Norrington, Andrew Deputy head of the central security division, Orley Enterprises. Responsible for the safety of the moon tour group.

Obiang, Teodoro Ruler of Equatorial Guinea until 2015.

O'Keefe, Finn Irish actor, became global superstar with *Perry Rhodan*. Critics' favourite, sex symbol, solitary and shy, with a reckless past. Nurtures his rebel image. Member of moon tour group.

Omura, Momoka Japanese actress, art film star, eccentric and arrogant. Wife of Warren Locatelli. Member of moon tour group.

Orley, Amber Tim Orley's wife, teacher. Capable and uncomplicated, tries to act as go-between for Tim and his father. Member of moon tour group.

Orley, Crystal Julian Orley's late wife, spent the last months of her life in a state of mental derangement.

Orley, Julian Former film producer, founder and CEO of technology empire Orley Enterprises and wealthiest man in the world. Unconventional, charismatic, with a pronounced instinct for power and a demonstrable dislike of nation states. Inventor of the space lift and host of moon tour group.

Orley, Lynn Julian Orley's daughter and CEO of Orley Travel, the tourism group of Orley Enterprises. Perfectionist, psychologically unstable, architect of the Gaia moon hotel and member of the moon tour group.

Orley, Tim Julian Orley's son, teacher, at loggerheads with his father. Tries to protect Lynn from collapse. Member of moon tour group.

Ögi, Heidrun Photographer, albino, former stripper and porn actress, calls a spade a spade. Wife of Walo Ögi and member of moon tour group.

Ögi, Walo Swiss investor, architect, man of the world and epicurean with a weakness for the music of the 1990s. Lovable, with tendency towards self-dramatisation and grand gestures. Husband of Heidrun Ögi. Member of moon tour group.

Palmer, Leland Commander of the American Peary Base, lunar North Pole.

Palstein, Gerald Head of strategy at EMCO oil company. Aesthete, numerate, spent years fighting for his company to switch focus to alternative energies. Narrowly escaped attempted assassination.

Parker-Edwards, Mimi Fashion designer and founder of the Mimi Kri label producing intelligent fashion. Diver, extreme sports fan, creationist views. Wife of Marc Edwards. Member of moon tour group.

Reardon, Mickey Ex-IRA man, specialist in alarm systems.

Rogachev, Oleg CEO of the Russian steel giant Rogamittal, with links to the Kremlin and the Russian Mafia. Martial arts and football enthusiast, places great stress on self-control, courteous, sometimes seems distant. Member of moon tour group.

Rogacheva, Olympiada Member of the Russian Parliament, daughter of the former Russian President Maxim Ginsburg and wife of Oleg Rogachev. Inconspicuous and dejected. Unhappy in her marriage, drinks. Member of moon tour group.

Ruiz, Alejandro Strategy manager of the Repsol oil company, vanished in South America in 2022.

Shaw, Jennifer Head of the central security division, Orley Enterprises. Competent and authoritarian, with a dry sense of humour.

Sina Editor, Society and Miscellaneous, at environmental broadcaster Greenwatch. Helps Loreena Keowa with her research.

Song, Joe Strategy manager of the Chinese oil company Sinopec, Beijing.

Sung, Tony Student, member of the internet dissident group 'the Guardians' and of the City Demons motorcycle club.

Tautou, Bernard CEO of the Franco-British water company Suez, politician. Charmer with a tendency to complacency. Member of moon tour group.

Tautou, Paulette Foreign language correspondent, wife of Bernard Tautou, condescending, weak stomach. Member of moon tour group.

Thiel, Sophie Deputy director of the Gaia moon hotel, responsible for housekeeping and life-support systems. Cheerful and open, detective instincts.

Thorn, Vic Commander of the first crew of the American Peary Base, lunar North Pole. Capable astronaut and playboy. Lost his life in an accident on Orley Space Station (OSS) in 2024.

Tu, Joanna Painter, ex-girlfriend of Owen Jericho and wife of Tu Tian. Elegant and urbane, observes the world with sardonic detachment.

Tu Tian Founder and CEO of Tu Technologies, a Shanghai company producing holograms and virtual environments. Skilled golfer and businessman, with unparallelled self-confidence. Confidant of Yoyo, companion of Chen Hongbing and close friend of Owen Jericho.

Vogelaar, Jan Kees Mercenary, sometime member of the government of Equatorial Guinea under General Mayé. Extremely cunning. Special characteristic: glass eye.

Voss, Marika Director of the Institute of Forensic Pathology at the Charité Hospital, Berlin.

Wachowski, Tommy Deputy commander of the American Peary Base, lunar North Pole.

Wang, Grand Cherokee Student, Yoyo's flatmate, self-dramatist, weak character. Operates the Silver Dragon ride at the Shanghai World Financial Center (WFC).

Winter, Miranda Ex-model, inheritor of billions and occasional actress. Naïve and uneducated, warm and strident. Has names for her breasts. Member of moon tour group.

Woodthorpe, Kay Director of the bioregenerative systems research group, Orley Space Station (OSS).

Xiao 'Maggie' Meiqi Student, member of the internet dissident group 'the Guardians' and of the City Demons motorcycle club.

Xin, Kenny Agent, aesthete and neurotic.

Yin Ziyi Student, member of the internet dissident group 'the Guardians' and of the City Demons motorcycle club.

Zhang Li Student, Yoyo's flatmate.

Zhao Bide Acquaintance and occasional helper of Owen Jericho from Quyu, like Jericho in search of Yoyo.

Zheng Pang-Wang Founder and CEO of the Chinese technology company Zheng Group, great hope of Chinese space travel.

Zhou Jinping Crew member of the Chinese helium-3 extraction station, Sinus Iridum, Moon.

Acknowledgements

Various textbooks, documentaries, photographs and films were a great help to me when I was writing this book – so many that it would be impossible for me to list them all here. I should like to thank the authors, journalists, scientists, photographers and directors whose discoveries flowed into my research all the more emphatically for their work.

But *Limit* would not have come into being if some remarkable people hadn't given up their time to me.

My knowledge of astronauts, space stations, spaceships, moon bases, satellites, interplanetary communication, the incidence of lunar helium-3 and the technology required for its extraction, space law, the Moon itself and the future of manned space travel was considerably enriched by:

Thomas Reiter, ISS and Mir astronaut, Chairman of the German Aerospace DLR Porz

Kerstin Rogon, Thomas Reiter office, DLR Porz

Dr Wolfgang Seboldt, Space missions and technology, DLR Porz

Dr Reinhold Ewald, Mir astronaut and physicist

Professor Ernst Messerschmidt, astronaut and physicist

Dr Eva Hassel-von Pock

Dr Paolo Ferri, head of solar and planetary missions, ESA Space Operations Centre, Darmstadt

Dr Frank-Jürgen Dieckmann, Spacecraft Operations Manager for Envisat and ERS-2, ESA Space Operations Centre, Darmstadt

Dr Manfred Warhaut, Head of Mission Operations, ESA Space Operations Centre, Darmstadt

Professor Dr Tilman Spohn, Head of the Institute of Planetary Research Management, DLR, Berlin

Dr Marietta Benkö, specialist in space law, Köln

Ranga Yogeshwar, physicist and presenter

The oil and gas sector, business structures and prognoses, but also the growing market in alternative energies, was brought closer to me by:

Werner Breuers, Chairman of LANXESS AG

Wahida Hammond, Skywalker, Köln – with extra thanks for contacts and *simply being Why*

I learned a lot about modern communication technology, the internet of tomorrow, IT security, holography and virtual environments from:

Dr Manfred Bogen, Head of Virtual Environments at the Fraunhofer Institute for Intelligent Analysis and Information Systems, Sankt Augustin

Paul Friessem, Head of Department, Secure Processes and Infrastructures, at the Fraunhofer Institute for Secure Information Technology, Sankt Augustin

Thorsten Holtkämper, Project Manager, Virtual Environments, at the Fraunhofer Institute for Intelligent Analysis and Information Systems, Sankt Augustin

Roland Kuck, Project Manager, Virtual Environments, at the Fraunhofer Institute for Intelligent Analysis and Information Systems, Sankt Augustin

Thomas Tikwinski, Project Manager, NetMedia, at the Fraunhofer Institute for Intelligent Analysis and Information Systems, Sankt Augustin

Jochen Haas, Simply Net Data Services, Köln

I was able to deepen my understanding of architecture and urban planning, particularly about urban development in China, but also about slums, thanks to:

Professor Dr Eckhard Ribbeck, City Planning Institute, Stuttgart University

Ingeborg Junge-Reyer, mayor of Berlin and Senator for Urban Development

The present and future state of forensic medicine were brought to life for me by:

Dr Michael Tsokos, Director of the Institute of Forensic Pathology at the Charité, Berlin

I was given information about the past, present and future of China, about Chinese manners and names, and the status quo of Chinese pop music by:

Mian Mian, author and scene icon, Shanghai

Wei Butter, Master of Arts, Asian Languages, Bonn

Facts about mercenaries, private security services, arms technology, police and detective work were communicated to me by:

Peter Nasse, Head of Personal Security Management Services, Köln

Uwe Steen, Public Relations, Köln Police

Special thanks to:

Gisela Tolk, judge and passionate sinologist, who tirelessly collected material about China for me

Maren Steingross, who summarised my Chinese research and thus got it into my head

Jürgen Muthmann, who read more newspapers in a week than I do in a whole year, and drew my attention to a lot of things that I would otherwise have missed

Larissa Kranz for being such a great dining companion

You can get a bit unsociable when you're writing fat books, which is down to a perceived distortion of space and time. For example, you could swear you'd been out with your best friend only the previous week, until he points out on the phone that you haven't seen each other in six months. Dear people who are important to you engage in dialogue with each other about the question of which galaxy their phys-ically and mentally absent friend, relation and husband may currently be travelling in. In fact I did go missing for a long time, but never heard a word of reproach. Instead I enjoyed two years of sympathy, support and patience. I owe my friends and family a debt of gratitude for that! More than anything else I'm glad to be able to spend more time with you all again – particularly since I hate sitting alone at my desk! If there were no laptops, high-performance batteries and extension leads, author would be the worst job imaginable for me. I like being around people too much, so I've got used to writing in public, surrounded by music, street noises and conversation. As a result, large parts of *Limit* were written in the establishments of restaurateur friends of mine, whose ministrations had considerable influence on the result.

I am particularly grateful to Thomas Wippenbeck and his great team at Restaurant Fonda in Südstadt, Köln, where I spent so much time that in the end I risked being mistaken for part of the furniture and stacked up with the chairs at night. I was also well looked after in the Spitz, whose friendly staff defended my regular table with knife and fork against all other guests. I was always given a welcome by the Sterns in the Vintage and Romain Wack in Wackes. Sometimes I simply had to get out of Köln and headed for the island of Sylt, where I received perfect treatment both from Johannes King and his team at the Söl'ring Hof and from Herbert Seckler, Ivo Köster and their team at the Sansibar.

I would like to thank the brilliant, committed staff at my publishing house, and quite particularly you, Helge, for your friendship and invaluable confidence.

But my ultimate thanks is for you, Sabina. However much I may have enjoyed travelling to the Moon in my mind – the best thing was always looking back at the Earth. Because that's where you are.